PENGUIN CLASSICS

THE GOLDEN AGE OF BRITISH
SHORT STORIES 1890–1914

Philip Hensher is the editor of *The Penguin Book of the British Short Story* (two volumes) and of *The Penguin Book of the Contemporary British Short Story*. His most recent novel is *A Small Revolution in Germany*.

D1336095

The Golden Age of British Short Stories 1890–1914

Edited by
PHILIP HENSHER

PENGUIN BOOKS

PENGUIN CLASSICS

UK | USA | Canada | Ireland | Australia
India | New Zealand | South Africa

Penguin Books is part of the Penguin Random House group of companies
whose addresses can be found at global.penguinrandomhouse.com.

This collection first published in hardback in Penguin Classics 2020
Paperback edition published 2021
001

Typeset by Jouve (UK), Milton Keynes
Printed and bound in Great Britain by Clays Ltd, Elcograf S.p.A.

A CIP catalogue record for this book is available from the British Library

The authorized representative in the EEA is Penguin Random House Ireland,
Morrison Chambers, 32 Nassau Street, Dublin D02 YH68

ISBN: 978-0-241-43431-4

www.greenpenguin.co.uk

Contents

Contents

Contents

Introduction

Literary genres have their heydays. Sometimes circumstances collide, and permit a particular literary form to rise to spectacular heights of expressive power. We can observe an explosion in English drama between the late 1580s and the 1620s, encompassing the careers of Marlowe, Jonson, Shakespeare and many others. Lyric poetry in England surpassed itself after the publication of *Lyrical Ballads* in 1798. Often, these periods prove quite short, rarely lasting more than thirty years in the first flush of excitement and brilliance.

It's the argument of this anthology that a comparable period of literary achievement occurred in the short story in Britain in the quarter century between 1890 and the outbreak of the First World War in 1914. This period encompassed the short story as practised by Kipling, Hardy, Lawrence, Joyce, Conrad, Bennett, Conan Doyle, Mansfield, Wells, Henry James, 'Saki', Forster and many others. There would be short fiction before, and there would be no shortage of masterpieces produced in the decades afterwards. But it was in those years that the most concentrated explosion of talent took place.

Such an explosion doesn't take place because of talent, or ability, alone. It takes place because the relationships between the people who write, and the people who read, take a particular and a propitious form, and because the means of distribution start to favour particular types of writing. The nature of the audience changes; the practicalities of publishing make things possible. In this case, talent was revealed by a propitious publishing environment; talent was given the opportunity to exercise itself repeatedly; repeated opportunities let writers develop and learn; the talent that had been revealed developed, quite often, into something much bigger. Writers see either that a readership on a large scale is achievable, or choose to produce something that defines itself in opposition to that large-scale readership. In either case, a literary form becomes more important than before. Whether the result is a hugely rewarded and enjoyed short story about Sherlock Holmes, a world-sweeping few pages about the future of science by H. G. Wells, or an exquisite, withdrawn vignette by George Egerton or Katherine Mansfield, only meant to appeal to the sophisticated few, space has been opened up that hardly existed before.

This anthology attempts to capture the sometimes bewildering variety in the short story in this period. Literary genres quickly took shape, were polished to perfection, turned upside down and reinvented – the detective story, the ghost story, the tale of fantasy. The short story would do for picaresque investigations of an entire society, like Bennett's 'The Death of Simon Fuge', or for the ravishingly cryptic expressions of inward delusions, like Henry James's 'The Figure in the Carpet'. It could be as specific about technology which does not yet exist as Wells's 'The Argonauts of the Air' or as studiously vague about those developments as Forster's 'The Celestial Omnibus'. Dense realism in the modest genius of Mary Mann or George Gissing; the unreal and impossible brought to the pitch of the reader's unquestioning belief in Kipling, M. R. James, or Saki. An author profoundly attuned to the most sophisticated international developments in fiction could produce Somerville and Ross, deeply inspired by Turgenev (and there were assessments of Chekhov's stories in England as early as 1891), Arnold Bennett with his obsession with French and Russian realists, or George Moore, closer to Flaubert and Maupassant than any English writer; other writers could not be more profoundly rooted in a specifically British aesthetic, such as Hardy's brutal myth, or W. S. Gilbert's flippant cynicism. The short story was used to talk to a readership about remote places and ways of doing things – Lawrence's terrible warning of the sexual frenzy underneath Prussian military culture, or Kipling's unforgettable evocation of the Indian climate, the last day before the monsoon, when 'now and again a spot of almost boiling water would fall on the dust with the flop of a frog'. Or it might just open up the true history of our neighbours – so unlike us, and until Israel Zangwill decided to write about the Jews in the East End, as unknown to us as Kipling's Pathans.

In short, this is one of the richest and most accomplished moments in literary history. If we now underestimate the colossal energy of the short story in this period, it may be because for decades now, most short stories have occupied a secondary place to the full-length novel in writers' oeuvres, and we have a tendency to project this personal hierarchy of genres into the careers of past writers. But, clearly, there were many more writers then who could create a substantial reputation without having to trouble with the full-length form, like M. R. James, Saki, George Egerton or Katherine Mansfield. For many others, there is no real reason to think the short story in this period a subordinate or inferior endeavour to their novels for writers as different as Kipling, Morrison, Lawrence, Beerbohm, Conan Doyle, Wells or Chesterton. Wells stopped writing short stories when he was rich enough to do so, but he certainly took the form very seriously before that. The place that the short story occupied in the careers of Henry James or Conrad is quite unprecedented. Although a Conrad short story or a James short story in a magazine is unlikely to have pulled in thousands of casual readers as a new Sherlock Holmes would, it's clear that it was a guarantee of a magazine's quality, and much of their best writing in this period came in periodical form – 'Heart of Darkness' and 'Typhoon', 'The Beast in the Jungle' and 'The Jolly Corner'. To go back to the period and try to read the short fiction, not as a trivial annex to the main achievement, but something through which names and fortunes were made, and where a huge readership could be achieved, is to understand quite why these great writers put the short story at the centre of their creative practice, and quite why they achieved so much through it.

The circumstances that enabled the achievement of the short story in these years are a combination of things. The first factor was the rapid approach to universal literacy after the introduction of compulsory free education. By the end of our period, literacy was universal. If, at the end of the 1830s, marriage registers show that literacy had reached only fifty-two per cent, by 1914 ninety-nine per cent of the population could read and write. This was at a period when only sixty per cent of the Italian population, for instance, were literate. The literary education that that generation had, moreover, was to our eyes astonishingly demanding. The 1871 *Grade Lesson Books in Six Standards, Especially Adapted to Meet the Requirements of the New Code* gave children 'Chaucer, Spenser, Shakespeare, Milton, Pope,

Cervantes, Goldsmith, Gilbert White and Dickens'.* If you want an explanation of the existence of a mass audience that could lap up a story as challenging and subtle as Kipling's 'Mrs Bathurst', the answer may lie in the ambitions of the parliamentary acts which, between 1870 and 1880, imposed universal compulsory elementary education. Of course, most children never reached the higher levels of Milton and Spenser; but a very much larger reading public than before was being created.

There was, too, a steady movement to give readers much more for much less money. David Vincent observes that 'A penny would buy a 250-word broadside in the 1840s, a fifty page songbook or a 7,000 word serial by the 1860s, a 20,000 word novelette by the 1880s, and from 1896, with the appearance of Newnes's Penny Library of Famous Books, unabridged versions of classic texts.'† One of the most striking developments of the period is that you didn't have to be rich to read exciting new literature, reliable editions of the classics, see great art in ideal conditions if you lived in a great city like London, Manchester, Leeds or Liverpool, or hear superb concerts (a shilling in 1912 to hear Sir Henry Wood introduce London to Schoenberg's *Five Orchestral Pieces*). As we shall see, degrees of elitism and patterns of exclusion would gather strength in time. But to a large extent, technology and education together gave much wider access to culture, both classic and contemporary. In E. M. Forster, Leonard Bast and Helen Schlegel sit in the same row at the Queen's Hall, in *Howards End*; Maurice and Alec meet in the British Museum in *Maurice*, standing before the treasures as if on equal ground. In the end, other forms of mass entertainment would draw people away, and the triumph of cinema and radio in the 1920s, of television in the 1950s, would diminish the width of appeal of what seems to us astonishingly sophisticated culture.

Most commentators between 1890 and 1914 were disappointingly keen to dismiss a good deal of writing of popular appeal, or to make the point that those products of universal education could not have a true appreciation of excellence. E. M. Forster's character Leonard Bast reads Ruskin, Richard Jeffries, Meredith and Stevenson, but it is somehow not good

---

* David Vincent, *Literacy and Popular Culture: England 1750–1914* (Cambridge, 1989), p. 224.
† *Ibid.*, p. 211.

enough that he should do so; he plays Grieg on the piano, but 'badly, and vulgarly'; he hasn't heard of Monet or Debussy and can't pronounce *Tannhäuser*. It doesn't seem to occur to Forster that Bast might have quite readily come to learn how to pronounce a German title, and might in due course have heard of Debussy. In commentaries on real life, the rise of the magazines that created the short story often seemed to need explanation in terms of inadequately cultured or educated readers, or in the brutal and new demands of their lives. In 1901, the *Cornhill Magazine* inquired into the taste for periodical literature in a dialogue between a literary figure and a commuter, and concluded that 'To be wearied at the day's end, and read nothing that demands more concentrated attention than an illustrated magazine, is only human nature.'* An American observer, ten years before, had already tied the enthusiasm for short periodical fiction to the demands of large-city life: 'The clerks and artisans, shopgirls, dressmakers, and milliners, who pour into London every morning by the early trains, have, each and every one, a choice specimen of penny fiction with which to beguile the short journey, and perhaps the few spare minutes of a busy day.'† The tendency to dismiss the writing that ordinary people most enjoy is nothing new; in 1889 the *Fortnightly Review* was stating a truism when it wearily remarked that 'the general results, then, of our inquiry are first, that there is an enormous demand for works of fiction, to the comparative neglect of other forms of literature, and secondly, that there is a decided preference for books of a highly sensational character.'‡ All that may be true, but it is also quite clear that those 'choice specimens' of 'works of fiction' might be rubbish, or might, at this time, be great masterpieces. What was about to happen was the result of education and literacy; some leisure time in busy lives; some limited money to spend on pleasures; some confidence in what they liked, and some awareness that literature could give immediate pleasure of an outrageous kind, or present a challenge, and give more lasting and serious enjoyment.§

* Lang and X, 'A Working Man', 'The Reading Public', *Cornhill Magazine* (1901), p. 794.
† A. Repplier, 'English Railway Fiction' in *Points of View* (Boston, 1891), cited by Vincent.
‡ W. M. Gattie, 'What English People Read', *Fortnightly Review*, 52 (1889), p. 320.
§ The working class voices surveyed by Jonathan Rose in his classic *The Intellectual Life of the British Working Classes* (New Haven, 2001) appear to us astonishingly comfortable with some very demanding writing, from Milton to Ruskin.

The single fact that enabled the achievements of the short story in these years was the creation of a very successful magazine devoted to the form. This decisive publication was *The Strand* magazine, first published in 1891. Both imitators of this magazine and people who despised everything it represented were inspired by it to create more outlets for writers, and a larger audience still for literature. Magazines before then had frequently run short fiction, though it's noticeable that until quite recently before *The Strand* started up, the difference between a serialized novel and a single short story had to be explained to readers. In the 1870s the prospectus for the *New Quarterly Magazine* explained that each issue would contain 'Two or more Tales . . . The Tales will invariably be completed in the numbers in which they appear.' *The Strand* was probably the first magazine to take the strong decision that it would contain nothing but single short stories, and it made a colossal success of it. Quite soon, with the help of the huge success of Conan Doyle's Sherlock Holmes stories, it was selling half a million copies an issue.

Other things about *The Strand* stood out. Unlike any other publication before or, I suspect, since, it paid authors on acceptance and not on publication. It was soon in a position to pay enormous sums, too – hundreds of pounds to star authors for single short stories, up to £100 per thousand words. That helped to ensure that it had first sight of stories by any ambitious newcomer. It benefited, too, from developments in printing technology that meant it could come close to an initial ambition to print a picture on every page, and print on heavy, good quality paper. (It is a pleasure, 130 years after their printing, to read the bound volumes of *The Strand*, so good is the quality.) It got all sorts of incidental things right; the price of sixpence must have seemed a splendid bargain for so much, and as it was only published once a month, it would not have seemed a too regular extravagance. Many imitators foundered by trying to create a weekly magazine. One of the very sudden developments of 1890s literary history is the sudden demise of the three-volume novel, which had ruled literature for decades. By the 1890s, the unvarying price of thirty-one shillings and sixpence appeared extortionate, and it was killed off by the demands of the circulating libraries, the extraordinary phenomenon of Hall Caine's *The Manxman* ('THERE WILL BE NO EDITION IN THREE VOLUMES,' Heinemann's advertisement boldly proclaimed, going on to sell 400,000 copies), and the concentrated ridicule of advanced taste. The disappearance of three-volume novels was startlingly rapid. Between 1894 and 1895 the publication of three-volume novels fell from 184 to 52; in 1896 it halved again, to 25; and in 1897 only 4 were published.* The sudden death of this venerable form of fiction reflected the rise of very different forms. Among these was the astonishingly modern and exciting form of the short story. *The Strand* was only clearing the first steps of the path.

The Strand was such a huge success due to its ruthless marketing strategies, which included demands about length, a fairly standard 6,000 words,† a heavy reliance on advertising, and even requirements on authors to apologize on the page for being in the place of a more popular author this month, and including puffs within the short story for other, forthcoming stories or other productions of the publisher. It published many masterpieces, without a doubt, from Conan Doyle to P. G. Wodehouse, but there could be no question about the brutal vulgarity of much of its ambition. It was clear and unembarrassed, however, about the new readership it had discovered, and both flattered and celebrated it. In 'The Naval Treaty', the first of the Sherlock Holmes stories to be confidently spread across two issues, Holmes and Watson are travelling into London when Holmes comments on the 'big, isolated clumps of buildings rising up above the slates, like brick islands in a lead-coloured sea'. Watson knows what they are – the Board Schools. 'Lighthouses, my boy! Beacons of the future! Capsules, with hundreds of bright little seeds in each, out of which will spring the wiser, better England of the future.'‡ *The Strand* knew what it was about. It was in a position to create an entirely different vision of the short story, and had created a market strong enough to support many alternatives.

---

* P. Waller, *Writers, Readers and Reputations: Literary Life in Britain 1870–1918* (Oxford, 2006), p. 668.

† Reginald Pound, an editor of *The Strand*, said 'English short story writers were in thrall to a convention of length, six thousand words minimum. A writer submitting a story of lesser length had almost no chance of acceptance.' Pound, *Mirror of the Century: The Strand Magazine, 1891–1950*.

‡ John Carey, *The Intellectuals and the Masses* (Faber, 1992), p. 16, rightly stresses the unusual nature of this confident statement in imaginative literature.

One such alternative has always been rightly seen by posterity as a pinnacle of the short story in artistic terms. *The Yellow Book* in its three years' existence sealed the understanding of the short story as a literary form. Many artistically ambitious writers, such as Henry James or even the young Arnold Bennett might have felt that the restrictions *The Strand* imposed would not be welcoming; a journal like *The Yellow Book* might well be more open to extravagant or exquisite novelties, publishing stories without resolution, comfortable with ambivalence, ambiguity and daringly advanced social positions. When *The Yellow Book* had come to an end, its editor, Henry Harland, published a piece putting forward his idea of the short story:

> You begin by taking an impression. That is to say, you look about the universe, and you see something; and the thing you see produces within you a certain state of mind and a certain state of emotion . . . if you are an artist, you are constantly possessed by a desire to give your impression expression in the particular form of art that it is your joy and your despair to cultivate. We are assuming that your particular form of art is fiction. Very good: that story is a short story, no matter how many pages it may cover, in which you have expressed your impression with the greatest possible economy of means.*

What Harland was hardly likely to admit was that his endeavour was made possible by the huge success of *The Strand*, and defined itself with great clarity against almost everything that magazine did. *The Yellow Book* was quarterly rather than monthly, and much more ambitiously priced at five shillings. It is certain that Harland wanted to create a publication that most of the half million *Strand* buyers would not be able to understand or appreciate, and that they certainly would not be able to afford. It made a point, of course, of the relative sophistication of its contents, and the art it contained was reverentially presented on individual pages, rather than with short stories wrapped around it. Nevertheless, it is fair to say that it is *The Strand*'s colossal success that made the idea of something like *The*

---

* Henry Harland, 'Concerning the Short Story', *Academy* (5 June 1897), p. 7.

Yellow Book possible, and both publications benefited from developments in printing technology that made lavish illustration possible.

And *The Yellow Book* was only one of many enterprises which responded to the huge success of *The Strand*, and the way it apparently created a huge and hitherto unsuspected readership for a unproved literary form out of nothing. There were at least twenty-three magazines founded in the 1890s that published short fiction either significantly or exclusively, according to Dean Baldwin.* The impact went well beyond the magazine industry alone. The publisher John Lane went on from *The Yellow Book* to promoting the hitherto unsupported and occasional form of the single-volume collection by a single author. The *Keynotes* series, named after its first volume, by 'George Egerton' (Mary Chavelita Bright's pseudonym) issued nineteen collections in its life between 1894 and 1897. With its design by *The Yellow Book*'s picture editor Aubrey Beardsley and its taste for the aesthetic 'impression', it might be seen as another direct reaction against popular mass-market short fiction. It is worth noting, however, that this enterprise of Lane's demonstrates that the different camps were not as exclusionary as one might assume; he published two volumes in the series by one of the pillars of *The Strand*, Grant Allen.

Given the explosion in outlets, and the keen competition between publishers and editors for talent, the opportunities for the short story writer were unmatched in the 1890s as never before. Established magazines such as *Cassell's Family Magazine* turned to short fiction; rivals to *The Strand* created their own recurrent detectives or comic 'knuts', as the Edwardians called the Bertie Wooster type. The atmosphere of keen competition, experienced by those within the market as good or bad luck, is beautifully captured by one of the regulars in the *Strand* rival *Black and White*, Barry Pain. In his story included here, 'The Autobiography of an Idea', success or failure is seen as a random and often unwelcome gift; from this gift a fortune and a reputation can be made.

As the period goes on, the multiple attempts to carve out a distinctive place in a very lively market start to have unpredictable artistic consequences. In 1992, John Carey published a compelling historical polemic, *The Intellectuals and the Masses*, which argued that the creation of

---

* Dean Baldwin, *Art and Commerce in the British Short Story, 1880–1950* (London, 2013).

modernism was fundamentally a matter of class. By examining the writings of people like Wyndham Lewis, Lawrence, Ortega y Gasset and Virginia Woolf, Carey was able to show convincingly that the increasing abstruseness of literary modernism was created by an irrational hatred of the products of the 1871 Education Act. Many writers undoubtedly wanted to create something that not only could not be understood by the board-school products, but also could not be afforded by them. The narrative has factors which make it less than ideally straightforward. *The Strand* was certainly not above appealing to an old-fashioned feudal snobbery, and the aesthetes and modernists were often at the forefront of democratic and, especially, feminist movements which would spread power. To take an individual example, H. G. Wells both despised the masses and wrote stories that had great mass appeal. (Interestingly, his stories were published across the board, by *The Strand, The Yellow Book* and *Black and White*, among many others.) Lawrence was a product of the generous spread of culture, while despising that spread.

Nevertheless, an examination of the tendency of the short story shows a clear development from the aesthetic reaction of *The Yellow Book* through the proto-modernist writings of Ford Madox Hueffer's *The English Review* from 1908 and John Middleton Murry's *Rhythm* from 1911. By the start of the First World War we have undoubted, full-scale, rebarbative modernism in the form of Wyndham Lewis and Ezra Pound's Vorticist magazine, *Blast*. It was published, like *The Yellow Book* of twenty years before, by John Lane, and lasted for two issues in 1914–15 – I've included a story from it by Rebecca West. These publishers found it very difficult to get the price of their magazines right – John Middleton Murry's *Rhythm* was priced at four shillings, and its successor *The Blue Review* at only one. A challenge, too, to all magazine publishers, was working out what the market would bear in terms of regularity of publication – *Black and White* struggled with weekly publication for an aesthetically minded journal. In short, most reactions to mass-market short fiction lasted two or three years at most. But two or three years is not nothing, and the huge market for short fiction that *The Strand* had opened up created an enormous number of possibilities for anyone wanting to try their luck.

The end result is what I have called it, a golden age of short story writing. I've concentrated on the practical and publishing arrangements which created such a flood of excellence, but the reader should be in no doubt that the excellence, and the variety of that excellence, is the thing that draws us back. What many editors and commentators at the time got wrong, or did not understand, was that literature is not a zero-sum game, and not a competition with first, second and third places. The success of one form of writing and publishing did not obliterate others; rather, it created huge new possibilities for readers. Probably some people only read the sort of short stories that gathered half a million eager readers. There was no reason then to suppose that someone who read Joseph Conrad's stories in *The English Review* or Katherine Mansfield's in *Rhythm* might not also be extremely attached to the Sherlock Holmes stories, or would come to be a Jeeves aficionado. Some of those popular productions of the time were highly sophisticated, and demanded a serious level of culture in their readers; one of E. F. Benson's *Lucia* stories turns on its heroine mistakenly referring to 'inverted fifths' in a Debussy prelude; she comically mistakes her phrase for 'consecutive fifths'. On the other hand the most sophisticated writers were not above engineering a vulgar thrill for their readers that would not have been beyond the range of a popular magazine's illustrators: Conrad's 'The Secret Sharer', one of the most alluringly ambiguous stories of a very subtle writer, contrives a barnstorming climax as the ship heads for the rocks and the captain keeps his secret. It was published in *Harper's Magazine* in 1910.

In putting this selection together, I hope to have avoided the danger of coming down on one side or another, and choosing between the crowd-pleaser and the withdrawn impression. Most of the best stories of the period have both an exquisite refinement of treatment and a definite quality of gusto – the stunning pastiche of dry-as-dust scholasticism with which the M. R. James story begins proceeds by steps to one of the most electrifying paragraphs in English literature. I begin with Kipling, whose literary artistry and ambition are astonishing, and who also acquired a huge popularity beyond the elite intellectual and political circles of his origins (Edward Burne-Jones and Stanley Baldwin were relations). This is one of the most complex and ambitious, as well as thrilling, of his stories. That outward-going, inquisitive, informative quality is one of the hallmarks of the short story in this period. Often, it takes the form of an investigation of what, to the ordinary reader, may be a very unfamiliar setting – Somerville and Ross's rural, feudal Ireland, Bennett's supremely accomplished and sybaritic provincial intellectuals, Zangwill's immigrant community. How things are done was a pillar of the informative non-fiction article in magazines for decades – it is one of the joys of Dickens's family journals, for instance – and it often spills over into fictional form. You would be very well informed about how ships can be steered from Conrad, or the practice of archaeology even from one of the most fantastic of M. R. James's stories. Evident authenticity about specific corners of human activity could reach outwards, or could be satisfied with a richly informative account of what it was like to be a writer, like Pain or Henry James. The possibilities of the literary or the publishing life have dramatic potential in George Egerton, and Kipling's wonderfully well-recalled setting of an Indian newspaper, too.

It is worth emphasizing, in the light of the short story's subsequent history, that it engaged with a good deal of energy with current political and social questions. I hope my selection goes some way to suggest what a significant part was played by short story writers in the question of women's lives, from the 'New Woman' of the 1890s, in Ella D'Arcy, George Egerton and Olive Schreiner, through suffrage movements and on to statements of women's sexual freedom in Charlotte Mew, Katherine Mansfield and Rebecca West. I thought West's torrid and excessive story an interesting counterpart to Lawrence's acknowledged classic of sexual sadism. Lawrence's story is not unusual in this period; unspoken homo-sexual passions are unmistakable in stories by Conrad, Saki, Forster, and even Joyce. Novels of the time by Musil, Mann, Gide, Proust and many others suggest that the subject was driving a much more universal anxiety than before or, perhaps, after.

That love of detail in support of authenticity enables a sublime vein of fantasy – Gilbert's extraordinary story, subsequently adapted and grossly toned down for one of his Sullivan collaborations, is followed by all sorts of bizarre impromptus. Quite a lot of these stories push the narrative staples of fiction to preposterous, self-parodying lengths – the tussle over the will in Arthur Morrison's glorious story, doom foretold in Beerbohm, or the secret life in Chesterton and Wilde. Hardy, Saki, Forster, M. R. James and E. F. Benson supply the impossible in a quotidian context. That pinnacle of horror in M. R. James's nerve-shredding story is attained in the physically specific, exactly described, in sentences whose grammar seems to be coming to pieces as the impossible becomes flesh. Horror grew to be one of the most compelling veins of the Edwardian short story; product of an age of great confidence that glimpsed something that would not be sated, lying in the corner, breathing heavily. I would have liked to have included Algernon Blackwood, too. I hope, nevertheless, that my selection conveys the feeling that I constantly had while reading through short stories of the period, that one could never be sure about what the next story in this month's issue was going to attempt. It is a period of remarkable confidence, with the confidence to do almost anything at all.

In making this selection, I've taken a broad view of what 'British' meant at the time, including writers from outside the British Isles whose career depended on London publishers, who often lived there, and who made an impact on British readers – Henry James, Olive Schreiner, Katherine Mansfield. I came close to including Bret Harte, too. Considering that the short story, especially in magazines, was a popular means of interesting British readers in ways of life in remote parts of the world, it would have distorted the picture to have omitted these authors. I have also included Irish writers, such as Somerville and Ross, George Moore and James Joyce – Ireland was, of course, a part of the United Kingdom in this period. After some thought, I left out short story writers whose best work was still to come, though they did publish in this period – Wodehouse, Walter de la Mare and Somerset Maugham.

This is the third anthology of the British short story I've published with Penguin, and the one that, I think, gave me the most pleasure to work on. It is a remarkable moment in literature, and one never likely to be repeated. It was a combination of happy accidents, unplanned but mutually helpful in unveiling talent, and helping that talent to a full flowering, one never envisaged before and hardly matched afterwards.

Philip Hensher

RUDYARD KIPLING

The Man Who Would be King

'Brother to a Prince and fellow to a beggar if he be found worthy.'

The Law, as quoted, lays down a fair conduct of life, and one not easy to follow. I have been fellow to a beggar again and again under circumstances which prevented either of us finding out whether the other was worthy. I have still to be brother to a Prince, though I once came near to kinship with what might have been a veritable King and was promised the reversion of a Kingdom – army, law-courts, revenue, and policy all complete. But, to-day, I greatly fear that my King is dead, and if I want a crown I must go hunt it for myself.

The beginning of everything was in a railway train upon the road to Mhow from Ajmir. There had been a Deficit in the Budget, which necessitated travelling, not Second-class, which is only half as dear as First-class, but by Intermediate, which is very awful indeed. There are no cushions in the Intermediate class, and the population are either Intermediate, which is Eurasian, or Native, which for a long night journey is nasty, or Loafer, which is amusing though Intoxicated. Intermediates do not buy from refreshment-rooms. They carry their food in bundles and pots, and buy sweets from the native sweetmeat-sellers, and drink the roadside water. That is why in the hot weather Intermediates are taken out of the carriages dead, and in all weathers are most properly looked down upon.

My particular Intermediate happened to be empty till I reached Nasirabad, when a big black-browed gentleman in shirt-sleeves entered, and, following the custom of Intermediates, passed the time of day. He was a wanderer and a vagabond like myself, but with an educated taste for whisky. He told tales of things he had seen and done, of out-of-the-way corners of the Empire into which he had penetrated, and of adventures in which he risked his life for a few days' food.

'If India was filled with men like you and me, not knowing more than the crows where they'd get their next day's rations, it isn't seven millions of revenue the land would be paying – it's seven hundred millions,' said he; and as I looked at his mouth and chin I was disposed to agree with him.

We talked politics – the politics of Loaferdom, that sees things from the underside where the lath and plaster is not smoothed off – and we talked postal arrangements because my friend wanted to send a telegram back from the next station to Ajmir, the turning-off place from the Bombay to the Mhow line as you travel westward. My friend had no money beyond eight annas, which he wanted for dinner, and I had no money at all, owing to the hitch in the Budget before mentioned. Further, I was going into a wilderness where, though I should resume touch with the Treasury, there were no telegraph offices. I was, therefore, unable to help him in any way.

'We might threaten a Station-master, and make him send a wire on tick,' said my friend, 'but that'd mean inquiries for you and for me, and I've got my hands full these days. Did you say you are travelling back along this line within any days?'

'Within ten,' I said.

'Can't you make it eight?' said he. 'Mine is rather urgent business.'

'I can send your telegram within ten days if that will serve you,' I said.

'I couldn't trust the wire to fetch him, now I think of it. It's this way. He leaves Delhi on the 23rd for Bombay. That means he'll be running through Ajmir about the night of the 23rd.'

'But I'm going into the Indian Desert,' I explained.

'Well *and* good,' said he. 'You'll be changing at Marwar Junction to get into Jodhpore territory – you must do that – and he'll be coming through Marwar Junction in the early morning of the 24th by the Bombay Mail. Can you be at Marwar Junction on that time? 'Twon't be inconveniencing you because I know that there's precious few pickings to be got out of these Central India States – even though you pretend to be correspondent of the *Backwoodsman*.'

'Have you ever tried that trick?' I asked.

'Again and again, but the Residents find you out, and then you get escorted to the border before you've time to get your knife into them. But

about my friend here. I *must* give him a word o' mouth to tell him what's
come to me or else he won't know where to go. I would take it more than
kind of you if you was to come out of Central India in time to catch him
at Marwar Junction, and say to him: "He has gone South for the week."
He'll know what that means. He's a big man with a red beard, and a great
swell he is. You'll find him sleeping like a gentleman with all his luggage
round him in a second-class compartment. But don't you be afraid. Slip
down the window, and say: "He has gone South for the week," and he'll
tumble. It's only cutting your time of stay in those parts by two days. I
ask you as a stranger – going to the West,' he said with emphasis.

'Where have *you* come from?' said I.

'From the East,' said he, 'and I am hoping that you will give him the
message on the Square – for the sake of my Mother as well as your own.'

Englishmen are not usually softened by appeals to the memory of their
mothers, but for certain reasons, which will be fully apparent I saw fit to
agree.

'It's more than a little matter,' said he, 'and that's why I asked you to
do it – and now I know that I can depend on you doing it. A second-class
carriage at Marwar Junction, and a red-haired man asleep in it. You'll be
sure to remember. I get out at the next station and I must hold on there
till he comes or sends me what I want.'

'I'll give the message if I catch him,' I said, 'and for the sake of your
Mother as well as mine I'll give you a word of advice. Don't try to run
the Central India States just now as the correspondent of the *Backwoodsman*. There's a real one knocking about there, and it might lead to trouble.'

'Thank you,' said he simply, 'and when will the swine be gone? I can't
starve because he's is ruining my work. I wanted to get hold of the Degumber Rajah down here about his father's widow, and give him a jump.'

'What did you do to his father's widow, then?'

'Filled her up with red pepper and slippered her to death as she hung
from a beam. I found that out myself, and I'm the only man that would
dare going into the State to get hush-money for it. They'll try to poison
me, same as they did in Chortumna when I went on the loot there. But
you'll give the man at Marwar Junction my message?'

He got out at a little roadside station, and I reflected. I had heard, more
than once, of men personating correspondents of newspapers and bleeding

small Native States with threats of exposure, but I had never met any of the caste before. They lead a hard life, and generally die with great suddenness. The Native States have a wholesome horror of English newspapers which may throw light on their peculiar methods of government, and do their best to choke correspondents with champagne, or drive them out of their mind with four-in-hand barouches. They do not understand that nobody cares a straw for the internal administration of Native States so long as oppression and crime are kept within decent limits, and the ruler is not drugged, drunk, or diseased from one end of the year to the other. They are the dark places of the earth, full of unimaginable cruelty, touching the Railway and Telegraph on one side, and, on the other, the days of Harun-al-Rasehid. When I left the train I did business with divers Kings, and in eight days passed through many changes of life. Sometimes I wore dress-clothes and consorted with Princes and Politicals, drinking from crystal and eating from silver. Sometimes I lay out upon the ground and devoured what I could get, from a plate made of leaves, and drank the running water, and slept under the same rug as my servant. It was all in the day's work.

Then I headed for the Great Indian Desert upon the proper date, as I had promised, and the night mail set me down at Marwar Junction, where a funny, little, happy-go-lucky, native-managed railway runs to Jodhpore. The Bombay Mail from Delhi makes a short halt at Marwar. She arrived as I got in, and I had just time to hurry to her platform and go down the carriages. There was only one second-class on the train. I slipped the window and looked down upon a flaming red beard, half covered by a railway rug. That was my man, fast asleep, and I dug him gently in the ribs. He woke with a grunt, and I saw his face in the light of the lamps. It was a great and shining face.

'Tickets again?' said he.

'No,' said I. 'I am to tell you that he has gone South for the week. He has gone South for the week!'

The train had begun to move out. The red man rubbed his eyes. 'He has gone South for the week,' he repeated. 'Now that's just like his impudence. Did he say that I was to give you anything? 'Cause I won't.'

'He didn't,' I said, and dropped away, and watched the red lights die out in the dark. It was horribly cold because the wind was blowing off the

4

sands. I climbed into my own train – not an Intermediate carriage this time – and went to sleep.

If the man with the beard had given me a rupee I should have kept it as a memento of a rather curious affair. But the consciousness of having done my duty was my only reward.

Later on I reflected that two gentlemen like my friends could not do any good if they forgathered and personated correspondents of newspapers, and might, if they blackmailed one of the little rat-trap states of Central India or Southern Rajputana, get themselves into serious difficulties. I therefore took some trouble to describe them as accurately as I could remember to people who would be interested in deporting them; and succeeded, so I was later informed, in having them headed back from the Degumber borders.

Then I became respectable, and returned to an office where there were no Kings and no incidents outside the daily manufacture of a newspaper. A newspaper office seems to attract every conceivable sort of person, to the prejudice of discipline. Zenana-mission ladies arrive, and beg that the Editor will instantly abandon all his duties to describe a Christian prize-giving in a back-slum of a perfectly inaccessible village; Colonels who have been overpassed for command sit down and sketch the outline of a series of ten, twelve, or twenty-four leading articles on Seniority *versus* Selection; Missionaries wish to know why they have not been permitted to escape from their regular vehicles of abuse and swear at a brother-missionary under special patronage of the editorial We; stranded theatrical companies troop up to explain that they cannot pay for their advertisements, but on their return from New Zealand or Tahiti will do so with interest; inventors of patent punkh-pulling machines, carriage couplings, and unbreakable swords and axle-trees, call with specifications in their pockets and hours at their disposal; tea-companies enter and elaborate their prospectuses with the office pens; secretaries of ball-committees clamour to have the glories of their last dance more fully described; strange ladies rustle in and say, 'I want a hundred lady's cards printed *at once*, please,' which is manifestly part of an Editor's duty; and every dissolute ruffian that ever tramped the Grand Trunk Road makes it his business to ask for employment as a proof-reader. And, all the time, the telephone-bell is ringing madly, and Kings are being killed on the

Continent, and Empires are saying, 'You're another,' and Mister Gladstone is calling down brimstone upon the British Dominions, and the little black copy-boys are whining, '*kaa-pi-chay-ha-yeh*' [copy wanted] like tired bees, and most of the paper is as blank as Modred's shield.

But that is the amusing part of the year. There are six other months when none ever comes to call, and the thermometer walks inch by inch up to the top of the glass, and the office is darkened to just above reading-light, and the press-machines are red-hot of touch, and nobody writes anything but accounts of amusements in the Hill-stations or obituary notices. Then the telephone becomes a tinkling terror, because it tells you of the sudden deaths of men and women that you knew intimately, and the prickly-heat covers you with a garment, and you sit down and writes 'A slight increase of sickness is reported from the Khuda Janta Khan District. The outbreak is purely sporadic in its nature, and, thanks to the energetic efforts of the District authorities, is now almost at an end. It is, however, with deep regret we record the death, etc.'

Then the sickness really breaks out, and the less recording and reporting the better for the peace of the subscribers. But the Empires and the Kings continue to divert themselves as selfishly as before, and the Foreman thinks that a daily paper really ought to come out once in twenty-four hours, and all the people at the Hill-stations in the middle of their amusements say: 'Good gracious! Why can't the paper be sparkling? I'm sure there's plenty going on up here.'

That is the dark half of the moon, and, as the advertisements say, 'must be experienced to be appreciated'.

It was in that season, and a remarkably evil season, that the paper began running the last issue of the week on Saturday night, which is to say Sunday morning, after the custom of a London paper. This was a great convenience, for immediately after the paper was put to bed, the dawn would lower the thermometer from 96° to almost 84° for half an hour, and in that chill – you have no idea how cold is 84° on the grass until you begin to pray for it – a very tired man could get off to sleep ere the heat roused him.

One Saturday night it was my pleasant duty to put the paper to bed alone. A King or courtier or a courtesan or a Community was going to die or get a new Constitution, or do something that was important on the other side of the world, and the paper was to be held open till the latest possible minute in order to catch the telegram.

It was a pitchy black night, as stifling as a June night can be, and the *loo*, the red-hot wind from the westward, was booming among the tinder-dry trees and pretending that the rain was on its heels. Now and again a spot of almost boiling water would fall on the dust with the flop of a frog, but all our weary world knew that was only pretence. It was a shade cooler in the press-room than the office, so I sat there, while the type ticked and clicked, and the night-jars hooted at the windows, and the all but naked compositors wiped the sweat from their foreheads, and called for water. The thing that was keeping us back, whatever it was, would not come off, though the *loo* dropped and the last type was set, and the whole round earth stood still in the choking heat, with its finger on its lip, to wait the event. I drowsed, and wondered whether the telegraph was a blessing, and whether this dying man, or struggling people, might be aware of the inconvenience the delay was causing. There was no special reason beyond the heat and worry to make tension, but, as the clock-hands crept up to three o'clock, and the machines spun their fly-wheels two or three times to see that all was in order before I said the word that would set them off, I could have shrieked aloud.

Then the roar and rattle of the wheels shivered the quiet into little bits. I rose to go away, but two men in white clothes stood in front of me. The first one said: 'It's him.' The second said: 'So it is!' And they both laughed almost as loudly as the machinery roared, and mopped their foreheads. 'We seed there was a light burning across the road, and we were sleeping in that ditch there for coolness, and I said to my friend here, "The office is open. Let's come along and speak to him as turned us back from the Degumber State,"' said the smaller of the two. He was the man I had met in the Mhow train, and his fellow was the red-haired man of Marwar Junction. There was no mistaking the eyebrows of the one or the beard of the other.

I was not pleased, because I wished to go to sleep, not to squabble with loafers. 'What do you want?' I asked.

'Half an hour's talk with you, cool and comfortable, in the office,' said the red-bearded man. 'We'd *like* some drink – the Contrack doesn't begin yet, Peachey, so you needn't look – but what we really want is advice. We

7

don't want money. We ask you as a favour, because we found out you did us a bad turn about Degumber State.'

I led them from the press-room to the stifling office with the maps on the walls, and the red-haired man rubbed his hands. 'That's something like,' said he. 'This was the proper shop to come to. Now, sir, let me introduce to you Brother Peachey Carnehan, that's him, and Brother Daniel Dravot, that is me, and the less said about our professions the better for we have been most things in our time. Soldier, sailor, compositor, photographer, proof-reader, street-preacher, *and* correspondent of the *Backwoodsman* when we thought the paper wanted one. Carnehan is sober, and so am I. Look at us first, and see that's sure. It will save you cutting into my talk. We'll take one of your cigars apiece, and you shall see us light up.'

I watched the test. The men were absolutely sober, so l gave them each a tepid whisky and soda.

'Well *and* good,' said Carnehan of the eyebrows, wiping the froth from his moustache. 'Let *me* talk now, Dan. We have been all over India, mostly on foot. We have been boiler-fitters, engine-drivers, petty contractors, and all that, and we have decided that India isn't big enough for such as us.'

They certainly were too big for the office. Dravot's beard seemed to fill half the room and Carnehan's shoulders the other half, as they sat on the big table. Carnehan continued: 'The country isn't half worked out because they that governs it won't let you touch it. They spend all their blessed time in governing it, and you can't lift a spade, not chip a rock, not look for oil, not anything like that, without all the Government saying, "Leave it alone, and let us govern." Therefore, such as it is, we will let it alone, and go away to some other place where a man isn't crowded and can come to his own. We are not little men, and there is nothing that we are afraid of except Drink, and we have signed a Contract on that. *Therefore*, we are going away to be Kings.'

'Kings in our own right,' muttered Dravot.

'Yes, of course,' I said. 'You've been tramping in the sun, and it's very warm night, and hadn't you better sleep over the notion? Come to-morrow.'

'Neither drunk nor sunstruck,' said Dravot. 'We have slept over the notion half a year, and require to see Books and Atlases, and we have decided that there is only one place now in the world that two strong men can Sar-a-*whack*. They call it Kafiristan. By my reckoning it's the top right-hand corner of Afghanistan, not more than three hundred miles from Peshawur. They have two-and-thirty heathen idols there, and we'll be the thirty-third and fourth. It's a mountaineous country, and the women of those parts are very beautiful.'

'But that is provided against in the Contrack,' said Carnehan. 'Neither Women nor Liquor, Daniel.'

'And that's all we know, except that no one has gone there, and they fight; and in any place where they fight, a man who knows how to drill men can always be a King. We shall go to those parts and say to any King we find – "D'you want to vanquish your foes?" and we will show him how to drill men; for that we know better than anything else. Then we will subvert that King and seize his Throne and establish a Dynasty.'

'You'll be cut to pieces before you're fifty miles across the Border,' I said. 'You have to travel through Afghanistan to get to that country. It's one mass of mountains and peaks and glaciers, and no Englishman has been through it. The people are utter brutes, and even if you reached them you couldn't do anything.'

'That's more like,' said Carnehan. 'If you could think us a little more mad we would be more pleased. We have come to you to know about this country, to read a book about it, and to be shown maps. We want you to tell us that we are fools and to show us your books.' He turned to the bookcases.

'Are you at all in earnest?' I said.

'A little,' said Dravot sweetly. 'As big a map as you have got, even if it's all blank where Kafiristan is, and any books you've got. We can read though we aren't very educated.'

I uncased the big thirty-two-miles-to-the-inch map of India, and two smaller Frontier maps, hauled down volume INF – KAN of the *Encyclopedia Britannica*, and the men consulted them.

'See here!' said Dravot, his thumb on the map. 'Up to Jagdallak, Peachey and me know the road. We was there with Roberts' Army. We'll have to turn off to the right at Jagdallak through Laghman territory. Then we get among the hills – fourteen thousand feet – fifteen thousand – it will be cold work there, but it don't look very far on the map.'

I handed him Wood on the *Sources of the Oxus*. Carnehan was deep in the *Encyclopedia*.

'They're a mixed lot,' said Dravot reflectively; 'and it won't help us to know the names of their tribes. The more tribes the more they'll fight, and the better for us. From Jagdallak to Ashang – H'mm!'

'But all the information about the country is as sketchy and inaccurate as can be,' I protested. 'No one knows anything about it really. Here's the file of the *United Services' Institute*. Read what Bellew says.'

'Blow Bellew!' said Carnehan. 'Dan, they're a stinkin' lot of heathens, but this book here says they think they're related to us English.'

I smoked while the men pored over Raverty, Wood, the maps, and the *Encyclopedia*.

'There is no use your waiting,' said Dravot politely. 'It's about four o'clock now. We'll go before six o'clock if you want to sleep, and we won't steal any of the papers. Don't you sit up. We're two harmless lunatics, and if you come to-morrow evening down to the Serai we'll say good-bye to you.'

'You *are* two fools,' I answered. 'You'll be turned back at the Frontier or cut up the minute you set foot in Afghanistan. Do you want any money or a recommendation down country? I can help you to the chance of work next week.'

'Next week we shall be hard at work ourselves, thank you,' said Dravot. 'It isn't so easy being a King as it looks. When we've got our Kingdom in going order we'll let you know, and you can come up and help us to govern it.'

'Would two lunatics make a Contrack like that?' said Carnehan, with subdued pride, showing me a greasy half-sheet of notepaper on which was written the following. I copied it, then and there, as a curiosity:

> *This contract between me and you persuing witnesseth in the name of*
> *God – Amen and so forth.*
> > *(One)*   *That me and you will settle this matter together; i.e. to be Kings*
> >   *of Kafiristan.*
> > *(Two)*   *That you and me will not, while this matter is being settled, look*
> >   *at any Liquor, nor any Woman black, white, or brown, so as*
> >   *to get mixed up with one or the other harmful.*
> > *(Three)* *That we conduct ourselves with Dignity and Discretion, and if*
> >   *one of us gets into trouble the other will stay by him.*

Signed by you and me this day,
　　Peachey Taliaferro Carnehan.
　　Daniel Dravot.
　　Both Gentlemen at Large.

'There was no need for the last article,' said Carnehan, blushing modestly; 'but it looks regular. Now you know the sort of men that loafers are – we *are* loafers, Dan, until we get out of India – and *do* you think that we would sign a Contrack like that unless we was in earnest? We have kept away from the two things that make life worth having.'

'You won't enjoy your lives much longer if you are going to try this idiotic adventure. Don't set the office on fire,' I said, 'and go away before nine o'clock.'

I left them still poring over the maps and making notes on the back of the 'Contrack'. 'Be sure to come down to the Serai to-morrow,' were their parting words.

The Kumharsen Serai is the great four-square sink of humanity where the strings of camels and horses from the North load and unload. All the nationalities of Central Asia may be found there, and most of the folk of India proper, Balkh and Bokhara there meet Bengal and Bombay, and try to draw eye-teeth. You can buy ponies, turquoises, Persian pussy-cats, saddle-bags, fat-tailed sheep and musk in the Kumharsen Serai, and get many strange things for nothing. In the afternoon I went down to see whether my friends intended to keep their word or were lying there drunk.

A priest attired in fragments of ribbons and rags stalked up to me, gravely twisting a child's paper whirligig. Behind him was his servant bending under the load of a crate of mud toys. The two were loading up two camels, and the inhabitants of the Serai watched them with shrieks of laughter.

'The priest is mad,' said a horse-dealer to me. 'He is going up to Kabul to sell toys to the Amir. He will either be raised to honour or have his head cut off. He came in here this morning and has been behaving madly ever since.'

'The witless are under the protection of God,' stammered a flat-cheeked Uzbeg in broken Hindi. 'They foretell future events.'

'Would they could have foretold that my caravan would have been cut up by the Shinwaris almost within shadow of the Pass!' grunted the Yusufzai agent of a Rajputana trading-house whose goods had been diverted into the hands of other robbers just across the Border, and whose misfortunes were the laughing stock of the bazar. 'Ohé, priest, whence come you and whither do you go?

'From Roum have I come,' shouted the priest, waving his whirligig; 'from Roum, blown by the breath of a hundred devils across the sea! O thieves, robbers, liars, the blessing of Pir Khan on pigs, dogs, and perjurers! Who will take the Protected of God to the North to sell charms that are never still to the Amir? The camels shall not gall, the sons shall not fall sick, and the wives shall remain faithful while they are away, of the men who give me place in their caravan. Who will assist me to slipper the King of the Roos with a golden slipper with a silver heel? The protection of Pir Khan be upon his labours!' He spread out the skirts of his gaberdine and pirouetted between the lines of tethered horses.

'There starts a caravan from Peshawur to Kabul in twenty days, *Huzrut*,' said the Yusufzai trader. 'My camels go therewith. Do thou also go and bring us good luck.'

'I will go even now!' shouted the priest. 'I will depart upon my winged camels, and be at Peshawur in a day! Ho! Hazar Mir Khan,' he yelled to his servant, 'drive out the camels, but let me first mount my own'

He leaped on the back of his beast as it knelt, and, turning round to me, cried: 'Come thou also, Sahib, a little along the road, and I will sell thee a charm – an amulet that shall make thee King of Kafiristan.'

Then the light broke upon me, and I followed the two camels out of the Serai till we reached open road and the priest halted.

'What d'you think o' that?' said he in English. 'Carnehan can't talk their patter, so I've made him my servant. He makes a handsome servant. 'Tisn't for nothing that I've been knocking about the country for fourteen years. Didn't I do that talk neat? We'll hitch on to a caravan at Peshawur till we get to Jagdallak, and then we'll see if we can get donkeys for our camels, and strike into Kafiristan. Whirligigs for the Amir, oh, Lor! Put your hand under the camel-bags and tell me what you feel.'

I felt the butt of a Martini, and another and another.

'Twenty of 'em,' said Dravot placidly. 'Twenty of 'em and ammunition to correspond, under the whirligigs and the mud dolls.'

'Heaven help you if you are caught with those things!' I said. 'A Martini is worth her weight in silver among the Pathans.'

'Fifteen hundred rupees of capital – every rupee we could beg, borrow, or steal – are invested on these two camels,' said Dravot. 'We won't get caught. We're going through the Khyber with a regular caravan. Who'd touch a poor mad priest?'

'Have you got everything you want?' I asked, overcome with astonishment.

'Not yet, but we shall soon. Give us a memento of your kindness *Brother*. You did me a service, yesterday, and that time in Marwar. Half my Kingdom shall you have, as the saying is.' I slipped a small charm compass from my watch-chain and handed it up to the priest.

'Good-bye,' said Dravot, giving me his hand cautiously. 'It's the last time we'll shake hands with an Englishman these many days. Shake hands with him, Carnehan,' he cried, as the second camel passed me.

Carnehan leaned down and shook hands. Then the camels passed away along the dusty road, and I was left alone to wonder. My eye could detect no failure in the disguises. The scene in the Serai proved that they were complete to the native mind. There was just the chance, therefore, that Carnehan and Dravot would be able to wander through, Afghanistan without detection. But, beyond, they would find death – certain and awful death.

Ten days later a native correspondent, giving me the news of the day from Peshawur, wound up his letter with: 'There has been much laughter here on account of a certain mad priest who is going in his estimation to sell petty gauds and insignificant trinkets which he ascribes as great charms to HH the Amir of Bokhara. He passed through Peshawur and associated himself to the Second Summer caravan that goes to Kabul. The merchants are pleased because through superstition they imagine that such mad fellows bring good fortune.'

The two, then, were beyond the Border. I would have prayed for them, but, that night, a real King died in Europe, and demanded an obituary notice.

The wheel of the world swings through the same phases again and again. Summer passed and winter thereafter, and came and passed again. The daily paper continued and I with it, and upon the third summer there fell a hot night, a night-issue, and a strained waiting for something to be telegraphed from the other side of the world, exactly as had happened before. A few great men had died in the past two years, the machines worked with more clatter, and some of the trees in the office garden were a few feet taller. But that was all the difference.

I passed over to the press-room, and went through just such a scene as I have already described. The nervous tension was stronger than it had been two years before, and I felt the heat more acutely. At three o'clock I cried, 'Print off,' and turned to go, when there crept to my chair what was left of a man. He was bent into a circle, his head was sunk between his shoulders, and he moved his feet one over the other like a bear. I could hardly see whether he walked or crawled – this rag-wrapped, whining cripple who addressed me by name, crying that he was come back. 'Can you give me a drink?' he whimpered, 'For the Lord's sake, give me a drink!'

I went back to the office, the man following with groans of pain, and I turned up the lamp.

'Don't you know me?' he gasped, dropping into a chair, and he turned his drawn face, surmounted by a shock of grey hair, to the light.

I looked at him intently. Once before had I seen eyebrows that met over the nose in an inch-broad black band, but for the life of me I could not recall where.

'I don't know you,' I said, handing him the whisky. 'What can I do for you?'

He took a gulp of the spirit raw, and shivered in spite of the suffocating heat.

'I've come back,' he repeated; 'and I was the King of Kafiristan – me and Dravot – crowned Kings we was. In this office we settled it – you setting there and giving us the books. I am Peachey – Peachey Taliaferro Carnehan, and you've been setting here ever since – oh, Lord!'

I was more than a little astonished, and expressed my feelings accordingly.

'It's true,' said Carnehan, with a dry cackle, nursing his feet, which were wrapped in rags. 'True as gospel. Kings we were, with crowns upon our heads – me and Dravot – poor Dan – oh, poor, poor Dan, that would never take advice, not though I begged of him!'

'Take the whisky,' I said, 'and take your own time. Tell me all you can recollect of everything from beginning to end. You got across the Border on your camels, Dravot dressed as a mad priest and you his servant. Do you remember that?'

'I ain't mad – yet, but I shall be that way soon. Of course I remember. Keep looking at me, or maybe my words will go all to pieces. Keep looking at me in my eyes and don't say anything.

I leaned forward and looked into his face as steadily as I could. He dropped one hand upon the table and I grasped it by the wrist. It was twisted like a bird's claw, and upon the back was a ragged red diamond-shaped scar.

'No, don't look there. Look at *me*,' said Carnehan. 'That comes afterwards, but for the Lord's sake don't distrack me. We left with that caravan, me and Dravot playing all sorts of antics to amuse the people we were with. Dravot used to make us laugh in the evenings when all the people was cooking their dinners – cooking their dinners, and . . . What did they do then? They lit little fires with sparks that went into Dravot's beard, and we all laughed – fit to die. Little red fires they was, going into Dravot's big red beard – so funny.' His eyes left mine and he smiled foolishly.

'You went as far as Jagdallak with that caravan,' I said at a venture, 'after you had lit those fires. To Jagdallak, where you turned off to try to get into Kafiristan.'

'No, we didn't neither. What are you talking about? We turned off before Jagdallak, because we heard the roads was good. But they wasn't good enough for our two camels – mine and Dravot's. When we left the caravan, Dravot took off all his clothes and mine too, and said we would be heathen, because the Kafirs didn't allow Mohammedans to talk to them. So we dressed betwixt and between, and such a sight as Daniel Dravot I never saw yet nor expect to see again. He burned half his beard, and slung a sheep-skin over his shoulder, and shaved his head into patterns. He shaved mine, too, and made me wear outrageous things to look like a heathen. That was in a most mountaineous country, and our camels couldn't go along any more because of the mountains. They were tall and black, and coming home I saw them fight like wild goats – there are lots of goats in Kafiristan. And these mountains, they never keep still, no more than the goats. Always fighting they are, and don't let you sleep at night.'

'Take some more whisky,' I said very slowly. 'What did you and Daniel Dravot do when the camels could go no farther because of the rough roads that led into Kafiristan?'

'What did which do? There was a party called Peachey Taliaferro Carnehan that was with Dravot. Shall I tell you about him? He died out there in the cold. Slap from the bridge fell old Peachey, turning and twisting in the air like a penny whirligig that you can sell to the Amir. – No; they was two for three ha'pence, those whirligigs, or I am much mistaken and woeful sore . . . And then these camels were no use, and Peachey said to Dravot – "For the Lord's sake let's get out of this before our heads are chopped off," and with that they killed the camels all among the mountains, not having anything in particular to eat, but first they took off the boxes with the guns and the ammunition, till two men came along driving four mules. Dravot up and dances in front of them, singing: "Sell me four mules." Says the first man: "If you are rich enough to buy, you are rich enough to rob"; but before ever he could put his hand to his knife, Dravot breaks his neck over his knee, and the other party runs away. So Carnehan loaded the mules with the rifles that was taken off the camels, and together we starts forward into those bitter cold mountaineous parts, and never a road broader than the back of your hand.'

He paused for a moment, while I asked him if he could remember the nature of the country through which he had journeyed.

'I am telling you as straight as I can, but my head isn't as good as it might be. They drove nails through it to make me hear better how Dravot died. The country was mountaineous, and the mules were most contrary, and the inhabitants was dispersed and solitary. They went up and up, and down and down, and that other party, Carnehan, was imploring of Dravot not to sing and whistle so loud, for fear of bringing down the tremenjus avalanches. But Dravot says that if a King couldn't sing it wasn't worth being King, and whacked the mules over the rump, and never took no heed for ten cold days. We came to a big level valley all among the mountains, and the mules were near dead, so we killed them, not having anything in special for them or us to eat. We sat upon the boxes, and played odd and even with the cartridges that was jolted out.

'Then ten men with bows and arrows ran down that valley, chasing twenty men with bows and arrows, and the row was tremenjus. They was fair men – fairer than you or me – with yellow hair and remarkable well built. Says Dravot, unpacking the guns: "This is the beginning of the business. We'll fight for the ten men," and with that he fires two rifles at the twenty men, and drops one of them at two hundred yards from the rock where he was sitting. The other men began to run, but Carnehan and Dravot sits on the boxes picking them off at all ranges, up and down the valley. Then we goes up to the ten men that had run across the snow too, and they fires a footy little arrow at us. Dravot he shoots above their heads and they all falls down flat. Then he walks over them and kicks them, and then he lifts them up and shakes hands all round to make them friendly like. He calls them and gives them the boxes to carry, and waves his hand for all the world as though he was King already. They takes the boxes and him across the valley and up the hill into a pine-wood on the top, where there was half-a-dozen big stone idols. Dravot he goes to the biggest – a fellow they call Imbra – and lays a rifle and a cartridge at his feet, rubbing his nose respectful with his own nose, patting him on the head, and saluting in front of it. He turns round to the men and nods his head, and says: "That's all right. I'm in the know too, and all these old jim-jams are my friends." Then he opens his mouth and points down it, and when the first man brings him food, he says: "No"; and when the second man brings him food, he says: "No"; but when one of the old priests and the boss of the village brings him food, he says: "Yes," very haughty, and eats it slow. That was how we came to our first village, without any trouble, just as though we had tumbled from the skies. But we tumbled from one of those damned rope-bridges, you see, and – you couldn't expect a man to laugh much after that?'

'Take some more whisky and go on,' I said. 'That was the first village you came into. How did you get to be King?'

'I wasn't King,' said Carnehan. 'Dravot he was the King, and a handsome man he looked with the gold crown on his head and all. Him and the other party stayed in that village, and every morning Dravot sat by the side of old Imbra, and the people came and worshipped. That was Dravot's order. Then a lot of men came into the valley, and Carnehan and Dravot picks them off with the rifles before they knew where they was, and runs down into the valley and up again the other side and finds another village, same as the first one, and the people all falls down flat on their faces, and Dravot says: "Now what is the trouble between you two villages?" and the people points to a woman, as fair as you or me, that was carried off, and Dravot takes her back to the first village and counts up the dead – eight there was. For each dead man Dravot pours a little milk on the ground and waves his arms like a whirligig, and "That's all right," says he. Then he and Carnehan takes the big boss of each village by the arm and walks them down into the valley, and shows them how to scratch a line with a spear right down the valley, and gives each a sod of turf from both sides of the line. Then all the people comes down and shouts like the devil and all, and Dravot says: "Go and dig the land, and be fruitful and multiply," which they did, though they didn't understand. Then we asks the names of things in their lingo – bread and water and fire and idols and such, and Dravot leads the priest of each village up to the idol, and says he must sit there and judge the people, and if anything goes wrong he is to be shot.

'Next week they was all turning up the land in the valley as quiet as bees and much prettier, and the priests heard all the complaints and told Dravot in dumb show what it was about. "That's just the beginning," says Dravot. "They think we're Gods." He and Carnehan picks out twenty good men and shows them how to click off a rifle, and form fours, and advance in line, and they was very pleased to do so, and clever to see the hang of it. Then he takes out his pipe and his baccy-pouch and leaves one at one village, and one at the other, and off we two goes to see what was to be done in the next valley. That was all rock, and there was a little village there, and Carnehan says: "Send 'em to the old valley to plant," and takes 'em there, and gives 'em some land that wasn't took before. They were a poor lot, and we blooded 'em with a kid before letting 'em into the new Kingdom. That was to impress the people, and then they settled down quiet, and Carnehan went back to Dravot, who had got into another valley, all snow and ice and most mountaineous. There was no people there and the Army got afraid, so Dravot shoots one of them, and goes on till he finds some people in a village, and the Army explains that unless the people wants to be killed they had better not shoot their little matchlocks; for they had matchlocks. We makes friends with the priest, and I stays there alone with two of the Army, teaching the men how to drill, and a thundering big Chief comes across the snow with kettle-drums and horns twanging, because he heard there was a new God kicking about. Carnehan sights for the brown of the men half a mile across the snow and wings one of them. Then he sends a message to the Chief that, unless he wished to be killed, he must come and shake hands with me and leave his arms behind. The Chief comes alone first, and Carnehan shakes hands with him and whirls his arms about, same as Dravot used, and very much surprised that Chief was, and strokes my eyebrows. Then Carnehan goes alone to the Chief, and asks him in dumb show if he had an enemy he hated. "I have," says the Chief. So Carnehan weeds out the pick of his men, and sets the two of the Army to show them drill, and at the end of two weeks the men can manoeuvre about as well as Volunteers. So he marches with the Chief to a great big plain on the top of a mountain, and the Chief's men rushes into a village and takes it; we three Martinis firing into the brown of the enemy. So we took that village too, and I gives the Chief a rag from my coat and says, "Occupy till I come"; which was scriptural. By way of a reminder, when me and the Army was eighteen hundred yards away, I drops a bullet near him standing on the snow, and all the people falls flat on their faces. Then I sends a letter to Dravot wherever he be by land or by sea.'

At the risk of throwing the creature out of train I interrupted: 'How could you write a letter up yonder?'

'The letter? – Oh! – The letter! Keep looking at me between the eyes, please. It was a string-talk letter; that we'd learned the way of it from a blind beggar in the Punjab.'

I remembered that there had once come to the office a blind man with a knotted twig and a piece of string which he wound round the twig according to some cipher of his own. He could, after the lapse of days or weeks, repeat the sentence which he had reeled up. He had reduced the alphabet to eleven primitive sounds, and tried to teach me his method, but I could not understand.

'I sent that letter to Dravot,' said Carnehan; 'and told him to come back because this Kingdom was growing too big for me to handle, and then I struck for the first valley, to see how the priests were working. They called the village we took along with the Chief, Bashkai, and the first village we took, Er-Heb. The priests at Er-Heb was doing all right, but they had a lot of pending cases about land to show me, and some men from another village had been firing arrows at night. I went out and looked for that village, and fired four rounds at it from a thousand yards. That used all the cartridges I cared to spend, and I waited for Dravot, who had been away two or three months, and I kept my people quiet.

'One morning I heard the devil's own noise of drums and horns, and Dan Dravot marches down the hill with his Army and a tail of hundreds of men, and, which was the most amazing, a great gold crown on his head. "My Gord, Carnehan," says Daniel, "this is a tremenjus business, and we've got the whole country as far as it's worth having. I am the son of Alexander by Queen Semiramis, and you're my younger brother and a God too! It's the biggest thing we've ever seen. I've been marching and fighting for six weeks with the Army, and every footy little village for fifty miles has come in rejoiceful; and more than that, I've got the key of the whole show, as you'll see, and I've got a crown for you! I told 'em to make two of 'em at a place called Shu, where the gold lies in the rock like suet in mutton. Gold I've seen, and turquoise I've kicked out of the cliffs, and there's garnets in the sands of the river, and here's a chunk of amber that a man brought me. Call up all the priests and, here, take your crown."

'One of the men opens a black hair bag, and I slips the crown on. It was too small and too heavy, but I wore it for the glory. Hammered gold it was – five pound weight, like a hoop of a barrel.

'"Peachey," says Dravot, "we don't want to fight no more. The Craft's the trick, so help me!" and he brings forward that same Chief that I left at Bashkai – Billy Fish we called him afterwards, because he was so like Billy Fish that drove the big tank-engine at Mach on the Bolen in the old days. "Shake hands with him," says Dravot, and I shook hands and nearly dropped, for Billy Fish gave me the Grip. I said nothing, but tried him with the Fellow Craft Grip. He answers all right, and I tried the Master's Grip, but that was a slip. "A Fellow Craft he is!" I says to Dan. "Does he know the Word?" – "He does," says Dan, "and all the priests know. It's a miracle! The Chiefs and the priests can work a Fellow Craft Lodge in a way that's very like ours, and they've cut the marks on the rocks, but they don't know the Third Degree, and they've come to find out. It's Gord's Truth. I've known these long years that the Afghans knew up to the Fellow Craft Degree, but this is a miracle. A God and a Grand-Master of the Craft am I, and a lodge in the Third Degree I will open, and we'll raise the head priests and the Chiefs of the villages."

'"It's against all the law," I says, "holding a Lodge without warrant from any one; and you know we never held office in any Lodge."

'"It's master-stroke o' policy," says Dravot. "It means running the country as easy as a four-wheeled bogie on a down grade. We can't stop to inquire now, or they'll turn against us. I've forty Chiefs at my heel, and passed and raised according to their merit they shall be. Billet these men on the villages, and see that we run up a Lodge of some kind. The temple of Imbra will do for the Lodge-room. The women must make aprons as you show them. I'll hold a levee of Chiefs to-night and Lodge to-morrow."

'I was fair run off my legs, but I wasn't such a fool as not to see what a pull this Craft business gave us. I showed the priests' families how to make aprons of the degrees, but for Dravot's apron the blue border and marks was made of turquoise lumps on white hide, not cloth. We took a great square stone in the temple for the Master's chair, and little stones for the officers' chairs, and painted the black pavement with white squares, and did what we could to make things regular.

'At the levee which was held that night on the hillside with big bonfires, Dravot gives out that him and me were Gods and sons of Alexander, and past Grand-Masters in the Craft, and was come to make Kafiristan a country where every man should eat in peace and drink in quiet, and 'specially obey us. Then the Chiefs come round to shake hands, and they were so hairy and white and fair it was just like shaking hands with old friends. We gave them names according as they was like men we had known in India – Billy Fish, Holly Dilworth, Pikky Kergan, that was Bazar-master when I was at Mhow, and so on, and so on.

'The most amazing miracles was at Lodge next night. One of the old priests was watching us continuous, and I felt uneasy, for I knew we'd have to fudge the Ritual, and I didn't know what the men knew. The old priest was a stranger come in from beyond the village of Bashkai. The minute Dravot puts on the Master's apron that the girls had made for him, the priest fetches a whoop and a howl, and tries to overturn the stone that Dravot was sitting on. "It's all up now," I says. "That comes of meddling with the Craft without warrant!" Dravot never winked an eye, not when ten priests took and tilted over the Grand-Master's chair – which was to say the stone of Imbra. The priest begins rubbing the bottom end of it to clear away the black dirt, and presently he shows all the other priests the Master's Mark, same as was on Dravot's apron, cut into the stone. Not even the priests of the temple of Imbra knew it was there. The old chap falls flat on his face at Dravot's feet and kisses 'em. "Luck again," says Dravot, across the Lodge to me; "they say it's the missing Mark that no one could understand the why of. We're more than safe now." Then he bangs the butt of his gun for a gavel and says: "By virtue of the authority vested in me by my own right hand and the help of Peachey, I declare myself Grand-Master of all Freemasonry in Kafiristan in this the Mother Lodge o' the country, and King of Kafiristan equally with Peachey!" At that he puts on his crown and I puts on mine – I was doing Senior Warden – and we opens the Lodge in most ample form. It was an amazing miracle! The priests moved in Lodge through the first two degrees almost without telling, as if the memory was coming back to them. After that, Peachey and Dravot raised such as was worthy – high priests and Chiefs of far-off villages. Billy Fish was the first, and I can tell you we scared the soul out of him. It was not in any way according to Ritual, but it served our turn. We didn't raise more than ten of the biggest men, because we didn't want to make the Degree common. And they was clamouring to be raised.

'"In another six months," says Dravot, "we'll hold another Communication, and see how you are working." Then he asks them about their villages, and learns that they was fighting one against the other, and was sick and tired of it. And when they wasn't doing that they was fighting with the Mohammedans. "You can fight those when they come into our country," says Dravot. "Tell off every tenth man of your tribes for a Frontier guard, and send two hundred at a time to this valley to be drilled. Nobody is going to be shot or speared any more so long as he does well, and I know that you won't cheat me, because you're white people – sons of Alexander – and not like common, black Mohammedans. You are *my* people, and by God," says he, running off into English at the end, "I'll make a damned fine Nation of you, or I'll die in the making!"

'I can't tell all we did for the next six months, because Dravot did a lot I couldn't see the hang of, and he learned their lingo in a way I never could. My work was to help the people plough, and now and again go out with some of the Army and see what the other villages were doing, and make 'em throw rope-bridges across the ravines which cut up the country horrid. Dravot was very kind to me, but when he walked up and down in the pine-wood pulling that bloody red beard of his with both fists I knew he was thinking plans I could not advise about, and I just waited for orders.

'But Dravot never showed me disrespect before the people. They were afraid of me and the Army, but they loved Dan. He was the best of friends with the priests and the Chiefs; but any one could come across the hills with a complaint, and Dravot would hear him out fair, and call four priests together and say what was to be done. He used to call in Billy Fish from Bashkai, and Pikky Kergan from Shu, and an old Chief we called Kafoozelum — it was like enough to his real name — and hold councils with 'em when there was any fighting to be done in small villages. That was his Council of War, and the four priests of Bashkai, Shu, Khawak, and Madora was his Privy Council. Between the lot of 'em they sent me, with forty men and twenty rifles and sixty men carrying turquoises, into the Ghorband country to buy those hand-made Martini rifles, that come out of the Amir's workshops at Kabul, from one of the Amir's Herati regiments that would have sold the very teeth out of their mouths for turquoises.

'I stayed in Ghorband a month, and gave the Governor there the pick of my baskets for hush-money, and bribed the Colonel of the regiment some more, and, between the two and the tribespeople, we got more than a hundred hand-made Martinis, a hundred good Kohat *jezails* that'll throw to six hundred yards, and forty man-loads of very bad ammunition for the rifles. I came back with what I had, and distributed 'em among the men that the Chiefs sent in to me to drill. Dravot was too busy to attend to those things, but the old Army that we first made helped me, and we turned out five hundred men that could drill, and two hundred that knew how to hold arms pretty straight. Even those corkscrewed, hand-made guns was a miracle to them. Dravot talked big about powder-shops and factories, walking up and down in the pine-wood when the winter was coming on.

'"I won't make a Nation," says he. "I'll make an Empire! These men aren't niggers; they're English! Look at their eyes — look at their mouths. Look at the way they stand up. They sit on chairs in their own houses.

They're the Lost Tribes, or something like it, and they've grown to be English. I'll take a census in the spring if the priests don't get frightened. There must be a fair two million of 'em in these hills. The villages are full o' little children. Two million people – two hundred and fifty thousand fighting men – and all English! They only want the rifles and a little drilling. Two hundred and fifty thousand men, ready to cut in on Russia's right flank when she tries for India! Peachey, man," he says, chewing his beard in great hunks, "we shall be Emperors – Emperors of the Earth! Rajah Brooke will be a suckling to us. I'll treat with the Viceroy on equal terms. I'll ask him to send me twelve picked English – twelve that I know of – to help us govern a bit. There's Mackray, Sergeant-pensioner at Segowli – many's the good dinner he's given me, and his wife a pair of trousers. There's Donkin, the Warder of Tounghoo jail. There's hundreds that I could lay my hand on if I was in India. The Viceroy shall do it for me. I'll send a man through in the spring for those men, and I'll write for a Dispensation from the Grand Lodge for what I've done as Grand-Master. That – and all the Sniders that'll be thrown out when the native troops in India take up the Martini. They'll be worn smooth, but they'll do for fighting in these hills. Twelve English and a hundred thousand Sniders run through the Amiris country in driblets – I'd be content with twenty thousand in one year – and we'd be an Empire. When everything was shipshape, I'd hand over the crown – this crown I'm wearing now – to Queen Victoria on my knees, and she'd say: 'Rise up, Sir Daniel Dravot.' Oh, it's big! it's big, I tell you! But there's so much to be done in every place – Bashkai, Khawak, Shu, and everywhere else."

'"What is it?" I says. "There are no more men coming in to be drilled this autumn. Look at those fat, black clouds. They're bringing the snow."

'"It isn't that," says Daniel, putting his hand very hard on my shoulder; "and I don't wish to say anything that's against you, for no other living man would have followed me and made me what I am as you have done. You're a first-class Commander-in-Chief, and the people know you; but – it's a big country, and somehow you can't help me, Peachey, in the way I want to be helped."

'"Go to your blasted priests, then!" I said, and I was sorry when I made that remark, but it did hurt me sore to find Daniel talking so superior when I'd drilled all the men, and done all he told me.

'"Don't let's quarrel, Peachey," says Daniel without cursing. "You're a King too, and the half of this Kingdom is yours; but can't you see, Peachey, we want cleverer men than us now – three or four of 'em, that we can scatter about for our Deputies. It's a hugeous great State, and I can't always tell the right thing to do, and I haven't time for all I want to do, and here's winter coming on and all." He stuffed half his beard into his mouth, all red like the gold of his crown.

'"I'm sorry, Daniel," says I. "I've done all I could. I've drilled the men and shown the people how to stack their oats better; and I've brought in those tinware rifles from Ghorband – but I know what you're driving at. I take it Kings always feel oppressed that way."

'"There's another thing too," says Dravot, walking up and down. "The winter's coming and these people won't be giving much trouble, and if they do we can't move about. I want a wife."

'"For God's sake, leave the women alone!" I says. "We've both got all the work we can, though I *am* a fool. Remember the Contrack, and keep clear o' women."

'"The Contrack only lasted till such time as we was Kings; and Kings we have been these months past," says Dravot, weighing his crown in his hand. "You go get a wife too, Peachey – a nice, strapping plump girl that'll keep you warm in the winter. They're prettier than English girls, and we can take the pick of 'em. Boil 'em once or twice in hot water and they'll come out like chicken and ham."

'"Don't tempt me!" I says. "I will not have any dealings with a woman not till we are a dam' sight more settled than we are now. I've been doing the work o' two men, and you've been doing the work o' three. Let's lie off a bit, and see if we can get some better tobacco from Afghan country and run in some good liquor; but no women."

'"Who's talking o' *women?*" says Dravot. "I said *wife* – a Queen to breed a King's son for the King. A Queen out of the strongest tribe, that'll make them your blood-brothers, and that'll lie by your side and tell you all the people thinks about you and their own affairs. That's what I want."

'"Do you remember that Bengali woman I kept at Mogul Serai when I was a platelayer?" says I. "A fat lot o' good she was to me. She taught me the lingo and one or two other things; but what happened? She ran away with the Station-master's servant and half my month's pay. Then she turned up at Dadur Junction in tow of a half-caste, and had the impidence to say I was her husband – all among the drivers in the running-shed too!"

'"We've done with that," says Dravot; "these women are whiter than you or me, and a Queen I will have for the winter months."

'"For the last time o' asking, Dan, do *not*," I says. "It'll only bring us harm. The Bible says that Kings ain't to waste their strength on women, 'specially when they've got a raw new Kingdom to work over."

'"For the last time of answering, I will," said Dravot, and he went away through the pine-trees looking like a big red devil, the sun being on his crown and beard and all.

'But getting a wife was not as easy as Dan thought. He put it before the Council, and there was no answer till Billy Fish said that he'd better ask the girls. Dravot damned them all round. "What's wrong with me?" he shouts, standing by the idol Imbra. "Am I a dog or am I not enough of a man for your wenches? Haven't I put the shadow of my hand over this country? Who stopped the last Afghan raid?" It was me really, but Dravot was too angry to remember. "Who bought your guns? Who repaired the bridges? Who's the Grand-Master of the Sign cut in the stone?" says he, and he thumped his hand on the block that he used to sit on in Lodge, and at Council, which opened like Lodge always. Billy Fish said nothing and no more did the others. "Keep your hair on, Dan," said I; "and ask the girls. That's how it's done at Home, and these people are quite English."

'"The marriage of the King is a matter of State," says Dan, in a red-hot rage, for he could feel, I hope, that he was going against his better mind. He walked out of the Council-room, and the others sat still, looking at the ground.

'"Billy Fish," says I to the Chief of Bashkai, "what's the difficulty here? A straight answer to a true friend."

'"You know," says Billy Fish. "How should a man tell you who knows everything? How can daughters of men marry Gods or Devils? It's not proper."

'I remembered something like that in the Bible; but if, after seeing us as long as they had, they still believed we were Gods 'twasn't for me to undeceive them.

'"A God can do anything," says I. "If the King is fond of a girl he'll not let her die." – "She'll have to," said Billy Fish. "There are all sorts of

Gods and Devils in these mountains, and now and again a girl marries one of them and isn't seen any more. Besides, you two know the Mark cut in the stone. Only the Gods know that. We thought you were men till you showed the sign of the Master."

'I wished then that we had explained about the loss of the genuine secrets of a Master-Mason at the first go-off; but I said nothing. All that night there was a blowing of horns in a little dark temple half-way down the hill, and I heard a girl crying fit to die. One of the priests told us that she was being prepared to marry the King.

'"I'll have no nonsense of that kind," says Dan. "I don't want to interfere with your customs, but I'll take my own wife." – "The girl's a little bit afraid," says the priest. "She thinks she's going to die, and they are a-heartening of her up down in the temple."

'"Hearten her very tender, then," says Dravot, "or I'll hearten you with the butt of a gun so you'll never want to be heartened again." He licked his lips, did Dan, and stayed up walking about more than half the night, thinking of the wife that he was going to get in the morning. I wasn't any means comfortable, for I knew that dealings with a woman in foreign parts, though you was a crowned King twenty times over, could not but be risky. I got up very early in the morning while Dravot was asleep, and I saw the priests talking together in whispers, and the Chiefs talking together too, and they looked at me out of the corners of their eyes.

'"What is up, Fish?" I says to the Bashkai man, who was wrapped up in his furs and looking splendid to behold.

'"I can't rightly say," says he; "but if you can make the King drop all this nonsense about marriage, you'll be doing him and me and yourself a great service."

'"That I do believe," says I. "But sure, you know, Billy, as well as me, having fought against and for us, that the King and me are nothing more than two of the finest men that God Almighty ever made. Nothing more, I do assure you."

'"That may be," says Billy Fish, "and yet I should be sorry if it was." He sinks his head upon his great fur cloak for a minute and thinks. "King," says he, "be you man or God or Devil, I'll stick by you to-day. I have twenty of my men with me, and they will follow me. We'll go to Bashkai until the storm blows over."

'A little snow had fallen in the night, and everything was white except the greasy fat clouds that blew down and down from the north. Dravot came out with his crown on his head, swinging his arms and stamping his feet, and looking more pleased than Punch.

'"For the last time, drop it, Dan," says I in a whisper. "Billy Fish here says that there will be a row."

'"A row among my people!" says Dravot. "Not much. Peachey, you're a fool not to get a wife too. Where's the girl?" says he with a voice as loud as the braying of a jackass. "Call up all the Chiefs and priests, and let the Emperor see if his wife suits him."

'There was no need to call any one. They were all there leaning on their guns and spears round the clearing in the centre of the pinewood. A lot of priests went down to the little temple to bring up the girl, and the horns blew fit to wake the dead. Billy Fish saunters round and gets as close to Daniel as he could, and behind him stood his twenty men with matchlocks. Not a man of them under six feet. I was next to Dravot, and behind me was twenty men of the regular Army. Up comes the girl, and a strapping wench she was, covered with silver and turquoises, but white as death, and looking back every minute at the priests.

'"She'll do," said Dan, looking her over. "What's to be afraid of, lass? Come and kiss me." He puts his arm round her. She shuts her eyes, gives a bit of a squeak, and down goes her face in the side of Dan's flaming red beard.

'"The slut's bitten me!" says he, clapping his hand to his neck, and, sure enough, his hand was red with blood. Billy Fish and two of his matchlock-men catches hold of Dan by the shoulders and drags him into the Bashkai lot, while the priests howl in their lingo: "Neither God nor Devil but a man!" I was all taken aback, for a priest cut at me in front, and the Army behind began firing into the Bashkai men.

'"God A'mighty!" says Dan. "What is the meaning o' this?"

'"Come back! Come away!" says Billy Fish. "Ruin and Mutiny's the matter. We'll break for Bashkai if we can."

'I tried to give some sort of orders to my men – the men o' the regular Army – but it was no use, so I fired into the brown of 'em with an English Martini and drilled three beggars in a line. The valley was full of shouting, howling people, and every soul was shrieking, "Not a God nor a Devil but only a man!" The Bashkai troops stuck to Billy Fish all they were worth, but their matchlocks wasn't half as good as the Kabul breech-loaders, and four of them dropped. Dan was bellowing like a bull, for he was very wrathy; and Billy Fish had a hard job to prevent him running out at the crowd.

'"We can't stand," says Billy Fish. "Make a run for it down the valley! The whole place is against us." The matchlock-men ran, and we went down the valley in spite of Dravot. He was swearing horrible and crying out he was a King. The priests rolled great stones on us, and the regular Army fired hard, and there wasn't more than six men, not counting Dan, Billy Fish, and me, that came down to the bottom of the valley alive.

'Then they stopped firing and the horns in the temple blew again. "Come away – for God's sake come away!" says Billy Fish. "They'll send runners out to all the villages before ever we get to Bashkai. I can protect you there, but I can't do anything now."

'My own notion is that Dan began to go mad in his head from that hour. He stared up and down like a stuck pig. Then he was all for walking back alone and killing the priests with his bare hands; which he could have done. "An Emperor am I," says Daniel, "and next year I shall be a Knight of the Queen."

'"All right, Dan," says I; "but come along now while there's time."

'"It's your fault," says he, "for not looking after your Army better. There was mutiny in the midst, and you didn't know – you damned engine-driving, plate-laying, missionary's-pass-hunting hound!" He sat upon a rock and called me every name he could lay tongue to. I was too heart-sick to care, though it was all his foolishness that brought the smash.

'"I'm sorry, Dan," says I, "but there's no accounting for natives. This business is our 'Fifty-Seven. Maybe we'll make something out of it yet, when we've got to Bashkai."

'"Let's get to Bashkai, then," says Dan, "and, by God, when I come back here again I'll sweep the valley so there isn't a bug in a blanket left!"

'We walked all that day, and all that night Dan was stumping up and down on the snow, chewing his beard and muttering to himself.

'"There's no hope o' getting clear," said Billy Fish. "The priests will have sent runners to the villages to say that you are only men. Why didn't you stick on as Gods till things was more settled? I'm a dead man," says

Billy Fish, and he throws himself down on the snow and begins to pray to his Gods.

'Next morning we was in a cruel bad country – all up and down, no level ground at all, and no food either. The six Bashkai men looked at Billy Fish hungry-ways as if they wanted to ask something, but they said never a word. At noon we came to the top of a flat mountain all covered with snow, and when we climbed up into it, behold, there was an Army in position waiting in the middle!

'"The runners have been very quick," says Billy Fish, with a little bit of a laugh. "They are waiting for us."

'Three or four men began to fire from the enemy's side, and a chance shot took Daniel in the calf of the leg. That brought him to his senses. He looks across the snow at the Army, and sees the rifles that we had brought into the country.

'"We're done for," says he. "They are Englishmen, these people, – and it's my blasted nonsense that has brought you to this. Get back, Billy Fish, and take your men away. You've done what you could, and now cut for it. Carnehan," says he, "shake hands with me and go along with Billy. Maybe they won't kill you. I'll go and meet 'em alone. It's me that did it. Me, the King!"

'"Go!" says I, "Go to Hell, Dan! I'm with you here. Billy Fish, you clear out, and we two will meet those folk."

'"I'm a Chief," says Billy Fish, quite quiet. "I stay with you. My men can go."

'The Bashkai fellows didn't wait for a second word, but ran off, and Dan and me and Billy Fish walked across to where the drums were drumming and the horns were horning. It was cold – awful cold. I've got that cold in the back of my head now. There's a lump of it there.'

The punkah-coolies had gone to sleep. Two kerosene lamps were blazing in the office, and the perspiration poured down my face and splashed on the blotter as I leaned forward. Carnehan was shivering, and I feared that his mind might go. I wiped my face, took a fresh grip of the piteously mangled hands, and said, 'What happened after that?'

The momentary shift of my eyes had broken the clear current.

'What was you pleased to say?' whined Carnehan. 'They took them without any sound. Not a little whisper all along the snow, not though the King knocked down the first man that set hand on him – not though old Peachey fired his last cartridge into the brown of 'em. Not a single solitary sound did those swines make. They just closed up tight, and I tell you their furs stunk. There was a man called Billy Fish, a good friend of us all, and they cut his throat, sir, then and there, like a pig: and the King kicks up the bloody snow and says: "We've had a dashed fine run for our money. What's coming next?" But Peachey, Peachey Taliaferro, I tell you, sir, in confidence as betwixt two friends, he lost his head, sir. No, he didn't neither. The King lost his head, so he did, all along o' one of those cunning rope-bridges. Kindly let me have the paper-cutter, sir. It tilted this way. They marched him a mile across that snow to a rope-bridge over a ravine with a river at the bottom. You may have seen such. They prodded him behind like an ox. "Damn your eyes!" says the King. "D'you suppose I can't die like a gentleman?" He turns to Peachey – Peachey that was crying like a child. "I've brought you to this, Peachey," says he. "Brought you out of your happy life to be killed in Kafiristan, where you was late Commander-in-Chief of the Emperor's forces. Say you forgive me, Peachey." – "I do," says Peachey. "Fully and freely do I forgive you, Dan." – "Shake hands, Peachey," says he. "I'm going now." Out he goes, looking neither right nor left, and when he was plumb in the middle of those dizzy dancing ropes – "Cut, you beggars," he shouts; and they cut, and old Dan fell, turning round and round and round, twenty thousand miles, for he took half an hour to fall till he struck the water, and I could see his body caught on a rock with the gold crown close beside.

'But do you know what they did to Peachey between two pine-trees? They crucified him, sir, as Peachey's hands will show. They used wooden pegs for his hands and his feet; and he didn't die. He hung there and screamed, and they took him down next day, and said it was a miracle that he wasn't dead. They took him down – poor old Peachey that hadn't done them any harm – that hadn't done them any – '

He rocked to and fro and wept bitterly, wiping his eyes with the back of his scarred hands and moaning like a child for some ten minutes.

'They was cruel enough to feed him up in the temple, because they said he was more of a God than old Daniel that was a man. Then they turned him out on the snow; and told him to go home, and Peachey came home in about a year, begging along the roads quite safe; for Daniel Dravot he walked before and said: "Come along, Peachey. It's a big thing we're doing." The mountains they danced at night, and the mountains they tried to fall on Peachey's head, but Dan he held up his hand, and Peachey came along bent double. He never let go of Dan's hand, he never let go of Dan's head. They gave it to him as a present in the temple, to remind him not to come again, and though the crown was pure gold, and Peachey was starving, never would Peachey sell the same. You knew Dravot, sir! You knew Right Worshipful Brother Dravot! Look at him now!'

He fumbled in the mass of rags round his bent waist; brought out a black horsehair bag embroidered with silver thread, and shook therefrom on to my table – the dried, withered head of Daniel Dravot! The morning sun that had long been paling the lamps struck the red beard and blind, sunken eyes; struck, too, a heavy circlet of gold studded with raw turquoises, that Carnehan placed tenderly on the battered temples.

'You behold now,' said Carnehan, 'the Emperor in his habit as he lived – the King of Kafiristan with his crown upon his head. Poor old Daniel that was a monarch once!'

I shuddered, for, in spite of defacements manifold, I recognized the head of the man of Marwar Junction. Carnehan rose to go. I attempted to stop him. He was not fit to walk abroad. 'Let me take away the whisky, and give me a little money,' he gasped. 'I was a King once. I'll go to the Deputy-Commissioner and ask to set in the Poorhouse till I get my health. No, thank you, I can't wait till you get a carriage for me. I've urgent private affairs – in the South – at Marwar.'

Ha shambled out of the office and departed in the direction of the Deputy-Commissioner's house. That day at noon I had occasion to go down the blinding hot Mall, and I saw a crooked man crawling along the white dust of the roadside, his hat in his hand, quavering dolorously after the fashion of street-singers at Home. There was not a soul in sight, and he was out of all possible earshot of the houses. And he sang through his nose, turning his head from right to left:

> 'The Son of God goes forth to war,
>   A kingly crown to gain;
> His blood-red banner streams afar!
>   Who follows in his train?'

I waited to hear no more, but put the poor wretch into my carriage and drove him off to the nearest missionary for eventual transfer to the Asylum. He repeated the hymn twice while he was with me, whom he did not in the least recognize, and I left him singing it to the missionary.

Two days later I inquired after his welfare of the Superintendent of the Asylum.

'He was admitted suffering from sunstroke. He died early yesterday morning,' said the Superintendent. 'Is it true that he was half an hour bare-headed in the sun at mid-day?'

'Yes,' said I, 'but do you happen to know if he had anything upon him by any chance when he died?'

'Not to my knowledge,' said the Superintendent.

And there the matter rests.

THOMAS HARDY

The Withered Arm

I

A LORN MILKMAID

It was an eighty-cow dairy, and the troop of milkers, regular and super-numerary, were all at work; for, though the time of the year was yet but early April, the feed lay entirely in water-meadows, and the cows were 'in full pail'. The hour was about six in the evening, and three-fourths of the large, red, rectangular animals having been finished off, there was opportunity for a little conversation.

'He brings home his bride to-morrow, I hear. They've come as far as Anglebury to-day.'

The voice seemed to proceed from the belly of the cow called Cherry, but the speaker was a milking-woman, whose face was buried in the flank of that motionless beast.

'Has anybody seen her?' said another.

There was a negative response from the first. 'Though they say she's a rosy-cheeked, tisty-tosty little body enough,' she added; and as the milk-maid spoke she turned her face so that she could glance past her cow's tail to the other side of the barton, where a thin, faded woman of thirty milked somewhat apart from the rest.

'Years younger than he, they say,' continued the second, with also a glance of reflectiveness in the same direction.

'How old do you call him, then?'

'Thirty or so.'

'More like forty,' broke in an old milkman near, in a long white pina-fore or 'wropper', and with the brim of his hat tied down so that he looked like a woman. 'A was born before our Great Weir was builded, and I hadn't man's wages when I laved water there.'

The discussion waxed so warm that the purr of the milk-streams became jerky, till a voice from another cow's belly cried with authority, 'Now then, what the Turk do it matter to us about Farmer Lodge's age, or Farmer Lodge's new mis'ess! I shall have to pay him nine pound a year for the rent of every one of these milchers, whatever his age or hers. Get on with your work, or 'twill be dark before we have done. The evening is pinking in a'ready.' This speaker was the dairy-man himself, by whom the milkmaids and men were employed.

Nothing more was said publicly about Farmer Lodge's wedding, but the first woman murmured, under her cow to her next neighbour, ' 'Tis hard for *she*,' signifying the thin, worn milkmaid aforesaid.

'Oh, no,' said the second. 'He hasn't spoke to Rhoda Brook for years.'

When the milking was done they washed their pails and hung them on a many-forked stand made of the peeled limb of an oak-tree, set upright in the earth, and resembling a colossal antlered horn. The majority then dispersed in various directions homeward. The thin woman who had not spoken was joined by a boy of twelve or thereabout, and the twain went away up the field also.

Their course lay apart from that of the others, to a lonely spot high above the water-meads, and not far from the border of Egdon Heath, whose dark countenance was visible in the distance as they drew nigh to their home.

'They've just been saying down in Barton that your father brings his young wife home from Anglebury to-morrow,' the woman observed. 'I shall want to send you for a few things to market, and you'll be pretty sure to meet 'em.'

'Yes, mother,' said the boy. 'Is father married, then?'

'Yes . . . You can give her a look, and tell me what she's like, if you do see her.'

'Yes, mother.'

'If she's dark or fair, and if she's tall – as tall as I. And if she seems like a woman who has ever worked for a living, or one that has always been well off, and has never done anything, and shows marks of the lady on her, as I expect she do.'

'Yes.'

They crept up the hill in the twilight, and entered the cottage. It was thatched, and built of mud-walls, the surface of which had been washed by many rains into channels and depressions that left none of the original flat surface visible, while here and there a rafter showed like a bone protruding through the skin.

She was kneeling down in the chimney-corner, before two pieces of turf laid together with the heather inward, blowing at the red-hot ashes with her breath till the turfs flamed. The radiance lit her pale cheek, and made her dark eyes, that had once been handsome, seem handsome anew. 'Yes,' she resumed, 'see if she is dark or fair; and if you can, notice if her hands are white; if not, see if they look as though she had ever done housework, or are milker's hands like mine.'

The boy again promised, inattentively this time, his mother not observing that he was cutting a notch with his pocket-knife in the beech-backed chair.

II

THE YOUNG WIFE

The road from Anglebury to Holmstoke is in general level; but there is one place where a sharp ascent breaks its monotony. Farmers homeward-bound from the former market-town, who trot all the rest of the way, walk their horses up this short incline.

The next evening, while the sun was yet bright, a handsome new gig, with a lemon-coloured body and red wheels, was spinning westward along the level highway at the heels of a powerful mare. The driver was a yeoman in the prime of life, cleanly shaven like an actor, his face being toned to that bluish-vermilion hue which so often graces a thriving farmer's features when returning home after successful dealings in the town. Beside him sat a woman, many years his junior – almost, indeed, a girl. Her face, too, was fresh in colour, but it was of a totally different quality – soft and evanescent, like the light under a heap of rose-petals.

Few people travelled this way, for it was not a turnpike-road; and the long white ribbon of gravel that stretched before them was empty, save of one small scarce-moving speck, which presently resolved itself into the figure of a boy, who was creeping on at a snail's pace, and continually looking behind him – the heavy bundle he carried being some excuse for, if not the reason of, his dilatoriness. When the bouncing gig-party slowed at the bottom of the incline before mentioned, the pedestrian was only a few yards in front. Supporting the large bundle by putting one hand on his hip, he turned and looked straight at the farmer's wife as though he would read her through and through, pacing along abreast of the horse.

The low sun was full in her face, rendering every feature, shade, and contour distinct, from the curve of her little nostril to the colour of her eyes. The farmer, though he seemed annoyed at the boy's persistent presence, did not order him to get out of the way; and thus the lad preceded them, his hard gaze never leaving her; till they reached the top of the ascent, when the farmer trotted on with relief in his lineaments – having taken no outward notice of the boy whatever.

'How that poor lad stared at me!' said the young wife.

'Yes, dear; I saw that he did.'

'He is one of the village, I suppose?'

'One of the neighbourhood. I think he lives with his mother a mile or two off.'

'He knows who we are, no doubt?'

'Oh, yes. You must expect to be stared at just at first, my pretty Gertrude.'

'I do – though I think the poor boy may have looked at us in the hope that we might relieve him of his heavy load, rather than from curiosity.'

'Oh, no,' said her husband, off-handedly. 'These country lads will carry a hundred-weight once they get it on their backs; besides, his pack had more size than weight in it. Now, then, another mile and I shall be able to show you our house in the distance – if it is not too dark before we get there.' The wheels spun round, and particles flew from their periphery as before, till a white house of ample dimensions revealed itself, with farm-buildings and ricks at the back.

Meanwhile the boy had quickened his pace, and turning up a by-lane some mile and a half short of the white farmstead, ascended towards the leaner pastures, and so on to the cottage of his mother.

She had reached home after her day's milking at the outlying dairy, and was washing cabbage at the doorway in the declining light. 'Hold up the net a moment,' she said, without preface, as the boy came up.

He flung down his bundle, held the edge of the cabbage-net, and as she filled its meshes with the dripping leaves she went on: 'Well, did you see her?'

'Yes, quite plain.'

'Is she lady-like?'

'Yes; and more. A lady complete.'

'Is she young?'

'Well, she's growed up, and her ways are quite a woman's.'

'Of course. What colour is her hair and face?'

'Her hair is lightish, and her face as comely as a live doll's.'

'Her eyes, then, are not dark like mine?'

'No – of a bluish turn; and her mouth is very nice and red, and when she smiles her teeth show white.'

'Is she tall?' said the woman, sharply.

'I couldn't see. She was sitting down.'

'Then do you go to Holmstoke Church to-morrow morning – e's sure to be there. Go early and notice her walking in, and come home and tell me if she's taller than I.'

'Very well, mother. But why don't you go and see for yourself?'

'*I* go to see her! I wouldn't look up at her if she were to pass my window this instant. She was with Mr Lodge, of course? What did he say or do?'

'Just the same as usual.'

'Took no notice of you?'

'None.'

Next day the mother put a clean shirt on the boy and started him off for Holmstoke Church. He reached the ancient little pile, when the door was just being opened, and he was the first to enter. Taking his seat by the font, he watched all the parishioners file in. The well-to-do Farmer Lodge came nearly last; and his young wife, who accompanied him, walked up the aisle with the shyness natural to a modest woman who had appeared thus for the first time. As all other eyes were fixed upon her, the youth's stare was not noticed now.

When he reached home his mother said 'Well?' before he had entered the room.

'She is not tall. She is rather short,' he replied.

'Ah!' said his mother, with satisfaction.

'But she's very pretty – very. In fact, she's lovely.' The youthful freshness of the yeoman's wife had evidently made an impression even on the somewhat hard nature of the boy.

'That's all I want to hear,' said his mother, quickly. 'Now spread the table-cloth. The hare you caught is very tender; but mind that nobody catches you. You've never told me what sort of hands she had.'

'I have never seen 'em. She never took off her gloves.'

'What did she wear this morning?'

'A white bonnet and a silver-coloured gown. It whewed and whistled so loud when it rubbed against the pews that the lady coloured up more than ever for very shame at the noise, and pulled it in to keep it from touching; but when she pushed into her seat it whewed more than ever. Mr Lodge, he seemed pleased, and his waistcoat stuck out, and his great golden seals hung like a lord's; but she seemed to wish her noisy gownd anywhere but on her.'

'Not she! However, that will do now.'

These descriptions of the newly married couple were continued from time to time by the boy at his mother's request, after any chance encounter he had had with them. But Rhoda Brook, though she might easily have seen young Mrs Lodge for herself by walking a couple of miles, would never attempt an excursion towards the quarter where the farm-house lay. Neither did she, at the daily milking in the dairy-man's yard on Lodge's outlying second farm, ever speak on the subject of the recent marriage. The dairy-man, who rented the cows of Lodge, and knew perfectly the tall milkmaid's history, with manly kindliness always kept the gossip in the cow-barton from annoying Rhoda. But the atmosphere thereabout was full of the subject during the first days of Mrs Lodge's arrival; and from her boy's description and the casual words of the other milkers, Rhoda Brook could raise a mental image of the unconscious Mrs Lodge that was realistic as a photograph.

III

A VISION

One night, two or three weeks after the bridal return, when the boy was gone to bed, Rhoda sat a long time over the turf-ashes that she had raked out in front of her to extinguish them. She contemplated so intently the new wife, as presented to her in her mind's eye, over the embers, that she forgot the lapse of time. At last, wearied with her day's work, she too retired.

But the figure which had occupied her so much during this and the previous days was not to be banished at night. For the first time Gertrude Lodge visited the supplanted woman in her dreams. Rhoda Brook dreamed – since her assertion that she really saw, before falling asleep, was not to be believed – that the young wife, in the pale silk dress and white bonnet, but with features shockingly distorted, and wrinkled as by age, was sitting upon her chest as she lay. The pressure of Mrs Lodge's person grew heavier; the blue eyes peered cruelly into her face; and then the figure thrust forward its left hand mockingly, so as to make the wedding-ring it wore glitter in Rhoda's eyes. Maddened mentally, and nearly suffocated by pressure, the sleeper struggled; the incubus, still regarding her, withdrew to the foot of the bed, only, however, to come forward by degrees, resume her seat, and flash her left hand as before.

Gasping for breath, Rhoda, in a last desperate effort, swung out her right hand, seized the confronting spectre by its obtrusive left arm, and whirled it backward to the floor, starting up herself, as she did so, with a low cry.

'Oh, merciful Heaven!' she cried, sitting on the edge of the bed in a cold sweat, 'that was not a dream – she was here!'

She could feel her antagonist's arm within her grasp even now – the very flesh and bone of it, as it seemed. She looked on the floor whither she had whirled the spectre, but there was nothing to be seen.

Rhoda Brook slept no more that night, and when she went milking at the next dawn they noticed how pale and haggard she looked. The milk that she drew quivered into her pail; her hand had not calmed even yet, and still retained the feel of the arm. She came home to breakfast as wearily as if it had been supper-time.

'What was that noise in your chimmer, mother, last night?' said her son. 'You fell off the bed, surely?'

'Did you hear anything fall? At what time?'

'Just when the clock struck two.'

She could not explain, and when the meal was done went silently about her housework, the boy assisting her, for he hated going afield on the farms, and she indulged his reluctance. Between eleven and twelve the garden gate clicked, and she lifted her eyes to the window. At the bottom of the garden, within the gate, stood the woman of her vision. Rhoda seemed transfixed.

'Ah, she said she would come!' exclaimed the boy, also observing her.

'Said so – when? How does she know us?'

'I have seen and spoken to her. I talked to her yesterday.'

'I told you,' said the mother, flushing indignantly, 'never to speak to anybody in that house, or go near the place.'

'I did not speak to her till she spoke to me. And I did not go near the place. I met her in the road.'

'What did you tell her?'

'Nothing. She said, "Are you the poor boy who had to bring the heavy load from market?" And she looked at my boots, and said they would not keep my feet dry if it came on wet, because they were so cracked. I told her I lived with my mother, and we had enough to do to keep ourselves, and that's how it was; and she said then, "I'll come and bring you some better boots, and see your mother." She gives away things to other folks in the meads besides us.'

Mrs Lodge was by this time close to the door – not in her silk, as Rhoda had seen her in the bedchamber, but in a morning hat, and gown of common light material, which became her better than silk. On her arm she carried a basket.

The impression remaining from the night's experience was still strong. Rhoda had almost expected to see the wrinkles, the scorn, and the cruelty on her visitor's face. She would have escaped an interview, had escape been possible. There was, however, no back door to the cottage, and in an instant the boy had lifted the latch to Mrs Lodge's gentle knock.

'I see I have come to the right house,' said she, glancing at the lad, and smiling. 'But I was not sure till you opened the door.'

The figure and action were those of the phantom; but her voice was so indescribably sweet, her glance so winning, her smile so tender, so unlike that of Rhoda's midnight visitant, that the latter could hardly believe the evidence of her senses. She was truly glad that she had not hidden away in sheer aversion, as she had been inclined to do. In her basket Mrs Lodge brought the pair of boots that she had promised to the boy, and other useful articles.

At these proofs of a kindly feeling towards her and hers, Rhoda's heart reproached her bitterly. This innocent young thing should have her blessing and not her curse. When she left them, a light seemed gone from the dwelling. Two days later she came again to know if the boots fitted; and less than a fortnight after that paid Rhoda another call. On this occasion the boy was absent.

'I walk a good deal,' said Mrs Lodge, 'and your house is the nearest outside our own parish. I hope you are well. You don't look quite well.'

Rhoda said she was well enough; and indeed, though the paler of the two, there was more of the strength that endures in her well-defined features and large frame than in the soft-cheeked young woman before her. The conversation became quite confidential as regarded their powers and weaknesses; and when Mrs Lodge was leaving, Rhoda said, 'I hope you will find this air agree with you, ma'am, and not suffer from the damp of the water-meads.'

The younger one replied that there was not much doubt of it, her general health being usually good. 'Though, now you remind me,' she added, 'I have one little ailment which puzzles me. It is nothing serious, but I cannot make it out.'

She uncovered her left hand and arm; and their outline confronted Rhoda's gaze as the exact original of the limb she had beheld and seized in her dream. Upon the pink round surface of the arm were faint marks of an unhealthy colour, as if produced by a rough grasp. Rhoda's eyes became riveted on the discolorations; she fancied that she discerned in them the shape of her own four fingers.

'How did it happen?' she said, mechanically.

'I cannot tell,' replied Mrs Lodge, shaking her head. 'One night when I was sound asleep, dreaming I was away in some strange place, a pain suddenly shot into my arm there, and was so keen as to awaken me. I must have struck it in the daytime, I suppose, though I don't remember doing so.' She added, laughing, 'I tell my dear husband that it looks just as if he had flown into a rage and struck me there. Oh, I dare say it will soon disappear.'

'Ha, ha! Yes! On what night did it come?'

Mrs Lodge considered, and said it would be a fortnight ago on the morrow. 'When I awoke I could not remember where I was,' she added, 'till the clock striking two reminded me.'

She had named the night and the hour of Rhoda's spectral encounter, and Brook felt like a guilty thing. The artless disclosure startled her; she did not reason on the freaks of coincidence; and all the scenery of that ghastly night returned with double vividness to her mind.

'Oh, can it be,' she said to herself, when her visitor had departed, 'that I exercise a malignant power over people against my own will?' She knew that she had been slyly called a witch since her fall; but never having understood why that particular stigma had been attached to her, it had passed disregarded. Could this be the explanation and had such things as this ever happened before?

IV

A SUGGESTION

The summer drew on, and Rhoda Brook almost dreaded to meet Mrs Lodge again, notwithstanding that her feeling for the young wife amounted wellnigh to affection. Something in her own individuality seemed to convict Rhoda of crime. Yet a fatality sometimes would direct the steps of the latter to the outskirts of Holmstoke whenever she left her house for any other purpose than her daily work; and hence it happened that their next encounter was out-of-doors. Rhoda could not avoid the subject which had so mystified her, and after the first few words she stammered, 'I hope your – arm is well again, ma'am?' She had perceived with consternation that Gertrude Lodge carried her left arm stiffly.

'No; it is not quite well. Indeed it is no better at all; it is rather worse. It pains me dreadfully sometimes.'

'Perhaps you had better go to a doctor, ma'am.'

She replied that she had already seen a doctor. Her husband had insisted upon her going to one. But the surgeon had not seemed to understand the afflicted limb at all; he had told her to bathe it in hot water, and she had bathed it, but the treatment had done no good.

'Will you let me see it?' said the milkwoman.

Mrs Lodge pushed up her sleeve and disclosed the place, which was a few inches above the wrist. As soon as Rhoda Brook saw it she could hardly preserve her composure. There was nothing of the nature of a wound, but the arm at that point had a shrivelled look, and the outline of the four fingers appeared more distinct than at the former time. More-over, she fancied that they were imprinted in precisely the relative position of her clutch upon the arm in the trance; the first finger towards Gertrude's wrist, and the fourth towards her elbow.

What the impress resembled seemed to have struck Gertrude herself since their last meeting. 'It looks almost like finger-marks,' she said, add-ing, with a faint laugh, 'My husband says it is as if some witch, or the devil himself, had taken hold of me there, and blasted the flesh.'

Rhoda shivered. 'That's fancy,' she said hurriedly. 'I wouldn't mind it, if I were you.'

'I shouldn't so much mind it,' said the younger, with hesitation, 'if – if I hadn't a notion that it makes my husband – dislike me – no, love me less. Men think so much of personal appearance.'

'Some do – he for one.'

'Yes; and he was very proud of mine, at first.'

'Keep your arm covered from his sight.'

'Ah, he knows the disfigurement is there!' She tried to hide the tears that filled her eyes.

'Well, ma'am, I earnestly hope it will go away soon.'

And so the milkwoman's mind was chained anew to the subject by a horrid sort of spell as she returned home. The sense of having been guilty of an act of malignity increased, affect as she might to ridicule her super-stition. In her secret heart Rhoda did not altogether object to a slight diminution of her successor's beauty, by whatever means it had come about; but she did not wish to inflict upon her physical pain. For though this pretty young woman had rendered impossible any reparation which Lodge might have made Rhoda for his past conduct, everything like resentment at the unconscious usurpation had quite passed away from the elder's mind.

If the sweet and kindly Gertrude Lodge only knew of the scene in the bedchamber, what would she think? Not to inform her of it seemed treachery in the presence of her friendliness; but tell she could not of her own accord, neither could she devise a remedy.

She mused upon the matter the greater part of the night; and the next day, after the morning milking, set out to obtain another glimpse of Gertrude Lodge if she could, being held to her by a grewsome fascination. By watching the house from a distance the milkmaid was presently able to discern the farmer's wife in a ride she was taking alone; probably to join her husband in some distant field. Mrs Lodge perceived her, and cantered in her direction.

'Good morning, Rhoda!' Gertrude said, when she had come up. 'I was going to call.'

Rhoda noticed that Mrs Lodge held the reins with some difficulty.

'I hope – the bad arm,' said Rhoda.

'They tell me there is possibly one way by which I might be able to find out the cause, and so perhaps the cure of it,' replied the other, anxiously. 'It is by going to some clever man over in Egdon Heath. They did not know if he was still alive – and I cannot remember his name at this moment; but they said that you knew more of his movements than anybody else hereabout, and could tell me if he were still to be consulted. Dear me – what was his name? But you know.'

'Not Conjuror Trendle?' said her thin companion, turning pale.

'Trendle – yes. Is he alive?'

'I believe so,' said Rhoda, with reluctance.

'Why do you call him conjuror?'

'Well – they say – they used to say he was a – he had powers other folks have not.'

'Oh, how could my people be so superstitious as to recommend a man of that sort? I thought they meant some medical man. I shall think no more of him.'

Rhoda looked relieved, and Mrs Lodge rode on. The milkwoman had inwardly seen, from the moment she heard of her having been mentioned as a reference for this man, that there must exist a sarcastic feeling among the work-folk that a sorceress would know the whereabouts of the exorcist. They suspected her, then. A short time ago this would have given no concern to a woman of her common sense. But she had a haunting reason to be superstitious now; and she had been seized with sudden dread that this Conjurer Trendle might name her as the malignant influence which was blasting the fair person of Gertrude, and so lead her friend to hate her forever, and to treat her as some fiend in human shape.

But all was not over. Two days after, a shadow intruded into the window-pattern thrown on Rhoda Brook's floor by the afternoon sun. The woman opened the door at once, almost breathlessly.

'Are you alone?' said Gertrude. She seemed to be no less harassed and anxious than Brook herself.

'Yes,' said Rhoda.

'The place on my arm seems worse, and troubles me!' the farmer's wife went on. 'It is so mysterious! I do hope it will not be a permanent blemish. I have again been thinking of what they said about Conjurer Trendle. I don't really believe in such men, but I should not mind just visiting him, from curiosity – though on no account must my husband know. Is it far to where he lives?'

'Yes – five miles,' said Rhoda, backwardly. 'In the heart of Egdon.'

'Well, I should have to walk. Could you not go with me to show me the way – say to-morrow afternoon?'

'Oh, not I – that is,' the milkwoman murmured, with a start of dismay. Again the dread seized her that something to do with her fierce act in the dream might be revealed, and her character in the eyes of the most useful friend she had ever had be ruined irretrievably.

Mrs Lodge urged, and Rhoda finally assented, though with much misgiving. Sad as the journey would be to her, she could not conscientiously stand in the way of a possible remedy for her patron's strange affliction. It was agreed that, to escape suspicion of their mystic intent, they should meet at the edge of the heath, at the corner of a plantation which was visible from the spot where they now stood.

V

CONJURER TRENDLE

By the next afternoon Rhoda would have done anything to escape this inquiry. But she had promised to go. Moreover, there was a horrid fascination at times in becoming instrumental in throwing such possible light on her own character as would reveal her to be something greater in the occult world than she had ever herself suspected.

She started just before the time of day mentioned between them, and half an hour's brisk walking brought her to the south-eastern extension of the Egdon tract of country, where the fir plantation was. A slight figure, cloaked and veiled, was already there. Rhoda recognized, almost with a shudder, that Mrs Lodge bore her left arm in a sling.

They hardly spoke to each other, and immediately set out on their climb into the interior of this solemn country, which stood high above the rich alluvial soil they had left half an hour before. It was a long walk; thick clouds made the atmosphere dark, though it was as yet only early afternoon; and the wind howled dismally over the hills of the heath – not improbably the same heath which had witnessed the agony of the Wessex King Ina, presented to after-ages as Lear. Gertrude Lodge talked most, Rhoda replying with monosyllabic preoccupation. She had a strange dislike to walking on the side of her companion where hung the afflicted arm, moving round to the other when inadvertently near it. Much heather had been brushed by their feet when they descended upon a cart-track, beside which stood the house of the man they sought.

He did not profess his remedial practices openly, or care anything about their continuance, his direct interests being those of a dealer in furze, turf, 'sharp sand', and other local products. Indeed, he affected not to believe largely in his own powers, and when warts that had been shown him for cure miraculously disappeared – which it must be owned they infallibly did – he would say lightly, 'Oh, I only drink a glass of grog upon 'em – perhaps it's all chance,' and immediately turn the subject.

He was at home when they arrived, having, in fact, seen them descending into his valley. He was a gray-bearded man, with a reddish face, and he looked singularly at Rhoda the first moment he beheld her. Mrs Lodge told him her errand, and then with words of self-disparagement he examined her arm.

'Medicine can't cure it,' he said, promptly. ' 'Tis the work of an enemy.'

Rhoda shrank into herself and drew back.

'An enemy? What enemy?' asked Mrs Lodge.

He shook his head. 'That's best known to yourself,' he said. 'If you like

I can show the person to you, though I shall not myself know who it is. I can do no more, and don't wish to do that.'

She pressed him; on which he told Rhoda to wait outside where she stood, and took Mrs Lodge into the room. It opened immediately from the door; and, as the latter remained ajar, Rhoda Brook could see the proceedings without taking part in them. He brought a tumbler from the dresser, nearly filled it with water, and fetching an egg, prepared it in some private way; after which he broke it on the edge of the glass, so that the white went in and the yolk remained. As it was getting gloomy, he took the glass and its contents to the window, and told Gertrude to watch them closely. They leaned over the table together, and the milkwoman could see the opaline hue of the egg-fluid changing form as it sank in the water, but she was not near enough to define the shape that it assumed.

'Do you catch the likeness of any face or figure as you look?' demanded the conjurer of the young woman.

She murmured a reply, in tones so low as to be inaudible to Rhoda, and continued to gaze intently into the glass. Rhoda turned, and walked a few steps away.

When Mrs Lodge came out, and her face was met by the light, it appeared exceedingly pale – as pale as Rhoda's – against the sad dun shades of the upland's garniture. Trendle shut the door behind her, and they at once started homeward together. But Rhoda perceived that her companion had quite changed.

'Did he charge much?' she asked, tentatively.

'Oh no – nothing. He would not take a farthing,' said Gertrude.

'And what did you see?' inquired Rhoda.

'Nothing I – care to speak of.' The constraint in her manner was remarkable; her face was so rigid as to wear an oldened aspect, faintly suggestive of the face in Rhoda's bedchamber.

'Was it you who first proposed coming here?' Mrs Lodge suddenly inquired, after a long pause. 'How very odd, if you did!'

'No. But I am not sorry we have come, all things considered,' she replied. For the first time a sense of triumph possessed her, and she did not altogether deplore that the young thing at her side should learn that their lives had been antagonized by other influences than their own.

The subject was no more alluded to during the long and dreary walk home. But in some way or other a story was whispered about the many-dairied Swenn Valley that winter that Mrs Lodge's gradual loss of the use of her left arm was owing to her being 'overlooked' by Rhoda Brook. The latter kept her own counsel about the incubus, but her face grew sadder and thinner; and in the spring she and her boy disappeared from the neighbourhood of Holmstoke.

VI

A SECOND ATTEMPT

Half a dozen years passed away, and Mr and Mrs Lodge's married experience sank into prosiness, and worse. The farmer was usually gloomy and silent; the woman whom he had wooed for her grace and beauty was contorted and disfigured in the left limb; moreover, she had brought him no child, which rendered it likely that he would be the last of a family who had occupied that valley for some two hundred years. He thought of Rhoda Brook and her son, and feared this might be a judgement from Heaven upon him.

The once blithe-hearted and enlightened Gertrude was changing into an irritable, superstitious woman, whose whole time was given to experimenting upon her ailment with every quack remedy she came across. She was honestly attached to her husband, and was ever secretly hoping against hope to win back his heart again by regaining some at least of her personal beauty. Hence it arose that her closet was lined with bottles, packets, and ointment-pots of every description – nay, bunches of mystic herbs, charms, and books of necromancy, which in her school-girl times she would have ridiculed as folly.

'D——d if you won't poison yourself with these apothecary messes and witch mixtures some time or other,' said her husband, when his eye chanced to fall upon the multitudinous array.

She did not reply, but turned her sad, soft glance upon him in such heart-swollen reproach that he looked sorry for his words, and added, 'I only meant it for your good, you know, Gertrude.'

'I'll clear out the whole lot, and destroy them,' said she, huskily, 'and attempt such remedies no more!'

'You want somebody to cheer you,' he observed. 'I once thought of adopting a boy; but he is too old now. And he is gone away I don't know where.'

She guessed to whom he alluded; for Rhoda Brook's story had in the course of years become known to her; though not a word had ever passed between her husband and herself on the subject. Neither had she ever spoken to him of her visit to Conjurer Trendle, and of what was revealed to her, or she thought was revealed to her, by that solitary heath-man.

She was now five-and-twenty; but she seemed older. 'Six years of marriage, and only a few months of love,' she sometimes whispered to herself. And then she thought of the apparent cause, and said, with a tragic glance at her withering limb, 'If I could only again be as I was when he first saw me!'

She obediently destroyed her nostrums and charms; but there remained a hankering wish to try something else – some other sort of cure altogether. She had never revisited Trendle since she had been conducted to the house of the solitary by Rhoda against her will; but it now suddenly occurred to Gertrude that she would, in a last desperate effort at deliverance from this seeming curse, again seek out the man, if he yet lived. He was entitled to a certain credence, for the indistinct form he had raised in the glass had undoubtedly resembled the only woman in the world who – as she now knew, though not then – could have a reason for bearing her ill-will. The visit should be paid.

This time she went alone, though she nearly got lost on the heath, and roamed a considerable distance out of her way. Trendle's house was reached at last, however; he was not indoors, and instead of waiting at the cottage she went to where his bent figure was pointed out to her at work a long way off. Trendle remembered her, and laying down the handful of furze-roots which he was gathering and throwing into a heap, he offered to accompany her in her homeward direction, as the distance was considerable and the days were short. So they walked together, his head bowed nearly to the earth, and his form of a colour with it.

'You can send away warts and other excrescences, I know,' she said; 'why can't you send away this?' And the arm was uncovered.

'You think too much of my powers!' said Trendle; 'and I am old and weak now, too. No, no; it is too much for me to attempt in my own person. What have ye tried?'

She named to him some of the hundred medicaments and counter-spells which she had adopted from time to time. He shook his head.

'Some were good enough,' he said, approvingly; 'but not many of them for such as this. This is of the nature of a blight, not of the nature of a wound; and if you ever do throw it off, it will be all at once.'

'If I only could!'

'There is only one chance of doing it known to me. It has never failed in kindred afflictions – that I can declare. But it is hard to carry out, and especially for a woman.'

'Tell me!' said she.

'You must touch with the limb the neck of a man who's been hanged.'

She started a little at the image he had raised.

'Before he's cold – just after he's cut down,' continued the conjurer, impassively.

'How can that do good?'

'It will turn the blood and change the constitution. But, as I say, to do it is hard. You must get into jail, and wait for him when he's brought off the gallows. Lots have done it, though perhaps not such pretty women as you. I used to send dozens for skin complaints. But that was in former times. The last I sent was in '13 – near twenty years ago.'

He had no more to tell her; and, when he had put her into a straight track homeward, turned and left her, refusing all money, as at first.

VII

A RIDE

The communication sank deep into Gertrude's mind. Her nature was rather a timid one; and probably of all remedies that the white wizard could have suggested there was not one which would have filled her with so much aversion as this, not to speak of the immense obstacles in the way of its adoption.

Casterbridge, the county-town, was a dozen or fifteen miles off; and though in those days, when men were executed for horse-stealing, arson, and burglary, an assize seldom passed without a hanging, it was not likely that she could get access to the body of the criminal unaided. And the fear of her husband's anger made her reluctant to breathe a word of Trendle's suggestion to him or to anybody about him.

She did nothing for months, and patiently bore her disfigurement as before. But her woman's nature, craving for renewed love, through the medium of renewed beauty (she was but twenty-five), was ever stimulating her to try what, at any rate, could hardly do her any harm. 'What came by a spell will go by a spell surely,' she would say. Whenever her imagination pictured the act she shrank in terror from the possibility of it; then the words of the conjurer, 'It will turn your blood,' were seen to be capable of a scientific no less than a ghastly interpretation; the mastering desire returned, and urged her on again.

There was at this time but one county-paper, and that her husband only occasionally borrowed. But old-fashioned days had old-fashioned means, and news was extensively conveyed by word of mouth from market to market or from fair to fair; so that, whenever such an event as an execution was about to take place, few within a radius of twenty miles were ignorant of the coming sight; and, so far as Holmstoke was concerned, some enthusiasts had been known to walk all the way to Casterbridge and back in one day, solely to witness the spectacle. The next assizes were in March; and when Gertrude Lodge heard that they had been held, she inquired stealthily at the inn as to the result, as soon as she could find opportunity.

She was, however, too late. The time at which the sentences were to be carried out had arrived, and to make the journey and obtain admission at such short notice required at least her husband's assistance. She dared not tell him, for she had found by delicate experiment that these smouldering village beliefs made him furious if mentioned, partly because he half entertained them himself. It was therefore necessary to wait for another opportunity.

Her determination received a fillip from learning that two epileptic children had attended from this very village of Holmstoke many years before with beneficial results, though the experiment had been strongly condemned by the neighbouring clergy. April, May, June passed; and it is no overstatement to say that by the end of the last-named month Gertrude wellnigh longed for the death of a fellow-creature.

Instead of her formal prayers each night, her unconscious prayer was, 'O Lord, hang some guilty or innocent person soon!' This time she made earlier inquiries, and was altogether more systematic in her proceedings. Moreover, the season was summer, between the haymaking and the harvest, and in the leisure thus afforded her husband had been holiday-taking away from home.

The assizes were in July, and she went to the inn as before. There was to be one execution – only one, for arson.

Her greatest problem was not how to get to Casterbridge, but what means she could adopt for obtaining admission to the jail. Though access for such purposes had formerly never been denied, the custom had fallen into desuetude; and in contemplating her possible difficulties she was again almost driven to fall back upon her husband. But, on sounding him about the assizes, he was so uncommunicative, so more than usually cold, that she did not proceed, and decided that whatever she did she would do alone.

Fortune, obdurate hitherto, showed her unexpected favour. On the Thursday before the Saturday fixed for the execution, Lodge remarked to her that he was going away from home for another day or two on business at a fair, and that he was sorry he could not take her with him.

She exhibited on this occasion so much readiness to stay at home that he looked at her in surprise. Time had been when she would have shown deep disappointment at the loss of such a jaunt. However, he lapsed into his usual taciturnity, and on the day named left Holmstoke.

It was now her turn. She at first had thought of driving, but on reflection held that driving would not do, since it would necessitate her keeping to the turnpike-road, and so increase by tenfold the risk of her ghastly errand being found out. She decided to ride, and avoid the beaten track, notwithstanding that in her husband's stables there was no animal just at present which by any stretch of imagination could be considered a lady's mount, in spite of his promise before marriage to always keep a mare for her. He had, however, many horses, fine ones of their kind; and among the rest was a serviceable creature, an equine Amazon, with a back as broad as a sofa, on which Gertrude had occasionally taken an airing when unwell. This horse she chose.

On Friday afternoon one of the men brought it round. She was dressed, and before going down looked at her shrivelled arm. 'Ah!' she said to it, 'if it had not been for you this terrible ordeal would have been saved me!'

When strapping up the bundle in which she carried a few articles of clothing, she took occasion to say to the servant, 'I take these in case I should not get back to-night from the person I am going to visit. Don't be alarmed if I am not in by ten, and close up the house as usual. I shall be at home to-morrow for certain.' She meant then to privately tell her husband; the deed accomplished was not like the deed projected. He would almost certainly forgive her.

And then the pretty palpitating Gertrude Lodge went from her husband's homestead; but though her goal was Casterbridge, she did not take the direct route thither through Stickleford. Her cunning course at first was in precisely the opposite direction. As soon as she was out of sight, however, she turned to the left, by a road which led into Egdon, and on entering the heath wheeled round, and set out in the true course, due westerly. A more private way down the county could not be imagined; and as to direction, she had merely to keep her horse's head to a point a little to the right of the sun. She knew that she would light upon a furze-cutter or cottager of some sort from time to time, from whom she might correct her bearing.

Though the date was comparatively recent, Egdon was much less fragmentary in character than now. The attempts – successful and otherwise – at cultivation on the lower slopes, which intrude and break up the original heath into small detached heaths, had not been carried far; Enclosure Acts had not taken effect, and the banks and fences which now exclude the cattle of those villagers who formerly enjoyed rights of commonage thereon, and the carts of those who had turbary privileges which kept them in firing all the year round, were not erected. Gertrude therefore rode along with no other obstacles than the prickly furze-bushes, the mats of heather, the white watercourses, and the natural steeps and declivities of the ground.

Her horse was sure, if heavy-footed and slow, and though a draught animal, was easy-paced; had it been otherwise, she was not a woman who could have ventured to ride over such a bit of country with a half-dead arm. It was therefore nearly eight-o'clock when she drew rein to breathe the mare on the last outlying high point of heath-land towards Casterbridge, previous to leaving Egdon for the cultivated valleys.

She halted before a pond flanked by the ends of two hedges; a railing ran through the centre of the pond, dividing it in half. Over the railing she saw the low green country; over the green trees the roofs of the town; over the roofs a white, flat façade, denoting the entrance to the county-jail. On the roof of this front specks were moving about; they seemed to be workmen erecting something. Her flesh crept. She descended slowly, and was soon amid cornfields and pastures. In another half-hour, when it was almost dusk, Gertrude reached the White Hart, the first inn of the town on that side.

Little surprise was excited by her arrival: farmers' wives rode on horseback then more than they do now – though, for that matter, Mrs Lodge was not imagined to be a wife at all; the inn-keeper supposed her some harum-scarum young woman who had come to attend 'hang-fair' next day. Neither her husband nor herself ever dealt in Casterbridge market, so that she was unknown. While dismounting she beheld a crowd of boys standing at the door of a harness-maker's shop just above the inn, looking inside it with deep interest.

'What is going on there?' she asked of the hostler.

'Making the rope for to-morrow.'

She throbbed responsively, and contracted her arm.

' 'Tis sold by the inch afterwards,' the man continued. 'I could get you a bit, miss, for nothing, if you'd like?'

She hastily repudiated any such wish, all the more from a curious creeping feeling that the condemned wretch's destiny was becoming interwoven with her own; and having engaged a room for the night, sat down to think.

Up to this time she had formed but the vaguest notions about her means of obtaining access to the prison. The words of the cunning man returned to her mind. He had implied that she should use her beauty, impaired though it was, as a pass-key. In her inexperience she knew little about jail functionaries; she had heard of a high-sheriff and an under-sheriff, but dimly only. She knew, however, that there must be a hangman, and to the hangman she determined to apply.

VIII

A WATER-SIDE HERMIT

At this date, and for several years after, there was a hangman to almost every jail. Gertrude found, on inquiry, that the Casterbridge official dwelt in a lonely cottage by a deep, slow river flowing under the cliff on which the prison buildings were situate – the stream being the self-same one, though she did not know it, which watered the Stickleford and Holmstoke meads lower down in its course.

Having changed her dress, and before she had eaten or drunk – for she could not take her ease till she had ascertained some particulars – Gertrude pursued her way by a path along the waterside to the cottage indicated. Passing thus the outskirts of the jail, she discerned on the level roof over the gateway three rectangular lines against the sky, where the specks had been moving in her distant view; she recognized what the erection was, and passed quickly on. Another hundred yards brought her to the executioner's house, which a boy pointed out. It stood close to the same stream, and was hard by a weir, the waters of which emitted a steady roar.

While she stood hesitating, a door opened and an old man came forth, shading a candle with one hand. Locking the door on the outside, he turned to a flight of wooden steps fixed against the end of the cottage, and began to ascend them, this being evidently the staircase to his bedroom. Gertrude hastened forward, but by the time she reached the foot of the ladder he was at the top. She called to him loudly enough to be heard above the roar of the weir; he looked down and said, 'What d'ye want here?'

'To speak to you a minute.'

The candlelight, such as it was, fell upon her imploring, pale, upturned face, and Davies (as the hangman was called) backed down the ladder. 'I was just going to bed,' he said; '"Early to bed and early to rise," but I don't mind stopping a minute for such a one as you. Come into the house.' He reopened the door, and preceded her to the room within.

The implements of his daily work, which was that of a jobbing gardener, stood in a corner, and seeing probably that she looked rural, he said, 'If you want me to undertake country work I can't come, for I never leave Casterbridge for gentle nor simple – not I. Though sometimes I make others leave,' he added, formally.

'Yes, yes! That's it! To-morrow!'

'Ah! I thought so. Well, what's the matter about that? 'Tis no use to come here about the knot – folks do come continually, but I tell 'em one knot is as merciful as another if ye keep it under the ear. Is the unfortunate man a relation; or, I should say, perhaps' (looking at her dress), 'a person who's been in your employ?'

'No. What time is the execution?'

'The same as usual – twelve o'clock, or as soon after as the London mail-coach gets in. We always wait for that, in case of a reprieve.'

'Oh – a reprieve – I hope not!' she said, involuntarily.

'Well – he, he! – as a matter of business, so do I! But still, if ever a young fellow deserved to be let off, this one does; only just turned eighteen, and only present by chance when the rick was fired. Howsoever, there's not much risk of it, as they are obliged to make an example of him, there having been so much destruction of property that way lately.'

'I mean,' she explained, 'that I want to touch him for a charm, a cure of an affliction, by the advice of a man who has proved the virtue of the remedy.'

'Oh yes, miss! Now I understand. I've had such people come in past years. But it didn't strike me that you looked of a sort to require blood-turning. What's the complaint? The wrong kind for this, I'll be bound.'

'My arm.' She reluctantly showed the withered skin.

'Ah! 'tis all a-scram!' said the hangman, examining it.

'Yes,' said she.

'Well,' he continued, with interest, 'this *is* the class o' subject, I'm bound to admit! I like the look of the place; it is truly as suitable for the cure as any I ever saw. 'Twas a knowing man that sent 'ee, whoever he was.'

'You can contrive for me all that's necessary?' she said, breathlessly.

'You should really have gone to the governor of the jail, and your doctor with 'ee, and given your name and address – that's how it used to be done, if I recollect. Still, perhaps I can manage it for a trifling fee.'

'Oh, thank you! I would rather do it this way, as I should like it kept private.'

'Lover not to know, eh?'

'No – husband.'

'Aha! Very well. I'll get 'ee a touch of the corpse.'

'Where is it now?' she said, shuddering.

'It? – *he*, you mean; he's living yet. Just inside that little small winder up there in the glum.' He signified the jail on the cliff above.

She thought of her husband and her friends. 'Yes, of course,' she said; 'and how am I to proceed?'

He took her to the door. 'Now, do you be waiting at the little wicket in the wall, that you'll find up there in the lane, not later than one o'clock.

I will open it from the inside, as I sha'n't come home to dinner till he's cut down. Good-night. Be punctual; and if you don't want anybody to know 'ee, wear a veil. Ah, once I had such a daughter as you!'

She went away, and climbed the path above, to assure herself that she would be able to find the wicket next day. Its outline was soon visible to her – a narrow opening in the outer wall of the prison precincts. The steep was so great that, having reached the wicket, she stopped a moment to breathe; and looking back upon the water-side cot, saw the hangman again ascending his out-door staircase. He entered the loft, or chamber, to which it led, and in a few minutes extinguished his light.

The town clock struck ten, and she returned to the White Hart as she had come.

IX

A RENCONTRE

It was one o'clock on Saturday. Gertrude Lodge, having been admitted to the jail as above described, was sitting in a waiting-room within the second gate, which stood under a classic archway of ashlar, then comparatively modern, and bearing the inscription, 'COUNTY JAIL: 1793'. This had been the façade she saw from the heath the day before. Near at hand was a passage to the roof on which the gallows stood.

The town was thronged, and the market suspended; but Gertrude had seen scarcely a soul. Having kept her room till the hour of the appointment, she had proceeded to the spot by a way which avoided the open space below the cliff where the spectators had gathered; but she could, even now, hear the multitudinous babble of their voices, out of which rose at intervals the hoarse croak of a single voice, uttering the words, 'Last dying speech and confession!' There had been no reprieve, and the execution was over; but the crowd still waited to see the body taken down.

Soon the persistent girl heard a trampling overhead, then a hand beckoned to her, and, following directions, she went out and crossed the inner paved court beyond the gate-house, her knees trembling so that she could scarcely walk. One of her arms was out of its sleeve, and only covered by her shawl.

On the spot to which she had now arrived were two trestles, and before she could think of their purpose she heard heavy feet descending stairs somewhere at her back. Turn her head she would not, or could not, and, rigid in this position, she was conscious of a rough coffin passing her shoulder, borne by four men. It was open, and in it lay the body of a young man, wearing the smock-frock of a rustic, and fustian breeches. It had been thrown into the coffin so hastily that the skirt of the smock-frock was hanging over. The burden was temporarily deposited on the trestles.

By this time the young woman's state was such that a grey mist seemed to float before her eyes, on account of which, and the veil she wore, she could scarcely discern anything; it was as though she had died but was held up by a sort of galvanism.

'Now,' said a voice close at hand, and she was just conscious that it had been addressed to her.

By a last strenuous effort she advanced, at the same time hearing persons approaching behind her. She bared her poor cursed arm; and Davies, uncovering the dead man's face, took her hand, and held it so that the arm lay across the neck of the corpse, upon a line the colour of an unripe blackberry which surrounded it.

Gertrude shrieked; 'the turn o' the blood,' predicted by the conjurer, had taken place. But at that moment a second shriek rent the air of the enclosure; it was not Gertrude's, and its effect upon her was to make her start round.

Immediately behind her stood Rhoda Brook, her face drawn, and her eyes red with weeping. Behind Rhoda stood her own husband; his countenance lined, his eyes dim, but without a tear.

'D——n you! what are you doing here?' he said, hoarsely.

'Hussy – to come between us and our child now!' cried Rhoda. 'This is the meaning of what Satan showed me in the vision! You are like her at last!' And clutching the bare arm of the younger woman, she pulled her unresistingly back against the wall. Immediately Brook had loosened her hold the fragile young Gertrude slid down against the feet of her husband. When he lifted her up she was unconscious.

The mere sight of the twain had been enough to suggest to her that the dead young man was Rhoda's son. At that time the relatives of an executed convict had the privilege of claiming the body for burial, if they chose to do so; and it was for this purpose that Lodge was awaiting the inquest with Rhoda. He had been summoned by her as soon as the young man was taken in the crime, and at different times since; and he had attended in court during the trial. This was the 'holiday' he had been indulging in of late. The two wretched parents had wished to avoid exposure; and hence had come themselves for the body, a wagon and a sheet for its conveyance and covering being in waiting outside.

Gertrude's case was so serious that it was deemed advisable to call to her the surgeon who was at hand. She was taken out of the jail into the town; but she never reached home alive. Her delicate vitality, sapped perhaps by the paralyzed arm, collapsed under the double shock that followed the severe strain, physical and mental, to which she had subjected herself during the previous twenty-four hours. Her blood had been 'turned' indeed – too far. Her death took place in the town three days after.

Her husband was never seen in Casterbridge again; once only in the old market-place at Anglebury, which he had so much frequented, and very seldom in public anywhere. Burdened at first with moodiness and remorse, he eventually changed for the better, and appeared as a chastened and thoughtful man. Soon after attending the funeral of his poor young wife, he took steps towards giving up the farms in Holmstoke and the adjoining parish, and, having sold every head of his stock, he went away to Port-Bredy, at the other end of the county, living there in solitary lodgings till his death, two years later, of a painless decline. It was then found that he had bequeathed the whole of his not inconsiderable property to a reformatory for boys, subject to the payment of a small annuity to Rhoda Brook, if she could be found to claim it.

For some time she could not be found; but eventually she reappeared in her old parish – absolutely refusing, however, to have anything to do with the provision made for her. Her monotonous milking at the dairy was resumed, and followed for many long years, till her form became bent, and her once abundant dark hair white and worn away at the forehead – perhaps by long pressure against the cows. Here, sometimes, those who knew her experiences would stand and observe her, and wonder what sombre thoughts were beating inside that impassive, wrinkled brow, to the rhythm of the alternating milk-streams.

W. S. GILBERT

An Elixir of Love

I

Ploverleigh was a picturesque little village in Dorsetshire, ten miles from anywhere. It lay in a pretty valley nestling amid clumps of elm trees, and a pleasant little trout stream ran right through it from end to end. The vicar of Ploverleigh was the Hon. and Rev. Mortimer De Becheville, third son of the forty-eighth Earl of Caramel. He was an excellent gentleman, and his living was worth £1,200 a-year. He was a graduate of Cambridge, and held a College Fellowship, besides which his father allowed him £500 a-year. So he was very comfortably 'off'.

Mr De Becheville had a very easy time of it, for he spent eleven-twelfths of the year away from the parish, delegating his duties to the Rev. Stanley Gay, an admirable young curate to whom he paid a stipend of £120 a-year, pocketing by this means a clear annual profit of £1,080. It was said by unkind and ungenerous people, that, as Mr. De Becheville had (presumably) been selected for his sacred duties at a high salary on account of his special and exceptional qualifications for their discharge, it was hardly fair to delegate them to a wholly inexperienced young gentleman of two-and-twenty. It was argued that if a colonel, or a stipendiary magistrate, or a superintendent of a county lunatic asylum, or any other person holding a responsible office (outside the Church of England), for which he was handsomely paid, were to do his work by cheap deputy, such a responsible official would be looked upon as a swindler. But this line of reasoning is only applied to the cure of souls by uncharitable and narrow-minded people who never go to church, and consequently can't know anything about it. Besides, who cares what people who never go to church think? If it comes to that, Mr De Becheville was *not* selected (as it happens) on account of his special and exceptional fitness for the cure of souls, inasmuch as the living was a family one, and went to De Becheville because his two elder brothers preferred the Guards. So that argument falls to the ground.

The Rev. Stanley Gay was a Leveller. I don't mean to say that he was a mere I'm-as-good-as-you Radical spouter, who advocated a redistribution of property from mere sordid motives. Mr Gay was an æsthetic Leveller. He held that as Love is the great bond of union between man and woman, no arbitrary obstacle should be allowed to interfere with its progress. He did not desire to abolish Rank, but he *did* desire that a mere difference in rank should not be an obstacle in the way of making two young people happy. He could prove to you by figures (for he was a famous mathematician) that, rank notwithstanding, all men are equal, and this is how he did it.

He began, as a matter of course, with x, because, as he said, x, whether it represents one or one hundred thousand, is always x, and do what you will, you cannot make w or y of it by any known process.

Having made this quite clear to you, he carried on his argument by means of algebra, until he got right through algebra to the 'cases' at the end of the book, and then he slid by gentle and imperceptible degrees into conic sections, where x, although you found it masquerading as the equation to the parabola, was still as much x as ever. Then if you were not too tired to follow him, you found yourself up to the eyes in plane and spherical trigonometry, where x again turned up in a variety of assumed characters, sometimes as 'cos α' sometimes as 'sin β', but generally with a $\sqrt[3]{}$ over it, and none the less x on that account. This singular character then made its appearance in a quaint binomial disguise, and was eventually run to earth in the very heart of differential and integral calculus, looking less like x, but being, in point of fact, more like x than ever. The force of his argument went to show that, do what you would, you could not stamp x out, and therefore it was better and wiser and more straightforward to call him x at once than to invest him with complicated sham dignities which meant nothing, and only served to bother and perplex people who met him for the first time. It's a very easy problem – anybody can do it.

Mr Gay was, as a matter of course, engaged to be married. He loved a pretty little girl of eighteen, with soft brown eyes, and bright silky brown hair. Her name was Jessie Lightly, and she was the only daughter of Sir Caractacus Lightly, a wealthy baronet who had a large place in the neighbourhood of Ploverleigh. Sir Caractacus was a very dignified old gentleman, whose wife had died two years after Jessie's birth. A well-bred, courtly old gentleman, too, with a keen sense of honour. He was very fond of Mr Gay, though he had no sympathy with his levelling views.

One beautiful moonlit evening Mr Gay and Jessie were sitting together on Sir Caractacus's lawn. Everything around them was pure and calm and still, so they grew sentimental.

'Stanley,' said Jessie, 'we are very, very happy, are we not?'

'Unspeakably happy,' said Gay. 'So happy that when I look around me, and see how many there are whose lives are embittered by disappointment – by envy, by hatred, and by malice' (when he grew oratorical he generally lapsed into the Litany) 'I turn to the tranquil and unruffled calm of my own pure and happy love for you with gratitude unspeakable.'

He really meant all this, though he expressed himself in rather flatulent periods.

'I wish with all my heart,' said Jessie, 'that every soul on earth were as happy as we two.'

'And why are they not?' asked Gay, who hopped on to his hobby whenever it was, so to speak, brought round to the front door. 'And why are they not, Jessie? I will tell you why they are not. Because – '

'Yes, darling,' said Jessie, who had often heard his argument before. 'I know why. It's dreadful.'

'It's as simple as possible,' said Gay. 'Take x to represent the abstract human being – '

'Certainly, dear,' said Jessie, who agreed with his argument heart and soul, but didn't want to hear it again. 'We took it last night.'

'Then,' said Gay, not heeding the interruption, 'let $x + 1$, $x + 2$, $x + 3$, represent three grades of high rank.'

'Exactly, it's contemptible,' said Jessie. 'How softly the wind sighs among the trees.'

'What is a duke?' asked Gay – not for information, but oratorically, with a view to making a point.

'A mere $x + 3$,' said Jessie. 'Could anything be more hollow. What a lovely evening!'

'The Duke of Buckingham and Chandos – it sounds well, I grant you,' continued Gay, 'but call him the $x + 3$ of Buckingham and Chandos, and you reduce him at once to – '

'I know,' said Jessie, 'to his lowest common denominator,' and her little upper lip curled with contempt.

'Nothing of the kind,' said Gay, turning red. 'Either hear me out, or let me drop the subject. At all events don't make ridiculous suggestions.'

'I'm very sorry, dear,' said Jessie, humbly. 'Go on, I'm listening, and I won't interrupt any more.'

But Gay was annoyed and wouldn't go on. So they returned to the house together. It was their first tiff.

II

In St Martin's Lane lived Baylis and Culpepper, magicians, astrologers, and professors of the Black Art. Baylis had sold himself to the Devil at a very early age, and had become remarkably proficient in all kinds of enchantment. Culpepper had been his apprentice, and having also acquired considerable skill as a necromancer, was taken into partnership by the genial old magician, who from the first had taken a liking to the frank and fair-haired boy. Ten years ago (the date of my story) the firm of Baylis and Culpepper stood at the very head of the London family magicians. They did what is known as a pushing trade, but although they advertised largely, and never neglected a chance, it was admitted even by their rivals, that the goods they supplied could be relied on as sound, useful articles. They had a special reputation for a class of serviceable family nativity, and they did a very large and increasing business in love philtres, 'The Patent Oxy-Hydrogen Love-at-First-Sight Draught' in bottles at 1*s.* 1½*d.* and 2*s.* 3*d.* ('our leading article,' as Baylis called it) was strong enough in itself to keep the firm going, had all its other resources failed them. But the establishment in St Martin's Lane was also a 'Noted House for Amulets,' and if you wanted a neat, well-finished divining-rod, I don't know any place to which I would sooner recommend you. Their Curses at a shilling per dozen were the cheapest things in the trade, and they sold thousands of them in the course of the year. Their Blessings – also very cheap indeed, and quite effective – were not much asked for. 'We always keep a few on hand as curiosities and for completeness, but we don't sell two in the twelvemonth,' said Mr Baylis. 'A gentleman bought one last week to send to his mother-in-law, but it turned out that he was afflicted in the head, and the persons who had charge of him declined to pay for it, and it's been returned to us. But the sale of penny curses, especially on Saturday nights, is tremendous. We can't turn 'em out fast enough.'

As Baylis and Culpepper were making up their books one evening, just at closing time, a gentle young clergyman with large violet eyes, and a beautiful girl of eighteen, with soft brown hair, and a Madonna-like purity of expression, entered the warehouse. These were Stanley Gay and Jessie Lightly. And this is how it came to pass that they found themselves in London, and in the warehouse of the worthy magicians.

As the reader knows, Stanley Gay and Jessie had for many months given themselves up to the conviction that it was their duty to do all in their power to bring their fellow men and women together in holy matrimony, without regard to distinctions of age or rank. Stanley gave lectures on the subject at mechanics' institutes, and the mechanics were unanimous in their approval of his views. He preached his doctrine in workhouses, in beer-shops, and in lunatic asylums, and his listeners supported him with enthusiasm. He addressed navvies at the roadside on the humanising advantages that would accrue to them if they married refined and wealthy ladies of rank, and not a navvy dissented. In short, he felt more and more convinced every day that he had at last discovered the secret of human happiness. Still he had a formidable battle to fight with class prejudice, and he and Jessie pondered gravely on the difficulties that were before them, and on the best means of overcoming them.

'It's no use disguising the fact, Jessie,' said Mr Gay, 'that the Countesses won't like it.' And little Jessie gave a sigh, and owned that she expected some difficulty with the Countesses. 'We must look these things in the face, Jessie, it won't do to ignore them. We have convinced the humble mechanics and artisans, but the aristocracy hold aloof.'

'The working-man is the true Intelligence after all,' said Jessie.

'He is a noble creature when he is quite sober,' said Gay. 'God bless him.'

Stanley Gay and Jessie were in this frame of mind when they came across Baylis and Culpepper's advertisement in the *Connubial Chronicle*.

'My dear Jessie,' said Gay, 'I see a way out of our difficulty.'

And dear little Jessie's face beamed with hope.

'These Love Philtres that Baylis and Culpepper advertise – they are very cheap indeed, and if we may judge by the testimonials, they are very effective. Listen, darling.'

And Stanley Gay read as follows: –

'From the Earl of Market Harborough. "I am a hideous old man of eighty, and everyone avoided me. I took a family bottle of your philtre, immediately on my accession to the title and estates a fortnight ago, and I can't keep the young women off. Please send me a pipe of it to lay down."'

'From Amelia Orange Blossom. – "I am a very pretty girl of fifteen. For upwards of fourteen years past I have been without a definitely declared admirer. I took a large bottle of your philtre yesterday, and within fourteen hours a young nobleman winked at me in church. Send me a couple of dozen."'

'What can the girl want with a couple of dozen young noblemen, darling?' asked Jessie.

'I don't know – perhaps she took it too strong. Now these men,' said Gay, laying down the paper', are benefactors indeed, if they can accomplish all they undertake. I would ennoble these men. They should have statues. I would enthrone them in high places. They would be $x + 3$.'

'My generous darling,' said Jessie, gazing into his eyes in a fervid ecstasy.

'Not at all,' replied Gay. 'They deserve it. We confer peerages on generals who plunge half a nation into mourning – shall we deny them to men who bring a life's happiness home to every door? Always supposing,' added the cautious clergyman, 'that they can really do what they profess.'

The upshot of this conversation was that Gay determined to lay in a stock of philtres for general use among his parishioners. If the effect upon them was satisfactory he would extend the sphere of their operations. So when Sir Caractacus and his daughter went to town for the season, Stanley Gay spent a fortnight with them, and thus it came to pass that he and Jessie went together to Baylis and Culpepper's.

'Have you any fresh Love Philtres to day?' said Gay.

'Plenty, sir,' said Mr. Culpepper. 'How many would you like?'

'Well – let me see,' said Gay. 'There are a hundred and forty souls in my parish, – say twelve dozen.'

'I think, dear,' said little Jessie, 'you are better to take a few more than you really want, in case of accidents.'

'In purchasing a large quantity, sir,' said Mr Culpepper, 'we would strongly advise you taking it in the wood, and drawing it off as you happen to want it. We have it in four-and-a-half and nine-gallon casks, and we deduct ten per cent. for cash payments.'

'Then, Mr Culpepper, be good enough to let me have a nine-gallon cask of Love Philtre as soon as possible. Send it to the Rev. Stanley Gay, Ploverleigh.'

He wrote a cheque for the amount, and so the transaction ended.

'Is there any other article?' said Mr Culpepper.

'Nothing to-day. Good afternoon.'

'Have you seen our new wishing-caps? They are lined with silk and very chastely quilted, sir. We sold one to the Archbishop of Canterbury not an hour ago. Allow me to put you up a wishing-cap.'

'I tell you that I want nothing more,' said Gay, going.

'Our Flying Carpets are quite the talk of the town, sir,' said Culpepper, producing a very handsome piece of Persian tapestry. 'You spread it on the ground and sit on it, and then you think of a place and you find yourself there before you can count ten. Our Abudah chests, sir, each chest containing a patent Hag, who comes out and prophecies disasters whenever you touch this spring, are highly spoken of. We can sell the Abudah chest complete for fifteen guineas.'

'I think you tradespeople make a great mistake in worrying people to buy things they don't want,' said Gay.

'You'd be surprised if you knew the quantity of things we get rid of by this means, sir.'

'No doubt, but I think you keep a great many people out of your shop. If x represents the amount you gain by it, and y the amount you lose by it, then if $\frac{x}{2} = y$ you are clearly out of pocket by it at the end of the year. Think this over. Good evening.'

And Mr Gay left the shop with Jessie.

'Stanley,' said she, 'what a blessing you are to mankind. You do good wherever you go.'

'My dear Jessie,' replied Gay, 'I have had a magnificent education, and if I can show these worthy but half-educated tradesmen that their ignorance of the profounder mathematics is misleading them, I am only dealing as I should deal with the blessings that have been entrusted to my care.'

As Messrs Baylis & Culpepper have nothing more to do with this story, it may be stated at once that Stanley Gay's words had a marked effect upon them. They determined never to push an article again, and within two years of this resolve they retired on ample fortunes, Baylis to a beautiful detached house on Clapham Common, and Culpepper to a handsome château on the Mediterranean, about four miles from Nice.

III

We are once more at Ploverleigh, but this time at the Vicarage. The scene is Mr Gay's handsome library, and in this library three persons are assembled – Mr Gay, Jessie, and old Zorah Clarke. It should be explained that Zorah is Mr Gay's cook and houseskeeper, and it is understood between him and Sir Caractacus Lightly that Jessie may call on the curate whenever she likes, on condition that Zorah is present during the whole time of the visit. Zorah is stone deaf and has to be communicated with through the medium of pantomime, so that while she is really no impediment whatever to the free flow of conversation, the chastening influence of her presence would suffice of itself to silence ill-natured comments, if such articles had an existence among the primitive and innocent inhabitants of Ploverleigh.

The nine-gallon cask of Love Philtre had arrived in due course, and Mr Gay had decided that it should be locked up in a cupboard in his library, as he thought it would scarcely be prudent to trust it to Zorah, whose curiosity might get the better of her discretion. Zorah (who believed that the cask contained sherry) was much scandalized at her master's action in keeping it in his library, and looked upon it as an evident and unmistakeable sign that he had deliberately made up his mind to take to a steady course of drinking. However, Mr Gay partly reassured the good old lady by informing her in pantomime (an art of expression in which long practice had made him singularly expert) that the liquid was not intoxicating in the ordinary sense of the word, but that it was a cunning and subtle essence, concocted from innocent herbs by learned gentlemen who had devoted a lifetime to the study of its properties. He added (still in pantomime) that he did not propose to drink a single drop of it himself, but that he intended to distribute it among his parishioners, whom it would benefit socially, mentally, and morally to a considerable extent. Master as he was of the art of expression by gesture, it took two days' hard work to make this clear to her, and even then she had acquired but a faint and feeble idea of its properties, for she always referred to it as sarsaparilla.

'Jessie,' said Gay, 'the question now arises, – How shall we most effectually dispense the great boon we have at our command? Shall we give a party to our friends, and put the Love Philtre on the table in decanters, and allow them to help themselves?'

'We must be very careful, dear,' said Jessie, 'not to allow any married people to taste it.'

'True,' said Gay, 'quite true. I never thought of that. It wouldn't do at all. I am much obliged to you for the suggestion. It would be terrible – quite terrible.'

And Stanley Gay turned quite pale and faint at the very thought of such a *contretemps*.

'Then,' said Jessie, 'there are the engaged couples. I don't think we ought to do anything to interfere with the prospects of those who have already plighted their troth.'

'Quite true,' said Gay, 'we have no right, as you say, to interfere with the arrangements of engaged couples. That narrows our sphere of action very considerably.'

'Then the widows and the widowers of less than one year's standing should be exempted from its influence.'

'Certainly, most certainly. That reflection did not occur to me, I confess. It is clear that the dispensing of the philtre will be a very delicate operation: it will have to be conducted with the utmost tact. Can you think of any more exceptions?'

'Let me see,' said Jessie. 'There's Tibbits, our gardener, who has fits; and there's Williamson, papa's second groom, who drinks, and oughtn't to be allowed to marry; and Major Crump, who uses dreadful language before ladies; and Dame Parboy, who is bed-ridden; and the old ladies in the almshouses – and little Tommy, the idiot – and, indeed, all children under – under what age shall we say?'

'All children who have not been confirmed,' said Gay. 'Yes, these exceptions never occurred to me.'

'I don't think we shall ever use the nine gallons, dear,' said Jessie. 'One tablespoonful is a dose.'

'I have just thought of another exception,' said Gay. 'Your papa.'

'Oh! papa *must* marry again! Poor dear old papa! Oh! You *must* let *him* marry.'

'My dear Jessie,' said Gay, 'Heaven has offered me the chance of entering into the married state unencumbered with a mother-in-law. And I am content to accept the blessing as I find it. Indeed, I prefer it so.'

'Papa *does* so want to marry – he is always talking of it,' replied the poor little woman, with a pretty pout. 'O indeed, *indeed*, my new mamma, whoever she may be, shall never interfere with us. Why, how thankless you are! My papa is about to confer upon you the most inestimable treasure in the world, a young, beautiful and devoted wife, and you withhold from him a priceless blessing that you are ready to confer on the very meanest of your parishioners.'

'Jessie,' said Gay, 'you have said enough. Sir Caractacus *shall* marry. I was wrong. If a certain burden to which I will not more particularly refer is to descend upon my shoulders, I will endeavour to bear it without repining.'

It was finally determined that there was only one way in which the philtre could be safely and properly distributed. Mr Gay was to give out that he was much interested in the sale of a very peculiar and curious old Amontillado, and small sample bottles of the wine were to be circulated among such of his parishioners as were decently eligible as brides and bridegrooms. The scheme was put into operation as soon as it was decided upon. Mr Gay sent to the nearest market-town for a gross of two-ounce phials, and Jessie and he spent a long afternoon bottling the elixir into these convenient receptacles. They then rolled them up in papers, and addressed them to the persons who were destined to be operated upon. And when all this was done Jessie returned to her papa, and Mr Gay sat up all night explaining in pantomime to Zorah that a widowed aunt of his, in somewhat straitened circumstances, who resided in a small but picturesque villa in the suburbs of Montilla, had been compelled to take a large quantity of the very finest sherry from a bankrupt wine-merchant, in satisfaction of a year's rent of her second floor, and that he had undertaken to push its sale in Ploverleigh in consideration of a commission of two-and-a-half per cent. on the sales effected – which commission was to be added to the fund for the restoration of the church steeple. He began his explanation at 9 P.M., and at 6 A.M. Zorah thought she began to understand him, and Stanley Gay, quite exhausted with his pantomimic exertions, retired, dead beat, to his chamber.

IV

The next morning as Sir Caractacus Lightly sat at breakfast with Jessie, the footman informed him that Mr Gay's housekeeper wished to speak to him on very particular business. The courtly old Baronet directed that she should be shown into the library, and at once proceeded to ask what she wanted.

'If you please Sir Caractacus, and beggin' your pardon,' said Zorah as he entered, 'I've come with a message from my master.'

'Pray be seated,' said Sir Caractacus. But the poor old lady could not hear him, so he explained his meaning to her in the best dumb show he could command. He pointed to a chair – walked to it – sat down in it – leant back, crossed his legs cosily, got up, and waved his hand to her in a manner that clearly conveyed to her that she was expected to do as he had done.

'My master's compliments and he's gone into the wine trade, and would you accept a sample?'

After all, Mr Gay's exertions had failed to convey his exact meaning to the deaf old lady.

'You astonish me,' said Sir Caractacus; then, finding that she did not understand him, he rumpled his hair, opened his mouth, strained his eye-balls, and threw himself into an attitude of the most horror-struck amazement. Having made his state of mind quite clear to her, he smiled pleasantly, and nodded to her to proceed.

'If you'll kindly taste it, sir, I'll take back any orders with which you may favour me.'

Sir Caractacus rang for a wineglass and proceeded to taste the sample.

'I don't know what it is, but it's not Amontillado,' said he, smacking his lips; 'still it is a pleasant cordial. Taste it.'

The old lady seemed to gather his meaning at once. She nodded, bobbed a curtsey, and emptied the glass.

Baylis and Culpepper had not over-stated the singular effects of the 'Patent Oxy-Hydrogen Love-at-First-Sight Draught.' Sir Caractacus's hard and firmly-set features gradually relaxed as the old lady sipped the contents of her glass. Zorah set it down when she had quite emptied it, and as she did so her eyes met those of the good old Baronet. She blushed under the ardour of his gaze, and a tear trembled on her old eyelid.

'You're a remarkably fine woman,' said Sir Caractacus, 'and singularly well preserved for your age.'

'Alas, kind sir,' said Zorah, 'I'm that hard of hearin' that cannons is whispers.'

Sir Caractacus stood up, stroked his face significantly, smacked his hands together, slapped them both upon his heart, and sank on one knee at her feet. He then got up and nodded smilingly at her to imply that he really meant it.

Zorah turned aside and trembled.

'I ain't no scollard, Sir Caractacus, and I don't rightly know how a poor old 'ooman like me did ought to own her likings for a lordly barrownight – but a true 'art is more precious than diamonds they do say, and a lovin' wife is a crown of gold to her husband. I ain't fashionable, but I'm a respectable old party, and can make you comfortable if nothing else.'

'Zorah, you are the very jewel of my hopes. My dear daughter will soon be taken from me. It lies with you to brighten my desolate old age. Will you be Lady Lightly?'

And he pointed to a picture of his late wife, and went through the pantomime of putting a ring on Zorah's finger. He then indicated the despair that would possess him if she refused to accept his offer. Having achieved these feats of silent eloquence, he smiled and nodded at her reassuringly, and waited for a reply with an interrogative expression of countenance.

'Yes, dearie,' murmured Zorah, as she sank into the Baronet's arms.

After a happy half-hour Zorah felt it was her duty to return to her master, so the lovers took a fond farewell of each other, and Sir Caractacus returned to the breakfast-room.

'Jessie,' said Sir Caractacus, 'I think you really love your poor old father?'

'Indeed, papa, I do.'

'Then you will, I trust, be pleased to hear that my declining years are not unlikely to be solaced by the companionship of a good, virtuous, and companionable woman.'

'My dear papa,' said Jessie, 'do you really mean that – that you are likely to be married?'

'Indeed, Jessie, I think it is more than probable! You know you are going to leave me very soon, and my dear little nurse must be replaced, or what will become of me?'

Jessie's eyes filled with tears – but they were tears of joy.

'I cannot tell you papa – dear, dear, papa – how happy you have made me.'

'And you will, I am sure, accept your new mamma with every feeling of respect and affection.'

'Any wife of yours is a mamma of mine,' said Jessie.

'My darling! Yes, Jessie, before very long I hope to lead to the altar a bride who will love and honour me as I deserve. She is no light and giddy girl, Jessie. She is a woman of sober age and staid demeanour, yet easy and comfortable in her ways. I am going to marry Mr Gay's cook, Zorah.'

'Zorah,' cried Jessie, 'dear, dear old Zorah! Oh, indeed, I am very, very glad and happy!'

'Bless you, my child,' said the Baronet. 'I knew my pet would not blame her poor old father for acting on the impulse of a heart that has never misled him. Yes, I think – nay, I am sure – that I have taken a wise and prudent step. Zorah is not what the world calls beautiful.'

'Zorah is very good, and very clean and honest, and quite, quite sober in her habits,' said Jessie warmly, 'and that is worth more – far more than beauty, dear papa. Beauty will fade and perish, but personal cleanliness is practically undying, for it can be renewed whenever it discovers symptoms of decay. Oh, I am sure you will be happy!' And Jessie hurried off to tell Stanley Gay how nobly the potion had done its work.

'Stanley, dear Stanley,' said she, 'I have such news – Papa and Zorah are engaged!'

'I am very glad to hear it. She will make him an excellent wife; it is a very auspicious beginning.'

'And have *you* any news to tell me?'

'None, except that all the bottles are distributed, and I am now waiting to see their effect. By the way, the Bishop has arrived unexpectedly, and is stopping at the Rectory, and I have sent him a bottle. I should like to find a nice little wife for the Bishop, for he has Crawleigh in his gift – the present incumbent is at the point of death, and the living is worth £1,800 a year. The duty is extremely light, and the county society unexceptional. I think I could be truly useful in such a sphere of action.'

V

The action of the 'Patent Oxy-Hydrogen Love-at-First-Sight Philtre' was rapid and powerful, and before evening there was scarcely a disengaged person (over thirteen years of age) in Ploverleigh. The Dowager Lady Fitz-Saracen, a fierce old lady of sixty, had betrothed herself to Alfred Creeper, of the 'Three Fiddlers,' a very worthy man, who had been engaged in the public trade all his life, and had never yet had a mark on his licence. Colonel Pemberton, of The Grove, had fixed his affections on dear little Bessie Lane, the pupil teacher, and his son Willie (who had returned from Eton only the day before) had given out his engagement to kind old Mrs Partlet, the widow of the late sexton. In point of fact there was only one disengaged person in the village – the good and grave old Bishop. He was in the position of the odd player who can't find a seat in the 'Family

Coach.' But, on the whole, Stanley Gay was rather glad of this, as he venerated the good old prelate, and in his opinion there was no one in the village at that time who was really good enough to be a Bishop's wife, except, indeed, the dear little brown-haired, soft-eyed maiden to whom Stanley himself was betrothed.

So far everything had worked admirably, and the unions effected through the agency of the philtre, if they were occasionally ill-assorted as regards the stations in life of the contracting parties, were all that could be desired in every other respect. Good, virtuous, straightforward, and temperate men were engaged to blameless women who were calculated to make admirable wives and mothers, and there was every prospect that Ploverleigh would become celebrated as the only Home of Perfect Happiness. There was but one sad soul in the village. The good old Bishop had drunk freely of the philtre, but there was no one left to love him. It was pitiable to see the poor love-lorn prelate as he wandered disconsolately through the smiling meadows of Ploverleigh, pouring out the accents of his love to an incorporeal abstraction.

'Something must be done for the Bishop,' said Stanley, as he watched him sitting on a stile in the distance. 'The poor old gentleman is wasting to a shadow.'

The next morning as Stanley was carefully reading through the manuscript sermon which had been sent to him by a firm in Paternoster Row for delivery on the ensuing Sabbath, little Jessie entered his library (with Zorah) and threw herself on a sofa, sobbing as if her heart would break.

'Why, Jessie – my own little love,' exclaimed Stanley. 'What in the world is the matter?'

And he put his arms fondly round her waist, and endeavoured to raise her face to his.

'Oh, no – no – Stanley – don't – you musn't – indeed, indeed, you musn't.'

'Why, my pet, what can you mean?'

'Oh, Stanley, Stanley – you will never, never forgive me.'

'Nonsense, child,' said he. 'My dear little Jessie is incapable of an act which is beyond the pale of forgiveness.' And he gently kissed her forehead.

'Stanley, you musn't do it – indeed you musn't.'

'No, you musn't do it, Muster Gay,' said Zorah.

'Why, confound you, what do you mean by interfering?' said Stanley in a rage.

'Ah, it's all very fine, I dare say, but I don't know what you're a-talking about.'

And Stanley, recollecting her infirmity, explained in pantomime the process of confounding a person, and intimated that it would be put into operation upon her if she presumed to cut in with impertinent remarks.

'Stanley – Mr Gay –' said Jessie.

'*Mr* Gay!' ejaculated Stanley.

'I musn't call you Stanley any more.'

'Great Heaven, why not?'

'I'll tell you all about it if you promise not to be violent.'

And Gay, prepared for some terrible news, hid his head in his hands, and sobbed audibly.

'I loved you – oh so, so much – you were my life – my heart,' said the poor little woman. 'By day and by night my thoughts were with you, and the love came from my heart as the water from a well!'

Stanley groaned.

'When I rose in the morning it was to work for your happiness, and when I lay down in my bed at night it was to dream of the love that was to weave itself through my life.'

He kept his head between his hands and moved not.

'My life was for your life – my soul for yours! I drew breath but for one end – to love, to honour, to reverence you.'

He lifted his head at last. His face was ashy pale.

'Come to the point,' he gasped.

'Last night,' said Jessie, 'I was tempted to taste a bottle of the Elixir. It was but a drop I took on the tip of my finger. I went to bed thinking but of you. I rose to-day, still with you in my mind. Immediately after breakfast I left home to call upon you, and as I crossed Bullthorn's meadow I saw the Bishop of Chelsea seated on a stile. At once I became conscious that I had placed myself unwittingly under the influence of the fatal potion. Horrified at my involuntary faithlessness – loathing my miserable weakness – hating myself for the misery I was about to weave around the life of a saint I had so long adored – I could not but own to myself that the love of my heart was given over, for ever, to that solitary and love-lorn prelate. Mr Gay (for by that name I must call you to the end), I have told you nearly all that you need care to know. It is enough to add that my love is, as a matter of course, reciprocated, and, but for the misery I have caused you, I am happy. But, full as my cup of joy may be, it will never be without a bitter after-taste, for I cannot forget that my folly – my wicked folly – has blighted the life of a man who, an hour ago, was dearer to me than the whole world!'

And Jessie fell sobbing on Zorah's bosom.

Stanley Gay, pale and haggard, rose from his chair, and staggered to a side table. He tried to pour out a glass of water, but as he was in the act of doing so the venerable Bishop entered the room.

'Mr Gay, I cannot but feel that I owe you some apology for having gained the affections of a young lady to whom you were attached – Jessie, my love, compose yourself.'

And the Bishop gently removed Jessie's arms from Zorah's neck, and placed them about his own.

'My Lord,' said Mr Gay, 'I am lost in amazement. When I have more fully realized the unparalleled misfortune that has overtaken me I shall perhaps be able to speak and act with calmness. At the present moment I am unable to trust myself to do either. I am stunned – quite, quite stunned.'

'Do not suppose, my dear Mr Gay,' said the Bishop, 'that I came here this morning to add to your reasonable misery by presenting myself before you in the capacity of a successful rival. No. I came to tell you that poor old Mr Chudd, the vicar of Crawleigh, has been mercifully removed. He is no more, and as the living is in my gift, I have come to tell you that, if it can compensate in any way for the terrible loss I have been the unintentional means of inflicting upon you, it is entirely at your disposal. It is worth £1,800 per annum – the duty is extremely light, and the local society is unexceptional.'

Stanley Gay pressed the kind old Bishop's hand.

'Eighteen hundred a year will not entirely compensate me for Jessie.'

'For Miss Lightly,' murmured the Bishop, gently.

'For Miss Lightly – but it will go some way towards doing so. I accept your lordship's offer with gratitude.'

'We shall always take an interest in you,' said the Bishop.

'Always – always,' said Jessie. 'And we shall be so glad to see you at the Palace – shall we not Frederick?'

'Well – ha – hum – yes – oh, yes, of course. Always,' said the Bishop. 'That is – oh, yes – always.'

The 14th of February was a great day for Ploverleigh, for on that date all the couples that had been brought together through the agency of the philtre were united in matrimony by the only bachelor in the place, the Rev. Stanley Gay. A week afterwards he took leave of his parishioners in an affecting sermon, and 'read himself in' at Crawleigh. He is still unmarried, and likely to remain so. He has quite got over his early disappointment, and he and the Bishop and Jessie have many a hearty laugh together over the circumstances under which the good old prelate wooed and won the bright-eyed little lady. Sir Caractacus died within a year of his marriage, and Zorah lives with her daughter-in-law at the Palace. The Bishop works hard at the art of pantomimic expression, but as yet with qualified success. He has lately taken to conversing with her through the medium of diagrams, many of which are very spirited in effect, though crude in design. It is not unlikely that they may be published before long. The series of twelve consecutive sketches, by which the Bishop informed his mother-in-law that, if she didn't mind her own business, and refrain from interfering between his wife and himself, he should be under the necessity of requiring her to pack up and be off, is likely to have a very large sale.

OLIVE SCHREINER

The Buddhist Priest's Wife

Cover her up! How still it lies! You can see the outline under the white. You would think she was asleep. Let the sunshine come in; it loved it so. She that had traveled so far, in so many lands, and done so much and seen so much, how she must like rest now! Did she ever love anything absolutely, this woman whom so many men loved, and so many women; who gave so much sympathy and never asked for anything in return! did she ever need a love she could not have? Was she never obliged to unclasp her fingers from anything to which they clung? Was she really so strong as she looked? Did she never wake up in the night crying for that which she could not have? Were thought and travel enough for her? Did she go about for long days with a weight that crushed her to earth? Cover her up! I do not think she would have liked us to look at her. In one way she was alone all her life; she would have liked to be alone now! . . . Life must have been very beautiful to her, or she would not look so young now. Cover her up! Let us go!

Many years ago in a London room, up long flights of stairs, a fire burned up in a grate. It showed the marks on the walls where pictures had been taken down, and the little blue flowers in the wall-paper and the blue felt carpet on the floor, and a woman sat by the fire in a chair at one side.

Presently the door opened, and the old woman came in who took care of the entrance hall downstairs.

'Do you not want anything to-night?' she said.

'No, I am only waiting for a visitor; when they have been, I shall go.'

'Have you got all your things taken away already?'

'Yes, only these I am leaving.'

The old woman went down again, but presently came up with a cup of tea in her hand.

'You must drink that; it's good for one. Nothing helps one like tea when one's been packing all day.'

The young woman at the fire did not thank her, but she ran her hand over the old woman's from the wrist to the fingers.

'I'll say good-bye to you when I go out.'

The woman poked the fire, put the last coals on, and went.

When she had gone the young one did not drink the tea, but drew her little silver cigarette case from her pocket and lighted a cigarette. For a while she sat smoking by the fire; then she stood up and walked the room.

When she had paced for a while she sat down again beside the fire. She threw the end of her cigarette away into the fire, and then began to walk again with her hands behind her. Then she went back to her seat and lit another cigarette, and paced again. Presently she sat down, and looked into the fire; she pressed the palms of her hands together, and then sat quietly staring into it.

Then there was a sound of feet on the stairs and someone knocked at the door.

She rose and threw the end into the fire and said without moving, 'Come in.'

The door opened and a man stood there in evening dress. He had a great-coat on, open in front.

'May I come in? I couldn't get rid of this downstairs; I didn't see where to leave it!' He took his coat off. 'How are you? This is a real bird's nest!'

She motioned to a chair.

'I hope you did not mind my asking you to come?'

'Oh no, I am delighted. I only found your note at my club twenty minutes ago.'

He sat down on a chair before the fire.

'So you really are going to India? How delightful! But what are you to do there? I think it was Grey told me six weeks ago you were going, but regarded it as one of those mythical stories which don't deserve credence. Yet I'm sure I don't know! Why, nothing would surprise me.'

He looked at her in a half-amused, half-interested way.

'What a long time it is since we met! Six months, eight?'

'Seven,' she said.

'I really thought you were trying to avoid me. What have you been doing with yourself all this time?'

'Oh, been busy. Won't you have a cigarette?' She held out the little case to him.

'Won't you take one yourself? I know you object to smoking with men, but you can make an exception in my case!'

'Thank you.' She lit her own and passed him the matches.

'But really what have you been doing with yourself all this time? You've entirely disappeared from civilized life. When I was down at the Grahams' in the spring, they said you were coming down there, and then at the last moment cried off. We were all quite disappointed. What is taking you to India now? Going to preach the doctrine of social and intellectual equality to the Hindu women and incite them to revolt? Marry some old Buddhist Priest, build a little cottage on the top of the Himalayas and live there, discuss philosophy and meditate? I believe that's what you'd like. I really shouldn't wonder if I heard you'd done it!'

She laughed and took out her cigarette case.

She smoked slowly.

'I've been here a long time, four years, and I want change. I was glad to see how well you succeeded in that election,' she said. 'You were much interested in it, were you not?'

'Oh, yes. We had a stiff fight. It tells in my favour, you know, though it was not exactly a personal matter. But it was a great worry.'

'Don't you think,' she said, 'you were wrong in sending that letter to the papers? It would have strengthened your position to have remained silent.'

'Yes, perhaps so; I think so now, but I did it under advice. However, we've won, so it's all right.' He leaned back in the chair.

'Are you pretty fit?'

'Oh, yes; pretty well; bored, you know. One doesn't know what all this working and striving is for sometimes.'

'Where are you going for your holiday this year?'

'Oh, Scotland, I suppose; I always do; the old quarters.'

'Why don't you go to Norway? It would be more change for you and rest you more. Did you get a book on sport in Norway?'

'Did you send it to me? How kind of you. I read it with much interest. I was almost inclined to start off there and then. I suppose it is the kind of *vis inertiae* that creeps over one as one grows older that sends one back to the old place. A change would he much better.'

'There's a list at the end of the book,' she said, 'of exactly the things one needs to take. I thought it would save trouble; you could just give it to your man, and let him get them all. Have you still got him?'

'Oh, yes. He's as faithful to me as a dog. I think nothing would induce him to leave me. He won't allow me to go out hunting since I sprained my foot last autumn. I have to do it surreptitiously. He thinks I can't keep my seat with a sprained ankle; but he's a very good fellow; takes care of me like a mother.' He smoked quietly with the firelight glowing on his black coat. 'But what are you going to India for? Do you know any one there?'

'No,' she said. 'I think it will be so splendid. I've always been a great deal interested in the East. It's a complex, interesting life.'

He turned and looked at her.

'Going to seek for more experience, you'll say, I suppose. I never knew a woman throw herself away as you do; a woman with your brilliant parts and attractions, to let the whole of life slip through your hands, and make nothing of it. You ought to be the most successful woman in London. Oh, yes; I know what you are going to say: "You don't care." That's just it; you don't. You are always going to get experience, going to get everything, and you never do. You are always going to write when you know enough, and you are never satisfied that you do. You ought to be making your two thousand a year, but you don't care. That's just it! Living, burying yourself here with a lot of old frumps. You will never do anything. You could have everything and you let it slip.'

'Oh, my life is very full,' she said. 'There are only two things that are absolute realities, love and knowledge, and you can't escape them.'

She had thrown her cigarette end away and was looking into the fire, smiling.

'I've let these rooms to a woman friend of mine.' She glanced round the room, smiling. 'She doesn't know I'm going to leave these things here for her. She'll like them because they were mine. The world's very beautiful, I think – delicious.'

'Oh, yes. But what do you do with it? What do you make of it? You ought to settle down and marry like other women, not go wandering about the world to India and China and Italy, and God knows where. You are simply making a mess of your life. You're always surrounding yourself with all sorts of extraordinary people. If I hear any man or woman is a great friend of yours, I always say: "What's the matter? Lost his money? Lost his character? Got an incurable disease?" I believe the only way in which any one becomes interesting to you is by having some complaint of mind or body. I believe you worship rags. To come and shut yourself up in a place like this away from everybody and everything! It's a mistake; it's idiotic, you know.'

'I'm very happy,' she said. 'You see,' she said, leaning forward towards the fire with her hands on her knees, 'what matters is that something should need you. It isn't a question of love. What's the use of being near a thing if other people could serve it as well as you can? If they could serve it better, it's pure selfishness. It's the need of one thing for another that makes the organic bond of union. You love mountains and horses, but they don't need you; so what's the use of saying anything about it! I suppose the most absolutely delicious thing in life is to feel a thing needs you, and to give at the moment it needs. Things that don't need you, you must love from a distance.'

'Oh, but a woman like you ought to marry, ought to have children. You go squandering yourself on every old beggar or forlorn female or escaped criminal you meet; it may be very nice for them, but it's a mistake from your point of view.'

He touched the ash gently with the tip of his little finger and let it fall.

'I intend to marry. It's a curious thing,' he said, resuming his pose with an elbow on one knee and his head bent forward on one side, so that she saw the brown hair with its close curls a little tinged with gray at the sides, 'that when a man reaches a certain age he wants to marry. He doesn't fall in love; it's not that he definitely plans anything; but he has a feeling that he ought to have a home and a wife and children. I suppose it is the same kind of feeling that makes a bird build nests at certain times of the year. It's not love; it's something else. When I was a young man I used to despise men for getting married; wondered what they did it for; they had everything to lose and nothing to gain. But when a man gets to be six-and-thirty his feeling changes. It's not love, passion, he wants; it's a home; it's a wife and children. He may have a house and servants; it isn't the same thing. I should have thought a woman would have felt it too.'

She was quiet for a minute, holding a cigarette between her fingers; then she said slowly:

'Yes, at times a woman has a curious longing to have a child, especially when she gets near to thirty or over it. It's something distinct from love for any definite person. But it's a thing one has to get over. For a woman, marriage is much more serious than for a man. She might pass her life without meeting a man whom she could possibly love, and, if she met him, it might not be right or possible. Marriage has become very complex now it has become so largely intellectual. Won't you have another?'

She held out the case to him. 'You can light it from mine.' She bent forward for him to light it.

'You are a man who ought to marry. You've no absorbing mental work with which the woman would interfere; it would complete you.' She sat back, smoking serenely.

'Yes,' he said, 'but life is too busy; I never find time to look for one, and I haven't a fancy for the pink-and-white prettiness so common and that some men like so. I need something else. If I am to have a wife I shall have to go to America to look for one.'

'Yes, an American would suit you best.'

'Yes,' he said, 'I don't want a woman to look after; she must be self-sustaining and she mustn't bore you. You know what I mean. Life is too full of cares to have a helpless child added to them.'

'Yes,' she said, standing up and leaning with her elbow against the fireplace. 'The kind of woman you want would be young and strong; she need not be excessively beautiful, but she must be attractive; she must have energy, but not too strongly marked an individuality; she must be largely neutral; she need not give you too passionate or too deep a devotion, but she must second you in a thoroughly rational manner. She must have the same aims and tastes that you have. No woman has the right to marry a man if she has to bend herself out of shape for him. She might wish to, but she could never be to him with all her passionate endeavour what the other woman could be to him without trying. Character will dominate over all and will come out at last.'

She looked down into the fire.

'When you marry you mustn't marry a woman who flatters you too much. It is always a sign of falseness somewhere. If a woman absolutely loves you as herself, she will criticize and understand you as herself. Two people who are to live through life together must be able to look into each other's eyes and speak the truth. That helps one through life. You would find many such women in America,' she said: 'women who would help you to succeed, who would not drag you down.'

'Yes, that's my idea. But how am I to obtain the ideal woman?'

'Go and look for her. Go to America instead of Scotland this year. It is perfectly right. A man has a right to look for what he needs. With a woman it is different. That's one of the radical differences between men and women.'

She looked downwards into the fire.

'It's a law of her nature and of sex relationship. There's nothing arbitrary or conventional about it any more than there is in her having to bear her child while the male does not. Intellectually we may both be alike. I suppose if fifty men and fifty women had to solve a mathematical problem, they would all do it in the same way; the more abstract and intellectual, the more alike we are. The nearer you approach to the personal and sexual, the more different we are. If I were to represent men's and women's natures,' she said, 'by a diagram, I would take two circular discs; the right side of each I should paint bright red; then I would shade the red away till in a spot on the left edge it became blue in the one and green in the other. That spot represents sex, and the nearer you come to it, the more the two discs differ in color. Well then, if you turn them so that the red sides touch, they seem to be exactly alike, but if you turn them so that the green and blue paint form their point of contact, they will seem to be entirely unlike. That's why you notice the brutal, sensual men invariably believe women are entirely different from men, another species of creature; and very cultured, intellectual men sometimes believe we are exactly alike. You see, sex love in its substance may be the same in both of us; in the form of its expression it must differ. It is not man's fault; it is nature's. If a man loves a woman, he has a right to try to make her love him because he can do it openly, directly, without bending. There need be no subtlety, no indirectness. With a woman it's not so; she can take no love that is not laid openly, simply, at her feet. Nature ordains that she should never show what she feels; the woman who had told a man she loved him would have put between them a barrier once and for ever that could not be crossed; and if she subtly drew him towards her, using the woman's means – silence, finesse, the dropped handkerchief, the surprise visit, the gentle assertion she had not thought to see him when she had come a long way to meet him, then she would be damned; she would hold the love, but she would have desecrated it by subtlety; it would have no value. Therefore she must always go with her arms folded sexually; only the love which lays itself down at her feet and implores of her to accept it is love she can ever rightly take up. That is the true difference between a man and a woman. You may seek for love because you can do it openly; we cannot because we must do it subtly. A woman should always walk with her arms folded. Of course friendship is different. You are on a perfect equality with man then; you can ask him to come and see you as I asked you. That's the beauty of the intellect and intellectual life to a woman, that she drops her shackles a little; and that is why she shrinks from sex so. If she were dying perhaps, or doing something equal to death, she might . . . Death means so much more to a woman than a man; when you knew you were dying, to look round on the world and feel the bond of sex that has broken and crushed you all your life gone, nothing but the human left, no woman any more, to meet everything on perfectly even ground. There's no reason why you shouldn't go to America and look for a wife perfectly deliberately. You will have to tell no lies. Look till you find a woman that you absolutely love, that you have not the smallest doubt suits you apart from love, and then ask her to marry you. You must have children; the life of an old childless man is very sad.'

'Yes, I should like to have children. I often feel now, what is it all for, this work, this striving, and no one to leave it to? It's a blank, suppose I succeed . . . ?'

'Suppose you get your title?'

'Yes; what is it all worth to me if I've no one to leave it to? That's my feeling. It's really very strange to be sitting and talking like this to you. But you are so different from other women. If all women were like you, all your theories of the equality of men and women would work. You're the only woman with whom I never realize that she is a woman.'

'Yes,' she said.

She stood looking down into the fire.

'How long will you stay in India?'

'Oh, I'm not coming back.'

'Not coming back! That's impossible. You will be breaking the hearts of half the people here if you don't. I never knew a woman who had such power of entrapping men's hearts as you have in spite of that philosophy of yours. I don't know,' he smiled, 'that I should not have fallen into the snare myself – three years ago I almost thought I should – if you hadn't always attacked me so incontinently and persistently on all and every point and on each and every occasion. A man doesn't like pain. A succession of slaps damps him. But it doesn't seem to have that effect on other men . . . There was that fellow down in the country when I was there last year, perfectly ridiculous. You know his name . . .' He moved his finger to try and remember it – 'big, yellow mustache, a major, gone to the east coast of Africa now; the ladies unearthed it that he was always carrying about a photograph of yours in his pocket; and he used to take out little scraps of things you printed and show them to people mysteriously. He almost had a duel with a man one night after dinner because he mentioned you; he seemed to think there was something incongruous between your name and – '

'I do not like to talk of any man who has loved me,' she said. 'However small and poor his nature may be, he has given me his best. There is nothing ridiculous in love. I think a woman should feel that all the love men have given her which she has not been able to return is a kind of crown set up above her which she is always trying to grow tall enough to wear. I can't bear to think that all the love that has been given me has been wasted on something unworthy of it. Men have been very beautiful and greatly honored me. I am grateful to them. If a man tells you he loves you,' she said, looking into the fire, 'with his breast uncovered before you for you to strike him if you will, the least you can do is to put out your hand and cover it up from other people's eyes. If I were a deer,' she said, 'and a stag got hurt following me, even though I could not have him for a companion, I would stand still and scrape the sand with my foot over the place where his blood had fallen; the rest of the herd should never know he had been hurt there following me. I would cover the blood up, if I were a deer,' she said, and then she was silent.

Presently she sat down in her chair and said, with her hand before her: 'Yet, you know, I have not the ordinary feeling about love. I think the one who is loved confers the benefit on the one who loves, it's been so great and beautiful that it should be loved. I think the man should be grateful to the woman or the woman to the man whom they have been able to love, whether they have been loved back or whether circumstances have divided them or not.' She stroked her knee softly with her hand.

'Well, really, I must go now.' He pulled out his watch. 'It's so fascinating sitting here talking that I could stay all night, but I've still two engagements.' He rose; she rose also and stood before him looking up at him for a moment.

'How well you look! I think you have found the secret of perpetual youth. You don't look a day older than when I first saw you just four years ago. You always look as if you were on fire and being burned up, but you never are, you know.'

He looked down at her with a kind of amused face as one does at an interesting child or a big Newfoundland dog.

'When shall we see you back?'

'Oh, not at all!'

'Not at all! Oh, we must have you back; you belong here, you know. You'll get tired of your Buddhist and come back to us.'

'You didn't mind my asking you to come and say good-bye?' she said in a childish manner unlike her determinateness when she discussed anything impersonal. 'I wanted to say good-bye to every one. If one hasn't said good-bye one feels restless and feels one would have to come back. If one has said good-bye to all one's friends, then one knows it is all ended.'

'Oh, this isn't a final farewell! You must come in ten years' time and we'll compare notes – you about your Buddhist Priest, I about my fair ideal American; and we'll see who succeeded best.'

She laughed.

'I shall always see your movements chronicled in the newspapers, so we shall not be quite sundered; and you will hear of me perhaps.'

'Yes, I hope you will be very successful.'

She was looking at him, with her eyes wide open, from head to foot. He turned to the chair where his coat hung.

'Can't I help you put it on?'

'Oh, no, thank you.'

He put it on.

'Button the throat,' she said, 'the room is warm.'

He turned to her in his great-coat and with his gloves. They were standing near the door.

'Well, good-bye. I hope you will have a very pleasant time.'

He stood looking down upon her, wrapped in his great-coat.

She put up one hand a little in the air. 'I want to ask you something,' she said quickly.

'Well, what is it?'

'Will you please kiss me?'

For a moment he looked down at her, then he bent over her.

In after years he could never tell certainly, but he always thought she put up her hand and rested it on the crown of his head, with a curious soft caress, something like a mother's touch when her child is asleep and she does not want to wake it. Then he looked round, and she was gone. The door had closed noiselessly. For a moment he stood motionless, then he walked to the fireplace and looked down into the fender at a little cigarette end lying there, then he walked quickly back to the door and opened it. The stairs were in darkness and silence. He rang the bell violently. The old woman came up. He asked her where the lady was. She said she had gone out, she had a cab waiting. He asked when she would be back. The old woman said, 'Not at all'; she had left. He asked where she had gone. The woman said she did not know; she had left orders that all her letters should be kept for six or eight months till she wrote and sent her address. He asked whether she had no idea where he might find her. The woman said no. He walked up to a space in the wall where a picture had hung and stood staring at it as though the picture were still hanging there. He drew his mouth as though he were emitting a long whistle, but no sound came. He gave the old woman ten shillings and went downstairs.

That was eight years ago.

How beautiful life must have been to it that it looks so young still!

OSCAR WILDE

The Sphinx without a Secret

One afternoon I was sitting outside the Café de la Paix, watching the splendour and shabbiness of Parisian life, and wondering over my vermouth at the strange panorama of pride and poverty that was passing before me, when I heard some one call my name. I turned round, and saw Lord Murchison. We had not met since we had been at college together, nearly ten years before, so I was delighted to come across him again, and we shook hands warmly. At Oxford we had been great friends. I had liked him immensely, he was so handsome, so high-spirited, and so honourable. We used to say of him that he would be the best of fellows, if he did not always speak the truth, but I think we really admired him all the more for his frankness. I found him a good deal changed. He looked anxious and puzzled, and seemed to be in doubt about something. I felt it could not be modern scepticism, for Murchison was the stoutest of Tories, and believed in the Pentateuch as firmly as he believed in the House of Peers; so I concluded that it was a woman, and asked him if he was married yet.

'I don't understand women well enough,' he answered.

'My dear Gerald,' I said, 'women are meant to be loved, not to be understood.'

'I cannot love where I cannot trust,' he replied.

'I believe you have a mystery in your life, Gerald,' I exclaimed; 'tell me about it.'

'Let us go for a drive,' he answered, 'it is too crowded here. No, not a yellow carriage, any other colour – there, that dark green one will do;' and in a few moments we were trotting down the boulevard in the direction of the Madeleine.

'Where shall we go to?' I said.

'Oh, anywhere you like!' he answered – 'to the restaurant in the Bois; we will dine there, and you shall tell me all about yourself.'

'I want to hear about you first,' I said. 'Tell me your mystery.'

He took from his pocket a little silver-clasped morocco case, and handed it to me. I opened it. Inside there was the photograph of a woman. She was tall and slight, and strangely picturesque with her large vague eyes and loosened hair. She looked like a clairvoyante, and was wrapped in rich furs.

'What do you think of that face?' he said; 'is it truthful?'

I examined it carefully. It seemed to me the face of some one who had a secret, but whether that secret was good or evil I could not say. Its beauty was a beauty moulded out of many mysteries – the beauty, in fact, which is psychological, not plastic – and the faint smile that just played across the lips was far too subtle to be really sweet.

'Well,' he cried impatiently, 'what do you say?'

'She is the Gioconda in sables,' I answered. 'Let me know all about her.'

'Not now,' he said; 'after dinner,' and began to talk of other things.

When the waiter brought us our coffee and cigarettes I reminded Gerald of his promise. He rose from his seat, walked two or three times up and down the room, and, sinking into an armchair, told me the following story:

'One evening,' he said, 'I was walking down Bond Street about five o'clock. There was a terrific crush of carriages, and the traffic was almost stopped. Close to the pavement was standing a little yellow brougham, which, for some reason or other, attracted my attention. As I passed by there looked out from it the face I showed you this afternoon. It fascinated me immediately. All that night I kept thinking of it, and all the next day. I wandered up and down that wretched Row, peering into every carriage, and waiting for the yellow brougham; but I could not find *ma belle inconnue*, and at last I began to think she was merely a dream. About a week afterwards I was dining with Madame de Rastail. Dinner was for eight o'clock; but at half-past eight we were still waiting in the drawing-room. Finally the servant threw open the door, and announced Lady Alroy. It was the woman I had been looking for. She came in very slowly, looking like a moon-beam in grey lace, and, to my intense delight, I was asked to take her in to dinner. After we had sat down, I remarked quite innocently:

"I think I caught sight of you in Bond Street some time ago, Lady Alroy."
She grew very pale, and said to me in a low voice: "Pray do not talk so
loud; you may be overheard." I felt miserable at having made such a bad
beginning, and plunged recklessly into the subject of the French plays.
She spoke very little, always in the same low musical voice, and seemed
as if she was afraid of some one listening. I fell passionately, stupidly in
love, and the indefinable atmosphere of mystery that surrounded her
excited my most ardent curiosity. When she was going away, which she
did very soon after dinner, I asked her if I might call and see her. She
hesitated for a moment, glanced round to see if any one was near us, and
then said: "Yes; to-morrow at a quarter to five." I begged Madame de
Rastail to tell me about her; but all that I could learn was that she was a
widow with a beautiful house in Park Lane, and as some scientific bore
began a dissertation on widows, as exemplifying the survival of the matri-
monially fittest, I left and went home.

'The next day I arrived at Park Lane punctual to the moment, but was
told by the butler that Lady Alroy had just gone out. I went down to the
club quite unhappy and very much puzzled, and after long consideration
wrote her a letter, asking if I might be allowed to try my chance some
other afternoon. I had no answer for several days, but at last I got a little
note saying she would be at home on Sunday at four, and with this extraordinary postscript: "Please do not write to me here again; I will explain
when I see you." On Sunday she received me, and was perfectly charming;
but when I was going away she begged of me, if I ever had occasion to
write to her again, to address my letter to "Mrs Knox, care of Whittaker's
Library, Green Street." "There are reasons," she said, "why I cannot receive
letters in my own house."

'All through the season I saw a great deal of her, and the atmosphere
of mystery never left her. Sometimes I thought that she was in the power
of some man, but she looked so unapproachable that I could not believe
it. It was really very difficult for me to come to any conclusion, for she
was like one of those strange crystals that one sees in museums, which
are at one moment clear, and at another clouded. At last I determined to
ask her to be my wife: I was sick and tired of the incessant secrecy that
she imposed on all my visits, and on the few letters I sent her. I wrote to
her at the library to ask her if she could see me the following Monday at

six. She answered yes, and I was in the seventh heaven of delight. I was infatuated with her: in spite of the mystery, I thought then – in consequence of it, I see now. No; it was the woman herself I loved. The mystery troubled me, maddened me. Why did chance put me in its track?'

'You discovered it, then?' I cried.

'I fear so,' he answered. 'You can judge for yourself.'

'When Monday came round I went to lunch with my uncle, and about four o'clock found myself in the Marylebone Road. My uncle, you know, lives in Regent's Park. I wanted to get to Piccadilly, and took a short cut through a lot of shabby little streets. Suddenly I saw in front of me Lady Alroy, deeply veiled and walking very fast. On coming to the last house in the street, she went up the steps, took out a latch-key, and let herself in. "Here is the mystery," I said to myself; and I hurried on and examined the house. It seemed a sort of place for letting lodgings. On the doorstep lay her handkerchief, which she had dropped. I picked it up and put it in my pocket. Then I began to consider what I should do. I came to the conclusion that I had no right to spy on her, and I drove down to the club. At six I called to see her. She was lying on a sofa, in a tea-gown of silver tissue looped up by some strange moonstones that she always wore. She was looking quite lovely. "I am so glad to see you," she said; "I have not been out all day." I stared at her in amazement, and pulling the handkerchief out of my pocket, handed it to her. "You dropped this in Cumnor Street this afternoon, Lady Alroy," I said very calmly. She looked at me in terror, but made no attempt to take the handkerchief. "What were you doing there?" I asked. "What right have you to question me?" she answered. "The right of a man who loves you," I replied; "I came here to ask you to be my wife." She hid her face in her hands, and burst into floods of tears. "You must tell me," I continued. She stood up, and, looking me straight in the face, said: "Lord Murchison, there is nothing to tell you." – "You went to meet some one," I cried; "this is your mystery." She grew dreadfully white, and said, "I went to meet no one." – "Can't you tell the truth?" I exclaimed. "I have told it," she replied. I was mad, frantic; I don't know what I said, but I said terrible things to her. Finally I rushed out of the house. She wrote me a letter the next day; I sent it back unopened, and started for Norway with Alan Colville. After a month I came back, and the first thing I saw in 'The Morning Post' was the death of Lady Alroy. She had caught a chill at the Opera, and had died in five days of congestion of the lungs. I shut myself up and saw no one. I had loved her so much, I had loved her so madly. Good God! how I had loved that woman!'

'You went to the street, to the house in it?' I said.

'Yes,' he answered. 'One day I went to Cumnor Street. I could not help it; I was tortured with doubt. I knocked at the door, and a respectable-looking woman opened it to me. I asked her if she had any rooms to let. "Well, sir," she replied, "the drawing-rooms are supposed to be let; but I have not seen the lady for three months, and as rent is owing on them, you can have them." – "Is this the lady?" I said, showing the photograph. "That's her, sure enough," she exclaimed; "and when is she coming back, sir?" – "The lady is dead," I replied. "Oh, sir, I hope not!" said the woman; "she was my best lodger. She paid me three guineas a week merely to sit in my drawing-rooms now and then." – "She met some one here?" I said; but the woman assured me that it was not so, that she always came alone, and saw no one. "What on earth did she do here?" I cried. "She simply sat in the drawing-room, sir, reading books, and sometimes had tea," the woman answered. I did not know what to say, so I gave her a sovereign and went away. Now, what do you think it all meant? You don't believe the woman was telling the truth?'

'I do.'

'Then why did Lady Alroy go there?'

'My dear Gerald,' I answered, 'Lady Alroy was simply a woman with a mania for mystery. She took these rooms for the pleasure of going there with her veil down, and imagining she was a heroine. She had a passion for secrecy, but she herself was merely a Sphinx without a secret.'

'Do you really think so?'

'I am sure of it,' I replied.

He took out the morocco case, opened it, and looked at the photograph. 'I wonder?' he said at last.

GEORGE MOORE

A Novel in a Nutshell

Mr Bryant was tall, slim, and not many years over thirty; his features were regular, but no one had ever mentioned him as a good-looking man. He lived with his mother in Bryanston Square, but he had chambers in Norman's Inn, where he wrote waltzes, received his friends, and practised wood-carving.

The service in Norman's Inn was performed by a retinue of maid-servants, working under the order of the porter and his wife; but these girls were idle, dirty, and slovenly; the porter's wife was an execrable cook, and Mr Bryant was very particular about what he ate, and could not bear the slightest speck of dust on the numerous knick-knacks that filled his sitting-room. So, after many complaints, he resolved to have a servant of his own. His mother had procured him one Clara Tompson, from King Edward's School, a young girl just turned seventeen, pale-complexioned, delicate features, and blue eyes, which seemed to tell of a delicate, senti-mental nature.

She stood now watching Mr Bryant eat his breakfast. He did not require her service, and wondered why she lingered.

'I'm thinking of leaving, Sir. If you don't mind, I should like to go at the end of the week.'

Mr Bryant looked up, surprised, 'Why do you want to leave, Clara?'

She told him she did not like Norman's Inn, and little by little he drew the story of her trouble from her. The porter's nephew had come to take the watchman's place until the old soldier returned from the hospital. Almost from the first he had begun to plague her with his attentions. Last week Fanny had asked her to come to the Turk's Head, a music-hall at the other end of the lane. Harry had sat with his arm round Fanny the whole time, and Mr Stokes's nephew had put his hand on her knee. She couldn't get away from him, and didn't want to make a fuss. At last she had to get up, but Harry had pulled her back and told her to drink some beer. The beer was poison; she thought they must have put something in it: she had only had a mouthful, and that made her feel quite giddy.

'And the singing that you heard at the Turk's Head?' asked Mr Bryant.

'It wasn't very nice, sir; but it wasn't quite so bad as what goes on in the kitchen of an evening when all the girls are there. I do all I can, sir, to keep out of his way, but he follows me down to the kitchen and kisses me by force. The others only laugh at me, and I'm insulted because I won't dance with him.'

'But what are these dances like?'

'Oh, sir! I can't tell you, sir! I try to see as little of it as I can. The other evening I said I'd stop there no longer, and walked up and down the inn until bedtime. That's how I got my cold.'

'I don't like to lose you, Clara. I can speak to Mr Stokes, and tell him that you must be let alone.'

'Oh, no, sir! don't do that – it would only set them more than ever against me. It isn't for me to find fault, but I'm not used to such company – it was so different in the school.' Tears started to her eyes; she turned aside to hide them.

Mr Bryant was touched.

'I won't have you go down into that kitchen any more, Clara. There's no reason why you should. It is all the same to me if I pay the porter for your food or if I put you on board wages. There's a kitchen here, you'll have coal and gas free. I'll give you ten shillings a week board wages.'

'Oh, sir, you're really too kind!'

'But you'll still have to sleep with Lizzie.'

'That doesn't matter, sir, so long as I haven't to go much to that kitchen. I was always there, sir, except when I was attending on you, sir, and that was so seldom.'

'You prefer to sit in these rooms?'

'Oh, sir!'

'You can sit in the back room and do your sewing when I'm here, and when I'm not here you can sit in this room. I'm afraid you'll find it lonely.'

'I sha'n't be lonely for their company. You're very good to me. I don't know how to thank you.'

When he returned from France he brought her back a shawl – a knitted silk shawl. The shawl meant that he had thought of her when he was away. She could hardly speak for happiness, and she spent hours thinking, wondering. It was such a pretty shawl; no other man would have chosen such a pretty shawl. There was no one like him. Her hands dropped on her knees, and she raised her eyes, now dim with dreams, and listened. He was singing, accompanying himself on the piano.

The days that he dined in the inn were red-letter days in her life, for he detained her during the meal with whatever conversation he thought would interest her, and she listened as a dog listens to its master, unmindful of the great love that consumed her or his indifference. One day there came a sharp double rap at the door which made them both start.

'That's the post,' she exclaimed.

'No: it is not the post,' she said, coming back, 'a messenger boy brought this letter, and he says there's an answer.'

Mr Bryant tore open the envelope, and Clara watched the eager expression on his face. He went to his desk and wrote a long letter. When he had fastened it she held out her hand, but he said he would speak to the boy himself.

Next morning there were several letters in the post-box: one was on perfumed paper, and she noticed that it bore the same perfume as the letter which the boy had brought yesterday.

'Any letter?'

'Yes, sir.'

Clara pulled up the blinds and prepared his bath. As she was leaving the room she looked back. He lay on his side, reading his letter, unconscious of everything but it. After breakfast he said –

'I want you to take a letter for me.'

'Do you want me to go at once, sir?'

'I want the letter to get there before twelve. There's plenty of time.'

'Is the letter finished, sir?'

'No, but it will be when you have done up my room.'

Mr Bryant was sitting in an attitude habitual to him when she came for the letter – with his left hand he held his chin, his right arm was thrown forward over the edge of the desk.

'Is the letter ready, sir?'

'Yes, here it is: Mrs Alexander, 37, Cadogan Gardens. You know how to get there?'

'No, sir.'

'You take the train to Sloane Square, and it is within a few minutes' walk of the station.'

She had often wondered if he were in love with any woman. None ever came to his chambers. But this Mrs Alexander, who was she? He had not told her not to leave the letter if she were out . . . Then why had he told the boy last night not to leave the letter? Mrs Alexander might be a widow. The thought frightened her; Mr Bryant might marry, give up his chambers in the inn, and send her away. Perhaps this was the very woman who would bring ruin upon her. She stopped, overcome by a sudden faintness, and when she raised her eyes she saw that a lady was watching her from a drawing-room window. Was this the number? Yes, this was 37. Before she had time to ring, the door was opened, and a lady said –

'I'm Mrs Alexander – is that letter for me?'

'Yes, Ma'am.'

Mrs Alexander was a small woman, dressed in a black woollen gown, well cut to her slight figure. The pallor of her face was heightened by the blackness of her hair. She stood reading the letter avidly, the black bow of a tiny slipper advanced beyond the skirt, her hand clasping the hand of a little child of four, who stood staring at Clara.

'She opened the door herself, so that the servants might not know that she received a letter,' Clara thought, as she sat in the train studying the handwriting so that she might know it again.

'She's no widow, for if she was she'd not take the trouble to watch from the window.' Clara was shocked at Mrs Alexander's wickedness. 'Living in that fine house, a good husband, no doubt, and that dear little girl to think of. But these sort of women don't think of anything but themselves.'

One morning she found a small lace handkerchief on one of the armchairs. Had Mrs Alexander given it to him, or had she been to his rooms late and forgotten it? It had been her pleasure not to allow a speck of dust to lie on the eighteenth-century tables, china vases, and the pictures in white frames. But another woman had been there, and all her pleasure in the room was destroyed. Mrs Alexander had sat on that chair: she had played on the piano; she had stood by the bookcase; she had taken down the books and leant over Mr Bryant's shoulder.

A month later the tea table wore a beautiful white cloth, worked over with red poppies, a bottle of smelling-salts appeared on his table, and, though it was winter, there were generally flowers in the vases. Clara noticed that the stamps on Mrs Alexander's letters were different from ordinary English stamps, and when the ordinary stamp reappeared on sweet-seented envelopes she knew that Mrs Alexander had come back.

'Clara. I should like you to dust and tidy up the place as much as possible.'

'Aren't the rooms clean, then, sir?'

'Well, I fancied they were getting rather dusty. I don't mean that it is your fault; the amount of smuts that come in from the chimney-pots opposite is something dreadful. I shall be going out in the afternoon; you'll have time for a thorough clean. You can get Lizzie to help you, and not only this room, but all the rooms. We are getting on into spring. I don't see why we should not have fresh curtains up in the bed-room, and don't forget to wash my brushes and to put a new toilet cover on the table. You might go to Covent Garden and order in some flowers – some bunches of lilac; they'll freshen up the place. I shall want some hyacinths, too, for the windows.'

Next morning the servants stopped as they went up the inn with their trays to admire Mr Bryant's window. He called to Clara for the watering-pot, and sent her to the restaurant for the bill of fare. At one o'clock the white-aproned cook-boys came up the inn with trays on their heads. The oysters, the bread and butter, and the Chablis were on the table. Everything was ready. The church clock had struck the half-hour, and Mr Bryant was beginning to complain – to express fear that the lady might have mistaken the day, when a slight interrogative knock was heard at the door. In a moment Mr Bryant was out of the sitting-room; he thrust his servant back into the kitchen, and she heard the swishing sound of a silk dress. A few moments after, the sitting-room door opened, and Mr Bryant called her.

'Is the lunch all ready, Clara? Is everything in the kitchen?'

'Yes, sir.'

'Then I'll get the things out myself, I sha'n't want you all the afternoon. You can go out for a walk if you like; but be back between five and six, in time to clear away.'

It was the sharp, peremptory tone of a master speaking to a servant, a tone which she had never heard from him before, and it made her feel that she was something below him, something that he was kind to because it was his nature to be kind.

Clara realized this with a distinctness which she was unaccustomed to, and in a sick paralysis of mind she took the dish of cutlets and placed it in the warmth, and was glad to leave the chambers; and meeting Lizzie as she went up the inn she told her she was feeling very bad, and was going to lie down. Would she kindly answer Mr Bryant if he called, and get him what he wanted? Lizzie promised that she would, and Clara went upstairs.

About five o'clock Lizzie came to her with the news that Mr Bryant was very sorry to hear she was unwell. Could he do anything for her? Was there anything he could send her? Would she see the doctor?

No, no, she wanted nothing, only to be alone. She caught the pillow, rolled herself over, and Lizzie heard her crying in the darkness, and when the coarse girl put her arms about her Clara turned round and sobbed upon her shoulder. Bessie was breathing hard, Fanny snored intermittently, and, speaking very low, Lizzie said –

'I suppose it is that you care for him?'

'I don't know; I don't know. He don't care to talk to me as he used. I feel that miserable – I can't stop here – I can't – '

'Yer ain't going to chuck your situation for him?'

'I don't know.'

'You'll be better to-morrow – them fancies wears off. Ah, that's why you wouldn't go out with Mr Stokes's nephew. Well, he was a low lot.'

'He was quite different.'

That was all the explanation Clara could give, but it seemed enough, for, as one animal understands another's inarticulate cry, so did Lizzie's common mind seem to divine the meaning of the words 'it was quite different'.

'A gentleman's nice soft speech and his beautiful clothes get on one somehow. I know what you means, yet Fanny says she likes Harry best when he's dirty.'

Next morning, when Clara went up with Mr Bryant's hot water, she saw that a letter from Mrs Alexander was in the post-box. He read it in bed, and he re-read it at breakfast – he did not seem even to know that she was in the room. She lingered, hoping that he would speak to her. She only wanted him to speak to her just as he used to – about herself, about himself. She did not wish to be wholly forgotten. But he was always reading letters from Mrs Alexander or writing letters to her. She hated having to take letters to Cadogan Gardens, and Mrs Alexander seemed to come more and more frequently to Norman's Inn. And every day she grew paler and thinner. She lost her strength, and at last could not accomplish her work. Mr Bryant complained of dust and untidiness. She listened to his reproofs like a sick person who has not strength to answer. One morning she said, as she was clearing the breakfast things –

'I'm thinking of leaving, sir.'

'Of leaving, Clara!' and, raising his eyes from the letter he was writing, Mr Bryant looked at her in blank astonishment. Then a smile began to appear on his face. 'Are you going to be married?' he said.

'No, sir.'

'Then why do you want to leave?'

'I think I'd like to go, sir.'

'You can get more wages elsewhere?'

'No, sir, it isn't that.'

'Then what is it? Haven't I been kind enough? Can I do anything? Do you want more money?'

'No, sir; it's nothing to do with money.'

'Then what is it?'

'I think I'd like to leave, sir.'

'When?'

'I should like to go at once.'

'At once! You don't think of the annoyance and trouble you're putting me to. I shall have to look out for another servant. Really, I think – of course, if you were going to get married, or if you had an offer of a better situation, I should say nothing; but to leave me in the lurch – some whim. I suppose you'd like a change?'

'I don't think that the inn agrees with me, sir.'

'You are looking poorly, If you'd like to go for a holiday – '

'No, sir; I think I'd like to leave.'

Mr Bryant's face grew suddenly overcast, and he muttered something about ingratitude. The word cut her to the heart; but there was no help for it – she had to go.

Her idol was taken from her – the idol that represented all that she could understand of grace, light, and beauty, and losing it, the whole world became for her a squalid kitchen, where coarse girls romped to a tune played on a concertina by a shoe-boy sitting on the dresser.

BARRY PAIN

The Autobiography of an Idea

I

BEFORE BIRTH

I am a literary idea. Unborn as yet, I have not the incarnation of paper and printing ink which will be mine hereafter. I am conscious. I have knowledge without the usual apparatus for its acquisition and storage. I see without eyes, and hear without ears. I move as I will, and material things cannot hinder my movements. They are swifter than light, and just as swift as thought. You know, of course, that if an idea is going to come to you, neither locked doors nor iron walls will prevent it; it arrives inevitably and insuperably; you are to be its parent and make it come into the world. You may be ranked as a genius because you are its parent, and (this amuses me) you will think that you are its parent because you are a genius.

To the large eyes of the imagination I might be pictured, in my unborn state, as a Puck-like phantom; only the imagination can see me until I select my parent. Ideas have that privilege. Human beings – on very slight evidence – believe that they do not select their parents; but, on the other hand, they believe – on no evidence at all – that they do select their ideas. I am not prescient, but I fancy that the man whom I select for my parent should be a very happy man. I am a perfectly brilliant idea. I am new, and I am a master; the world will say it. I shall bring fortune and fame to my parent. Even now – when I am unborn and cannot tell the precise form that I shall take – I exult in my own utter goodness. This is, of course, vain. But then humility is only one of the impositions of the weak majority upon the strong minority, to enable the weak majority to keep up a self-respect to which facts do not entitle it.

I decided to come here. Before me lies a vast mass of building materials, sorted out into houses and the like, and known on the eighteenpenny folding map as 'London and its Environs.' It swarms. It is too large. Let me see what is immediately before me.

Before me is No. 23 Harriet Terrace, Fulham. It is a new terrace of thirty-pound houses, and there is no external difference, except the number, between 23 and the rest. It is the residence of Albert Weeks, literary hack. Shall I enter, and bid Albert Weeks be my parent? I should bring him money and reputation. He would be able to live in a better house than this; people would come to him and say, 'Albert Weeks, where *did* you get that perfectly splendid idea?' He would taste popularity, smile complacently, and subscribe to a press-cutting agency. Shall I select him or not? He might possibly, after he had become my parent, be unable to reach the same level again. But that disaster rarely happens. Ideas and sheep follow where there are ideas and sheep in front of them; genius is more often chronic than acute. I do not think that I should have to reproach myself with having caused him ultimately the bitterest failure – the failure of a man who once succeeded. But shall I select him?

Albert Weeks is married, of course, and has three children. His wife is well-meaning, but, I fear, a trifle under-educated. He met her in the old days when he was on a kind of a spree; his love-making was a kind of a spree; there was a touch of sheer spree even in his marriage. It was all irresponsible – enthusiastic – desperate; and the spree is well out of their lives for ever and ever – unless I interfere. They are still heart-fond of each other, though she has ceased to remark on his cleverness and sometimes is almost snappish, and he has no time to pet her because he is so busy for so little remuneration.

The front room in which he is sitting is rather sordid. They call it the drawing-room, sometimes substitute it for the nursery, and habitually use it as his study. There is a quaint gathering of antagonistic furniture. He bought as little furniture as possible at first – because he was no fool and knew that they would have to be economical – and he has added to it since on occasions when he could not possibly afford it. There are, for instance, two chairs from a drawing-room suite – two only. These are covered with pale green velvet, and the velvet is covered with dust. On the chair nearest to the table at which he is writing stands a chipped cup of cold tea, surmounting the dust and the velvet. The cold tea seems to be looking upward with a grey, patient eye at the gaudy paper lamp-shade, the photogravure of 'The Prodigal Son,' and the smoked ceiling. It is a room that must always have had crumbs in it. House-flies go long distances in order to die in this room. They have died conspicuously and frequently in it. In one corner broken and bygone bamboo has now definitely despaired of ever signifying refinement; and in the one piano-sconce which is not broken lingers the stump of a candle that has wept its composite heart out over the stained keyboard – wept for the death of the flies, and the despair of the bad bamboo, and the general deadliness of everything.

There is on the table a handsome, black-spotted wedding present of an inkstand. In front of it sits Albert Weeks at work. He is rather a small man with sandy hair, and the frock-coat which he has given up wearing out-of-doors, or when, as his wife says, 'there are people.' There are not any now, for he is alone in the room. The expression of his face is careful. He has to be careful, because the editor of *The Inner Circle* was by no means satisfied with his last batch of paragraphs, and he cannot afford to be deprived of the guinea a week which he receives from that very fashionable journal.

The editor had said – though more rudely, technically and briefly – that either Mr Albert Weeks would have to convey a more convincing impression of his intimate acquaintance with high society or *The Inner Circle* would dispense with his valuable services. The words that the Editor – who was rather less fashionable than his penny panting paper – actually used were, 'More *savvy*, or outside only, my dear boy, and don't you forget it.'

What are you to do when you are too good to know the butler, and not good enough for the butler's master to know you? This is what, I perceive, Albert Weeks is doing, writing laboriously:

'The season is dying fast, and I am sure that most of my readers will agree with me that it has been an unusually brilliant one. So everybody was saying to me at Lady Ballingham's last night. By the way, Lady Ballingham must have the secret of eternal youth; last night she looked more beautiful than ever. As for her house in Park Lane, I have always considered it to be quite the most charming town house that I have seen in the whole course of my experience. Well, the long round of delightful and luxurious – '

Here he is interrupted, because his worn-out, striving, vulgar, respectable, loving, sharpish wife had come into the room with a blue paper in her hand.

'Supper, Albert; come on now. Oh, you ain't touched your tea, and I was particular to bring it. Are you comin'? 'Ennery 'as broke the soap-dish in the nursery; that's what the cryin' was about. This here is Bilderspin's for what he did to the kitchen range. It's high – one-seventeen-six.'

That is the last straw. His editor has bothered him. His work has bothered him. He is very tired. A paragraph – which was really coming out very nicely – has been interrupted. Money is very scarce. And supper is mere mutton, and his wife looks rather ill, and Bilderspin is one-seventeen-six. The combination over-powers him. The little man throws down his pen, stamps his foot, and swears like a mad blackguard – swears profusely.

His wife takes a step backward, as if to get out of the room. Then her face becomes twisted, she sits down on the music-stool, and suddenly begins to cry. She is shaken with sobs. 'Oh, Albert! Oh, Albert!' she says, over and over again, and then: 'How can you be so cruel? Aren't things bad enough without that?'

Then he goes quickly to her, and is remorseful. He is not angry with her, of course. It is only that things are going so badly. He takes her hand. She regains her composure. She is sure that he is quite overworked, but he ought not to give way; on the contrary, he should 'ope for the best. There is a good deal of make-believe cheerfulness over the mere mutton subsequently.

Now, then, shall I make this man my parent? If I crept through that sandy hair into the whitey-grey brain, what a change there would be. He would be conscious that he had got a new, tremendous, imperial idea. He would put down his knife and fork, finish the beer in his glass at one gulp, explain hurriedly to his wife that he was really inspired this time, and rush wildly at the handsome inkstand and his work. By the following midday I should be in manuscript. In six weeks Albert would be famous. In six months he would have real money and no debts, and there would be more money to come. There would be a new soap-dish, new furniture, new dresses for his wife. 'Ennery would have toys and a go-cart; Albert would, on little occasions, have Heidsieck. They would be off to the seaside for a fortnight, and do the thing well, and the personal paragraphs would say that Mr Weeks and his family were spending the winter in Brighton, 'where it is to be hoped that this new and brilliant author will not allow his pen to be idle.' No, I definitely decide that I will *not* make Albert Weeks my parent. I am not a philanthropist; I am only an idea. I do not want to benefit Albert Weeks, and I do want to satisfy my own whim. My own whim definitely refuses Albert Weeks.

At the same time, I am in a great hurry to be born. I have knowledge, but it is limited. For instance, I believe that I am an idea for a short story, but I am not sure. I know I am a miraculously good idea, but I do not know in what way I am miraculously good. I yearn to see myself in my final form. I must positively get born.

Well, let me examine elsewhere.

Here, I observe, the traffic is being partially disturbed by a long funeral procession coming briskly back from the cemetery. In the first coach is a young man alone. He is in deep mourning. He has drawn the window-blinds down. His hat is placed on the front seat. He himself is kneeling on the floor of the coach; his arms sprawl over the back seat; his eyes are glaring, hot with unshed tears; he bends his head and bites the wrist of one hand. I knew his name at once and something about him. He is the Hon. Charles Turnour Wylmot. Away in the cemetery lies the still body of Maud Farradyce, whom Wylmot was to have married two months hence if she had lived. The agony of his grief would not be doubted by anyone who saw him now.

Yet Wylmot is a man who has always doubted himself. He is haunted with the thought that he is a sham. He once doubted his love for his books, and had himself put up for a sporting club which neither interested him nor desired his membership. The reactionary fit was bitter, but it was short. As with his books so with his writing. In proud moments he believes that he is going to be a leader; he pays for his pride with days of depression when he doubts whether he is even capable of being a decent follower. As with his writing so with his love. A few weeks ago he asked himself seriously if he was not merely trying to be romantic, if he really loved this Maud Farradyce who was to be his wife. That doubt went before the pretty yellow-headed girl died. And now he does not doubt his sorrow.

Yes, the Hon. Charles Turnour Wylmot shall be my parent. He shall bring me into the world. Now, as he sprawls in that mourning-coach, his wild, aching brain shall become possessed of me. It is a delightful whim.

In I go.

II

BIRTH

The Hon. Charles Turnour Wylmot has, later in the same day, in the solitude of his comfortable chambers overlooking Piccadilly, just recovered from rather an unpleasant fit of hysteria. Albert Weeks would have thanked God for me, but Wylmot positively does not want to be my parent. He would cheerfully sacrifice a year's income if by so doing he could definitely get me out of his head. But he cannot. I am going to be born, and this is the first part of the process.

The trouble is that I am inappropriate – horribly and grotesquely inappropriate; for I have discovered more about myself, and I find that I am a humorous idea. I am the newest, the most delicious, the most inevitably humorous idea that ever has been or ever will be. The bare thought of me brings a deep satisfaction right away down in the very pit of one's appreciations. At first I am too great for laughter, but the laughter comes. It comes in chuckles; it swells and grows to shaking paroxysms. Here, in this room, but half an hour ago, Wylmot at last reached the full appreciation of me. It had been growing upon him ever since the moment in the mourning-coach when I first came to him. There had been at intervals sudden smiles over his face, succeeded by an expression of agonized shame and contrition. But at the full appreciation of me he gave up the struggle and began to laugh. He threw back his head; he stamped one foot; he held his sides with both hands; he roared; he howled helplessly. He staggered about the room, doubled up with convulsions of laughter; he tried to stop, but could not; he tried again, and for one moment gravity secured a foothold; then it slipped and off he went once more, worse than ever, roaring, howling, screaming, purple in the face.

His laughter stopped quite suddenly, as great fits of laughter often do, as if it had been cut short with a clean stroke of a knife. He took out his watch, glanced at it, and – just as he had realized the full humour of me – realized the full horror of the situation. Three short hours before he had stood beside an open grave, wherein he did then most truly believe that all his interest and all the brightness of his life lay. He had wanted the world to stop because Maud Farradyce was gone, and there was nothing else of importance. He had heard the robed priest, Maud's cousin, reciting in a voice that tried to be steadier than it was: 'From henceforth blessed are the dead which die in the Lord.' He had become unconscious then of the service, unconscious of anything but the burning in his heart. Someone had touched him on the shoulder when it was time to go.

That was three hours ago.

And yet he had just finished a fit of the wildest, most uncontrollable laughter. He had been allowing himself to be amused. It was just here that Wylmot had that unpleasant attack of hysteria.

He has recovered from it, and has composed himself. His face is very white now, and he looks rather like a man under a curse. He gets out his writing materials. 'Maud,' he says softly, 'you are not minding, are you? This damned thing has got into my head. I didn't want to think of anything humorous, but this came to me. Maud, it would make the dead laugh – it is *too* funny – and I don't want to think about it any more. That is why I am going to write it all out. Then perhaps I may be able to put it aside. Oh, Maud, don't think that I'm irreverent and unfeeling. My heart is dead and with you. I hate myself for having laughed, but I had to. I will get rid of this idea that's haunting me, and then I don't think I shall ever laugh again.'

He sits down, and at the top of the page writes in a large hand, 'Ellen.' It is the title of the story which is to embody me. He writes fast for half an hour, and then a servant brings in the lighted lamps.

'Will you dine in to-night, sir?' he asks, when Wylmot looks up from the paper.

'Yes – no – I don't know.' He speaks a little absent-mindedly, with one hand on his forehead, shading his eyes, as though he held the idea there and were afraid that it would escape. I have no intention of escaping. 'I'm busy; if I want to dine I'll go to the club. That will be all to-night.'

'Very good, sir.'

The moment the servant has gone, the pen dashes down on the paper again, as though it had gained an additional impetus by being kept back for a minute. He does not dine out; he does not go to the club. He writes at lightning speed, only pausing to laugh from time to time more wildly than ever. He laughs and writes, writes and laughs, on and on, until he finds that the lamps are going out, and glances at his watch. It is five o'clock in the morning, and the stack of paper in front of him is the finished story – me myself – me, the magnificently humorous idea.

He draws back the curtain and lets the wan London daylight into the room. He realizes that he feels very exhausted and shaky, goes to the sideboard in an adjoining room, and gets himself some brandy. He drinks two glasses of it in rapid succession; then he goes off to bed. He is too tired for any further emotion. Laughter and tears alike will be a closed book to him until he has slept. He falls to sleep at once, and sleeps long – heavily, dreamlessly.

And I lie on the table in the study, new-born, in a snow-white manuscript incarnation. Will my reluctant parent burn me in the morning?

III

AFTER BIRTH

No, I am safe – safe in a foolscap envelope, directed, sufficiently stamped, whirled about by postal arrangements.

It happened in this way. Wylmot came into the study rather late next morning. He looked beaten, humiliated, tired, and half-starved. He cast one vindictive glance at me, and passed into the next room, where breakfast was ready for him. He was rather a long time over breakfast. When the emotional heart is completely broken up, the ordinary blood-pumping heart will still go on with its work. So with the other organs. Sorrow postpones appetite rather than destroys it. Wylmot had no dinner on the day of Maud's funeral; he had quite a nice breakfast on the following morning.

He came back to me at last, and I knew that he meant to destroy me. His face was intentionally rigid, the lip set firm, the eye merciless. Yet somewhere at the back of that merciless eye lurked a quite different, milder expression. The fried sole and eggs had done their carnal work; an incongruous geniality was struggling upward in him; he was going through the disgusting experience of feeling the better for his food. However, he poked the fire fiercely; then he lit a pipe, with the air that he did not care about it, but did not think it worth while to omit it. And then he picked me up, to hurl me in the fire. As he held me in his hand, his eye rested for one second on the front page.

In that one second my young life hung in the balance. It was a moment of terrible excitement for me. The eye glanced through a few lines, and I felt a shade safer. The eye twinkled. Then I knew that it was all over, and that my future was assured; Wylmot would not burn me. His habit of doubting himself had triumphed once more.

Of course, after that he had nothing to do but to sit down before the fire and argue it out with himself. The story should be published in *The Cosmopolitan*. Why not? It was unhappy, incongruous, wretched that a humorous idea should have come to him yesterday of all days. But he had not sought for it. He had even struggled to the utmost to put the thing out of his head. After all, if there was any harm done – if there had been any sign of want of feeling on his part – that lay far more in the writing than in the publication of the story. He would never put his name to it, of course. No one should be able to say that Maud's lover took the loss of her lightly. And he would take no remuneration for it. He would forward the amount of the cheque that he received from *The Cosmopolitan* to some charity. Besides, what right had he to keep that story from the public? It might not be – probably was not – so splendidly and amazingly good as he had imagined, but still he knew something of his business, and he knew that it would be likely to be popular. It might cheer many who were ill and depressed, and add something to the sum of human happiness. And he did not think that the critics, with their Athenian longing to see and to hear some new thing, would miss noticing the novelty and spirit of it. Indeed he had mingled feelings of philanthropy and self-abnegation as he sat down to write (on deep-edged paper) a little note to the editor of *The Cosmopolitan*.

To a certain extent he deceived himself. If Albert Weeks had voluntarily surrendered, on sentimental grounds, his honorarium for a short story, there would have been something in the sacrifice. But Wylmot had a private income, more than sufficient for all his needs, and to him the surrender of the cheque meant nothing. His surrender of the reputation which he believed would attach to the author of 'Ellen' did amount to something, for he had the weakness *cui etiam saepe boni indulgent;* but it did not amount to very much, because it is an exceedingly rare thing for a single short story to attract any attention at all, and although Wylmot believed in the chance of 'Ellen,' he knew that it was not more than a thousand-to-one chance. Nor was there very much in his doubt whether he had the right, for the sake of his personal sorrow, to deny the public an enjoyment.

The real reason that swayed him was paternal love. He had made me and seen that I was very good. He could not commit infanticide. He liked to explain himself, but his curious mixture of intense humility and some subtle vanities always made a desperate business of it whenever the real explanation was some simple thing.

His note to the editor of *The Cosmopolitan* ran as follows:

My dear Roger, – If you will read the enclosed story, you will understand how gladly I could have sent it to you a few weeks ago. As I did not do so then, I do so now – but, as you will imagine, with the greatest possible reluctance. I send it, because I do really think that it is the kind of thing that I have often heard you say you want. The only condition I make is that my name shall not be put to it, or disclosed in connection with it. I send it you to-day, instead of waiting, because I am leaving England, and I am trying to put my house in order before I go, and to clear up such business as I have on hand. But I am sure you will appreciate how eager I am to get to some place – any place – where solitude and silence are possible. I fear that this will be my last contribution to The Cosmopolitan. If it were not so melodramatic to say so, I would tell you that from henceforth I am practically dead. – Yours ever,　　　　　　　　　C. T. WYLMOT.

Now I think it must be acknowledged that, for a man who was not, as a rule, a liar, this letter is from a liar's point of view distinctly creditable.

I hold that letter in my own, somewhat corpulent, manuscript embrace.

It and I together, in the twilight seclusion of a foolscap envelope, are at present being whirled through postal machinery.

It is all over. My embodiments have been multiplied, since *The Cosmopolitan* has sold out seven editions of the number which contains me, to a marvellous extent. I have been a phenomenal and unprecedented success. In the library of the country-house, in the rectory, in Mayfair drawing-rooms, in Bloomsbury parlours, in working-men's clubs, in public-house bars, in England, in America, in the Colonies – everywhere where English, or an approximation to it, is spoken – I am the subject of discussion. There is a touch of the universal about me, and already the translators are busy. Enthusiastic critics have been more screamingly enthusiastic than ever before about me; the severest critics have unbent. I have the additional attraction of a mystery. Only two people really know who wrote me – Wylmot, my author, and Roger Birman, his editor – and neither of them will tell. On the authorship of 'Ellen' only two people have dared to question Birman: his assistant-editor and his proprietor. Birman has told neither, and quarrelled with both; it is the day of his glory, and he can afford to quarrel with almost anybody. *Canards* on the subject of my authorship have flown over the country in dense flocks. Albert Weeks has, as usual, drawn his long-bow at a venture; and, as usual, missed the joints of the harness. This is his little paragraph on the subject:

'The secret of the authorship of "Ellen" has been wonderfully well kept. There are probably not more than twenty people in London who really know it. When the secret is told, and – unless unforeseen circumstances occur – it will be told very soon, there will be howling and gnashing of teeth among various uninformed paragraphists who have been spreading their rumours on the subject. As an instance of the importance which the author attaches to the secret, I may say that one of the twenty "in the know" is a butler who became possessed of the information by accident, and that he is to be rewarded for his silence with an annuity of £200. More than this I am, unfortunately, not permitted to say at present.'

Of course, I knew from the first that I was exceedingly good, but still it is very pleasant to have it acknowledged. My success is a joy to me; it is also a joy to Birman; it is also a joy – and this is really terrible – to the

Hon. Charles Turnour Wylmot. For in this latter case I fear the reaction. Letters, forwarded by the secret hand of Birman, have come to him from the office of *The Cosmopolitan*. For many editors have been anxious to communicate with the author of 'Ellen,' care of *The Cosmopolitan*. He has answered none of them. Yet, just for a minute, he has hesitated. At this time he carefully abstains from any thought of Maud; if such a thought arises, he puts it out of his head again feverishly. That is the trouble – he dare not think about Maud.

Maud is apparently not to be denied. The power of the dead has come forth. Wylmot's heart and brain are filled with Maud now. He sees her eyes on him, and hears her voice in day-dreams and night-dreams. He is alone in his rooms, doing nothing, frightened, sickened, humiliated; it seems to him that he had once the belief that, with all his faults, he was at least a man of feeling and honour, and that he has now lost the belief, and that he cannot live without it.

He starts from the chair, and paces the room slowly in utter agony; his brows are contracted; his eyes ache; sometimes his hands close convulsively; sometimes he draws a deep breath, like one who is enduring a torture that kills.

It is the reaction. It began yesterday.

Yesterday he noticed that he felt uneasy whenever he looked at the little oil-painting of Maud that hung above his mantelpiece. He thought that must be because the portrait did no true justice to her, or because it distressed him that any other eyes but his own should see Maud's picture. During the whole period of joy in the funny successful story that he wrote on the night that Maud was buried, he had been ready with shoals of euphemistic cheerful arguments to prove that he was acting finely. Yet, as a matter of fact, the uneasiness that he felt arose from a kind of fear. He decided to lock the portrait away with her letters in the bureau. As he was doing so, his eye fell on the first note that he had ever received from Maud – merely an invitation to dinner, written to save her mother the trouble, written in shy, formal language, and commencing with 'Dear Mr Wylmot.' An impulse seized him to look again, by way of contrast, at the last letter that he had ever had from her. It was written in pencil, just at the beginning of Maud's sudden and fatal illness. It began thus:

'They tell me I am very ill, Charley, and they won't let me write more than just a little letter. They say that they will send you a longer letter themselves all about the illness. Oh, my poor dear one, I must tell you! I got it out of the doctors that they think I am going to die, perhaps. But I'm not! You've made my life so sweet that I won't leave it. I can't die and be taken away from you. Do not be despairing, my lover; doctors so often make mistakes, you know, and I am sure that I shall get better. How could I die when you've made living so well worth while? Oh, dear lover, did any man ever love so finely and nobly as you! I don't deserve you – no, I don't.'

The letter shook in Wylmot's trembling hand. It was with difficulty that he read on:

'I cried so much last night, and you weren't there to comfort me, and I was so lonely. Why – '

He had to stop there. His throat moved involuntarily, and he was on the verge of sobbing. Moving slowly and quietly, he put the letters back in the bureau and the portrait back in its place on the wall. He sat down in front of the portrait and gazed at it – a pretty, yellow-haired girl with mournful eyes, who had loved him well and thought him noble. And God had taken her and left him to the composition of an intensely humorous story. Now that he has lost the belief in himself as a man of feeling and honour he cannot live without it. Late at night he goes out. He goes down to the Embankment with the intention of killing himself.

He does not do it because he arrives there just in time to stop another man from killing himself. The other man, a stranger to Wylmot, is a young man with sandy hair – to wit, Mr Albert Weeks.

'I think,' says Wylmot, speaking firmly, but with a curious smile on his face, 'you had better come back with me to my rooms and talk this over.' He stops a passing cab.

'What's it got to do with you?' Weeks begins.

'You happen to have saved my life.'

'That's a lie. You saved mine, though I didn't want your damned interference. You pulled me back as I was on the parapet. What do you mean by saying *I* saved *your* life?'

'Ah!' Wylmot says, with the same dreary smile, 'that is what I want you to come and talk about. I also had intended to commit suicide. Surely that is sufficient introduction. Come now; get into the cab.'

At Wylmot's chambers the servant, with an anxious expression on his face, let them in. It vanished as he saw Wylmot. He had been nervous about his master, and he was glad to see him no longer alone and looking in better spirits.

'Have you dined?' Wylmot asked Weeks.

'I don't care for it,' Weeks answered doggedly.

'No? Nor do I. We will suppose dinner. Francis, bring coffee. Yes, and we will have a bottle of the port.' Francis recognized the force of the definite article.

Albert Weeks felt mazed and wondering. Were the events of the last few days that had driven him to desperation unreal, or was this unreal? The two men had drawn their chairs up in front of the fire. Albert Weeks sipped the fragrant coffee and blinked his eyes; he was in a kind of dream. Through it he heard Wylmot speaking.

'Yes, if it had not been for you, I should have drowned myself to-night. The sight of another man on the verge of committing exactly the same act suddenly showed me that suicide was running away. One should not run away. It is not brave, though brave men have done it through sudden panic. You have placed me under a very great obligation to you.'

Weeks shook his head. 'You saved me too.'

'No, no, I saved you from an isolated act. You saved me from an entirely wrong principle. I do not know whether I make myself clear. But I feel the obligation deeply, and I will speak of it again afterwards. In the meantime you should know my name.' He handed Weeks a card.

Weeks glanced at it and said: 'I have no card, but my name is Albert Weeks, and I used to live at No. 23 Harriet Terrace, Fulham. I was a journalist. I failed. I used to be on *The Inner Circle* but I got kicked off. Do you know *The Inner Circle?*'

'I've seen the posters, but I cannot say that I've ever read it.'

'It's nothing much to read, but it was all I had to live on. I'm married, with children. It was very difficult to get along. Sometimes I got a short thing taken elsewhere, not often. I borrowed a little money on my furniture. When I got kicked off *The Inner Circle* I couldn't pay the interest due, and so the Jews took the furniture. My wife and the children have gone to her married sister – a Mrs Warboys. She wouldn't have me, and she grudges the shelter that she gives my wife and children; they'll come to the workhouse. So I haven't lived anywhere the last two days. To-night I sold the last thing I had. It was my mother's wedding-ring. I thought I'd buy myself a good dinner before I died.'

'Then why didn't you?'

'Oh, I'd got into the habit of giving my wife anything that I happened to make, so I went into a post-office and sent it off to her without thinking.'

'Go on,' said Wylmot.

'Well, there wasn't much more. In the letter I sent from the post-office, I told her I had a berth to go abroad, and if I *could* make anything I would send it. I've cut my name off the linen. If I'd once got into the river, there would have been nothing to identify me by. So she'd have got used gradually to being without me. And her married sister would have felt she'd more claim for support if she had no husband.'

'Now I must tell you about myself.'

'Well, of course, I know a little about you. I've seen signed things by you in *The Cosmopolitan*. I was never one of the lucky ones – they wouldn't take me on the swell magazines.'

'Did you read "Ellen"?'

'Read it and roared over it.'

'So did I.'

'They kept the secret well. I suppose they didn't tell you who wrote it?'

'No, they never told me. Fill your glass again.'

Albert Weeks did so. The wine was warming him, giving him a little more self-confidence and geniality.

'This is beautiful port,' he said, 'really beautiful port. I can't understand why you should have wanted to commit suicide. You have no money troubles?'

'None.'

'You live in these comfortable chambers in perfect luxury, with a butler and everything. You can get your stuff taken by the very best papers. I don't say that you've made a real hit, like the man who wrote "Ellen," but you must be good to get into *The Cosmopolitan*.'

'It's so much better, you know, Weeks, to be a good man than to be a good author. I had done a disgraceful thing. It did not involve public disgrace; it was not, in the eyes of the law, an offence at all. But it took away my self-respect, and I did not feel as if I could live without it. It was driving me mad. I would rather not speak of the details.'

'Certainly not,' said Weeks.

'Now I want to talk over some plans for you, but I must first write a letter. Will you excuse me?' The letter was soon written, and given to Francis to post.

'Now then,' said Wylmot, standing before the fire, 'as we have finished our wine we will smoke. A cigar? It seems to me indicated. As I said before, without intending it, you have placed me under a very great obligation. I feel sure that you, as a gentleman, will understand that I should like to show my sense of the position. As some slight acknowledgment of the great service that you have rendered me, I have just sent in instructions to my solicitors by which you will, on my decease, receive a legacy of one thousand pounds. You want money now, and I want to give it you, but of course you would not consent to the humiliation of receiving a present of money. A legacy is a different matter; and one can take a legacy.'

'I – I do not know how to thank you,' said Weeks. 'I could not, of course, have accepted a present of money.'

'Now I must tell you my plans for you. You love your wife?'

'She and the children are – well, they're naturally the principal thing.'

'Now it is quite evident to me that it is your duty to take them into the country for a holiday. You look over-worked.'

'Oh, I worked pretty hard, but it didn't come to anything. I failed.'

'Very likely from over-work. Your wife and children, too, will want a change. You must be away at least two months. When you come back, I will give you a letter to the editor of *The Cosmopolitan*; he will do, I may say, a good deal for me. If you can write, he will let you write. If not, he will find some other remunerative occupation for you. And, I think, you would probably like to discharge any pecuniary obligation that you may be under to Mrs Warboys.'

'I should. But it is impossible. There is no money.'

'Oh, some arrangement can easily be made. Let me see. Why not borrow a hundred from me, giving me your I.O.U.? Even if it is not convenient for you to pay before my decease, the sum to which you are entitled under my will –'

'Stop,' said Weeks. 'It doesn't take me in. You're giving me money; I take it with gratitude. You've saved my life, and you've made it possible for me to go on living. And you've done it all so kindly, treating me as an equal, and no one's been like this to me for a long time – and, damn it, I can't even speak about it!' He rose and turned to the window with a sob in his throat.

Albert Weeks holds a sub-editorial post on *The Cosmopolitan* now. He has a very comfortable little flat in South Kensington. Wylmot did his best to live without self-respect. He lasted a few years, wearing himself out with work. He died of something quite commonplace.

But I am still remembered. I am still the standard of humour to which nothing more recent approaches.

ELLA D'ARCY

Irremediable

A young man strolled along a country road one August evening after a long delicious day – a day of that blessed idleness the man of leisure never knows: one must be a bank clerk forty-nine weeks out of the fifty-two before one can really appreciate the exquisite enjoyment of doing nothing for twelve hours at a stretch. Willoughby had spent the morning lounging about a sunny rickyard; then, when the heat grew unbearable, he had retreated to an orchard, where, lying on his back in the long cool grass, he had traced the pattern of the apple-leaves diapered above him upon the summer sky; now that the heat of the day was over he had come to roam whither sweet fancy led him, to lean over gates, view the prospect, and meditate upon the pleasures of a well-spent day. Five such days had already passed over his head, fifteen more remained to him. Then farewell to freedom and clean country air! Back again to London and another year's toil.

He came to a gate on the right of the road. Behind it a footpath meandered up over a grassy slope. The sheep nibbling on its summit cast long shadows down the hill almost to his feet. Road and fieldpath were equally new to him, but the latter offered greener attractions; he vaulted lightly over the gate and had so little idea he was taking thus the first step towards ruin that he began to whistle 'White Wings' from pure joy of life.

The sheep stopped feeding and raised their heads to stare at him from pale-lashed eyes; first one and then another broke into a startled run, until there was a sudden woolly stampede of the entire flock. When Willoughby gained the ridge from which they had just scattered, he came in sight of a woman sitting on a stile at the further end of the field. As he advanced towards her he saw that she was young, and that she was not what is called 'a lady' – of which he was glad: an earlier episode in his career having indissolubly associated in his mind ideas of feminine refinement with those of feminine treachery.

He thought it probable this girl would be willing to dispense with the formalities of an introduction, and that he might venture with her on some pleasant foolish chat.

As she made no movement to let him pass he stood still, and, looking at her, began to smile.

She returned his gaze from unabashed dark eyes, and then laughed, showing teeth white, sound, and smooth as split hazel-nuts.

'Do you wanter get over?' she remarked familiarly.

'I'm afraid I can't without disturbing you.'

'Dontcher think you're much better where you are?' said the girl, on which Willoughby hazarded:

'You mean to say looking at you? Well, perhaps I am!'

The girl at this laughed again, but nevertheless dropped herself down into the further field; then, leaning her arms upon the cross-bar, she informed the young man: 'No, I don't wanter spoil your walk. You were goin' p'raps ter Beacon Point? It's very pretty that wye.'

'I was going nowhere in particular,' he replied; 'just exploring, so to speak. I'm a stranger in these parts.'

'How funny! Imer stranger here too. I only come down larse Friday to stye with a Naunter mine in Horton. Are you stying in Horton?'

Willoughby told her he was not in Orton, but at Povey Cross Farm out in the other direction.

'Oh, Mrs Payne's, ain't it? I've heard aunt speak ovver. She takes summer boarders, don't chee? I egspeck you come from London, heh?'

'And I expect you come from London too?' said Willoughby, recognizing the familiar accent.

'You're as sharp as a needle,' cried the girl with her unrestrained laugh; 'so I do. I'm here for a hollerday 'cos I was so done up with the work and the hot weather. I don't look as though I'd bin ill, do I? But I was, though: for it was just stiflin' hot up in our workrooms all larse month, an' tailorin's awful hard work at the bester times.'

Willoughby felt a sudden accession of interest in her. Like many intelligent young men, he had dabbled a little in Socialism, and at one time had wandered among the dispossessed; but since then, had caught up and held loosely the new doctrine – it is a good and fitting thing that Woman also should earn her bread by the sweat of her brow. Always in reference to the woman who, fifteen months before, had treated him ill, he had said to himself that even the breaking of stones in the road should be considered a more feminine employment than the breaking of hearts.

He gave way therefore to a movement of friendliness for this working daughter of the people, and joined her on the other side of the stile in token of his approval. She, twisting round to face him, leaned now with her back against the bar, and the sunset fires lent a fleeting glory to her face. Perhaps she guessed how becoming the light was, for she took off her hat and let it touch to gold the ends and fringes of her rough abundant hair. Thus and at this moment she made an agreeable picture, to which stood as background all the beautiful, wooded Southshire view.

'You don't really mean to say you are a tailoress?' said Willoughby, with a sort of eager compassion.

'I do, though! An' I've bin one ever since I was fourteen. Look at my fingers if you don't b'lieve me.'

She put out her right hand, and he took hold of it, as he was expected to do. The finger-ends were frayed and blackened by needle-pricks, but the hand itself was plump, moist, and not unshapely. She meanwhile examined Willoughby's fingers enclosing hers.

'It's easy ter see you've never done no work!' she said, half admiring, half envious. 'I s'pose you're a tip-top swell, ain't you?'

'Oh, yes! I'm a tremendous swell indeed!' said Willoughby, ironically. He thought of his hundred and thirty pounds' salary; and he mentioned his position in the British and Colonial Banking house, without shedding much illumination on her mind, for she insisted:

'Well, anyhow, you're a gentleman. I've often wished I was a lady. It must be so nice ter wear fine clo'es an' never have ter do any work all day long.'

Willoughby thought it innocent of the girl to say this; it reminded him of his own notion as a child – that kings and queens put on their crowns the first thing on rising in the morning. His cordiality rose another degree.

'If being a gentleman means having nothing to do,' said he, smiling, 'I can certainly lay no claim to the title. Life isn't all beer and skittles with me, any more than it is with you. Which is the better reason for enjoying the present moment, don't you think? Suppose, now, like a kind little girl, you were to show me the way to Beacon Point, which you say is so pretty?'

She required no further persuasion. As he walked beside her through the upland fields where the dusk was beginning to fall, and the white evening moths to emerge from their daytime hiding-places, she asked him many personal questions, most of which he thought fit to parry. Taking no offence thereat, she told him, instead, much concerning herself and her family. Thus he learned her name was Esther Stables, that she and her people lived Whitechapel way; that her father was seldom sober, and her mother always ill; and that the aunt with whom she was staying kept the post-office and general shop in Orton village. He learned, too, that Esther was discontented with life in general; that, though she hated being at home, she found the country dreadfully dull; and that, consequently, she was extremely glad to have made his acquaintance. But what he chiefly realized when they parted was that he had spent a couple of pleasant hours talking nonsense with a girl who was natural, simple-minded, and entirely free from that repellently protective atmosphere with which a woman of the 'classes' so carefully surrounds herself. He and Esther had 'made friends' with the ease and rapidity of children before they have learned the dread meaning of 'etiquette,' and they said good-night, not without some talk of meeting each other again.

Obliged to breakfast at a quarter to eight in town, Willoughby was always luxuriously late when in the country, where he took his meals also in leisurely fashion, often reading from a book propped up on the table before him. But the morning after his meeting with Esther Stables found him less disposed to read than usual. Her image obtruded itself upon the printed page, and at length grew so importunate he came to the conclusion the only way to lay it was to confront it with the girl herself.

Wanting some tobacco, he saw a good reason for going into Orton. Esther had told him he could get tobacco and everything else at her aunt's. He found the post-office to be one of the first houses in the widely spaced village street. In front of the cottage was a small garden ablaze with old-fashioned flowers; and in a larger garden at one side were apple-trees, raspberry and currant bushes, and six thatched beehives on a bench. The bowed windows of the little shop were partly screened by sunblinds; nevertheless the lower panes still displayed a heterogeneous collection of goods – lemons, hanks of yarn, white linen buttons upon blue cards, sugar cones, churchwarden pipes, and tobacco jars. A letter-box opened its narrow mouth low down in one wall, and over the door swung the sign, 'Stamps and money-order office,' in black letters on white enamelled iron.

The interior of the shop was cool and dark. A second glass-door at the back permitted Willoughby to see into a small sitting-room, and out again through a low and square-paned window to the sunny landscape beyond. Silhouetted against the light were the heads of two women; the rough young head of yesterday's Esther, the lean outline and bugled cap of Esther's aunt.

It was the latter who at the jingling of the doorbell rose from her work and came forward to serve the customer; but the girl, with much mute meaning in her eyes, and a finger laid upon her smiling mouth, followed behind. Her aunt heard her footfall. 'What do you want here, Esther?' she said with thin disapproval; 'get back to your sewing.'

Esther gave the young man a signal seen only by him and slipped out into the side-garden, where he found her when his purchases were made. She leaned over the privet-hedge to intercept him as he passed.

'Aunt's an awful ole maid,' she remarked apologetically; 'I b'lieve she'd never let me say a word to enny one if she could help it.'

'So you got home all right last night?' Willoughby inquired; 'what did your aunt say to you?'

'Oh, she arst me where I'd been, and I tolder a lotter lies.' Then, with a woman's intuition, perceiving that this speech jarred, Esther made haste to add, 'She's so dreadful hard on me. I dursn't tell her I'd been with a gentleman or she'd never have let me out alone again.'

'And at present I suppose you'll be found somewhere about that same stile every evening?' said Willoughby foolishly, for he really did not much care whether he met her again or not. Now he was actually in her company, he was surprised at himself for having given her a whole morning's thought; yet the eagerness of her answer flattered him, too.

'To-night I can't come, worse luck! It's Thursday, and the shops here close of a Thursday at five. I'll havter keep aunt company. But to-morrer? I can be there to-morrer. You'll come, say?'

'Esther!' cried a vexed voice, and the precise, right-minded aunt emerged through a row of raspberry-bushes; 'whatever are you thinking about, delayin' the gentleman in this fashion?' She was full of rustic and official civility for 'the gentleman,' but indignant with her niece. 'I don't want none of your London manners down here,' Willoughby heard her say as she marched the girl off.

He himself was not sorry to be released from Esther's too friendly eyes, and he spent an agreeable evening over a book, and this time managed to forget her completely.

Though he remembered her first thing next morning, it was to smile wisely and determine he would not meet her again. Yet by dinner-time the day seemed long; why, after all, should he not meet her? By tea-time prudence triumphed anew – no, he would not go. Then he drank his tea hastily and set off for the stile.

Esther was waiting for him. Expectation had given an additional colour to her cheeks, and her red-brown hair showed here and there a beautiful glint of gold. He could not help admiring the vigorous way in which it waved and twisted, or the little curls which grew at the nape of her neck, tight and close as those of a young lamb's fleece. Her neck here was admirable, too, in its smooth creaminess; and when her eyes lighted up with such evident pleasure at his coming, how avoid the conviction she was a good and nice girl after all?

He proposed they should go down into the little copse on the right, where they would be less disturbed by the occasional passer-by. Here, seated on a felled tree-trunk, Willoughby began that bantering, silly, meaningless form of conversation known among the 'classes' as flirting. He had but the wish to make himself agreeable, and to while away the time. Esther, however, misunderstood him.

Willoughby's hand lay palm downwards on his knee, and she, noticing a ring which he wore on his little finger, took hold of it.

'What a funny ring!' she said; 'let's look?'

To disembarrass himself of her touch, he pulled the ring off and gave it her to examine.

'What's that ugly dark green stone?' she asked.

'It's called a sardonyx.'

'What's it for?' she said, turning it about.

'It's a signet ring, to seal letters with.'

'An' there's a sorter king's head scratched on it, an' some writin' too, only I carnt make it out?'

'It isn't the head of a king, although it wears a crown,' Willoughby explained, 'but the head and bust of a Saracen against whom my ancestor of many hundred years ago went to fight in the Holy Land. And the words cut round it are our motto, "Vertue vaunceth," which means virtue prevails.'

Willoughby may have displayed some accession of dignity in giving this bit of family history, for Esther fell into uncontrolled laughter, at which he was much displeased. And when the girl made as though she would put the ring on her own finger, asking, 'Shall I keep it?' he coloured up with sudden annoyance.

'It was only my fun!' said Esther hastily, and gave him the ring back, but his cordiality was gone. He felt no inclination to renew the idle-word pastime, said it was time to go, and, swinging his cane vexedly, struck off the heads of the flowers and the weeds as he went. Esther walked by his side in complete silence, a phenomenon of which he presently became conscious. He felt rather ashamed of having shown temper.

'Well, here's your way home,' said he with an effort at friendliness. 'Good-bye; we've had a nice evening anyhow. It was pleasant down there in the woods, eh?'

He was astonished to see her eyes soften with tears, and to hear the real emotion in her voice as she answered, 'It was just heaven down there with you until you turned so funny-like. What had I done to make you cross? Say you forgive me, do!'

'Silly child!' said Willoughby, completely mollified, 'I'm not the least angry. There, good-bye!' and like a fool he kissed her.

He anathematized his folly in the white light of next morning, and, remembering the kiss he had given her, repented it very sincerely. He had an uncomfortable suspicion she had not received it in the same spirit in which it had been bestowed, but, attaching more serious meaning to it, would build expectations thereon which must be left unfulfilled. It was best indeed not to meet her again; for he acknowledged to himself that, though he only half liked, and even slightly feared her, there was a certain attraction about her – was it in her dark unflinching eyes or in her very red lips? – which might lead him into greater follies still.

Thus it came about that for two successive evenings Esther waited for him in vain, and on the third evening he said to himself, with a grudging relief, that by this time she had probably transferred her affections to some one else.

It was Saturday, the second Saturday since he left town. He spent the day about the farm, contemplated the pigs, inspected the feeding of the stock, and assisted at the afternoon milking. Then at evening, with a refilled pipe, he went for a long lean over the west gate, while he traced fantastic pictures and wove romances in the glories of the sunset clouds.

He watched the colours glow from gold to scarlet, change to crimson, sink at last to sad purple reefs and isles, when the sudden consciousness of some one being near him made him turn round. There stood Esther, and her eyes were full of eagerness and anger.

'Why have you never been to the stile again?' she asked him. 'You promised to come faithful, and you never came. Why have you not kep' your promise? Why? Why?' she persisted, stamping her foot because Willoughby remained silent.

What could he say? Tell her she had no business to follow him like this; or own, what was, unfortunately, the truth, he was just a little glad to see her?

'P'raps you don't care for me any more?' she said. 'Well, why did you kiss me, then?'

Why, indeed! thought Willoughby, marvelling at his own idiocy, and yet – such is the inconsistency of man – not wholly without the desire to kiss her again. And while he looked at her she suddenly flung herself down on the hedge-bank at his feet and burst into tears. She did not cover up her face, but simply pressed one cheek down upon the grass while the water poured from her eyes with astonishing abundance. Willoughby saw the dry earth turn dark and moist as it drank the tears in. This, his first experience of Esther's powers of weeping, distressed him horribly; never in his life before had he seen any one weep like that, he should not have believed such a thing possible; he was alarmed, too, lest she should be noticed from the house. He opened the gate; 'Esther!' he begged, 'don't cry. Come out here, like a dear girl, and let us talk sensibly.'

Because she stumbled, unable to see her way through wet eyes, he gave her his hand, and they found themselves in a field of corn, walking along the narrow grass-path that skirted it, in the shadow of the hedgerow.

'What is there to cry about because you have not seen me for two days?' he began; 'why, Esther, we are only strangers, after all. When we have been at home a week or two we shall scarcely remember each other's names.'

Esther sobbed at intervals, but her tears had ceased. 'It's fine for you to talk of home,' she said to this. 'You've got something that is a home, I s'pose? But me! my home's like hell, with nothing but quarrellin' and cursin', and a father who beats us whether sober or drunk. Yes!' she repeated shrewdly, seeing the lively disgust on Willoughby's face, 'he beat me, all ill as I was, jus' before I come away. I could show you the bruises on my arms still. And now to go back there after knowin' you! It'll be worse than ever. I can't endure it, and I won't! I'll put an end to it or myself somehow, I swear!'

'But, my poor Esther, how can I help it? what can I do?' said Willoughby. He was greatly moved, full of wrath with her father, with all the world which makes women suffer. He had suffered himself at the hands of a woman and severely, but this, instead of hardening his heart, had only rendered it the more supple. And yet he had a vivid perception of the peril in which he stood. An interior voice urged him to break away, to seek safety in flight even at the cost of appearing cruel or ridiculous; so, coming to a point in the field where an elm-bole jutted out across the path, he saw with relief he could now withdraw his hand from the girl's, since they must walk singly to skirt round it.

Esther took a step in advance, stopped and suddenly turned to face him; she held out her two hands and her face was very near his own.

'Don't you care for me one little bit?' she said wistfully, and surely sudden madness fell upon him. For he kissed her again, he kissed her many times, he took her in his arms, and pushed all thoughts of the consequences far from him.

But when, an hour later, he and Esther stood by the last gate on the road to Orton, some of these consequences were already calling loudly to him.

'You know I have only £130 a year?' he told her; 'it's no very brilliant prospect for you to marry me on that.'

For he had actually offered her marriage, although to the mediocre man such a proceeding must appear incredible, uncalled for. But to Willoughby, overwhelmed with sadness and remorse, it seemed the only atonement possible.

Sudden exultation leaped at Esther's heart.

'Oh! I'm used to managin',' she told him confidently, and mentally resolved to buy herself, so soon as she was married, a black feather boa, such as she had coveted last winter.

Willoughby spent the remaining days of his holiday in thinking out and planning with Esther the details of his return to London and her own, the secrecy to be observed, the necessary legal steps to be taken, and the quiet suburb in which they would set up housekeeping. And, so successfully did he carry out his arrangements, that within five weeks from the day on which he had first met Esther Stables, he and she came out one morning from a church in Highbury, husband and wife. It was a mellow September day, the streets were filled with sunshine, and Willoughby, in reckless high spirits, imagined he saw a reflection of his own gaiety on the indifferent faces of the passers-by. There being no one else to perform the office, he congratulated himself very warmly, and Esther's frequent laughter filled in the pauses of the day.

Three months later Willoughby was dining with a friend, and the hour-hand of the clock nearing ten, the host no longer resisted the guest's growing anxiety to be gone. He arose and exchanged with him good wishes and good-byes.

'Marriage is evidently a most successful institution,' said he, half-jesting, half-sincere; 'you almost make me inclined to go and get married myself. Confess now your thoughts have been at home the whole evening.'

Willoughby thus addressed turned red to the roots of his hair, but did not deny it.

The other laughed. 'And very commendable they should be,' he continued, 'since you are scarcely, so to speak, out of your honeymoon.'

With a social smile on his lips, Willoughby calculated a moment before replying, 'I have been married exactly three months and three days.' Then, after a few words respecting their next meeting, the two shook hands and parted – the young host to finish the evening with books and pipe, the young husband to set out on a twenty minutes' walk to his home.

It was a cold, clear December night following a day of rain. A touch of frost in the air had dried the pavements, and Willoughby's footfall ringing upon the stones re-echoed down the empty suburban street Above his head was a dark, remote sky thickly powdered with stars, and as he turned westward Alpherat hung for a moment '*comme le point sur un* i,' over the slender spire of St John's. But he was insensible to the worlds about him; he was absorbed in his own thoughts, and these, as his friend had surmised, were entirely with his wife. For Esther's face was always before his eyes, her voice was always in his ears, she filled the universe for him; yet only four months ago he had never seen her, had never heard her name. This was the curious part of it – here in December he found himself the husband of a girl who was completely dependent upon him not only for food, clothes, and lodging, but for her present happiness, her whole future life; and last July he had been scarcely more than a boy himself, with no greater care on his mind than the pleasant difficulty of deciding where he should spend his annual three weeks' holiday.

But it is events, not months or years, which age. Willoughby, who was only twenty-six, remembered his youth as a sometime companion irrevocably lost to him; its vague, delightful hopes were now crystallized into definite ties, and its happy irresponsibilities displaced by a sense of care, inseparable perhaps from the most fortunate of marriages.

As he reached the street in which he lodged his pace involuntarily slackened. While still some distance off, his eye sought out and distinguished the windows of the room in which Esther awaited him. Through the broken slats of the Venetian blinds he could see the yellow gaslight within. The parlour beneath was in darkness; his landlady had evidently gone to bed, there being no light over the hall-door either. In some apprehension he consulted his watch under the last street-lamp he passed, to find comfort in assuring himself it was only ten minutes after ten. He let himself in with his latch-key, hung up his hat and overcoat by the sense of touch, and, groping his way upstairs, opened the door of the first floor sitting-room.

At the table in the centre of the room sat his wife, leaning upon her elbows, her two hands thrust up into her ruffled hair; spread out before her was a crumpled yesterday's newspaper, and so interested was she to all appearance in its contents that she neither spoke nor looked up as Willoughby entered. Around her were the still uncleared tokens of her last meal: tea-slops, bread-crumbs, and an eggshell crushed to fragments upon a plate, which was one of those trifles that set Willoughby's teeth on edge, – whenever his wife ate an egg she persisted in turning the egg-cup upside down upon the tablecloth, and pounding the shell to pieces in her plate with her spoon.

The room was repulsive in its disorder. The one lighted burner of the gaselier, turned too high, hissed up into a long tongue of flame. The fire smoked feebly under a newly administered shovelful of 'slack,' and a heap of ashes and cinders littered the grate. A pair of walking boots, caked in dry mud, lay on the hearthrug just where they had been thrown off. On the mantelpiece, amidst a dozen other articles which had no business there, was a bedroom-candlestick; and every single article of furniture stood crookedly out of its place.

Willoughby took in the whole intolerable picture, and yet spoke with kindliness. 'Well, Esther! I'm not so late, after all. I hope you did not find the time dull by yourself?' Then he explained the reason of his absence. He had met a friend he had not seen for a couple of years, who had insisted on taking him home to dine.

His wife gave no sign of having heard him; she kept her eyes riveted on the paper before her.

'You received my wire, of course,' Willoughby went on, 'and did not wait?'

Now she crushed the newspaper up with a passionate movement, and threw it from her. She raised her head, showing cheeks blazing with anger, and dark, sullen, unflinching eyes.

'I did wyte then!' she cried. 'I wyted till near eight before I got your old telegraph! I s'pose that's what you call the manners of a "gentleman," to keep your wife mewed up here, while you go gallivantin' off with your fine friends?'

Whenever Esther was angry, which was often, she taunted Willoughby with being 'a gentleman,' although this was the precise point about him which at other times found most favour in her eyes. But to-night she was envenomed by the idea he had been enjoying himself without her, stung by fear lest he should have been in company with some other woman.

Willoughby, hearing the taunt, resigned himself to the inevitable. Nothing that he could do might now avert the breaking storm; all his words would only be twisted into fresh griefs. But sad experience had taught him that to take refuge in silence was more fatal still. When Esther was in such a mood as this it was best to supply the fire with fuel, that, through the very violence of the conflagration, it might the sooner burn itself out.

So he said what soothing things he could, and Esther caught them up, disfigured them, and flung them back at him with scorn. She reproached him with no longer caring for her; she vituperated the conduct of his family in never taking the smallest notice of her marriage; and she detailed the insolence of the landlady who had told her that morning she pitied 'poor Mr Willoughby,' and had refused to go out and buy herrings for Esther's early dinner.

Every affront or grievance, real or imaginary, since the day she and Willoughby had first met, she poured forth with a fluency due to frequent repetition, for, with the exception of to-day's added injuries, Willoughby had heard the whole litany many times before.

While she raged and he looked at her, he remembered he had once thought her pretty. He had seen beauty in her rough brown hair, her strong colouring, her full red mouth. He fell into musing . . . a woman may lack beauty, he told himself, and yet be loved . . .

Meanwhile Esther reached white heats of passion, and the strain could no longer be sustained. She broke into sobs and began to shed tears with the facility peculiar to her. In a moment her face was all wet with the big drops which rolled down her cheeks faster and faster, and fell with audible splashes on to the table, on to her lap, on to the floor. To this tearful abundance, formerly a surprising spectacle, Willoughby was now acclimatized; but the remnant of chivalrous feeling not yet extinguished in his bosom forbade him to sit stolidly by while a woman wept, without seeking to console her. As on previous occasions, his peace-overtures were eventually accepted. Esther's tears gradually ceased to flow, she began to exhibit a sort of compunction, she wished to be forgiven, and, with the kiss of reconciliation, passed into a phase of demonstrative affection perhaps more trying to Willoughby's patience than all that had preceded it. 'You don't love me?' she questioned, 'I'm sure you don't love me?' she reiterated; and he asseverated that he loved her until he despised himself. Then at last, only half satisfied, but wearied out with vexation – possibly, too, with a movement of pity at the sight of his haggard face – she consented to leave him. Only, what was he going to do? she asked suspiciously; write those rubbishing stories of his? Well, he must promise not to stay up more than half-an-hour at the latest – only until he had smoked one pipe.

Willoughby promised, as he would have promised anything on earth to secure to himself a half-hour's peace and solitude. Esther groped for her slippers, which were kicked off under the table; scratched four or five matches along the box and threw them away before she succeeded in lighting her candle; set it down again to contemplate her tear-swollen reflection in the chimney-glass, and burst out laughing.

'What a fright I do look, to be sure!' she remarked complacently, and again thrust her two hands up through her disordered curls. Then, holding the candle at such an angle that the grease ran over on to the carpet, she gave Willoughby another vehement kiss and trailed out of the room with an ineffectual attempt to close the door behind her.

Willoughby got up to shut it himself, and wondered why it was that Esther never did any one mortal thing efficiently or well. Good God! how irritable he felt. It was impossible to write. He must find an outlet for his impatience, rend or mend something. He began to straighten the room, but a wave of disgust came over him before the task was fairly commenced. What was the use? To-morrow all would be bad as before. What was the use of doing anything? He sat down by the table and leaned his head upon his hands.

The past came back to him in pictures: his boyhood's past first of all. He saw again the old home, every inch of which was familiar to him as his own name; he reconstructed in his thought all the old well-known furniture, and replaced it precisely as it had stood long ago. He passed again a childish finger over the rough surface of the faded Utrecht velvet chairs, and smelled again the strong fragrance of the white lilac tree, blowing in through the open parlour-window. He savoured anew the pleasant mental atmosphere produced by the dainty neatness of cultured women, the companionship of a few good pictures, of a few good books. Yet this home had been broken up years ago, the dear familiar things had been scattered far and wide, never to find themselves under the same roof again; and from those near relatives who still remained to him he lived now hopelessly estranged.

Then came the past of his first love-dream, when he worshipped at the feet of Nora Beresford, and, with the whole-heartedness of the true fanatic, clothed his idol with every imaginable attribute of virtue and tenderness. To this day there remained a secret shrine in his heart wherein the Lady of his young ideal was still enthroned, although it was long since he had come to perceive she had nothing whatever in common with the Nora of reality. For the real Nora he had no longer any sentiment, she had passed altogether out of his life and thoughts; and yet, so permanent is all influence, whether good or evil, that the effect she wrought upon his character remained. He recognized to-night that her treatment of him in the past did not count for nothing among the various factors which had determined his fate.

Now, the past of only last year returned, and, strangely enough, this seemed farther removed from him than all the rest. He had been particularly strong, well, and happy this time last year. Nora was dismissed from his mind, and he had thrown all his energies into his work. His tastes were sane and simple, and his dingy, furnished rooms had become through habit very pleasant to him. In being his own, they were invested with a greater charm than another man's castle. Here he had smoked and studied, here he had made many a glorious voyage into the land of books. Many a home-coming, too, rose up before him out of the dark ungenial streets, to a clear blazing fire, a neatly laid cloth, an evening of ideal enjoyment; many a summer twilight when he mused at the open window, plunging his gaze deep into the recesses of his neighbour's lime-tree, where the unseen sparrows chattered with such unflagging gaiety.

He had always been given to much day-dreaming, and it was in the silence of his rooms of an evening that he turned his phantasmal adventures into stories for the magazines; here had come to him many an editorial refusal, but here, too, he had received the news of his first unexpected success. All his happiest memories were embalmed in those shabby, badly-furnished rooms.

Now all was changed. Now might there be no longer any soft indulgence of the hour's mood. His rooms and everything he owned belonged now to Esther, too. She had objected to most of his photographs, and had removed them. She hated books, and were he ever so ill-advised as to open one in her presence, she immediately began to talk, no matter how silent or how sullen her previous mood had been. If he read aloud to her she either yawned despairingly, or was tickled into laughter where there was no reasonable cause. At first Willoughby had tried to educate her, and had gone hopefully to the task. It is so natural to think you may make what you will of the woman who loves you. But Esther had no wish to improve. She evinced all the self-satisfaction of an illiterate mind. To her husband's gentle admonitions she replied with brevity that she thought her way quite as good as his; or, if he didn't approve of her pronunciation, he might do the other thing, she was too old to go to school again. He gave up the attempt, and, with humiliation at his previous fatuity, perceived that it was folly to expect that a few weeks of his companionship could alter or pull up the impressions of years, or rather of generations.

Yet here he paused to admit a curious thing: it was not only Esther's bad habits which vexed him, but habits quite unblameworthy in themselves which he never would have noticed in another, irritated him in her. He disliked her manner of standing, of walking, of sitting in a chair, of folding her hands. Like a lover, he was conscious of her proximity without seeing her. Like a lover, too, his eyes followed her every movement, his ear noted every change in her voice. But then, instead of being charmed by everything as the lover is, everything jarred upon him.

What was the meaning of this? To-night the anomaly pressed upon him: he reviewed his position. Here was he, quite a young man, just twenty-six years of age, married to Esther, and bound to live with her so long as life should last – twenty, forty, perhaps fifty years more. Every day of those years to be spent in her society; he and she face to face, soul to soul; they two alone amid all the whirling, busy, indifferent world. So near together in semblance; in truth, so far apart as regards all that makes life dear.

Willoughby groaned. From the woman he did not love, whom he had never loved, he might not again go free; so much he recognized. The feeling he had once entertained for Esther, strange compound of mistaken chivalry and flattered vanity, was long since extinct; but what, then, was the sentiment with which she inspired him? For he was not indifferent to her – no, never for one instant could he persuade himself he was indifferent, never for one instant could he banish her from his thoughts. His mind's eye followed her during his hours of absence as pertinaciously as his bodily eye dwelt upon her actual presence. She was the principal object of the universe to him, the centre around which his wheel of life revolved with an appalling fidelity.

What did it mean? What could it mean? he asked himself with anguish.

And the sweat broke out upon his forehead and his hands grew cold, for on a sudden the truth lay there like a written word upon the tablecloth before him. This woman, whom he had taken to himself for better, for worse, inspired him with a passion, intense indeed, all – masterful, soul-subduing as Love itself . . . But when he understood the terror of his Hatred, he laid his head upon his arms and wept, not facile tears like Esther's, but tears wrung out from his agonizing, unavailing regret.

H. G. WELLS

The Argonauts of the Air

One saw Monson's flying-machine from the windows of the trains passing either along the South-Western main line or along the line between Wimbledon and Worcester Park, – to be more exact, one saw the huge scaffoldings which limited the flight of the apparatus. They rose over the tree-tops, a massive alley of interlacing iron and timber, and an enormous web of ropes and tackle, extending the best part of two miles. From the Leatherhead branch this alley was foreshortened and in part hidden by a hill with villas; but from the main line one had it in profile, a complex tangle of girders and curving bars, very impressive to the excursionists from Portsmouth and Southampton and the West. Monson had taken up the work where Maxim had left it, had gone on at first with an utter contempt for the journalistic wit and ignorance that had irritated and hampered his predecessor, and had spent (it was said) rather more than half his immense fortune upon his experiments. The results, to an impatient generation, seemed inconsiderable. When some five years had passed after the growth of the colossal iron groves at Worcester Park, and Monson still failed to put in a fluttering appearance over Trafalgar Square, even the Isle of Wight trippers felt their liberty to smile. And such intelligent people as did not consider Monson a fool stricken with the mania for invention, denounced him as being (for no particular reason) a self-advertising quack.

Yet now and again a morning trainload of season-ticket holders would see a white monster rush headlong through the airy tracery of guides and bars, and hear the further stays, nettings, and buffers snap, creak, and groan with the impact of the blow. Then there would be an efflorescence of black-set white-rimmed faces along the sides of the train, and the morning papers would be neglected for a vigorous discussion of the possibility of flying (in which nothing new was ever said by any chance), until the train reached Waterloo, and its cargo of season-ticket holders dispersed themselves over London. Or the fathers and mothers in some multitudinous train of weary excursionists returning exhausted from a day of rest by the sea, would find the dark fabric, standing out against the evening sky, useful in diverting some bilious child from its introspection, and be suddenly startled by the swift transit of a huge black flapping shape that strained upward against the guides. It was a great and forcible thing beyond dispute, and excellent for conversation; yet, all the same, it was but flying in leading-strings, and most of those who witnessed it scarcely counted its flight as flying. More of a switchback it seemed to the run of the folk.

Monson, I say, did not trouble himself very keenly about the opinions of the press at first. But possibly he, even, had formed but a poor idea of the time it would take before the tactics of flying were mastered, the swift assured adjustment of the big soaring shape to every gust and chance movement of the air; nor had he clearly reckoned the money this prolonged struggle against gravitation would cost him. And he was not so pachydermatous as he seemed. Secretly he had his periodical bundles of cuttings sent him by Romeike, he had his periodical reminders from his banker; and if he did not mind the initial ridicule and scepticism, he felt the growing neglect as the months went by and the money dribbled away. Time was when Monson had sent the enterprising journalist, keen after readable matter, empty from his gates. But when the enterprising journalist ceased from troubling, Monson was anything but satisfied in his heart of hearts. Still day by day the work went on, and the multitudinous subtle difficulties of the steering diminished in number. Day by day, too, the money trickled away, until his balance was no longer a matter of hundreds of thousands, but of tens. And at last came an anniversary.

Monson, sitting in the little drawing-shed, suddenly noticed the date on Woodhouse's calendar.

'It was five years ago to-day that we began,' he said to Woodhouse suddenly.

'Is it?' said Woodhouse.

'It's the alterations play the devil with us,' said Monson, biting a paper-fastener.

The drawings for the new vans to the hinder screw lay on the table before him as he spoke. He pitched the mutilated brass paper-fastener into the waste-paper basket and drummed with his fingers. 'These alterations! Will the mathematicians ever be clever enough to save us all this patching and experimenting. Five years – learning by rule of thumb, when one might think that it was possible to calculate the whole thing out beforehand. The cost of it! I might have hired three senior wranglers for life. But they'd only have developed some beautifully useless theorems in pneumatics. What a time it has been, Woodhouse!'

'These mouldings will take three weeks,' said Woodhouse. 'At special prices.'

'Three weeks!' said Monson, and sat drumming.

'Three weeks certain,' said Woodhouse, an excellent engineer, but no good as a comforter. He drew the sheets towards him and began shading a bar.

Monson stopped drumming and began to bite his finger-nails, staring the while at Woodhouse's head.

'How long have they been calling this Monson's Folly?' he said suddenly.

'*Oh!* Year or so,' said Woodhouse, carelessly, without looking up.

Monson sucked the air in between his teeth, and went to the window. The stout iron columns carrying the elevated rails upon which the start of the machine was made rose up close by, and the machine was hidden by the upper edge of the window. Through the grove of iron pillars, red painted and ornate with rows of bolts, one had a glimpse of the pretty scenery towards Esher. A train went gliding noiselessly across the middle distance, its rattle drowned by the hammering of the workmen overhead. Monson could imagine the grinning faces at the windows of the carriages. He swore savagely under his breath, and dabbed viciously at a blowfly that suddenly became noisy on the window-pane.

'What's up?' said Woodhouse, staring in surprise at his employer.

'I'm about sick of this.'

Woodhouse scratched his cheek. 'Oh!' he said, after an assimilating pause. He pushed the drawing away from him.

'Here these fools – I'm trying to conquer a new element – trying to do a thing that will revolutionize life. And instead of taking an intelligent interest, they grin and make their stupid jokes, and call me and my appliances names.'

'Asses! 'said Woodhouse, letting his eye fall again on the drawing.

The epithet, curiously enough, made Monson wince. 'I'm about sick of it, Woodhouse, anyhow,' he said, after a pause.

Woodhouse shrugged his shoulders.

'There's nothing for it but patience, I suppose,' said Monson, sticking his hands in his pockets. 'I've started. I've made my bed, and I've got to lie on it. I can't go back. I'll see it through, and spend every penny I have and every penny I can borrow. But I tell you, Woodhouse, I'm infernally sick of it, all the same. If I'd paid a tenth part of the money towards some political greaser's expenses – I'd have been a baronet before this.'

Monson paused. Woodhouse stared in front of him with a blank expression he always employed to indicate sympathy, and tapped his pencil-case on the table. Monson stared at him for a minute.

'Oh, *damn!*' said Monson, suddenly, and abruptly rushed out of the room.

Woodhouse continued his sympathetic rigour for perhaps half a minute. Then he sighed and resumed the shading of the drawings. Something had evidently upset Monson. Nice chap, and generous, but difficult to get on with. It was the way with every amateur who had anything to do with engineering – wanted everything finished at once. But Monson had usually the patience of the expert. Odd he was so irritable. Nice and round that aluminium rod did look now! Woodhouse threw back his head, and put it, first this side and then that, to appreciate his bit of shading better.

'Mr Woodhouse,' said Hooper, the foreman of the labourers, putting his head in at the door.

'Hullo!' said Woodhouse, without turning round.

'Nothing happened, sir?' said Hooper.

'Happened?' said Woodhouse.

'The governor just been up the rails swearing like a tornader.'

'*Oh!*' said Woodhouse.

'It ain't like him, sir.'

'No?'

'And I was thinking perhaps – '

'Don't think,' said Woodhouse, still admiring the drawings.

Hooper knew Woodhouse, and he shut the door suddenly with a vicious slam. Woodhouse stared stonily before him for some further minutes, and then made an ineffectual effort to pick his teeth with his pencil. Abruptly he desisted, pitched that old, tried, and stumpy servitor across the room, got up, stretched himself, and followed Hooper.

He looked ruffled – it was visible to every workman he met. When a millionaire who has been spending thousands on experiments that employ quite a little army of people suddenly indicates that he is sick of the undertaking, there is almost invariably a certain amount of mental friction in the ranks of the little army he employs. And even before he indicates his intentions there are speculations and murmurs, a watching of faces and a study of straws. Hundreds of people knew before the day was out that Monson was ruffled, Woodhouse ruffled, Hooper ruffled. A workman's wife, for instance (whom Monson had never seen), decided to keep her money in the savings-bank instead of buying a velveteen dress. So far-reaching are even the casual curses of a millionaire.

Monson found a certain satisfaction in going on the works and behaving disagreeably to as many people as possible. After a time even that palled upon him, and he rode off the grounds, to every one's relief there, and through the lanes south-eastward, to the infinite tribulation of his house steward at Cheam.

And the immediate cause of it all, the little grain of annoyance that had suddenly precipitated all this discontent with his life-work was – these trivial things that direct all our great decisions! – half a dozen ill-considered remarks made by a pretty girl, prettily dressed, with a beautiful voice and something more than prettiness in her soft grey eyes. And of these half-dozen remarks, two words especially – 'Monson's Folly.' She had felt she was behaving charmingly to Monson; she reflected the next day how exceptionally effective she had been, and no one would have been more amazed than she, had she learned the effect she had left on Monson's mind. I hope, considering everything, that she never knew.

'How are you getting on with your flying-machine?' she asked. ('I wonder if I shall ever meet any one with the sense not to ask that,' thought Monson.) 'It will be very dangerous at first, will it not?' ('Thinks I'm afraid.') 'Jorgon is going to play presently; have you heard him before?'

('My mania being attended to, we turn to rational conversation.') Gush about Jorgon; gradual decline of conversation, ending with – 'You must let me know when your flying-machine is finished, Mr Monson, and then I will consider the advisability of taking a ticket.' ('One would think I was still playing inventions in the nursery.') But the bitterest thing she said was not meant for Monson's ears. To Phlox, the novelist, she was always conscientiously brilliant. 'I have been talking to Mr Monson, and he can think of nothing, positively nothing, but that flying-machine of his. Do you know, all his workmen call that place of his "Monson's Folly"? He is quite impossible. It is really very, very sad. I always regard him myself in the light of sunken treasure – the Lost Millionaire, you know.'

She was pretty and well educated, – indeed, she had written an epigrammatic novelette; but the bitterness was that she was typical. She summarized what the world thought of the man who was working sanely, steadily, and surely towards a more tremendous revolution in the appliances of civilization, a more far-reaching alteration in the ways of humanity than has ever been effected since history began. They did not even take him seriously. In a little while he would be proverbial. 'I *must* fly now,' he said on his way home, smarting with a sense of absolute social failure. 'I must fly soon. If it doesn't come off soon, by God! I shall run amuck.'

He said that before he had gone through his pass-book and his litter of papers. Inadequate as the cause seems, it was that girl's voice and the expression of her eyes that precipitated his discontent. But certainly the discovery that he had no longer even one hundred thousand pounds' worth of realizable property behind him was the poison that made the wound deadly.

It was the next day after this that he exploded upon Woodhouse and his workmen, and thereafter his bearing was consistently grim for three weeks, and anxiety dwelt in Cheam and Ewell, Malden, Morden, and Worcester Park, places that had thriven mightily on his experiments.

Four weeks after that first swearing of his, he stood with Woodhouse by the reconstructed machine as it lay across the elevated railway, by means of which it gained its initial impetus. The new propeller glittered a brighter white than the rest of the machine, and a gilder, obedient to a whim of Monson's, was picking out the aluminium bars with gold. And looking down the long avenue between the ropes (gilded now with the sunset), one saw red signals, and two miles away an anthill of workmen busy altering the last falls of the run into a rising slope.

'I'll *come*,' said Woodhouse. 'I'll come right enough. But I tell you it's infernally foolhardy. If only you would give another year – '

'I tell you I won't. I tell you the thing works. I've given years enough – '

'It's not that,' said Woodhouse. 'We're all right with the machine. But it's the steering – '

'Haven't I been rushing, night and morning, backwards and forwards, through this squirrel's cage? If the thing steers true here, it will steer true all across England. It's just funk, I tell you, Woodhouse. We could have gone a year ago. And besides – '

'Well?' said Woodhouse.

'The money!' snapped Monson, over his shoulder.

'Hang it! I never thought of the money,' said Woodhouse, and then, speaking now in a very different tone to that with which he had said the words before, he repeated, 'I'll come. Trust me.'

Monson turned suddenly, and saw all that Woodhouse had not the dexterity to say, shining on his sunset-lit face. He looked for a moment, then impulsively extended his hand. 'Thanks,' he said.

'All right,' said Woodhouse, gripping the hand, and with a queer softening of his features. 'Trust me.'

Then both men turned to the big apparatus that lay with its flat wings extended upon the carrier, and stared at it meditatively. Monson, guided perhaps by a photographic study of the flight of birds, and by Lilienthal's methods, had gradually drifted from Maxim's shapes towards the bird form again. The thing, however, was driven by a huge screw behind in the place of the tail; and so hovering, which needs an almost vertical adjustment of a flat tail, was rendered impossible. The body of the machine was small, almost cylindrical, and pointed. Forward and aft on the pointed ends were two small petroleum engines for the screw, and the navigators sat deep in a canoe-like recess, the foremost one steering, and being protected by a low screen, with two plate-glass windows, from the blinding rush of air. On either side a monstrous flat framework with a curved front border could be adjusted so as either to lie horizontally, or to be tilted upward or down. These wings worked rigidly together, or, by releasing a pin, one could be tilted through a small angle independently of its fellow.

The front edge of either wing could also be shifted back so as to diminish the wing-area about one-sixth. The machine was not only not designed to hover, but it was also incapable of fluttering. Monson's idea was to get into the air with the initial rush of the apparatus, and then to skim, much as a playing-card may be skimmed, keeping up the rush by means of the screw at the stern. Rooks and gulls fly enormous distances in that way with scarcely a perceptible movement of the wings. The bird really drives along on an aërial switch-back. It glides slanting downward for a space, until it has gained considerable momentum, and then altering the inclination of its wings, glides up again almost to its original altitude. Even a Londoner who has watched the birds in the aviary in Regent's Park knows that.

But the bird is practising this art from the moment it leaves its nest. It has not only the perfect apparatus, but the perfect instinct to use it. A man off his feet has the poorest skill in balancing. Even the simple trick of the bicycle costs him some hours of labour. The instantaneous adjustments of the wings, the quick response to a passing breeze, the swift recovery of equilibrium, the giddy, eddying movements that require such absolute precision – all that he must learn, learn with infinite labour and infinite danger, if ever he is to conquer flying. The flying-machine that will start off some fine day, driven by neat 'little levers,' with a nice open deck like a liner, and all loaded up with bomb-shells and guns, is the easy dreaming of a literary man. In lives and in treasure the cost of the conquest of the empire of the air may even exceed all that has been spent in man's great conquest of the sea. Certainly it will be costlier than the greatest war that has ever devastated the world.

No one knew these things better than these two practical men. And they knew they were in the front rank of the coming army. Yet there is hope even in a forlorn hope. Men are killed outright in the reserves sometimes, while others who have been left for dead in the thickest corner crawl out and survive.

'If we miss these meadows – ' said Woodhouse, presently in his slow way.

'My dear chap,' said Monson, whose spirits had been rising fitfully during the last few days, 'we mustn't miss these meadows. There's a quarter of a square mile for us to hit, fences removed, ditches levelled. We shall come down all right – rest assured. And if we don't – '

'Ah!' said Woodhouse. 'If we don't!'

Before the day of the start, the newspaper people got wind of the alterations at the northward end of the framework, and Monson was cheered by a decided change in the comments Romeike forwarded him. 'He will be off some day,' said the papers. 'He will be off some day,' said the South-Western season-ticket holders one to another; the seaside excursionists, the Saturday-to-Monday trippers from Sussex and Hampshire and Dorset and Devon, the eminent literary people from Hazlemere, all remarked eagerly one to another, 'He will be off some day,' as the familiar scaffolding came in sight. And actually, one bright morning, in full view of the ten-past-ten train from Basingstoke, Monson's flying-machine started on its journey.

They saw the carrier running swiftly along its rail, and the white-and-gold screw spinning in the air. They heard the rapid rumble of wheels, and a thud as the carrier reached the buffers at the end of its run. Then a whirr as the flying-machine was shot forward into the networks. All that the majority of them had seen and heard before. The thing went with a drooping flight through the framework and rose again, and then every beholder shouted, or screamed, or yelled, or shrieked after his kind. For instead of the customary concussion and stoppage, the flying-machine flew out of its five years' cage like a bolt from a crossbow, and drove slantingly upward into the air, curved round a little, so as to cross the line, and soared in the direction of Wimbledon Common.

It seemed to hang momentarily in the air and grow smaller, then it ducked and vanished over the clustering blue tree-tops to the east of Coombe Hill, and no one stopped staring and gasping until long after it had disappeared.

That was what the people in the train from Basingstoke saw. If you had drawn a line down the middle of that train, from engine to guard's van, you would not have found a living soul on the opposite side to the flying-machine. It was a mad rush from window to window as the thing crossed the line. And the engine-driver and stoker never took their eyes off the low hills about Wimbledon, and never noticed that they had run clean through Coombe and Malden and Raynes Park, until, with returning animation, they found themselves pelting, at the most indecent pace, into Wimbledon station.

From the moment when Monson had started the carrier with a '*Now!*' neither he nor Woodhouse said a word. Both men sat with clenched teeth. Monson had crossed the line with a curve that was too sharp, and Woodhouse had opened and shut his white lips; but neither spoke. Woodhouse simply gripped his seat, and breathed sharply through his teeth, watching the blue country to the west rushing past, and down, and away from him. Monson knelt at his post forward, and his hands trembled on the spoked wheel that moved the wings. He could see nothing before him but a mass of white clouds in the sky.

The machine went slanting upward, travelling with an enormous speed still, but losing momentum every moment. The land ran away underneath with diminishing speed.

'*Now!*' said Woodhouse at last, and with a violent effort Monson wrenched over the wheel and altered the angle of the wings. The machine seemed to hang for half a minute motionless in mid-air, and then he saw the hazy blue house-covered hills of Kilburn and Hampstead jump up before his eyes and rise steadily, until the little sunlit dome of the Albert Hall appeared through his windows. For a moment he scarcely understood the meaning of this upward rush of the horizon, but as the nearer and nearer houses came into view, he realized what he had done. He had turned the wings over too far, and they were swooping steeply downward towards the Thames.

The thought, the question, the realization were all the business of a second of time. 'Too much!' gasped Woodhouse. Monson brought the wheel half-way back with a jerk, and forthwith the Kilburn and Hampstead ridge dropped again to the lower edge of his windows. They had been a thousand feet above Coombe and Malden station; fifty seconds after they whizzed, at a frightful pace, not eighty feet above the East Putney station, on the Metropolitan District line, to the screaming astonishment of a platformful of people. Monson flung up the vans against the air, and over Fulham they rushed up their atmospheric switchback again, steeply – too steeply. The 'busses went floundering across the Fulham Road, the people yelled.

Then down again, too steeply still, and the distant trees and houses about Primrose Hill leapt up across Monson's window, and then suddenly he saw straight before him the greenery of Kensington Gardens and the towers of the Imperial Institute. They were driving straight down upon South Kensington. The pinnacles of the Natural History Museum rushed up into view. There came one fatal second of swift thought, a moment of hesitation. Should he try and clear the towers, or swerve eastward?

He made a hesitating attempt to release the right wing, left the catch half released, and gave a frantic clutch at the wheel.

The nose of the machine seemed to leap up before him. The wheel pressed his hand with irresistible force, and jerked itself out of his control.

Woodhouse, sitting crouched together, gave a hoarse cry, and sprang up towards Monson. 'Too far!' he cried, and then he was clinging to the gunwale for dear life, and Monson had been jerked clean overhead, and was falling backwards upon him.

So swiftly had the thing happened that barely a quarter of the people going to and fro in Hyde Park, and Brompton Road, and the Exhibition Road saw anything of the aërial catastrophe. A distant winged shape had appeared above the clustering houses to the south, had fallen and risen, growing larger as it did so; had swooped swiftly down towards the Imperial Institute, a broad spread of flying wings, had swept round in a quarter circle, dashed eastward, and then suddenly sprang vertically into the air. A black object shot out of it, and came spinning downward. A man! Two men clutching each other! They came whirling down, separated as they struck the roof of the Students' Club, and bounded off into the green bushes on its southward side.

For perhaps half a minute, the pointed stem of the big machine still pierced vertically upward, the screw spinning desperately. For one brief instant, that yet seemed an age to all who watched, it had hung motionless in mid-air. Then a spout of yellow flame licked up its length from the stern engine, and swift, swifter, swifter, and flaring like a rocket, it rushed down upon the solid mass of masonry which was formerly the Royal College of Science. The big screw of white and gold touched the parapet, and crumpled up like wet linen. Then the blazing spindle-shaped body smashed and splintered, smashing and splintering in its fall, upon the north westward angle of the building.

But the crash, the flame of blazing paraffin that shot heavenward from the shattered engines of the machine, the crushed horrors that were found in the garden beyond the Students' Club, the masses of yellow parapet and red brick that fell headlong into the roadway, the running to and fro of people like ants in a broken anthill, the galloping of fire-engines, the gathering of crowds – all these things do not belong to this story, which was written only to tell how the first of all successful flying-machines was launched and flew. Though he failed, and failed disastrously, the record of Monson's work remains – a sufficient monument – to guide the next of that band of gallant experimentalists who will sooner or later master this great problem of flying. And between Worcester Park and Malden there still stands that portentous avenue of iron-work, rusting now, and dangerous here and there, to witness to the first desperate struggle for man's right of way through the air.

HENRY JAMES

The Figure in the Carpet

I

I had done a few things and earned a few pence – I had perhaps even had
time to begin to think I was finer than was perceived by the patronizing;
but when I take the little measure of my course (a fidgety habit, for it's
none of the longest yet) I count my real start from the evening George
Corvick, breathless and worried, came in to ask me a service. He had
done more things than I, and earned more pence, though there were
chances for cleverness I thought he sometimes missed. I could only however that evening declare to him that he never missed one for kindness.
There was almost rapture in hearing it proposed to me to prepare for *The
Middle*, the organ of our lucubrations, so called from the position in the
week of its day of appearance, an article for which he had made himself
responsible, and of which, tied up with a stout string, he laid on my table
the subject. I pounced upon my opportunity – that is on the first volume
of it – and paid scant attention to my friend's explanation of his appeal.
What explanation could be more to the point than my obvious fitness for
the task? I had written on Hugh Vereker, but never a word in *The Middle*,
where my dealings were mainly with the ladies and the minor poets. This
was his new novel, an advance copy, and whatever much or little it should
do for his reputation I was clear on the spot as to what it should do for
mine. Moreover if I always read him as soon as I could get hold of him I
had a particular reason for wishing to read him now: I had accepted an
invitation to Bridges for the following Sunday, and it had been mentioned
in Lady Jane's note that Mr Vereker was to be there. I was young enough
for a flutter at meeting a man of his renown, and innocent enough to

believe the occasion would demand the display of an acquaintance with his 'last'.

Corvick, who had promised a review of it, had not even had time to read it; he had gone to pieces in consequence of news requiring – as on precipitate reflection he judged – that he should catch the night-mail to Paris. He had had a telegram from Gwendolen Erme in answer to his letter offering to fly to her aid. I knew already about Gwendolen Erme; I had never seen her, but I had my ideas, which were mainly to the effect that Corvick would marry her if her mother would only die. That lady seemed now in a fair way to oblige him; after some dreadful mistake about a climate or a 'cure' she had suddenly collapsed on the return from abroad. Her daughter, unsupported and alarmed, desiring to make a rush for home but hesitating at the risk, had accepted our friend's assistance, and it was my secret belief that at sight of him Mrs Erme would pull round. His own belief was scarcely to be called secret, it discernibly at any rate differed from mine. He had showed me Gwendolen's photograph with the remark that she wasn't pretty but was awfully interesting; she had published at the age of nineteen a novel in three volumes, 'Deep Down', about which, in *The Middle*, he had been really splendid. He appreciated my present eagerness and undertook that the periodical in question should do no less; then at the last, with his hand on the door, he said to me: 'Of course you'll be all right, you know.' Seeing I was a trifle vague he added: 'I mean you won't be silly.'

'Silly – about Vereker! Why, what do I ever find him but awfully clever?'

'Well, what's that but silly? What on earth does "awfully clever" mean? For God's sake try to get *at* him. Don't let him suffer by our arrangement. Speak of him, you know, if you can, as *I* should have spoken of him.'

I wondered an instant. 'You mean as far and away the biggest of the lot – that sort of thing?'

Corvick almost groaned. 'Oh you know, I don't put them back to back that way; it's the infancy of art! But he gives me a pleasure so rare; the sense of' – he mused a little – 'something or other.'

I wondered again. 'The sense, pray, of what?'

'My dear man, that's just what I want *you* to say!'

Even before he had banged the door I had begun, book in hand, to prepare myself to say it. I sat up with Vereker half the night; Corvick couldn't have done more than that. He was awfully clever – I stuck to that, but he wasn't a bit the biggest of the lot. I didn't allude to the lot, however; I flattered myself that I emerged on this occasion from the infancy of art. 'It's all right,' they declared vividly at the office; and when the number appeared I felt there was a basis on which I could meet the great man. It gave me confidence for a day or two – then that confidence dropped. I had fancied him reading it with relish, but if Corvick wasn't satisfied how could Vereker himself be? I reflected indeed that the heat of the admirer was sometimes grosser even than the appetite of the scribe. Corvick at all events wrote me from Paris a little ill-humouredly. Mrs Erme was pulling round, and I hadn't at all said what Vereker gave him the sense of.

II

The effect of my visit to Bridges was to turn me out for more profundity. Hugh Vereker, as I saw him there, was of a contact so void of angles that I blushed for the poverty of imagination involved in my small precautions. If he was in spirits it wasn't because he had read my review; in fact on the Sunday morning I felt sure he hadn't read it, though *The Middle* had been out three days and bloomed, I assured myself, in the stiff garden of periodicals which gave one of the ormolu tables the air of a stand at a station. The impression he made on me personally was such that I wished him to read it, and I corrected to this end with a surreptitious hand what might be wanting in the careless conspicuity of the sheet. I'm afraid I even watched the result of my manoeuvre, but up to luncheon I watched in vain.

When afterwards, in the course of our gregarious walk, I found myself for half an hour, not perhaps without another manoeuvre, at the great man's side, the result of his affability was a still livelier desire that he shouldn't remain in ignorance of the peculiar justice I had done him. It wasn't that he seemed to thirst for justice; on the contrary I hadn't yet caught in his talk the faintest grunt of a grudge – a note for which my young experience had already given me an ear. Of late he had had more recognition, and it was pleasant, as we used to say in *The Middle*, to see how it drew him out. He wasn't of course popular, but I judged one of the sources of his good humour to be precisely that his success was independent of that. He had none the less become in a manner the fashion; the critics at least had put on a spurt and caught up with him. We had found out at last how clever he was, and he had had to make the best of the loss of his mystery. I was strongly tempted, as I walked beside him, to let him know how much of that unveiling was my act; and there was a moment when I probably should have done so had not one of the ladies of our party, snatching a place at his other elbow, just then appealed to him in a spirit comparatively selfish. It was very discouraging: I almost felt the liberty had been taken with myself.

I had had on my tongue's end, for my own part, a phrase or two about the right word at the right time, but later on I was glad not to have spoken, for when on our return we clustered at tea I perceived Lady Jane, who had not been out with us, brandishing *The Middle* with her longest arm. She had taken it up at her leisure; she was delighted with what she had found, and I saw that, as a mistake in a man may often be a felicity in a woman, she would practically do for me what I hadn't been able to do for myself. 'Some sweet little truths that needed to be spoken,' I heard her declare, thrusting the paper at rather a bewildered couple by the fireplace. She grabbed it away from them again on the reappearance of Hugh Vereker, who after our walk had been upstairs to change something. 'I know you don't in general look at this kind of thing, but it's an occasion really for doing so. You *haven't* seen it? Then you must. The man has actually got *at* you, at what *I* always feel, you know.' Lady Jane threw into her eyes a look evidently intended to give an idea of what she always felt; but she added that she couldn't have expressed it. The man in the paper expressed it in a striking manner. 'Just see there, and there, where I've dashed it, how he brings it out.' She had literally marked for him the brightest patches of my prose, and if I was a little amused Vereker himself may well have been. He showed how much he was when before us all Lady Jane wanted to read something aloud. I liked at any rate the way he defeated her purpose by jerking the paper affectionately out of her clutch. He'd take it upstairs with him and look at it on going to dress. He did this half an hour later – I saw it in his hand when he repaired to his room. That was the moment at which, thinking to give her pleasure, I mentioned to Lady Jane that I was the author of the review. I did give her pleasure, I judged, but perhaps not quite so much as I had expected. If the author was 'only me' the thing didn't seem quite so remarkable. Hadn't I had the effect rather of diminishing the lustre of the article than of adding to my own? Her ladyship was subject to the most extraordinary drops. It didn't matter; the only effect I cared about was the one it would have on Vereker up there by his bedroom fire.

At dinner I watched for the signs of this impression, tried to fancy some happier light in his eyes; but to my disappointment Lady Jane gave me no chance to make sure. I had hoped she'd call triumphantly down the table, publicly demand if she hadn't been right. The party was large – there were people from outside as well, but I had never seen a table long enough to deprive Lady Jane of a triumph. I was just reflecting in truth that this interminable board would deprive *me* of one when the guest next me, dear woman – she was Miss Poyle, the vicar's sister, a robust unmodulated person – had the happy inspiration and the unusual courage to address herself across it to Vereker, who was opposite, but not directly, so that when he replied they were both leaning forward. She enquired, artless body, what he thought of Lady Jane's 'panegyric', which she had read – not connecting it however with her right-hand neighbour; and while I strained my ear for his reply I heard him, to my stupefaction, call back gaily, his mouth full of bread: 'Oh it's all right – the usual twaddle!'

I had caught Vereker's glance as he spoke, but Miss Poyle's surprise was a fortunate cover for my own. 'You mean he doesn't do you justice?' said the excellent woman.

Vereker laughed out, and I was happy to be able to do the same. 'It's a charming article,' he tossed us.

Miss Poyle thrust her chin half across the cloth. 'Oh you're so deep!' she drove home.

'As deep as the ocean! All I pretend is that the author doesn't see – ' But a dish was at this point passed over his shoulder, and we had to wait while he helped himself.

'Doesn't see what?' my neighbour continued.

'Doesn't see anything.'

'Dear me – how very stupid!'

'Not a bit,' Vereker laughed again. 'Nobody does.'

The lady on his further side appealed to him and Miss Poyle sank back to myself. 'Nobody sees anything!' she cheerfully announced; to which I replied that I had often thought so too, but had somehow taken the thought for a proof on my own part of a tremendous eye. I didn't tell her the article was mine; and I observed that Lady Jane, occupied at the end of the table, had not caught Vereker's words.

I rather avoided him after dinner, for I confess he struck me as cruelly conceited, and the revelation was a pain. 'The usual twaddle' – my acute little study! That one's admiration should have had a reserve or two could gall him to that point? I had thought him placid, and he was placid enough; such a surface was the hard polished glass that encased the bauble of his vanity. I was really ruffled, and the only comfort was that if nobody saw anything George Corvick was quite as much out of it as I. This comfort however was not sufficient, after the ladies had dispersed, to carry me in the proper manner – I mean in a spotted jacket and humming an air – into the smoking-room. I took my way in some dejection to bed; but in the passage I encountered Mr Vereker, who had been up once more to change, coming out of his room. *He* was humming an air and had on a spotted jacket, and as soon as he saw me his gaiety gave a start.

'My dear young man,' he exclaimed. 'I'm so glad to lay hands on you! I'm afraid I most unwittingly wounded you by those words of mine at dinner to Miss Poyle. I learned but half an hour ago from Lady Jane that you're the author of the little notice in *The Middle*.'

I protested that no bones were broken; but he moved with me to my own door, his hand, on my shoulder, kindly feeling for a fracture; and on hearing that I had come up to bed he asked leave to cross my threshold and just tell me in three words what his qualification of my remarks had represented. It was plain he really feared I was hurt, and the sense of his solicitude suddenly made all the difference to me. My cheap review fluttered off into space, and the best things I had said in it became flat enough beside the brilliancy of his being there. I can see him there still, on my rug, in the firelight and his spotted jacket, his fine clear face all bright with the desire to be tender to my youth. I don't know what he had at first meant to say, but I think the sight of my relief touched him, excited him, brought up words to his lips from far within. It was so these words presently conveyed to me something that, as I afterwards knew, he had never uttered to anyone. I've always done justice to the generous impulse that made him speak; it was simply compunction for a snub unconsciously administered to a man of letters in a position inferior to his own, a man of letters moreover in the very act of praising him. To make the thing right he talked to me exactly as an equal and on the ground of what we both loved best. The hour, the place, the unexpectedness deepened the impression: he couldn't have done anything more intensely effective.

III

'I don't quite know how to explain it to you,' he said, 'but it was the very fact that your notice of my book had a spice of intelligence, it was just your exceptional sharpness, that produced the feeling – a very old story with me, I beg you to believe – under the momentary influence of which I used in speaking to that good lady the words you so naturally resent. I don't read the things in the newspapers unless they're thrust upon me as that one was – it's always one's best friend who does it! But I used to read them sometimes – ten years ago. I dare say they were in general rather stupider then; at any rate it always struck me they missed my little point with a perfection exactly as admirable when they patted me on the back as when they kicked me in the shins. Whenever since I've happened to have a glimpse of them they were still blazing away – still missing it, I mean, deliciously. *You* miss it, my dear fellow, with inimitable assurance; the fact of your being awfully clever and your article's being awfully nice doesn't make a hair's breadth of difference. It's quite with you rising young men,' Vereker laughed, 'that I feel most what a failure I am!'

I listened with keen interest; it grew keener as he talked. '*You* a failure – heavens! What then may your "little point" happen to be?'

'Have I got to *tell* you, after all these years and labours?' There was something in the friendly reproach of this – jocosely exaggerated – that made me, as an ardent young seeker for truth, blush to the roots of my hair. I'm as much in the dark as ever, though I've grown used in a sense to my obtuseness; at that moment, however, Vereker's happy accent made me appear to myself, and probably to him, a rare dunce. I was on the point of exclaiming 'Ah yes, don't tell me: for my honour, for that of the craft, don't!' when he went on in a manner that showed he had read my thoughts and had his own idea of the probability of our some day redeeming ourselves. 'By my little point I mean – what shall I call it? – the particular thing I've written my books most *for*. Isn't there for every writer a particular thing of that sort, the thing that most makes him apply himself, the thing without the effort to achieve which he wouldn't write at all, the very passion of his passion, the part of the business in which, for him, the flame of art burns most intensely? Well, it's *that*!'

I considered a moment – that is I followed at a respectful distance, rather gasping. I was fascinated – easily, you'll say; but I wasn't going after all to be put off my guard. 'Your description's certainly beautiful, but it doesn't make what you describe very distinct.'

'I promise you it would be distinct if it should dawn on you at all.' I saw that the charm of our topic overflowed for my companion into an emotion as lively as my own. 'At any rate,' he went on, 'I can speak for myself: there's an idea in my work without which I wouldn't have given a straw for the whole job. It's the finest fullest intention of the lot, and the application of it has been, I think, a triumph of patience, of ingenuity. I ought to leave that to somebody else to say; but that nobody does say it is precisely what we're talking about. It stretches, this little trick of mine, from book to book, and every thing else, comparatively, plays over the surface of it. The order, the form, the texture of my books will perhaps some day constitute for the initiated a complete representation of it. So it's naturally the thing for the critic to look for. It strikes me,' my visitor added, smiling, 'even as the thing for the critic to find.'

This seemed a responsibility indeed. 'You call it a little trick?'

'That's only my little modesty. It's really an exquisite scheme.'

'And you hold that you've carried the scheme out?'

'The way I've carried it out is the thing in life I think a bit well of myself for.'

I had a pause. 'Don't you think you ought – just a trifle – to assist the critic?'

'Assist him? What else have I done with every stroke of my pen? I've shouted my intention in his great blank face!' At this, laughing out again, Vereker laid his hand on my shoulder to show the allusion wasn't to my personal appearance.

'But you talk about the initiated. There must therefore, you see, *be* initiation.'

'What else in heaven's name is criticism supposed to be?'

I'm afraid I coloured at this too; but I took refuge in repeating that his account of his silver lining was poor in something or other that a plain man knows things by. 'That's only because you've never had a glimpse of it,' he returned. 'If you had had one the element in question would soon have become practically all you'd see. To me it's exactly as palpable as the marble of this chimney. Besides, the critic just *isn't* a plain man: if he were, pray, what would he be doing in his neighbour's garden? You're anything but a plain man yourself, and the very *raison d'être* of you all is that you're little demons of subtlety. If my great affair's a secret, that's only because it's a secret in spite of itself – the amazing event has made it one. I not only never took the smallest precaution to keep it so, but never dreamed of any such accident. If I had I shouldn't in advance have had the heart to go on. As it was, I only became aware little by little, and meanwhile I had done my work.'

'And now you quite like it?' I risked.

'My work?'

'Your secret. It's the same thing.'

'Your guessing that,' Vereker replied, 'is a proof that you're as clever as I say!' I was encouraged by this to remark that he would clearly be pained to part with it, and he confessed that it was indeed with him now the great amusement of life. 'I live almost to see if it will ever be detected.' He looked at me for a jesting challenge; something far within his eyes seemed to peep out. 'But I needn't worry – it won't!'

'You fire me as I've never been fired,' I declared; 'you make me determined to do or die.' Then I asked: 'Is it a kind of esoteric message?'

His countenance fell at this – he put out his hand as if to bid me good night. 'Ah my dear fellow, it can't be described in cheap journalese!'

I knew of course he'd be awfully fastidious, but our talk had made me feel how much his nerves were exposed. I was unsatisfied – I kept hold of his hand. 'I won't make use of the expression then,' I said, 'in the article which I shall eventually announce my discovery, though I dare say I shall have hard work to do without it. But meanwhile, just to hasten that difficult birth, can't you give a fellow a clue?' I felt much more at my ease.

'My whole lucid effort gives him the clue – every page and line and letter. The thing's as concrete there as a bird in a cage, a bait on a hook, a piece of cheese in a mouse-trap. It's stuck into every volume as your foot is stuck into your shoe. It governs every line, it chooses every word, it dots every i, it places every comma.'

I scratched my head. 'Is it something in the style or something in the thought? An element of form or an element of feeling?'

He indulgently shook my hand again, and I felt my questions to be crude and my distinctions pitiful. 'Good night, my dear boy – don't bother about it. After all, you do like a fellow.'

'And a little intelligence might spoil it?' I still detained him.

He hesitated. 'Well, you've got a heart in your body. Is that an element of form or an element of feeling? What I contend that nobody has ever mentioned in my work is the organ of life.'

'I see – it's some idea *about* life, some sort of philosophy. Unless it be,' I added with the eagerness of a thought perhaps still happier, 'some kind of game you're up to with your style, something you're after in the language. Perhaps it's a preference for the letter P!' I ventured profanely to break out. 'Papa, potatoes, prunes – that sort of thing?' He was suitably indulgent: he only said I hadn't got the right letter. But his amusement was over; I could see he was bored. There was nevertheless something else I had absolutely to learn. 'Should you be able, pen in hand, to state it clearly yourself – to name it, phrase it, formulate it?'

'Oh,' he almost passionately sighed, 'if I were only, pen in hand, one of *you* chaps!'

'That would be a great chance for you of course. But why should you despise us chaps for not doing what you can't do yourself?'

'Can't do?' He opened his eyes. 'Haven't I done it in twenty volumes? I do it in my way,' he continued. 'Go *you* and don't do it in yours.'

'Ours is so devilish difficult,' I weakly observed.

'So's mine! We each choose our own. There's no compulsion. You won't come down and smoke?'

'No. I want to think this thing out.'

'You'll tell me then in the morning that you've laid me bare?'

'I'll see what I can do; I'll sleep on it. But just one word more,' I added. We had left the room – I walked again with him a few steps along the passage. 'This extraordinary "general intention", as you call it – for that's the most vivid description I can induce you to make of it – is then, generally, a sort of buried treasure?'

His face lighted. 'Yes, call it that, though it's perhaps not for me to do so.'

'Nonsense!' I laughed. 'You know you're hugely proud of it.'

'Well, I didn't propose to tell you so; but it *is* the joy of my soul!'

'You mean it's a beauty so rare, so great?'

He waited a little again. 'The loveliest thing in the world!' We had stopped, and on these words he left me; but at the end of the corridor, while I looked after him rather yearningly, he turned and caught sight of my puzzled face. It made him earnestly, indeed I thought quite anxiously, shake his head and wave his finger. 'Give it up – give it up!'

This wasn't a challenge – it was fatherly advice. If I had had one of his books at hand I'd have repeated my recent act of faith – I'd have spent half the night with him. At three o'clock in the morning, not sleeping, remembering moreover how indispensable he was to Lady Jane, I stole down to the library with a candle. There wasn't, so far as I could discover, a line of his writing in the house.

IV

Returning to town I feverishly collected them all; I picked out each in its order and held it up to the light. This gave me a maddening month, in the course of which several things took place. One of these, the last, I may as well immediately mention, was that I acted on Vereker's advice: I renounced my ridiculous attempt. I could really make nothing of the business; it proved a dead loss. After all I had always, as he had himself noted, liked him; and what now occurred was simply that my new intelligence and vain preoccupation damaged my liking. I not only failed to run a general intention to earth, I found myself missing the subordinate intentions I had formerly enjoyed. His books didn't even remain the charming things they had been for me; the exasperation of my search put me out of conceit of them. Instead of being a pleasure the more they became a resource the less; for from the moment I was unable to follow up the author's hint I of course felt it a point of honour not to make use professionally of my knowledge of them. I *had* no knowledge – nobody had any. It was humiliating, but I could bear it – they only annoyed me now. At last they even bored me, and I accounted for my confusion – perversely, I allow – by the idea that Vereker had made a fool of me. The buried treasure was a bad joke, the general intention a monstrous *pose*.

The great point of it all is, however, that I told George Corvick what had befallen me and that my information had an immense effect on him. He had at last come back, but so, unfortunately, had Mrs Erme, and there was as yet, I could see, no question of his nuptials. He was immensely stirred up by the anecdote I had brought from Bridges; it fell in so completely with the sense he had had from the first that there was more in Vereker than met the eye. When I remarked that the eye seemed what the printed page had been expressly invented to meet he immediately accused me of being spiteful because I had been foiled. Our commerce had always that pleasant latitude. The thing Vereker had mentioned to me was exactly the thing he, Corvick, had wanted me to speak of in my review. On my suggesting at last that with the assistance I had now given him he would doubtless be prepared to speak of it himself he admitted freely that before doing this there was more he must understand. What he would have said, had he reviewed the new book, was that there was evidently in the writer's inmost art something to *be* understood. I hadn't so much as hinted at that: no wonder the writer hadn't been flattered! I asked Corvick what he really considered he meant by his own supersubtlety, and, unmistakably kindled, he replied: 'It isn't for the vulgar – it isn't for the vulgar!' He had hold of the tail of something: he would pull hard, pull it right out. He pumped me dry on Vereker's strange confidence and, pronouncing me the luckiest of mortals, mentioned half a dozen questions he wished to goodness I had had the gumption to put. Yet on the other hand he didn't want to be told too much – it would spoil the fun of seeing what would come. The failure of *my* fun was at the moment of our meeting not complete, but I saw it ahead, and Corvick saw that I saw it. I, on my side, saw likewise that one of the first things he would do would be to rush off with my story to Gwendolen.

On the very day after my talk with him I was surprised by the receipt of a note from Hugh Vereker, to whom our encounter at Bridges had been recalled, as he mentioned, by his falling, in a magazine, on some article to which my signature was attached. 'I read it with great pleasure,' he wrote, 'and remembered under its influence our lively conversation by your bedroom fire. The consequence of this has been that I begin to measure the temerity of my having saddled you with a knowledge that you may find something of a burden. Now that the fit's over I can't imagine how I came to be moved so much beyond my wont. I had never before mentioned, no matter in what state of expansion, the fact of my little secret, and I shall never speak of the mystery again. I was accidentally so much more explicit with you than it had ever entered into my game to be, that I find this game – I mean the pleasure of playing it – suffers considerably. In short, if you can understand it, I've rather spoiled my sport. I really don't want to give anybody what I believe you clever young men call the tip. That's of course a selfish solicitude, and I name it to you for what it may be worth to you. If you're disposed to humour me don't repeat my revelation. Think me demented – it's your right; but don't tell anybody why.'

The sequel to this communication was that as early on the morrow as I dared I drove straight to Mr Vereker's door. He occupied in those years one of the honest old houses in Kensington Square. He received me immediately, and as soon as I came in I saw I hadn't lost my power to minister to his mirth. He laughed out at sight of my face, which doubtless expressed my perturbation. I had been indiscreet – my compunction was great. 'I *have* told somebody,' I panted, 'and I'm sure that person will by this time have told somebody else! It's a woman, into the bargain.'

'The person you've told?'

'No, the other person. I'm quite sure he must have told her.'

'For all the good it will do her – or do *me*! A woman will never find out.'

'No, but she'll talk all over the place: she'll do just what you don't want.'

Vereker thought a moment, but wasn't so disconcerted as I had feared: he felt that if the harm was done it only served him right. 'It doesn't matter – don't worry.'

'I'll do my best, I promise you, that your talk with me shall go no further.'

'Very good; do what you can.'

'In the meantime,' I pursued, 'George Corvick's possession of the tip may, on his part, really lead to something.'

'That will be a brave day.'

I told him about Corvick's cleverness, his admiration, the intensity of his interest in my anecdote; and without making too much of the divergence of our respective estimates mentioned that my friend was already of opinion that he saw much further into a certain affair than most people. He was quite as fired as I had been at Bridges. He was moreover in love with the young lady: perhaps the two together would puzzle something out.

Vereker seemed struck with this. 'Do you mean they're to be married?'

'I dare say that's what it will come to.'

'That may help them,' he conceded, 'but we must give them time!'

I spoke of my own renewed assault and confessed my difficulties; whereupon he repeated his former advice: 'Give it up, give it up!' He evidently didn't think me intellectually equipped for the adventure. I stayed half an hour, and he was most good-natured, but I couldn't help pronouncing him a man of unstable moods. He had been free with me in a mood, he had repented in a mood, and now in a mood he had turned indifferent. This general levity helped me to believe that, so far as the subject of the tip went, there wasn't much in it. I contrived however to make him answer a few more questions about it, though he did so with visible impatience. For himself, beyond doubt, the thing we were all so blank about was vividly there. It was something, I guessed, in the primal plan; something like a complex figure in a Persian carpet. He highly approved of this image when I used it, and he used another himself. 'It's the very string,' he said, 'that my pearls are strung on!' The reason of his note to me had been that he really didn't want to give us a grain of succour – our density was a thing too perfect in its way to touch. He had formed the habit of depending on it, and if the spell was to break it must break by some force of its own. He comes back to me from that last occasion – for I was never to speak to him again – as a man with some safe preserve for sport. I wondered as I walked away where he had got *his* tip.

V

When I spoke to George Corvick of the caution I had received he made me feel that any doubt of his delicacy would be almost an insult. He had instantly told Gwendolen, but Gwendolen's ardent response was in itself a pledge of discretion. The question would now absorb them and would offer them a pastime too precious to be shared with the crowd. They appeared to have caught instinctively at Vereker's high idea of enjoyment. Their intellectual pride, however, was not such as to make them indifferent to any further light I might throw on the affair they had in hand. They were indeed of the 'artistic temperament', and I was freshly struck with my colleague's power to excite himself over a question of art. He'd call it letters, he'd call it life, but it was all one thing. In what he said I now seemed to understand that he spoke equally for Gwendolen, to whom, as soon as Mrs Erme was sufficiently better to allow her a little leisure, he made a point of introducing me. I remember our going together one Sunday in August to a huddled house in Chelsea, and my renewed envy of Corvick's possession of a friend who had some light to mingle with his own. He could say things to her that I could never say to him. She had indeed no sense of humour and, with her pretty way of holding her head on one side, was one of those persons whom you want, as the phrase is, to shake, but who have learnt Hungarian by themselves. She conversed perhaps in Hungarian with Corvick; she had remarkably little English for his friend. Corvick afterwards told me that I had chilled her by my apparent indisposition to oblige them with the detail of what Vereker had said to me. I allowed that I felt I had given thought enough to that indication: hadn't I even made up my mind that it was vain and would lead nowhere? The importance they attached to it was irritating and quite envenomed my doubts.

That statement looks unamiable, and what probably happened was that I felt humiliated at seeing other persons deeply beguiled by an experiment that had brought me only chagrin. I was out in the cold while, by the evening fire, under the lamp, they followed the chase for which I myself had sounded the horn. They did as I had done, only more deliberately and sociably – they went over their author from the beginning. There was no hurry, Corvick said – the future was before them and the fascination could only grow; they would take him page by page, as they would take one of the classics, inhale him in slow draughts and let him sink all the way in. They would scarce have got so wound up, I think, if they hadn't been in love: poor Vereker's inner meaning gave them endless occasion to put and to keep their young heads together. None the less it represented the kind of problem for which Corvick had a special aptitude, drew out the particular pointed patience of which, had he lived, he would have given more striking and, it is to be hoped, more fruitful examples. He at least was, in Vereker's words, a little demon of subtlety. We had begun by disputing, but I soon saw that without my stirring a finger his infatuation would have its bad hours. He would bound off on false scents as I had done – he would clap his hands over new lights and see them blown out by the wind of the turned page. He was like nothing, I told him, but the maniacs who embrace some bedlamitical theory of the cryptic character of Shakespeare. To this he replied that if we had had Shakespeare's own word for his being cryptic he would at once have accepted it. The case there was altogether different – we had nothing but the word of Mr Snooks. I returned that I was stupefied to see him attach such importance even to the word of Mr Vereker. He wanted thereupon to know if I treated Mr Vereker's word as a lie. I wasn't perhaps prepared, in my unhappy rebound, to go so far as that, but I insisted that till the contrary was proved I should view it as too fond an imagination. I didn't, I confess, say – I didn't at that time quite know – all I felt. Deep down, as Miss Erme would have said, I was uneasy, I was expectant. At the core of my disconcerted state – for my wonted curiosity lived in its ashes – was the sharpness of a sense that Corvick would at last probably come out somewhere. He made, in defence of his credulity, a great point of the fact that from of old, in his study of this genius, he had caught whiffs and hints of he didn't know what, faint wandering notes of a hidden music. That was just the rarity, that was the charm: it fitted so perfectly into what I reported.

If I returned on several occasions to the little house in Chelsea I dare say it was as much for news of Vereker as for news of Miss Erme's ailing parent. The hours spent there by Corvick were present to my fancy as those of a chessplayer bent with a silent scowl, all the lamplit winter, over his board and his moves. As my imagination filled it out the picture held me fast. On the other side of the table was a ghostlier form, the faint figure of an antagonist good-humouredly but a little wearily secure – an antagonist who leaned back in his chair with his hands in his pockets and a smile on his fine clear face. Close to Corvick, behind him, was a girl who had begun to strike me as pale and wasted and even, on more familiar view, as rather handsome, and who rested on his shoulder and hung on his moves. He would take up a chessman and hold it poised a while over one of the little squares, and then would put it back in its place with a long sigh of disappointment. The young lady, at this, would slightly but uneasily shift her position and look across, very hard, very long, very strangely, at their dim participant. I had asked them at an early stage of the business if it mightn't contribute to their success to have some closer communication with him. The special circumstances would surely be held to have given me a right to introduce them. Corvick immediately replied that he had no wish to approach the altar before he had prepared the sacrifice. He quite agreed with our friend both as to the delight and as to the honour of the chase – he would bring down the animal with his own rifle. When I asked him if Miss Erme were as keen a shot he said after thinking: 'No, I'm ashamed to say she wants to set a trap. She'd give anything to see him; she says she requires another tip. She's really quite morbid about it. But she must play fair – she *shan't* see him!' he emphatically added. I wondered if they hadn't even quarrelled a little on the subject – a suspicion not corrected by the way he more than once exclaimed to me: 'She's quite incredibly literary, you know – quite fantastically!' I remember his saying of her that she felt in italics and thought in capitals. 'Oh when I've run him to earth,' he also said, 'then, you know, I shall knock at his door. Rather – I beg you to believe. I'll have it from his own lips: "Right you are, my boy; you've done it this time!" He shall crown me victor – with the critical laurel.'

Meanwhile he really avoided the chances London life might have given him of meeting the distinguished novelist; a danger, however, that disappeared with Vereker's leaving England for an indefinite absence, as the newspapers announced – going to the south for motives connected with the health of his wife, which had long kept her in retirement. A year – more than a year – had elapsed since the incident at Bridges, but I had had no further sight of him. I think I was at bottom rather ashamed – I hated to remind him that, though I had irremediably missed his point, a reputation for acuteness was rapidly overtaking me. This scruple led me a dance; kept me out of Lady Jane's house, made me even decline, when in spite of my bad manners she was a second time so good as to make me a sign, an invitation to her beautiful seat. I once became aware of her under Vereker's escort at a concert, and was sure I was seen by them, but I slipped out without being caught. I felt, as on that occasion I splashed along in the rain, that I couldn't have done anything else; and yet I remember saying to myself that it was hard, was even cruel. Not only had I lost the books, but I had lost the man himself: they and their author had been alike spoiled for me. I knew too which was the loss I most regretted. I had taken to the man still more than I had ever taken to the books.

VI

Six months after our friend had left England George Corvick, who made his living by his pen, contracted for a piece of work which imposed on him an absence of some length and a journey of some difficulty, and his undertaking of which was much of a surprise to me. His brother-in-law had become editor of a great provincial paper, and the great provincial paper, in a fine flight of fancy, had conceived the idea of sending a 'special commissioner' to India. Special commissioners had begun, in the 'metropolitan press', to be the fashion, and the journal in question must have felt it had passed too long for a mere country cousin. Corvick had no hand, I knew, for the big brush of the correspondent, but that was his brother-in-law's affair, and the fact that a particular task was not in his line was apt to be with himself exactly a reason for accepting it. He was prepared to out-Herod the metropolitan press; he took solemn precautions against priggishness, he exquisitely outraged taste. Nobody ever knew it – that offended principle was all his own. In addition to his expenses he was to be conveniently paid, and I found myself able to help him, for the usual fat book, to a plausible arrangement with the usual fat publisher. I naturally inferred that his obvious desire to make a little money was not unconnected with the prospect of a union with Gwendolen Erme. I was aware that her mother's opposition was largely addressed to his want of means and of lucrative abilities, but it so happened that, on my saying the last time I saw him something that bore on the question of his separation from our young lady, he brought out with an emphasis that startled me: 'Ah, I'm not a bit engaged to her, you know!'

'Not overtly,' I answered, 'because her mother doesn't like you. But I've always taken for granted a private understanding.'

'Well, there *was* one. But there isn't now.' That was all he said save something about Mrs Erme's having got on her feet again in the most extraordinary way – a remark pointing, as I supposed, the moral that private understandings were of little use when the doctor didn't share them. What I took the liberty of more closely inferring was that the girl might in some way have estranged him. Well, if he had taken the turn of jealousy for instance it could scarcely be jealousy of me. In that case – over and above the absurdity of it – he wouldn't have gone away just to leave us together. For some time before his going we had indulged in no allusion to the buried treasure, and from his silence, which my reserve simply emulated, I had drawn a sharp conclusion. His courage had dropped, his ardour had gone the way of mine – this appearance at least he left me to scan. More than that he couldn't do; he couldn't face the triumph with which I might have greeted an explicit admission. He needn't have been afraid, poor dear, for I had by this time lost all need to triumph. In fact I considered I showed magnanimity in not reproaching him with his collapse, for the sense of his having thrown up the game made me feel more than ever how much I at last depended on him. If Corvick had broken down I should never know; no one would be of any use if *he* wasn't. It wasn't a bit true I had ceased to care for knowledge; little by little my curiosity not only had begun to ache again, but had become the familiar torment of my days and my nights. There are doubtless people to whom torments of such an order appear hardly more natural than the contortions of disease; but I don't after all know why I should in this connection so much as mention them. For the few persons, at any rate, abnormal or not, with whom my anecdote is concerned, literature was a game of skill, and skill meant courage, and courage meant honour, and honour meant passion, meant life. The stake on the table was of a special substance and our roulette the revolving mind, but we sat round the green board as intently as the grim gamblers at Monte Carlo. Gwendolen Erme, for that matter, with her white face and her fixed eyes, was of the very type of the lean ladies one had met in the temples of chance. I recognized in Corvick's absence that she made this analogy vivid. It was extravagant, I admit, the way she lived for the art of the pen. Her passion visibly preyed on her, and in her presence I felt almost tepid. I got hold of *Deep Down* again: it was a desert in which she had lost herself, but in which too she had dug a wonderful hole in the sand – a cavity out of which Corvick had still more remarkably pulled her.

Early in March I had a telegram from her, in consequence of which I repaired immediately to Chelsea, where the first thing she said to me was 'He has got it, he has got it!'

She was moved, as I could see, to such depths that she must mean the great thing. 'Vereker's idea?'

'His general intention. George has cabled from Bombay.'

She had the missive open there; it was emphatic though concise. 'Eureka. Immense.' That was all – he had saved the cost of the signature. I shared her emotion, but I was disappointed. 'He doesn't say what it is.'

'How could he – in a telegram? He'll write it.'

'But how does he know?'

'Know it's the real thing? Oh I'm sure that when you see it you do know. *Vera incessu patuit dea!*'

'It's you, Miss Erme, who are a "dear" for bringing me such news!' – I went all lengths in my high spirits. 'But fancy finding our goddess in the temple of Vishnu! How strange of George to have been able to go into the thing again in the midst of such different and such powerful solicitations!'

'He hasn't gone into it, I know; it's the thing itself, let severely alone for six months, that has simply sprung out at him like a tigress out of the jungle. He didn't take a book with him – on purpose; indeed he wouldn't have needed to – he knows every page, as I do, by heart. They all worked in him together, and some day somewhere, when he wasn't thinking, they fell, in all their superb intricacy, into the one right combination. The figure in the carpet came out. That's the way he knew it would come and the real reason – you didn't in the least understand, but I suppose I may tell you now – why he went and why I consented to his going. We knew the change would do it – that the difference of thought, of scene, would give the needed touch, the magic shake. We had perfectly, we had admirably calculated. The elements were all in his mind, and in the *secousse* of a new and intense experience they just struck light.' She positively struck light herself – she was literally, facially luminous. I stammered something about unconscious cerebration, and she continued: 'He'll come right home – this will bring him.'

'To see Vereker, you mean?'

'To see Vereker – and to see *me*. Think what he'll have to tell me!'

I hesitated. 'About India?'

'About fiddlesticks! About Vereker – about the figure in the carpet.'

'But, as you say, we shall surely have that in a letter.'

She thought like one inspired, and I remembered how Corvick had told me long before that her face was interesting. 'Perhaps it can't be got into a letter if it's "immense".'

'Perhaps not if it's immense bosh. If he has hold of something that can't be got into a letter he hasn't hold of *the* thing. Vereker's own statement to me was exactly that the "figure" *would* fit into a letter.'

'Well, I cabled to George an hour ago – two words,' said Gwendolen.

'Is it indiscreet of me to ask what they were?'

She hung fire, but at last brought them out. '"Angel, write."'

'Good!' I cried. 'I'll make it sure – I'll send him the same.'

VII

My words however were not absolutely the same – I put something instead of 'angel'; and in the sequel my epithet seemed the more apt, for when eventually we heard from our traveller it was merely, it was thoroughly to be tantalized. He was magnificent in his triumph, he described his discovery as stupendous; but his ecstasy only obscured it – there were to be no particulars till he should have submitted his conception to the supreme authority. He had thrown up his commission, he had thrown up his book, he had thrown up everything but the instant need to hurry to Rapallo, on the Genoese shore, where Vereker was making a stay. I wrote him a letter which was to await him at Aden – I besought him to relieve my suspense. That he had found my letter was indicated by a telegram which, reaching me after weary days and in the absence of any answer to my laconic dispatch to him at Bombay, was evidently intended as a reply to both communications. Those few words were in familiar French, the

French of the day, which Corvick often made use of to show he wasn't a prig. It had for some persons the opposite effect, but his message may fairly be paraphrased. 'Have patience; I want to see, as it breaks on you, the face you'll make!' '*Tellement envie de voir ta tête!*' – that was what I had to sit down with. I can certainly not be said to have sat down, for I seem to remember myself at this time as rattling constantly between the little house in Chelsea and my own. Our impatience, Gwendolen's and mine, was equal, but I kept hoping her light would be greater. We all spent during this episode, for people of our means, a great deal of money in telegrams and cabs, and I counted on the receipt of news from Rapallo immediately after the junction of the discoverer with the discovered. The interval seemed an age, but late one day I heard a hansom precipitated to my door with the crash engendered by a hint of liberality. I lived with my heart in my mouth and accordingly bounded to the window – a movement which gave me a view of a young lady erect on the footboard of the vehicle and eagerly looking up at my house. At sight of me she flourished a paper with a movement that brought me straight down, the movement with which, in melodramas, handkerchiefs and reprieves are flourished at the foot of the scaffold.

'Just seen Vereker – not a note wrong. Pressed me to bosom – keeps me a month.' So much I read on her paper while the cabby dropped a grin from his perch. In my excitement I paid him profusely and in hers she suffered it; then as he drove away we started to walk about and talk. We had talked, heaven knows, enough before, but this was a wondrous lift. We pictured the whole scene at Rapallo, where he would have written, mentioning my name, for permission to call; that is *I* pictured it, having more material than my companion, whom I felt hang on my lips as we stopped on purpose before shop-windows we didn't look into. About one thing we were clear: if he was staying on for fuller communication we should at least have a letter from him that would help us through the dregs of delay. We understood his staying on, and yet each of us saw, I think, that the other hated it. The letter we were clear about arrived; it was for Gwendolen, and I called on her in time to save her the trouble of bringing it to me. She didn't read it out, as was natural enough; but she repeated to me what it chiefly embodied. This consisted of the remarkable statement that he'd tell her after they were married exactly what she wanted to know.

'Only *then*, when I'm his wife – not before,' she explained. 'It's tantamount to saying – isn't it? – that I must marry him straight off!' She smiled at me while I flushed with disappointment, a vision of fresh delay that made me at first unconscious of my surprise. It seemed more than a hint that on me as well he would impose some tiresome condition. Suddenly, while she reported several more things from his letter, I remembered what he had told me before going away. He had found Mr Vereker deliriously interesting and his own possession of the secret a real intoxication. The buried treasure was all gold and gems. Now that it was there it seemed to grow and grow before him; it would have been, through all time and taking all tongues, one of the most wonderful flowers of literary art. Nothing, in especial, once you were face to face with it, could show for more consummately *done*. When once it came out it came out, was there with a splendour that made you ashamed; and there hadn't been, save in the bottomless vulgarity of the age, with every one tasteless and tainted, every sense stopped, the smallest reason why it should have been overlooked. It was great, yet so simple, was simple, yet so great, and the final knowledge of it was an experience quite apart. He intimated that the charm of such an experience, the desire to drain it, in its freshness, to the last drop, was what kept him there close to the source. Gwendolen, frankly radiant as she tossed me these fragments, showed the elation of a prospect more assured than my own. That brought me back to the question of her marriage, prompted me to ask if what she meant by what she had just surprised me with was that she was under an engagement.

'Of course I am!' she answered. 'Didn't you know it?' She seemed astonished, but I was still more so, for Corvick had told me the exact contrary. I didn't mention this, however; I only reminded her how little I had been on that score in her confidence, or even in Corvick's and that moreover I wasn't in ignorance of her mother's interdict. At bottom I was troubled by the disparity of the two accounts; but after a little I felt Corvick's to be the one I least doubted. This simply reduced me to asking myself if the girl had on the spot improvised an engagement – vamped up an old one or dashed off a new – in order to arrive at the satisfaction she desired. She must have had resources of which I was destitute, but she made her case slightly more intelligible by returning presently: 'What the state of things has been is that we felt of course bound to do nothing in mamma's lifetime.'

'But now you think you'll just dispense with mamma's consent?'

'Ah it mayn't come to that!' I wondered what it might come to, and she went on: 'Poor dear, she may swallow the dose. In fact, you know,' she added with a laugh, 'she really *must*!' – a proposition of which, on behalf of every one concerned, I fully acknowledged the force.

VIII

Nothing more vexatious had ever happened to me than to become aware before Corvick's arrival in England that I shouldn't be there to put him through. I found myself abruptly called to Germany by the alarming illness of my younger brother, who, against my advice, had gone to Munich to study, at the feet indeed of a great master, the art of portraiture in oils. The near relative who made him an allowance had threatened to withdraw it if he should, under specious pretexts, turn for superior truth to Paris – Paris being somehow, for a Cheltenham aunt, the school of evil, the abyss. I deplored this prejudice at the time, and the deep injury of it was now visible – first in the fact that it hadn't saved the poor boy, who was clever, frail and foolish, from congestion of the lungs, and second in the greater break with London to which the event condemned me. I'm afraid that what was uppermost in my mind during several anxious weeks was the sense that if we had only been in Paris I might have run over to see Corvick. This was actually out of the question from every point of view: my brother, whose recovery gave us both plenty to do, was ill for three months, during which I never left him and at the end of which we had to face the absolute prohibition of a return to England. The consideration of climate imposed itself, and he was in no state to meet it alone. I took him to Meran and there spent the summer with him, trying to show him by example how to get back to work and nursing a rage of another sort that I tried *not* to show him.

The whole business proved the first of a series of phenomena so strangely interlaced that, taken all together – which was how I had to take them – they form as good an illustration as I can recall of the manner in which, for the good of his soul doubtless, fate sometimes deals with a man's avidity. These incidents certainly had larger bearings than the comparatively meagre consequence we are here concerned with – though I feel that consequence also a thing to speak of with some respect. It's mainly in such a light, I confess, at any rate, that the ugly fruit of my exile is at this hour present to me. Even at first indeed the spirit in which my avidity, as I have called it, made me regard that term owed no element of case to the fact that before coming back from Rapallo George Corvick addressed me in a way I objected to. His letter had none of the sedative action I must today profess myself sure he had wished to give it, and the march of occurrences was not so ordered as to make up for what it lacked. He had begun on the spot, for one of the quarterlies, a great last word on Vereker's writings, and this exhaustive study, the only one that would have counted, have existed, was to turn on the new light, to utter – oh so quietly! – the unimagined truth. It was in other words to trace the figure in the carpet through every convolution, to reproduce it in every tint. The result, according to my friend, would be the greatest literary portrait ever painted, and what he asked of me was just to be so good as not to trouble him with questions till he should hang up his masterpiece before me. He did me the honour to declare that, putting aside the great sitter himself, all aloft in his indifference, I was individually the connoisseur he was most working for. I was therefore to be a good boy and not try to peep under the curtain before the show was ready: I should enjoy it all the more if I sat very still.

I did my best to sit very still, but I couldn't help giving a jump on seeing in *The Times,* after I had been a week or two in Munich and before, as I knew, Corvick had reached London, the announcement of the sudden death of poor Mrs Erme. I instantly, by letter, appealed to Gwendolen for particulars, and she wrote me that her mother had yielded to long-threatened failure of the heart. She didn't say, but I took the liberty of reading into her words, that from the point of view of her marriage and also of her eagerness, which was quite a match for mine, this was a solution more prompt than could have been expected and more radical than waiting for the old lady to swallow the dose. I candidly admit indeed that at the time – for I heard from her repeatedly – I read some singular things into Gwendolen's words and some still more extraordinary ones into her silences. Pen in hand, this way, I live the time over, and it brings back the oddest sense of my having been, both for months and in spite of myself, a kind of coerced spectator. All my life had taken refuge in my eyes, which the procession of events appeared to have committed itself to keep astare. There were days when I thought of writing to Hugh Vereker and simply throwing myself on his charity. But I felt more deeply that I hadn't fallen quite so low – besides which, quite properly, he would send me about my business. Mrs Erme's death brought Corvick straight home, and within the month he was united 'very quietly' – as quietly, I seemed to make out, as he meant in his article to bring out his *trouvaille* – to the young lady he had loved and quitted. I use this last term, I may parenthetically say, because I subsequently grew sure that at the time he went to India, at the time of his great news from Bombay, there had been no positive pledge between them whatever. There had been none at the moment she was affirming to me the very opposite. On the other hand he had certainly become engaged the day he returned. The happy pair went down to Torquay for their honeymoon, and there, in a reckless hour, it occurred to poor Corvick to take his young bride for a drive. He had no command of that business: this had been brought home to me of old in a little tour we had once made together in a dog-cart. In a dog-cart he perched his companion for a rattle over Devonshire hills, on one of the likeliest of which he brought his horse, who, it was true, had bolted, down with such violence that the occupants of the cart were hurled forward and that he fell horribly on his head. He was killed on the spot; Gwendolen escaped unhurt.

I pass rapidly over the question of this unmitigated tragedy, of what the loss of my best friend meant for me, and I complete my little history of my patience and my pain by the frank statement of my having, in a postscript to my very first letter to her after the receipt of the hideous news, asked Mrs Corvick whether her husband mightn't at least have finished the great article on Vereker. Her answer was as prompt as my question: the article, which had been barely begun, was a mere heartbreaking scrap. She explained that our friend, abroad, had just settled down to it when interrupted by her mother's death, and that then, on his return, he had been kept from work by the engrossments into which that calamity was to plunge them. The opening pages were all that existed; they were striking, they were promising, but they didn't unveil the idol. That great intellectual feat was obviously to have formed his climax. She said nothing more, nothing to enlighten me as to the state of her own knowledge – the knowledge for the acquisition of which I had fancied her prodigiously acting. This was above all what I wanted to know: had *she* seen the idol unveiled? Had there been a private ceremony for a palpitating audience of one? For what else but that ceremony had the nuptials taken place? I didn't like as yet to press her, though when I thought of what had passed between us on the subject in Corvick's absence her reticence surprised me. It was therefore not till much later, from Meran, that I risked another appeal, risked it in some trepidation, for she continued to tell me nothing. 'Did you hear in those few days of your blighted bliss,' I wrote, 'what we desired so to hear?' I said 'we' as a little hint; and she showed me she could take a little hint. 'I heard everything,' she replied, 'and I mean to keep it to myself!'

IX

It was impossible not to be moved with the strongest sympathy for her, and on my return to England I showed her every kindness in my power. Her mother's death had made her means sufficient, and she had gone to live in a more convenient quarter. But her loss had been great and her visitation cruel; it never would have occurred to me moreover to suppose she could come to feel the possession of a technical tip, of a piece of literary experience, a counterpoise to her grief. Strange to say, none the less, I couldn't help believing after I had seen her a few times that I caught a glimpse of some such oddity. I hasten to add that there had been other things I couldn't help believing, or at least imagining; and as I never felt I was really clear about these, so, as to the point I here touch on, I give her memory the benefit of the doubt. Stricken and solitary, highly accomplished and now, in her deep mourning, her maturer grace and her uncomplaining sorrow, incontestably handsome, she presented herself as leading a life of singular dignity and beauty. I had at first found a way to persuade myself that I should soon get the better of the reserve formulated, the week after the catastrophe, in her reply to an appeal as to which I was not unconscious that it might strike her as mistimed. Certainly that reserve was something of a shock to me – certainly it puzzled me the more I thought of it and even though I tried to explain it (with moments of success) by an imputation of exalted sentiments, of superstitious scruples, of a refinement of loyalty. Certainly it added at the same time hugely to the price of Vereker's secret, precious as this mystery already appeared. I may as well confess abjectly that Mrs Corvick's unexpected attitude was the final tap on the nail that was to fix fast my luckless idea, convert it into the obsession of which I'm for ever conscious.

But this only helped me the more to be artful, to be adroit, to allow time to elapse before renewing my suit. There were plenty of speculations for the interval, and one of them was deeply absorbing. Corvick had kept his information from his young friend till after the removal of the last barrier to their intimacy – then only had he let the cat out of the bag. Was it Gwendolen's idea, taking a hint from him, to liberate this animal only on the basis of the renewal of such a relation? Was the figure in the carpet traceable or describable only for husbands and wives – for lovers supremely united? It came back to me in a mystifying manner that in Kensington Square, when I mentioned that Corvick would have told the girl he loved, some word had dropped from Vereker that gave colour to this possibility. There might be little in it, but there was enough to make me wonder if I should have to marry Mrs Corvick to get what I wanted. Was I prepared to offer her this price for the blessing of her knowledge? Ah that way madness lay! – so I at least said to myself in bewildered hours. I could see meanwhile the torch she refused to pass on flame away in her chamber of memory – pour through her eyes a light that shone in her lonely house. At the end of six months I was fully sure of what this warm presence made up to her for. We had talked again and again of the man who had brought us together – of his talent, his character, his personal charm, his certain career, his dreadful doom, and even of his clear purpose in that great study which was to have been a supreme literary portrait, a kind of critical Vandyke or Velasquez. She had conveyed to me in abundance that she was tongue-tied by her perversity, by her piety, that she would never break the silence it had not been given to the 'right person', as she said, to break. The hour however finally arrived. One evening when I had been sitting with her longer than usual I laid my hand firmly on her arm. 'Now at last what *is* it?'

She had been expecting me and was ready. She gave a long slow sound-less headshake, merciful only in being inarticulate. This mercy didn't prevent its hurling at me the largest finest coldest 'Never!' I had yet, in the course of a life that had known denials, had to take full in the face. I took it and was aware that with the hard blow the tears had come into my eyes. So for a while we sat and looked at each other; after which I slowly rose. I was wondering if some day she would accept me; but this was not what I brought out. I said as I smoothed down my hat: 'I know what to think then. It's nothing!'

A remote disdainful pity for me gathered in her dim smile; then she spoke in a voice that I hear at this hour. 'It's my *life*!' As I stood at the door she added: 'You've insulted him!'

'Do you mean Vereker?'

'I mean the Dead!'

I recognized when I reached the street the justice of her charge. Yes, it was her life – I recognized that too; but her life none the less made room with the lapse of time for another interest. A year and a half after Corvick's death she published in a single volume her second novel, *Over-mastered*, which I pounced on in the hope of finding in it some tell-tale echo or some peeping face. All I found was a much better book than her younger performance, showing I thought the better company she had kept. As a tissue tolerably intricate it was a carpet with a figure of its own; but the figure was not the figure I was looking for. On sending a review of it to *The Middle* I was surprised to learn from the office that a notice was already in type. When the paper came out I had no hesitation in attributing this article, which I thought rather vulgarly overdone, to Drayton Deane, who in the old days had been something of a friend of Corvick's, yet had only within a few weeks made the acquaintance of his widow. I had had an early copy of the book, but Deane had evidently had an earlier. He lacked all the same the light hand with which Corvick had gilded the gingerbread – he laid on the tinsel in splotches.

X

Six months later appeared *The Right of Way*, the last chance, though we didn't know it, that we were to have to redeem ourselves. Written wholly during Vereker's sojourn abroad, the book had been heralded, in a hundred paragraphs, by the usual ineptitudes. I carried it, as early a copy as any, I this time flattered myself, straightway to Mrs Corvick. This was the only use I had for it; I left the inevitable tribute of *The Middle* to some more ingenious mind and some less irritated temper. 'But I already have it,' Gwendolen said. 'Drayton Deane was so good as to bring it to me yesterday, and I've just finished it.'

'Yesterday? How did he get it so soon?'

'He gets everything so soon! He's to review it in *The Middle*.'

'He – Drayton Deane – review Vereker?' I couldn't believe my ears.

'Why not? One fine ignorance is as good as another.'

I winced but I presently said: 'You ought to review him yourself!'

'I don't "review",' she laughed. 'I'm reviewed!'

Just then the door was thrown open. 'Ah yes, here's your reviewer!' Drayton Deane was there with his long legs and his tall forehead: he had come to see what she thought of *The Right of Way*, and to bring news that was singularly relevant. The evening papers were just out with a telegram on the author of that work, who, in Rome, had been ill for some days with an attack of malarial fever. It had at first not been thought grave, but had taken, in consequence of complications, a turn that might give rise to anxiety. Anxiety had indeed at the latest hour begun to be felt.

I was struck in the presence of these tidings with the fundamental detachment that Mrs Corvick's overt concern quite failed to hide: it gave me the measure of her consummate independence. That independence rested on her knowledge, the knowledge which nothing now could destroy and which nothing could make different. The figure in the carpet might take on another twist or two, but the sentence had virtually been written. The writer might go down to his grave: she was the person in the world to whom – as if she had been his favoured heir – his continued existence was least of a need. This reminded me how I had observed at a particular moment – after Corvick's death – the drop of her desire to see him face to face. She had got what she wanted without that. I had been sure that if she hadn't got it she wouldn't have been restrained from the endeavour to sound him personally by those superior reflections, more conceivable on a man's part than on a woman's, which in my case had served as a deterrent. It wasn't however, I hasten to add, that my case, in spite of this invidious comparison, wasn't ambiguous enough. At the thought that Vereker was perhaps at that moment dying there rolled over me a wave of anguish – a poignant sense of how inconsistently I still depended on him. A delicacy that it was my one compensation to suffer to rule me had left the Alps and the Apennines between us, but the sense of the waning occasion suggested that I might in my despair at last have gone to him. Of course I should really have done nothing of the sort. I remained five minutes, while my companions talked of the new book, and when Drayton Deane appealed to me for my opinion of it I made answer, getting up, that I detested Hugh Vereker and simply couldn't read him. I departed with the moral certainty that as the door closed behind me Deane would brand me for awfully superficial. His hostess wouldn't contradict *that* at least.

I continue to trace with a briefer touch our intensely odd successions. Three weeks after this came Vereker's death, and before the year was out the death of his wife. That poor lady I had never seen, but I had had a futile theory that, should she survive him long enough to be decorously accessible, I might approach her with the feeble flicker of my plea. Did she know and if she knew would she speak? It was much to be presumed that for more reasons than one she would have nothing to say; but when she passed out of all reach I felt renunciation indeed my appointed lot. I was shut up in my obsession for ever – my gaolers had gone off with the key. I find myself quite as vague as a captive in a dungeon about the time that further elapsed before Mrs Corvick became the wife of Drayton Deane. I had foreseen, through my bars, this end of the business, though there was no indecent haste and our friendship had rather fallen off. They were both so 'awfully intellectual' that it struck people as a suitable match, but I had measured better than any one the wealth of understanding the bride would contribute to the union. Never, for a marriage in literary circles – so the newspapers described the alliance – had a lady been so bravely dowered. I began with due promptness to look for the fruit of the affair – that fruit, I mean, of which the premonitory symptoms would be peculiarly visible in the husband. Taking for granted the splendour of the other party's nuptial gift, I expected to see him make a show commensurate with his increase of means. I knew what his means had been – his article on *The Right of Way* had distinctly given one the figure. As he was now exactly in the position in which still more exactly I was not I watched from month to month, in the likely periodicals, for the heavy message poor Corvick had been unable to deliver and the responsibility of which would have fallen on his successor. The widow and wife would have broken by the rekindled hearth the silence that only a widow and wife might break, and Deane would be as aflame with the knowledge as Corvick in his own hour, as Gwendolen in hers, had been. Well, he was aflame doubtless, but the fire was apparently not to become a public blaze. I scanned the periodicals in vain: Drayton Deane filled them with exuberant pages, but he withheld the page I most feverishly sought. He wrote on a thousand subjects, but never on the subject of Vereker. His special line was to tell truths that other people either 'funked,' as he said, or overlooked, but he never told the only truth that seemed to me in these days to signify. I met the couple in those literary circles referred to in the papers: I have sufficiently intimated that it was only in such circles we were all constructed to revolve. Gwendolen was more than ever committed to them by the publication of her third novel, and I myself definitely classed by holding the opinion that this work was inferior to its immediate predecessor. Was it worse because she had been keeping worse company? If her secret was, as she had told me, her life – a fact discernible in her increasing bloom, an air of conscious privilege that, cleverly corrected by pretty charities, gave distinction to her appearance – it had yet not a direct influence on her work. That only made one – everything only made one – yearn the more for it; only rounded it off with a mystery finer and subtler.

XI

It was therefore from her husband I could never remove my eyes: I beset him in a manner that might have made him uneasy. I went even so far as to engage him in conversation. *Didn't* he know, hadn't he come into it as a matter of course? – that question hummed in my brain. Of course he knew; otherwise he wouldn't return my stare so queerly. His wife had told him what I wanted and he was amiably amused at my impotence. He didn't laugh – he wasn't a laugher: his system was to present to my irritation, so that I should crudely expose myself, a conversational blank as vast as his big bare brow. It always happened that I turned away with a settled conviction from these unpeopled expanses, which seemed to complete each other geographically and to symbolize together Drayton Deane's want of voice, want of form. He simply hadn't the art to use what he knew, he literally was incompetent to take up the duty where Corvick had left it. I went still further – it was the only glimpse of happiness I had. I made up my mind that the duty didn't appeal to him. He wasn't interested, he didn't care. Yes, it quite comforted me to believe him too stupid to have joy of the thing I lacked. He was as stupid after as he had been before, and that deepened for me the golden glory in which the mystery was wrapped. I had of course none the less to recollect that his wife might have imposed her conditions and exactions. I had above all to remind myself that with Vereker's death the major incentive dropped. He was still there to be honoured by what might be done – he was no longer there to give it his sanction. Who alas but he had the authority?

Two children were born to the pair, but the second cost the mother her life. After this stroke I seemed to see another ghost of a chance. I jumped at it in thought, but I waited a certain time for manners, and at last my opportunity arrived in a remunerative way. His wife had been dead a year when I met Drayton Deane in the smoking-room of a small club of which we both were members, but where for months – perhaps because I rarely entered it – I hadn't seen him. The room was empty and the occasion propitious. I deliberately offered him, to have done with the matter for ever, that advantage for which I felt he had long been looking.

'As an older acquaintance of your late wife's than even you were,' I began, 'you must let me say to you something I have on my mind. I shall be glad to make any terms with you that you see fit to name for the information she must have had from George Corvick – the information, you know, that had come to *him*, poor chap, in one of the happiest hours of his life, straight from Hugh Vereker.'

He looked at me like a dim phrenological bust. 'The information – ?'

'Vereker's secret, my dear man – the general intention of his books: the string the pearls were strung on, the buried treasure, the figure in the carpet.'

He began to flush – the numbers on his bumps to come out. 'Vereker's books had a general intention?'

I started in my turn. 'You don't mean to say you don't know it?' I thought for a moment he was playing with me. 'Mrs Deane knew it; she had it, as I say, straight from Corvick, who had, after infinite search and to Vereker's own delight, found the very mouth of the cave. Where *is* the mouth? He told after their marriage – and told alone – the person who, when the circumstances were reproduced, must have told *you*. Have I been wrong in taking for granted that she admitted you, as one of the highest privileges of the relation in which you stood to her, to the knowledge of which she was after Corvick's death the sole depositary? All *I* know is that that knowledge is infinitely precious, and what I want you to understand is that if you'll in your turn admit me to it you'll do me a kindness for which I shall he lastingly grateful.'

He had turned at last very red; I dare say he had begun by thinking I had lost my wits. Little by little he followed me; on my own side I stared with a livelier surprise. Then he spoke. 'I don't know what you're talking about.'

He wasn't acting – it was the absurd truth. 'She *didn't* tell you – ?'

'Nothing about Hugh Vereker.'

I was stupefied; the room went round. It had been too good even for that! 'Upon your honour?'

'Upon my honour. What the devil's the matter with you?' he growled.

'I'm astounded – I'm disappointed. I wanted to get it out of you.'

'It isn't *in* me!' he awkwardly laughed. 'And even if it were – '

'If it were you'd let me have it – oh yes, in common humanity. But I believe you. I see – I see!' I went on, conscious, with the full turn of the wheel, of my great delusion, my false view of the poor man's attitude. What I saw, though I couldn't say it, was that his wife hadn't thought him worth enlightening. This struck me as strange for a woman who had thought him worth marrying. At last I explained it by the reflection that she couldn't possibly have married him for his understanding. She had married him for something else.

He was to some extent enlightened now, but he was even more astonished, more disconcerted: he took a moment to compare my story with his quickened memories. The result of his meditation was his presently saying with a good deal of rather feeble form: 'This is the first I hear of what you allude to. I think you must be mistaken as to Mrs Drayton Deane's having had any unmentioned, and still less any unmentionable, knowledge of Hugh Vereker. She'd certainly have wished it – should it have borne on his literary character – to be used.'

'It *was* used. She used it herself. She told me with her own lips that she "lived" on it.'

I had no sooner spoken than I repented of my words; he grew so pale that I felt as if I had struck him. 'Ah "lived" – !' he murmured, turning short away from me.

My compunction was real; I laid my hand on his shoulder. 'I beg you to forgive me – I've made a mistake. You *don't* know what I thought you knew. You could, if I had been right, have rendered me a service; and I had my reasons for assuming that you'd be in a position to meet me.'

'Your reasons?' he echoed. 'What were your reasons?'

I looked at him well; I hesitated; I considered. 'Come and sit down with me here and I'll tell you.' I drew him to a sofa, I lighted another cigar and, beginning with the anecdote of Vereker's one descent from the clouds, I recited to him the extraordinary chain of accidents that had, in spite of the original gleam, kept me till that hour in the dark. I told him in a word just what I've written out here. He listened with deepening attention, and I became aware, to my surprise, by his ejaculations, by his questions, that he would have been after all not unworthy to be trusted by his wife. So abrupt an experience of her want of trust had now a disturbing effect on him; but I saw the immediate shock throb away little by little and then gather again into waves of wonder and curiosity – waves that promised, I could perfectly judge, to break in the end with the fury of my own highest tides. I may say that today as victims of unappeased desire there isn't a pin to choose between us. The poor man's state is almost my consolation, there are really moments when I feel it to be quite my revenge.

GEORGE EGERTON

A Nocturne

I have rather nice diggings. I got them last year, just after you went on that Egyptian racket. They are on the Embankment, within sight of Cleopatra's Needle. I like that anachronism of a monument; it has a certain fascination for me. I can see it at night, if I lean out of my window, outlined above the light-flecked river sacred to our sewer goddess that runs so sullenly under its canopy of foggy blue.

To me the Embankment has beauties unsurpassed in any city in Europe. I never tire of it at night. The opaque blotches of the plane-trees' foliage, the glistening water, the dotted lines of golden light, the great blocks of buildings rearing to the clouds like shadow monuments, the benches laden with human flotsam and jetsam.

I was leaning out of my window one night in November, in a lull in the rainfall; Big Ben had just boomed out one, when I noticed a woman rise from a seat below. She had been sitting there an hour, for I had seen the light shine on her hair, yellow hair like a child's, when I went down to the pillar-box at midnight.

Her carriage was that of a gentlewoman. Curious how gait tells. She walked a little way, stumbled, stood with her hand pressed to her heart, – a drunken woman would have lurched again. Then she went to the parapet, and leant against it, staring into the water.

A good many women I have known could not gaze steadily into running water, or look down from a height without feeling more than an impulse to throw themselves over – something impelled them to it, so they have assured me. I don't know the reason for it any more than I know why a man always buttons from left to right; a woman from right to left. It's a fact, though. The button-holes on a woman's garments are always made on the right side, never on the left; and it is just as awkward for her to button our way, as for us to try hers. – Hang it, man, I know it's so. I got a poor woman to make me some pyjamas, and she put the darned buttonholes wrong side. I had to get the beastly things changed. – Well, to come back to the story, I didn't like the way that lady looked into the river; it had rained all day, the streets glistened with water, and a northeast wind scooped round the corners. I went down to have a look at her. Just as I crossed over she dropped her head in an odd sort of way, took a step out, then fell back against the wall. The measured beat of a policeman's step struck the pavement a little farther down. I steadied her, and asked:

'Are you ill, madam; can I help you?'

She lifted the strangest face I ever saw to mine. It was like some curious mask – more than a flesh and blood phiz. Her eyes were beautifully set and burned sombrely; they looked as live eyes might through the sockets of a mask. Her yellow hair seemed like a wig against her forehead and temples. She started and shrank as I touched her; her teeth chattered.

'Yes, I *am* ill; I feel faint, strangely faint . . .'

She evidently suffered from some heart trouble. There was a bluish tinge around her mouth. She rocked on her feet, her lids drooped. I put my arm through hers; the steps came nearer; she roused and moaned mutteringly: 'Yes, I'm only resting; I'll move on in a few minutes.'

'Come with me,' I said; 'you can't stay here; try and walk.'

She came all right, in a dazed sort of way, though. All the under floors of the building in which I have my rooms are offices, so we met no one. She panted a bit as she mounted the stairs. I kept close behind, in case of a fall. Her boots must have been broken, for she left little wet splotches on each step. I showed her into the room. The electric light roused her; she hesitated and coloured up, – it was the most curious thing I ever saw, the way her face thawed and quickened. She turned round, and looked straight at me; I braced myself to meet her eyes, miserable, honest eyes they were too, that probed me like steel; she would have detected the least sign of bad faith, like a shot.

I pushed an arm-chair nearer the fire; she sat down, leant back her head against the cushion, and before she could say whatever she intended to, fainted dead away. Faith, it gave me an uncomfortable sensation. I forced some brandy between her teeth and tried to pull her round. I like doing things for women, – any kind of woman almost, – they all interest me tremendously. I don't think I do them. Women seem at fault some way in their choice of men, they so often give themselves to brutes or sneaks – it may be these types don't scruple to seize the opportune moment with them.

I took off her hat, a quiet little black felt affair, positively soaked with rain. She had lovely hair, glossy yellow, not 'brown at the roots' kind, you know; it had a crinkle in it, and the line down the middle of her head was white as an almond. I hate the type of blonde that has a pink skin to her scalp. I concluded she couldn't have been long in the streets, for the bit of white at her neck and the handkerchief in her lap were clean, – a day's soil at most. She wore woollen gloves; I pulled them off; she opened her eyes, closed them again. She wore an old-fashioned thin wedding-ring on her right hand, perhaps her mother's; she had pretty, long hands; but hands don't attract me like feet or ears. I belong to the race of men to whom temptation comes in the guise of little feet. An instep or ankle appeals irresistibly to my senses; I acknowledge it frankly; it's damned odd, but I can't help it – the appeal, I mean. My friend Foote says, delicately perfumed *lingerie* is his weak spot; his fall is sure at a flutter of lace and ribbon. To be virtuous, he would have to live in a land where the drying of women's frillikins on a clothes-line would be prohibited by law. Her feet were not pretty, although her boots were decently cut. What an odd face she had; I can see it in white relief on the red of the leather. A bit like Christine Nilsson about the forehead, big clever nose, tremendous jaw, – a devil or a saint, or I'm no judge. She opened her eyes at last. I held out the glass; she shuddered, pushed it away almost roughly, and said:

'No, please not that, I am afraid of it; I daren't touch it, it would be so easy to get to want it – when one is miserable.'

'Quite right; suppose you have some tea instead.'

She flushed and smiled; the saint was certainly uppermost just then.

'You are *very* good; yes, I should like some.'

I am rather a dab at making tea. Lloyd gets me the best in the market; never get good tea in a woman's house, – afraid of the price or something.

'You had better take off that wet jacket.'

Odd woman that; she stood up at once – she was still shaking – and took it off, hanging it over an oak stool. She was a well set up woman, of the thorough-bred flat, spare English type; getting on for the age the lady novelists find interesting, – thirty, perhaps. They may say what they like though, there is nothing like milk-fresh youth. By the Lord Harry, it's a beauty in itself! The plainest fresh-skinned wench with the dew of life in her eyes is worth ten of any beauty of thirty-five. Her dress was literally soaked, it hung heavily about her ankles; there were two wet patches too, where her feet had rested. I dug the poker into the fire, and said, without looking round:

'You'll be laid up to-morrow if you keep that skirt on; go into the other room and take it off; don't mind me, I've seen petticoats before now. Hang it to dry before the fire and put your boots in the fender. You'll see a collection of Eastern footwear – it's rather a fad of mine – on the wall, find a pair to fit and slip them on . . .'

Didn't see her face, busy with the kettle. A moment's silence, then I heard the door shut softly. Admirable woman that! when I come to think of it, the only woman I ever met who could do a thing without arguing about it; never wanted a reason, never gave any. It's curious, the inclination women have to gab about everything; they spoil a caress by asking you if you liked it. The weather had not improved; I felt quite glad I had kept on my diggings. The adventure was one after my own heart. I would honour my unknown lady with my best china. I took down an old Worcester cup and saucer, tipped the sugar into my prettiest lacquer bowl, put out some sandwiches and biscuits, and was surveying my arrangements when the door behind me opened. By Jove, how rarely that woman changed when she smiled! it reminded me of the first spray of almond bloom one sees in spring in some dingy, sordid London street. It youthened her, melted the stark, hungry grip about her mouth. I suppose the petticoat was too short or something – women are so devilishly illogical. I have seen half-way down a woman's back and bosom, and she didn't mind in the least; yet she'd have fainted at the idea of showing the calf of her decently stockinged leg.

She had taken down an old Jap kimono, once a gorgeous affair, but time had faded the flowery broidery on the plum-blue ground to mellow half-tones.

Her embarrassment was pretty to see; what a fetching thing a woman is when she is perfectly natural. I pointed to the chair, and uncovered the teapot.

She sat down and poured out the tea rather awkwardly, I don't fancy it lay much in her line. She drank it eagerly, but paled a bit when I offered her a sandwich. I know that sensation, I had it during the last days of the Siege of Paris; ask me to tell you about that some other time – the poor thing was faint with hunger, the very sight of food made her feel sick, she put her handkerchief to her mouth; I took the sandwiches away and got out some dry biscuits.

'Have some more tea?' I said, 'and try these dry biscuits by and by, when you feel better.

She leant back; she had the prettiest line of throat I ever saw, quite white and soft, under that jaw, too. I poured out some more tea for her.

'You have been fasting too long; when did you eat last? . . .'

'Not since yesterday morning!'

Good God! She forgot that the hour made it over two days.

She put the tea down and said simply: 'May I ask you for a cigarette? I think I should feel better if I were to smoke one or two. I don't feel as if I could eat just now.'

'Of course,' I said; 'how jolly that you smoke! You must have some of my special baccy.' She was smoking tranquilly when a gust of wind howled and shook the window-sash viciously, and the rain rattled like gravel thrown against the panes. She started and looked at the clock, the hands pointed to 1.45; the colour rushed to her face; I took the bull by the horns.

'My dear lady, don't bother about the hour, time is an entirely artificial arrangement. You can't go out in that rain, it's not to be thought of. You wouldn't be out on that seat, if you had any shelter to go to. I don't want to know anything you don't volunteer to tell me. You do me proud in accepting my hospitality, such as it is; indeed you do, it's a charity; I hate going to bed. When you have had a good rest you'll think of some way out of the snarl, whatever it is. Good baccy, ain't it?'

She held out her hand and gave mine an honest grip, as a nice lad might have done. Those big, grey eyes of hers got black when the tears filled them.

She was a vexatious sort of contradictory person; there was a tantalizing lack of finality about her – just as you had made up your mind that she was really deuced ugly, she flushed and bloomed and sparkled into down-right charm, and before you had time to drink it in she was plain again. Her voice too was twin to her face. It was deep, and at times harsh with sudden soft rushing inflections and tender lilts in it.

'You have Irish blood in you?' I ventured.

'Yes, on the distaff side; how did you know?'

'Oh, voice, and I suppose it's the kin feeling of race.'

We talked of a good many things during the next hour. I noticed that her eyes wandered wistfully to my books. I rather pride myself on some of my specimens of rare binding – two little shelves represent a good many years' income.

'Do you like books?' I asked. She caught what I meant at once, and her face lit up. I gave her my only heirloom, an, from me at least, unpurchas-able, Aldine classic. She positively handled it lovingly. The more I think of that woman, the more I am persuaded of her rarity; one is almost afraid to give one of one's book pets into most women's hands. She knew it at once – didn't say anything banal or gushing, only, 'I love the peculiar olive colour of the leather.'

'Have you ever seen any of Le Gaston's work? Look how well the lines of gold dot-work tell upon the scarlet of the morocco. How it has kept its colour. Machinery and cloth have played the deuce with the art of it.'

'If I were a rich woman I'd have any book I cared to keep especially bound for myself.'

Funny situation! Well, I suppose it was, rather. But if you come to think of it, the rummiest situations and most unlikely incidents in life are just those that don't get treated in fiction. Most poor devils have to write with one eye fixed on the mental limitations of their publisher or the index expurgatorius of the booksellers; that is, if they want to pay income tax.

She dropped off to sleep with a book in her lap. I covered her knees with a rug, turned out the light; the glow of the fire surrounded her with a magic circle. I went and lay down; I can sleep or wake at will. I decided to sleep till five. She had never stirred. I made up the fire; it was jolly to think of her there in the warmth instead of being out in that awful night, perhaps bobbing under a barge or knocking against the arches in the swirl of that filthy water.

I went back and slept till seven, tubbed, and took a peep at her. Her face looked good as a child's in her sleep, but a child that had suffered under bad treatment and grown prematurely old. It was dreadfully haggard; that woman had been slowly starving to death.

It was one of those beastly mornings, fine under protest, with a sun that looked as if he had been making a night of it. I hate the mornings, except out in wild nature; someway in civilization they are always a sort of ill-natured comment on the night before. Like some excellent women, there is a brutal lack of semitone about them. I slipped the bolt on the door; Bates never came up unless I rang for him, but sometimes fellows drop in for a pick-me-up or a devil, – by the way, a red herring done in whisky isn't half bad.

She woke in a fright with a fearsome sort of half cry. I expect she thought she had been asleep on that seat. I knew the beastly morning would unsettle her, she was right as a trivet the night before. She flushed horribly when she realized where she was, and the time, and stammered: 'I'm so sorry, oh, I *am* so sorry! I was so tired, I really couldn't help myself. I haven't slept for many nights, you know, and one gets so stupid – '

'That's all right. I've been asleep, slept like a top; always do. Suppose you freshen up a bit in my dressing-room; your frock is dry. You will find hot water and things if you look about, – help yourself. I am going to lock you in if you don't mind: I want my man to fix things up a bit . . .'

She flushed again. I'll stake my oath that kind of blush hurts a woman.

My usual hour is eleven, but Bates cleared up and laid breakfast without an atom of expression in his face or voice. Odd man, Bates! He brought enough for two; makes a good living, that fellow, by an expedient regulation of the organs of sight and hearing. He finished at last, never knew him take so long; he asked :

'Shall you want me again, sir?'

'No, I'll shove the tray outside, I am going out later on, not in to anyone.'

'All right, sir.'

I knocked at the door as I unlocked it. She came out, self-possessed, straight and somewhat stiffly slim in her black frock. I bet she could ride.

'You look better already,' I cried; 'would you like tea better than coffee? No! come, then.'

She took her seat, outwardly unembarrassed, anyhow. I opened the papers and glanced at the headings. The *Globe* was lying on a chair; I don't know why I got it; she asked me might she see it. She glanced at the first page, and whatever she saw pleased her. I dawdled through my meal, for I did not know how to get any further with her. She was not the sort, you see, one could give a kiss and a quid and say, 'Now, run along Polly, and don't get into any more trouble than you can help.' However, she gave me a lead herself, for when we had finished she came over, put out her hand and – well what she said don't matter, anyway, it made me feel a bally idiot. I put her into the arm-chair without any ceremony and pushed over the cigarettes, saying:

'Can't talk unless I smoke. Now, my dear lady, granted you consider you owe me something, suppose you take it out in as much confidence as you care to give away. How did you come to be without a bed last night?'

'Simply enough; to explain, I must go back a bit. Some years ago a younger brother and I were left almost penniless. Neither of us had been brought up to do anything except to get rid of money in the most happy-go-lucky way. That makes it difficult to get a living when even the trained people are crowded out. We got it as best we could. I've played the piano at bean feasts, "devilled" at 6d. an hour, done whatever offered itself, don't you know,' she had a trick of ending her statement that way. 'We kept together, were saving to emigrate. Then he was ill for months; he died at Christmas. That broke me up, don't you know; I was very fond of him; and left me without a penny. I went as nurse companion to a Christian gentlewoman in Bath at £12 a year; pay for my own washing. I broke down under it in six months. Came to town ill, and went into the fever hospital three days after, stayed there six weeks; had to go to a convalescent home for a month. It was very cheap, but it took all I had left. I couldn't get anything to do. I tried for a place as a domestic; I didn't look it, so they said. Things have been going steadily from bad to worse, don't you know? I used to work at the British Museum. A fortnight ago my landlady gave me notice; she wasn't a bad sort, but she had the brokers in herself, and there was a sale. I had to leave; she let me take my box to her sister's for a few days. I sat in St James' Park the night before last, and sent a description of it to a paper – ' She hesitated. 'I have been trying journalism, paragraphs, and articles,' and with the most abject tone of apology, 'verse, rubbish, you know; but sometimes it gets taken. Only one has to wait such a time before one knows. I have had a turn-over in the *Globe*; it's a guinea, and there was another last night . . .'

(I had skimmed it, not half a bad one on 'Adder lore in the Fens' . . .) 'I'll get along all right now; it was rather bad last night; I was overtired or . . .'

I interrupted her.

'My dear woman, you can't go far on a guinea with arrears of rent, however small, to pay out of it.'

To cut it all short, I proposed to give her a note to an editress I know, a jolly, good little woman, who would stretch more than a point to serve me. I hinted as delicately as I could that she had better not let her feelings rush her ever, and give away the genesis of our acquaintance; sort of thing, you know, might be annotated badly. She gave me her word of honour that she would let me know the result, and see me next day if nothing came of the interview. She took my pasteboard. I got Bates out of the way with an empty Gladstone bag and a note to Paddy Foote, to take it in and say nothing. She put on her things whilst I wrote the note; I watched her put on her hat; she looked better without it.

'I am going to speak of you as "bearer",' I said. 'I won't ask your name now; I'd like to learn it just when you like – or leave it to chance – I've an idea you'd rather . . .'

She nodded gravely; we shook hands – she has lovely eyes, as I said before – and went, leaving one the poorer by herself.

I haven't a thing belonging to her except the ashes of her cigarette. I tipped it into my match-box; I suppose I am a damned fool; most Irishmen are, in one way or another.

It's curious how things have a knack of running twos; I had never met her before that night, and yet, that same evening, as I came out of the Charing Cross post-office, I felt a touch on my arm, turned round, and, by Jove, there she was. The little woman had fixed her up all right, and things were going to hum, so she said.

Sometimes, when the rain beats, and that beastly old river yawns like a grave, I stand up at the window and look down. I never felt a want in my old digs before. It was jolly to have a woman – a woman of that kind, you know – taking an interest in one's first editions.

ARTHUR MORRISON

Old Cater's Money

I

The firm of Dorrington & Hicks had not been constructed at the time when this case came to Dorrington's hand. Dorrington had barely emerged from the obscurity that veils his life before some ten years ago, and he was at this time a needier adventurer than he had been at the period of any other of the cases I have related. Indeed, his illicit gains on this occasion would seem first to have set him on his feet and enabled him first to cut a fair exterior figure. Whether or not he had developed to the full the scoundrelism that first brought me acquainted with his trade I do not know; but certain it is that he was involved at the time in transactions wretchedly ill paid, on behalf of one Flint, a ship-stores dealer at Deptford; an employer whose record was never a very clean one. This Flint was one of an unpleasant family. He was nephew to old Cater the wharfinger (and private usurer) and cousin to another Cater, whose name was Paul, and who was also a usurer, though he variously described himself as a 'commission agent' or 'general dealer'. Indeed, he was a general dealer, if the term may be held to include a dealer in whatever would bring him gain, and who made no great punctilio in regard to the honesty or otherwise of his transactions. In fact, all three of these pleasant relatives had records of the shadiest, and all three did whatever in the way of money-lending, mortgaging, and blood-sucking came in their way. It is, however, with old Cater – Jerry Cater, he was called – that this narrative is in the first place concerned. I got the story from a certain Mr Sinclair, who for many years acted as his clerk and debt-collector.

Old Jerry Cater lived in the crooked and decaying old house over his wharf by Bermondsey Wall, where his father had lived before him. It was a grim and strange old house, with long-shut loft-doors in upper floors, and hinged flaps in sundry rooms that, when lifted, gave startling glimpses of muddy water washing among rotten piles below. Not once in six months now did a barge land its load at Cater's Wharf, and no coasting brig ever lay alongside. For, in fact, the day of Cater's Wharf was long past; and it seemed indeed that few more days were left for old Jerry Cater himself. For seventy-eight years old Jerry Cater had led a life useless to himself and to everybody else, though his own belief was that he had profited considerably. Truly if one counted nothing but the money the old miser had accumulated, then his profit was large indeed; but it had brought nothing worth having, neither for himself nor for others, and he had no wife nor child who might use it more wisely when he should at last leave it behind him; no other relative indeed than his two nephews, each in spirit a fair copy of himself, though in body a quarter of a century younger. Seventy-eight years of every mean and sordid vice and of every virtue that had pecuniary gain for its sole object left Jerry Cater stranded at last in his cheap iron bedstead with its insufficient coverings, with not a sincere friend in the world to sit five minutes by his side. Down below, Sinclair, his unhappy clerk, had the accommodation of a wooden table and a chair; and the clerk's wife performed what meagre cooking and cleaning service old Cater would have. Sinclair was a man of forty-five, rusty, starved, honest, and very cheap. He was very cheap because it had been his foolishness, twenty years ago, when in City employ, to borrow forty pounds of old Cater to get married with, and to buy furniture, together with forty pounds he had of his own. Sinclair was young then, and knew nothing of the ways of the two hundred per cent. money-lender. When he had, by three or four years' pinching, paid about a hundred and fifty pounds on account of interest and fines, and only had another hundred or two still due to clear everything off, he fell sick and lost his place. The payment of interest ceased, and old Jerry Cater took his victim's body, soul, wife, sticks, and chairs together. Jerry Cater discharged his own clerk, and took Sinclair, with a saving of five shillings a week on the nominal salary, and out of the remainder he deducted, on account of the debt and ever-accumulating interest, enough to keep his man thin and broken-spirited, without absolutely incapacitating him from work, which would have been bad finance. But the rest of the debt, capital and interest, was made into a capital debt, with usury on the whole. So that for sixteen years or more Sinclair had been paying something every week off the eternally increasing sum, and might have kept on for sixteen centuries at the same rate without getting much nearer freedom. If only there had been one more room in the house old Cater might have compulsorily lodged his clerk, and have deducted something more for rent. As it was he might have used the office for the purpose, but he could never have brought himself to charge a small rent for it, and a large one would have swallowed most of the rest of Sinclair's salary, thus bringing him below starvation point, and impairing his working capacity. But Mrs Sinclair, now gaunt and scraggy, did all the housework, so that that came very cheap. Most of the house was filled with old bales and rotting merchandise which old Jerry Cater had seized in payment for wharfage dues and other debts, and had held to, because his ideas of selling prices were large, though his notion of buying prices were small. Sinclair was out of doors more than in, dunning and threatening debtors as hopeless as himself. And the household was completed by one Samuel Greer, a squinting man of grease and rags, within ten years of the age of old Jerry Cater himself. Greer was wharf-hand, messenger, and personal attendant on his employer, and, with less opportunity, was thought to be near as bad a scoundrel as Cater. He lived and slept in the house, and was popularly supposed to be paid nothing at all; though his patronage of the 'Ship and Anchor', hard by, was as frequent as might be.

Old Jerry Cater was plainly not long for this world. Ailing for months, he at length gave in and took to his bed. Greer watched him anxiously and greedily, for it was his design, when his master went at last, to get what he could for himself. More than once during his illness old Cater had sent Greer to fetch his nephews. Greer had departed on these errands, but never got farther than the next street. He hung about a reasonable time – perhaps in the 'Ship and Anchor', if funds permitted – and then returned to say that the nephews could not come just yet. Old Cater had quarrelled with his nephews, as he had with everybody else, some time before, and Greer was resolved, if he could, to prevent any meeting now, for that would mean that the nephews would take possession of the place, and he would lose his chance of convenient larceny when the end came. So it was that neither nephew knew of old Jerry Cater's shaky condition.

Before long, finding that the old miser could not leave his bed – indeed he could scarcely turn in it – Greer took courage, in Sinclair's absence, to poke about the place in search of concealed sovereigns. He had no great time for this, because Jerry Cater seemed to have taken a great desire for his company, whether for the sake of his attendance or to keep him out of mischief was not clear. At any rate Greer found no concealed sovereigns, nor anything better than might be sold for a few pence at the rag-shop. Until one day, when old Cater was taking alternate fits of restlessness and sleep, Greer ventured to take down a dusty old pickle-jar from the top shelf in the cupboard of his master's bedroom. Cater was dozing at the moment, and Greer, tilting the jar toward the light, saw within a few doubled papers, very dusty. He snatched the papers out, stuffed them into his pocket, replaced the jar, and closed the cupboard door hastily. The door made some little noise, and old Cater turned and woke, and presently he made a shift to sit up in bed, while Greer scratched his head as innocently as he could, and directed his divergent eyes to parts of the room as distant from the cupboard as possible.

'Sam'l Greer,' said old Cater in a feeble voice, while his lower jaw waggled and twitched, 'Sam'l Greer, I think I'll 'ave some beef-tea.' He groped tremulously under his pillow, turning his back to Greer, who tip-toed and glared variously over his master's shoulders. He saw nothing, however, though he heard the chink of money. Old Cater turned, with a shilling in his shaking hand. 'Git 'alf a pound o' shin o' beef,' he said, 'an' go to Green's for it at the other end o' Grange Road, d'ye hear? It's – it's a penny a pound cheaper there than it is anywhere nearer, and – and I ain't in so much of a 'urry for it, so the distance don't matter. Go 'long.' And old Jerry Cater subsided in a fit of coughing.

Greer needed no second bidding. He was anxious to take a peep at the papers he had secreted. Sinclair was out collecting, or trying to collect, but Greer did not stop to examine his prize before he had banged the street door behind him, lest Cater, listening above, should wonder what detained him. But in a convenient court-yard a hundred yards away he drew out the papers and inspected them eagerly. First, there was the policy of insurance of the house and premises. Then there was a bundle of receipts for the yearly insurance premiums. And then – there was old Jerry Cater's will.

There were two foolscap sheets, written all in Jerry Cater's own straggling handwriting. Greer hastily scanned the sheets, and his dirty face grew longer and his squint intensified as he turned over the second sheet, found nothing behind it, and stuffed the papers back in his pocket. For it was plain that not a penny of old Jerry Cater's money was for his faithful servant, Samuel Greer. 'Ungrateful ole wagabone!' mused the faithful servant as he went his way. 'Not a blessed 'a'peny; not a 'a'peny! An' them as don't want it gets it, o' course. That's always the way – it's like a-greasing' of a fat pig. I shall 'ave to get what I can while I can, that's all.' And so ruminating he pursued his way to the butcher's in Grange Road.

Once more on his way there, and twice on his way back, Samuel Greer stepped into retired places to look at those papers again, and at each inspection he grew more thoughtful. There might be money in it yet. Come, he must think it over.

The front door being shut, and Sinclair probably not yet returned, he entered the house by a way familiar to the inmates – a latched door giving on to the wharf. The clock told him that he had been gone nearly an hour, but Sinclair was still absent. When he entered old Cater's room upstairs he found a great change. The old man lay in a state of collapse, choking with a cough that exhausted him; and for this there seemed little wonder, for the window was open, and the room was full of the cold air from the river.

'Wot jer bin openin' the winder for?' asked Greer in astonishment. 'It's enough to give ye yer death.' He shut it and returned to the bedside. But though he offered his master the change from the shilling the old man seemed not to see it nor to hear his voice.

'Well, if you won't – don't,' observed Greer with some alacrity, pocketing the coppers. 'But I'll bet he'll remember right enough presently.' 'D'y'ear,' he added, bending over the bed, 'I've got the beef. Shall I bile it now?'

But old Jerry Cater's eyes still saw nothing and he heard not, though his shrunken chest and shoulders heaved with the last shudders of the cough that had exhausted him. So Greer stepped lightly to the cupboard and restored the fire policy and the receipts to the pickle-jar. He kept the will.

Greer made preparations for cooking the beef, and as he did so he encountered another phenomenon. 'Well, he have bin a goin' of it!' said Greer. 'Blow me if he ain't bin readin' the Bible now!'

A large, ancient, worn old Bible, in a rough calf-skin cover, lay on a chair by old Cater's hand. It had probably been the family Bible of the Caters for generations back, for certainly old Jerry Cater would never have bought such a thing. For many years it had accumulated dust on a distant shelf among certain out-of-date account-books, but Greer had never heard of its being noticed before. 'Feels he goin', that's about it,' Greer mused as he pitched the Bible back on the shelf to make room for his utensils. 'But I shouldn't ha' thought 'e'd take it sentimental like that – readin' the Bible an' lettin' in the free air of 'eaven to make 'im cough 'isself blind.'

The beef-tea was set simmering, and still old Cater lay impotent. The fit of prostration was longer than any that had preceded it, and presently Greer thought it might be well to call the doctor. Call him he did accordingly (the surgery was hard by), and the doctor came. Jerry Cater revived a little, sufficiently to recognize the doctor, but it was his last effort. He lived another hour and a half. Greer kept the change and had the beef-tea as well. The doctor gave his opinion that the old man had risen in delirium and had expended his last strength in moving about the room and opening the window.

II

Samuel Greer found somewhere near two pounds in silver in the small canvas bag under the dead man's pillow. No more money, however, rewarded his hasty search about the bedroom, and when Sinclair returned Greer set off to carry the news to Paul Cater, the dead man's nephew.

The respectable Greer had considered well the matter of the will, and saw his way, he fancied, at least to a few pounds by way of compensation for his loss of employment and the ungrateful forgetfulness of his late employer. The two sheets comprised, in fact, not a simple will merely, but a will and a codicil, each on one of the sheets, the codicil being a year or two more recent than the will. Nobody apparently knew anything of these papers, and it struck Greer that it was now in his power to prevent anybody learning, unless an interested party were disposed to pay for the disclosure. That was why he now took his way toward the establishment of Paul Cater, for the will made Paul Cater not only sole executor, but practically sole legatee. Wherefore Greer carefully separated the will from the codicil, intending the will alone for sale to Paul Cater. Because, indeed, the codicil very considerably modified it, and might form the subject of independent commerce.

Paul Cater made a less miserly show than had been the wont of his uncle. His house was in a street in Pimlico, the ground-floor front room of which was made into an office, with a wire blind carrying his name in gilt letters. Perhaps it was that Paul Cater carried his covetousness to a greater refinement than his uncle had done, seeing that a decent appearance is a commercial advantage by itself, bringing a greater profit than miserly habits could save.

The man of general dealings was balancing his books when Greer arrived, but at the announcement of his uncle's death he dropped everything. He was not noticeably stricken with grief, unless a sudden seizure of his hat and a roaring aloud for a cab might be considered as indications of affliction; for in truth Paul Cater knew well that it was a case in which much might depend on being first at Bermondsey Wall. The worthy Greer had scarce got the news out before he found himself standing in the street while Cater was giving directions to a cabman. 'Here – you come in too,' said Cater, and Greer was bustled into the cab.

It was plainly a situation in which half-crowns should not be too reluctantly parted with. So Paul Cater produced one and presented it. Cater was a strong-faced man of fifty odd, with a tight-drawn mouth that proclaimed everywhere a tight fist; so that the unaccustomed passing over of a tip was a noticeably awkward and unspontaneous performance, and Greer pocketed the money with little more acknowledgment than a growl.

'Do you know where he put the will?' asked Paul Cater with a keen glance.

'Will?' answered Greer, looking him blankly in the face – the gaze of one eye passing over Cater's shoulder and that of the other seeming to seek his boots. 'Will? P'raps 'e never made one.'

'Didn't he?'

'That 'ud mean, lawfully, as the property would come to you an' Mr

Flint – 'arves. Bein' all personal property. So I'd think.' And Greer's composite gaze blankly persisted.

'But how do you know whether he made a will or not?'

' 'Ow do I know? Ah, well, p'raps I dunno. It's only fancy like. I jist put it to you – that's all. It 'ud be divided atween the two of you.' Then, after a long pause, he added: 'But lor! it 'ud be a pretty fine thing for you if he did leave a will, and willed it all to you, wouldn't it? Mighty fine thing! An' it 'ud be a mighty fine thing for Mr Flint if there was a will leaving it all to him, wouldn't it? Pretty fine thing!'

Cater said nothing, but watched Greer's face sharply. Greer's face, with its greasy features and its irresponsible squint, was as expressive as a brick. They travelled some distance in silence. Then Greer said musingly, 'Ah, a will like that 'ud be a mighty fine thing! What 'ud you be disposed to give for it now?'

'Give for it? What do you mean? If there's a will there's an end to it. Why should I give anything for it?'

'Jist so – jist so,' replied Greer, with a complacent wave of the hand. 'Why should you? No reason at all, unless you couldn't find it without givin' something.'

'See here, now,' said Cater sharply, 'let us understand this. Do you mean that there is a will, and you know that it is hidden, and where it is?'

Greer's squint remained impenetrable. 'Hidden? Lor! – 'ow should I know if it was hidden? I was a-puttin' of a case to you.'

'Because,' Cater went on, disregarding the reply, 'if that's the case, the sooner you out with the information the better it'll be for you. Because there are ways of making people give up information of that sort for nothing.'

'Yes – o' course,' replied the imperturbable Greer. 'O' course there is. An' quite right too. Ah, it's a fine thing is the lawr – a mighty fine thing!'

The cab rattled over the stones of Bermondsey Wall, and the two alighted at the door through which old Jerry Cater was soon to come feet first. Sinclair was back, much disturbed and anxious. At sight of Paul Cater the poor fellow, weak and broken-spirited, left the house as quietly as he might. For years of grinding habit had inured him to the belief that in reality old Cater had treated him rather well, and now he feared the probable action of the heirs.

'Who was that?' asked Paul Cater of Greer. 'Wasn't it the clerk that owed my uncle the money?'

Greer nodded.

'Then he's not to come here again – do you hear? I'll take charge of the books and things. As to the debt – well, I'll see about that after. And now look here.' Paul Cater stood before Greer and spoke with decision. 'About that will, now. Bring it.'

Greer was not to be bluffed. 'Where from?' he asked innocently.

'Will you stand there and tell me you don't know where it is?'

'Maybe I'd best stand here and tell you what pays me best.'

'Pay you? How much more do you want? Bring me that will, or I'll have you in gaol for stealing it!'

'Lor!' answered Greer composedly, conscious of holding another trump as well as the will. 'Why, if there *was* anybody as knowed where the will was, and you talked to him as woilent as that 'ere, why, you'd frighten him so much he'd as likely as not go out and get a price from your cousin, Mr Flint. Whatever was in the will it might pay him to get hold of it.'

At this moment there came a furious knocking at the front door. 'Why,' Greer continued, 'I bet that's him. It can't be nobody else – I bet the doctor's told him, or summat.'

They were on the first-floor landing, and Greer peeped from a broken-shuttered window that looked on the street. 'Yes,' he said, 'that's Mr Flint sure enough. Now, Mr Paul Cater, business. Do you want to see that will before I let Mr Flint in?'

'Yes!' exclaimed Cater furiously, catching at his arm. 'Quick – where is it?'

'I want twenty pound.'

'Twenty pound! You're mad! What for?'

'All right, if I'm mad, I'll go an' let Mr Flint in.'

The knocking was repeated, louder and longer.

'No,' cried Cater, getting in his way. 'You know you mustn't conceal a will – that's law. Give it up.'

'What's the law that says I must give it up to you, 'stead of yer cousin? *If* there's a will it may say anythin' – in yer favour or out of it. If there ain't, you'll git 'alf. The will might give you more, or it might give you less, or it might give you nothink. Twenty pound for first look at it 'fore

Flint comes in, and do what you like with it 'fore he knows anythink about it.'

Again the knocking came at the door, this time supplemented by kicks.

'But I don't carry twenty pound about with me!' protested Cater, waving his fists. 'Give me the will and come to my office for the money to-morrow!'

'No tick for this sort of job,' answered Greer decisively. 'Sorry I can't oblige you – I'm goin' down to the front door.' And he made as though to go.

'Well, look here!' said Cater desperately, pulling out his pocket-book. 'I've got a note or two, I think –'

' 'Ow much?' asked Greer, calmly laying hold of the pocket-book. 'Two at least. Two fivers. Well, I'll let it go at that. Give us hold.' He took the notes, and pulled out the will from his pocket. Flint, outside, battered the door once more.

'Why,' exclaimed Cater as he glanced over the sheet, 'I'm sole executor and I get the lot! Who are these witnesses?'

'Oh, they're all right. Longshore hands just hereabout. You'll get 'em any day at the "Ship and Anchor".'

Cater put the will in his breast-pocket. 'You'd best get out o' this, my man,' he said. 'You've had me for ten pound, and the further you get from me the safer you'll be.'

'What?' said Greer with a chuckle. 'Not even grateful! Shockin'!' He took his way downstairs, and Cater followed. At the door Flint, a counterpart of Cater, except that his dress was more slovenly, stood ragefully.

'Ah, cousin,' said Cater, standing on the threshold and preventing his entrance, 'this is a very sad loss!'

'Sad loss!' Flint replied with disgust. 'A lot you think of the loss – as much as I do, I reckon. I want to come in.'

'Then you sha'n't!' Cater replied, with a prompt change of manner. 'You sha'n't! I'm sole executor, and I've got the will in my pocket.' He pulled it out sufficiently far to show the end of the paper, and then returned it. 'As executor I'm in charge of the property, and responsible. It's vested in me till the will's put into effect. That's law. And it's a bad thing for anybody to interfere with an executor. That's law too.'

Flint was angry, but cautious. 'Well,' he said, 'you're uncommon high,

with your will and your executor's law and your "sad loss," I must say.
What's your game?'

For answer Cater began to shut the door.

'Just you look out!' cried Flint. 'You haven't heard the last of this! You
may be executor or it may be a lie. You may have the will or you may not;
anyway I know better than to run the risk of putting myself in the wrong
now. But I'll watch you, and I'll watch this house, and I'll be about when
the will comes to be proved! And if that ain't done quick, I'll apply for
administration myself, and see the thing through!'

III

Samuel Greer sheered off as the cousinly interview ended, well satisfied
with himself. Ten pounds was a fortune to him, and he meant having a
good deal more. He did nothing further till the following morning, when
he presented himself at the shop of Jarvis Flint.

'Good mornin', Mr Flint,' said Samuel Greer, grinning and squinting
affably. 'I couldn't help noticin' as you had a few words yesterday with Mr
Cater after the sad loss.'

'Well?'

'It 'appens as I've seen the will as Mr Cater was talkin' of, an' I thought
p'raps it 'ud save you makin' mistakes if I told you of it.'

'What about it?' Jarvis Flint was not disposed to accept Greer altogether
on trust.

'Well it *do* seem a scandalous thing, certainly, but what Mr Cater said
was right. He *do* take the personal property, subjick to debts, an' he do
take the freehold prim'ses. An' he is the 'xecutor.'

'Was the will witnessed?'

'Yes – two waterside chaps well know'd thereabouts.'

'Was it made by a lawyer?'

'No – all in the lamented corpse's 'and-writin'.'

'Umph!' Flint maintained his hard stare in Greer's face. 'Anything else?'

'Well, no, Mr Flint, sir, p'raps not. But I wonder if there might be sich
a thing as a codicil?'

'Is there?'

'Oh, I was a-wonderin', that's all. It might make a deal o' difference in the will, mightn't it? And p'raps Mr Cater mightn't know anythink about the codicil.'

'What do you mean? Is there a codicil?'

'Well, reely, Mr Flint,' answered Greer with a deprecatory grin –'reely it ain't business to give information for nothink, is it?'

'Business or not, if you know anything you'll find you'll have to tell it. I'm not going to let Cater have it all his own way, if he *is* executor. My lawyer'll be on the job before you're a day older, my man, and you won't find it pay to keep things too quiet.'

'But it can't pay worse than to give information, for nothink,' persisted Greer. 'Come, now Mr Flint, s'pose (I don't say there is, mind – I only say *s'pose*) – s'pose there *was* a codicil, and s'pose that codicil meant a matter of a few thousand pound in your pocket. And s'pose some person could tell you where to put your hand on that codicil, what might you be disposed to pay that person?'

'Bring me the codicil,' answered Flint, 'and if it's all right I'll give you – well, say five shillings.'

Greer grinned again and shook his head. 'No, reely, Mr Flint,' he said, 'we can't do business on terms like them. Fifty pound down in my hand now, and it's done. Fifty 'ud be dirt cheap. And the longer you are a-considerin' – well, you know, Mr Cater might get hold of it, and then, why, s'pose it got burnt and never 'eard of agen?'

Flint glared with round eyes. 'You get out!' he said. 'Go on! Fifty pound, indeed! Fifty pound, without my knowing whether you're telling lies or not! Out you go! I know what to do now, my man!'

Greer grinned once more, and slouched out. He had not expected to bring Flint to terms at once. Of course the man would drive him away at first, and, having got scent of the existence of the codicil, and supposing it to be somewhere concealed about the old house at Bermondsey Wall, he would set his lawyer to warn his cousin that the thing was known, and that he, as executor, would be held responsible for it. But the trump card, the codicil itself, was carefully stowed in the lining of Greer's hat, and Cater knew nothing about it. Presently Flint, finding Cater obdurate, would approach the wily Greer again, and then he could be squeezed. Meanwhile the hat-lining was as safe a place as any in which to keep the paper. Perhaps Flint might take a fancy to have him waylaid at night and searched, in which case a pocket would be an unsafe repository.

Flint, on his part, was in good spirits. Plainly there *was* a codicil, favourable to himself. Certainly he meant neither to pay Greer for discovering it – at any rate no such sum as fifty pounds – nor to abate a jot of his rights. Flint had a running contract with a shady solicitor, named Lugg, in accordance with which Lugg received a yearly payment and transacted all his legal business – consisting chiefly of writing threatening letters to unfortunate debtors. Also, as I think I have mentioned, Dorrington was working for him at the time, and working at very cheap rates. Flint resolved, to begin with, to set Dorrington and Lugg to work. But first Dorrington – who, as a matter of fact, was in Flint's back office during the interview with Greer. Thus it was that in an hour or two Dorrington found himself in active pursuit of Samuel Greer, with instructions to watch him closely, to make him drunk if possible, and to get at his knowledge of the codicil by any means conceivable.

IV

On the morning of the day after his talk with Flint, Samuel Greer ruminated doubtfully on the advisability of calling on the ship-store dealer again, or waiting in dignified silence till Flint should approach him. As he ruminated he rubbed his chin, and so rubbing it found it very stubbly. He resolved on the luxury of a penny shave, and, as he walked the street, kept his eyes open for a shop where the operation was performed at that price. Mr Flint, at any rate, could wait till his chin was smooth. Presently, in a turning by Abbey Street, Bermondsey, he came on just such a barber's shop as he wanted. Within, two men were being shaved already, and another waiting; and Greer felt himself especially fortunate in that three more followed at his heels. He was ahead of their turns, anyhow. So he waited patiently.

The man whose turn was immediately before his own did not appear to be altogether sober. A hiccough shook him from time to time; he grinned with a dull glance at a comic paper held upside down in his hand, and when he went to take his turn at a chair his walk was unsteady. The barber had to use his skill to avoid cutting him, and he opened his mouth to make remarks at awkward times. Then Greer's turn came at the other chair, and when his shave was half completed he saw the unsteady customer rise, pay his penny, and go out.

'Beginnin' early in the mornin'!' observed one customer.

The barber laughed. 'Yes,' he said. 'He wants to get a proper bust on before he goes to bed, I s'pose.'

Samuel Greer's chin being smooth at last, he rose and turned to where he had hung his hat. His jaw dropped, and his eyes almost sprang out to meet each other as he saw – a bare peg! The unsteady customer had walked off with the wrong hat – his hat, and – the paper concealed inside!

'Lor!' cried the dismayed Greer, 'he's took my hat!'

All the shopful of men set up a guffaw at this. 'Take 'is then,' said one. 'It's a blame sight better one than yourn!'

But Greer, without a hat, rushed into the street, and the barber, without his penny, rushed after him. 'Stop 'im!' shouted Greer distractedly. 'Stop thief!'

Thus it was that Dorrington, at this time of a far less well-groomed appearance than was his later wont, watching outside the barber's, observed the mad bursting forth of Greer, followed by the barber. After the barber came the customers, one grinning furiously beneath a coating of lather.

'Stop 'im!' cried Greer. ' 'E's got my 'at! Stop 'im!'

'You pay me my money,' said the barber, catching his arm. 'Never mind yer 'at – you can 'ave 'is. But just you pay me first.'

'Leave go! You're responsible for lettin' 'im take it, I tell you! It's a special 'at – valuable; leave go!'

Dorrington stayed to hear no more. Three minutes before he had observed a slightly elevated navvy emerge from the shop and walk solemnly across the street under a hat manifestly a size or two too small for him. Now Dorrington darted down the turning which the man had taken. The hat was a wretched thing, and there must be some special reason for Greer's wild anxiety to recover it, especially as the navvy must have left another, probably better, behind him. Already Dorrington had conjectured that Greer was carrying the codicil about with him, for he had no place else to hide it, and he would scarcely have offered so confidently to negotiate over it if it had been in the Bermondsey Wall house, well in reach of Paul Cater. So he followed the elevated navvy with all haste. He might never have seen him again were it not that the unconscious bearer of the fortunes of Flint (and, indeed, Dorrington) hesitated for a little while whether or not to enter the door of a public-house near St Saviour's Dock. In the end he decided to go on, and it was just as he had started that Dorrington sighted him again.

The navvy walked slowly and gravely on, now and again with a swerve to the wall or the curb, but generally with a careful and laboured directness. Presently he arrived at a dock-bridge, with a low iron rail. An incoming barge attracted his eye, and he stopped and solemnly inspected it. He leaned on the low rail for this purpose, and as he did so the hat, all too small, fell off. Had he been standing two yards nearer the centre of the bridge it would have dropped into the water. As it was it fell on the quay, a few feet from the edge, and a dockman, coming toward the steps by the bridge-side, picked it up and brought it with him.

'Here y'are, mate,' said the dockman, offering the hat.

The navvy took it in lofty silence, and inspected it narrowly. Then he said, ' 'Ere – wot's this? This ain't my 'at!' And he glared suspiciously at the dockman.

Ain't it?' answered the dockman carelessly. 'Aw right then, keep it for the bloke it b'longs to. I don't want it.'

'No,' returned the navvy with rising indignation, 'but I want mine, though! Wotcher done with it? Eh? It ain't a rotten old 'un like this 'ere. None o' yer 'alf-larks. Jist you 'and it over, come on!'

' 'And wot over?' asked the dockman, growing indignant in his turn. 'You drops yer 'at over the bridge like some kid as can't take care of it, and I brings it up for ye. 'Stead o' sayin' "thank ye", like a man, y' asks me for another 'at! Go an' bile yer face!' And he turned on his heel.

'No, ye don't!' bawled the navvy, dropping the battered hat and making a complicated rush at the other's retreating form. 'Not much! You gimme my 'at!' And he grabbed the dockman anywhere, with both hands.

The dockman was as big as the navvy, and no more patient. He immediately punched his assailant's nose; and in three seconds a mingled bunch of dockman and navvy was floundering about the street. Dorrington saw no more. He had the despised hat in his hand, and, general attention being directed to the action in progress he hurried quietly up the nearest court.

V

Samuel Greer, having got clear of the barber by paying his penny, was in much perplexity, and this notwithstanding his acquisition of the navvy's hat, a very decent bowler, which covered his head generously and rested on his ears. What should be the move now? His hat was clean gone, and the codicil with it. To find it again would be a hopeless task, unless by chance the navvy should discover his mistake and return to the barber's to make a rectification of hats. So Samuel Greer returned once more to the barber's, and for the rest of the day called again and again fruitlessly. At first the barber was vastly amused, and told the story to his customers, who laughed. Then the barber got angry at the continual worrying, and at the close of the day's barbering he earned his night's repose by pitching Samuel Greer neck and crop into the gutter. Samuel Greer gathered himself up disconsolately, surrounded his head with the navvy's hat, and shuffled off to the 'Ship and Anchor.'

At the 'Ship and Anchor' he found one Barker, a decayed and sodden lawyer's clerk out of work. Greer's temporary affluence enabling him to stand drinks, he was presently able, by putting artfully hypothetical cases, to extract certain legal information from Barker. Chiefly he learned that if a will or a codicil were missing, it might nevertheless be possible to obtain probate of it by satisfying the court with evidence of its contents and its genuineness. Here, at any rate, was a certain hope. He alone, apparently, of all persons, knew the contents of the codicil and the names of the witnesses; and since it was impossible to sell the codicil, now that it was gone, he might at least sell his evidence. He resolved to offer his evidence for sale to Flint at once, and take what he could get. There must be no delay, for possibly the navvy might find the paper in the hat and carry it to Flint, seeing that his name was beneficially mentioned in it, and his address given. Plainly the hat would not go back to the barber's now. If the drunken navvy had found out his mistake he probably had not the least notion where he had been nor where the hat had come from, else he would have returned it during the day, and recovered his own superior property. So Samuel Greer went at once, late as it was, and knocked up Mr Flint.

Flint congratulated himself, feeling sure that Greer had thought better of his business and had come to give his information for anything he could get. Greer, on his part, was careful to conceal the fact that the codicil had been in his possession and had been lost. All he said was that he had seen the codicil, that its date was nine months later than that of the will, and that it benefited Jarvis Flint to the extent of some ten thousand pounds; leaving Flint to suppose, if he pleased, that Cater, the executor, had the codicil, but would probably suppress it. Indeed this was the conclusion that Flint immediately jumped at.

And the result of the interview was this: Flint, with much grudging and reluctance, handed over as a preliminary fee the sum of one pound, the most he could be screwed up to. Then it was settled that Greer should come on the morrow and consult with Flint and his solicitor Lugg, the object of the consultation being the construction of a consistent tale and a satisfactory *soi-disant* copy of the codicil, which Greer was to swear to, if necessary, and armed with which Paul Cater might be confronted and brought to terms.

It may be wondered why, ere this, Flint had not received the genuine codicil itself, recovered by Dorrington from Greer's hat. The fact was that Dorrington, as was his wont, was playing a little game of his own. Having possessed himself of the codicil, he was now in a position to make the most from both sides, and in a far more efficient manner than the clumsy Greer. People of Jarvis Flint's sordid character are apt, with all their sordid keenness, to be wonderfully short-sighted in regard to what might seem fairly obvious to a man of honest judgment. Thus it never occurred to Flint that a man like Dorrington, willing, for a miserable wage, to apply his exceptional subtlety to the furtherance of his employer's rascally designs, would be at least as ready to swindle that master on his own account when the opportunity offered; would be, in fact, the more ready, in proportion to the stinginess wherewith his master had treated him.

Having found the codicil, Dorrington's procedure was not to hand it over forthwith to Flint. It was this: first he made a careful and exact copy of the codicil; then he procured two men of his acquaintance, men of good credit, to read over the copy, word for word, and certify it as being an exact copy of the original by way of a signed declaration written on the back of the copy. Then he was armed at all points.

He packed the copy carefully away in his pocket-book, and with the original in his coat pocket, he called at the house in Bermondsey Wall, where Paul Cater had taken up his quarters to keep guard over everything till the will should be proved. So it happened that while Samuel Greer, Jarvis Flint, and Lugg, the lawyer, were building their scheme, Dorrington was talking to Paul Cater at Cater's Wharf.

On the assurance that he had business of extreme importance, Cater took Dorrington into the room in which the old man had died. Cater was using this room as an office in which to examine and balance his uncle's books, and the corpse had been carried to a room below to await the funeral. Dorrington's clothes at this time, as I have hinted, were not distinguished by the excellence of cut and condition that was afterwards noticeable; in point of fact, he was seedy. But his assurance and his presence of mind were fully developed, and it was this very transaction that was to put the elegant appearance within his reach.

'Mr Cater,' he said, 'I believe you are sole executor of the will of your uncle, Mr Jeremiah Cater, who lived in this house.' Cater assented.

'That will is one extremely favourable to yourself. In fact, by it you become not only sole executor, but practically sole legatee.'

'Well?'

'I am here as a man of business and as a man of the world to give you certain information. There is a codicil to that will.'

Cater started. Then he shrugged his shoulders and shook his head as though he knew better.

'There is a codicil,' Dorrington went on, imperturbably, 'executed in strict form, all in the handwriting of the testator, and dated nine months later than the will. That codicil benefits your cousin, Mr Jarvis Flint, to the extent of ten thousand pounds. To put it in another way, it deprives *you* of ten thousand pounds.'

Cater felt uneasy, but he did his best to maintain a contemptuous appearance. 'You're rushing ahead pretty fast,' he said, 'talking about the terms of this codicil, as you call it. What I want to know is, where is it?'

'That,' replied Dorrington, smilingly, 'is a question very easily answered. The codicil is in my pocket.' He tapped his coat as he spoke.

Paul Cater started again, and now he was plainly discomposed. 'Very well,' he said, with some bravado, 'if you've got it you can show it to me, I suppose.'

'Nothing easier,' Dorrington responded affably. He stepped to the fire-place and took the poker. 'You won't mind my holding the poker while you inspect the paper, will you?' he asked politely. 'The fact is, the codicil is of such a nature that I fear a man of your sharp business instincts might be tempted to destroy it, there being no other witness present, unless you had the assurance (which I now give you) that if you as much as touch it I shall stun you with the poker. There is the codicil, which you may read with your hands behind you.' He spread the paper out on the table, and Cater bent eagerly and read it, growing paler as his eye travelled down the sheet.

Before raising his eyes, however, he collected himself, and as he stood up he said, with affected contempt, 'I don't care a brass farthing for this thing! It's a forgery on the face of it.'

'Dear me!' answered Dorrington placidly, recovering the paper and folding it up; 'that's very disappointing to hear. I must take it round to Mr Flint and see if that is his opinion.'

'No, you mustn't!' exclaimed Cater, desperately. 'You say that's a genuine document. Very well. I'm still executor, and you are bound to give it to me.'

'Precisely,' Dorrington replied sweetly. 'But in the strict interests of justice I think Mr Flint, as the person interested, ought to have a look at it first, *in case* any accident should happen to it in your hands. Don't you?'

Cater knew he was in a corner, and his face betrayed it.

'Come,' said Dorrington in a more business-like tone. 'Here is the case in a nutshell. It is my business, just as it is yours, to get as much as I can for nothing. In pursuance of that business I quietly got hold of this codicil. Nobody but yourself knows I have it, and as to *how* I got it you needn't ask, for I sha'n't tell you. Here is the document, and it is worth ten thousand pounds to either of two people, yourself and Mr Flint, your worthy cousin. I am prepared to sell it at a very great sacrifice – to sell it dirt cheap, in fact, and I give you the privilege of first refusal, for which you ought to be grateful. One thousand pounds is the price, and that gives you a profit of nine thousand pounds when you have destroyed the codicil – a noble profit of nine hundred per cent. at a stroke! Come, is it a bargain?'

'What?' ejaculated Cater, astounded. 'A thousand pounds?'

'One thousand pounds exactly,' replied Dorrington complacently, 'and a penny for the receipt stamp – if you want a receipt.'

'Oh,' said Cater, 'you're mad. A thousand pounds! Why, it's absurd!'

'Think so?' remarked Dorrington, reaching for his hat. 'Then I must see if Mr Flint agrees with you, that's all. He's a man of business, and I never heard of his refusing a certain nine hundred per cent. profit yet. Good-day!'

'No, stop!' yelled the desperate Cater. 'Don't go. Don't be unreasonable now – say five hundred and I'll write you a cheque.'

'Won't do,' answered Dorrington, shaking his head. 'A thousand is the price, and not a penny less. And not by cheque, mind. I understand all moves of that sort. Notes or gold. I wonder at a smart man like yourself expecting me to be so green.'

'But I haven't the money here.'

'Very likely not. Where's your bank? We'll go there and get it.'

Cater, between his avarice and his fears, was at his wits' end. 'Don't be so hard on me, Mr Dorrington,' he whined. 'I'm not a rich man, I assure you. You'll ruin me!'

'Ruin you? What *do* you mean? I give you ten thousand pounds for one thousand and you say I ruin you! Really, it seems too ridiculously cheap. If you don't settle quickly, Mr Cater, I shall raise my terms, I warn you!'

So it came about that Dorrington and Cater took a cab together for a branch bank in Pimlico, whence Dorrington emerged with one thousand pounds in notes and gold, stowed carefully about his person, and Cater with the codicil to his uncle's will, which half an hour later he had safely burnt.

VI

So much for the first half of Dorrington's operation. For the second half he made no immediate hurry. If he had been aware of Samuel Greer's movements and Lugg's little plot he might have hurried, but as it was he busied himself in setting up on a more respectable scale by help of his newly acquired money. But he did not long delay. He had the attested copy of the codicil, which would be as good as the original if properly backed with evidence in a court of law. The astute Cater, wise in his own conceit, just as was his equally astute cousin Flint, had clean over-looked the possibility of such a trick as this. And now all Dorrington had to do was to sell the copy for one more thousand pounds to Jarvis Flint.

It was on the morning of old Jerry Cater's funeral that he made his way to Deptford to do this, and he chuckled as he reflected on the probable surprise of Flint, who doubtless wondered what had become of his sweated inquiry agent, when confronted with his offer. But when he arrived at the ship-store shop he found that Flint was out, so he resolved to call again in the evening.

At that moment Jarvis Flint, Samuel Greer, and Lugg the lawyer were at the house in Bermondsey Wall attacking Paul Cater. Greer, foreseeing probable defiance by Cater from a window, had led the party in by the wharf door and so had taken Cater by surprise. Cater was in a suit of decent black, as befitted the occasion, and he received the news of the existence of a copy of the codicil he had destroyed with equal fury and apprehension.

'What do you mean?' he demanded. 'What do you mean? I'm not to be bluffed like this! You talk about a codicil – where is it? Where is it, eh?'

'My dear sir,' said Lugg peaceably – he was a small, snuffy man – 'we are not here to make disturbances or quarrels, or breaches of the peace; we are here on a strictly business errand, and I assure you it will be for your best interests if you listen quietly to what we have to say. Ahem! It seems that Mr Samuel Greer here has frequently seen the codicil –'

'Greer's a rascal – a thief – a scoundrel!' cried the irate Cater, shaking his fist in the thick of Greer's squint. 'He swindled me out of ten pounds! He –'

'Really, Mr Cater,' Lugg interposed, 'you do no good by such outbursts, and you prevent my putting the case before you. As I was saying, Mr Greer has frequently seen the codicil, and saw it, indeed, on the very day of the late Mr Cater's decease. You may not have come across it, and, indeed, there may be some temporary difficulty in finding the original. But fortunately Mr Greer took notes of the contents and of the witnesses' names, and from those notes I have been able to draw up this statement, which Mr Greer is prepared to subscribe to, by affidavit or declaration, if by any chance you may be unable to produce the original codicil.'

Cater, seeing his thousand pounds to Dorrington going for nothing, and now confronted with the fear of losing ten thousand pounds more, could scarce speak for rage. 'Greer's a liar, I tell you!' he spluttered out. 'A liar, a thief, a scoundrel! His word – his affidavit – his oath – anything of his – isn't worth a straw!'

'That, my dear sir,' Lugg proceeded equably, 'is a thing that may remain for the probate court, and possibly a jury, to decide upon. In the meantime permit me to suggest that it will be better for all parties – cheaper in fact – if this matter be settled out of court. I think, if you will give the matter a little calm and unbiased thought, you will admit that the balance of strength is altogether with our case. Would you like to look at the statement? Its effect, you will see, is, roughly speaking, to give my client a legacy of say about ten thousand pounds in value. The witnesses are easily produced, and really, I must say, for my part, if Mr Greer, who has nothing to gain or lose either way, is prepared to take the serious responsibility of swearing a declaration –'

'I don't believe he will!' cried Cater, catching at the straw. 'I don't believe he will. Mind, Greer,' he went on, 'there's penal servitude for perjury!'

'Yes,' Greer answered, speaking for the first time, with a squint and a chuckle, 'so there is. And for stealin' an' suppressin' dockyments, I'm told. I'm ready to make that 'ere declaration.'

'I don't believe he is!' Cater said, with an attempt to affect indifference. 'And anyhow, I needn't take any notice of it till he does.'

'Well,' said Lugg accommodatingly, 'there need be no difficulty or delay about that. The declaration's all written out, and I'm a commissioner to administer oaths. I think that's a Bible I see on the shelf there, isn't it?' He stepped across to where the old Bible had lain since Greer flung it there, just before Jerry Cater's death. He took the book down and opened it at the title-page. 'Yes,' he said, 'a Bible; and now – why – what? what?'

Mr Lugg stood suddenly still and stared at the fly-leaf. Then he said quietly, 'Let me see, it was on Monday last that Mr Cater died, was it not?'

'Yes.'

'Late in the afternoon?'

'Yes.'

'Then, gentlemen, you must please prepare yourselves for a surprise. Mr Cater evidently made another will, revoking all previous wills and codicils, on the very day of his death. And here it is!' He extended the Bible before him, and it was plain to see that the fly-leaf was covered with the weak, straggling handwriting of old Jerry Cater – a little weaker and a little more straggling than that in the other will, but unmistakably his.

Flint stared, perplexed and bewildered, Greer scratched his head and squinted blankly at the lawyer. Paul Cater passed his hand across his forehead and seized a tuft of hair over one temple as though he would pull it out. The only book in the house that he had not opened or looked at during his stay was the Bible.

'The thing is very short,' Lugg went on, inclining the writing to the light. '*"This is the last will and testament of me, Jeremiah Cater, of Cater's Wharf. I give and bequeath the whole of the estate and property of which I may die possessed, whether real or personal, entirely and absolutely to – to –"* what is the name? Oh yes – *"to Henry Sinclair, my clerk –"'*

'What?' yelled Cater and Flint in chorus, each rising and clutching at the Bible. 'Not Sinclair! No! Let me see!'

'I think, gentlemen,' said the solicitor, putting their hands aside, 'that you will get the information quickest by listening while I read. *"– to Henry Sinclair, my clerk. And I appoint the said Henry Sinclair my sole executor. And I wish it to be known that I do this, not only by way of reward to an honest servant, and to recompense him for his loss in loan transactions with me, but also to mark my sense of the neglect of my two nephews. And I revoke all former wills and codicils."* Then follows date and signature and the signatures of witnesses – both apparently men of imperfect education.'

'But you're mad – it's impossible!' exclaimed Cater, the first to find his tongue. 'He *couldn't* have made a will then – he was too weak. Greer knows he couldn't.'

Greer, who understood better than anybody else present the allusion in the will to the nephews' neglect, coughed dubiously, and said, 'Well, he did get up while I was out. An' when I got back he had the Bible beside him, an' he seemed pretty well knocked up with something. An' the winder was wide open – I expect he opened it to holler out as well as he could to some chaps on the wharf or somewhere to come up by the wharf door and do the witnessing. An' now I think of it I expect he sent me out a-purpose in case – well, in case if I knowed I might get up to summat with the will. He told me not to hurry. An' I expect he about used himself up with the writin' an' the hollerin' an' the cold air an' what not.'

Cater and Flint, greatly abashed, exchanged a rapid glance. Then Cater, with a preliminary cough, said hesitatingly, 'Well now, Mr Lugg, let us consider this. It seems quite evident to me – and no doubt it will to you, as my cousin's solicitor – it seems quite evident to me that my poor uncle could not have been in a sound state of mind when he made this very ridiculous will. Quite apart from all questions of genuineness, I've no doubt that a court would set it aside. And in view of that it would be very cruel to allow this poor man Sinclair to suppose himself to be entitled to a great deal of money, only to find himself disappointed and ruined after all. You'll agree with that, I'm sure. So I think it will be best for all parties if we keep this thing to ourselves, and just tear out that fly-leaf and burn it, to save trouble. And on my part I shall be glad to admit the copy of the codicil you have produced, and no doubt my cousin and I will be pre-pared to pay you a fee which will compensate you for any loss of business in actions – eh?'

Mr Lugg was tempted, but he was no fool. Here was Samuel Greer at his elbow knowing everything, and without a doubt, no matter how well bribed, always ready to make more money by betraying the arrangement to Sinclair. And that would mean inevitable ruin to Lugg himself, and probably a dose of gaol. So he shook his head virtuously and said, 'I couldn't think of anything of the sort, Mr Cater, not for an instant. I am a solicitor, and I have my strict duties. It is my duty immediately to place this will in the hands of Mr Henry Sinclair, as sole executor. I wish you a good-day, gentlemen.'

And so it was that old Jerry Cater's money came at last to Sinclair. And the result was a joyful one, not only for Sinclair and his wife, but also for a number of poor debtors whose 'paper' was part of the property. For Sinclair knew the plight of these wretches by personal experience, and was merciful, as neither Flint nor Paul Cater would have been. The two witnesses to the Bible will turned out to be bargemen. They had been mightily surprised to be hailed from Jerry Cater's window by the old man himself, already looking like a corpse. They had come up, however, at his request, and had witnessed the will, though neither knew anything of its contents. But they were ready to testify that it was written in a Bible, that they saw Cater sign it, and that the attesting signatures were theirs. They had helped the old man back into bed, and next day they heard that he was dead.

As for Dorrington, he had a thousand pounds to set him up in a gentlemanly line of business and villainy. Ignorant of what had happened, he attempted to tap Flint for another thousand pounds as he had designed, but was met with revilings and an explanation. Seeing that the game was finished, Dorrington laughed at both the cousins and turned his attention to his next case.

And old Jerry Cater's funeral was attended, as nobody would have expected, by two very genuine mourners – Paul Cater and Jarvis Flint. But they mourned, not the old man, but his lost fortune, and Paul Cater also mourned a sum of one thousand and ten pounds of his own. They had followed Lugg to the door when he walked off with the Bible in hope to persuade him, but he saw a wealthy client in prospect in Mr Henry Sinclair, and would not allow his virtue to be shaken.

Samuel Greer walked away from the old house in moody case. Plainly there were no more pickings available from old Jerry Cater's wills and codicils. As he trudged by St Saviour's Dock he was suddenly confronted by a large navvy with a black eye. The navvy stooped and inspected a peacock's feather-eye that adorned the band of the hat Greer was wearing. Then he calmly grabbed and inspected the hat itself, inside and outside. 'Why, blow me if this ain't my 'at!' said the navvy. 'Take that, ye dirty squintin' thief! And that too! And that!'

GEORGE GISSING

The Peace Bringer

It was a disease with a long name; at times the man could totter into his garden and sit there for an hour, at others he lay helpless on the elaborate piece of mechanism called an invalid's couch; his mind had perhaps begun to fail, but in talk with intimates he was still the old Jaffray, whimsical, imaginative, by turns a satirist and a mystic. To stoicism he had never pretended; pain he bore ill, and the poor fellow had a good deal of it to bear. He wrote a little poem called 'The Operation', and much wanted to publish it; but an editor, one of his friends, called the thing blasphemous. And his wife, after with difficulty obtaining a sight of it, looked at him with her soft, intelligent, pitiful eyes and shook her head. Jaffray admitted that his days of verse-making were over. At prose he had never tried his hand, and it was too late now.

Naturally, the house grew dull. Not many persons made a point of coming frequently to Sevenoaks, to sit with an invalid who might or might not even seem grateful, or to call upon a woman subdued by sadness. There was money in abundance, but nowadays it could purchase little that Jaffray or his wife desired. Change of climate had been tried, but was useless. The sufferer chose to live in this out-of-the-way spot, saying that it saved his friends either an annoyance or a hypocrisy. And as for Mrs Jaffray, she had her garden, where she tended the first flowers of spring, as though they were babies that could smile in her face.

She had no child; that was the worst of it. She, of all women, should have had a child. Overflowing with tenderness and compassion, very wise in the ways of a household, brilliant not at all, but of delicate understanding, of fine perceptiveness, she would have been one of those mothers who are worshipped by offspring worthy of them. As it was, she perfected herself in wifehood; at all events, in those qualities of wifehood which her position called for. Nine years she had been wedded: at the end of the third, Jaffray's health gave way, and he had never recovered. Bitter enough, for him, such an issue of a marriage promising greatly – a marriage, he was wont to say in confidence, a good deal better than he deserved. He had his sleeping partnership in a sleepy city house, and his toy reputation as the author of *Vignettes and Blotches* he had his one great scandal (duly outlived) and his posy of fragrant memories; he had his fine, pale face and his admired fingers. Mrs Jaffray brought him a fortune, and her virtues. About the latter he rhymed for a twelvemonth, and rhymed so sincerely that he never cared to print the verses – probably his best. When he did once more publish an effusion, it was about a young woman who played to him one day in an hotel in Bordighera, a young Englishwoman, by name Mrs Lanyon, of whom he wished to see more than fate at that time permitted.

Unfortunately, Mrs Jaffray did not excel as a musician. She touched the piano, indeed, but ineffectively; for song she had no voice. Jaffray regretted these things. He weighed against them, however, her admirable reading, whether of verse or prose.

And, as time went on, that gift was abundantly exercised. Mrs Jaffray read to her husband, read through no small library, until she began to notice that her voice seemed to have a wearying effect upon him. He no longer stopped her with a comment, still less with praise; his eyes wandered, his long fingers beat a silent tattoo. The hours of reading were reduced, and at length, after purposely intermitting the habit for several days, she found that he did not desire its resumption, and so she read not at all.

Had there been children, it would not so much have mattered. Mrs Jaffray was tolerant of her husband's humours; she had studied him with loving assiduity: she often read his mind with admirable intelligence. Without more than a natural sigh, she could have recognized the danger of being too much about him, and have waited, amid other duties, the revival of his need for her. But her duties were so few, and discharged so easily. If she left her husband, she for the most part sat alone, and had no choice but to sorrow.

'Can't you get a few people together?' he asked her, rather drearily, one morning when for several days he had not been able to walk across the room.

'Two or three will be coming this afternoon,' she replied, glad that her action had anticipated his wish.

'Who?'

'Mr and Mrs Dyer, and perhaps Mr Hurst – '

A groan interrupted her. She thought it meant a spasm of pain, but Jaffray explained himself. These Dyers and Hursts were all very well in their way, decent folk, but it drove him crazy to think of having to talk with them.

'Who would you like to have, dear?'

He looked at her dreamily, before speaking.

'I suppose the Watmores are still away? – Yes, yes, I know we can't bore people with our invitations. By-the-bye, why don't you go to town oftener? Because I'm done for, that's no reason why you should be cut off from society. Do go and enjoy yourself.'

'It's very kind of you; but I have no mind to go.'

'I know. But you must. It's quite absurd – at your age. It makes me worse, to see you fretting and mooning. – No, I know you don't do that. But you're too good. Go and enjoy yourself, or try to. Tell me about things when you come back. I should like it; upon my soul I should.'

He returned to the subject next day, and at last persuaded her to make calls in town. After that he was always begging, entreating, ordering her to go; it was as though he desired her absence for some special reason. Yet, as Mrs Jaffray perceived, the reason could only be that he was weary of her proximity; of that she was growing too well aware. Once or twice it gave him moderate entertainment to hear the news she brought back, but afterwards he heard it with a forced show of interest. It was difficult to understand how he passed his time. The man-servant who was always within call reported that he scarcely read even the newspaper; that for the most part he lay motionless, sometimes muttering to himself, sometimes trying to sing.

'Perhaps he is composing poetry,' thought his wife, and felt a moment's solace.

His friend Watmore, the dramatist, came to see him – returned from some twenty thousand miles of travel. And Watmore, in his large talk, chanced to mention a rather interesting woman he had met on the steamer, returning from the Cape, her name Mrs Lanyon. At once Jaffray brightened with curiosity. This was the Mrs Lanyon he had known at Bordighera. Watmore's account of her left her circumstances a matter of doubt; ostensibly she still had a husband, a professional musician, but it seemed probable that she led an adventurous life; the women on board would have little to do with her, but with certain of the men she was in great request. He spoke of her singing to the guitar, o' nights, when the sea was still, and the tropic heaven throbbed with starlight. She had impressed him as being superior to her chances, a woman who might have figured rather well in the world of orderly things, had fate permitted. In short, she suggested a central character for Watmore's dramatic handling, and with that in view he was going to call upon her, in London.

Jaffray asked her address, and made a mental note of it.

Three days after, he began lamenting to his wife that he could so seldom hear music. It would be such a solace to him.

'I've half a mind to engage someone to play,'

'Why not?' acquiesced Mrs Jaffray. And she encouraged the idea, offered to seek a suitable person. Half a year ago she would have added a regret concerning her own inability to serve him; to-day the thought found no expression, for she knew the look (averted, unquiet) with which it would be received.

'I think I know someone who will do,' said Jaffray absently. 'There's a Mrs Lanyon – a friend of Watmore's – why you remember her don't you? At Bordighera, you know – '

Yes, Mrs Jaffray remembered her, and very quietly, said so. By chance, too, she knew that a letter from her husband had been posted to Mrs Lanyon a day or two ago.

'Perhaps she could come over now and then,' Jaffray pursued, his eyes on the ceiling. 'You see, one must have fairly good music – else, why not hire a piano-organ? I daresay it'll be expensive – '

'What does that matter?' said his wife, with a flitting smile.

And the conversation ceased.

Mrs Lanyon came down to Sevenoaks. Apprised of her coming, Mrs Jaffray received her as she would have received any other lady with whom she was slightly acquainted – entire courtesy, the welcome of a country house; nothing more and nothing less. An opportunity was given for private talk between the visitor and Jaffray. Returning to the room, the hostess heard notes of the piano; she entered and seated herself to listen whilst Mrs Lanyon played, careful, the while, not to observe her husband's countenance. Nor did she, save for a glance or so, pay heed to the musician. To-day Mrs Jaffray was dressed with more than ordinary simplicity; she looked older than her wont, and showed very distinctly the results of her life of care and seclusion. Mrs Lanyon, on the other hand, had every advantage of costume, and her half-beauty showed at its best as she played and sang. She was about the same age as her hostess, four or five-and-thirty. Something of the adventuress appeared in her, but she had the orthodox accent, and bore herself inoffensively. Her visit lasted for a couple of hours, and she returned to town.

'That has done me good,' said Jaffray, in the course of the evening. 'She must come as often as possible.'

'I am glad she is at your disposal,' replied his wife, gently.

'Capital, isn't it? It just happens that her time is free. It has really done me good: Saul and David, you know – '

He laughed; Mrs Jaffray smiled; and they parted for the night rather earlier than usual.

At Mrs Lanyon's second visit, the hostess did not appear; she excused herself on the plea of a headache. The day after she went early to London, and was away till dinner-time. On her return she found Jaffray seated in the garden, a small blotter and a sheet or two of paper on his knee: he welcomed her merrily, and seemed in better health than for a long time.

'Would you mind,' she asked presently, 'If I offered our garden – say one or two days a week – to a society that gives little holidays to children of the East End?'

'Mind? An excellent idea, and like yourself. Just let me know the dates, that's all.'

'Thank you.'

Thenceforth, Mrs Jaffray was very often away. She spoke now and then of the business that took her townward; she had found what more pretentious people call a 'sphere of usefulness', and did a good deal of quiet work of a helpful kind. Jaffray praised her warmly, but she gave no sign of pleasure in his approval, talking to him much as a quiet, good-natured sister might have done, and never giving him more than half an hour of her society.

Mrs Lanyon came three times a week, and her visits were of longer duration. It was her habit at length to arrive about eleven o'clock, and remain till six; and on these days Mrs Jaffray was never at home. Music sounded very soon after the visitor's arrival, and from time to time throughout her stay; but there were long intervals occupied with conversation. Jaffray lay on his couch, which was wheeled to one room or another, as he desired; latterly his attempts to walk had been futile, and the watchers of his physical condition saw that he grew worse. Between his regular medical attendant and Mrs Jaffray there was confidential talk; the patient had harmed himself by encouraging a mood of excitement, and was pursuing the best way to bring on a crisis which would probably be fatal. Mrs Jaffray would not herself warn him – could not bring herself even to speak to him of his health; but the doctor did his duty, and with medical directness. It availed him nothing, Mrs Lanyon came four days a week, instead of three.

One morning when the leaves had begun to fall, the musician drove as usual from Sevenoaks station to the house, and as usual was led into the drawing-room. But Jaffray was not awaiting her: his man-nurse came to beg that she would amuse herself for a short time. until the invalid felt able to be wheeled in. He had passed a very bad night, and seemed very ill this morning, but had insisted on being dressed as usual for his visitor. He would probably be able to join her in half an hour.

So Mrs Lanyon waited, not at all impatiently, glancing at books and pictures, but for the most part musing. She had never been in better health and spirits; a soft warmth lay upon her cheeks, her lips were ruddy, her eyes bright. She hummed an air and smiled at her own thoughts.

The door opened: the couch was wheeled in. Jaffray looked so ghostlike. The first sight of him startled Mrs Lanyon. He fixed his eyes upon her, eyes of suffering and desire, but spoke no word till they were alone.

'I couldn't – I've had a bad attack – I know you'll forgive me.'

'For what?' asked the musician, with a puzzled air.

'The verses I promised you.'

'Oh, never mind! What does it matter! I'm so awfully sorry – '

The hand she gave him he raised to his wrinkled lips, and held it there for some moments, Mrs Lanyon. the while, glancing uneasily about the room.

'I'll write them to-day,' he promised. 'You do care for my poetry, don't you?'

'Of course I do. Charming always! I shall keep all you have given me, as long as I live.'

'Don't go away. Sit by me – talk – '

'Don't you think it's better for you when I play?'

'Yes – yes – presently. Your voice is music enough, just now. Tell me what you did yesterday.'

Mrs Lanyon gave a little laugh, and in spite of his resistance extricated her hand. She sat by him, but beyond his reach, and began to talk gaily of social amusements.

'By-the-bye, I go away on Monday,' she let fall, as if it were a matter of no consequence.

'What do you mean?'

He tried to raise himself in his excitement, and all but groaned with pain.

'I'm going to Bordighera for the winter. And I ought to thank you before I go: but for you, I don't quite see how I should have managed it. You told me, you know' – she gave him a playful look – 'that money was of no consequence whatever to you. To me it's of a good deal, and it was awfully good of you to give me the chance of earning a nice little sum.'

Jaffray's visage had gone cadaverous; the sight of it gave Mrs Lanyon what she might have called a 'turn', and she shrank away from him.

'You're not going to treat me like that?' he said, in a thick voice.

'I have told you again and again that I couldn't come for very long. Is it my fault if you wouldn't believe me?'

'Another week – '

'I must go on Monday.'

'Anything you like – any sum – '

'Thank you: I am not scheming for profit. And, to tell you the truth, I see no chance of doing you good. You *will* excite yourself so, though I have done my best to make you reasonable. I have nothing to reproach myself with. If I could have done you good, I should have been delighted,

as you know. I feel really sorry for you. Take my advice, now: make friends
with your wife again – '

Jaffray made a wild gesture of irritation.

'It's you that I want – you! No one else can help me, either to live or
to die. Stay with me to the end, and you won't be sorry you did. Any terms
you like to make – I'm not so foolish as to think you care a snap of the
fingers about me; but I can't do without you – your talk and your playing
and singing. Look here: if you leave me, I shall kill myself. I won't bear
this hell of a life for one day after you are gone.'

Mrs Lanyon seemed to reflect. Instead of answering, she went to the
piano, and played for nearly an hour, such music as might give the spirit
rest. In an interval she heard sobbing: to drown the sound she played on,
her face affording proof that she was not insensible to the misery of the
situation. When she looked round at length, Jaffray lay in a posture of
wearied self-forgetfulness, his eyes red, his thin lips parted. She
approached him.

'Better now?'

He nodded carelessly.

'It's no business of mine, you know, about you and your wife,' she went
on, in a pleasant voice. 'I was engaged to come here, and I had nothing
to do with your private affairs. So far as I can see, Mrs Jaffray has behaved
just as I should have done myself in her position; she has let you have your
own way, and made no trouble. But it isn't every woman, you know – at
least, not of that kind. When you think it over, you'll see that it's best to
call her back again. Don't be afraid. She'll come, if you give her the
chance.'

'It won't matter,' croaked Jaffray, with a sinister look.

'Just as you like about that,' was the calm rejoinder. 'But, in that case,
I had better have my cheque before I leave.'

Jaffray stared at her, and could not determine whether she exhibited her true self, or affected a cold brutality in order to have done with
him.

'And you don't care a curse,' he faltered, 'whether I live or not.'

'Of course I do. I think you are a very interesting man, and I should
be really sorry to hear of your death. But I have my own life to live, you
see. I've been quite honest with you all along; it's your fault if you wouldn't

take me at my word. I don't mind telling you, in confidence, that I'm going to Bordighera because somebody I know will be there. We all have our troubles; we have to get all we can out of life, before it's too late; to tell you the truth. I don't think you have done badly; I really don't think you ought to grumble. But I know it's no use preaching. We all know what we want better than any one else can. I'm sorry for you, and I can't say any more.'

The man hid his face.

'Sing me something.'

She returned to the piano, and sang noble things, verse and music that touch the heart, that raise the soul: then she sat in silence, waiting.

'If you are going,' sounded Jaffray's voice, 'go at once.'

'Certainly.'

'The cheque will be posted you to-night.'

'Thank you.'

Scarce a moment's hesitation, and she walked straight from the room without a word, without a look.

When the mistress of the house returned that evening, Jaffray had gone to bed. She inquired concerning him, but did not see him. The next day she remained at home, and sat with her husband for a little, now and then; speaking for the most part of her own work in London, and giving no sign of discontent. In the night that followed he was again very ill. Mrs Jaffray sat up and gave directions to those in attendance, but did not herself minister to the sick man.

Next morning, early, he sent a message to her: he wished her to stay at home, and she replied that she would do so.

'Doesn't your musician come to-day?' Mrs Jaffray asked, when she had been sitting beside him for a few minutes after breakfast.

'She isn't coming again; she has gone away – out of England.'

'Would you like me to read to you?'

'No, thank you. Later on, if you will.'

She did so, and the old habit was resumed. Mrs Jaffrey ceased her journeys to London, saying, when he questioned her, that the weather was too bad. To Jaffray, searching her features and listening intently to her voice, the strange thing seemed to be that she was quite placid; he could detect no resentment, and no trace of tender emotion. When he suffered, she spoke kindly, nothing more. Their eyes never met, and they conversed no more intimately than patient and nurse.

After long gazing at her, one day, he said abruptly: 'Why do you trouble about me?'

'Because I pity you.'

'Only that?'

'Only that.'

He turned his face away, and, when Mrs Jaffray resumed her reading, kept silence. Her voice had not its wonted steadiness, and once or twice she paused, as if with a catching of the breath.

'I am like a stranger to you?' he said, when the book was closed.

'No; simply someone I have known a long time.'

'I don't see that. You are not so to me.'

'It would be truer to say that I feel only a certain duty to you. How should I feel more? I was never able – never in my life – to have affection for anyone who had none for me. I don't reproach you, of course. Love exists, or it does not. If you turn from me to some one else, I can say nothing. You were quite frank with me – the only thing I have a right to ask.'

'And' – asked Jaffray, quietly – 'you have no wifely feeling for me?'

'No wifely love for you. How can you expect it?'

'Because I have so much love for you, I suppose,' he answered, with bent head.

Mrs Jaffray smiled, but said nothing more, and went away before he again spoke. Later, he sent for her. As she drew near, he held out a hand; she gave her own.

'Am I to go out of the world without love?'

'Whose love do you want?' she asked gently.

'I want the love of the only woman who will, or can, give it. There's only one. I got it into my head that someone else – but I've learnt my lesson. There's no one else, if *you* can't love me. It comes to that, now I'm lying here.'

'You mean,' she said, softly and forbearingly, 'that, such as it is, you must make the best of it. But I could have told you that before; I could have told you that, my husband.'

'I shan't burden you long,' he said, simply and sincerely. 'There will be a new beginning of life for you.'

'Dear,' Mrs Jaffray answered, through her tears, 'the new beginning would have the old end. Ten years of marriage teach one all one has to learn about that side of life. I know you, and I know myself. The one is just as much and *just* as little to blame as the other. Only the foolish embitter life with reproaches.'

He held out both his hands to her, and Mrs Jaffray took them softly in her own, and smiled as she had smiled before.

ARTHUR CONAN DOYLE

The Brazilian Cat

It is hard luck on a young fellow to have expensive tastes, great expectations, aristocratic connections, but no actual money in his pocket, and no
profession by which he may earn any. The fact was that my father, a good,
sanguine, easy-going man, had such confidence in the wealth and benevolence of his bachelor elder brother, Lord Southerton, that he took it for
granted that I, his only son, would never be called upon to earn a living
for myself. He imagined that if there were not a vacancy for me on the
great Southerton Estates, at least there would be found some post in that
diplomatic service which still remains the special preserve of our privil-
eged classes. He died too early to realize how false his calculations had
been. Neither my uncle nor the State took the slightest notice of me, or
showed any interest in my career. An occasional brace of pheasants, or
basket of hares, was all that ever reached me to remind me that I was heir
to Otwell House and one of the richest estates in the country. In the
meantime, I found myself a bachelor and man about town, living in a
suite of apartments in Grosvenor Mansions, with no occupation save that
of pigeon-shooting and polo-playing at Hurlingham. Month by month I
realized that it was more and more difficult to get the brokers to renew
my bills, or to cash any further post-obits upon an unentailed property.
Ruin lay right across my path, and every day I saw it clearer, nearer, and
more absolutely unavoidable.

What made me feel my own poverty the more was that, apart from the
great wealth of Lord Southerton, all my other relations were fairly well-
to-do. The nearest of these was Everard King, my father's nephew and
my own first cousin, who had spent an adventurous life in Brazil, and had
now returned to this country to settle down on his fortune. We never

knew how he made his money, but he appeared to have plenty of it, for he bought the estate of Greylands, near Clipton-on-the-Marsh, in Suffolk. For the first year of his residence in England he took no more notice of me than my miserly uncle; but at last one summer morning, to my very great relief and joy, I received a letter asking me to come down that very day and spend a short visit at Greylands Court. I was expecting a rather long visit to Bankruptcy Court at the time, and this interruption seemed almost providential. If I could only get on terms with this unknown relative of mine, I might pull through yet. For the family credit he could not let me go entirely to the wall. I ordered my valet to pack my valise, and I set off the same evening for Clipton-on-the-Marsh.

After changing at Ipswich, a little local train deposited me at a small, deserted station lying amidst a rolling grassy country, with a sluggish and winding river curving in and out amidst the valleys, between high, silted banks, which showed that we were within reach of the tide. No carriage was awaiting me (I found afterwards that my telegram had been delayed), so I hired a dog-cart at the local inn. The driver, an excellent fellow, was full of my relative's praises, and I learned from him that Mr Everard King was already a name to conjure with in that part of the country. He had entertained the school-children, he had thrown his grounds open to visitors, he had subscribed to charities – in short, his benevolence had been so universal that my driver could only account for it on the supposition that he had Parliamentary ambitions.

My attention was drawn away from my driver's panegyric by the appearance of a very beautiful bird which settled on a telegraph-post beside the road. At first I thought that it was a jay, but it was larger, with a brighter plumage. The driver accounted for its presence at once by saying that it belonged to the very man whom we were about to visit. It seems that the acclimatization of foreign creatures was one of his hobbies, and that he had brought with him from Brazil a number of birds and beasts which he was endeavouring to rear in England. When once we had passed the gates of Greylands Park we had ample evidence of this taste of his. Some small spotted deer, a curious wild pig known, I believe, as a peccary, a gorgeously feathered oriole, some sort of armadillo, and a singular lumbering intoed beast like a very fat badger, were among the creatures which I observed as we drove along the winding avenue.

Mr Everard King, my unknown cousin, was standing in person upon the steps of his house, for he had seen us in the distance, and guessed that it was I. His appearance was very homely and benevolent, short and stout, forty-five years old perhaps, with a round, good-humoured face, burned brown with the tropical sun, and shot with a thousand wrinkles. He wore white linen clothes, in true planter style, with a cigar between his lips, and a large Panama hat upon the back of his head. It was such a figure as one associates with a verandahed bungalow, and it looked curiously out of place in front of this broad, stone English mansion, with its solid wings and its Palladio pillars before the doorway.

'My dear!' he cried, glancing over his shoulder; 'my dear, here is our guest! Welcome, welcome to Greylands! I am delighted to make your acquaintance, Cousin Marshall, and I take it as a great compliment that you should honour this sleepy little country place with your presence.'

Nothing could be more hearty than his manner, and he set me at my ease in an instant. But it needed all his cordiality to atone for the frigidity and even rudeness of his wife, a tall, haggard woman, who came forward at his summons. She was, I believe, of Brazilian extraction, though she spoke excellent English, and I excused her manners on the score of her ignorance of our customs. She did not attempt to conceal, however, either then or afterwards, that I was no very welcome visitor at Greylands Court. Her actual words were, as a rule, courteous, but she was the possessor of a pair of particularly expressive dark eyes, and I read in them very clearly from the first that she heartily wished me back in London once more.

However, my debts were too pressing and my designs upon my wealthy relative were too vital for me to allow them to be upset by the ill-temper of his wife, so I disregarded her coldness and reciprocated the extreme cordiality of his welcome. No pains had been spared by him to make me comfortable. My room was a charming one. He implored me to tell him anything which could add to my happiness. It was on the tip of my tongue to inform him that a blank cheque would materially help towards that end, but I felt that it might be premature in the present state of our acquaintance. The dinner was excellent, and as we sat together afterwards over his Havanas and coffee, which latter he told me was specially prepared upon his own plantation, it seemed to me that all my driver's eulogies were justified, and that I had never met a more large-hearted and hospitable man.

But, in spite of his cheery good nature, he was a man with a strong will and a fiery temper of his own. Of this I had an example upon the following morning. The curious aversion which Mrs Everard King had conceived towards me was so strong, that her manner at breakfast was almost offensive. But her meaning became unmistakable when her husband had quitted the room.

'The best train in the day is at twelve fifteen,' said she.

'But I was not thinking of going to-day,' I answered, frankly – perhaps even defiantly, for I was determined not to be driven out by this woman.

'Oh, if it rests with you – ' said she, and stopped, with a most insolent expression in her eyes.

'I am sure,' I answered 'that Mr Everard King would tell me if I were outstaying my welcome.'

'What's this? What's this?' said a voice, and there he was in the room. He had overheard my last words, and a glance at our faces had told him the rest. In an instant his chubby, cheery face set into an expression of absolute ferocity.

'Might I trouble you to walk outside, Marshall,' said he. (I may mention that my own name is Marshall King.)

He closed the door behind me, and then, for an instant, I heard him talking in a low voice of concentrated passion to his wife. This gross breach of hospitality had evidently hit upon his tenderest point. I am no eavesdropper, so I walked out on to the lawn. Presently I heard a hurried step behind me, and there was the lady, her face pale with excitement, and her eyes red with tears.

'My husband has asked me to apologize to you, Mr Marshall King,' said she, standing with downcast eyes before me.

'Please do not say another word, Mrs King.'

Her dark eyes suddenly blazed out at me.

'You fool!' she hissed, with frantic vehemence, and turning on her heel swept back to the house.

The insult was so outrageous, so insufferable, that I could only stand staring after her in bewilderment. I was still there when my host joined me. He was his cheery, chubby self once more.

'I hope that my wife has apologized for her foolish remarks,' said he.

'Oh, yes – yes, certainly!'

He put his hand through my arm and walked with me up and down the lawn.

'You must not take it seriously,' said he. 'It would grieve me inexpressibly if you curtailed your visit by one hour. The fact is – there is no reason why there should be any concealment between relatives – that my poor dear wife is incredibly jealous. She hates that any one – male or female – should for an instant come between us. Her ideal is a desert island and an eternal *tête-à-tête*. That gives you the clue to her actions, which are, I confess, upon this particular point, not very far removed from mania. Tell me that you will think no more of it.'

'No, no; certainly not.'

'Then light this cigar and come round with me and see my little menagerie.'

The whole afternoon was occupied by this inspection, which included all the birds, beasts, and even reptiles which he had imported. Some were free, some in cages, a few actually in the house. He spoke with enthusiasm of his successes and his failures, his births and his deaths, and he would cry out in his delight, like a schoolboy, when, as we walked, some gaudy bird would flutter up from the grass, or some curious beast slink into the cover. Finally he led me down a corridor which extended from one wing of the house. At the end of this there was a heavy door with a sliding shutter in it, and beside it there projected from the wall an iron handle attached to a wheel and a drum. A line of stout bars extended across the passage.

'I am about to show you the jewel of my collection,' said he. 'There is only one other specimen in Europe, now that the Rotterdam cub is dead. It is a Brazilian cat.'

'But how does that differ from any other cat?'

'You will soon see that,' said he, laughing. 'Will you kindly draw that shutter and look through?'

I did so, and found that I was gazing into a large, empty room, with stone flags, and small, barred windows upon the farther wall.

In the centre of this room, lying in the middle of a golden patch of sunlight, there was stretched a huge creature, as large as a tiger, but as black and sleek as ebony. It was simply a very enormous and very well-kept black cat, and it cuddled up and basked in that yellow pool of light exactly as a cat would do. It was so graceful, so sinewy, and so gently and smoothly diabolical, that I could not take my eyes from the opening.

'Isn't he splendid?' said my host, enthusiastically.

'Glorious! I never saw such a noble creature.'

'Some people call it a black puma, but really it is not a puma at all. That fellow is nearly eleven feet from tail to tip. Four years ago he was a little ball of black fluff, with two yellow eyes staring out of it. He was sold me as a new-born cub up in the wild country at the head-waters of the Rio Negro. They speared his mother to death after she had killed a dozen of them.'

'They are ferocious, then?'

'The most absolutely treacherous and blood-thirsty creatures upon earth. You talk about a Brazilian cat to an up-country Indian, and see him get the jumps. They prefer humans to game. This fellow has never tasted living blood yet, but when he does he will be a terror. At present he won't stand any one but me in his den. Even Baldwin, the groom, dare not go near him. As to me, I am his mother and father in one.'

As he spoke he suddenly, to my astonishment, opened the door and slipped in, closing it instantly behind him. At the sound of his voice the huge, lithe creature rose, yawned, and rubbed its round, black head affectionately against his side, while he patted and fondled it.

'Now, Tommy, into your cage!' said he.

The monstrous cat walked over to one side of the room and coiled itself up under a grating. Everard King came out, and taking the iron handle which I have mentioned, he began to turn it. As he did so the line of bars in the corridor began to pass through a slot in the wall and closed up the front of this grating, so as to make an effective cage. When it was in position he opened the door once more and invited me into the room, which was heavy with the pungent, musty smell peculiar to the great carnivora.

'That's how we work it,' said he. 'We give him the run of the room for exercise, and then at night we put him in his cage. You can let him out by turning the handle from the passage, or you can, as you have seen, coop him up in the same way. No, no, you should not do that!'

I had put my hand between the bars to pat the glossy, heaving flank. He pulled it back, with a serious face.

'I assure you that he is not safe. Don't imagine that because I can take liberties with him any one else can. He is very exclusive in his friends – aren't you, Tommy? Ah, he hears his lunch coming to him! Don't you, boy?'

A step sounded in the stone-flagged passage, and the creature had sprung to his feet, and was pacing up and down the narrow cage, his yellow eyes gleaming, and his scarlet tongue rippling and quivering over the white line of his jagged teeth. A groom entered with a coarse joint upon a tray, and thrust it through the bars to him. He pounced lightly upon it, carried it off to the corner, and there, holding it between his paws, tore and wrenched at it, raising his bloody muzzle every now and then to look at us. It was a malignant and yet fascinating sight.

'You can't wonder that I am fond of him, can you?' said my host, as we left the room, 'especially when you consider that I have had the rearing of him. It was no joke bringing him over from the centre of South America; but here he is safe and sound – and, as I have said, far the most perfect specimen in Europe. The people at the Zoo are dying to have him, but I really can't part with him. Now, I think that I have inflicted my hobby upon you long enough, so we cannot do better than follow Tommy's example, and go to our lunch.'

My South American relative was so engrossed by his grounds and their curious occupants, that I hardly gave him credit at first for having any interests outside them. That he had some, and pressing ones, was soon borne in upon me by the number of telegrams which he received. They arrived at all hours, and were always opened by him with the utmost eagerness and anxiety upon his face. Sometimes I imagined that it must be the turf, and sometimes the Stock Exchange, but certainly he had some very urgent business going forwards which was not transacted upon the Downs of Suffolk. During the six days of my visit he had never fewer than three or four telegrams a day, and sometimes as many as seven or eight.

I had occupied these six days so well, that by the end of them I had succeeded in getting upon the most cordial terms with my cousin. Every night we had sat up late in the billiard-room, he telling me the most extraordinary stories of his adventures in America – stories so desperate and reckless, that I could hardly associate them with the brown little, chubby man before me. In return, I ventured upon some of my own reminiscences of London life, which interested him so much, that he vowed he would come up to Grosvenor Mansions and stay with me. He was anxious to see the faster side of city life, and certainly, though I say it, he could not have chosen a more competent guide. It was not until the last day of my visit that I ventured to approach that which was on my mind. I told him frankly about my pecuniary difficulties and my impending ruin, and I asked his advice – though I hoped for something more solid. He listened attentively, puffing hard at his cigar.

'But surely,' said he, 'you are the heir of our relative, Lord Southerton?'

'I have every reason to believe so, but he would never make me any allowance.'

'No, no, I have heard of his miserly ways. My poor Marshall, your position has been a very hard one. By the way, have you heard any news of Lord Southerton's health lately?'

'He has always been in a critical condition ever since my childhood.'

'Exactly – a creaking hinge, if ever there was one. Your inheritance may be a long way off. Dear me, how awkwardly situated you are!'

'I had some hopes, sir, that you, knowing all the facts, might be inclined to advance –'

'Don't say another word, my dear boy,' he cried, with the utmost cordiality; 'we shall talk it over to-night, and I give you my word that whatever is in my power shall be done.'

I was not sorry that my visit was drawing to a close, for it is unpleasant to feel that there is one person in the house who eagerly desires your departure. Mrs King's sallow face and forbidding eyes had become more and more hateful to me. She was no longer actively rude – her fear of her husband prevented her – but she pushed her insane jealousy to the extent of ignoring me, never addressing me, and in every way making my stay at Greylands as uncomfortable as she could. So offensive was her manner during that last day, that I should certainly have left had it not been for that interview with my host in the evening which would, I hoped, retrieve my broken fortunes.

It was very late when it occurred, for my relative, who had been receiving even more telegrams than usual during the day, went off to his study after dinner, and only emerged when the household had retired to bed. I heard him go round locking the doors, as his custom was of a night, and finally he joined me in the billiard-room. His stout figure was wrapped in a dressing-gown, and he wore a pair of red Turkish slippers without any heels. Settling down into an arm-chair, he brewed himself a glass of grog, in which I could not help noticing that the whisky considerably predominated over the water.

'My word!' said he, 'what a night!'

It was, indeed. The wind was howling and screaming round the house, and the latticed windows rattled and shook as if they were coming in. The glow of the yellow lamps and the flavour of our cigars seemed the brighter and more fragrant for the contrast.

'Now, my boy,' said my host, 'we have the house and the night to ourselves. Let me have an idea of how your affairs stand, and I will see what can be done to set them in order. I wish to hear every detail.'

Thus encouraged, I entered into a long exposition, in which all my tradesmen and creditors, from my landlord to my valet, figured in turn. I had notes in my pocket-book, and I marshalled my facts, and gave, I flatter myself, a very business-like statement of my own unbusiness-like ways and lamentable position. I was depressed, however, to notice that my companion's eyes were vacant and his attention elsewhere. When he did occasionally throw out a remark, it was so entirely perfunctory and pointless, that I was sure he had not in the least followed my remarks. Every now and then he roused himself and put on some show of interest, asking me to repeat or to explain more fully, but it was always to sink once more into the same brown study. At last he rose and threw the end of his cigar into the grate.

'I'll tell you what, my boy,' said he. 'I never had a head for figures, so you will excuse me. You must jot it all down upon paper, and let me have a note of the amount. I'll understand it when I see it in black and white.'

The proposal was encouraging. I promised to do so.

'And now it's time we were in bed. By Jove, there's one o'clock striking in the hall.'

The tinging of the chiming clock broke through the deep roar of the gale. The wind was sweeping past with the rush of a great river.

'I must see my cat before I go to bed,' said my host. 'A high wind excites him. Will you come?'

'Certainly,' said I.

'Then tread softly and don't speak, for every one is asleep.'

We passed quietly down the lamp-lit Persian-rugged hall, and through the door at the farther end. All was dark in the stone corridor, but a stable lantern hung on a hook, and my host took it down and lit it. There was no grating visible in the passage, so I knew that the beast was in its cage.

'Come in!' said my relative, and opened the door.

A deep growling as we entered showed that the storm had really excited the creature. In the flickering light of the lantern, we saw it, a huge black mass, coiled in the corner of its den and throwing a squat, uncouth shadow upon the whitewashed wall. Its tail switched angrily among the straw.

'Poor Tommy is not in the best of tempers,' said Everard King, holding up the lantern and looking in at him. 'What a black devil he looks, doesn't he? I must give him a little supper to put him in a better humour. Would you mind holding the lantern for a moment?'

I took it from his hand and he stepped to the door.

'His larder is just outside here,' said he. 'You will excuse me for an instant, won't you?' He passed out, and the door shut with a sharp metallic click behind him.

That hard crisp sound made my heart stand still. A sudden wave of terror passed over me. A vague perception of some monstrous treachery turned me cold. I sprang to the door, but there was no handle upon the inner side.

'Here!' I cried. 'Let me out!'

'All right! Don't make a row!' said my host from the passage. 'You've got the light all right.'

'Yes, but I don't care about being locked in alone like this.'

'Don't you?' I heard his hearty, chuckling laugh. 'You won't be alone long.'

'Let me out, sir!' I repeated angrily. 'I tell you I don't allow practical jokes of this sort.'

'Practical is the word,' said he, with another hateful chuckle. And then suddenly I heard, amidst the roar of the storm, the creak and whine of the winch handle turning, and the rattle of the grating as it passed through the slot. Great God, he was letting loose the Brazilian cat!

In the light of the lantern I saw the bars sliding slowly before me. Already there was an opening a foot wide at the farther end. With a scream I seized the last bar with my hands and pulled with the strength of a madman. I *was* a madman with rage and horror. For a minute or more I held the thing motionless. I knew that he was straining with all his force upon the handle, and that the leverage was sure to overcome me. I gave inch by inch, my feet sliding along the stones, and all the time I begged and prayed this inhuman monster to save me from this horrible death. I conjured him by his kinship. I reminded him that I was his guest; I begged to know what harm I had ever done him. His only answers were the tugs and jerks upon the handle, each of which, in spite of all my struggles, pulled another bar through the opening. Clinging and clutching, I was dragged across the whole front of the cage, until at last, with aching wrists and lacerated fingers, I gave up the hopeless struggle. The grating clanged back as I released it, and an instant later I heard the shuffle of the Turkish slippers in the passage, and the slam of the distant door. Then everything was silent.

The creature had never moved during this time. He lay still in the corner, and his tail had ceased switching. This apparition of a man adhering to his bars and dragged screaming across him had apparently filled him with amazement. I saw his great eyes staring steadily at me. I had dropped the lantern when I seized the bars, but it still burned upon the floor, and I made a movement to grasp it, with some idea that its light might protect me. But the instant I moved, the beast gave a deep and menacing growl. I stopped and stood still, quivering with fear in every limb. The cat (if one may call so fearful a creature by so homely a name) was not more than ten feet from me. The eyes glimmered like two discs of phosphorus in the darkness. They appalled and yet fascinated me. I could not take my own eyes from them. Nature plays strange tricks with us at such moments of intensity, and those glimmering lights waxed and waned with a steady rise and fall. Sometimes they seemed to be tiny points of extreme brilliancy – little electric sparks in the black obscurity – then they would widen and widen until all that corner of the room was filled with their shifting and sinister light. And then suddenly they went out altogether.

The beast had closed its eyes. I do not know whether there may be any truth in the old idea of the dominance of the human gaze, or whether the huge cat was simply drowsy, but the fact remains that, far from showing any symptom of attacking me, it simply rested its sleek, black head upon its huge forepaws and seemed to sleep. I stood, fearing to move lest I should rouse it into malignant life once more. But at least I was able to think clearly now that the baleful eyes were off me. Here I was shut up for the night with the ferocious beast. My own instincts, to say nothing of the words of the plausible villain who laid this trap for me, warned me that the animal was as savage as its master. How could I stave it off until morning? The door was hopeless, and so were the narrow, barred windows. There was no shelter anywhere in the bare, stone-flagged room. To cry for assistance was absurd. I knew that this den was an outhouse, and that the corridor which connected it with the house was at least a hundred feet long. Besides, with that gale thundering outside, my cries were not likely to be heard. I had only my own courage and my own wits to trust to.

And then, with a fresh wave of horror, my eyes fell upon the lantern. The candle had burned low, and was already beginning to gutter. In ten minutes it would be out. I had only ten minutes then in which to do something, for I felt that if I were once left in the dark with that fearful beast I should be incapable of action. The very thought of it paralyzed me. I cast my despairing eyes round this chamber of death, and they rested upon one spot which seemed to promise I will not say safety, but less immediate and imminent danger than the open floor.

I have said that the cage had a top as well as a front, and this top was left standing when the front was wound through the slot in the wall. It consisted of bars at a few inches' interval, with stout wire netting between, and it rested upon a strong stanchion at each end. It stood now as a great barred canopy over the crouching figure in the corner. The space between this iron shelf and the roof may have been from two to three feet. If I could only get up there, squeezed in between bars and ceiling, I should have only one vulnerable side. I should be safe from below, from behind, and from each side. Only on the open face of it could I be attacked. There, it is true, I had no protection whatever; but, at least, I should be out of the brute's path when he began to pace about his den. He would have to come out of his way to reach me. It was now or never, for if once the light were out it would be impossible. With a gulp in my throat I sprang up, seized the iron edge of the top, and swung myself panting on to it. I writhed in face downwards, and found myself looking straight into the terrible eyes and yawning jaws of the cat. Its fetid breath came up into my face like the steam from some foul pot.

It appeared, however, to be rather curious than angry. With a sleek ripple of its long, black back it rose, stretched itself, and then rearing itself on its hind legs, with one fore paw against the wall, it raised the other, and drew its claws across the wire meshes beneath me. One sharp, white hook tore through my trousers – for I may mention that I was still in evening dress – and dug a furrow in my knee. It was not meant as an attack, but rather as an experiment, for upon my giving a sharp cry of pain he dropped down again, and springing lightly into the room, he began walking swiftly round it, looking up every now and again in my direction. For my part I shuffled backwards until I lay with my back against the wall, screwing myself into the smallest space possible. The farther I got the more difficult it was for him to attack me.

He seemed more excited now that he had begun to move about, and he ran swiftly and noiselessly round and round the den, passing continually underneath the iron couch upon which I lay. It was wonderful to see so great a bulk passing like a shadow, with hardly the softest thudding of velvety pads. The candle was burning low – so low that I could hardly see the creature. And then, with a last flare and splutter it went out altogether. I was alone with the cat in the dark!

It helps one to face a danger when one knows that one has done all that possibly can be done. There is nothing for it then but to quietly await the result. In this case, there was no chance of safety anywhere except the precise spot where I was. I stretched myself out, therefore, and lay silently, almost breathlessly, hoping that the beast might forget my presence if I did nothing to remind him. I reckoned that it must already be two o'clock. At four it would be full dawn. I had not more than two hours to wait for daylight.

Outside, the storm was still raging, and the rain lashed continually against the little windows. Inside, the poisonous and fetid air was overpowering. I could neither hear nor see the cat. I tried to think about other things – but only one had power enough to draw my mind from my terrible position. That was the contemplation of my cousin's villainy, his unparalleled hypocrisy, his malignant hatred of me. Beneath that cheerful face there lurked the spirit of a mediæval assassin. And as I thought of it I saw more clearly how cunningly the thing had been arranged. He had apparently gone to bed with the others. No doubt he had his witnesses to prove it. Then, unknown to them, he had slipped down, had lured me into this den and abandoned me. His story would be so simple. He had left me to finish my cigar in the billiard-room. I had gone down on my own account to have a last look at the cat. I had entered the room without observing that the cage was opened, and I had been caught. How could such a crime be brought home to him? Suspicion, perhaps – but proof, never!

How slowly those dreadful two hours went by! Once I heard a low, rasping sound, which I took to be the creature licking its own fur. Several times those greenish eyes gleamed at me through the darkness, but never in a fixed stare, and my hopes grew stronger that my presence had been forgotten or ignored. At last the least faint glimmer of light came through the windows – I first dimly saw them as two grey squares upon the black wall, then grey turned to white, and I could see my terrible companion once more. And he, alas, could see me!

It was evident to me at once that he was in a much more dangerous and aggressive mood than when I had seen him last. The cold of the morning had irritated him, and he was hungry as well. With a continual growl he paced swiftly up and down the side of the room which was far-thest from my refuge, his whiskers bristling angrily, and his tail switching and lashing. As he turned at the corners his savage eyes always looked upwards at me with a dreadful menace. I knew then that he meant to kill me. Yet I found myself even at that moment admiring the sinuous grace of the devilish thing, its long, undulating, rippling movements, the gloss of its beautiful flanks, the vivid, palpitating scarlet of the glistening tongue which hung from the jet-black muzzle. And all the time that deep, threat-ening growl was rising and rising in an unbroken crescendo. I knew that the crisis was at hand.

It was a miserable hour to meet such a death – so cold, so comfortless, shivering in my light dress clothes upon this gridiron of torment upon which I was stretched. I tried to brace myself to it, to raise my soul above it, and at the same time, with the lucidity which comes to a perfectly desperate man, I cast round for some possible means of escape. One thing was clear to me. If that front of the cage was only back in its position once more, I could find a sure refuge behind it. Could I possibly pull it back? I hardly dared to move for fear of bringing the creature upon me. Slowly, very slowly, I put my hand forward until it grasped the edge of the front, the final bar which protruded through the wall. To my surprise it came quite easily to my jerk. Of course the difficulty of drawing it out arose from the fact that I was clinging to it. I pulled again, and three inches of it came through. It ran apparently on wheels. I pulled again . . . and then the cat sprang!

It was so quick, so sudden, that I never saw it happen. I simply heard the savage snarl, and in an instant afterwards the blazing yellow eyes, the flattened black head with its red tongue and flashing teeth, were within reach of me. The impact of the creature shook the bars upon which I lay, until I thought (as far as I could think of anything at such a moment) that they were coming down. The cat swayed there for an instant, the head and front paws quite close to me, the hind paws clawing to find a grip upon the edge of the grating. I heard the claws rasping as they clung to the wire netting, and the breath of the beast made me sick. But its bound had been miscalculated. It could not retain its position. Slowly, grinning with rage and scratching madly at the bars, it swung backwards and dropped heavily upon the floor. With a growl it instantly faced round to me and crouched for another spring.

I knew that the next few moments would decide my fate. The creature had learned by experience. It would not miscalculate again. I must act promptly, fearlessly, if I were to have a chance for life. In an instant I had formed my plan. Pulling off my dress-coat, I threw it down over the head of the beast. At the same moment I dropped over the edge, seized the end of the front grating, and pulled it frantically out of the wall.

It came more easily than I could have expected. I rushed across the room, bearing it with me; but, as I rushed, the accident of my position put me upon the outer side. Had it been the other way, I might have come off scatheless. As it was, there was a moment's pause as I stopped it and tried to pass in through the opening which I had left. That moment was enough to give time to the creature to toss off the coat with which I had blinded him and to spring upon me. I hurled myself through the gap and pulled the rails to behind me, but he seized my leg before I could entirely withdraw it. One stroke of that huge paw tore off my calf as a shaving of wood curls off before a plane. The next moment, bleeding and fainting, I was lying among the foul straw with a line of friendly bars between me and the creature which ramped so frantically against them.

Too wounded to move, and too faint to be conscious of fear, I could only lie, more dead than alive, and watch it. It pressed its broad, black chest against the bars and angled for me with its crooked paws as I have seen a kitten do before a mouse-trap. It ripped my clothes, but, stretch as it would, it could not quite reach me. I have heard of the curious numbing effect produced by wounds from the great carnivora, and now I was destined to experience it, for I had lost all sense of personality, and was as interested in the cat's failure or success as if it were some game which I was watching. And then gradually my mind drifted away into strange, vague dreams, always with that black face and red tongue coming back into them, and so I lost myself in the nirvana of delirium, the blessed relief of those who are too sorely tried.

Tracing the course of events afterwards, I conclude that I must have been insensible for about two hours. What roused me to consciousness once more was that sharp metallic click which had been the precursor of my terrible experience. It was the shooting back of the spring lock. Then, before my senses were clear enough to entirely apprehend what they saw, I was aware of the round, benevolent face of my cousin peering in through the opened door. What he saw evidently amazed him. There was the cat crouching on the floor. I was stretched upon my back in my shirt-sleeves within the cage, my trousers torn to ribbons and a great pool of blood all round me. I can see his amazed face now, with the morning sunlight upon it. He peered at me, and peered again. Then he closed the door behind him, and advanced to the cage to see if I were really dead.

I cannot undertake to say what happened. I was not in a fit state to witness or to chronicle such events. I can only say that I was suddenly conscious that his face was away from me – that he was looking towards the animal.

'Good old Tommy!' he cried. 'Good old Tommy!'

Then he came near the bars, with his back still towards me.

'Down, you stupid beast!' he roared. 'Down, sir! Don't you know your master?'

Suddenly even in my bemuddled brain a remembrance came of those words of his when he had said that the taste of blood would turn the cat into a fiend. My blood had done it, but he was to pay the price.

'Get away!' he screamed. 'Get away, you devil! Baldwin! Baldwin! Oh, my God!'

And then I heard him fall, and rise, and fall again, with a sound like the ripping of sacking. His screams grew fainter until they were lost in the worrying snarl. And then, after I thought that he was dead, I saw, as in a nightmare, a blinded, tattered, blood-soaked figure running wildly round the room – and that was the last glimpse which I had of him before I fainted once again.

I was many months in my recovery – in fact, I cannot say that I have ever recovered, for to the end of my days I shall carry a stick as a sign of my night with the Brazilian cat. Baldwin, the groom, and the other servants could not tell what had occurred when, drawn by the death cries of their master, they found me behind the bars, and his remains – or what they afterwards discovered to be his remains – in the clutch of the creature which he had reared. They stalled him off with hot irons, and afterwards shot him through the loophole of the door before they could finally extricate me. I was carried to my bedroom, and there, under the roof of my would-be murderer, I remained between life and death for several weeks. They had sent for a surgeon from Clipton and a nurse from London, and in a month I was able to be carried to the station, and so conveyed back once more to Grosvenor Mansions.

I have one remembrance of that illness, which might have been part of the ever-changing panorama conjured up by a delirious brain were it not so definitely fixed in my memory. One night, when the nurse was absent, the door of my chamber opened, and a tall woman in blackest mourning slipped into the room. She came across to me, and as she bent her sallow face I saw by the faint gleam of the night-light that it was the Brazilian woman whom my cousin had married. She stared intently into my face, and her expression was more kindly than I had ever seen it.

'Are you conscious?' she asked.

I feebly nodded – for I was still very weak.

'Well, then, I only wished to say to you that you have yourself to blame. Did I not do all I could for you? From the beginning I tried to drive you from the house. By every means, short of betraying my husband, I tried to save you from him. I knew that he had a reason for bringing you here. I knew that he would never let you get away again. No one knew him as I knew him, who had suffered from him so often. I did not dare to tell you all this. He would have killed me. But I did my best for you. As things have turned out, you have been the best friend that I have ever had. You have set me free, and I fancied that nothing but death would do that. I am sorry if you are hurt, but I cannot reproach myself. I told you that you were a fool – and a fool you have been.' She crept out of the room, the bitter, singular woman, and I was never destined to see her again. With what remained from her husband's property she went back to her native land, and I have heard that she afterwards took the veil at Pernambuco.

It was not until I had been back in London for some time that the doctors pronounced me to be well enough to do business. It was not a very welcome permission to me, for I feared that it would be the signal for an inrush of creditors; but it was Summers, my lawyer, who first took advantage of it.

'I am very glad to see that your lordship is so much better,' said he. 'I have been waiting a long time to offer my congratulations.'

'What do you mean, Summers? This is no time for joking.'

'I mean what I say,' he answered. 'You have been Lord Southerton for the last six weeks, but we feared that it would retard your recovery if you were to learn it.'

Lord Southerton! One of the richest peers in England! I could not believe my ears. And then suddenly I thought of the time which had elapsed, and how it coincided with my injuries.

'Then Lord Southerton must have died about the same time that I was hurt?'

'His death occurred upon that very day.' Summers looked hard at me as I spoke, and I am convinced – for he was a very shrewd fellow – that he had guessed the true state of the case. He paused for a moment as if awaiting a confidence from me, but I could not see what was to be gained by exposing such a family scandal.

'Yes, a very curious coincidence,' he continued, with the same knowing look. 'Of course, you are aware that your cousin Everard King was the next heir to the estates. Now, if it had been you instead of him who had been torn to pieces by this tiger, or whatever it was, then of course he would have been Lord Southerton at the present moment.'

'No doubt,' said I.

'And he took such an interest in it,' said Summers. 'I happen to know that the late Lord Southerton's valet was in his pay, and that he used to have telegrams from him every few hours to tell him how he was getting on. That would be about the time when you were down there. Was it not strange that he should wish to be so well informed, since he knew that he was not the direct heir?'

'Very strange,' said I. 'And now, Summers, if you will bring me my bills and a new cheque-book, we will begin to get things into order.'

E. W. HORNUNG

Gentlemen and Players

Old Raffles may or may not have been an exceptional criminal, but as a cricketer I dare swear he was unique. Himself a dangerous bat, a brilliant field, and perhaps the very finest slow bowler of his decade, he took incredibly little interest in the game at large. He never went up to Lord's without his cricket-bag, or showed the slightest interest in the result of a match in which he was not himself engaged. Nor was this mere hateful egotism on his part. He professed to have lost all enthusiasm for the game, and to keep it up only from the very lowest motives.

'Cricket,' said Raffles, 'like everything else, is good enough sport until you discover a better. As a source of excitement it isn't in it with other things you wot of, Bunny, and the involuntary comparison becomes a bore. What's the satisfaction of taking a man's wicket when you want his spoons? Still, if you can bowl a bit your low cunning won't get rusty, and always looking for the weak spot's just the kind of mental exercise one wants. Yes, perhaps there's some affinity between the two things after all. But I'd chuck up cricket to-morrow, Bunny, if it wasn't for the glorious protection it affords a person of my proclivities.'

'How so?' said I. 'It brings you before the public, I should have thought, far more than is either safe or wise.'

'My dear Bunny, that's exactly where you make a mistake. To follow crime with reasonable impunity you simply must have a parallel ostensible career – the more public the better. The principle is obvious. Mr Peace, of pious memory, disarmed suspicion by acquiring a local reputation for playing the fiddle and taming animals, and it's my profound conviction that Jack the Ripper was a really eminent public man, whose speeches were very likely reported alongside his atrocities. Fill the bill in some prominent part, and you'll never be suspected of doubling it with another of equal prominence. That's why I want you to cultivate journalism, my boy, and sign all you can. And it's the one and only reason why I don't burn my bats for firewood.'

Nevertheless, when he did play there was no keener performer on the field, nor one more anxious to do well for his side. I remember how he went to the nets, before the first match of the season, with his pocket full of sovereigns, which he put on the stumps instead of bails. It was a sight to see the professionals bowling like demons for the hard cash, for whenever a stump was hit a pound was tossed to the bowler and another balanced in its stead, while one man took £3 with a ball that spread-eagled the wicket. Raffles' practice cost him either eight or nine sovereigns; but he had absolutely first-class bowling all the time and he made fifty-seven runs next day.

It became my pleasure to accompany him to all his matches, to watch every ball he bowled, or played, or fielded, and to sit chatting with him in the pavilion when he was doing none of these three things. You might have seen us there, side by side, during the greater part of the Gentlemen's first innings against the Players (who had lost the toss) on the second Monday in July. We were to be seen, but not heard, for Raffles had failed to score, and was uncommonly cross for a player who cared so little for the game. Merely taciturn with me, he was positively rude to more than one member who wanted to know how it had happened, or who ventured to commiserate him on his luck; there he sat, with a straw hat tilted over his nose and a cigarette stuck between lips that curled disagreeably at every advance. I was, therefore, much surprised when a young fellow of the exquisite type came and squeezed himself in between us and met with a perfectly civil reception despite the liberty. I did not know the boy by sight, nor did Raffles introduce us; but their conversation proclaimed at once a slightness of acquaintanceship and a licence on the lad's part which combined to puzzle me. Mystification reached its height when Raffles was informed that the other's father was anxious to meet him, and he instantly consented to gratify that whim.

'He's in the Ladies' Enclosure. Will you come round now?'

'With pleasure,' says Raffles. 'Keep a place for me, Bunny.'

And they were gone.

'Young Crowley,' said some voice farther back. 'Last year's Harrow Eleven.'

'I remember him. Worst man in the team.'

'Keen cricketer, however. Stopped till he was twenty to get his colours. Governor made him. Keen breed. Oh, pretty, sir! Very pretty!'

The game was boring me. I only came to see old Raffles perform. Soon I was looking wistfully for his return, and at length I saw him beckoning me from the palings to the right.

'Want to introduce you to old Amersteth,' he whispered, when I joined him. 'They've a cricket week next month, when this boy Crowley comes of age, and we've both got to go down and play.'

'Both!' I echoed. 'But I'm no cricketer!'

'Shut up,' says Raffles. 'Leave that to me. I've been lying for all I'm worth,' he added sepulchrally, as we reached the bottom of the steps. 'I trust to you not to give the show away.'

There was the gleam in his eye that I knew well enough elsewhere, but was unprepared for in those healthy, sane surroundings; and it was with very definite misgivings and surmises that I followed the Zingari blazer through the vast flower-bed of hats that bloomed beneath the ladies' awning.

Lord Amersteth was a fine-looking man with a short moustache and a double chin. He received me with much dry courtesy, through which, however, it was not difficult to read a less flattering tale. I was accepted as the inevitable appendage of the invaluable Raffles, with whom I felt deeply incensed as I made my bow.

'I have been bold enough,' said Lord Amersteth, 'to ask one of the Gentlemen of England to come down and play some rustic cricket for us next month. He is kind enough to say that he would have liked nothing better, but for this little fishing expedition of yours, Mr – , Mr – ,' and Lord Amersteth succeeded in remembering my name.

It was, of course, the first I had ever heard of that fishing expedition, but I made haste to say that it could easily, and should certainly, be put off. Raffles gleamed approval through his eyelashes. Lord Amersteth bowed and shrugged.

'You're very good, I'm sure,' said he. 'But I understand you're a cricketer yourself?'

'He was one at school,' said Raffles, with infamous readiness.

'Not a real cricketer,' I was stammering meanwhile.

'In the eleven?' said Lord Amersteth.

'I'm afraid not,' said I.

'But only just out of it,' declared Raffles, to my horror.

'Well, well, we can't all play for the Gentlemen,' said Lord Amersteth slyly. 'My son Crowley only just scraped into the eleven at Harrow, and he's going to play. I may even come in myself at a pinch; so you won't be the only duffer, if you are one, and I shall be very glad if you will come down and help us too. You shall flog a stream before breakfast and after dinner, if you like.'

'I should be very proud,' I was beginning, as the mere prelude to reso-lute excuses; but the eye of Raffles opened wide upon me; and I hesitated weakly, to be duly lost.

'Then that's settled,' said Lord Amersteth, with the slightest suspicion of grimness. 'It's to be a little week, you know, when my son comes of age. We play the Free Foresters, the Dorsetshire Gentlemen, and probably some local lot as well. But Mr Raffles will tell you all about it, and Crow-ley shall write. Another wicket! By Jove, they're all out! Then I rely on you both.' And, with a little nod, Lord Amersteth rose and sidled to the gangway.

Raffles rose also, but I caught the sleeve of his blazer.

'What are you thinking of?' I whispered savagely, 'I was nowhere near the eleven. I'm no sort of cricketer. I shall have to get out of this!'

'Not you,' he whispered back. 'You needn't play, but come you must. If you wait for me after half-past six, I'll tell you why.'

But I could guess the reason; and I am ashamed to say that it revolted me much less than did the notion of making a public fool of myself on a cricket-field. My gorge rose at this as it no longer rose at crime, and it was in no tranquil humour that I strolled about the ground while Raffles disappeared in the pavilion. Nor was my annoyance lessened by a little meeting I witnessed between young Crowley and his father, who shrugged as he stopped and stooped to convey some information which made the young man look a little blank. It may have been pure self-consciousness on my part, but I could have sworn that the trouble was their inability to secure the great Raffles without his insignificant friend.

Then the bell rang, and I climbed to the top of the pavilion to watch Raffles bowl. No subtleties are lost up there; and if ever a bowler was full of them, it was A. J. Raffles on this day, as, indeed, all the cricket world remembers. One had not to be a cricketer oneself to appreciate his perfect command of pitch and break, his beautifully easy action, which never varied with the varying pace, his great ball on the leg-stump – his dropping head-ball – in a word, the infinite ingenuity of that versatile attack. It was no mere exhibition of athletic prowess, it was an intellectual treat, and one with a special significance in my eyes. I saw the 'affinity between the two things,' saw it in that afternoon's tireless warfare against the flower of professional cricket. It was not that Raffles took many wickets for few runs; he was too fine a bowler to mind being hit; and time was short, and the wicket good. What I admired, and what I remember, was the combination of resource and cunning, of patience and precision, of head-work and handiwork, which made every over an artistic whole. It was all so characteristic of that other Raffles whom I alone knew!

'I felt like bowling this afternoon,' he told me later – in the cab. 'With a pitch to help me, I'd have done something big; as it is, three for forty-one, out of the four that fell, isn't so bad for a slow bowler on a plumb wicket against those fellows. But I felt venomous! Nothing riles me more than being asked about for my cricket as though I were a pro. myself.'

'Then why on earth go?'

'To punish them, and – because we shall be jolly hard up, Bunny, before the season's over!'

'Ah!' said I. 'I thought it was that.'

'Of course it was! It seems they're going to have the very devil of a week of it – balls – dinner-parties – swagger house-party – general junketings – and obviously a houseful of diamonds as well. Diamonds galore! As a general rule nothing would induce me to abuse my position as a guest. I've never done it, Bunny. But in this case we're engaged like the waiters and the band, and by heaven we'll take our toll! Let's have a quiet dinner somewhere and talk it over.'

'It seems rather a vulgar sort of theft,' I could not help saying; and to this, my single protest, Raffles instantly assented.

'It is a vulgar sort,' said he; 'but I can't help that. We're getting vulgarly hard up again, and there's an end on't. Besides, these people deserve it and can afford it. And don't you run away with the idea that all will be plain sailing; nothing will be easier than getting some stuff, and nothing harder than avoiding all suspicion, as, of course, we must. We may come away with no more than a good working plan of the premises. Who knows? In any case there's weeks of thinking in it for you and me.'

But with those weeks I will not weary you further than by remarking that the 'thinking' was done entirely by Raffles, who did not always trouble to communicate his thoughts to me. His reticence, however, was no longer an irritant. I began to accept it as a necessary convention of these little enterprises. And, after our last adventure of this kind, more especially after its *dénouement*, my trust in Raffles was much too solid to be shaken by a want of trust in me, which I still believe to have been more the instinct of the criminal than the judgment of the man.

It was on Monday, August 10, that we were due at Milchester Abbey, Dorset; and the beginning of the month found us cruising about that very county, with fly-rods actually in our hands. The idea was that we should acquire at once a local reputation as decent fishermen, and some knowledge of the country-side, with a view to further and more deliberate operations in the event of an unprofitable week. There was another idea which Raffles kept to himself until he had got me down there. Then one day he produced a cricket-ball in a meadow we were crossing, and threw me catches for an hour together. More hours he spent in bowling to me on the nearest green; and, if I was never a cricketer, at least I came nearer to being one, by the end of that week, than ever before or since.

Incident began early on the Monday. We had sallied forth from a desolate little junction within quite a few miles of Milchester, had been caught in a shower, had run for shelter to a wayside inn. A florid, over-dressed man was drinking in the parlour, and I could have sworn it was at the sight of him that Raffles recoiled on the threshold, and afterwards insisted on returning to the station through the rain. He assured me, however, that the odour of stale ale had almost knocked him down. And I had to make what I could of his speculative, downcast eyes and knitted brows.

Milchester Abbey is a grey, quadrangular pile, deep-set in rich woody country, and twinkling with triple rows of quaint windows, every one of which seemed alight as we drove up just in time to dress for dinner. The carriage had whirled us under I know not how many triumphal arches in process of construction, and past the tents and flag-poles of a juicy-looking cricket field, on which Raffles undertook to bowl up to his reputation. But the chief signs of festival were within, where we found an enormous house party assembled, including more persons of pomp, majesty, and dominion than I had ever encountered in one room before. I confess I felt overpowered. Our errand and my own pretences combined to rob me of an address upon which I had sometimes plumed myself; and I have a grim recollection of my nervous relief when dinner was at last announced. I little knew what an ordeal it was to prove.

I had taken in a much less formidable young lady than might have fallen to my lot. Indeed I began by blessing my good fortune in this respect. Miss Melhuish was merely the rector's daughter, and she had only been asked to make an even number. She informed me of both facts before the soup reached us, and her subsequent conversation was characterized by the same engaging candour. It exposed what was little short of a mania for imparting information. I had simply to listen, to nod, and to be thankful. When I confessed to knowing very few of those present, even by sight, my entertaining companion proceeded to tell me who everybody was, beginning on my left and working conscientiously round to her right. This lasted quite a long time, and really interested me; but a great deal that followed did not; and, obviously to recapture my unworthy attention, Miss Melhuish suddenly asked me, in a sensational whisper, whether I could keep a secret.

I said I thought I might, whereupon another question followed, in still lower and more thrilling accents:

'Are you afraid of burglars?'

Burglars! I was roused at last. The word stabbed me. I repeated it in horrified query.

'So I've found something to interest you at last!' said Miss Melhuish, in naive triumph. 'Yes – burglars! But don't speak so loud. It's supposed to be kept a great secret. I really oughtn't to tell you at all!'

'But what is there to tell?' I whispered with satisfactory impatience.

'You promise not to speak of it?'

'Of course!'

'Well, then, there are burglars in the neighbourhood.'

'Have they committed any robberies?'

'Not yet.'

'Then how do you know?'

'They've been seen. In the district. Two well-known London thieves!'

Two! I looked at Raffles. I had done so often during the evening, envying him his high spirits, his iron nerve, his buoyant wit, his perfect ease and his self-possession. But now I pitied him; through all my own terror and consternation, I pitied him as he sat eating and drinking, and laughing, and talking, without a cloud of fear or of embarrassment on his handsome, taking, dare-devil face. I caught up my champagne and emptied the glass.

'Who has seen them?' I then asked calmly.

'A detective. They were traced down from town a few days ago. They are believed to have designs on the Abbey!'

'But why aren't they run in?'

'Exactly what I asked papa on the way here this evening; he says there is no warrant out against the men at present, and all that can be done is to watch their movements.'

'Oh! so they are being watched?'

'Yes, by a detective who is down here on purpose. And I heard Lord Amersteth tell papa that they had been seen this afternoon at Warbeck Junction.'

The very place where Raffles and I had been caught in the rain! Our stampede from the inn was now explained; on the other hand, I was no longer to be taken by surprise by anything that my companion might have to tell me; and I succeeded in looking her in the face with a smile.

'This is really quite exciting, Miss Melhuish,' said I. 'May I ask how you come to know so much about it?'

'It's papa,' was the confidential reply. 'Lord Amersteth consulted him, and he consulted me. But for goodness' sake don't let it get about! I can't think what tempted me to tell you!'

'You may trust me, Miss Melhuish. But – aren't you frightened?'

Miss Melhuish giggled.

'Not a bit! They won't come to the rectory. There's nothing for them there. But look round the table; look at the diamonds. Look at old Lady Melrose's necklace alone!'

The Dowager-Marchioness of Melrose was one of the few persons whom it had been unnecessary to point out to me. She sat on Lord Amersteth's right flourishing her ear-trumpet, and drinking champagne with her usual notorious freedom, as dissipated and kindly a dame as the world has ever seen. It was a necklace of diamonds and sapphires that rose and fell about her ample neck.

'They say it's worth five thousand pounds at least,' continued my companion. 'Lady Margaret told me so this morning (that's Lady Margaret next your Mr Raffles, you know); and the old dear will wear them every night. Think what a haul they would be! No; we don't feel in immediate danger at the rectory.'

When the ladies rose, Miss Melhuish bound me to fresh vows of secrecy; and left me, I should think, with some remorse for her indiscretion, but more satisfaction at the importance which it had undoubtedly given her in my eyes. The opinion may smack of vanity, though, in reality, the very springs of conversation reside in that same human, universal itch to thrill the auditor. The peculiarity of Miss Melhuish was that she must be thrilling at all costs. And thrilling she had surely been.

I spare you my feelings of the next two hours. I tried hard to get a word with Raffles, but again and again I failed. In the dining-room he and Crowley lit their cigarettes with the same match, and had their heads together all the time. In the drawing-room I had the mortification of hearing him talk interminable nonsense into the trumpet-ear of Lady Melrose, whom he knew in town. Lastly, in the billiard-room, they had a great and lengthy pool, while I sat aloof and chafed more than ever in the company of a very serious Scotsman, who had arrived since dinner, and who would talk of nothing but the recent improvements in instantaneous photography. He had not come to play in the matches (he told me), but to obtain for Lord Amersteth such a series of cricket photographs as had never been taken before; whether as an amateur or a professional photographer I was unable to determine. I remember, however, seeking distraction in little bursts of resolute attention to the conversation of this bore. And so at last the long ordeal ended; glasses were emptied, men said good night, and I followed Raffles to his room.

'It's all up!' I gasped, as he turned up the gas and I shut the door. 'We're being watched. We've been followed down from town. There's a detective here on the spot!'

'How do you know?' asked Raffles, turning upon me quite sharply, but without the least dismay. And I told him how I knew.

'Of course,' I added, 'it was the fellow we saw in the inn this afternoon.'

'The detective?' said Raffles. 'Do you mean to say you don't know a detective when you see one, Bunny?'

'If that wasn't the fellow, which is?'

Raffles shook his head.

'To think that you've been talking to him for the last hour in the billiard-room and couldn't spot what he was!'

'The Scotch photographer – '

I paused aghast.

'Scotch he is,' said Raffles, 'and photographer he may be. He is also Inspector Mackenzie of Scotland Yard – the very man I sent the message to that night last April. And you couldn't spot who he was in a whole hour! Oh, Bunny, Bunny, you were never built for crime!'

'But,' said I, 'if that was Mackenzie, who was the fellow you bolted from at Warbeck?'

'The man he's watching.'

'But he's watching us!'

Raffles looked at me with a pitying eye, and shook his head again before handing me his open cigarette-case.

'I don't know whether smoking's forbidden in one's bedroom, but you'd better take one of these and stand tight, Bunny, because I'm going to say something offensive.'

I helped myself with a laugh.

'Say what you like, my dear fellow, if it really isn't you and I that Mackenzie's after.'

'Well, then, it isn't, and it couldn't be, and nobody but a born Bunny would suppose for a moment that it was! Do you seriously think he would sit there and knowingly watch his man playing pool under his nose? Well, he might; he's a cool hand, Mackenzie; but I'm not cool enough to win a pool under such conditions. At least, I don't think I am; it would be interesting to see. The situation wasn't free from strain as it was, though I knew he wasn't thinking of us. Crowley told me all about it after dinner, you see, and then I'd seen one of the men for myself this afternoon. You thought it was a detective who made me turn tail at that inn. I really don't know why I didn't tell you at the time, but it was just the opposite. That loud, red-faced brute is one of the cleverest thieves in London, and I once had a drink with him and our mutual fence. I was an East-ender from tongue to toe at the moment, but you will understand that I don't run unnecessary risks of recognition by a brute like that.'

'He's not alone, I hear.'

'By no means; there's at least one other man with him; and it's suggested that there may be an accomplice here in the house.'

'Did Lord Crowley tell you so?'

'Crowley and the champagne between them. In confidence, of course, just as your girl told you; but even in confidence he never let on about Mackenzie. He told me there was a detective in the background, but that was all. Putting him up as a guest is evidently their big secret, to be kept from the other guests because it might offend them, but more particularly from the servants whom he's here to watch. That's my reading of the situation, Bunny, and you will agree with me that it's infinitely more interesting than we could have imagined it would prove.'

'But infinitely more difficult for us,' said I, with a sigh of pusillanimous relief. 'Our hands are tied for this week, at all events.'

'Not necessarily, my dear Bunny, though I admit that the chances are against us. Yet I'm not so sure of that either. There are all sorts of possibilities in these three-cornered combinations. Set A to watch B, and he won't have an eye left for C. That's the obvious theory, but then Mackenzie's a very big A. I should be sorry to have any boodle about me with that man in the house. Yet it would be great to nip in between A and B and score off them both at once! It would be worth a risk, Bunny, to do that; it would be worth risking something merely to take on old hands like B and his men at their own old game! Eh, Bunny? That would be something like a match. Gentlemen and Players at single wicket, by Jove!'

His eyes were brighter than I had known them for many a day. They shone with the perverted enthusiasm which was roused in him only by the contemplation of some new audacity. He kicked off his shoes and began pacing his room with noiseless rapidity; not since the night of the Old Bohemian dinner to Reuben Rosenthall had Raffles exhibited such excitement in my presence; and I was not sorry at the moment to be reminded of the fiasco to which that banquet had been the prelude.

'My dear A.J.,' said I in his very own tone, 'you're far too fond of the uphill game; you will eventually fall a victim to the sporting spirit and nothing else. Take a lesson from our last escape, and fly lower as you value our skins. Study the house as much as you like, but do – not – go and shove your head into Mackenzie's mouth!'

My wealth of metaphor brought him to a standstill, with his cigarette between his fingers and a grin beneath his shining eyes.

'You're quite right, Bunny. I won't. I really won't. Yet – you saw old Lady Melrose's necklace? I've been wanting it for years! But I'm not going to play the fool, honour bright, I'm not; yet – by Jove! – to get to windward of the professors and Mackenzie too! It would be a great game, Bunny, it would be a great game!'

'Well, you mustn't play it this week.'

'No, no, I won't. But I wonder how the professors think of going to work? That's what one wants to know. I wonder if they've really got an accomplice in the house? How I wish I knew their game! But it's all right, Bunny; don't you be jealous; it shall be as you wish.'

And with that assurance I went off to my own room and so to bed with an incredibly light heart. I had still enough of the honest man in me to welcome the postponement of our actual felonies, to dread their performance, and to deplore their necessity: which is merely another way of stating the too patent fact that I was an incomparably weaker man than Raffles, while every whit as wicked. I had, however, one rather strong point. I possessed the gift of dismissing unpleasant considerations, not intimately connected with the passing moment, entirely from my mind. Through the exercise of this faculty I had lately been living my frivolous life in town with as much ignoble enjoyment as I had derived from it the year before; and similarly, here at Milchester, in the long-dreaded cricket week, I had after all a quite excellent time.

It is true that there were other factors in this pleasing disappointment. In the first place, *mirabile dictu*, there were one or two even greater duffers than I on the Abbey cricket field. Indeed, quite early in the week, when it was of most value to me, I gained considerable kudos for a lucky catch; a ball, of which I had merely heard the hum, stuck fast in my hand, which

Lord Amersteth himself grasped in public congratulation. This happy accident was not to be undone even by me, and, as nothing succeeds like success, and the constant encouragement of the one great cricketer on the field was in itself an immense stimulus, I actually made a run or two in my very next innings. Miss Melhuish said pretty things to me that night at the great ball in honour of Viscount Crowley's majority; she also told me that was the night on which the robbers would assuredly make their raid, and was full of arch tremors when we sat out in the garden, though the entire premises were illuminated all night long. Meanwhile the quiet Scotsman took countless photographs by day, which he developed by night in a dark room admirably situated in the servants' part of the house; and it is my firm belief that only two of his fellow guests knew Mr Clephane of Dundee for Inspector Mackenzie of Scotland Yard.

The week was to end with a trumpery match on the Saturday, which two or three of us intended abandoning early in order to return to town that night. The match, however, was never played. In the small hours of the Saturday morning a tragedy took place at Milchester Abbey.

Let me tell of the thing as I saw and heard it. My room opened upon the central gallery, and was not even on the same floor as that on which Raffles – and I think all the other men – were quartered. I had been put, in fact, into the dressing-room of one of the grand suites, and my two near neighbours were old Lady Melrose and my host and hostess. Now, by the Friday evening the actual festivities were at an end, and, for the first time that week, I must have been sound asleep since midnight, when all at once I found myself sitting up breathless. A heavy thud had come against my door, and now I heard hard breathing and the dull stamp of muffled feet.

'I've got ye,' muttered a voice. 'It's no use struggling.'

It was the Scotch detective, and a new fear turned me cold. There was no reply, but the hard breathing grew harder still, and the muffled feet beat the floor to a quicker measure. In sudden panic I sprang out of bed and flung open my door. A light burnt low on the landing, and by it I could see Mackenzie swaying and staggering in a silent tussle with some powerful adversary.

'Hold this man!' he cried, as I appeared. 'Hold the rascal!'

But I stood like a fool until the pair of them backed into me, when, with a deep breath, I flung myself on the fellow, whose face I had seen at last. He was one of the footmen who waited at table; and no sooner had I pinned him than the detective loosed his hold.

'Hang on to him,' he cried. 'There's more of 'em below.'

And he went leaping down the stairs, as other doors opened and Lord Amersteth and his son appeared simultaneously in their pyjamas. At that my man ceased struggling; but I was still holding him when Crowley turned up the gas.

'What the devil's all this?' asked Lord Amersteth, blinking. 'Who was that ran downstairs?'

'MacClephane!' said I hastily.

'Aha!' said he, turning to the footman. 'So you're the scoundrel, are you? Well done! Well done! Where was he caught?'

I had no idea.

'Here's Lady Melrose's door open,' said Crowley. 'Lady Melrose! Lady Melrose!'

'You forget she's deaf,' said Lord Amersteth. 'Ah! that'll be her maid.'

An inner door had opened; next instant there was a little shriek, and a white figure gesticulated on the threshold.

'*Où donc est l'écrin de Madame la Marquise? La fenêtre est ouverte, Il a disparu!*'

'Window open and jewel-case gone, by Jove!' exclaimed Lord Amersteth. '*Mais comment est Madame la Marquise? Est-elle bien?*'

'*Oui*, milor. *Elle dort.*'

'Sleeps through it all,' said my lord. 'She's the only one, then!'

'What made Mackenzie – Clephane – bolt?' young Crowley asked me.

'Said there were more of them below.'

'Why the devil couldn't you tell us so before?' he cried, and went leaping downstairs in his turn.

He was followed by nearly all the cricketers, who now burst upon the scene in a body, only to desert it for the chase. Raffles was one of them, and I would gladly have been another, had not the footman chosen this moment to hurl me from him, and to make a dash in the direction from which they had come. Lord Amersteth had him in an instant; but the fellow fought desperately, and it took the two of us to drag him downstairs amid a terrified chorus from half-open doors. Eventually we handed him over to two other footmen who appeared with their night-shirts tucked into their trousers, and my host was good enough to compliment me as he led the way outside.

'I thought I heard a shot,' he added. 'Didn't you?'

'I thought I heard three.'

And out we dashed into the darkness.

I remember how the gravel pricked my feet, how the wet grass numbed them as we made for the sound of voices on an outlying lawn. So dark was the night that we were in the cricketers' midst before we saw the shimmer of their pyjamas, and then Lord Amersteth almost trod on Mackenzie as he lay prostrate in the dew.

'Who's this?' he cried. 'What on earth's happened?'

'It's Clephane,' said a man who knelt over him. 'He's got a bullet in him somewhere.'

'Is he alive?'

'Barely.'

'Good God! Where's Crowley?'

'Here I am,' called a breathless voice. 'It's no good, you fellows. There's nothing to show which way they've gone. Here's Raffles; he's chucked it, too.' And they ran up panting.

'Well, we've got one of them, at all events,' muttered Lord Amersteth. 'The next thing is to get this poor fellow indoors. Take his shoulders somebody. Now his middle. Join hands under him. Altogether now; that's the way. Poor fellow! Poor fellow! His name isn't Clephane at all. He's a Scotland Yard detective, down here for these very villains!'

Raffles was the first to express surprise; but he had also been the first to raise the wounded man. Nor had any of them a stronger or more tender hand in the slow procession to the house. In a little we had the senseless man stretched on a sofa in the library. And there, with ice on his wound and brandy in his throat, his eyes opened and his lips moved.

Lord Amersteth bent down to catch the words.

'Yes, yes,' said he; 'we've got one of them safe and sound. The brute you collared upstairs.' Lord Amersteth bent lower. 'By Jove! Lowered the jewel-case out of the window, did he? And they've got clean away with it! Well, well! I only hope we'll be able to pull this good fellow through. He's off again.'

An hour passed; the sun was rising.

It found a dozen young fellows on the settees in the billiard-room, drinking whisky and soda-water in their overcoats and pyjamas, and still talking excitedly in one breath. A time-table was being passed from hand to hand: the doctor was still in the library. At last the door opened and Lord Amersteth put in his head.

'It isn't hopeless,' said he, 'but it's bad enough. There'll be no cricket to-day.'

Another hour, and most of us were on our way to catch the early train; between us we filled a compartment almost to suffocation. And still we talked all together of the night's event; and still I was a little hero in my way, for having kept my hold of the one ruffian who had been taken; and my gratification was subtle and intense. Raffles watched me under lowered lids. Not a word had we had together; not a word did we have until we had left the others at Paddington, and were skimming through the streets in a hansom with noiseless tyres and a tinkling bell.

'Well, Bunny,' said Raffles, 'so the professors have it, eh?'

'Yes,' said I. 'And I'm jolly glad!'

'That poor Mackenzie has a bullet in his chest?'

'That you and I have been on the decent side for once.'

He shrugged his shoulders.

'You're hopeless, Bunny, quite hopeless! I take it you wouldn't have refused your share if the boodle had fallen to us? Yet you positively enjoy coming off second best – for the second time running! I confess, however, that the professors' methods were full of interest to me. I, for one, have probably gained as much in experience of I have lost in other things. That lowering the jewel-case out of the window was a very simple and effective expedient; two of them had been waiting below for it for hours.'

'How do you know?' I asked.

'I saw them from my own window, which was just above the dear old lady's. I was fretting for that necklace in particular, when I went up to turn in for our last night – and I happened to look out of the window. In point of fact, I wanted to see whether the one below was open, and whether there was the slightest chance of working the oracle with my sheet for a rope. Of course I took the precaution of turning my light off first, and it was a lucky thing I did. I saw the pros. right down below, and they never saw me. I saw a little tiny luminous disc just for an instant, and then again for an instant a few minutes later. Of course I knew what it was, for I have my own watch-dial daubed with luminous paint; it makes a lantern of sorts when you can get no better. But these fellows were not using theirs as a lantern. They were under the old lady's window. They were watching the time. The whole thing was arranged with their accomplice inside. Set a thief to catch a thief: in a minute I had guessed what the whole thing proved to be.'

'And you did nothing!' I exclaimed.

'On the contrary, I went downstairs and straight into Lady Melrose's room –'

'You did?'

'Without a moment's hesitation. To save her jewels. And I was prepared to yell as much into her ear-trumpet for all the house to hear. But the dear lady is too deaf and too fond of her dinner to wake easily.'

'Well?'

'She didn't stir.'

'And yet you allowed the professors, as you call them, to take her jewels, case and all!'

'All but this,' said Raffles, thrusting his fist into my lap. 'I would have shown it you before, but really, old fellow, your face all day has been worth a fortune to the firm!'

And he opened his fist, to shut it next instant on the bunch of diamonds and of sapphires that I had last seen encircling the neck of Lady Melrose.

SOMERVILLE AND ROSS

Trinket's Colt

It was petty sessions day in Skebawn, a cold, grey day of February. A case of trespass had dragged its burden of cross summonses and cross swearing far into the afternoon, and when I left the bench my head was singing from the bellowings of the attorneys, and the smell of their clients was heavy upon my palate.

The streets still testified to the fact that it was market day, and I evaded with difficulty the sinuous course of carts full of soddenly screwed people, and steered an equally devious one for myself among the groups anchored round the doors of the public-houses. Skebawn possesses, among its legion of public-houses, one establishment which timorously, and almost imperceptibly, proffers tea to the thirsty. I turned in there, as was my custom on court days, and found the little dingy den, known as the Ladies' Coffee-Room, in the occupancy of my friend Mr Florence McCarthy Knox, who was drinking strong tea and eating buns with serious simplicity. It was a first and quite unexpected glimpse of that domesticity that has now become a marked feature in his character.

'You're the very man I wanted to see,' I said as I sat down beside him at the oilcloth-covered table; 'a man I know in England who is not much of a judge of character has asked me to buy him a four-year-old down here, and as I should rather be stuck by a friend than a dealer, I wish you'd take over the job.'

Flurry poured himself out another cup of tea, and dropped three lumps of sugar into it in silence.

Finally he said, 'There isn't a four-year-old in this country that I'd be seen dead with at a pig fair.'

This was discouraging, from the premier authority on horse-flesh in the district.

'But it isn't six weeks since you told me you had the finest filly in your stables that was ever foaled in the County Cork,' I protested; 'what's wrong with her?'

'Oh, is it that filly?' said Mr Knox with a lenient smile; 'she's gone these three weeks from me. I swapped her and £6 for a three-year-old Iron-monger colt, and after that I swapped the colt and £19 for that Bandon horse I rode last week at your place, and after that again I sold the Bandon horse for £75 to old Welply, and I had to give him back a couple of sovereigns luck-money. You see I did pretty well with the filly after all.'

'Yes, yes – oh rather,' I assented, as one dizzily accepts the propositions of a bimetallist; 'and you don't know of anything else – ?'

The room in which we were seated was closely screened from the shop by a door with a muslin-curtained window in it; several of the panes were broken, and at this juncture two voices that had for some time carried on a discussion forced themselves upon our attention.

'Begging your pardon for contradicting you, ma'am,' said the voice of Mrs McDonald, proprietress of the tea-shop, and a leading light in Ske-bawn Dissenting circles, shrilly tremulous with indignation, 'if the servants I recommend you won't stop with you, it's no fault of mine. If respectable young girls are set picking grass out of your gravel, in place of their proper work, certainly they will give warning!'

The voice that replied struck me as being a notable one, well-bred and imperious.

'When I take a barefooted slut out of a cabin, I don't expect her to dictate to me what her duties are!'

Flurry jerked up his chin in a noiseless laugh. 'It's my grandmother!' he whispered. 'I bet you Mrs McDonald don't get much change out of her!'

'If I set her to clean the pig-sty I expect her to obey me,' continued the voice in accents that would have made me clean forty pig-sties had she desired me to do so.

'Very well, ma'am,' retorted Mrs McDonald, 'if that's the way you treat your servants, you needn't come here again looking for them. I consider your conduct is neither that of a lady nor a Christian!'

'Don't you, indeed?' replied Flurry's grandmother. 'Well, your opinion doesn't greatly distress me, for, to tell you the truth, I don't think you're much of a judge.'

'Didn't I tell you she'd score?' murmured Flurry, who was by this time applying his eye to a hole in the muslin curtain. 'She's off,' he went on, returning to his tea. 'She's a great character! She's eighty-three if she's a day, and she's as sound on her legs as a three-year-old! Did you see that old shandrydan of hers in the street a while ago, and a fellow on the box with a red beard on him like Robinson Crusoe? That old mare that was on the near side – Trinket her name is – is mighty near clean bred. I can tell you her foals are worth a bit of money.'

I had heard of old Mrs Knox of Aussolas; indeed, I had seldom dined out in the neighbourhood without hearing some new story of her and her remarkable ménage, but it had not yet been my privilege to meet her.

'Well, now,' went on Flurry in his slow voice, 'I'll tell you a thing that's just come into my head. My grandmother promised me a foal of Trinket's the day I was one-and-twenty, and that's five years ago, and deuce a one I've got from her yet. You were at Aussolas? No, you were not. Well, I tell you the place there is like a circus with horses. She has a couple of score of them running wild in the woods, like deer.'

'Oh, come,' I said, 'I'm a bit of a liar myself – '

'Well, she has a dozen of them anyhow, rattling good colts too, some of them, but they might as well be donkeys for all the good they are to me or any one. It's not once in three years she sells one, and there she has them walking after her for bits of sugar, like a lot of dirty lapdogs,' ended Flurry with disgust.

'Well, what's your plan? Do you want me to make her a bid for one of the lapdogs?'

'I was thinking,' replied Flurry, with great deliberation, 'that my birthday's this week, and maybe I could work a four-year-old colt of Trinket's she has out of her in honour of the occasion.'

'And sell your grandmother's birthday present to me?'

'Just that, I suppose,' answered Flurry with a slow wink.

A few days afterwards a letter from Mr Knox informed me that he had 'squared the old lady, and it would be all right about the colt.' He further told me that Mrs Knox had been good enough to offer me, with him, a day's snipe shooting on the celebrated Aussolas bogs, and he proposed to drive me there the following Monday, if convenient. Most people found it convenient to shoot the Aussolas snipe bog when they got the chance. Eight o'clock on the following Monday morning saw Flurry, myself, and a groom packed into a dogcart, with portmanteaus, gun-cases, and two rampant red setters.

It was a long drive, twelve miles at least, and a very cold one. We passed through long tracts of pasture country, fraught, for Flurry, with memories of runs, which were recorded for me, fence by fence, in every one of which the biggest dog-fox in the country had gone to ground, with not two feet – measured accurately on the handle of the whip – between him and the leading hound; through bogs that imperceptibly melted into lakes, and finally down and down into a valley, where the fir-trees of Aussolas clustered darkly round a glittering lake, and all but hid the grey roofs and pointed gables of Aussolas Castle.

'There's a nice stretch of a demesne for you,' remarked Flurry, pointing downwards with the whip, 'and one little old woman holding it all in the heel of her fist. Well able to hold it she is, too, and always was, and she'll live twenty years yet, if it's only to spite the whole lot of us, and when all's said and done goodness knows how she'll leave it!'

'It strikes me you were lucky to keep her up to her promise about the colt,' I said.

Flurry administered a composing kick to the ceaseless strivings of the red setters under the seat.

'I used to be rather a pet with her,' he said, after a pause; 'but mind you, I haven't got him yet, and if she gets any notion I want to sell him I'll never get him, so say nothing about the business to her.'

The tall gates of Aussolas shrieked on their hinges as they admitted us, and shut with a clang behind us, in the faces of an old mare and a couple of young horses, who, foiled in their break for the excitements of the outer world, turned and galloped defiantly on either side of us. Flurry's admirable cob hammered on, regardless of all things save his duty.

'He's the only one I have that I'd trust myself here with,' said his master, flicking him approvingly with the whip; 'there are plenty of people afraid to come here at all, and when my grandmother goes out driving she has a boy on the box with a basket full of stones to peg at them. Talk of the dickens, here she is herself!'

A short, upright old woman was approaching, preceded by a white woolly dog with sore eyes and a bark like a tin trumpet; we both got out of the trap and advanced to meet the lady of the manor.

I may summarize her attire by saying that she looked as if she had robbed a scarecrow; her face was small and incongruously refined, the skinny hand that she extended to me had the grubby tan that bespoke the professional gardener, and was decorated with a magnificent diamond ring. On her head was a massive purple velvet bonnet.

'I am very glad to meet you, Major Yeates,' she said with an old-fashioned precision of utterance; 'your grandfather was a dancing partner of mine in old days at the Castle, when he was a handsome young aide-de-camp there, and I was – you may judge for yourself what I was.'

She ended with a startling little hoot of laughter, and I was aware that she quite realized the world's opinion of her, and was indifferent to it.

Our way to the bogs took us across Mrs Knox's home farm, and through a large field in which several young horses were grazing.

'There now, that's my fellow,' said Flurry, pointing to a fine-looking colt, 'the chestnut with the white diamond on his forehead. He'll run into three figures before he's done, but we'll not tell that to the old lady!'

The famous Aussolas bogs were as full of snipe as usual, and a good deal fuller of water than any bogs I had ever shot before. I was on my day, and Flurry was not, and as he is ordinarily an infinitely better snipe shot than I, I felt at peace with the world and all men as we walked back, wet through, at five o'clock.

The sunset had waned, and a big white moon was making the eastern tower of Aussolas look like a thing in a fairy tale or a play when we arrived at the hall door. An individual, whom I recognized as the Robinson Crusoe coachman, admitted us to a hall, the like of which one does not often see. The walls were panelled with dark oak up to the gallery that ran round three sides of it, the balusters of the wide staircase were heavily carved, and blackened portraits of Flurry's ancestors on the spindle side stared sourly down on their descendant as he tramped upstairs with the bog mould on his hobnailed boots.

We had just changed into dry clothes when Robinson Crusoe shoved his red beard round the corner of the door, with the information that the mistress said we were to stay for dinner. My heart sank. It was then barely half-past five. I said something about having no evening clothes and having to get home early.

'Sure the dinner'll be in another half-hour,' said Robinson Crusoe, joining hospitably in the conversation; 'and as for evening clothes – God bless ye!'

The door closed behind him.

'Never mind,' said Flurry, 'I dare say you'll be glad enough to eat another dinner by the time you get home.' He laughed. 'Poor Slipper!' he added inconsequently, and only laughed again when I asked for an explanation.

Old Mrs Knox received us in the library, where she was seated by a roaring turf fire, which lit the room a good deal more effectively than the pair of candles that stood beside her in tall silver candlesticks. Ceaseless and implacable growls from under her chair indicated the presence of the woolly dog. She talked with confounding culture of the books that rose all round her to the ceiling; her evening dress was accomplished by means of an additional white shawl, rather dirtier than its congeners; as I took her into dinner she quoted Virgil to me, and in the same breath screeched an objurgation at a being whose matted head rose suddenly into view from behind an ancient Chinese screen, as I have seen the head of a Zulu woman peer over a bush.

Dinner was as incongruous as everything else. Detestable soup in a splendid old silver tureen that was nearly as dark in hue as Robinson Crusoe's thumb; a perfect salmon, perfectly cooked, on a chipped kitchen dish; such cut glass as is not easy to find nowadays; sherry that, as Flurry subsequently remarked, would burn the shell off an egg; and a bottle of port, draped in immemorial cobwebs, wan with age, and probably priceless. Throughout the vicissitudes of the meal Mrs Knox's conversation flowed on undismayed, directed sometimes at me – she had installed me in the position of friend of her youth, and talked to me as if I were my own grandfather – sometimes at Crusoe, with whom she had several heated arguments, and sometimes she would make a statement of remarkable frankness on the subject of her horse-farming affairs to Flurry, who, very much on his best behaviour, agreed with all she said, and risked no original remark. As I listened to them both, I remembered with infinite amusement how he had told me once that 'a pet name she had for him was "Tony Lumpkin", and no one but herself knew what she meant by it.' It seemed strange that she made no allusion to Trinket's colt or to Flurry's birthday, but, mindful of my instructions, I held my peace.

As, at about half-past eight, we drove away in the moonlight, Flurry congratulated me solemnly on my success with his grandmother. He was good enough to tell me that she would marry me to-morrow if I asked her, and he wished I would, even if it was only to see what a nice grandson he'd be for me. A sympathetic giggle behind me told me that Michael, on the back seat, had heard and relished the jest.

We had left the gates of Aussolas about half a mile behind when, at the corner of a by-road, Flurry pulled up. A short squat figure arose from the black shadow of a furze bush and came out into the moonlight, swinging its arms like a cab-man and cursing audibly.

'Oh murdher, oh murdher, Misther Flurry! What kept ye at all? 'Twould perish the crows to be waiting here the way I am these two hours – '

'Ah, shut your mouth, Slipper!' said Flurry, who, to my surprise, had turned back the rug and was taking off his driving coat, 'I couldn't help it. Come on, Yeates, we've got to get out here.'

'What for?' I asked, in not unnatural bewilderment.

'It's all right. I'll tell you as we go along,' replied my companion, who was already turning to follow Slipper up the by-road. 'Take the trap on, Michael, and wait at the River's Cross.' He waited for me to come up with him, and then put his hand on my arm. 'You see, Major, this is the way it is. My grandmother's given me that colt right enough, but if I waited for her to send him over to me I'd never see a hair of his tail. So I just thought that as we were over here we might as well take him back with us, and maybe you'll give us a help with him; he'll not be altogether too handy for a first go off.'

I was staggered. An infant in arms could scarcely have failed to discern the fishiness of the transaction, and I begged Mr Knox not to put himself to this trouble on my account, as I had no doubt I could find a horse for my friend elsewhere. Mr Knox assured me that it was no trouble at all, quite the contrary, and that, since his grandmother had given him the colt, he saw no reason why he should not take him when he wanted him; also, that if I didn't want him he'd be glad enough to keep him himself; and finally, that I wasn't the chap to go back on a friend, but I was welcome to drive back to Shreelane with Michael this minute if I liked.

Of course I yielded in the end. I told Flurry I should lose my job over the business, and he said I could then marry his grandmother, and the discussion was abruptly closed by the necessity of following Slipper over a locked five-barred gate.

Our pioneer took us over about half a mile of country, knocking down stone gaps where practicable and scrambling over tall banks in the deceptive moonlight. We found ourselves at length in a field with a shed in one corner of it; in a dim group of farm buildings a little way off a light was shining.

'Wait here,' said Flurry to me in a whisper; 'the less noise the better. It's an open shed, and we'll just slip in and coax him out.'

Slipper unwound from his waist a halter, and my colleagues glided like spectres into the shadow of the shed, leaving me to meditate on my duties as Resident Magistrate, and on the questions that would be asked in the House by our local member when Slipper had given away the adventure in his cups.

In less than a minute three shadows emerged from the shed, where two had gone in. They had got the colt.

'He came out as quiet as a calf when he winded the sugar,' said Flurry; 'it was well for me I filled my pockets from grandmamma's sugar basin.'

He and Slipper had a rope from each side of the colt's head; they took him quickly across a field towards a gate. The colt stepped daintily between them over the moonlit grass; he snorted occasionally, but appeared on the whole amenable.

The trouble began later, and was due, as trouble often is, to the beguilements of a short cut. Against the maturer judgment of Slipper, Flurry insisted on following a route that he assured us he knew as well as his own pocket, and the consequence was that in about five minutes I found myself standing on top of a bank hanging on to a rope, on the other end of which the colt dangled and danced, while Flurry, with the other rope, lay prone in the ditch, and Slipper administered to the bewildered colt's hindquarters such chastisement as could be ventured on.

I have no space to narrate in detail the atrocious difficulties and disasters of the short cut. How the colt set to work to buck, and went away across a field, dragging the faithful Slipper, literally *ventre-à-terre,* after him, while I picked myself in ignominy out of a briar patch, and Flurry cursed himself black in the face. How we were attacked by ferocious cur dogs, and I lost my eyeglass; and how, as we neared the River's Cross, Flurry espied the police patrol on the road, and we all hid behind a rick of turf, while I realized in fullness what an exceptional ass I was, to have been beguiled into an enterprise that involved hiding with Slipper from the Royal Irish Constabulary.

Let it suffice to say that Trinket's infernal offspring was finally handed over on the high-road to Michael and Slipper, and Flurry drove me home in a state of mental and physical overthrow.

I saw nothing of my friend Mr Knox for the next couple of days, by the end of which time I had worked up a high polish on my misgivings, and had determined to tell him that under no circumstances would I have anything to say to his grandmother's birthday present. It was like my usual luck that, instead of writing a note to this effect, I thought it would be good for my liver to walk across the hills to Tory Cottage and tell Flurry so in person.

It was a bright, blustery morning, after a muggy day. The feeling of spring was in the air, the daffodils were already in bud, and crocuses showed purple in the grass on either side of the avenue. It was only a couple of miles to Tory Cottage by the way across the hills; I walked fast, and it was barely twelve o'clock when I saw its pink walls and clumps of evergreens below me. As I looked down at it the chiming of Flurry's hounds in the kennels came to me on the wind; I stood still to listen, and could almost have sworn that I was hearing again the clash of Magdalen bells, hard at work on May morning.

The path that I was following led downwards through a larch plantation to Flurry's back gate. Hot wafts from some hideous caldron at the other side of a wall apprised me of the vicinity of the kennels and their cuisine, and the fir-trees round were hung with gruesome and unknown joints. I thanked Heaven that I was not a master of hounds, and passed on as quickly as might be to the hall door.

I rang two or three times without response; then the door opened a couple of inches and was instantly slammed in my face. I heard the hurried paddling of bare feet on oilcloth, and a voice, 'Hurry, Bridgie, hurry! There's quality at the door!'

Bridgie, holding a dirty cap on with one hand, presently arrived and informed me that she believed Mr Knox was out about the place. She seemed perturbed, and she cast scared glances down the drive while speaking to me.

I knew enough of Flurry's habits to shape a tolerably direct course for his whereabouts. He was, as I had expected, in the training paddock, a field behind the stable-yard, in which he had put up practice jumps for his horses. It was a good-sized field with clumps of furze in it, and Flurry was standing near one of these with his hands in his pockets, singularly unoccupied. I supposed that he was prospecting for a place to put up another jump. He did not see me coming, and turned with a start as I spoke to him. There was a queer expression of mingled guilt and what I can only describe as divilment in his grey eyes as he greeted me. In my dealings with Flurry Knox, I have since formed the habit of sitting tight, in a general way, when I see that expression.

'Well, who's coming next, I wonder!' he said, as he shook hands with me; 'it's not ten minutes since I had two of your d——d peelers here searching the whole place for my grandmother's colt!'

'What!' I exclaimed, feeling cold all down my back; 'do you mean the police have got hold of it?'

'They haven't got hold of the colt anyway,' said Flurry, looking sideways at me from under the peak of his cap, with the glint of the sun in his eye. 'I got word in time before they came.'

'What do you mean?' I demanded; 'where is he? For Heaven's sake don't tell me you've sent the brute over to my place!'

'It's a good job for you I didn't,' replied Flurry, 'as the police are on their way to Shreelane this minute to consult you about it. *You!*' He gave utterance to one of his short diabolical fits of laughter. 'He's where they'll not find him, anyhow. Ho! ho! It's the funniest hand I ever played!'

'Oh yes, it's devilish funny, I've no doubt,' I retorted, beginning to lose my temper, as is the manner of many people when they are frightened; 'but I give you fair warning that if Mrs Knox asks me any questions about it, I shall tell her the whole story.'

'All right,' responded Flurry; 'and when you do, don't forget to tell her how you flogged the colt out on to the road over her own bounds ditch.'

'Very well,' I said hotly, 'I may as well go home and send in my papers. They'll break me over this – '

'Ah, hold on, Major,' said Flurry soothingly, 'it'll be all right. No one knows anything. It's only on spec the old lady sent the bobbies here. If you'll keep quiet it'll all blow over.'

'I don't care,' I said, struggling hopelessly in the toils; 'if I meet your grandmother, and she asks me about it, I shall tell her all I know.'

'Please God you'll not meet her! After all, it's not once in a blue moon that she – ' began Flurry. Even as he said the words his face changed. 'Holy fly!' he ejaculated, 'isn't that her dog coming into the field? Look at her bonnet over the wall ! Hide, hide for your life!' He caught me by the shoulder and shoved me down among the furze bushes before I realized what had happened.

'Get in there! I'll talk to her.'

I may as well confess that at the mere sight of Mrs Knox's purple bonnet my heart had turned to water. In that moment I knew what it would be like to tell her how I, having eaten her salmon, and capped her quotations, and drunk her best port, had gone forth and helped to steal her horse. I abandoned my dignity, my sense of honour; I took the furze prickles to my breast and wallowed in them.

Mrs Knox had advanced with vengeful speed; already she was in high altercation with Flurry at no great distance from where I lay; varying sounds of battle reached me, and I gathered that Flurry was not – to put it mildly – shrinking from that economy of truth that the situation required.

'Is it that curby, long-backed brute? You promised him to me long ago, but I wouldn't be bothered with him!'

The old lady uttered a laugh of shrill derision. 'Is it likely I'd promise you my best colt? And still more, is it likely that you'd refuse him if I did?'

'Very well, ma'am.' Flurry's voice was admirably indignant. 'Then I suppose I'm a liar and a thief.'

'I'd be more obliged to you for the information if I hadn't known it before,' responded his grandmother with lightning speed; 'if you swore to me on a stack of Bibles you knew nothing about my colt I wouldn't believe you! I shall go straight to Major Yeates and ask his advice. I believe *him* to be a gentleman, in spite of the company he keeps!'

I writhed deeper into the furze bushes, and thereby discovered a sandy rabbit run, along which I crawled, with my cap well over my eyes, and the furze needles stabbing me through my stockings. The ground shelved a little, promising profounder concealment, but the bushes were very thick, and I laid hold of the bare stem of one to help my progress. It lifted out of the ground in my hand, revealing a freshly-cut stump. Something snorted, not a yard away; I glared through the opening, and was confronted by the long, horrified face of Mrs Knox's colt, mysteriously on a level with my own.

Even without the white diamond on his forehead I should have divined the truth; but how in the name of wonder had Flurry persuaded him to couch like a woodcock in the heart of a furze brake? For a full minute I lay as still as death for fear of frightening him, while the voices of Flurry and his grandmother raged on alarmingly close to me. The colt snorted, and blew long breaths through his wide nostrils, but he did not move. I crawled an inch or two nearer, and after a few seconds of cautious peering I grasped the position. They had buried him.

A small sandpit among the furze had been utilized as a grave; they had filled him in up to his withers with sand, and a few furze bushes, artistically disposed round the pit, had done the rest. As the depth of Flurry's guile was revealed, laughter came upon me like a flood; I gurgled and shook apoplectically, and the colt gazed at me with serious surprise, until a sudden outburst of barking close to my elbow administered a fresh shock to my tottering nerves.

Mrs Knox's woolly dog had tracked me into the furze, and was now baying the colt and me with mingled terror and indignation. I addressed him in a whisper, with perfidious endearments, advancing a crafty hand towards him the while, made a snatch for the back of his neck, missed it badly, and got him by the ragged fleece of his hind-quarters as he tried to flee. If I had flayed him alive he could hardly have uttered a more deafening series of yells, but, like a fool, instead of letting him go, I dragged him towards me, and tried to stifle the noise by holding his muzzle. The tussle lasted engrossingly for a few seconds, and then the climax of the nightmare arrived.

Mrs Knox's voice, close behind me, said, 'Let go my dog this instant, sir ! Who are you – '

Her voice faded away, and I knew that she also had seen the colt's head.

I positively felt sorry for her. At her age there was no knowing what effect the shock might have on her. I scrambled to my feet and confronted her.

'Major Yeates!' she said. There was a deathly pause. 'Will you kindly tell me,' said Mrs Knox slowly, 'am I in Bedlam, or are you? And *what is that?*'

She pointed to the colt, and that unfortunate animal, recognizing the voice of his mistress, uttered a hoarse and lamentable whinny. Mrs Knox felt around her for support, found only furze prickles, gazed speechlessly at me, and then, to her eternal honour, fell into wild cackles of laughter.

So, I may say, did Flurry and I. I embarked on my explanation and broke down; Flurry followed suit and broke down too. Overwhelming laughter held us all three, disintegrating our very souls. Mrs Knox pulled herself together first.

'I acquit you, Major Yeates, I acquit you, though appearances are against you. It's clear enough to me you've fallen among thieves.' She stopped and glowered at Flurry. Her purple bonnet was over one eye. 'I'll thank you, sir,' she said, 'to dig out that horse before I leave this place. And when you've dug him out you may keep him. I'll be no receiver of stolen goods!'

She broke off and shook her fist at him. 'Upon my conscience, Tony, I'd give a guinea to have thought of it myself!'

CHARLOTTE MEW

Mark Stafford's Wife

I

I had promised her mother, blindly, as one makes such promises, to 'look after' Kate, but never found myself quite fitted for the task.

To say that, at the outset, there were moments when she seemed to hang between two worlds, is to make her out less brightly human than she was, but now and then she gave a hint of unreality, or rather of intangibility, which set me wondering how she was equipped to meet those problems which present themselves to most young women of remarkable attraction and substantial fortune, in the course of time.

If she had been, as she was said to be, a perfect copy of my beautiful dead friend, that would have turned the key on all perplexities, but as it was, the likeness ended with her face. The rare tranquillity which had reflected faithfully her mother's temperament, with Kate served merely to screen off an unsuspected fire. One knew it was there; one couldn't know what it was burning or might burn, that reticent little flame, so hidden that it was common for a certain coldness and inanimation to be noted as her chief distinction or defect.

She made the most of her reputation, she lived up to it, partly, no doubt, believed in it; at any rate she liked us all to take this view. It was her pose, though no one ever posed less consciously, to despise the stuff of dreams; yet I believe she walked sometimes clad wholly in that gossamer; the air of gay indifference, almost of insensibility, which she perversely wore, while it imposed on casual spectators, remained for me an exquisite mask, a thin protection possibly, but unreliable as unrealities invariably are. If anyone had ventured to remind her how excessively romantic the real

Katharine Relton was, she would have given him the lie with fine effect – refuted such a calumny as stoutly to herself as to her accuser's face.

No one can smile more readily than she, poor child, would once have smiled at this presentment of what she was pleased to call her 'simple self.'

'You know, dearest duenna,' she would say, 'you take amazing pains to make a puzzle of me. I can see you turning the inoffensive picture upside down to find poor Napoleon standing by his tomb. He isn't there!'

But it was just this sense of some intention in the picture missed, that made her difficult, even dangerous, to touch.

Her splendid health seemed a sufficient spell against the fashionable curse of nerves. I no more dreaded them for Kate, than I dreaded kleptomania. She was beautifully sound; but in her very soundness there was the suggestive quality of flawless glass, a frailness, a transparency, even a hardness of the finer sort. She would never, under a strain, I fancied, slowly and pitifully fail, but simply break. At her mother's death, one of the cruellest endings to a gentle life, though they had lived entirely in and for each other, she went through those indescribable days with something like a smile, a bright and, as I thought, unnatural sanity; until, going one evening with some message to her room, I learnt how terribly for Kate the night undid the day. From that moment I feared really nothing for her but the test of her own extraordinary self-control.

Afterwards, at once, she wished to travel, not under my wing I plainly understood, but with someone more remote from immediate memories, who hadn't cared and didn't know.

With more reluctance than I showed, I let her go, nominally in charge of a lively American widow, who was not, as she put it, 'one of those terribly concrete creatures who can't see that a tree will make a table,' and who proposed to develop her companion on the newest lines with 'rollicking success.' I was not alarmed, and submitted to their long silences and a certain freedom in their choice of people and of places as part of the adventure. After nine months' absence, Kate returned – avowedly 'penitent and improved.' She no longer evaded, she declared, the guardianship of angels, and to put herself in the way of it, agreed to come and live under my roof, at my suggestion; childless and solitary woman that I was, she seemed to throw back the shutters of the long-closed house, letting in patches of the bluest sky, freshening it with a rush of youthful air, and opening my doors to all sorts of charming people, for whom she displayed so admirable an impartiality, that before I had well begun to take the measure of their assiduity or to buckle on my shining armour for their benefit, behold! under my heedless eye, she had become engaged to Charlie Darch.

They had foreseen, these two young people, they protested with confident effrontery, that I was capable of producing some sober, gifted and impossibly eligible person, and in view of such a blunder, to spare me and the shadowy fourth our disillusionment, had settled it themselves.

Prepared perhaps for eventful surprises, I had meanwhile been negligently trusting in a kindly guiding star; and that it was now shining over a young man of no particular brilliance or distinction, did not disquiet me.

Charlie Darch was a surprise but by no means a disaster. For my ideal he was too young, and at first I was inclined to look on him as a nice enough, but rather plain, unvarnished fact. On a nearer view, however, there was a pleasing side to his honest unpretentiousness, his lack of the modern intellectual veneer.

He was so modestly aware that he wasn't, as he phrased it, 'showy,' and his recognition that Kate, in 'putting up' with him, was missing chances infinitely showier was touchingly sincere.

'I'm not, and of course I know it,' he said in his literal way, 'your notion, or anywhere near it – of what Kate might have done. She might have done, it's easily understood, immensely better, except,' he added simply, 'that I can't believe any man could think so much of her, or be more bent on giving her, every way, his best. I daresay she seems to you, like a delicate bit of china put into rather clumsy hands, not at all, in fact, into the hands of a connoisseur; but you've no idea how tremendously careful and considerate and all that, I shall be. You'll see.'

This was, I think, the only profession he ever made to me. A thing once said and done, with him was apt to be dismissed as needing no retrospect nor reinforcement. He was, as became his youth, a little final, and I had imagined that for me at any rate he would probably stand still. But he advanced. Once on the road to your goodwill, he made his way; you liked him better, found it easier to believe in, to accept him; and not difficult, as time went on, to discover that he shone, though unobtrusively, in human dealings. He got rough but remarkably good impressions; he was apt to catch them instinctively from the sunny side and to be, too, very prompt and positive in his judgment and decisions and appreciations.

Only in one instance he was noticeably vague. He had met Mark Stafford at my house; we had presented our celebrity, not perhaps without some flourishes, and Darch's view of him seemed singularly indistinct; he slipped in speaking of him behind borrowed phrases and struck persistently the impersonal note. His mind – if it was clear to him in this particular – remained for us a perfect smudge.

Stafford was then emerging steadily, though 'The Forest and the Market Place' had yet to make its memorable stir. Kate had come across him at Mentone; later he found us out in London and came to frequent our little weekly 'At Homes' with, I was told, a flattering regularity. He made a point of being very nice to Darch. He liked him, he explained, for what he called his bold indifference to subtleties, his breadth of line. 'And incidentally, perhaps,' he said, 'because he hasn't read, and doesn't mean to read, our precious books. He's splendidly illiterate; his scorn of current values is a real distinction.'

I wasn't so distinguished. I had submissively run through Mark Stafford's books and didn't care for them. They gave me too much the idea of a vivisectionist at work, the man with the knife, with, in his case, no great end to serve, though I had the assurance of Kate and worthier critics than this incisive touch – this pitiless impartiality was, properly understood, superb.

I grew indeed a little weary of his trumpeted superiority, his unique methods and results and all the rest; clinging more stubbornly, in the full blare of it, to my own obsolete ideals of his craft.

But though, personally, I might prefer the literary artist to the literary surgeon, the man himself was another matter, one with which preference had less to do.

You might hold out, you did for a time, intractably, against the charm which, sooner or later, he would delicately impose, yielding at last more to a sense of your own ungraciousness than to any urgency of his. While in a manner detaining you, until you found the inevitable recognition, he put you exquisitely at your ease, seeming to cover your reticences, your reluctances, and incertitudes towards him with a strong, unfluttering wing. He never swooped, as you felt he could quite gracefully and effectively have done, to hold you in the grip of a mind that knew no stumbling movements nor halting flights, nor any state of unpreparedness. He understood and didn't mind your hesitations, meeting and smoothing them with a rich patience, which assured you that it could afford to wait. So gradual was the influence, winning on you by imperceptible inches, that till quite the end I never guessed to what extent I had given in. He suppressed himself to give you room, kept in the shadow not to disturb your flickering lights; his own, one suspected, burned extremly clear, defined things perfectly though he had the air of moving about like the rest of us with a delightful vagueness, involved in the general mist.

'If he didn't ignore so charmingly,' Kate pointed out, 'his own importance, you wouldn't be grudgingly giving him the benefit of a doubt which doesn't practically exist. He would get from you his due. And I believe he really does. Admit that, in your treacherous, timorous heart, you are half afraid of him, and to meet the case have fallen back on your religious instincts, and are burning little private candles on his altar in self-defence? I burn them too, but openly and with a difference; not to propitiate my deity, merely to come in for a share of the reflected glory – to shine a little too.'

'But isn't superstition,' I suggested, 'one of your great man's pet ninepins – the chief one, in fact – that he's so elaborately setting up for the pleasure of so neatly knocking down?'

'Oh! he won't draw the line as close as that,' she inconsistently turned round; 'he won't count himself a superstition. They don't, you know.'

He was not then, I mildly urged, too much above and beyond us all to believe immensely in himself.

'Only with him' – she saved herself – 'there is a solid basis of belief. He can't help knowing that he is bound – whatever he's driving at – in the end, to win.'

'Are you answering for it, that he will in time get Charlie over to his side?'

'He doesn't for a moment want to. Charlie is too straight a path, he hasn't any windings – not the shadow of a turning, and when Mark Stafford's walking in a garden, he makes instinctively for the maze.'

'He finds your young man interesting all the same.'

'For just such glimpses, as unwarily, and incidentally, he may afford of me. That's all.'

'And you don't mind?'

'Not in the least. I enjoy it, wouldn't you – posing for a master?'

'Do you mean he will have the assurance to put you down in black and white?'

'Nothing so crude! There is the deeper joy of pure discovery – and the passion of the chase. The sport comes for me, in knowing that he will never perfectly "get" me. We shall wake up one fine morning to find he "has softly and suddenly vanished away, for the snark was a Boojum, you see".'

'Have you made sure of that?'

'It was made sure for me, long ago; when I was born perhaps, that I must *be* myself and stay myself and belong, in a fashion, to myself alone. Even marriage – ' she suddenly broke off.

'Yes,' I prompted, 'even marriage – ?'

'Well, I can't to anyone open every door; whoever owns the poor little house, there must be rooms of which, to the end, I keep the key.'

'And this is the person who used to talk of her "simple self"!'

'The simplest selves have, haven't they, private corners, quiet nooks?'

'The simplest people don't deliberately pose to their favourite painters, for the purposes of mystification.'

'They don't,' she smiled, 'always get the chance, with the rare experience thrown in, of watching them at work, surprising their little tricks; and his little tricks are sometimes, let me tell you, quite inspired.'

It is difficult at this distance, and in the light, or darkness, of all that has come and gone, to be sure if she really thought as much of him as she made out; whether in face of Darch's evasive attitude and my pretence – it was merely that – of antagonism, she wasn't 'standing up' to us from sheer perversity. I am inclined to think she was. One is so apt, in looking back, to tint the glass to the shade of subsequent experience and to see things through it, not in the white glare of fact.

In those early days of their engagement, it is nearly clear to me that the only prominent figure in the landscape was Charlie Darch. There may have been a patch of sky above, and a strip of earth beneath his broad, beaming, genial figure, but the intervening space was inconsiderable. There was no mistaking them, for all their show of taking each other very much for granted, for anything but the happiest pair; their eyes, half-humorously, half-seriously bent on their amazing future, their feet in perfect step – marching, poor children, with a gaiety, a confidence, a blind felicity towards their obscure parting of the ways. Then Darch was unexpectedly called upon to superintend some engineering work in Spain.

Kate declared herself ready for a hasty marriage and the wilds, a scheme which he pronounced impracticable. It was, he insisted, a choice between throwing up the business, or going out for a year, he hoped it wouldn't run to more, alone. Finally, supported by our promise to join him later at some fairly civilized point in Andalusia, if he could manage to snatch a few weeks' holiday, he went.

For four or five months, the bulk and frequency of their correspondence was remarkable. Then it inexplicably flagged and dropped. This turn in their affairs, for me was complicated by Kate's alternate anxiety and reluctance to mature our plans for Spain. Nothing, with her, of course was obvious, only subtly, like a coming change of temperature, in the air. Without allusion to it, one could see, or rather feel her, raising and removing barriers to our departure, weeks before it could feasibly take place.

I can't say how she produced the effect, but simply that she did, for me, produce it, of a person listening and looking for something she hoped not to find, walking on tip-toe, opening and shutting doors. Her fine composure was not outwardly impaired, but running through it like a twisted thread, one divined a flaw in its smooth surface, wondering from what jar in the machinery it came. At length, making a bold attempt at some unravelment, I asked when we should actually start, what we were going to do. She came out quite distinctly with a plan, a prompt –

'Well, if it's manageable and agreeable for you, what would you say to Biarritz next week, and gently on from there?'

'Gently – but definitely where?' I wished to know.

'Oh! somewhere – can't that be settled later? – within easy range of his outlandish quarters. It's to come for him, by way of a surprise. Isn't it enough for us, just now, that he'll be immensely pleased to see us?'

For me, this presumption was not so entirely sufficing. It came to me, at least, as a surprise, her charming vagueness, her confidence that I should, as I seemed to do, incuriously embrace it. We got as far as Paris, even as far as our last evening there, when suddenly she called a halt. I had gone upstairs to pack, leaving her with some friends, whom she had found in the hotel, to settle the question of the Opera or the Français, when the message was brought up to me that a gentleman had called, and would I, Miss Relton asked, kindly, at my convenience, descend? I was not greatly surprised to recognize Mark Stafford in our visitor. Paris was a place where he would naturally, if unexpectedly, turn up. He had, he explained, only that morning learnt from mutual friends, that we were passing through, *en route* for Spain. He had hastened at the first possible moment to present himself, tentatively to suggest that, as he was also working round to Madrid, we might be able to make use of him. He hoped we should. His plans were elastic, perfectly adaptable, could contract or expand, if we delightfully permitted it, in sympathy with ours. Kate had been standing by the window with her back half turned, a slight white figure, motionless, with something almost rigid in the erectness of its pose – while he was making me his explanations; but at this, she turned with the slow grace of all her movements; with an air of serene premeditation, like an actor taking up his cue. 'I think,' she said, with an odd deliberation meant to reach something beyond my ear, 'that it is the nicest proposition imaginable, one of the most alluring, only unfortunately, after all it isn't to be Spain. At the last moment, we have had to give it up.' She paused, and without looking across at me, more rapidly proceeded: 'This is just a little extravagant splash – and we are absurdly going back to – Scotland. Spain, if it's ever to be Spain, is – well – not yet.'

'Yes,' I backed her up, and I felt that I was forcing it, as she had exquisitely failed to do, 'we've had to block it out when it seemed fitted in.'

'But for me,' he faced her, while, though I was obviously out of it, he took me in with an inclusive smile, 'this is a real blow. It takes the wind out of the little sail I was so gaily spreading. What – I am falling back on dreams! – I might have shown you, for I know some of the untrodden ways – what we might have done!'

'Ah, yes,' she assented, with a little deprecatory wave of the hand, and quoted lightly –

> '"They sailed across the silent main,
>   And reached the great Grombrolian plain,
>   And there they play for ever more
>   At battlecock and shuttledore –"'

and we are slinking tamely back to – golf! It's very stupid.'

'It's extremely sad,' he substituted.

'No' she returned with a faint flash, 'it's not altogether sad, because it's so courageous. Don't you think it is?'

He glanced swiftly across at her, and the flush died out, leaving her unusually pale.

'It's too courageous,' he said, his eyes in full possession of her lovely, inexpressive face, 'since it leaves me out in the cold.'

'It leaves you precisely where you were,' she threw back, meeting his glance with a sort of smiling stare, 'for weren't we, in the first instance, going quite alone?'

'But I had the hope –' he protested.

'Oh, the hope,' she interposed, '"Hope is a timid friend." You prefer, admit it, something braver – more definite – even to the definiteness of disappointment.'

'Miss Relton means,' he hazarded, addressing himself to me, 'that you wouldn't have had me after all.'

'Oh, I never answer for Kate. Though for myself –' I left it flatteringly open.

'No one is rash enough to answer for "Kate,"' she challenged him. 'Even you – venturous as you are!'

He laughed.

'I am never that. I am, as you know, the most unconscionable plodder. I potter and crawl. I go extremely slow.'

'Then – that,' she concluded, 'must have settled it, if it hadn't been already settled. You needn't be told that my normal state is quiescent, but when I do move, I want to fly.'

'That parts the clouds. I shall scan the sky –' he risked, 'on the chance that eventually you may catch me up. Meanwhile I am keeping you from Calvé, you mustn't let me do that. Down below, I can feel them champing, your impatient friends; feverishly buttoning gloves and consulting clocks.'

'Aren't you coming, too,' her tone, never vivid, was at the moment, singularly colourless, but his put on a warmer tint.

'I? – yes – of course. I am coming, too.' She went, at this, to fetch her cloak, leaving a hush behind her in the loud, overlit, flamboyant room.

After a short concession to it, he broke it lightly with –

'So while I pursue my lonely way, the poor young man over there has got to wait?'

'Oh, Kate – ' I suggested, 'is a person to be waited for, not by any means to be whistled for, to be snatched.'

'She might so easily be scared, you mean, or spirit herself away? Yes, and one imagines, too, it must be a waiting, in a sense, in ambush; as it were behind one's tree, since fairies don't come out when mortals are abroad. She has, hasn't she, a touch of the sprite, a vague atmosphere of mist, of moonlight, which makes of Darch still more emphatically an embodiment of, well – of the broad glare of day?'

'In spite of which, she will come out for him – she has; it's part, perhaps, of her charming waywardness, that it's for him she has come out.'

'Though for me,' he returned, 'she won't, she hasn't. I shan't, however,' he concluded softly, 'despondently believe that she never will.'

The ensuing silence was for me intensified by the acquiescence, the absorption in it of Kate herself, who had come back and stood reflected in a mirror facing me, but not within his view. She had noiselessly pushed open the half-closed door and paused there, framed in the high opening, erect, elated, with a strange air of victory, sure and silent, her lips just parted in a faint, unwavering smile. Thinking herself unseen, she stayed a moment watching us remotely; puppets, from her dispassionate regard, we might have been, inaudibly discoursing on a distant stage.

So curiously detached, exclusively, intensely in possession of herself, and aloof from us, she seemed, that I couldn't naturally make a sign of recognition. Stafford, however, as though aware of it, broke the spell by abruptly rising, turning and confronting her, upon which she advanced a step or two, coming down suddenly as it were, by some, to us, inaccessible private stair.

'It's not to be Calvé,' she announced immediately. 'It's to be Réjane.'

'Your final choice?' he asked.

'Our unanimous decision.'

'And she was giving *Carmen*,' he protested, 'you won't go back?'

'It's too late to go back; and more than time to be going on.' At which he joined her and they left me to make what I might of the new tangle.

Briefly, I made little of it; and Kate, to whom I looked eventually for enlightenment, was disappointing.

She knocked at my door shortly after midnight, entered, sat down, deliberately drew off her gloves and waited apparently for comments I was not prepared to offer. At length, accepting my not unnatural reluctance to launch in untried waters, with her slow, tranquil stroke, she pushed off herself.

'You are justly vexed?'

'I am reasonably puzzled.'

'And of course it won't simplify things to tell you, late enough in the day, that my engagement with Charlie Darch is "off"?'

I caught as closely as I could her level tone:

'This happened – ?'

'It happened, dear friend, six weeks ago.'

'All the same, we were, so I supposed, on our way out to him – ?'

'It's incredible, indecent,' she assented evenly; 'but as you say, we were. You have every right to exclaim that I have behaved, continue to behave, unpardonably; though it's on your patience, your indulgence, I have so much counted for – for' – she paused, got up, walked to the window and came back, 'for breathing space, for room to twist and turn as easily as I may.'

'You can,' I assured her, conscious nevertheless that she was stretching them, 'count on them still, I hope indefinitely.'

'I know; you are perfect, which makes me monstrous; but I can't bring the figures out of the mist for you. That was,' she pursued reflectively, remotely, 'my notion, in getting incredibly and indecently, as I said, at Charlie – who is not a thing of shadows – of uncertainties, and who might – but now I see, who couldn't' – she broke off and ended with a note of new decision – 'He mustn't be involved.'

'Involved, my dearest child,' I asked, 'in what?'

'In my intolerable vapours, my precious mist.'

'Decidedly,' I concluded, 'we had better, after all, make for definiteness and daylight by way of Biarritz to-morrow.'

'No,' she shut it out with a prompt, final gesture. 'Not if you are going to be immensely considerate and kind. And if I can't to-night, nor perhaps to-morrow, make things clear, well – you will give me time? Later, you'll let me return to it; we'll repack and restart – that's roughly my idea – quite peaceably by ourselves.'

II

It was not long before the figure which she could not or would not, that night, bring out of the mist, emerged unmistakably in the shape of Stafford.

She had suggested I should give her time: I did, taking it there had been some temporary hitch, not easily explainable, which time would adjust without my interference; her attitude during our stay in Scotland lent colour to this view.

'It's not imperative,' she said, 'since he's so far off – so fortunately out of it, poor boy! – that the lights should be turned on us just yet. I want a few weeks quietly in the shade.'

I acquiesced: it worked in well with my idea that she should want it: Darch, whom I illogically acquitted, would be shortly coming back and they would patch it up. But, at once on our return, she declared her readiness to become for a day or two a subject of discussion, insisting quietly that now it must come out.

'Oh! if it's final – ?'

I wouldn't press her, but I didn't hide my difficulty and reluctance.

'You think me horribly light – a leaf in the wind!'

'They have sometimes a way of blowing back?' I hazarded.

'No; they blow on.' She was too positive, and her conclusion had an unusual touch of bitterness. 'After all, if we are as light as that – as inconsequent – as detached – it doesn't greatly matter, our vagrant way!'

'But you are not, my child,' I was throwing at the moment hands out in the darkness, 'as light as that – and if I believed it – '

'Wait!' she interposed. 'You'll see.'

I saw not then, but soon enough, that the door was definitely shut on Darch, and that any movement towards it reopening was blocked by Stafford. He was not aggressively in the way; he was simply there – a substantial, stationary figure which she couldn't or wouldn't pass and made no effort to dislodge. They both seemed to be standing very still, facing each other, waiting, with the space between them not yet bridged – cut clear. My first impulse was to step in and strike out blindly for the poor young man behind the door, but I realized that I had missed my moment, amiably blinking, sitting, it proved, ridiculously still. Now, it was not so much Stafford who tripped me up in my attempt to rise, as Kate herself, with whom I was less than ever on solid ground. She was taking me uncomfortably off my feet. Nothing about her was stranger, when at length they made their plunge, than what, for want of a better term, I must call her assurance. She offered no excuses, for the inexcusable, and appeared to cast no shadow of thought upon a change of front, which, however easily effected, is supposed to have its pensive side. She seemed to have no shadows, no pensive side, so suddenly had she ceased to be the Kate I knew or guessed at. I had said of her once that she seemed to hang between two worlds, giving her then, in thought perhaps, a vague companionship with spirits of a lighter air, but at last she had come down and planted herself on a patch of earth. She hadn't etherealized, she had materialized. Stopping determinately from the path of dreams, shaking away the mists, she stood out an intensely actual figure shining with a hard, new brightness.

For my old-fashioned views, I told her, it was too much of a jump, when almost in the same breath with the announcement of her break with Darch, she wished her new engagement given out.

'But I am quite indifferent,' she returned, dismissing me with a brilliant smile, 'to the gaping crowd – the public stare.'

'And to me too;' I couldn't help reminding her. 'To my private stare, which up to now, my dear, I have considerately kept down.'

'If I am not indifferent to it, I can face it. Am I the first woman who has changed her mind? I know it's reckoned more picturesque to change it to slow music, but if I prefer to do without the modulation, to start at once with a crash on the new chord – ?'

'It doesn't occur to you that that may strike Charlie as rather harsh – ?'

'Happily he hasn't a "temperament"! He will survive; when one knows the worst one can. I liked and like him, of course, amazingly, but – well – God, you know, eventually disposes – '

'Oh, if you mean me to look on Mark as a divine provision – !'

'Can't you? But I see you can't. I wonder why? He is going to be a "personage," and by the same token I – ' she paused.

'You,' I reminded her, 'will "shine a little too." He will give you, of course, as Charles would put it, "A much better show."'

'A share, for what it's worth, of his little row of footlights, yes – but you are not reconciled, you are undisguisedly displeased. Am I too practical or too perfidious? And behind it all, you are still looking for our old friend the spectre – you won't find him – you never will!'

'You admit at last then, that it's there – ?'

'Produce it, annihilate it, and I'll own everything,' she challenged me, and with that I had to be content.

They spent the honeymoon – a matter of some months – in Egypt, and the letters which she wrote from there, one by one, as I put them by – and together, as I took them out to re-read and reconsider – produced the same crude, unnatural effect: the effect, in fine, of glare.

They showed a curious lack of the half-lights and quiet tones and human touches which had been noticeably hers; telling me everything and nothing, they were mercilessly bright; as though for the time, her personality, steeped in and even hypnotized by the immutable relentless sunshine, had caught the tireless, shadeless brilliance and detachment of the East. I was to find, however, on her return, that she hadn't left it there.

Within the year, for Mark, who had just brought out what is said to be his masterpiece, the little row of footlights was for the first time in full flare; but it was Kate who at once stepped up to them, taking, with an ease, a certainty, the centre of the stage. Interested, amused, her husband genially retreated.

'It's not Mark Stafford's book, it's Mark Stafford's wife,' he remarked quietly, one evening, looking round his uncomfortably encumbered rooms, 'which explains and justifies this distinguished crowd. It's not to something like two years of pious toil, but to the happy accident of the happiest choice, that I owe my little hour of fame. You can see for yourself, if in the first instance it was for me they ventured forth, it's for Kate they stay, and it's for her they come again. And you never prepared me! Was it fair – ?'

'Didn't she,' I asked, 'ever confront you with the warning that, in a given case, she meant to shine?'

'Not a whisper, not a breath! She sprang it on me. Don't you remember our old notion of her as a shy, reluctant fay, not to be rudely tempted into the vulgarities, the mortalities of daylight?'

'All the same,' I risked, with a sense of touching upon certainty, 'you *were*, as a matter of fact, prepared for – anything!'

'I am now,' he admitted smiling, 'for everything, aren't you? And definitely, for the rapid fall of the curtain' – and, as I didn't catch his drift, he added – 'for her backing out of it – suddenly refusing to keep it up.'

From our comparatively unobstructed corner, I followed the glance he shot across at her, over the buzzing, faintly scented, somewhat congested company – to be, for the first time forcibly, painfully struck by the unexpectedness, the incredibility of it all. Kate planted there, so vividly reminiscent of, so impenetrably unlike herself, the conspicuous centre of a group of men, for the most part strangers or quite new-comers, intimately held, detained by an influence which I somehow divined to be as far from the spirit of the girl I had known and sheltered as high, quiet stars from the lamps of town.

Never had she looked more beautiful; whatever she had lost – and I can't say how it became chillingly plain to me that some vague virtue had gone out of her – she had gained to a supreme degree, what she had never lacked – distinction.

In her severe white and silver draperies, with her wonderfully dressed fair hair, her erect carriage, her slow, gracious movements, she wore the air of an exiled queen. Her familiar inexpressiveness seemed to be more pronounced, more studied; the repose of her attitude, her voice, her infrequent gestures, was profound – and in its intensity almost provocative of the impression she was obviously and, as I unwillingly conceded to myself, consciously producing.

Her beauty apparently commanded an attention absorbed enough to waive the usual claims of speech, She was listening perfectly, talking little, giving her quiescent charm full play. With an extraordinary rapidity, she had surrendered to some nameless need of prominence, and was finally mounted on her pedestal exposing an insentient surface, while inwardly – I couldn't doubt it – she was breathing some secret flame.

I turned to Mark with an answer pitched as nearly as I could manage it in his own easy key.

'Why shouldn't she keep it up? She has matured; as you say "come out"; she wasn't naturally, going to be left behind. You are both, and I suppose you are mutually aware of it, a wonderful – a joint success.'

I had never prevaricated with a clearer conscience or a more clouded mind. If she were going to keep it up, if this was what she meant by shining, it became for me an important question whether the background wouldn't grow appreciably darker with the increased definiteness of her luminosity. How long – to put it plainly – would it take to turn Mark's indulgent smile into an intelligible frown? Already I was beginning to hear a shade too much and to see too little of 'the beautiful Mrs Stafford.'

I saw more of her gowns, though it was not to her I owed the privilege. Her dressmaker, who happened also to be mine, was not, on my occasional visits, to be deterred from thrusting on me an acquaintance, which I should not otherwise have enjoyed, with her extravagant sequence of 'creations.' Her tastes had been so simple, her expenditure so modest in this direction that, without exaggerating the significance of trifles, I was compelled to add this new departure to the list of her surprises. Later, I sometimes met with the gowns again, but Kate herself was not now, in any sense, to be come upon in *déshabillé*, in the intimacy, so to speak, of the morning wrapper. She was rarely to be found alone; with the wave, as it were, of an invisible wand, she had summoned round her a deterrent band, set up an elaborate human barrier, against old privacies and old associations.

She went everywhere and she never seemed to come really back; her few free hours were merely interludes; she was always going on again. She lived, to my view, at the foot or at the head of stairs, getting in and out of carriages, and relaxing, if she relaxed at all, under the eyes and hands of an heroic maid in the intervals between receptions. As time went on, one or two men – mere names to me – were accidentally referred to in my hearing as being distinguished by her friendship, and Mark himself had casually responded to my interest in the one I picked out at random – a young Frenchman – with – 'Oh! a rising sprig, a painter, one of Kate's retainers.'

The phrase, while its complacency was, in a measure, reassuring, had inconsequently jarred.

Her husband's work – I heard it on all sides – monopolized him, he was too preoccupied apparently to be critical of his wife's distractions, but to what extent his negligence accounted for their latitude I saw too little of either of them to decide. They had taken a house in Scotland for the shooting, and in the autumn for a week or two I was to join their party there. Meanwhile conclusion halted; looking at the whole blurred business through what remained to me of her mother's eyes, I was watching rather anxiously for daylight, when Charlie Darch broke in upon the scene.

On my return from a round of visits, I found his card among the little pile awaiting me, and later heard from Mark that in my absence he had cropped up and they had seen a fair amount of him.

'You'll meet him,' he added, 'with the rest, I hope, in September, if he doesn't look you up before. He's just the same old Philistine; an exhilarating chap!'

If this was how he affected Mark, his presence in the big, strange country house subsequently inspired me with frank mistrust.

He was not the same: he was distinctly older and more finished: he had grown the least bit formidable in the process of throwing off the boyish diffidence which, in the old days, had made him more accessible and, perhaps too, more easily dismissible. A day or two sufficed to show me that his interest in Kate had steadfastly survived, but what she made of the discovery was obscure. If she distinguished him at all, it was by a peculiar stillness in his company, as though she were keeping recognition in reserve, while he stopped short of any intimate approach.

The detestably keen eye I kept on both of them disclosed at length that he too was watching her, intently but discreetly and reluctantly. Poor Kate! What were we looking for? It may have been a conscience-stricken fancy that, for all its stealth, she felt our scrutiny and faced it – beat it off with her unclouded gaze, her remote serenity. There was one moment in the dusk, when there seemed to be something like a lurking horror in it.

The nights were sultry, and I hadn't slept. The house was full and, as usual, she was more or less surrounded; the little Frenchman, at close quarters, proved to be no more a matter for uneasiness than the acquisition of a lap-dog, though at the end of a ribbon held by Kate, he was as much a matter for surprise. She seemed to find his relaxed fidelity, the air of weary ardour with which he hovered round her, mildly entertaining. Mark, when he wasn't shooting, drifted, as his way was, to the background; Darch, too, held himself somewhat aloof; he was obviously not concerned with her immediate circle; these people didn't count, he was looking over their heads indifferently, like a tall man in a crowd.

My visit reached its term a day or two before Mark's birthday, for which some elaborate tableaux had been arranged; and on the plea that since I had brought my camera, I must stay on to photograph the party and be generally useful, I was persuaded to extend it.

Kate was to posture as Ophelia to the Hamlet of the little Frenchman, who had been languid as an invalid and difficult as a spoiled child until the idea, his own, of impersonating the morbid Dane served partially to restore his lost deportment and vitality. Darch backed out, protesting it was much more in his line to do the limelight. Afterwards there was to be a dance.

The night was fine, but heavy, airless, with the heat that comes before a storm, and contemplating an escape from the hot rooms, with the precaution of my years I had gone up to fetch a wrap, was on the point of going down, when I turned back to throw up my closed window. It looked down upon the shrubbery, festooned to-night with paper lanterns. As I glanced out, I was aware of two figures stationed opposite, against the wall of green. Their presence rather than their attitude, for passion has its magnetism even for those who have out-distanced it, suggested my retreat. I was about to make it when the man bent forward, seizing the woman's hands insistently, thwarting what might have been a movement of refusal or withdrawal. It was Darch, and without waiting for her to turn her head, I knew too, that it was Kate. They spoke so low, I couldn't hear what they were saying – I didn't want, or need, I thought, to hear.

Below, I found Mark asking for her and she presently appeared among the dancers. She hadn't changed the gown she had worn for the 'Hamlet' tableau, copied from some picture of Rossetti's.

'It suits her uncommonly well,' Mark commented, 'but, under our breath, let us confess she beautifully missed the part. Kate has her qualities, but pliancy isn't one of them. You don't get Pure Reason condescending even to look distraught.'

'Is she so purely reasonable?'

'Call it balance. She would be worth watching in a panic – but for this sort of thing,' he laughed, 'if she had had her way, I believe she would have done Ophelia with her hair up! Didn't you hear her, but perhaps you weren't behind the scenes? – I don't know what's your elegant equivalent – damning the straws?'

She had come up behind, and made her own defence:

'Naturally; a woman's more or less at a disadvantage, and a shade disreputable with her hair down. So I was shocking? But of course I knew it. If there had been tragedy in me I must have shown it; I was thinking of supper, and the cook who has an inveterate habit of getting drunk on these occasions. You have your shawl.' She turned to me. 'You are going out? But who's taking you?'

'Only a step or two, and I am not being taken.'

She followed me out on to the illuminated lawn.

'I am not sure if I altogether like this painting of the night,' she began, looking round upon the mass of hanging coloured lights. 'One ought to be able to command the moon, it's more distinguished and satisfactory. But on the whole, wouldn't you call it a success?'

I was not in the mood to talk inanities, or to wait for a fitter moment, or to question the wisdom of direct attack.

'What has become of Charlie?' I asked irrelevantly. 'I have hardly seen him all the evening.'

'He doesn't dance, but it may be taken for granted he's doing his duty somewhere. He was out here just now.'

'With you?'

'Yes.' Her inflection hinted faint surprise. 'With me.'

'It hasn't occurred to you' – I made my plunge – 'that you see too much of him, that he's not a person quickly to resign himself – to forget – and that even if it's wise, it mayn't be kind?'

There was a long and rather painful pause, in which she stood staring at the lit windows, the moving figures, and beating time with her fingers on the back of a seat to the waltz which had just struck up. At length she relieved it with –

'I understand. It's an unflattering inference, but I am not afraid of corrupting my old friend – or of shaking his fine stability.'

'Or of causing him useless pain?'

'You are assuming – what?' she asked dispassionately.

'Nothing; surely my affection for you both is reason enough – excuse enough – if I have over-anxiously misread the situation – '

She interposed:

'If you want facts, it was not I who suggested his coming here; it was Mark. The "situation," whatever that implies, is Mark's affair.'

I didn't pretend, I couldn't, wholly to believe it.

'He was not a friend of Mark's,' I reminded her. 'He never frankly liked him. Do you imagine he likes him better – now?'

She was still staring past me at the lit windows. The waltz had stopped, but she went on fingering the memory of it.

'I haven't the least idea; but why not – when it's all over?'

'Is it all over?' I persisted gently.

She turned round and showed me beneath the unreal, festive lights, a white face, intensely familiar, intensely strange – a young face suddenly grown old.

'Is anything ever over?' she broke out, with the first spark of passion I had ever seen struck from her. 'Is even death itself the end? We can't see – can't possibly see – though we *are seen*, and not by any means in a glass darkly. If one was sure – but nothing's sure – that there was at the close – deliverance from this awful light, this uplifting darkness, that we are in the grip of – blind – blind stumblers – !'

Catching at the only thread in this bewildering tangle which I thought I could make use of, I said rather unsteadily –

'We can, at least, see far enough to save ourselves, and others too, from walking crookedly. And Charlie – '

She thrust in swiftly, as if to intercept a threatening blow:

'Before God – I am clear of Charlie. If there's truth in anything, there's truth in friendship; it's a refuge and not a danger; his hands are safe.'

'My poor child,' I said, her vehemence moved, while it alarmed me, 'you are owning that, to some extent, you are in them.'

'With an abrupt return to her old expressionless detachment, she discriminated:

'Mayn't one, for instance, own to being in the hands of God without dismay? But all this is extremely lurid; it's more to the point, since we are talking confidences, that I am not particularly, as you see, myself. I can't – to define the symptoms – always think consecutively, and I don't remember my engagements.'

I was successfully diverted. Such an admission, on her lips, with her unblotted record – she had invariably scoffed at ailments – suggested something which might be grave.

'Have you seen anyone?'

'No. You know exactly what they are. We flock to them in our thousands and they wave us off with a great deal of "dear lady" and rest, or massage, or change of scene, according to our purse!'

'I shall take you to Sir Matthew Fenton.'

'A delightful man, and a profound admirer of Mark's. I know; you would arrange to see him privately and elicit the valuable information that Mrs Stafford was an ideal hostess and her husband a first-rate pathologist – spoiled; with the genial afterthought that you couldn't get these charming women to embrace St Paul's doctrine "moderation, moderation!" A pause for the inspection of his new Mauve – or is it Maris he collects? and he would amiably bow you out. We eat too many sweets – in fine – and take ourselves too seriously. *Voilà tout!*'

'But you will see him?'

'Possibly, or someone else – if I don't pull myself together. But I mean to!'

She touched my arm with a light pressure of dismissal:

'Are you coming in? You know I ought to be dancing.'

My night's outlook was sufficiently confused, and the events of the morrow didn't tend to clear it.

Mark and I breakfasted alone together; Darch had been up with the lark, he said, and had gone out early; and when, an hour or so later, he came upon me in Kate's little sitting-room, where I had taken refuge from the general dishevelment, he brought in a breath of outdoor freshness with a vaguely uneasy manner and a look of sleeplessness.

He was promptly definite, blankly candid: it was Kate he wanted to talk over, and his unembarrassed assumption of his right to do so, temporarily overcame my impulse to dispute it.

He closed the door and sat down and came out at once with the bald question:

'Have you any idea how bad she really is?'

I had learned in the past that my conversational strategies were no match for his direct simplicity.

'It was only last night she let me suspect that there was anything the matter, and from what she said – it wasn't much – I concluded that she was thoroughly run down.'

'Is that your name for it – or hers?' He seemed to be summoning patience for the potterer he had to deal with, and went on indulgently, 'but probably she has not been open with you if you haven't decided on any step – '

'Isn't her husband – ?' I began rather pointedly.

He cut me short.

'What is the good of these – these absurd pretences? We are old friends, and we are in possession of what, I take it, is common property. Her husband is probably the last person to whom she is likely to confess a weakness, the first, in fact, from whom she would ingeniously hide it. It's no affair of mine, their mutual attitude, except so far as there must be someone to act. You don't suppose it's my choice to move in the miserable business?'

'Don't you think that all round you may be taking an exaggerated view?'

He got up and began pacing up and down the little room with slow, short strides, stopping at length and resolutely facing me.

'I am breaking faith – but it's clear you aren't aware – and you ought to be – that for some time she's been under a delusion, an obsession – I got it out of her. She thinks, poor child! that there's something, some shapeless horror, looking over her shoulder straight, as she hideously persists, into her soul. Not,' he went on, with a sort of forced irrelevancy, 'that it won't bear looking into – the clearest pool! – but it's the what – the monstrous thing that's doing it, that's shattering her. And it's not recent. She won't say how long – she says reluctantly – "some time" – '

'She told me last night she couldn't think coherently – wasn't remembering her engagements.'

'That's the threat, if we can't avert it, of a catastrophe: she is beginning not to have any thought outside it, not to remember anything but that. She has made an inconceivably splendid fight, but it can't go on; it's for us to prevent her great success from becoming a great disaster. You have seen her, she's been literally smiling through it; but what a nightmare!'

He made a movement which revealed to me how completely she had impressed him with the actuality of the unreal, how appallingly clear, how irrationally reasonable, she must have been. He was visibly, almost physically oppressed; he looked haunted, too. I laid a hand upon his arm.

'It's all terrible, incredible, but you mustn't look almost as if you shared it.'

'Wait,' he said, 'until she tells you herself. Perhaps then you'll be shaken, you'll be inclined to share it too. She must see someone, at once – you are the fittest person to insist. I was pledged on my honour not – as she put it – to betray her, but it's too serious!'

'I must speak to Mark.'

'Didn't he tell you? He had a wire – some business muddle – he's gone up to town. It's a matter, so I understood, of a day or two.'

He made the announcement with a certain grim relief which drew from me:

'You waited – ?'

'No,' he checked me. 'I simply didn't think of him. I took my cue, I suppose, from – from everybody; they are not spoken of, even paragraphed together; they are independent – ' he paused for a word and finally braved it out – 'notorieties: will that do?'

'Mark, I remember, used to admire you for your indifference to fine shades. It isn't subtle.'

'No, thank God!' he broke out, 'it isn't subtle! That's not my line; if it were, I shouldn't be pleading for her now. She would be in my hands not in his – and partially in yours. She wouldn't have been brought to this extremity. Have you never asked yourself,' he went on more steadily, 'what broke our compact? Have you ever mistaken her, since then, for a happy woman? What is it, do you suppose, that has twisted the Kate we knew into – well, the woman who allows that French poodle to patter at her heels? Kate – our Kate, the Mrs Stafford of shop windows – the "beautiful Mrs Stafford!" What is the key to the whole unthinkable change, if it's not some blind instinct of flight, of escape from some intolerable influence or atmosphere? Call it subtlety, if you like! I haven't found, and I'm not particularly keen to find its name.'

'My dear boy,' I protested, 'I can't follow you. You are naturally distressed, upset, and you are taking the most grotesque and unjustifiable view of the whole sad business. I was on the spot and I believe, although, at the time, I couldn't of course approve of it, that she made her choice deliberately. She was dazzled, one doesn't know how a girl's head is turned, by what – you know how the world looks at things – seemed to her a brilliant opportunity. But why go back to it? As to her husband – and oughtn't he surely just now to have our sympathy? – if he is in any sense to blame, it is simply in having left her perhaps too much to herself. And if she, poor child, hasn't used her freedom altogether wisely, it's after all an intelligible weakness. Wasn't she bound, under the circumstances, to make some stir? Mark himself admitted that she was his finest discovery. He was frankly proud of it, that he didn't miss, even in her, his "little human praise."'

He gave me a look which suddenly, decisively, divided us – put an impassable space between us.

'I give it up,' was his brief conclusion. 'You are all beyond me – I haven't, as you say, a head for subtleties. What do you mean to do?'

'Mark must be told – consulted.' For the moment I saw no further.

'Damn consultations!' he said quietly. 'What is to hinder your taking her up to-day?'

'For one thing, Kate herself. And then there are these tableaux people to be photographed this afternoon. Half of them will be gone to-morrow. Don't you see how inexplicable, with Mark too away, it must appear even if Kate would agree to a plausible excuse? She wouldn't – she won't in any case be easy. She is not, you know, a person to be forced.'

'It's in your hands.' He was speaking now from a distance, trying to make his voice carry – to reach me – to move me. 'If it were in mine –'

'If it were,' I urged, 'you wouldn't before it's absolutely unavoidable provoke the inevitable chatter?'

He deliberately turned his back on me, went to the window and stood cheerlessly looking out. There was nothing more to say – nothing to stay for; I got up and moved towards the door. He hastened to open it, remarking as he did so, dully – distantly:

'I am one of the inconvenient people who will be gone to-morrow.' Shutting me out with it – turning into the room again before I bad shaped my lips to a conventional regret.

At luncheon, I found it difficult – almost impossible – to fit the picture of my startled thought into the frame of his pitiful disclosure. Her whole aspect of tranquil brilliance, her perfect manipulation of the pieces in the social game, had it not been for Darch's corroborative presence, would have made the dreaded thing unthinkable; but later in the afternoon, the shadow of the cloud took shape. The stage had been left up. Most of the tableaux had been taken, when Kate, who had not come in to tea, and was being asked for, appeared and had her scene set up. She mounted the platform and began rather automatically to strike her pose, when a murmur reached her from below. She had forgotten to change her dress. For a moment she stared, stood still, as if she didn't catch the point of the remonstrance – wasn't going to – when a glance from Darch seemed to recall her to herself, and meeting it, she at once stepped down with a timid, absent –

'So I have. I am sorry. Does it matter? Then we are out of it.'

'Not hopelessly,' said Darch, who was bent, I understood, on keeping her attention on the stretch. 'M. Devereux – Hamlet must be done anyway – in solitary distinction.'

'Of course,' she rose to it at once, 'he mustn't be missed, and after all he gains immensely. Please,' she called up to him, 'stay where you are.'

He untractably descended.

'But no,' he objected, 'without you – it becomes meaningless, and it must not be that Mrs Stafford alone remains uncommemorated. Impossible!'

'Oh! for that' – she had regained entire possession of herself – 'it easily arranges itself. You shall commemorate my stupidity! Will this do?'

She walked across the room and placed herself against a *portière* – a white figure erect and admirably posed – smiling out from the crimson folds.

It seemed as if in this momentary presentment, for the first time since her marriage she confronted me alone, cut off. She stood, to my sense, in a cleared, hushed space, the centre of a far-reaching muteness, indefinable and uninvaded by the chattering crowd. With the click of the camera, she was once more of it, a moving, shining part – a sunlit presence with all clouds dispersed.

I had no more speech with her that day. I never, now I come to think of it, had speech with her again. Whether, that evening, she really evaded me, or whether my own uneasy, indeterminate movements towards her – too hesitant to be frankly met – let down between us the final curtain, I can never be quite sure.

I awoke next morning with a firmer mind, less faltering purposes. Too late! She had slipped through my irresolute fingers. Her maid brought me a note at noon. 'Madame had wished me not to be disturbed.'

I took the envelope from the woman's hand, and, loth to open it under her attentive, initiated eye, dismissed her, divining a disposition to loiter – to be questioned. She left me startled by the simple commentary with which she withdrew. 'Madame had accompanied Mr Darch to the station last night and had not yet returned.'

I closed the door on her and turned to the letter which was going to explain itself. But it was not explicit.

'I have left Mark,' it started with that abrupt announcement. 'Charlie is taking me away. I cannot explain or justify our action; but in time the inevitable justifies itself. The world will have ugly thoughts of us; will you be able to find something truer? I am sure only of one sufficient thing, that God will not condemn us – if it were only God!'

And that was all. I sat staring stupidly at the little sheet with its meagre, startling statement, waiting perhaps for some light to flash out from between the lines, upon those two elusive, receding images, of Kate, of Darch, which slowly, strangely enough, as the minutes passed, became obscured, over-shadowed by another; till at length it was Mark alone I distinctly saw. For me, for themselves, they had taken flight, but he remained and I – I who must singly and immediately face him, be arraigned possibly before him and vicariously stripped and judged. It came over me with a force which left me almost indifferent to the other exigencies of the moment, the dismissal or entertainment of his lingering unenlightened guests, of whom I finally disposed as rapidly and adroitly as I could.

Travelling all night, I arrived in London unreasonably early, but as soon as I felt myself presentable, I set forth and knocked at the familiar door. He was out. The man knew nothing of his movements beyond a probability of his being home to dinner. I left a note and went home and waited the better part of the intolerable day.

When at last, late, he was shown in, the tense silence which served for greeting served too to show me that it was not now on me that sentence was to be pronounced. If it was on her, I was ready with my testimony – my plea.

'You wished to see me?' he said at length, in the tone of one gravely, patiently wondering why.

'I wanted you, without delay, to know all the facts, because they must prove to you that it's not, even now, too late to recall – to save her.'

'Kate,' he said, slowly, reflectively, seeming, with this utterance of her name, to summon her, set her visibly, tangibly there between us. 'You have not heard? but how should you? She has saved herself.'

'By coming back?'

'No, by going on' – he paused – 'by dying!' He spoke considerately, deliberately, as if – called upon: brutally to strike – he found no means to humanize the blow. 'She died last night.'

'How?' It broke from me, an articulate dread, not of the event, but of the manner of it.

'Quite simply and suddenly. They had got as far as Dover – and there, with scarcely any warning, she failed – and ended. They give, of course, some plausible name to it, but it was, as you know, her habit – her nature – to do things very quietly, and this – this step of hers was too violent, too unnatural. She felt herself falling – she did fall, and practically – it killed her.'

'The effort, you mean, to recover herself, the will to return, was there, but ineffectual?'

'We shall never know. She has eluded us to the end. It's terrible, but it's perfect. It's Kate herself!'

His thought seemed to be folded in the present, voluntarily bounded by the day so near its close, as though he had schooled himself to press no further; but I was looking back from this strange deliverance to the unintelligible past, and on to that future with its threatening dusk – averted. She *had* been spared.

'As it is,' I managed to say, 'she *is* safe – her memory – herself – ?'

'Absolutely. It's in her face.'

'You have seen her?'

'I could almost believe I had never before seen her.' He stopped, and added after an interval, 'but that's unspeakable. Death is an appalling silence.'

'And an absolution?' I wished to know it.

He didn't answer at once, and when he did, it was with a sort of finality, a weight as of last words:

'They are beyond that – the dead. They are divinely indifferent.'

'If you mean we can't reach them, I don't believe it.'

'It is better to. There is that poor young man trying hard not to believe it. He won't succeed.'

'You have forgiven him?'

'I am bound to feel immensely sorry for him. He will move his heaven and his earth to call her back, and she won't come.' He held out his hand; he *was* final. 'You were anxious to tell me things, but I shall, please remember it, never want to hear them. They are profoundly immaterial, now, the things that can be told. Good-night.'

It was some weeks later that poor Charlie wrote to me, making vivid, in his simple, troubled note, Mark's image of him, vainly moving his two worlds to call her back.

He was the last person, he knew, he wrote, to ask or be granted any sort of favour – but he was asking one – perhaps the most unpardonable. He wanted, of my charity, the photograph of Kate – the last – he supposed I had it – taken that afternoon in Scotland. He had long since destroyed the earlier ones, his own, and had nothing for what – for want of a better word – he would call remembrance. He would take my silence, if it must be, for refusal, and fully understand it. But perhaps I too might understand and – not refuse.

After a momentary hesitation, I replied telling him I had as yet done nothing with it, but if he cared to come and see in about a week's time, I hoped to have it ready for his acceptance. My attitude, which might intelligibly have been less friendly, was partly determined by Mark's sympathetic sketch of him, and partly by a sense of my own shortcoming in having perhaps met earlier and more impersonal appeal, I believe too, I hoped he might have something to tell me, be able to throw some light upon the edges of the cloud by which, in thought, they were both still, for me, somewhat over-shadowed.

I had meant some time to elapse before I touched the portrait, – that poignant reopening of a too recent wound, for which, with the grim self-torture of youth, he pleaded. For me, its associations were too tragic, and the curious muteness, the sense almost of suspended breath which I remembered to have felt in it, was too premonitory of what had so shortly afterwards come to pass.

That afternoon, however, I took out the plate and proceeded to develop it. It came slowly, and eventually, as I held it up, I slightly recoiled – was suddenly struck with something wrong about it, unexpected, strange! Beside the face I was looking for there appeared, not – and yet after all it was another – or the semblance of another face; twisting round, immediately behind her, close over her shoulder; not at first to me a thing human or recognizable, but gradually growing hideously distinct, monstrously familiar – the face of her husband – of Mark himself!

For a second I stood frozenly staring at it, and then with a violence, involuntary, uncontrollable, I threw up the window and flung it out, down, on to the pavement below, where it fell in shattered fragments.

My first instinct during the days and nights which followed, as the horror defined itself – unbearably persisted – was to share it – to shift the weight of it, in defiance of reason, in defiance of everything; and it was naturally Darch to whom, in those hours of disorder and oppression, I was prepared to turn, for whom, in fact, I was tremulously waiting.

But when, punctually at the end of his week, he came, his burdened presence steadied me and I forbore.

As he stood there before me so altered, so spent, so inarticulate, my own selfish need declined, my intention of relief at his expense receded; and I understood that that intolerable revelation must be finally and for ever consigned to silence – to the limbo of unutterable things.

He talked for a time inanimately, evasively, of the weather, the opera, the changes in the Cabinet, but while I listened to that lifeless voice of his uttering its unprofitable commonplaces, I was aware of another, a living voice, lifted above it in insistent supplication.

'Not of Kate,' it reiterated, 'let us speak of anything, of everything but her.'

And she was not named between us, she was simply, mutely, inconquerably present – a haunting shade.

At length he got up to go, standing before he made farewell, silently, submissively expectant.

'You will find it difficult to forgive me,' I told him gently, 'but after all, you were not to have it – none of us were to have it, the precious thing you are waiting for. I have – I had – I hardly know how to confess it – irretrievably spoiled the plate.'

He remained silent, looking at me lingeringly, intently, questioningly in the face, and for an instant, I shrank back before that disturbing scrutiny. Was it possible, imaginable – that he guessed – he knew?

But as soon as I found courage enough to meet, to return his gaze, I saw in it merely the fixity, the pain, the incredulity of acute failure and something like despair.

'It was hopeless, impossible?' he asked at last reluctantly.

'It was quite hopeless, quite impossible,' I said.

M. R. JAMES

The Treasure of Abbot Thomas

I

'Verum usque in præsentem diem multa garriunt inter se Canonici de abscondito quodam istius Abbatis Thomæ thesauro, quem sæpe, quanquam adhuc incassum, quæsiverunt Steinfeldenses. Ipsum enim Thomam adhuc florida in ætate existentem ingentem auri massam circa monasterium defodisse perhibent; de quo multoties interrogatus ubi esset, cum risu respondere solitus erat: "Job, Johannes, et Zacharias vel vobis vel posteris indicabunt"; idemque aliquando adiicere se inventuris minime invisurum. Inter alia huius Abbatis opera, hoc memoria præcipue dignum iudico quod fenestram magnam in orientali parte alæ australis in ecclesia sua imaginibus optime in vitro depictis impleverit: id quod et ipsius effigies et insignia ibidem posita demonstrant. Domum quoque Abbatialem fere totam restauravit: puteo in atrio ipsius effosso et lapidibus marmoreis pulchre cælatis exornato. Decessit autem, morte aliquantulum subitanea perculsus, ætatis suæ anno lxxiido, incarnationis vero Dominicæ mdxxixo.'

'I suppose I shall have to translate this,' said the antiquary to himself, as he finished copying the above lines from that rather rare and exceedingly diffuse book, the '*Sertum Steinfeldense Norbertinum.*'* 'Well, it may as well be done first as last,' and accordingly the following rendering was very quickly produced:

---

* An account of the Premonstratensian abbey of Steinfeld, in the Eiffel, with lives of the Abbots, published at Cologne in 1712 by Christian Albert Erhard, a resident in the district. The epithet *Nobertinum* is due to the fact that St Norbert was founder of the Premonstratensian Order.

'Up to the present day there is much gossip among the Canons about a certain hidden treasure of this Abbot Thomas, for which those of Steinfeld have often made search, though hitherto in vain. The story is that Thomas, while yet in the vigour of life, concealed a very large quantity of gold somewhere in the monastery. He was often asked where it was, and always answered, with a laugh: "Job, John, and Zechariah will tell either you or your successors." He sometimes added that he should feel no grudge against those who might find it. Among other works carried out by this Abbot I may specially mention his filling the great window at the east end of the south aisle of the church with figures admirably painted on glass, as his effigy and arms in the window attest. He also restored almost the whole of the Abbot's lodging, and dug a well in the court of it, which he adorned with beautiful carvings in marble. He died rather suddenly in the seventy-second year of his age, A.D. 1529.'

The object which the antiquary had before him at the moment was that of tracing the whereabouts of the painted windows of the Abbey Church of Steinfeld. Shortly after the Revolution, a very large quantity of painted glass made its way from the dissolved abbeys of Germany and Belgium to this country, and may now be seen adorning various of our parish churches, cathedrals, and private chapels. Steinfeld Abbey was among the most considerable of these involuntary contributors to our artistic possessions (I am quoting the somewhat ponderous preamble of the book which the antiquary wrote), and the greater part of the glass from that institution can be identified without much difficulty by the help, either of the numerous inscriptions in which the place is mentioned, or of the subjects of the windows, in which several well-defined cycles or narratives were represented.

The passage with which I began my story had set the antiquary on the track of another identification. In a private chapel – no matter where – he had seen three large figures, each occupying a whole light in a window, and evidently the work of one artist. Their style made it plain that that artist had been a German of the sixteenth century; but hitherto the more exact localizing of them had been a puzzle. They represented – will you be surprised to hear it? – Job Patriarcha, Johannes Evangelista, Zacharias Propheta, and each of them held a book or scroll, inscribed with a sentence from his writings. These, as a matter of course, the antiquary had noted, and he had been struck by the curious way in which they differed from any text of the Vulgate that he had been able to examine. Thus the scroll in Job's hand was inscribed: 'Auro est locus in quo absconditur' (for 'conflatur');* on the book of John was: 'Habent in vestimentis suis scripturam quam nemo novit'† (for 'in vestimento scriptum,' the following words being taken from another verse); and Zacharias had: 'Super lapidem unum septem oculi sunt'‡ (which alone of the three presents an unaltered text).

A sad perplexity it had been to our investigator to think why these three personages should have been placed together in one window. There was no bond of connection between them, either historic, symbolic, or doctrinal, and he could only suppose that they must have formed part of a very large series of Prophets and Apostles, which might have filled, say, all the clerestory windows of some capacious church. But the passage from the *Sertum* had altered the situation by showing that the names of the actual personages represented in the glass now in Lord D——'s chapel had been constantly on the lips of Abbot Thomas von Eschenhausen of Steinfeld, and that this Abbot had put up a painted window, probably about the year 1520, in the south aisle of his abbey church. It was no very wild conjecture that the three figures might have formed part of Abbot Thomas's offering; it was one which, moreover, could probably be confirmed or set aside by another careful examination of the glass. And, as Mr Somerton was a man of leisure, he set out on pilgrimage to the private chapel with very little delay. His conjecture was confirmed to the full. Not only did the style and technique of the glass suit perfectly with the date and place required, but in another window of the chapel he found some glass, known to have been bought along with the figures, which contained the arms of Abbot Thomas von Eschenhausen.

At intervals during his researches Mr Somerton had been haunted by the recollection of the gossip about the hidden treasure, and, as he thought the matter over, it became more and more obvious to him that if the Abbot meant anything by the enigmatical answer which he gave

---

* There is a place for gold where it is hidden.

† They have on their raiment a writing which no man knoweth.

‡ Upon one stone are seven eyes.

to his questioners, he must have meant that the secret was to be found somewhere in the window he had placed in the abbey church. It was undeniable, furthermore, that the first of the curiously-selected texts on the scrolls in the window might be taken to have a reference to hidden treasure.

Every feature, therefore, or mark which could possibly assist in elucidating the riddle which, he felt sure, the Abbot had set to posterity he noted with scrupulous care, and, returning to his Berkshire manor-house, consumed many a pint of the midnight oil over his tracings and sketches. After two or three weeks, a day came when Mr Somerton announced to his man that he must pack his own and his master's things for a short journey abroad, whither for the moment we will not follow him.

II

Mr Gregory, the Rector of Parsbury, had strolled out before breakfast, it being a fine autumn morning, as far as the gate of his carriage-drive, with intent to meet the postman and sniff the cool air. Nor was he disappointed of either purpose. Before he had had time to answer more than ten or eleven of the miscellaneous questions propounded to him in the lightness of their hearts by his young offspring, who had accompanied him, the postman was seen approaching; and among the morning's budget was one letter bearing a foreign postmark and stamp (which became at once the objects of an eager competition among the youthful Gregorys), and was addressed in an uneducated, but plainly an English hand.

When the Rector opened it, and turned to the signature, he realized that it came from the confidential valet of his friend and squire, Mr Somerton. Thus it ran:

Honourd Sir, –

Has I am in a great anxeity about Master I write at is Wish to Beg you Sir if you could be so good as Step over. Master Has add a Nastey Shock and keeps His Bedd. I never Have known Him like this but No wonder and Nothing will serve but you Sir. Master says would I mintion the Short Way Here is Drive to Cobblince and take a Trap. Hopeing I Have maid

*all Plain, but am much Confused in Myself what with Anxiatey and
Weakfulness at Night. If I might be so Bold Sir it will be a Pleasure to see
a Honnest Brish Face among all These Forig ones.*

> *I am Sir*
>> *Your obedt Servt*
>>> *WILLIAM BROWN.*

P.S. – The Villiage for Town I will not Turm It is name Steenfeld.

The reader must be left to picture to himself in detail the surprise,
confusion, and hurry of preparation into which the receipt of such a letter
would be likely to plunge a quiet Berkshire parsonage in the year of grace
1859. It is enough for me to say that a train to town was caught in the
course of the day, and that Mr Gregory was able to secure a cabin in the
Antwerp boat and a place in the Coblentz train. Nor was it difficult to
manage the transit from that centre to Steinfeld.

I labour under a grave disadvantage as narrator of this story in that I
have never visited Steinfeld myself, and that neither of the principal actors
in the episode (from whom I derive my information) was able to give me
anything but a vague and rather dismal idea of its appearance. I gather
that it is a small place, with a large church despoiled of its ancient fittings;
a number of rather ruinous great buildings, mostly of the seventeenth
century, surround this church; for the abbey, in common with most of
those on the Continent, was rebuilt in a luxurious fashion by its inhabitants
at that period. It has not seemed to me worth while to lavish money on
a visit to the place, for though it is probably far more attractive than either
Mr Somerton or Mr Gregory thought it, there is evidently little, if anything, of first-rate interest to be seen – except, perhaps, one thing, which
I should not care to see.

The inn where the English gentleman and his servant were lodged is,
or was, the only 'possible' one in the village. Mr Gregory was taken to it
at once by his driver, and found Mr Brown waiting at the door. Mr
Brown, a model when in his Berkshire home of the impassive whiskered
race who are known as confidential valets, was now egregiously out of his
element, in a light tweed suit, anxious, almost irritable, and plainly anything but master of the situation. His relief at the sight of the 'honest

British face' of his Rector was unmeasured, but words to describe it were denied him. He could only say:

'Well, I ham pleased, I'm sure, sir, to see you. And so I'm sure, sir, will master.'

'How *is* your master, Brown?' Mr Gregory eagerly put in.

'I think he's better, sir, thank you; but he's had a dreadful time of it. I 'ope he's gettin' some sleep now, but – '

'What has been the matter – I couldn't make out from your letter? Was it an accident of any kind?'

'Well, sir, I 'ardly know whether I'd better speak about it. Master was very partickler he should be the one to tell you. But there's no bones broke – that's one thing I'm sure we ought to be thankful – '

'What does the doctor say?' asked Mr Gregory.

They were by this time outside Mr Somerton's bedroom door, and speaking in low tones. Mr Gregory, who happened to be in front, was feeling for the handle, and chanced to run his fingers over the panels. Before Brown could answer, there was a terrible cry from within the room.

'In God's name, who is that?' were the first words they heard. 'Brown, is it?'

'Yes, sir – me, sir, and Mr Gregory,' Brown hastened to answer, and there was an audible groan of relief in reply.

They entered the room, which was darkened against the afternoon sun, and Mr Gregory saw, with a shock of pity, how drawn, how damp with drops of fear, was the usually calm face of his friend, who, sitting up in the curtained bed, stretched out a shaking hand to welcome him.

'Better for seeing you, my dear Gregory,' was the reply to the Rector's first question, and it was palpably true.

After five minutes of conversation Mr Somerton was more his own man, Brown afterwards reported, than he had been for days. He was able to eat a more than respectable dinner, and talked confidently of being fit to stand a journey to Coblentz within twenty-four hours.

'But there's one thing,' he said, with a return of agitation which Mr Gregory did not like to see, 'which I must beg you to do for me, my dear Gregory. Don't,' he went on, laying his hand on Gregory's to forestall any interruption – 'don't ask me what it is, or why I want it done. I'm not up to explaining it yet; it would throw me back – undo all the good you have done me by coming. The only word I will say about it is that you run no risk whatever by doing it, and that Brown can and will show you to-morrow what it is. It's merely to put back – to keep – something – No; I can't speak of it yet. Do you mind calling Brown?'

'Well, Somerton,' said Mr Gregory, as he crossed the room to the door; 'I won't ask for any explanations till you see fit to give them. And if this bit of business is as easy as you represent it to be, I will very gladly undertake it for you the first thing in the morning.'

'Ah, I was sure you would, my dear Gregory; I was certain I could rely on you. I shall owe you more thanks than I can tell. Now, here is Brown. Brown, one word with you.'

'Shall I go?' interjected Mr Gregory.

'Not at all. Dear me, no. Brown, the first thing to-morrow morning – (you don't mind early hours, I know, Gregory) – you must take the Rector to – *there*, you know' (a nod from Brown, who looked grave and anxious), 'and he and you will put that back. You needn't be in the least alarmed; it's *perfectly* safe in the daytime. You know what I mean. It lies on the step, you know, where – where we put it.' (Brown swallowed dryly once or twice, and, failing to speak, bowed.) 'And – yes, that's all. Only this one other word, my dear Gregory. If you *can* manage to keep from questioning Brown about this matter, I shall be still more bound to you. To-morrow evening, at latest, if all goes well, I shall be able, I believe, to tell you the whole story from start to finish. And now I'll wish you good night. Brown will be with me – he sleeps here – and if I were you, I should lock my door. Yes, be particular to do that. They – they like it, the people here, and it's better. Good night, good night.'

They parted upon this, and if Mr Gregory woke once or twice in the small hours and fancied he heard a fumbling about the lower part of his locked door, it was, perhaps, no more than what a quiet man, suddenly plunged into a strange bed and the heart of a mystery, might reasonably expect. Certainly he thought, to the end of his days, that he had heard such a sound twice or three times between midnight and dawn.

He was up with the sun, and out in company with Brown soon after. Perplexing as was the service he had been asked to perform for Mr Somerton, it was not a difficult or an alarming one, and within half an hour from his leaving the inn it was over. What it was I shall not as yet divulge.

Later in the morning Mr Somerton, now almost himself again, was able to make a start from Steinfeld; and that same evening, whether at Coblentz or at some intermediate stage on the journey I am not certain, he settled down to the promised explanation. Brown was present, but how much of the matter was ever really made plain to his comprehension he would never say, and I am unable to conjecture.

III

This was Mr Somerton's story:

'You know roughly, both of you, that this expedition of mine was undertaken with the object of tracing something in connection with some old painted glass in Lord D——'s private chapel. Well, the starting-point of the whole matter lies in this passage from an old printed book, to which I will ask your attention.'

And at this point Mr Somerton went carefully over some ground with which we are already familiar.

'On my second visit to the chapel,' he went on, 'my purpose was to take every note I could of figures, lettering, diamond-scratchings on the glass, and even apparently accidental markings. The first point which I tackled was that of the inscribed scrolls. I could not doubt that the first of these, that of Job – "There is a place for the gold where it is hidden" – with its intentional alteration, must refer to the treasure; so I applied myself with some confidence to the next, that of St John – "They have on their vestures a writing which no man knoweth." The natural question will have occurred to you: Was there an inscription on the robes of the figures? I could see none; each of the three had a broad black border to his mantle, which made a conspicuous and rather ugly feature in the window. I was nonplussed, I will own, and but for a curious bit of luck I think I should have left the search where the Canons of Steinfeld had left it before me. But it so happened that there was a good deal of dust on the surface of the glass, and Lord D——, happening to come in, noticed my blackened hands, and kindly insisted on sending for a Turk's head broom to clean down the window. There must, I suppose, have been a rough piece in the broom; anyhow, as it passed over the border of one of the mantles, I noticed that it left a long scratch, and that some yellow stain instantly showed up. I asked the man to stop his work for a moment, and ran up the ladder to examine the place. The yellow stain was there, sure enough, and what had come away was a thick black pigment, which had evidently been laid on with the brush after the glass had been burnt, and could therefore be easily scraped off without doing any harm. I scraped, accordingly, and you will hardly believe – no, I do you an injustice; you will have guessed already – that I found under this black pigment two or three clearly-formed capital letters in yellow stain on a clear ground. Of course, I could hardly contain my delight.

'I told Lord D—— that I had detected an inscription which I thought might be very interesting, and begged to be allowed to uncover the whole of it. He made no difficulty about it whatever, told me to do exactly as I pleased, and then, having an engagement, was obliged – rather to my relief, I must say – to leave me. I set to work at once, and found the task a fairly easy one. The pigment, disintegrated, of course, by time, came off almost at a touch, and I don't think that it took me a couple of hours, all told, to clean the whole of the black borders in all three lights. Each of the figures had, as the inscription said, "a writing on their vestures which nobody knew."

'This discovery, of course, made it absolutely certain to my mind that I was on the right track. And, now, what was the inscription? While I was cleaning the glass I almost took pains not to read the lettering, saving up the treat until I had got the whole thing clear. And when that *was* done, my dear Gregory, I assure you I could almost have cried from sheer disappointment. What I read was only the most hopeless jumble of letters that was ever shaken up in a hat. Here it is:

Job.	DREVICIOPEDMOOMSMVIVLISLCAVI
	BASBATAOVT
St. John.	RDIIEAMRLESIPVSPODSEEIRSETTAA
	ESGIAVNNR
Zechariah.	FTEEAILNQDPVAIVMTLEEATTOHIO
	ONVMCAAT.H.Q.E.

'Blank as I felt and must have looked for the first few minutes, my disappointment didn't last long. I realized almost at once that I was dealing with a cipher or cryptogram; and I reflected that it was likely to be of a pretty simple kind, considering its early date. So I copied the letters with the most anxious care. Another little point, I may tell you, turned up in the process which confirmed my belief in the cipher. After copying the letters on Job's robe I counted them, to make sure that I had them right. There were thirty-eight; and, just as I finished going through them, my eye fell on a scratching made with a sharp point on the edge of the border. It was simply the number xxxviii in Roman numerals. To cut the matter short, there was a similar note, as I may call it, in each of the other lights; and that made it plain to me that the glass-painter had had very strict orders from Abbot Thomas about the inscription, and had taken pains to get it correct.

'Well, after that discovery you may imagine how minutely I went over the whole surface of the glass in search of further light. Of course, I did not neglect the inscription on the scroll of Zechariah – "Upon one stone are seven eyes," but I very quickly concluded that this must refer to some mark on a stone which could only be found *in situ*, where the treasure was concealed. To be short, I made all possible notes and sketches and tracings, and then came back to Parsbury to work out the cipher at leisure. Oh, the agonies I went through! I thought myself very clever at first, for I made sure that the key would be found in some of the old books on secret writing. The "*Steganographia*" of Joachim Trithemius, who was an earlier contemporary of Abbot Thomas, seemed particularly promising; so I got that, and Selenius's "*Cryptographia*" and Bacon "*de Augmentis Scientiarum,*" and some more. But I could hit upon nothing. Then I tried the principle of the "most frequent letter," taking first Latin and then German as a basis. That didn't help, either; whether it ought to have done so, I am not clear. And then I came back to the window itself, and read over my notes, hoping almost against hope that the Abbot might himself have somewhere supplied the key I wanted. I could make nothing out of the colour or pattern of the robes. There were no landscape backgrounds with subsidiary objects; there was nothing in the canopies. The only resource possible seemed to be in the attitudes of the figures. "Job," I read: "scroll in left hand, forefinger of right hand extended upwards. John: holds inscribed book in left hand; with right hand blesses, with two fingers. Zechariah: scroll in left hand; right hand extended upwards, as Job, but with three fingers pointing up." In other words, I reflected, Job has *one* finger extended, John has *two*, Zechariah has *three*. May not there be a numeral key concealed in that? My dear Gregory,' said Mr Somerton, laying his hand on his friend's knee, 'that *was* the key. I didn't get it to fit at first, but after two or three trials I saw what was meant. After the first letter of the inscription you skip *one* letter, after the next you skip *two*, and after that skip *three*. Now look at the result I got. I've underlined the letters which form words:

<u>D</u>REVICIOPED<u>M</u>OO<u>M</u>SMV<u>I</u>V<u>L</u>IS<u>L</u>CAV<u>IB</u>AS<u>B</u>A
TA<u>O</u>V<u>T</u>

<u>R</u>DIIEAM<u>R</u>LESIP<u>V</u>SP<u>OD</u>SEE<u>I</u>RS<u>ETT</u>A<u>A</u>ESGIA
V<u>NN</u>R

F<u>TEE</u>AI<u>L</u>N<u>QD</u>PVAI<u>V</u>MTLEEAT<u>TO</u>HIOONVMC
<u>AAT</u>.H.Q.E.

'Do you see it? *"Decent millia auri reposita sunt in puteo in at . . ."* (Ten thousand [pieces] of gold are laid up in a well in . . .), followed by an incomplete word beginning *at*. So far so good. I tried the same plan with the remaining letters; but it wouldn't work, and I fancied that perhaps the placing of dots after the three last letters might indicate some difference of procedure. Then I thought to myself, "Wasn't there some allusion to a well in the account of Abbot Thomas in that book the '*Sertum*'?" Yes, there was: he built a *puteus in atrio* (a well in the court). There, of course, was my word *atrio*. The next step was to copy out the remaining letters of the inscription, omitting those I had already used. That gave what you will see on this slip:

RVIIOPDOOSMVVISCAVBSBTAOTDIEAMLSIVSPD
EERSETAEGIANRFEEALQDVAIMLEATTHOOVMCA.
H.Q.E.

'Now, I knew what the three first letters I wanted were – namely, *rio* – to complete the word *atrio*; and, as you will see, these are all to be found in the first five letters. I was a little confused at first by the occurrence of two *i*'s but very soon I saw that every alternate letter must be taken in the remainder of the inscription. You can work it out for yourself; the result, continuing where the first "round" left off, is this:

"*rio domus abbatialis de Steinfeld a me, Thoma, qui posui custodem super ea. Gare à qui la touche.*"

'So the whole secret was out:

"Ten thousand pieces of gold are laid up in the well in the court of the Abbot's house of Steinfeld by me, Thomas, who have set a guardian over them. *Gare à qui la touche.*"

'The last words, I ought to say, are a device which Abbot Thomas had adopted. I found it with his arms in another piece of glass at Lord D——'s, and he drafted it bodily into his cipher, though it doesn't quite fit in point of grammar.

'Well, what would any human being have been tempted to do, my dear Gregory, in my place? Could he have helped setting off, as I did, to Steinfeld, and tracing the secret literally to the fountain-head? I don't believe he could. Anyhow, I couldn't, and, as I needn't tell you, I found myself at Steinfeld as soon as the resources of civilization could put me there, and installed myself in the inn you saw. I must tell you that I was not altogether free from forebodings – on one hand of disappointment, on the other of danger. There was always the possibility that Abbot Thomas's well might have been wholly obliterated, or else that someone, ignorant of cryptograms, and guided only by luck, might have stumbled on the treasure before me. And then' – there was a very perceptible shaking of the voice here – 'I was not entirely easy, I need not mind confessing, as to the meaning of the words about the guardian of the treasure. But, if you don't mind, I'll say no more about that until – until it becomes necessary.

'At the first possible opportunity Brown and I began exploring the place. I had naturally represented myself as being interested in the remains of the abbey, and we could not avoid paying a visit to the church, impatient as I was to be elsewhere. Still, it did interest me to see the windows where the glass had been, and especially that at the east end of the south aisle. In the tracery lights of that I was startled to see some fragments and coats-of-arms remaining – Abbot Thomas's shield was there, and a small figure with a scroll inscribed "*Oculos habent, et non videbunt*" (They have eyes, and shall not see), which, I take it, was a hit of the Abbot at his Canons.

'But, of course, the principal object was to find the Abbot's house. There is no prescribed place for this, so far as I know, in the plan of a monastery; you can't predict of it, as you can of the chapter-house, that it will be on the eastern side of the cloister, or, as of the dormitory, that it will communicate with a transept of the church. I felt that if I asked many questions I might awaken lingering memories of the treasure, and I thought it best to try first to discover it for myself. It was not a very long or difficult search. That three-sided court south-east of the church, with deserted piles of building round it, and grass-grown pavement, which you saw this morning, was the place. And glad enough I was to see that it was put to no use, and was neither very far from our inn nor overlooked by any inhabited building; there were only orchards and paddocks on the slopes east of the church. I can tell you that fine stone glowed wonderfully in the rather watery yellow sunset that we had on the Tuesday afternoon.

'Next, what about the well? There was not much doubt about that, as you can testify. It is really a very remarkable thing. That curb is, I think, of Italian marble, and the carving I thought must be Italian also. There were reliefs, you will perhaps remember, of Eliezer and Rebekah, and of Jacob opening the well for Rachel, and similar subjects; but, by way of disarming suspicion, I suppose, the Abbot had carefully abstained from any of his cynical and allusive inscriptions.

'I examined the whole structure with the keenest interest, of course – a square well-head with an opening in one side; an arch over it, with a wheel for the rope to pass over, evidently in very good condition still, for it had been used within sixty years, or perhaps even later, though not quite recently. Then there was the question of depth and access to the interior. I suppose the depth was about sixty to seventy feet; and as to the other point, it really seemed as if the Abbot had wished to lead searchers up to the very door of his treasure-house, for, as you tested for yourself, there were big blocks of stone bonded into the masonry, and leading down in a regular staircase round and round the inside of the well.

'It seemed almost too good to be true. I wondered if there was a trap – if the stones were so contrived as to tip over when a weight was placed on them; but I tried a good many with my own weight and with my stick, and all seemed, and actually were, perfectly firm. Of course, I resolved that Brown and I would make an experiment that very night.

'I was well prepared. Knowing the sort of place I should have to explore, I had brought a sufficiency of good rope and bands of webbing to surround my body, and crossbars to hold to, as well as lanterns and candles and crowbars, all of which would go into a single carpet-bag and excite no suspicion. I satisfied myself that my rope would be long enough, and that the wheel for the bucket was in good working order, and then we went home to dinner.

'I had a little cautious conversation with the landlord, and made out that he would not be overmuch surprised if I went out for a stroll with my man about nine o'clock, to make (Heaven forgive me!) a sketch of the abbey by moonlight. I asked no questions about the well, and am not likely to do so now. I fancy I know as much about it as anyone in Steinfeld: at least' – with a strong shudder – 'I don't want to know any more.

'Now we come to the crisis, and, though I hate to think of it, I feel sure, Gregory, that it will be better for me in all ways to recall it just as it happened. We started, Brown and I, at about nine with our bag, and attracted no attention; for we managed to slip out at the hinder end of the inn-yard into an alley which brought us quite to the edge of the village. In five minutes we were at the well, and for some little time we sat on the edge of the well-head to make sure that no one was stirring or spying on us. All we heard was some horses cropping grass out of sight farther down the eastern slope. We were perfectly unobserved, and had plenty of light from the gorgeous full moon to allow us to get the rope properly fitted over the wheel. Then I secured the band round my body beneath the arms. We attached the end of the rope very securely to a ring in the stonework. Brown took the lighted lantern and followed me; I had a crowbar. And so we began to descend cautiously, feeling every step before we set foot on it, and scanning the walls in search of any marked stone.

'Half aloud I counted the steps as we went down, and we got as far as the thirty-eighth before I noted anything at all irregular in the surface of the masonry. Even here there was no mark, and I began to feel very blank, and to wonder if the Abbot's cryptogram could possibly be an elaborate hoax. At the forty-ninth step the staircase ceased. It was with a very sinking heart that I began retracing my steps, and when I was back on the thirty-eighth – Brown, with the lantern, being a step or two above me – I scrutinized the little bit of irregularity in the stonework with all my might; but there was no vestige of a mark.

'Then it struck me that the texture of the surface looked just a little smoother than the rest, or, at least, in some way different. It might possibly be cement and not stone. I gave it a good blow with my iron bar. There was a decidedly hollow sound, though that might be the result of our being in a well. But there was more. A great flake of cement dropped on to my feet, and I saw marks on the stone underneath. I had tracked the Abbot down, my dear Gregory; even now I think of it with a certain pride. It took but a very few more taps to clear the whole of the cement away, and I saw a slab of stone about two feet square, upon which was engraven a cross. Disappointment again, but only for a moment. It was you, Brown, who reassured me by a casual remark. You said, if I remember right:

'"It's a funny cross; looks like a lot of eyes."

'I snatched the lantern out of your hand, and saw with inexpressible pleasure that the cross *was* composed of seven eyes, four in a vertical line, three horizontal. The last of the scrolls in the window was explained in the way I had anticipated. Here was my "stone with the seven eyes." So far the Abbot's data had been exact, and, as I thought of this, the anxiety about the "guardian" returned upon me with increased force. Still, I wasn't going to retreat now.

'Without giving myself time to think, I knocked away the cement all round the marked stone, and then gave it a prise on the right side with my crowbar. It moved at once, and I saw that it was but a thin light slab, such as I could easily lift out myself, and that it stopped the entrance to a cavity. I did lift it out unbroken, and set it on the step, for it might be very important to us to be able to replace it. Then I waited for several minutes on the step just above. I don't know why, but I think to see if any dreadful thing would rush out. Nothing happened. Next I lit a candle, and very cautiously I placed it inside the cavity, with some idea of seeing whether there were foul air, and of getting a glimpse of what was inside. There *was* some foulness of air which nearly extinguished the flame, but in no long time it burned quite steadily. The hole went some little way back, and also on the right and left of the entrance, and I could see some rounded light-coloured objects within which might be bags. There was no use in waiting. I faced the cavity, and looked in. There was nothing immediately in the front of the hole. I put my arm in and felt to the right, very gingerly . . .

'Just give me a glass of cognac, Brown. I'll go on in a moment, Gregory . . .

'Well, I felt to the right, and my fingers touched something curved, that felt – yes – more or less like leather; dampish it was, and evidently part of a heavy, full thing. There was nothing, I must say, to alarm one. I grew bolder, and putting both hands in as well as I could, I pulled it to me, and it came. It was heavy, but moved more easily than I had expected. As I pulled it towards the entrance, my left elbow knocked over and extinguished the candle. I got the thing fairly in front of the mouth and began drawing it out. Just then Brown gave a sharp ejaculation and ran quickly up the steps with the lantern. He will tell you why in a moment. Startled as I was, I looked round after him, and saw him stand for a minute at the top and then walk away a few yards. Then I heard him call softly, "All right, sir," and went on pulling out the great bag, in complete darkness. It hung for an instant on the edge of the hole, then slipped forward on to my chest, and *put its arms round my neck*.

'My dear Gregory, I am telling you the exact truth. I believe I am now acquainted with the extremity of terror and repulsion which a man can endure without losing his mind. I can only just manage to tell you now the bare outline of the experience. I was conscious of a most horrible smell of mould, and of a cold kind of face pressed against my own, and moving slowly over it, and of several – I don't know how many – legs or arms or tentacles or something clinging to my body. I screamed out, Brown says, like a beast, and fell away backward from the step on which I stood, and the creature slipped downwards, I suppose, on to that same step. Providentially the band round me held firm. Brown did not lose his head, and was strong enough to pull me up to the top and get me over the edge quite promptly. How he managed it exactly I don't know, and I think he would find it hard to tell you. I believe he contrived to hide our implements in the deserted building near by, and with very great difficulty he got me back to the inn. I was in no state to make explanations, and Brown knows no German; but next morning I told the people some tale of having had a bad fall in the abbey ruins, which, I suppose, they believed. And now, before I go further, I should just like you to hear what Brown's experiences during those few minutes were. Tell the Rector, Brown, what you told me.'

'Well, sir,' said Brown, speaking low and nervously, 'it was just this way. Master was busy down in front of the 'ole, and I was 'olding the lantern and looking on, when I 'eard somethink drop in the water from the top, as I thought. So I looked up, and I see someone's 'ead lookin' over at us. I s'pose I must ha' said somethink, and I 'eld the light up and run up the steps, and my light shone right on the face. That was a bad un, sir, if ever I see one! A holdish man, and the face very much fell in, and larfin, as I thought. And I got up the steps as quick pretty nigh as I'm tellin' you, and when I was out on the ground there warn't a sign of any person. There 'adn't been the time for anyone to get away, let alone a hold chap, and I made sure he warn't crouching down by the well, nor nothink. Next thing I hear master cry out something 'orrible, and hall I see was him hanging out by the rope, and, as master says, 'owever I got him up I couldn't tell you.'

'You hear that, Gregory?' said Mr Somerton. 'Now, does any explanation of that incident strike you?'

'The whole thing is so ghastly and abnormal that I must own it puts me quite off my balance; but the thought did occur to me that possibly the – well, the person who set the trap might have come to see the success of his plan.'

'Just so, Gregory, just so. I can think of nothing else so – *likely*. I should say, if such a word had a place anywhere in my story. I think it must have been the Abbot . . . Well, I haven't much more to tell you. I spent a miserable night, Brown sitting up with me. Next day I was no better; unable to get up; no doctor to be had; and, if one had been available, I doubt if he could have done much for me. I made Brown write off to you, and spent a second terrible night. And, Gregory, of this I am sure, and I think it affected me more than the first shock, for it lasted longer: there was someone or something on the watch outside my door the whole night. I almost fancy there were two. It wasn't only the faint noises I heard from time to time all through the dark hours, but there was the smell – the hideous smell of mould. Every rag I had had on me on that first evening I had stripped off and made Brown take it away. I believe he stuffed the things into the stove in his room; and yet the smell was there, as intense as it had been in the well; and, what is more, it came from outside the door. But with the first glimmer of dawn it faded out, and the sounds ceased, too; and that convinced me that the thing or things were creatures of darkness, and could not stand the daylight; and so I was sure that if anyone could put back the stone, it or they would be powerless until someone else took it away again. I had to wait until you came to get that done. Of course, I couldn't send Brown to do it by himself, and still less could I tell anyone who belonged to the place.

'Well, there is my story; and if you don't believe it, I can't help it. But I think you do.'

'Indeed,' said Mr Gregory, 'I can find no alternative. I *must* believe it! I saw the well and the stone myself, and had a glimpse, I thought, of the bags or something else in the hole. And, to be plain with you, Somerton, I believe my door was watched last night, too.'

'I dare say it was, Gregory; but, thank goodness, that is over. Have you, by the way, anything to tell about your visit to that dreadful place?'

'Very little,' was the answer. 'Brown and I managed easily enough to get the slab into its place, and he fixed it very firmly with the irons and wedges you had desired him to get, and we contrived to smear the surface with mud so that it looks just like the rest of the wall. One thing I did notice in the carving on the well-head, which I think must have escaped you. It was a horrid, grotesque shape – perhaps more like a toad than anything else, and there was a label by it inscribed with the two words, *"Depositum custodi."'*

G. K. CHESTERTON

The Awful Reason of the Vicar's Visit

The revolt of Matter against Man (which I believe to exist) has now been reduced to a singular condition. It is the small things rather than the large things which make war against us and, I may add, beat us. The bones of the last mammoth have long ago decayed, a mighty wreck; the tempests no longer devour our navies, nor the mountains with hearts of fire heap hell over our cities. But we are engaged in a bitter and eternal war with small things; chiefly with microbes and with collar studs. The stud with which I was engaged (on fierce and equal terms) as I made the above reflections, was one which I was trying to introduce into my shirt collar when a loud knock came at the door.

My first thought was as to whether Basil Grant had called to fetch me. He and I were to turn up at the same dinner-party (for which I was in the act of dressing), and it might be that he had taken it into his head to come my way, though we had arranged to go separately. It was a small and confidential affair at the table of a good but unconventional political lady, an old friend of his. She had asked us both to meet a third guest, a Captain Fraser, who had made something of a name and was an authority on chimpanzees. As Basil was an old friend of the hostess and I had never seen her, I felt that it was quite possible that he (with his usual social sagacity) might have decided to take me along in order to break the ice. The theory, like all my theories, was complete; but as a fact it was not Basil.

I was handed a visiting card inscribed: 'Rev. Ellis Shorter', and underneath was written in pencil, but in a hand in which even hurry could not conceal a depressing and gentlemanly excellence, 'Asking the favour of a few moments' conversation on a most urgent matter.'

I had already subdued the stud, thereby proclaiming that the image of God has supremacy over all matters (a valuable truth), and throwing on my dress-coat and waistcoat, hurried into the drawing-room. He rose at my entrance, flapping like a seal; I can use no other description. He flapped a plaid shawl over his right arm; he flapped a pair of pathetic black gloves; he flapped his clothes; I may say, without exaggeration, that he flapped his eyelids, as he rose. He was a bald-browed, white-haired, white-whiskered old clergyman, of a flappy and floppy type. He said:

'I am so sorry. I am so very sorry. I am so extremely sorry. I come – I can only say – I can only say in my defence, that I come – upon an important matter. Pray forgive me.'

I told him I forgave perfectly and waited.

'What I have to say,' he said brokenly, 'is so dreadful – it is so dreadful – I have lived a quiet life.'

I was burning to get away, for it was already doubtful if I should be in time for dinner. But there was something about the old man's honest air of bitterness that seemed to open to me the possibilities of life larger and more tragic than my own.

I said gently: 'Pray go on.'

Nevertheless the old gentleman, being a gentleman as well as old, noticed my secret impatience and seemed still more unmanned.

'I'm so sorry,' he said meekly; 'I wouldn't have come – but for – your friend Major Brown recommended me to come here.'

'Major Brown!' I said, with some interest.

'Yes,' said the Reverend Mr Shorter, feverishly flapping his plaid shawl about. 'He told me you helped him in a great difficulty – and my difficulty! Oh, my dear sir, it's a matter of life and death.'

I rose abruptly, in an acute perplexity. 'Will it take long, Mr Shorter?' I asked. 'I have to go out to dinner almost at once.'

He rose also, trembling from head to foot, and yet somehow, with all his moral palsy, he rose to the dignity of his age and his office.

'I have no right, Mr Swinburne – I have no right at all,' he said. 'If you have to go out to dinner, you have of course – a perfect right – of course a perfect right. But when you come back – a man will be dead.'

And he sat down, quaking like a jelly.

The triviality of the dinner had been in those two minutes dwarfed and drowned in my mind. I did not want to go and see a political widow, and a captain who collected apes; I wanted to hear what had brought this dear, doddering old vicar into relation with immediate perils.

'Will you have a cigar?' I said.

'No, thank you,' he said, with indescribable embarrassment, as if not smoking cigars was a social disgrace.

'A glass of wine?' I said.

'No, thank you, no, thank you; not just now,' he repeated with that hysterical eagerness with which people who do not drink at all often try to convey that on any other night of the week they would sit up all night drinking rum-punch. 'Not just now, thank you.'

'Nothing else I can get for you?' I said, feeling genuinely sorry for the well-mannered old donkey. 'A cup of tea?'

I saw a struggle in his eye and I conquered. When the cup of tea came he drank it like a dipsomaniac gulping brandy. Then he fell back and said:

'I have had such a time, Mr Swinburne. I am not used to these excitements. As Vicar of Chuntsey, in Essex' – he threw this in with an indescribable airiness of vanity – 'I have never known such things happen.'

'What things happen?' I asked.

He straightened himself with sudden dignity.

'As Vicar of Chuntsey, in Essex,' he said, 'I have never been forcibly dressed up as an old woman and made to take part in a crime in the character of an old woman. Never once. My experience may be small. It may be insufficient. But it has never occurred to me before.'

'I have never heard of it,' I said, 'as among the duties of a clergyman. But I am not well up in church matters. Excuse me if perhaps I failed to follow you correctly. Dressed up – as what?'

'As an old woman,' said the vicar solemnly, 'as an old woman.'

I thought in my heart that it required no great transformation to make an old woman of him, but the thing was evidently more tragic than comic, and I said respectfully:

'May I ask how it occurred?'

'I will begin at the beginning,' said Mr Shorter, 'and I will tell my story with the utmost possible precision. At seventeen minutes past eleven this morning I left the vicarage to keep certain appointments and pay certain visits in the village. My first visit was to Mr Jervis, the treasurer of our League of Christian Amusements, with whom I concluded some business touching the claim made by Parkes the gardener in the matter of the rolling of our tennis lawn. I then visited Mrs Arnett, a very earnest churchwoman, but permanently bedridden. She is the author of several small works of devotion, and of a book of verse, entitled (unless my memory misleads me) *Eglantine*.'

He uttered all this not only with deliberation, but with something that can only be called, by a contradictory phrase, eager deliberation. He had, I think, a vague memory in his head of the detectives in the detective stories, who always sternly require that nothing should be kept back.

'I then proceeded,' he went on, with the same maddening conscientiousness of manner, 'to Mr Carr (not Mr James Carr, of course; Mr Robert Carr) who is temporarily assisting our organist, and having consulted with him (on the subject of a choir boy who is accused, I cannot as yet say whether justly or not, of cutting holes in the organ pipes), I finally dropped in upon a Dorcas meeting at the house of Miss Brett. The Dorcas meetings are usually held at the vicarage, but my wife being unwell, Miss Brett, a newcomer in our village, but very active in church work, had very kindly consented to hold them. The Dorcas society is entirely under my wife's management as a rule, and except for Miss Brett, who, as I say, is very active, I scarcely know any members of it. I had, however, promised to drop in on them, and I did so.

'When I arrived there were only four other maiden ladies with Miss Brett, but they were sewing very busily. It is very difficult, of course, for any person, however strongly impressed with the necessity in these matters of full and exact exposition of the facts, to remember and repeat the actual details of a conversation, particularly a conversation which (though inspired with a most worthy and admirable zeal for good work) was one which did not greatly impress the hearer's mind at the time and was, in fact – er – mostly about socks. I can, however, remember distinctly that one of the spinster ladies (she was a thin person with a woollen shawl, who appeared to feel the cold, and I am almost sure she was introduced to me as Miss James) remarked that the weather was very changeable. Miss Brett then offered me a cup of tea, which I accepted, I cannot recall in what words. Miss Brett is a short and stout lady with white hair. The only other figure in the group that caught my attention was a Miss Mowbray, a small and neat lady of aristocratic manners, silver hair, and a high voice and colour. She was the most emphatic member of the party; and her views on the subject of pinafores, though expressed with a natural deference to myself, were in themselves strong and advanced. Beside her (although all five ladies were dressed simply in black) it could not be denied that the others looked in some way what you men of the world would call dowdy.

'After about ten minutes' conversation I rose to go, and as I did so I heard something which – I cannot describe it – something which seemed to – but I really cannot describe it.'

'What did you hear?' I asked, with some impatience.

'I heard,' said the vicar solemnly, 'I heard Miss Mowbray (the lady with the silver hair) say to Miss James (the lady with the woollen shawl), the following extraordinary words. I committed them to memory on the spot, and as soon as circumstances set me free to do so, I noted them down on a piece of paper. I believe I have it here.' He fumbled in his breast-pocket, bringing out mild things, note-books, circulars and programmes of village concerts. 'I heard Miss Mowbray say to Miss James, the following words: "Now's your time, Bill."'

He gazed at me for a few moments after making this announcement, gravely and unflinchingly, as if conscious that here he was unshaken about his facts. Then he resumed, turning his bald head more towards the fire.

'This appeared to me remarkable. I could not by any means understand it. It seemed to me first of all peculiar that one maiden lady should address another maiden lady as "Bill". My experience, as I have said, may be incomplete; maiden ladies may have among themselves and in exclusively spinster circles wilder customs than I am aware of. But it seemed to me odd, and I could almost have sworn (if you will not misunderstand the phrase), I should have been strongly impelled to maintain at the time that the words, "Now's your time, Bill", were by no means pronounced with that upper-class intonation which, as I have already said, had up to now characterized Miss Mowbray's conversation. In fact, the words, "Now's your time, Bill", would have been, I fancy, unsuitable if pronounced with that upper-class intonation.

'I was surprised, I repeat, then, at the remark. But I was still more surprised when, looking round me in bewilderment, my hat and umbrella in hand, I saw the lean lady with the woollen shawl leaning upright against the door out of which I was just about to make my exit. She was still knitting, and I supposed that this erect posture against the door was only an eccentricity of spinsterhood and an oblivion of my intended departure.

'I said genially, "I am so sorry to disturb you, Miss James, but I must really be going. I have – er – " I stopped here, for the words she had uttered in reply, though singularly brief and in tone extremely business-like, were such as to render that arrest of my remarks, I think, natural and excusable. I have these words also noted down. I have not the least idea of their meaning; so I have only been able to render them phoneti-cally. But she said,' and Mr Shorter peered short-sightedly at his papers, 'she said: "Chuck it, fat 'ead," and she added something that sounded like "It's a kop", or (possibly) "a kopt". And then the last cord, either of my sanity or the sanity of the universe, snapped suddenly. My esteemed friend and helper, Miss Brett, standing by the mantelpiece, said: "Put 'is old 'ead in a bag, Sam, and tie 'im up before you start jawin'. You'll be kopt yourselves some o' these days with this way of doin' things, har lar theater."

'My head went round and round. Was it really true, as I had suddenly fancied a moment before, that unmarried ladies had some dreadful riotous society of their own from which all others were excluded? I remembered dimly in my classical days (I was a scholar in a small way once, but now, alas! rusty), I remembered the mysteries of the Bona Dea and their strange female freemasonry. I remembered the witches' Sabbaths. I was just, in my absurd lightheadedness, trying to remember a line of verse about Diana's nymphs, when Miss Mowbray threw her arm round me from behind. The moment it held me I knew it was not a woman's arm.

'Miss Brett – or what I had called Miss Brett – was standing in front of me with a big revolver in her hand and a broad grin on her face. Miss James was still leaning against the door, but had fallen into an attitude so totally new, and so totally unfeminine, that it gave one a shock. She was kicking her heels, with her hands in her pockets and her cap on one side. She was a man. I mean he was a wo – no, that is I saw that instead of being a woman she – he, I mean – that is, it was a man.'

Mr Shorter became indescribably flurried and flapping in endeavouring to arrange these genders and his plaid shawl at the same time. He resumed with a higher fever of nervousness:

'As for Miss Mowbray, she – he, held me in a ring of iron. He had her arm – that is she had her arm – round her neck – my neck I mean – and I could not cry out. Miss Brett – that is, Mr Brett, at least Mr something who was not Miss Brett – had the revolver pointed at me. The other two ladies – or er – gentlemen, were rummaging in some bag in the background. It was all clear at last: they were criminals dressed up as women, to kidnap me! To kidnap the Vicar of Chuntsey, in Essex. But why? Was it to be Nonconformists?

'The brute leaning against the door called out carelessly, " 'Urry up, 'Arry. Show the old bloke what the game is, and let's get off."

'"Curse 'is eyes," said Miss Brett – I mean the man with the revolver – "why should we show 'im the game?"

'"If you take my advice you bloomin' well will," said the man at the door, whom they called Bill. "A man wot knows wot 'e's doin' is worth ten wot don't, even if 'e's a potty old parson."

'"Bill's right enough," said the coarse voice of the man who held me (it had been Miss Mowbray's). "Bring out the picture, 'Arry."

'The man with the revolver walked across the room to where the other two women – I mean men – were turning over baggage, and asked them for something which they gave him. He came back with it across the room and held it out in front of me. And compared to the surprise of that display, all the previous surprises of this awful day shrank suddenly.

'It was a portrait of myself. That such a picture should be in the hands of these scoundrels might in any case have caused a mild surprise; but no more. It was no mild surprise that I felt. The likeness was an extremely good one, worked up with all the accessories of the conventional photographic studio. I was leaning my head on my hand and was relieved against a painted landscape of woodland. It was obvious that it was no snapshot; it was clear that I had sat for this photograph. And the truth was that I had never sat for such a photograph. It was a photograph that I had never had taken.

'I stared at it again and again. It seemed to me to be touched up a good deal; it was glazed as well as framed, and the glass blurred some of the details. But there unmistakably was my face, my eyes, my nose and mouth, my head and hand, posed for a professional photographer. And I had never posed so for any photographer.

'"Be'old the bloomin' miracle," said the man with the revolver, with ill-timed facetiousness. "Parson, prepare to meet your God." And with this he slid the glass out of the frame. As the glass moved, I saw that part of the picture was painted on it in Chinese white, notably a pair of white whiskers and a clerical collar. And underneath was a portrait of an old lady in a quiet black dress, leaning her head on her hand against the woodland landscape. The old lady was as like me as one pin is like another. It had required only the whiskers and the collar to make it me in every hair.

'"Entertainin', ain't it?" said the man described as 'Arry, as he shot the glass back again. "Remarkable resemblance, parson. Gratifyin' to the lady. Gratifyin' to you. And hi may hadd, particlery gratifyin' to us, as bein' the probable source of a very tolerable haul. You know Colonel Hawker, the man who's come to live in these parts, don't you?"

'I nodded.

'"Well," said the man 'Arry, pointing to the picture, "that's 'is mother. 'Oo ran to catch 'im when 'e fell? She did," and he flung his fingers in a general gesture towards the photograph of the old lady who was exactly like me.

'"Tell the old gent wot 'e's got to do and be done with it," broke out Bill from the door. "Look 'ere, Reverend Shorter, we ain't goin' to do you no 'arm. We'll give you a sov. for your trouble if you like. And as for the old woman's clothes – why, you'll look lovely in 'em."

'"You ain't much of a 'and at a description, Bill," said the man behind me. "Mr Shorter, it's like this. We've got to see this man Hawker tonight. Maybe 'e'll kiss us all and 'ave up the champagne when 'e sees us. Maybe on the other 'and – 'e won't. Maybe 'e'll be dead when we goes away. Maybe not. But we've got to see 'im. Now as you know, 'e shuts 'isself up and never opens the door to a soul; only you don't know why and we does. The only one as can ever get at 'im is 'is mother. Well, it's a confounded funny coincidence," he said, accenting the penultimate, "it's a very unusual piece of good luck, but you're 'is mother."

'"When first I saw 'er picture," said the man Bill, shaking his head in a ruminant manner, "when I first saw it I said – old Shorter. Those were my exact words – old Shorter."

'"What do you mean, you wild creatures?" I gasped. "What am I to do?"

'"That's easy said, your 'oliness," said the man with the revolver, good-humouredly; "you've got to put on those clothes," and he pointed to a poke-bonnet and a heap of female clothes in the corner of the room.

'I will not dwell, Mr Swinburne, upon the details of what followed. I had no choice. I could not fight five men, to say nothing of a loaded pistol. In five minutes, sir, the Vicar of Chuntsey was dressed as an old woman – as somebody else's mother, if you please – and was dragged out of the house to take part in a crime.

'It was already late in the afternoon, and the nights of winter were closing in fast. On a dark road, in a blowing wind, we set out towards the lonely house of Colonel Hawker, perhaps the queerest cortège that ever straggled up that or any other road. To every human eye, in every external, we were six very respectable old ladies of small means, in black dresses and refined but antiquated bonnets; and we were really five criminals and a clergyman.

'I will cut a long story short. My brain was whirling like a windmill as I walked, trying to think of some manner of escape. To cry out, so long as we were far from houses, would be suicidal, for it would be easy for the ruffians to knife me or to gag me and fling me into a ditch. On the other hand, to attempt to stop strangers and explain the situation was impossible, because of the frantic folly of the situation itself. Long before I had persuaded the chance postman or carrier of so absurd a story, my companions would certainly have got off themselves, and in all probability would have carried me off, as a friend of theirs who had the misfortune to be mad or drunk. The last thought, however, was an inspiration; though a very terrible one. Had it come to this, that the Vicar of Chuntsey must pretend to be mad or drunk? It had come to this.

'I walked along with the rest up the deserted road, imitating and keeping pace, as far as I could, with their rapid and yet lady-like step, until at length I saw a lamp-post and a policeman standing under it. I had made up my mind. Until we reached them we were all equally demure and silent and swift. When we reached them I suddenly flung myself against the railings and roared out: "Hooray! Hooray! Hooray! Rule Britannia! Get your 'air cut. Hoop-la! Boo!" It was a condition of no little novelty for a man in my position.

'The constable instantly flashed his lantern on me, or the draggled, drunken old woman that was my travesty. "Now then, mum," he began gruffly.

'"Come along quiet, or I'll eat your heart," cried Sam in my ear hoarsely. "Stop, or I'll flay you." It was frightful to hear the words and see the neatly shawled old spinster who whispered them.

'I yelled, and yelled – I was in for it now. I screamed comic refrains that vulgar young men had sung, to my regret, at our village concerts; I rolled to and fro like a ninepin about to fall.

'"If you can't get your friend on quiet, ladies," said the policeman, "I shall have to take 'er up. Drunk and disorderly she is right enough."

'I redoubled my efforts. I had not been brought up to this sort of thing; but I believe I eclipsed myself. Words that I did not know I had ever heard of seemed to come pouring out of my open mouth.

'"When we get you past," whispered Bill, "you'll howl louder; you'll howl louder when we're burning your feet off."

'I screamed in my terror those awful songs of joy. In all the nightmares that men have ever dreamed, there has never been anything so blighting and horrible as the faces of those five men, looking out of their poke-bonnets; the figures of district visitors with the faces of devils. I cannot think there is anything so heart-breaking in hell.

'For a sickening instant I thought that the bustle of my companions and the perfect respectability of all our dresses would overcome the police-man and induce him to let us pass. He wavered, so far as one can describe anything so solid as a policeman as wavering. I lurched suddenly forward and ran my head into his chest, calling out (if I remember correctly), "Oh, crikey, blimey, Bill." It was at that moment that I remembered most clearly that I was the Vicar of Chuntsey, in Essex.

'My desperate coup saved me. The policeman had me hard by the back of the neck.

'"You come along with me," he began, but Bill cut in with his perfect imitation of a lady's finnicking voice.

'"Oh, pray, constable, don't make a disturbance with our poor friend.

335

We will get her quietly home. She does drink too much, but she is quite a lady – only eccentric."

'"She butted me in the stomach," said the policeman briefly.

'"Eccentricities of genius," said Sam earnestly.

'"Pray let me take her home," reiterated Bill, in the resumed character of Miss James, "she wants looking after."

'"She does," said the policeman, "but I'll look after her."

'"That's no good," cried Bill feverishly. "She wants her friends. She warns a particular medicine we've got."

'"Yes," assented Miss Mowbray, with excitement, "no other medicine any good, constable. Complaint quite unique."

'"I'm all righ'. Cutchy, cutchy, coo!" remarked, to his eternal shame, the Vicar of Chuntsey.

'"Look here, ladies," said the constable sternly, "I don't like the eccentricity of your friend, and I don't like 'er songs, or 'er 'ead in my stomach. And now I come to think of it, I don't like the looks of you. I've seen many as quiet dressed as you as was wrong 'uns. Who are you?"

'"We've not our cards with us," said Miss Mowbray, with indescribable dignity. "Nor do we see why we should be insulted by any Jack-in-office who chooses to be rude to ladies, when he is paid to protect them. If you choose to take advantage of the weakness of our unfortunate friend, no doubt you are legally entitled to take her. But if you fancy you have any legal right to bully us, you will find yourself in the wrong box."

'The truth and dignity of this staggered the policeman for a moment. Under cover of their advantage my five persecutors turned for an instant on me faces like faces of the damned and then swished off into the darkness. When the constable first turned his lantern and his suspicions on to them, I had seen the telegraphic look flash from face to face saying that only retreat was possible now.

'By this time I was sinking slowly to the pavement, in a state of acute reflection. So long as the ruffians were with me, I dared not quit the role of drunkard. For if I had begun to talk reasonably and explain the real case, the officer would merely have thought that I was slightly recovered and would have put me in charge of my friends. Now, however, if I liked I might safely undeceive him.

'But I confess I did not like. The chances of life are many, and it may doubtless sometimes lie in the narrow path of duty for a clergyman of the Church of England to pretend to be a drunken old woman; but such necessities are, I imagine, sufficiently rare to appear to many improbable. Suppose the story got about that I had pretended to be drunk. Suppose people did not all think it was pretence!

'I lurched up, the policeman half-lifting me. I went along weakly and quietly for about a hundred yards. The officer evidently thought that I was too sleepy and feeble to effect an escape, and so held me lightly and easily enough. Past one turning, two turnings, three turnings, four turnings, he trailed me with him, a limp and slow and reluctant figure. At the fourth turning, I suddenly broke from his hand and tore down the street like a maddened stag. He was unprepared, he was heavy, and it was dark. I ran and ran and ran, and in five minutes' running, found I was gaining. In half an hour I was out in the fields under the holy and blessed stars, where I tore off my accursed shawl and bonnet and buried them in clean earth.'

'The old gentleman had finished his story and leant back in his chair. Both the matter and the manner of his narration had, as time went on, impressed me favourably. He was an old duffer and pedant, but behind these things he was a country-bred man and gentleman, and had showed courage and a sporting instinct in the hour of desperation. He had told his story with many quaint formalities of diction, but also with a very convincing realism.

'And now – ' I began.

'And now,' said Shorter, leaning forward again with something like servile energy, 'and now, Mr Swinburne, what about that unhappy man Hawker. I cannot tell what those men meant, or how far what they said was real. But surely there is danger. I cannot go to the police, for reasons that you perceive. Among other things, they wouldn't believe me. What is to be done?'

I took out my watch. It was already half past twelve.

'My friend Basil Grant,' I said, 'is the best man we can go to. He and I were to have gone to the same dinner tonight; but he will just have come back by now. Have you any objection to taking a cab?'

'Not at all,' he replied, rising politely, and gathering up his absurd plaid shawl.

A rattle in a hansom brought us underneath the sombre pile of work-men's flats in Lambeth which Grant inhabited; a climb up a wearisome wooden staircase brought us to his garret. When I entered that wooden and scrappy interior, the white gleam of Basil's shirt-front and the lustre of his fur coat flung on the wooden settle, struck me as a contrast. He was drinking a glass of wine before retiring. I was right; he had come back from the dinner-party.

He listened to the repetition of the story of the Rev. Ellis Shorter with the genuine simplicity and respect which he never failed to exhibit in dealing with any human being. When it was over he said simply:

'Do you know a man named Captain Fraser?'

I was so startled at this totally irrelevant reference to the worthy col-lector of chimpanzees with whom I ought to have dined that evening, that I glanced sharply at Grant. The result was that I did not look at Mr Shorter. I only heard him answer, in his most nervous tone, 'No.'

Basil, however, seemed to find something very curious about his answer or his demeanour generally, for he kept his big blue eyes fixed on the old clergyman, and though the eyes were quite quiet they stood out more and more from his head.

'You are quite sure, Mr Shorter,' he repeated, 'that you don't know Captain Fraser?'

'Quite,' answered the vicar, and I was certainly puzzled to find him returning so much to the timidity, not to say the demoralization, of his tone when he first entered my presence.

Basil sprang smartly to his feet.

'Then our course is clear,' he said. 'You have not even begun your inves-tigation, my dear Mr Shorter; the first thing for us to do is to go together to see Captain Fraser.'

'When?' asked the clergyman, stammering.

'Now,' said Basil, putting one arm in his fur coat.

The old clergyman rose to his feet, quaking all over.

'I really do not think that it is necessary,' he said.

Basil took his arm out of the fur coat, threw it over the chair again, and put his hands in his pockets.

'Oh,' he said, with emphasis. 'Oh – you don't think it necessary; then,' and he added the words with great clearness and deliberation, 'then, Mr

Ellis Shorter, I can only say that I would like to see you without your whiskers.'

And at these words I also rose to my feet, for the great tragedy of my life had come. Splendid and exciting as life was in continual contact with an intellect like Basil's, I had always the feeling that that splendour and excitement were on the borderland of sanity. He lived perpetually near the vision of the reason of things which makes men lose their reason. And I felt of his insanity as men feel of the death of friends with heart disease. It might come anywhere, in a field, in a hansom cab, looking at a sunset, smoking a cigarette. It had come now. At the very moment of delivering a judgement for the salvation of a fellow creature, Basil Grant had gone mad.

'Your whiskers,' he cried, advancing with blazing eyes. 'Give me your whiskers. And your bald head.'

The old vicar naturally retreated a step or two. I stepped between.

'Sit down, Basil,' I implored, 'you're a little excited. Finish your wine.'

'Whiskers,' he answered sternly, 'whiskers.'

And with that he made a dash at the old gentleman, who made a dash for the door, but was intercepted. And then, before I knew where I was the quiet room was turned into something between a pantomime and a pandemonium by those two. Chairs were flung over with a crash, tables were vaulted with a noise like thunder, screens were smashed, crockery scattered in smithereens, and still Basil Grant bounded and bellowed after the Rev. Ellis Shorter.

And now I began to perceive something else, which added the last half-witted touch to my mystification. The Rev. Ellis Shorter, of Chuntsey, in Essex, was by no means behaving as I had previously noticed him to behave, or as, considering his age and station, I should have expected him to behave. His power of dodging, leaping, and fighting would have been amazing in a lad of seventeen, and in this doddering old vicar looked like a sort of farcical fairy-tale. Moreover, he did not seem to be so much astonished as I had thought. There was even a look of something like enjoyment in his eyes; so there was in the eye of Basil. In fact, the unintelligible truth must be told. They were both laughing.

At length Shorter was cornered.

'Come, come, Mr Grant,' he panted, 'you can't do anything to me.

339

It's quite legal. And it doesn't do any one the least harm. It's only a social fiction. A result of our complex society, Mr Grant.'

'I don't blame you, my man,' said Basil coolly. 'But I want your whiskers. And your bald head. Do they belong to Captain Fraser?'

'No, no,' said Mr Shorter, laughing, 'we provide them ourselves. They don't belong to Captain Fraser.'

'What the deuce does all this mean?' I almost screamed. 'Are you all in an infernal nightmare? Why should Mr Shorter's bald head belong to Captain Fraser? How could it? What the deuce has Captain Fraser to do with the affair? What is the matter with him? You dined with him, Basil.'

'No,' said Grant, 'I didn't.'

'Didn't you go to Mrs Thornton's dinner-party?' I asked, staring. 'Why not?'

'Well,' said Basil, with a slow and singular smile, 'the fact is I was detained by a visitor. I have him, as a point of fact, in my bedroom.'

'In your bedroom?' I repeated; but my imagination had reached that point when he might have said in his coal scuttle or his waistcoat pocket.

Grant stepped to the door of an inner room, flung it open and walked in. Then he came out again with the last of the bodily wonders of that wild night. He introduced into the sitting-room, in an apologetic manner, and by the nape of the neck, a limp clergyman with a bald head, white whiskers and a plaid shawl.

'Sit down, gentlemen,' cried Grant, striking his hands heartily. 'Sit down all of you and have a glass of wine. As you say, there is no harm in it, and if Captain Fraser had simply dropped me a hint I could have saved him from dropping a good sum of money. Not that you would have liked that, eh?'

The two duplicate clergymen, who were sipping their Burgundy with two duplicate grins, laughed heartily at this, and one of them carelessly pulled off his whiskers and laid them on the table.

'Basil,' I said, 'if you are my friend, save me. What is all this?'

He laughed again.

'Only another addition, Cherub, to your collection of Queer Trades. These two gentlemen (whose health I have now the pleasure of drinking) are Professional Detainers.'

'And what on earth's that?' I asked.

'It's really very simple, Mr Swinburne,' began he who had once been the Rev. Ellis Shorter, of Chuntsey, in Essex; and it gave me a shock indescribable to hear out of that pompous and familiar form come no longer its own pompous and familiar voice, but the brisk sharp tones of a young city man. 'It is really nothing very important. We are paid by our clients to detain in conversation, on some harmless pretext, people whom they want out of the way for a few hours. And Captain Fraser –' and with that he hesitated and smiled.

Basil smiled also. He intervened.

'The fact is that Captain Fraser, who is one of my best friends, wanted us both out of the way very much. He is sailing tonight for East Africa, and the lady with whom we were all to have dined is – er – what is I believe described as "the romance of his life". He wanted that two hours with her, and employed these two reverend gentlemen to detain us at our houses so as to let him have the field to himself.'

'And of course,' said the late Mr Shorter apologetically to me, 'as I had to keep a gentleman at home from keeping an appointment with a lady, I had to come with something rather hot and strong – rather urgent. It wouldn't have done to be tame.'

'Oh,' I said, 'I acquit you of tameness.'

'Thank you, sir,' said the man respectfully, 'always very grateful for any recommendation, sir.'

The other man idly pushed back his artificial bald head, revealing close red hair, and spoke dreamily, perhaps under the influence of Basil's admirable Burgundy.

'It's wonderful how common it's getting, gentlemen. Our office is busy from morning till night. I've no doubt you've often knocked up against us before. You just take no notice. When an old bachelor goes on boring you with hunting stories when you're burning to be introduced to somebody, he's from our bureau. When a lady calls on parish work and stops hours, just when you wanted to go to the Robinsons', she's from our bureau. The Robinson hand, sir, may be darkly seen.'

'There is one thing I don't understand,' I said. 'Why you are both vicars.'

A shade crossed the brow of the temporary incumbent of Chuntsey, in Essex.

'That may have been a mistake, sir,' he said. 'But it was not our fault. It was all the munificence of Captain Fraser. He requested that the highest price and talent on our tariff should be employed to detain you gentlemen. Now the highest payment in our office goes to those who impersonate vicars, as being the most respectable and more of a strain. We are paid five guineas a visit. We have had the good fortune to satisfy the firm with our work; and we are now permanently vicars. Before that we had two years as colonels, the next in our scale. Colonels are four guineas.'

MAY SINCLAIR

Wilkinson's Wife

I

Nobody ever understood why he married her.

You expected calamity to pursue Wilkinson – it always had pursued him – ; but that Wilkinson should have gone out of his way to pursue calamity (as if he could never have enough of it) really seemed a most unnecessary thing.

For there had been no pursuit on the part of the lady. Wilkinson's wife had the quality of her defects, and revealed herself chiefly in a formidable reluctance. It was understood that Wilkinson had prevailed only after an austere struggle. Her appearance sufficiently refuted any theory of unholy fascination or disastrous charm.

Wilkinson's wife was not at all nice to look at. She had an insignificant figure, a small, square face, colourless hair scraped with difficulty to the top of her head, eyes with no lashes to protect you from their stare, a mouth that pulled at an invisible curb, a sallow skin stretched so tight over her cheek-bones that the red veins stood stagnant there; and with it all, poor lady, a dull, strained expression hostile to further intimacy.

Even in her youth she never could have looked young, and she was years older than Wilkinson. Not that the difference showed, for his marriage had made Wilkinson look years older than he was; at least, so it was said by people who had known him before that unfortunate event.

It was not even as if she had been intelligent. Wilkinson had a gentle passion for the things of intellect; his wife seemed to exist on purpose to frustrate it. In no department of his life was her influence so penetrating and malign. At forty he no longer counted; he had lost all his brilliance, and had replaced it by a shy, unworldly charm. There was something in Wilkinson that dreamed or slept, with one eye open, fixed upon his wife. Of course, he had his blessed hours of deliverance from the woman. Sometimes he would fly in her face and ask people to dine at his house in Hampstead, to discuss Roman remains, or the Troubadours, or Nietzsche. He never could understand why his wife couldn't 'enter,' as he expressed it, into these subjects. He smiled at you in the dimmest, saddest way when he referred to it. 'It's extraordinary,' he would say, 'the little interest she takes in Nietzsche.'

Mrs Norman found him once wandering in the High Street, with his passion full on him. He was a little absent, a little flushed; his eyes shone behind his spectacles; and there were pleasant creases in his queer, clean-shaven face.

She inquired the cause of his delight.

'I've got a man coming to dine this evening, to have a little talk with me. He knows all about the Troubadours.'

And Wilkinson would try and make you believe that they had threshed out the Troubadours between them. But when Mrs Norman, who was a little curious about Wilkinson, asked the Troubadour man what they *had* talked about, he smiled and said it was something – some extraordinary adventure – that had happened to Wilkinson's wife.

People always smiled when they spoke of her. Then, one by one, they left off dining with Wilkinson. The man who read Nietzsche was quite rude about it. He said he wasn't going there to be gagged by that woman. He would have been glad enough to ask Wilkinson to dine with him, if he would go without his wife.

If it had not been for Mrs Norman the Wilkinsons would have vanished from the social scene. Mrs Norman had taken Wilkinson up, and it was evident that she did not mean to let him go. That, she would have told you with engaging emphasis, was not her way. She had seen how things were going, socially, with Wilkinson, and she was bent on his deliverance.

If anybody could have carried it through, it would have been Mrs Norman, she was clever; she was charming; she had a house in Fitzjohn's Avenue, where she entertained intimately. At forty she had preserved the best part of her youth and prettiness, and an income insufficient for Mr

Norman, but enough for her. As she said in her rather dubious pathos, she had nobody but herself to please now.

You gathered that if Mr Norman had been living he would not have been pleased with her cultivation of the Wilkinsons. She was always asking them to dinner. They turned up punctually at her delightful Friday evenings (her little evenings) from nine to eleven. They dropped in to tea on Sunday afternoons. Mrs Norman had a wonderful way of drawing Wilkinson out; while Evey, her unmarried sister, made prodigious efforts to draw Wilkinson's wife in. 'If you could only make her,' said Mrs Norman, 'take an interest in something.'

But Evey couldn't make her take an interest in anything. Evey had no sympathy with her sister's missionary adventure. She saw what Mrs Norman wouldn't see – that, if they forced Mrs Wilkinson on people who were trying to keep away from her, people would simply keep away from them. Their Fridays were not so well attended, so delightful, as they had been. A heavy cloud of dulness seemed to come into the room, with Mrs Wilkinson, at nine o'clock. It hung about her chair, and spread slowly, till everybody was wrapped in it.

Then Evey protested. She wanted to know why Cornelia allowed their evenings to be blighted thus. 'Why ask Mrs Wilkinson?'

'I wouldn't,' said Cornelia, 'if there was any other way of getting him.'

'Well,' said Evey, 'he's nice enough, but it's rather a large price to have to pay.'

'And is he,' cried Cornelia passionately, 'to be cut off from everything because of that one terrible mistake?'

Evey said nothing. If Cornelia were going to take him that way, there was nothing to be said!

So Mrs Norman went on drawing Wilkinson out more and more, till one Sunday afternoon, sitting beside her on the sofa, he emerged positively splendid. There were moments when he forgot about his wife.

They had been talking together about his blessed Troubadours. (It was wonderful the interest Mrs Norman took in them!) Suddenly his gentleness and sadness fell from him, a flame sprang up behind his spectacles, and the something that slept or dreamed in Wilkinson awoke. He was away with Mrs Norman in a lovely land, in Provence of the thirteenth century. A strange chant broke from him; it startled Evey, where she sat at the other end of the room. He was reciting his own translation of a love-song of Provence.

At the first words of the refrain his wife, who had never ceased staring at him, got up and came across the room. She touched his shoulder just as he was going to say '*Ma mie.*'

'Come, Peter,' she said, 'it's time to be going home.'

Wilkinson rose on his long legs. '*Ma mie,*' he said, looking down at her; and the flaming dream was still in his eyes behind his spectacles.

He took the little cloak she held out to him, a pitiful and rather vulgar thing. He raised it with the air of a courtier handling a royal robe; then he put it on her, smoothing it tenderly about her shoulders.

Mrs Norman followed them to the porch. As he turned to her on the step, she saw that his eyes were sad, and that his face, as she put it, had gone to sleep again.

When she came back to her sister, her own eyes shone and her face was rosy.

'Oh, Evey,' she said, 'isn't it beautiful?'

'Isn't what beautiful?'

'Mr Wilkinson's behaviour to his wife.'

II

It was not an easy problem that Mrs Norman faced. She wished to save Wilkinson; she also wished to save the character of her Fridays, which Wilkinson's wife had already done her best to destroy. Mrs Norman could not think why the woman came, since she didn't enjoy herself, since she was impenetrable to the intimate, peculiar charm. You could only suppose that her object was to prevent its penetrating Wilkinson, to keep the other women off. Her eyes never left him.

It was all very well for Evey to talk. She *might*, of course, have been wiser in the beginning. She might have confined the creature to their big monthly crushes, where, as Evey had suggested, she would easily have been mislaid and lost. But so, unfortunately, would Wilkinson; and the whole point was how not to lose him.

Evey said she was tired of being told off to entertain Mrs Wilkinson.

She was beginning to be rather disagreeable about it. She said Cornelia was getting to care too much about that Wilkinson man. She wouldn't have minded playing up to her if she had approved of the game; but Mrs Wilkinson was, after all, you know, Mr Wilkinson's wife.

Mrs Norman cried a little. She told Evey she ought to have known it was his spirit that she cared about. But she owned that it wasn't right to sacrifice poor Evey. Neither, since he *had* a wife, was it altogether right for her to care about Wilkinson's spirit to the exclusion of her other friends.

Then, one Friday, Mrs Norman, relieving her sister for once, made a discovery while Evey, who was a fine musician, played. Mrs Wilkinson did, after all, take an interest in something; she was accessible to the throbbing of Evey's bow across the strings.

She had started; her eyes had turned from Wilkinson and fastened on the player. There was a light in them, beautiful and piercing, as if her soul had suddenly been released from some hiding-place in its unlovely house. Her face softened, her mouth relaxed, her eyes closed. She lay back in her chair, at peace, withdrawn from them, positively lost.

Mrs Norman slipped across the room to the corner where Wilkinson sat alone. His face lightened as she came.

'It's extraordinary,' he said, 'her love of music.'

Mrs Norman assented. It *was* extraordinary, if you came to think of it. Mrs Wilkinson had no understanding of the art. What did it mean to her? Where did it take her? You could see she was transported, presumably to some place of chartered stupidity, of condoned oblivion, where nobody could challenge her right to enter and remain.

'So soothing,' said Wilkinson, 'to the nerves.'

Mrs Norman smiled at him. She felt that, under cover of the music, his spirit was seeking communion with hers.

He thanked her at parting; the slight hush and mystery of his manner intimated that she had found a way.

'I hope,' she said, 'you'll come often – often.'

'May we? May we? 'He seemed to leap at it – as if they hadn't come often enough before!

Certainly she had found the way – the way to deliver him, the way to pacify his wife, to remove her gently to her place and keep her there.

The dreadful lady thus creditably disposed of, Wilkinson was no longer backward in the courting of his opportunity. He proved punctual to the first minute of the golden hour.

Hampstead was immensely interested in his blossoming forth. It found a touching simplicity in the way he lent himself to the sympathetic eye. All the world was at liberty to observe his intimacy with Mrs Norman.

It endured for nine weeks. Then suddenly, to Mrs Norman's bewilderment, it ceased. The Wilkinsons left off coming to her Friday evenings. They refused her invitations. Their behaviour was so abrupt and so mysterious that Mrs Norman felt that something must have happened to account for it. Somebody, she had no doubt, had been talking. She was much annoyed with Wilkinson in consequence, and, when she met him accidentally in the High Street, her manner conveyed to him her just resentment.

He called in Fitzjohn's Avenue the next Sunday. For the first time, he was without his wife.

He was so downcast, and so penitent, and so ashamed of himself that Mrs Norman met him halfway with a little rush of affection.

'Why have you not been to see us all this time?' she said.

He looked at her unsteadily; his whole manner betrayed an extreme embarrassment.

'I've come,' he said, 'on purpose to explain. You mustn't think I don't appreciate your kindness, but, the fact is, my poor wife' – (She knew that woman was at the bottom of it!) – 'is no longer – up to it.'

'What is the wretch up to, I should like to know?' thought Mrs Norman.

He held her with his melancholy, unsteady eyes. He seemed to be endeavouring to approach a subject intimately and yet abstrusely painful.

'She finds the music – just at present – a little too much for her; the vibrations, you know. It's extraordinary how they affect her. She feels them – most unpleasantly – just here.' Wilkinson laid two delicate fingers on the middle buttons of his waistcoat.

Mrs Norman was very kind to him. He was not very expert, poor fellow, in the fabrication of excuses. His look seemed to implore her pardon for the shifts he had been driven to; it appealed to her to help him out, to stand by him in his unspeakable situation.

'I see,' she said.

He smiled, in charming gratitude to her for seeing it.

That smile raised the devil in her. Why, after all, should she help him out?

'And are you susceptible to music – in the same unpleasant way?'

'Me? Oh, no – no. I like it; it gives me the very greatest pleasure.' He stared at her in bewilderment and distress.

'Then why,' said Mrs Norman sweetly, 'if it gives you pleasure, should you cut yourself off from it?'

'My dear Mrs Norman, we have to cut ourselves off from a great many things – that give us pleasure. It can't be helped.'

She meditated. 'Would it be any good,' she said, 'if I were to call on Mrs Wilkinson?'

Wilkinson looked grave. 'It is most kind of you, but – just at present – I think it might be wiser not. She really, you know, isn't very fit.'

Mrs Norman's silence neither accepted nor rejected the preposterous pretext. Wilkinson went on, helping himself out as best he could:

'I can't talk about it; but I thought I ought to let you know. We've just got to give everything up.'

She held herself in. A terrible impulse was upon her to tell him straight out that she did not see it; that it was too bad; that there was no reason why *she* should be called upon to give everything up.

'So, if we don't come,' he said, 'you'll understand? It's better – it really is better not.' His voice moved her, and her heart cried to him, 'Poor Peter!'

'Yes,' she said; 'I understand.'

Of course she understood. Poor Peter! so it had come to that?

'Can't you stay for tea?' she said.

'No; I must be going back to her.'

He rose. His hand found hers. Its slight pressure told her that he gave and took the sadness of renunciation.

That winter Mrs Wilkinson fell ill in good earnest, and Wilkinson became the prey of a pitiful remorse that kept him a prisoner by his wife's bedside.

He had always been a good man; it was now understood that he avoided Mrs Norman because he desired to remain what he had always been.

III

There was also an understanding, consecrated by the piety of their renunciation, that Wilkinson was only waiting for his wife's death to marry Mrs Norman.

And Wilkinson's wife was a long time in dying. It was not to be supposed that she would die quickly, as long as she could interfere with his happiness by living.

With her genius for frustrating and tormenting, she kept the poor man on tenter-hooks with perpetual relapses and recoveries. She jerked him on the chain. He was always a prisoner on the verge of his release. She was at death's door in March. In April she was to be seen, convalescent, in a bath-chair, being wheeled slowly up and down the Spaniard's Road. And Wilkinson walked by the chair, his shoulders bent, his eyes fixed on the ground, his face set in an expression of illimitable patience.

In the summer she gave it up and died; and in the following spring Wilkinson resumed his converse with Mrs Norman. All things considered, he had left a decent interval.

By autumn Mrs Norman's friends were all on tiptoe and craning their necks with expectation. It was assumed among them that Wilkinson would propose to her the following summer, when the first year of his widowhood should be ended. When summer came, there was nothing between them that anybody could see. But it by no means followed that there was nothing to be seen. Mrs Norman seemed perfectly sure of him. In her intense sympathy for Wilkinson, she knew how to account for all his hesitations and delays. She could not look for any passionate, decisive step from the broken creature he had become; she was prepared to accept him as he was, with all his humiliating fears and waverings. The tragic things his wife had done to him could not be undone in a day.

Another year divided Wilkinson from his tragedy, and still he stood trembling weakly on the verge. Mrs Norman began to grow thin. She lost her bright air of defiance, and showed herself vulnerable by the hand of time. And nothing, positively nothing, stood between them, except Wilkinson's morbid diffidence. So absurdly manifest was their case that somebody (the Troubadour man, in fact) interposed discreetly. In the most delicate manner possible, he gave Wilkinson to understand that he would not necessarily make himself obnoxious to Mrs Norman were he to approach her with – well, with a view to securing their joint happiness – happiness which they had both earned by their admirable behaviour.

That was all that was needed: a tactful friend of both parties to put it to Wilkinson simply and in the right way. Wilkinson rose from his abasement. There was a light in his eye that rejoiced the tactful friend; his face had a look of sudden, virile determination.

'I will go to her,' he said, 'now.'

It was a dark, unpleasant evening, full of cold and sleet.

Wilkinson thrust his arms into an overcoat, jammed a cap down on his forehead, and strode into the weather. He strode into Mrs Norman's drawing-room.

When Mrs Norman saw that look on his face, she knew that it was all right. Her youth rose in her again to meet it.

'Forgive me,' said Wilkinson. 'I had to come.'

'Why not?' she said.

'It's so late.'

'Not too late for me.'

He sat down, still with his air of determination, in the chair she indicated. He waved away, with unconcealed impatience, the trivialities she used to soften the violence of his invasion.

'I've come,' he said, 'because I've had something on my mind. It strikes me that I've never really thanked you.'

'Thanked me?'

'For your great kindness to my wife.'

Mrs Norman looked away,

'I shall always be grateful to you,' said Wilkinson. 'You were very good to her.'

'Oh, no, no,' she moaned.

'I assure you,' he insisted, 'she felt it very much. I thought you would like to know that.'

'Oh, yes.' Mrs Norman's voice went very low with the sinking of her heart.

'She used to say you did more for her – you and your sister, with her beautiful music – than all the doctors. You found the thing that eased her. I suppose *you* knew how ill she was – all the time? I mean before her last illness.'

'I don't think,' said she, 'I did know.'

His face, which had grown grave, brightened. 'No? Well, you see, she was so plucky. Nobody could have known; I didn't always realize it myself.'

Then he told her that for five years his wife had suffered from a nervous malady that made her subject to strange excitements and depressions.

'We fought it,' he said, 'together. Through it all, even on her worst days, she was always the same to me.'

He sank deeper into memory.

'Nobody knows what she was to me. She wasn't one much for society. She went into it' (his manner implied that she had adorned it) 'to please me, because I thought it might do her good. It was one of the things we tried.'

Mrs Norman stared at him. She stared through him and beyond him, and saw a strange man. She listened to a strange voice that sounded far off, from somewhere beyond forgetfulness,

'There were times,' she heard him saying, 'when we could not go out or see any one. All we wanted was to be alone together. We could sit, she and I, a whole evening without saying a word. We each knew what the other wanted to say without saying it. I was always sure of her; she understood me as nobody else ever can.' He paused. 'All that's gone.'

'Oh, no,' Mrs Norman said, 'it isn't.'

'It is.' He illuminated himself with a faint flame of passion.

'Don't say that, when you have friends who understand.'

'They don't. They can't. And,' said Wilkinson, 'I don't want them to.'

Mrs Norman sat silent, as in the presence of something sacred and supreme.

She confessed afterward that what had attracted her to Peter Wilkinson was his tremendous capacity for devotion. Only (this she did not confess) she never dreamed that it had been given to his wife.

ISRAEL ZANGWILL

The Tug of Love

When Elias Goldenberg, Belcovitch's head cutter, betrothed himself to Fanny Fersht, the prettiest of the machinists, the Ghetto blessed the match, always excepting Sugarman the *Shadchan* (whom love matches shocked), and Goldenberg's relatives (who considered Fanny flighty and fond of finery).

'That Fanny of yours was cut out for a rich man's wife,' insisted Goldenberg's aunt, shaking her pious wig.

'He who marries Fanny *is* rich,' retorted Elias.

'"Pawn your hide, but get a bride,"' quoted the old lady savagely.

As for the slighted marriage-broker, he remonstrated almost like a relative.

'But I didn't want a negotiated marriage,' Elias protested.

'A love marriage I could also have arranged for you,' replied Sugarman indignantly.

But Elias was quite content with his own arrangement, for Fanny's glance was melting and her touch transporting. To deck that soft warm hand with an engagement-ring, a month's wages had not seemed disproportionate, and Fanny flashed the diamond bewitchingly. It lit up the gloomy workshop with its signal of felicity. Even Belcovitch, bent over his press-iron, sometimes omitted to rebuke Fanny's badinage.

The course of true love seemed to run straight to the Canopy – Fanny had already worked the bridegroom's praying-shawl – when suddenly a storm broke. At first the cloud was no bigger than a man's hand – in fact, it was a man's hand. Elias espied it groping for Fanny's in the dim space between the two machines. As Fanny's fingers fluttered towards it, her other hand still guiding the cloth under the throbbing needle, Elias felt

353

the needle stabbing his heart up and down, through and through. The very finger that held his costly ring lay in this alien paw gratis.

The shameless minx! Ah, his relatives were right. He snapped the scissors savagely like a dragon's jaw.

'Fanny, what dost thou?' he gasped in Yiddish.

Fanny's face flamed; her guilty fingers flew back.

'I thought thou wast on the other side,' she breathed.

Elias snorted incredulously.

As soon as Sugarman heard of the breaking of the engagement he flew to Elias, his blue bandanna streaming from his coat-tail.

'If you had come to me,' he crowed, 'I should have found you a more reliable article. However, Heaven has given you a second helping. A well-built wage-earner like you can look as high as a greengrocer's daughter even.'

'I never wish to look upon a woman again,' Elias groaned.

'*Schtuss!*' said the great marriage-broker. 'Three days after the Fast of Atonement comes the Feast of Tabernacles. The Almighty, blessed be He, who created both light and darkness, has made obedient females as well as pleasure-seeking jades.' And he blew his nose emphatically into his bandanna.

'Yes; but she won't return me my ring,' Elias lamented.

'What!' Sugarman gasped. 'Then she considers herself still engaged to you.'

'Not at all. She laughs in my face.'

'And she has given you back your promise?'

'My promise – yes. The ring – no.'

'But on what ground?'

'She says I gave it to her.'

Sugarman clucked his tongue. 'Tututu! Better if we had followed our old custom, and the man had worn the engagement-ring, not the woman!'

'In the workshop,' Elias went on miserably, 'she flashes it in my eyes. Everybody makes mock. Oh, the Jezebel!'

'I should summons her!'

'It would only cost me more. Is it not true I gave her the ring?'

Sugarman mopped his brow. His vast experience was at fault. No maiden had ever refused to return his client's ring; rather had she flung it in the wooer's false teeth.

'This comes of your love matches!' he cried sternly. 'Next time there must be a proper contract.'

'Next time!' repeated Elias. 'Why, how am I to afford a new ring? Fanny was ruinous in cups of chocolate and the pit of the Pavilion Theatre!'

'I should want my fee down!' said Sugarman sharply.

Elias shrugged his shoulders. 'If you bring me the ring.'

'I do not get old rings, but new maidens,' Sugarman reminded him haughtily. 'However, as you are a customer – ' and crying 'Five per cent. on the greengrocer's daughter,' he hurried away ere Elias had time to dissent from the bargain.

Donning his sealskin vest to overawe the Fershts, Sugarman ploughed his way up the dark staircase to their room. His attire was wasted on the family, for Fanny herself opened the door.

'Peace to you,' he cried. 'I have come on behalf of Elias Goldenberg.'

'It is useless. I will not have him.' And she was shutting the door. Her misconception, wilful or not, scattered all Sugarman's prepared diplomacies. 'He does not want you, he wants the ring,' he cried hastily.

Fanny indecorously put a finger to her nose. The diamond glittered mockingly on it. Then she turned away giggling. 'But look at this photograph!' panted Sugarman desperately through the closing door.

Surprise and curiosity brought her eyes back. She stared at the sheepish features of a frock-coated stranger.

'Four pounds a week all the year round, head cutter at S. Cohn's,' said Sugarman, pursuing this advantage. 'A good old English family; Benjamin Beckenstein is his name, and he is dying to step into Elias's shoes.'

'His feet are too large!' And she flicked the photograph floorwards with her bediamonded finger.

'But why waste the engagement-ring?' pleaded Sugarman, stooping to pick up the suitor.

'What an idea! A new man, a new ring!' And Fanny slammed the door.

'Impudence-face! Would you become a jewellery shop!' the baffled *Shadchan* shrieked through the woodwork.

He returned to Elias, brooding darkly.

'Well?' queried Elias.

'O, your love matches!' And Sugarman shook them away with shuddersome palms.

'Then she won't – '

'No, she won't. Ah, how blessed you are to escape from that daughter of Satan! The greengrocer's daughter, now – '

'Speak me no more matches. I risk no more rings.'

'I will get you one on the hire system.'

'A maiden?'

'Guard your tongue! A ring, of course.'

Elias shook an obdurate head. 'No. I must have the old ring back.'

'That is impossible – unless you marry her to get it back. Stay! Why should I not arrange that for you?'

'Leave me in peace! Heaven has opened my eyes.'

'Then see how economical she is!' urged Sugarman. 'A maiden who sticks to a ring like that is not likely to be wasteful of your substance.'

'You have not seen her swallow "stuffed monkeys,"' said Elias grimly. 'Make an end! I have done with her.'

'No, you have not! You can still give yourself a counsel.' And Sugarman looked a conscious sphinx. 'You may yet get back the ring.'

'How?'

'Of course, I have the next disposal of it?' said Sugarman.

'Yes, yes. Go on.'

'To-morrow in the workshop pretend to steal loving glances all day long when she's not looking. When she catches you – '

'But she won't be looking!'

'Oh, yes, she will. When she catches you, you must blush.'

'But I can't blush at will,' Elias protested.

'I know it is hard. Well, look foolish. That will be easier for you.'

'But why shall I look foolish?'

'To make her think you are in love with her after all.'

'I should look foolish if I were.'

'Precisely. That is the idea. When she leaves the workshop in the evening follow her, and as she passes the cake-shop, sigh and ask her if she will not eat a "stuffed monkey" for the sake of peace-be-upon-him times.'

'But she won't.'

'Why not? She is still in love.'

'With stuffed monkeys,' said Elias cynically.

'With you too.'

Elias blushed quite easily. 'How do you know?'

'I offered her another man, and she slammed the door in my face!'

'You – you offered –' Elias stuttered angrily.

'Only to test her,' said Sugarman soothingly. He continued:

'Now, when she has eaten the cake and drunk a cup of chocolate, too (for one must play high with such a ring at stake), you must walk on by her side, and when you come to a dark corner, take her hand and say "My treasure," or "My angel," or whatever nonsense you modern young men babble to your maidens – with the results you see! – and while she is drinking it all in like more chocolate, her fingers in yours, give a sudden tug, and off comes the ring!'

Elias gazed at him in admiration. 'You are as crafty as Jacob, our father.'

'Heaven has not denied everybody brains,' replied Sugarman modestly. 'Be careful to seize the left hand.'

The admiring Elias followed the scheme to the letter.

Even the blush he had boggled at came to his cheeks punctually whenever his sheep's-eyes met Fanny's He was so surprised to find his face burning that he looked foolish into the bargain.

They dallied long in the cake-shop, Elias trying to summon up courage for the final feint. He would get a good grip on the ring finger. The tug-of-war should be brief.

Meantime the couple clinked chocolate cups, and smiled into each other's eyes.

'The good-for-nothing!' thought Elias hotly. 'She will make the same eyes at the next man.'

And he went on gorging her, every speculative 'stuffed monkey' increasing his nervous tension. Her white teeth, biting recklessly into the cake, made him itch to slap her rosy cheek. Confectionery palled at last, and Fanny led the way out. Elias followed, chattering with feverish gaiety. Gradually he drew up even with her.

They turned down the deserted Fishmonger's Alley, lit by one dull gas-lamp. Elias's limbs began to tremble with the excitement of the critical moment. He felt like a footpad. Hither and thither he peered – nobody was about. But – was he on the right side of her? 'The right is the left,' he told himself, trying to smile, but his pulses thumped, and in the tumult of heart and brain he was not sure he knew her right hand from her left. Fortunately he caught the glitter of the diamond in the gloom, and instinctively his robber hand closed upon it.

But as he felt the warm responsive clasp of those soft fingers, that ancient delicious thrill pierced every vein. Fool that he had been to doubt that dear hand! And it was wearing his ring still – she could not part with it! O blundering male ingrate!

'My treasure! My angel!' he murmured ecstatically.

ARNOLD BENNETT

The Death of Simon Fuge

I

It was in the train that I learnt of his death. Although a very greedy eater
of literature, I can only enjoy reading when I have little time for reading.
Give me three hours of absolute leisure, with nothing to do but read, and
I instantly become almost incapable of the act. So it is always on railway
journeys, and so it was that evening. I was in the middle of Wordsworth's
Excursion; I positively gloated over it, wondering why I should have
allowed a mere rumour that it was dull to prevent me from consuming it
earlier in my life. But do you suppose I could continue with Wordsworth
in the train? I could not. I stared out of the windows; I calculated the
speed of the train by my watch; I thought of my future and my past; I
drew forth my hopes, examined them, polished them, and put them back
again; I forgave myself for my sins; and I dreamed of the exciting conquest
of a beautiful and brilliant woman that I should one day achieve. In short,
I did everything that men habitually do under such circumstances. The
Gazette was lying folded on the seat beside me: one of the two London
evening papers that a man of taste may peruse without humiliating himself. How appetizing a morsel, this sheet new and smooth from the press,
this sheet written by an ironic, understanding, small band of men for just
a few thousand persons like me, ruthlessly scornful of the big circulations
and the idols of the people! If the *Gazette* and its sole rival ceased to
appear, I do believe that my existence and many similar existences would
wear a different colour. Could one dine alone in Jermyn Street or Panton
Street without this fine piquant evening commentary on the gross newspapers of the morning? (Now you perceive what sort of a man I am, and

you guess, rightly, that my age is between thirty and forty.) But the train had stopped at Rugby and started again, and more than half of my journey was accomplished, ere at length I picked up the *Gazette*, and opened it with the false calm of a drunkard who has sworn that he will not wet his lips before a certain hour. For, well knowing from experience that I should suffer acute *ennui* in the train, I had, when buying the *Gazette* at Euston, taken oath that I would not even glance at it till after Rugby; it is always the final hour of these railway journeys that is the nethermost hell.

The second thing that I saw in the *Gazette* (the first was of course the 'Entremets' column of wit, humour, and parody, very uneven in its excellence) was the death of Simon Fuge. There was nearly a column about it, signed with initials, and the subheading of the article ran, 'Sudden death of a great painter'. That was characteristic of the *Gazette*. That Simon Fuge was indeed a great painter is now admitted by most dilettantes, though denied by a few. But to the great public he was not one of the few great names. To the great public he was just a medium name. Ten to one that in speaking of him to a plain person you would feel compelled to add: 'The painter, you know,' and the plain person would respond: 'Oh yes,' falsely pretending that he was perfectly familiar with the name. Simon Fuge had many friends on the press, and it was solely owing to the loyalty of these friends in the matter of obituary notices that the great public heard more of Simon Fuge in the week after his death than it had heard of him during the thirty-five years of his life. It may be asked: Why, if he had so many and such loyal friends in the press, these friends did not take measures to establish his reputation before he died? The answer is that editors will not allow journalists to praise a living artist much in excess of the esteem in which the public holds him; they are timid. But when a misunderstood artist is dead the editors will put no limit on laudation. I am not on the press, but it happens that I know the world.

Of all the obituary notices of Simon Fuge, the *Gazette*'s was the first. Somehow the *Gazette* had obtained exclusive news of the little event, and some one high up on the *Gazette*'s staff had a very exalted notion indeed of Fuge, and must have know him personally. Fuge received his deserts as a painter in that column of print. He was compared to Sorolla y Bastida for vitality; the *morbidezza* of his flesh-tints was stated to be unrivalled even by – I forget the name, painting is not my speciality. The

writer blandly inquired why examples of Fuge's work were to be seen in
the Luxembourg, at Vienna, at Florence, at Dresden; and not, for instance,
at the Tate Gallery, or in the Chantrey collection. The writer also inquired,
with equal blandness, why a painter who had been on the hanging committee of the Société Nationale des Beaux Arts at Paris should not have
been found worthy to be even an A.R.A. in London. In brief, old England
'caught it', as occurred somewhere or other most nights in the columns of
the *Gazette*. Fuge also received his deserts as a man. And the *Gazette* did
not conceal that he had not been a man after the heart of the British
public. He had been too romantically and intensely alive for that. The
writer gave a little pen-portrait of him. It was very good, recalling his tricks
of manner, his unforgettable eyes, and his amazing skill in talking about
himself and really interesting everybody in himself. There was a special
reference to one of Fuge's most dramatic recitals – a narration of a night
spent in a boat on Ilam Lake with two beautiful girls, sisters, natives of
the Five Towns, where Fuge was born. Said the obituarist: 'Those two
wonderful creatures who played so large a part in Simon Fuge's life.'

This death was a shock to me. It took away my *ennui* for the rest of the
journey. I too had known Simon Fuge. That is to say, I had met him once,
at a *soirée*, and on that single occasion, as luck had it, he had favoured the
company with the very narration to which the *Gazette* contributor referred.
I remembered well the burning brilliance of his blue-black eyes, his touching assurance that all of us were necessarily interested in his adventures,
and the extremely graphic and convincing way in which he reconstituted
for us the nocturnal scene on Ilam Lake – the two sisters, the boat, the
rustle of trees, the lights on shore, and his own difficulty in managing
the oars, one of which he lost for half-an-hour and found again. It was
by such details as that about the oar that, with a tint of humour, he added
realism to the romantic quality of his tales. He seemed to have no reticences concerning himself. Decidedly he allowed things to be
understood . . . ! Yes, his was a romantic figure, the figure of one to whom
every day, and every hour of the day, was coloured by the violence of his
passion for existence. His pictures had often an unearthly beauty, but for
him they were nothing but faithful renderings of what he saw.

My mind dwelt on those two beautiful sisters. Those two beautiful
sisters appealed to me more than anything else in the *Gazette*'s obituary.

Surely – Simon Fuge had obviously been a man whose emotional suscep-
tibility and virile impulsiveness must have opened the door for him to
multifarious amours – but surely he had not made himself indispensable
to both sisters simultaneously. Surely even he had not so far forgotten that
Ilam Lake was in the middle of a country called England, and not the
ornamental water in the Bois de Boulogne! And yet . . . The delicious
possibility of ineffable indiscretions on the part of Simon Fuge monopolized my mind till the train stopped at Knype, and I descended.
Nevertheless, I think I am a serious and fairly insular Englishman. It is
truly astonishing how a serious person can be obsessed by trifles that, to
speak mildly, do not merit sustained attention.

I wondered where Ilam Lake was. I knew merely that it lay somewhere
in the environs of the Five Towns. What put fuel on the fire of my interest
in the private affairs of the dead painter was the slightly curious coincidence that on the evening of the news of his death I should be travelling
to the Five Towns – and for the first time in my life. Here I was at Knype,
which, as I had gathered from Bradshaw, and from my acquaintance
Brindley, was the traffic centre of the Five Towns.

II

My knowledge of industrial districts amounted to nothing. Born in
Devonshire, educated at Cambridge, and fulfilling my destiny as curator
of a certain department of antiquities at the British Museum, I had never
been brought into contact with the vast constructive material activities of
Lancashire, Yorkshire, and Staffordshire. I had but passed through them
occasionally on my way to Scotland, scorning their necessary grime with
the perhaps too facile disdain of the clean-faced southerner, who is apt to
forget that coal cannot walk up unaided out of the mine, and that the
basin in which he washes his beautiful purity can only be manufactured
amid conditions highly repellent. Well, my impressions of the platform
of Knype station were unfavourable. There was dirt in the air; I could feel
it at once on my skin. And the scene was shabby, undignified, and rude.
I use the word 'rude' in all its senses. What I saw was a pushing, exclama-
tory, ill-dressed, determined crowd, each member of which was bent on

the realization of his own desires by the least ceremonious means. If an item of this throng wished to get past me, he made me instantly aware of his wish by abruptly changing my position in infinite space; it was not possible to misconstrue his meaning. So much crude force and naked will-to-live I had not before set eyes on. In truth, I felt myself to be a very brittle, delicate bit of intellectual machinery in the midst of all these physical manifestations. Yet I am a tallish man, and these potters appeared to me to be undersized, and somewhat thin too! But what elbows! What glaring egoistic eyes! What terrible decisiveness in action!

'Now then, get in if ye're going!' said a red-haired porter to me curtly.

'I'm not going. I've just got out,' I replied.

'Well, then, why dunna' ye stand out o' th' wee and let them get in as wants to?'

Unable to offer a coherent answer to this crushing demand, I stood out of the way. In the light of further knowledge I now surmise that that porter was a very friendly and sociable porter. But at the moment I really believed that, taking me for the least admirable and necessary of God's creatures, he meant to convey his opinion to me for my own good. I glanced up at the lighted windows of the train, and saw the composed, careless faces of haughty persons who were going direct from London to Manchester, and to whom the Five Towns was nothing but a delay. I envied them. I wanted to return to the shelter of the train. When it left, I fancied that my last link with civilization was broken. Then another train puffed in, and it was simply taken by assault in a fraction of time, to an incomprehensible bawling of friendly sociable porters. Season-ticket holders at Finsbury Park think they know how to possess themselves of a train; they are deceived. So this is where Simon Fuge came from (I reflected)! The devil it is (I reflected)! I tried to conceive what the invaders of the train would exclaim if confronted by one of Simon Fuge's pictures. I could imagine only one word, and that a monosyllable, that would meet the case of their sentiments. And his dalliance, his tangential nocturnal deviations in gondolas with exquisite twin odalisques! There did not seem to be much room for amorous elegance in the lives of these invaders. And his death! What would they say of his death? Upon my soul, as I stood on that dirty platform, in a *milieu* of advertisement of soap, boots, and aperients, I began to believe that Simon Fuge never had lived, that he was a mere illusion of his friends and his small public. All that I saw around me was a violent negation of Simon Fuge, that entity of rare, fine, exotic sensibilities, that perfectly mad gourmet of sensations, that exotic seer of beauty.

I caught sight of my acquaintance and host, Mr Robert Brindley, coming towards me on the platform. Hitherto I had only met him in London, when, as chairman of the committee of management of the Wedgwood Institution and School of Art at Bursley, he had called on me at the British Museum for advice as to loan exhibits. He was then dressed like a self-respecting tourist. Now, although an architect by profession, he appeared to be anxious to be mistaken for a sporting squire. He wore very baggy knickerbockers, and leggings, and a cap. This raiment was apparently the agreed uniform of the easy classes in the Five Towns; for in the crowd I had noticed several such consciously superior figures among the artisans. Mr Brindley, like most of the people in the station, had a slightly pinched and chilled air, as though that morning he had by inadvertence omitted to don those garments which are not seen. He also, like most of the people there, but not to the same extent, had a somewhat suspicious and narrowly shrewd regard, as who should say: 'If any person thinks he can get the better of me by a trick, let him try – that's all.' But the moment his eye encountered mine, this expression vanished from his face, and he gave me a candid smile.

'I hope you're well,' he said gravely, squeezing my hand in a sort of vice that he carried at the end of his right arm.

I reassured him.

'Oh, *I'm* all right,' he said, in response to the expression of *my* hopes.

It was a relief to me to see him. He took charge of me. I felt, as it were, safe in his arms. I perceived that, unaided and unprotected, I should never have succeeded in reaching Bursley from Knype.

A whistle sounded.

'Better get in,' he suggested; and then in a tone of absolute command: 'Give me your bag.'

I obeyed. He opened the door of a first-class carriage.

'I'm travelling second,' I explained.

'Never mind. Get *in*.'

In his tones was a kindly exasperation.

I got in; he followed. The train moved.

'Ah!' breathed Mr Brindley, blowing out much air and falling like a sack of coal into a corner seat. He was a thin man, aged about thirty, with brown eyes, and a short blonde beard.

Conversation was at first difficult. Personally I am not a bubbling fount of gay nothings when I find myself alone with a comparative stranger. My drawbridge goes up as if by magic, my postern is closed, and I peer cautiously through the narrow slits of my turret to estimate the chances of peril. Nor was Mr Brindley offensively affable. However, we struggled into a kind of chatter. I had come to the Five Towns, on behalf of the British Museum, to inspect and appraise, with a view to purchase by the nation, some huge slip-decorated dishes, excessively curious according to photographs, which had been discovered in the cellars of the Conservative Club at Bursley. Having shared in the negotiations for my visit, Mr Brindley had invited me to spend the night at his house. We were able to talk about all this. And when we had talked about all this we were able to talk about the singular scenery of coal dust, potsherds, flame and steam, through which the train wound its way. It was squalid ugliness, but it was squalid ugliness on a scale so vast and overpowering that it became sublime. Great furnaces gleamed red in the twilight, and their fires were reflected in horrible black canals; processions of heavy vapour drifted in all directions across the sky, over what acres of mean and miserable brown architecture! The air was alive with the most extraordinary, weird, gigantic sounds. I do not think the Five Towns will ever be described: Dante lived too soon. As for the erratic and exquisite genius, Simon Fuge, and his odalisques reclining on silken cushions on the enchanted bosom of a lake – I could no longer conjure them up even faintly in my mind.

'I suppose you know Simon Fuge is dead?' I remarked, in a pause.

'No! Is he?' said Mr Brindley, with interest. 'Is it in the paper?'

He did not seem to be quite sure that it would be in the paper.

'Here it is,' said I, and I passed him the *Gazette*.

'Ha!' he exclaimed explosively. This 'Ha!' was entirely different from his 'Ah!' Something shot across his eyes, something incredibly rapid – too rapid for a wink; yet it could only be called a wink. It was the most subtle transmission of the beyond-speech that I have ever known any man accomplish, and it endeared Mr Brindley to me. But I knew not its significance.

'What do they think of Fuge down here?' I asked.

'I don't expect they think of him,' said my host.

He pulled a pouch and a packet of cigarette papers from his pocket.

'Have one of mine,' I suggested, hastily producing my case.

He did not even glance at its contents.

'No, thanks,' he said curtly.

I named my brand.

'My dear sir,' he said, with a return to his kindly exasperation, 'no cigarette that is not fresh made can be called a cigarette.' I stood corrected. 'You may pay as much as you like, but you can never buy cigarettes as good as I am make out of an ounce of fresh B.D.V. tobacco. Can you roll one?' I had to admit that I could not, I who in Bloomsbury was accepted as an authority on cigarettes as well as on porcelain. 'I'll roll you one, and you shall try it.'

He did so.

I gathered from his solemnity that cigarettes counted in the life of Mr Brindley. He could not take cigarettes other than seriously. The worst of it was that he was quite right. The cigarette which he constructed for me out of his wretched B.D.V. tobacco was adorable, and I have made my own cigarettes ever since. You will find B.D.V. tobacco all over the haunts frequented by us of the Museum now-a-days, solely owing to the expertise of Mr Brindley. A terribly capable and positive man! He *knew,* and he knew that he knew.

He said nothing further as to Simon Fuge. Apparently he had forgotten the deceased.

'Do you often see the *Gazette*?' I asked, perhaps in the hope of attracting him back to Fuge.

'No,' he said; 'the musical criticism is too rotten.'

Involuntarily I bridled. It was startling, and it was not agreeable, to have one's favourite organ so abruptly condemned by a provincial architect in knickerbockers and a cap, in the midst of all that industrial ugliness. What could the Five Towns know about art? Yet here was this fellow condemning the *Gazette* on artistic grounds. I offered no defence, because he was right – again. But I did not like it.

'Do you ever see the *Manchester Guardian*?' he questioned, carrying the war into my camp.

'No,' I said.

'Pity!' he ejaculated.

'I've often heard that it's a very good paper,' I said politely.

'It isn't a very good paper,' he laid me low. 'It's the best paper in the world. Try it for a month – it gets to Euston at half-past eight – and then tell me what you think.'

I saw that I must pull myself together. I had glided into the Five Towns in a mood of gentle, wise condescension. I saw that it would be as well, for my own honour and safety, to put on another mood as quickly as possible, otherwise I might be left for dead on the field. Certainly the fellow was provincial, curt, even brutal in his despisal of diplomacy. Certainly he exggerated the importance of cigarettes in the great secular scheme of evolution. But he was a man; he was a very tonic dose. I thought it would be safer to assume that he knew everything, and that the British Museum knew very little. Yet at the British Museum he had been quite different, quite deferential and rather timid. Still, I liked him. I liked his eyes.

The train stopped at an incredible station situated in the centre of a rolling desert whose surface consisted of broken pots and cinders. I expect no one to believe this.

'Here we are,' said he blithely. 'No, give me the bag. Porter!'

His summons to the solitary porter was like a clap of thunder.

III

He lived in a low, blackish-crimson heavy-browed house at the corner of a street along which electric cars were continually thundering. There was a thin cream of mud on the pavements and about two inches of mud in the roadway, rich, nourishing mud like Indian ink half-mixed. The prospect of carrying a pound or so of that unique mud into a civilized house affrighted me, but Mr Brindley opened his door with his latchkey and entered the abode as unconcernedly as if some fair repentent had cleansed his feet with her tresses.

'Don't worry too much about the dirt,' he said. 'You're in Bursley.'

The house seemed much larger inside than out. A gas-jet burnt in the hall, and sombre *portières* gave large mysterious hints of rooms. I could hear, in the distance, the noise of frizzling over a fire, and of a child crying. Then a tall, straight, well-made, energetic woman appeared like a conjuring trick from behind a *portière*.

'How do you do, Mr Loring?' she greeted me, smiling. 'So glad to meet you.'

'My wife,' Mr Brindley explained gravely.

'Now, I may as well tell you now, Bob,' said she, still smiling at me. 'Bobbie's got a sore throat and it may be mumps; the chimney's been on fire and we're going to be summoned; and you owe me sixpence.'

'Why do I owe you sixpence?'

'Because Annie's had her baby and it's a girl.'

'That's all right. Supper ready?'

'Supper is waiting for you.'

She laughed. 'Whenever I have anything to tell my husband, I always tell him at *once*!' she said. 'No matter who's there.' She pronounced 'once' with a wholehearted enthusiasm for its vowel sound that I have never heard equalled elsewhere, and also with a very magnified '*w*' at the beginning of it. Often when I hear the word 'once' pronounced in less downright parts of the world, I remember how they pronounce it in the Five Towns, and there rises up before me a complete picture of the district, its atmosphere, its spirit.

Mr Brindley led me to a large bathroom that had a faint odour of warm linen. In addition to a lot of assorted white baby-clothes there were millions of towels in that bathroom. He turned on a tap and the place was instantly full of steam from a jet of boiling water.

'Now, then,' he said, 'you can start.'

As he showed no intention of leaving me, I did start. 'Mind you don't scald yourself,' he warned me, 'that water's *hot*.' While I was washing, he prepared to wash. I suddenly felt as if I had been intimate with him and his wife for about ten years.

'So this is Bursley!' I murmured, taking my mouth out of a towel.

'Bosley, we call it,' he said. 'Do you know the limerick – "There was a young woman of Bosley"?'

'No.'

He intoned the local limerick. It was excellently good; not meet for a mixed company, but a genuine delight to the true amateur. One good limerick deserves another. It happened that I knew a number of the unprinted Rossetti limericks, precious things, not at all easy to get at. I detailed them to Mr Brindley, and I do not exaggerate when I say that I impressed him. I recovered all the ground I had lost upon cigarettes and newspapers. He appreciated those limericks with a juster taste than I should have expected. So, afterwards, did his friends. My belief is that I am to this day known and revered in Bursley, not as Loring the porcelain expert from the British Museum, but as the man who first, as it were, brought the good news of the Rossetti Limericks from Ghent to Aix.

'Now, Bob,' an amicable voice shrieked femininely up from the ground-floor, 'am I to send the soup to the bathroom or are you coming down?'

A limerick will make a man forget even his dinner.

Mr Brindley performed once more with his eyes that something that was, not a wink, but a wink unutterably refined and spiritualized. This time I comprehended its import. Its import was to the effect that women are women.

We descended, Mr Brindley still in his knickerbockers.

'This way,' he said, drawing aside a portière. Mrs Brindley, as we entered the room, was trotting a male infant round and round a table charged with everything digestible and indigestible. She handed the child, who was in its nightdress, to a maid.

'Say good night to father.'

'Good ni', faver,' the interesting creature piped.

'By-bye, sonny,' said the father, stooping to tickle. 'I suppose,' he added, when maid and infant had gone, 'if one's going to have mumps, they may as well all have it together.'

'Oh, of course,' the mother agreed cheerfully. 'I shall stick them all into a room.'

'How many children have you?' I inquired with polite curiosity.

'Three,' she said; 'that's the eldest that you've seen.'

What chiefly struck me about Mrs Brindley was her serene air of capableness, of having a self-confidence which experience had richly justified. I could see that she must be an extremely sensible mother. And yet she had quite another aspect too – how shall I explain it? – as though she had only had children in her spare time.

We sat down. The room was lighted by four candles, on the table. I am rather short-sighted, and so I did not immediately notice that there were low book-cases all round the walls. Why the presence of these book-cases should have caused me a certain astonishment I do not know, but it did. I thought of Knype station, and the scenery, and then the other little station, and the desert of pots and cinders, and the mud in the road and on the pavement and in the hall, and the baby-linen in the bathroom, and three children all down with mumps, and Mr Brindley's cap and knickerbockers and cigarettes; and somehow the books – I soon saw there were at least a thousand of them, and not circulating-library books, either, but *books* – well, they administered a little shock to me.

To Mr Brindley's right hand was a bottle of Bass and a corkscrew.

'Beer!' he exclaimed, with solemn ecstasy, with an ecstasy gross and luscious. And, drawing the cork, he poured out a glass, with fine skill in the management of froth, and pushed it towards me.

'No, thanks,' I said.

'No beer!' he murmured, with benevolent, puzzled disdain. 'Whisky?'

'No, thanks,' I said. 'Water.'

'I know what Mr Loring would like,' said Mrs Brindley, jumping up. 'I *know* what Mr Loring would like.' She opened a cupboard and came back to the table with a bottle, which she planted in front of me. 'Wouldn't you, Mr Loring?'

It was a bottle of mercurey, a wine which has given me many dreadful dawns, but which I have never known how to refuse.

'I should,' I admitted; 'but it's very bad for me.'

'Nonsense!' said she. She looked at her husband in triumph.

'Beer!' repeated Mr Brindley with undiminished ecstasy, and drank about two-thirds of a glass at one try. Then he wiped the froth from his moustache. 'Ah!' he breathed low and soft. 'Beer!'

They called the meal supper. The term is inadequate. No term that I can think of would be adequate. Of its kind the thing was perfect. Mrs Brindley knew that it was perfect. Mr Brindley also knew that it was perfect. There were prawns in aspic. I don't know why I should single out that dish, except that it seemed strange to me to have crossed the desert of pots and cinders in order to encounter prawns in aspic. Mr Brindley ate more cold roast beef than I had ever seen any man eat before, and more pickled walnuts. It is true that the cold roast beef transcended all the cold roast beef of my experience. Mrs Brindley regaled herself largely on trifle, which Mr Brindley would not approach, preferring a most glorious Stilton cheese. I lost touch, temporarily, with the intellectual life. It was Mr Brindley who recalled me to it.

'Jane,' he said. (This was at the beef and pickles stage.)

No answer.

'Jane!'

Mrs Brindley turned to me. 'My name is not Jane,' she said, laughing, and making a *moue* simultaneously. 'He only calls me that to annoy me. I told him I wouldn't answer to it, and I won't. He thinks I shall give in because we've got "company"! But I won't treat you as "company", Mr Loring, and I shall expect you to take my side. What dreadful weather we're having, aren't we?'

'Dreadful!' I joined in the game.

'Jane!'

'Did you have a comfortable journey down?'

'Yes, thank you.'

'Well, then, Mary!' Mr Brindley yielded.

'Thank you very much, Mr Loring, for your kind assistance,' said his wife. 'Yes, dearest?'

Mr Brindley glanced at me over his second glass of beer.

'If those confounded kids are going to have mumps,' he addressed his words apparently into the interior of the glass, 'it probably means the doctor, and the doctor means money, and I shan't be able to afford the *Hortulus Animae*.'

I opened my ears.

'My husband goes stark staring mad sometimes,' said Mrs Brindley to me. 'It lasts for a week or so, and pretty nearly lands us in the workhouse. This time it's the *Hortulus Animae*. Do you know what it is? I don't.'

'No,' I said, and the prestige of the British Museum trembled. Then I had a vague recollection. 'There's an illuminated manuscript of that name in the Imperial Library of Vienna, isn't there?'

'You've got it in one,' said Mr Brindley. 'Wife, pass those walnuts.'

'You aren't by any chance buying it?' I laughed.

'No,' he said. 'A Johnny at Utrecht is issuing a facsimile of it, with all the hundred odd miniatures in colour. It will be the finest thing in reproduction ever done. Only seventy-five copies for England.'

'How much?' I asked.

'Well,' said he, with a preliminary look at his wife, 'thirty-three pounds.'

'Thirty-three *pounds*!' she screamed. 'You never told me.'

'My wife never will understand,' said Mr Brindley, 'that complete confidence between two human beings is impossible.'

'I shall go out as a milliner, that's all,' Mrs Brindley returned. 'Remember, the *Dictionary of National Biography* isn't paid for yet.'

'I'm glad I forgot that, otherwise I shouldn't have ordered the *Hortulus*.'

'You've not ordered it?'

'Yes, I have. It'll be here tomorrow – at least the first part will.'

Mrs Brindley affected to fall back dying in her chair.

'Quite mad!' she complained to me. 'Quite mad. It's a hopeless case.'

But obviously she was very proud of the incurable lunatic.

'But you're a book-collector!' I exclaimed, so struck by these feats of extravagance in a modest house that I did not conceal my amazement.

'Did you think I collected postage-stamps?' the husband retorted. 'No, *I'm* not a book-collector, but our doctor is. He *has* a few books, if you like. Still, I wouldn't swop him; he's much too fond of fashionable novels.'

'You know you're always up his place,' said the wife; 'and I wonder what *I* should do if it wasn't for the doctor's novels!' The doctor was evidently a favourite of hers.

'I'm not always up at his place,' the husband contradicted. 'You know perfectly well I never go there before midnight. And *he* knows perfectly well that I only go because he has the beat whisky in the town. By the way, I wonder whether he knows that Simon Fuge is dead. He's got one of his etchings. I'll go up.'

'Who's Simon Fuge?' asked Mrs Brindley.

'Don't you remember old Fuge that kept the Blue Bell at Cauldon?'

'What? Simple Simon?'

'Yes. Well, his son.'

'Oh! I remember. He ran away from home once, didn't he, and his mother had a port-wine stain on her left cheek? Oh, of course. I remember him perfectly. He came down to the Five Towns some years ago for his aunt's funeral. So he's dead. Who told you?'

'Mr Loring.'

'Did you know him?' she glanced at me.

'I scarcely knew him,' said I. 'I saw it in the paper.'

'What, the *Signal*?'

'The *Signal*'s the local rag,' Mr Brindley interpolated. 'No. It's in the *Gazette*.'

'The *Birmingham Gazette*?'

'No, bright creature – the *Gazette*,' said Mr Brindley.

'Oh!' She seemed puzzled.

'Didn't you know he was a painter?' the husband condescendingly catechized.

'I knew he used to teach at the Hanbridge School of Art,' said Mrs Brindley stoutly. 'Mother wouldn't let me go there because of that. Then he got the sack.'

'Poor defenseless thing! How old were you?'

'Seventeen, I expect.'

'I'm much obliged to your mother.'

'Where did he die?' Mrs Brindley demanded.

'At San Remo,' I answered. 'Seems queer him dying at San Remo in September, doesn't it?'

'Why?'

'San Remo is a winter place. No one ever goes there before December.'

'Oh, is it?' the lady murmured negligently. 'Then that would be just like Simon Fuge. *I* was never afraid of him,' she added, in a defiant tone, and with a delicious inconsequence that choked her husband in the midst of a draught of beer.

'You can laugh,' she said sturdily.

At that moment there was heard a series of loud explosive sounds in the street. They continued for a few seconds apparently just outside the dining-room window. Then they stopped, and the noise of the bumping electric cars resumed its sway over the ear.

'That's Oliver!' said Mr Brindley, looking at his watch. 'He must have come from Manchester in an hour and a half. He's a terror.'

'Glass! Quick!' Mrs Brindley exclaimed. She sprang to the sideboard, and seized a tumbler, which Mr Brindley filled from a second bottle of Bass. When the door of the room opened she was standing close to it, laughing, with the full, frothing glass in her hand.

A tall, thin man, rather younger than Mr Brindley and his wife, entered. He wore a long dust-coat and leggings, and he carried a motorist's cap in a great hand. No one spoke; but little puffs of laughter escaped all Mrs Brindley's efforts to imprison her mirth. Then the visitor took the glass with a magnificent broad smile, and said, in a rich and heavy Midland voice –

'Here's to moy wife's husband!'

And drained the nectar.

'Feel better now, don't you?' Mrs Brindley inquired.

'Aye, Mrs Bob, I do!' was the reply. 'How do, Bob?'

'How do?' responded my host laconically. And then with gravity: 'Mr Loring – Mr Oliver Colclough – thinks he knows something about music.'

'Glad to meet you, sir,' said Mr Colclough, shaking hands with me. He had a most attractively candid smile, but he was so long and lanky that he seemed to pervade the room like an omnipresence.

'Sit down and have a bit of cheese, Oliver,' said Mrs Brindley, as she herself sat down.

'No, thanks, Mrs Bob. I must be getting towards home.'

He leaned on her chair.

'Trifle, then?'

'No, thanks.'

'Machine going all right?'

'Like oil. Never stopped th' engine once.'

'Did you get the *Sinfonia Domestica*, Ol?' Mr Brindley inquired,

'Didn't I say as I should get it, Bob?'

'You *said* you would.'

'Well, I've got it.'

'In Manchester?'

'Of course.'

Mr Brindley's face shone with desire and Mr Oliver Colclough's face shone with triumph.

'Where is it?'

'In the hall.'

'My hall?'

'Aye!'

'We'll play it, Ol.'

'No, really, Bob! I can't stop now. I promised the wife –'

'We'll *play* it, Ol! You'd no business to make promises. Besides, suppose you'd had a puncture!'

'I expect you've heard Strauss's *Sinfonia Domestica*, Mr Loring, up in the village?' Mr Colclough addressed me. He had surrendered to the stronger will.

'In London?' I said. 'No. But I've heard of it.'

'Bob and I heard it in Manchester last week, and we thought it 'ud be a bit of a lark to buy the arrangement for pianoforteduet.'

'Come and listen to it,' said Mr Brindley. 'That is, if nobody wants any more beer.'

IV

The drawing-room was about twice as large as the dining-room, and it contained about four times as much furniture. Once again there were books all round the walls. A grand piano, covered with music, stood in a corner, and behind was a cabinet full of bound music.

Mr Brindley, seated on one corner of the bench in front of the piano, cut the leaves of the *Sinfonia Domestica*.

'It's the devil!' he observed.

'Aye, lad!' agreed Mr Colclough, standing over him. 'It's difficult.'

'Come on,' said Mr Brindley, when he had finished cutting.

'Better take your dust-coat off, hadn't you?' Mrs Brindley suggested to the friend. She and I were side by side on a sofa at the other end of the room.

'I may as well,' Mr Colclough admitted, and threw the long garment on to a chair. 'Look here, Bob, my hands are stiff with steering.'

'Don't find fault with your tools,' said Mr Brindley; 'and sit down. No, my boy, I'm going to play the top part. Shove along.'

'I want to play the top part because it's easiest,' Mr Colclough grumbled.

'How often have I told you the top part is never easiest? Who do you suppose is going to keep this symphony together – you or me?'

'Sorry I spoke.'

They arranged themselves on the bench, and Mr Brindley turned up the lower corners of every alternate leaf of the music.

'Now,' said he. 'Ready?'

'Let her zip,' said Mr Colclough.

They began to play. And then the door opened, and a servant, whose white apron was starched as stiff as cardboard, came in carrying a tray of coffee and unholy liqueurs, which she deposited with a rattle on a small table near the hostess.

'Curse!' muttered Mr Brindley, and stopped.

'Life's very complex, ain't it, Bob?' Mr Colclough murmured.

'Aye, lad.' The host glanced round to make sure that the rattling servant had entirely gone. 'Now start again.'

'Wait a minute, wait a minute!' cried Mrs Brindley excitedly. 'I'm just pouring out Mr Loring's coffee. There!' As she handed me the cup she whispered, 'We daren't talk. It's more than our place is worth.'

The performance of the symphony proceeded. To me, who am not a performer, it sounded excessively brilliant and incomprehensible. Mr Colclough stretched his right hand to turn over the page, and fumbled it. Another stoppage.

'Damn you, Ol!' Mr Brindley exploded. 'I wish you wouldn't make yourself so confoundedly busy. Leave the turning to me. It takes a great artist to turn over, and you're only a blooming chauffeur. We'll begin again.'

'Sackcloth!' Mr Colclough whispered.

I could not estimate the length of the symphony; but my impression was one of extreme length. Halfway through it the players both took their coats off. There was no other surcease.

'What dost think of it, Bob?' asked Mr Colclough in the weird silence that reigned after they bad finished. They were standing up and putting on their coats and wiping their faces.

'I think what I thought before,' said Mr Brindley. 'It's childish.'

'It isn't childish,' the other protested. 'It's ugly, but it isn't childish.'

'It's childishly clever,' Mr Brindley modified his description. He did not ask my opinion.

'Coffee's cold,' said Mrs Brindley.

'I don't want any coffee. Give me some Chartreuse, please. Have a drop o' green, Ol?'

'A split soda 'ud be more in my line. Besides, I'm just going to have my supper. Never mind, I'll have a drop, miss's, and chance it. I've never tried Chartreuse as an appetizer.'

At this point commenced a sanguinary conflict of wills to settle whether or not I also should indulge in green Chartreuse. I was defeated. Besides the Chartreuse, I accepted a cigar. Never before or since have I been such a buck.

'I must book it,' said Mr Colclough, picking up his dust-coat.

'Not yet you don't,' said Mr Brindley. 'I've got to get the taste of that infernal Strauss out of my mouth. We'll play the first movement of the G minor? *La-la-la – la-la-la – la-la-la-ta.*' He whistled a phrase.

Mr Colclough obediently sat down again to the piano.

The Mozart was like an idyll after a farcical melodrama. They played it with an astounding delicacy. Through the latter half of the movement I could hear Mr Brindley breathing regularly and heavily through his nose, exactly as though he were being hypnotized. I had a tickling sensation in the small of my back, a sure sign of emotion in me. The atmosphere was charged.

'What a heavenly thing!' I exclaimed enthusiastically, when they had finished.

Mr Brindley looked at me sharply, and just nodded in silence. 'Well, good night, Ol.'

'I say,' said Mr Colclough; 'if you've nothing doing later on, bring Mr Loring round to my place. Will you come, Mr Loring? Do! Us'll have a drink.'

These Five Towns people certainly had a simple, sincere way of offering hospitality that was quite irresistible. One could see that hospitality was among their chief and keenest pleasures.

We all went to the front door to see Mr Colclough depart homewards in his automobile. The two great acetylene headlights sent long glaring shafts of light down the side street. Mr Colclough, throwing the score of the *Sinfonia Domestica* into the tonneau of the immense car, put on a pair of gloves and began to circulate round the machine, tapping here, screwing there, as chauffeurs will. Then he bent down in front to start the engine.

'By the way, Ol,' Mr Brindley shouted from the doorway. 'it seems Simon Fuge is dead.'

We could see the man's stooping form between the two headlights. He turned his head towards the house.

'Who the dagger is Simon Fuge?' he inquired. 'There's about five thousand Fuges in th' Five Towns.'

'Oh! I thought you knew him.'

'I might, and I mightn't. It's not one o' them Fuge brothers saggar-makers at Longshaw, is it?'

'No, It's – '

Mr Colclough had succeeded in starting his engine, and the air was rent with gun-shots. He jumped lightly into the driver's seat.

'Well, see you later,' he cried, and was off, persuading the enormous beast under him to describe a semicircle in the narrow street backing, forcing forward, and backing again, to the accompaniment of the continuous fusillade. At length he got away, drew up within two feet of an electric tram that slid bumping down the main street, and vanished round the corner. A little ragged boy passed, crying, *'Signal,* extra,' and Mr Brindley hailed him.

'What *is* Mr Colclough?' I asked in the drawing-room.

'Manufacturer – sanitary ware,' said Mr Brindley. 'He's got one of the best businesses in Hanbridge. I wish I'd half his income. Never buys a book, you know.'

'He seems to play the piano very well.'

'Well, as to that, he doesn't what you may call *play,* but he's the best sight-reader in this district, bar me. I never met his equal. When you come across any one who can read a thing like the Domestic Symphony right off and never miss his place, you might send me a telegram. Colclough's got a Steinway. Wish I had.'

Mrs Brindley had been looking through the *Signal.*

'I don't see anything about Simon Fuge here,' said she.

'Oh, nonsense!' said her husband. 'Buchanan's sure to have got something in about it. Let's look.'

He received the paper from his wife, but failed to discover in it a word concerning the death of Simon Fuge.

'Dashed if I don't ring Buchanan up and ask him what he means! Here's a paper with an absolute monopoly in the district, and brings in about five thousand a year clear to somebody, and it doesn't give the news! There never is anything but advertisements and sporting results in the blessed thing.'

He rushed to his telephone, which was in the hall. Or rather, he did not rush; he went extremely quickly, with aggressive footsteps that seemed to symbolize just retribution. We could hear him at the telephone.

'Hello! No. Yes. Is that you, Buchanan? Well, I want Mr Buchanan. Is that you, Buchanan? Yes, I'm all right. What in thunder do you mean by having nothing in tonight about Simon Fuge's death? Eh? Yes, the *Gazette*. Well, I suppose you aren't Scotch for nothing. Why the devil couldn't you stop in Scotland and edit papers there?' Then a laugh. 'I see. Yes. What did you think of those cigars? Oh! See you at the dinner. Ta-ta.' A final ring.

'The real truth is, he wanted some advice as to the tone of his obituary notice,' said Mr Brindley, coming back into the drawing-room. 'He's got it, seemingly. He says he's writing it now, for tomorrow. He didn't put in the mere news of the death, because it was exclusive to the *Gazette*, and he's been having some difficulty with the *Gazette* lately. As he says, tomorrow afternoon will be quite soon enough for the Five Towns. It isn't as if Simon Fuge was a cricket match. So now you see how the wheels go round, Mr Loring.'

He sat down to the piano and began to play softly the Castle motive from the *Nibelung's Ring*. He kept repeating it in different keys.

'What about the mumps, wife?' he asked Mrs Brindley, who had been out of the room and now returned.

'Oh! I don't think it is mumps,' she replied. 'They're all asleep.'

'Good!' he murmured, still playing the Castle motive.

'Talking of Simon Fuge,' I said determined to satisfy my curiosity, 'who *were* the two sisters?'

'What two sisters?'

'That he spent the night in the boat with, on Ilam Lake.'

'Was that in the *Gazette*? I didn't read all the article.'

He changed abruptly into the Sword motive, which he gave with a violent flourish, and then he left the piano.

'I do beg you not to wake my children,' said his wife.

'Your children must get used to my piano,' said he. 'Now, then, what about these two sisters?'

I pulled the *Gazette* from my pocket and handed it to him.

He read aloud the passage describing the magic night on the lake.

'I don't know who they were,' he said. 'Probably something tasty from the Hanbridge Empire.'

We both observed a faint, amused smile on the face of Mrs Brindley, the smile of a woman who has suddenly discovered in her brain a piece of knowledge rare and piquant.

'I can guess who they were,' she said. 'In fact, I'm sure.'

'Who?'

'Annie Brett and – you know who.'

'What, down at the Tiger?'

'Certainly. Hush!' Mrs Brindley ran to the door and, opening it, listened. The faint, fretful cry of a child reached us. 'There! You've done it! I told you you would!'

She disappeared. Mr Brindley whistled.

'And who is Annie Brett?' I inquired.

'Look here,' said he, with a peculiar inflection. 'Would you like to see her?'

'I should,' I said with decision.

'Well, come on, then. We'll go down to the Tiger and have a drop of something.'

'And the other sister?' I asked.

'The other sister is Mrs Oliver Colclough,' he answered. 'Curious, ain't it?'

Again there was that swift, scarcely perceptible phenomenon in his eyes.

V

We stood at the corner of the side-street and the main road, and down the main road a vast, white rectangular cube of bright light came plunging – its head rising and dipping – at express speed, and with a formidable roar. Mr Brindley imperiously raised his stick; the extraordinary box of light stopped as if by a miracle, and we jumped into it, having splashed through mud, and it plunged off again – bump, bump, bump – into the town of Bursley. As Mr Brindley passed into the interior of the car, he said laconically to two men who were smoking on the platform –

'How do, Jim? How do, Jo?'

And they responded laconically –

'How do, Bob?'

'How do, Bob?'

We sat down. Mr Brindley pointed to the condition of the floor.

'Cheerful, isn't it?' he observed to me, shouting above the din of vibrating glass.

Our fellow-passengers were few and unromantic, perhaps half-a-dozen altogether on the long, shiny, yellow seats of the car, each apparently lost in gloomy reverie.

'It's the advertisements and notices in these cars that are the joy of the super-man like you and me,' shouted Mr Brindley. 'Look there, "Passengers are requested not to spit on the floor." Simply an encouragement to lie on the seats and spit on the ceiling, isn't it? "Wear only Noble's wonderful boots." Suppose we did! Unless they came well up above the waist we should be prosecuted. But there's no sense of humour in this district.'

Greengrocers' shops and public-houses were now flying past the windows of the car. It began to climb a hill, and then halted.

'Here we are!' ejaculated Mr Brindley.

And he was out of the car almost before I had risen.

We strolled along a quiet street, and came to a large building with many large lighted windows, evidently some result of public effort.

'What's that place?' I demanded.

'That's the Wedgwood Institution.'

'Oh! So that's the Wedgwood Institution, is it?'

'Yes. Commonly called the Wedgwood. Museum, reading-room, public library – dirtiest books in the world, I mean physically – art school, science school. I've never explained to you why I'm chairman of the Management Committee, have I? Well, it's because the Institution is meant to foster the arts, and I happen to know nothing about 'em. I needn't tell you that architecture, literature, and music are not arts within the meaning of the act. Not much! Like to come in and see the museum for a minute? You'll have to see it in your official capacity tomorrow.'

We crossed the road, and entered an imposing portico. Just as we did so a thick stream of slouching men began to descend the steps, like a waterfall of treacle. Mr Brindley they appeared to see, but evidently I made no impression on their retinas. They bore down the steps, hands deep in pockets, sweeping over me like Fate. Even when I bounced off one of them to a lower step, he showed by no sign that the fact of my existence had reached his consciousness – simply bore irresistibly downwards. The crowd was absolutely silent. At last I gained the entrance hall.

'It's closing-time for the reading room,' said Mr Brindley.

'I'm glad I survived it,' I said.

'The truth is,' said he, 'that people who can't look after themselves don't flourish in these latitudes. But you'll be acclimatized by tomorrow. See that?'

He pointed to an alabaster tablet on which was engraved a record of the historical certainty that Mr Gladstone opened the Institution in 1868, also an extract from the speech which he delivered on that occasion.

'What do you think of Gladstone down here?' I demanded.

'In my official capacity I think that these deathless words are the last utterance of wisdom on the subject of the influence of the liberal arts on life. And I should advise you, in your official capacity, to think the same, unless you happen to have a fancy for having your teeth knocked down your throat.'

'I see,' I said, not sure how to take him.

'Lest you should go away with the idea that you have been visiting a rude and barbaric people, I'd better explain that that was a joke. As a matter of fact, we're rather enlightened here. The only man who stands a chance of getting his teeth knocked down his throat here is the ingenious person who started the celebrated legend of the man-and-dog fight at Hanbridge. It's a long time ago, a very long time ago; but his grey hairs won't save him from horrible tortures if we catch him. We don't mind being called immoral, we're above a bit flattered when London newspapers come out with shocking details of debauchery in the Five Towns, but we

pride ourselves on our manners. I say, Aked!' His voice rose command-
ingly, threateningly, to an old bent, spectacled man who was ascending a
broad white staircase in front of us.

'Sir!' The man turned.

'Don't turn the lights out yet in the museum.'

'No, sir! Are you coming up?' The accents were slow and tremulous.

'Yes. I have a gentleman here from the British Museum who wants to
look round.'

The oldish man came deliberately down the steps, and approached us.
Then his gaze, beginning at my waist, gradually rose to my hat.

'From the *British* Museum?' he drawled, 'I'm sure I'm very glad to meet
you, sir. I'm sure it's a very great honour.'

He held out a wrinkled hand, which I shook.

'Mr Aked,' said Mr Brindley, by way of introduction. 'Been caretaker
here for pretty near forty years.'

'Ever since it opened, sir,' said Aked.

We went up the white stone stairway, rather a grandiose construction
for a little industrial town. It divided itself into doubling curving flights
at the first landing, and its walls were covered with pictures and designs.
The museum itself, a series of three communicating rooms, was about as
large as a pocket-handkerchief.

'Quite small,' I said.

I gave my impression candidly, because I had already judged Mr Brindley to be the rare and precious individual who is worthy of the high honour
of frankness.

'Do you think so?' he demanded quickly. I had shocked him, that was
clear. His tone was unmistakable; it indicated an instinctive, involuntary
protest. But he recovered himself in a flash. 'That's jealousy,' he laughed.
'All you British Museum people are the same.' Then be added, with an
unsuccessful attempt to convince me that he meant what he was saying:
'Of course it *is* small. It's nothing, simply nothing.'

Yes, I had unwittingly found the joint in the armour of this extraordinary Midland personage. With all his irony, with all his violent humour,
with all his just and unprejudiced perceptions, he had a tenderness for the
Institution of which he was the dictator. He loved it. He could laugh like
a god at everything in the Five Towns except this one thing. He would

try to force himself to regard even this with the same lofty detachment, but he could not do it naturally.

I stopped at a case of Wedgwood ware, marked 'Perkins Collection.'

'By Jove!' I exclaimed, pointing to a vase. 'What a body!'

He was enchanted by my enthusiasm.

'Funny you should have hit on that,' said he. 'Old Daddy Perkins always called it his ewe-lamb.'

Thus spoken, the name of the greatest authority on Wedgwood ware that Europe has ever known curiously impressed me.

'I suppose you knew him?' I questioned.

'Considering that I was one of the pall-bearers at his funeral, and caught the champion cold of my life!'

'What sort of a man was he?'

'Outside Wedgwood ware he wasn't any sort of a man. He was that scourge of society, a philanthropist,' said Mr Brindley. 'He was an upright citizen, and two thousand people followed him to his grave. I'm an upright citizen, but I have no hope that two thousand people will follow me to my grave.'

'You never know what may happen,' I observed, smiling.

'No.' He shook his head. 'If you undermine the moral character of your fellow-citizens by a long course of unbridled miscellaneous philanthropy, you can have a funeral procession as long as you like, at the rate of about forty shillings a foot. But you'll never touch the great heart of the enlightened public of these boroughs in any other way. Do you imagine anyone cared a twopenny damn for Perkins' Wedgwood ware?'

'It's like that everywhere,' I said.

'I suppose it is,' he assented unwillingly.

Who can tell what was passing in the breast of Mr Brindley? I could not. At least I could not tell with any precision. I could only gather, vaguely, that what he considered the wrong-headedness, the blindness, the lack of true perception, of *his* public was beginning to produce in his individuality a faint trace of permanent soreness. I regretted it. And I showed my sympathy with him by asking questions about the design and construction of the museum (a late addition to the Institution), of which I happened to know that he had been the architect.

He at once became interested and interesting. Although he perhaps insisted a little too much on the difficulties which occur when original talent encounters stupidity, he did, as he walked me up and down, contrive to convey to me a notion of the creative processes of the architect in a way that was in my experience entirely novel. He was impressing me anew, and I was wondering whether he was unique of his kind or whether there existed regiments of him in this strange parcel of England.

'Now, you see this girder,' he said, looking upwards.

'That's surely something of Fuge's, isn't it?' I asked, indicating a small picture in a corner, after he had finished his explanation of the functions of the girder.

As on the walls of the staircase and corridors, so on the walls here, there were many paintings, drawings, and engravings. And of course the best were here in the museum. The least uninteresting items of the collection were, speaking generally, reproductions in monotint of celebrated works, and a few second- or third-rate loan pictures from South Kensington. Aside from such matters I had noticed nothing but the usual local trivialities, gifts from one citizen or another, travel-jottings of some artmaster, careful daubs of apt students without a sense of humour. The aspect of the place was exactly the customary aspect of the small provincial museum, as I have seen it in half-a-hundred towns that are not among 'the great towns'. It had the terrible trite 'museum' aspect, the aspect that brings woe and desolation to the heart of the stoutest visitor, and which seems to form part of the purgatorio of Bank-holidays, wide mouths, and stiff clothes. The movement for opening museums on Sundays is the most natural movement that could be conceived. For if ever a resort was invented and fore-ordained to chime with the true spirit of the British sabbath, that resort is the avenge museum. I ought to know. I do know.

But there was the incomparable Wedgwood ware, and there was the little picture by Simon Fuge. I am not going to lose my sense of perspective concerning Simon Fuge. He was not the greatest painter that ever lived, or even of his time. He had, I am ready to believe, very grave limitations. But he was a painter by himself, as all line painters are. He had his own vision. He was unique. He was exclusively preoccupied with the beauty and the romance of the authentic. The little picture showed all this. It was a painting, unfinished, of a girl standing at a door and evidently hesitating whether to open the door or not: a very young girl, very thin, with long legs in black stockings, and short, white, untidy frock; thin bare arms; the head thrown on one side, and the hands raised, and one foot raised, in a wonderful childish gesture – the gesture of an undecided fox-terrier. The face was an infant's face, utterly innocent; and yet Simon Fuge had somehow caught in that face a glimpse of all the future of the woman that the girl was to be, he had displayed with exquisite insolence the essential naughtiness of his vision of things. The thing was not much more than a sketch! it was a happy accident, perhaps, in some day's work of Simon Fuge's. But it was genius. When once you had yielded to it, there was no other picture in the room. It killed everything else. But, wherever it had found itself, nothing could have killed it. Its success was undeniable, indestructible. And it glowed sombrely there on the wall, a few splashes of colour on a morsel of canvas, and it was Simon Fuge's unconscious, proud challenge to the Five Towns. It *was* Simon Fuge, at any rate all of Simon Fuge that was worth having, masterful, imperishable. And not merely was it his challenge, it was his scorn, his aristocratic disdain, his positive assurance that in the battle between them he had annihilated the Five Towns. It hung there in the very midst thereof, calmly and contemptuously waiting for the acknowledgement of his victory.

'Which?' said Mr Brindley.

'That one.'

'Yes, I fancy it is,' he negligently agreed. 'Yes, it is.'

'It's not signed,' I remarked.

'It ought to be,' said Mr Brindley; then laughed, 'Too late now!'

'How did it get here?'

'Don't know. Oh! I think Mr Perkins won it in a raffle at a bazaar, and then hung it here. He did as he liked here, you know.'

I was just going to become vocal in its praise, when Mr Brindley said –

'That thing under it is a photograph of a drinking-cup for which one of our pupils won a national scholarship last year!'

Mr Aked appeared in the distance.

'I fancy the old boy wants to be off to bed,' Mr Brindley whispered kindly.

So we left the Wedgwood Institution. I began to talk to Mr Brindley about music. The barbaric attitude of the Five Towns towards great music was the theme of some very lively animadversions on his part.

VI

The Tiger was very conveniently close to the Wedgwood Institution. The Tiger had a 'yard', one of those long, shapeless expanses of the planet, partly paved with uneven cobbles and partly unsophisticated planet, without which no provincial hotel can call itself respectable. We came into it from the hinterland through a wooden doorway in a brick wall. Far off I could see one light burning. We were in the centre of Bursley, the gold angel of its Town Hall rose handsomely over the roof of the hotel in the diffused moonlight, but we might have been in the purlieus of some dubious establishment on the confines of a great seaport, where anything may happen. The yard was so deserted, so mysterious, so shut in, so silent, that, really, infamous characters ought to have rushed out at us from the obscurity of shadows, and felled us to the earth with no other attendant phenomenon than a low groan. There are places where one seems to feel how thin and brittle is the crust of law and order. Why one should be conscious of this in the precincts of such a house as the Tiger, which I was given to understand is as respectable as the parish church, I do not know. But I have experienced a similar feeling in the yards of other provincial hotels that were also as correct as parish churches. We passed a dim fly, with its shafts slanting forlornly to the ground, and a wheelbarrow. Both looked as though they had been abandoned for ever. Then we came to the lamp, which illuminated a door, and on the door was a notice: 'Private Bar. Billiards.'

I am not a frequenter of convivial haunts. I should not dare to penetrate alone into a private bar; when I do enter a private bar it is invariably under the august protection of an *habitué*, and it is invariably with the idea that at last I am going to see life. Often has this illusion been shattered, but each time it perfectly renewed itself. So I followed the bold Mr Brindley into the private bar of the Tiger.

It was a small and low room. I instinctively stooped, though there was no necessity for me to stoop. The bar had no peculiarity. It can be described in a breath: Three perpendicular planes. Back plane, bottles arranged exactly like books on book shelves; middle plane, the upper halves of two women dressed in tight black; front plane, a counter, dotted with glasses, and having strange areas of zinc. Reckon all that as the stage, and the rest of the room as auditorium. But the stage of a private bar is more mysterious than the stage of a theatre. You are closer to it, and yet it is far less approachable. The edge of the counter is more sacred than the footlights. Impossible to imagine yourself leaping over it. Impossible to imagine yourself in that cloistered place behind it. Impossible to imagine how the priestesses got themselves into that place, or that they ever leave it. They are always there; they are always the same. You may go into a theatre when it is empty and dark; but did you ever go into a private bar that was empty and dark? A private bar is as eternal as the hills, as changeless as the monomania of a madman, as mysterious as sorcery. Always the same order of bottles, the same tinkling, the same popping, the same time tables, and the same realistic pictures of frothing champagne on the walls, the same advertisements on the same ash-trays on the counter, the same odour that wipes your face like a towel the instant you enter; and the same smiles, the same gestures, the same black fabric stretched to tension over the same impressive mammiferous phenomena of the same inexplicable creatures who apparently never eat and never sleep, imprisoned for life in the hallowed and mystic hollow between the bottles and the zinc.

In a tone almost inaudible in its discretion, Mr Brindley let fall to me as he went in –

'This is she.'

She was not quite the ordinary barmaid. Nor, as I learnt afterwards, was she considered to be the ordinary barmaid. She was something midway in importance between the wife of the new proprietor and the younger woman who stood beside her in the cloister talking to a being that resembled a commercial traveller. It was the younger woman who was the ordinary barmaid; she had bright hair, and the bright vacant stupidity which, in my narrow experience, barmaids so often catch like an infectious disease from their clients. But Annie Brett was different. I can best explain how she impressed me by saying that she had the mien of a handsome married woman of forty with a coquettish and superficially emotional past, but also with a daughter who is just going into long skirts. I have known one or two such women. They have been beautiful; they are still handsome at a distance of twelve feet. They are rather effusive; they think they know life, when as a fact their instinctive repugnance for any form of truth has prevented them from acquiring even the rudiments of the knowledge of life. They are secretly preoccupied by the burning question of obesity. They flatter, and they will pay any price for flattery. They are never sincere, not even with themselves; they never, during the whole of their existence, utter a sincere word; even in anger they coldly exaggerate. They are always frothing at the mouth with ecstasy. They adore everything, including God; go to church carrying a prayer-book and hymn-book in separate volumes, and absolutely fawn on the daughter. They are stylish – and impenetrable. But there is something about them very wistful and tragic.

In another social stratum, Miss Annie Brett might have been such a woman. Without doubt nature had intended her for the *rôle*. She was just a little ample, with broad shoulders and a large head and a lot of dark chestnut hair; a large mouth, and large teeth. She had earrings, a brooch, and several rings; also a neat originality of cuffs that would not have been permitted to an ordinary barmaid. As for her face, there were crow's-feet, and a mole (which had selected with infinite skill a site on her chin), and a general degeneracy of complexion; but it was an effective face. The little thing of twenty-three or so by her side had all the cruel advantages of youth, and was not ugly; but she was 'killed' by Annie Brett. Miss Brett had a maternal bust. Indeed, something of the maternal resided in all of her that was visible above the zinc. She must have been about forty; that is to say, apparently older than the late Simon Fuge. Nevertheless, I could conceive her, even now, speciously picturesque in a boat at midnight on a moonstruck water. Had she been on the stage she would have been looking forward to *ingénue* parts for another five years yet – such was her durable sort of effectiveness. Yes, she indubitably belonged to the ornamental half of the universe.

'So this is one of them!' I said to myself.

I tried to be philosophical; but at heart I was profoundly disappointed. I did not know what I had expected; but I had not expected *that*. I was well aware that a thing written always takes on a quality which does not justly appertain to it. I had not expected, therefore, to see an odalisque, a houri, an ideal toy or the remains of an ideal toy; I had not expected any kind of obvious brilliancy, nor a subtle charm that would haunt my memory for evermore. On the other hand, I had not expected the banal, the perfectly commonplace. And I think that Miss Annie Brett was the most banal person that it has pleased Fate to send into my life. I knew that instantly. She was a condemnation of Simon Fuge. *She* was one of the 'wonderful creatures who had played so large a part' in the career of Simon Fuge! *Sapristi!* Still, she *was* one of the wonderful creatures, etc. She *had* floated o'er the bosom of the lake with a great artist. She *had* received his homage. She *had* stirred his feelings. She *had* shared with him the magic of the night. I might decry her as I would; she had known how to cast a spell over him – she and the other one! Something there was in her which had captured him and, seemingly, held him captive.

'Good-*evening*, Mr Brindley,' she expanded. 'You're quite a stranger.' And she embraced me also in the largeness of her welcome.

'It just happens,' said Mr Brindley, 'that I was here last night. But you weren't.'

'Were you now!' she exclaimed, as though learning a novel fact of the most passionate interest. 'The truth is, I had to leave the bar to Miss Slaney last night. Mrs Moorcroft was ill – and the baby only six weeks old, you know – and I wouldn't leave her. No, I wouldn't.'

It was plain that in Miss Annie Brett's opinion there was only one really capable intelligence in the Tiger. This glimpse of her capability, this out-leaping of the latent maternal in her, completely destroyed for the moment my vision of her afloat on the bosom of the lake.

'I see,' said Mr Brindley kindly. Then he rurned to me with character-istic abruptness. 'Well, give it a name, Mr Loring.'

Such is my simplicity that I did not immediately comprehend his mean-ing. For a fraction of a second I thought of the baby. Then I perceived that he was merely employing one of the sacred phrases, sanctified by centuries of usage, of the private bar. I had already drunk mercurey, green Char-treuse, and coffee. I had a violent desire not to drink anything more. I knew my deplorable tomorrows. Still, I would have drunk hot milk, cold water, soda water, or tea. Why should I not have had what I did not object to having? Herein lies another mystery of the private bar. One could surely order tea or milk or soda water from a woman who left everything to tend a mother with a six-weeks-old baby! But no. One could not. As Miss Annie Brett smiled at me pointedly, and rubbed her ringed hands, and kept on smiling with her terrific mechanical effusiveness, I lost all my self-control; I would have resigned myself to a hundred horrible tomorrows under the omnipotent, inexplicable influence of the private bar. I ejaculated, as though to the manner born –

'Irish.'

It proved to have been rather clever of me, showing as it did a due regard for convention combined with a pretty idiosyncrasy. Mr Brindley was clearly taken aback. The idea struck him as a new one. He reflected, and then enthusiastically exclaimed –

'Dashed if I don't have Irish too!'

And Miss Brett, delighted by this unexpected note of Irish in the long, long symphony of Scotch, charged our glasses with gusto. I sipped, death in my heart, and rakishness in my face and gesture. Mr Brindley raised his glass respectfully to Miss Annie Brett, and I did the same. Those two were evidently good friends.

She led the conversation with hard, accustomed ease. When I say 'hard' I do not in the least mean unsympathetic. But her sympathetic quality was toughened by excessive usage, like the hand of a charwoman. She spoke of the vagaries of the Town Hall clock, the health of Mr Brindley's children, the price of coal, the incidence of the annual wakes, the bankruptcy of the draper next door, and her own sciatica, all in the same tone of metallic tender solicitude. Mr Brindley adopted an entirely serious attitude towards her. If I had met him there and nowhere else I should have taken him for a dignified mediocrity, little better than a fool, but with just enough discretion not to give himself away. I said nothing. I was shy. I always am shy in a bar. Out of her cold, cold roving eye Miss Brett watched me, trying to add me up and not succeeding. She must have perceived, however, that I was not like a fish in water.

There was a pause in the talk, due, I think, to Miss Annie Brett's preoccupation with what was going on between Miss Slaney, the ordinary barmaid, and her commercial traveller. The commercial traveller, if he was one, was reading something from a newspaper to Miss Slaney in an indistinct murmur, and with laughter in his voice.

'By the way,' said Mr Brindley, 'you used to know Simon Fuge, didn't you?'

'Old Simon Fuge!' said Miss Brett. 'Yes; after the brewery company took the Blue Bell at Cauldon over from him, I used to be there. He would come in sometimes. Such a nice queer old man!'

'I mean the son,' said Mr Brindley.

'Oh yes,' she answered. 'I knew young Mr Simon too.' A slight hesitation, and then: 'Of course!' Another hesitation. 'Why?'

'Nothing,' said Mr Brindley. 'Only he's dead.'

'You don't mean to say he's dead?' she exclaimed.

'Day before yesterday, in Italy,' said Mr Brindley ruthlessly.

Miss Annie Brett's manner certainly changed. It seemed almost to become natural and unecstatic.

'I suppose it will be in the papers?' she ventured.

'It's in the London paper.'

'Well I never!' she muttered.

'A long time, I should think, since he was in this part of the world,' said Mr Brindley. 'When did *you* last see him?'

He was exceedingly skilful, I considered.

She put the back of her hand over her mouth, and bending her head slightly and lowering her eyelids, gazed reflectively at the counter.

'It was once when a lot of us went to Ilam,' she answered quietly. 'The St Luke's lot, *you* know.'

'Oh!' cried Mr Brindley, apparently startled. 'The St Luke's lot?'

'Yes.'

'How came he to go with you?'

'He didn't go with us. He was there – stopping there, I suppose.'

'Why, I believe I remember hearing something about that,' said Mr Brindley cunningly. 'Didn't he take you out in a boat?'

A very faint dark crimson spread over the face of Miss Annie Brett. It could not be called a blush, but it was as like a blush as was possible to her. The phenomenon, as I could see from his eyes, gave Mr Brindley another shock.

'Yes,' she replied. 'Sally was there as well.'

Then a silence, during which the commercial traveller could be heard reading from the newspaper.

'When was that?' gently asked Mr Brindley.

'Don't ask *me* when it was, Mr Brindley,' she answered nervously. 'It's ever so long ago. What did he die of?'

'Don't know.'

Miss Annie Brett opened her mouth to speak, and did not speak. There were tears in her reddened eyes. I felt very awkward, and I think that Mr Brindley also felt awkward. But I was glad. Those moist eyes caused me a thrill. There was after all some humanity in Miss Annie Brett. Yes, she had after all floated on the bosom of the lake with Simon Fuge. The least romantic of persons, she had yet felt romance. If she had touched Simon Fuge, Simon Fuge had touched her. She had memories. Once she had lived. I pictured her younger. I sought in her face the soft remains of youthfulness, I invented languishing poses for her in the boat. My imagination was equal to the task of seeing her as Simon Fuge saw her. I did so see her. I recalled Simon Fuge's excited description of the long night in the boat, and I could reconstitute the night from end to end. And there the identical creature stood before me, the creature who had set fire to Simon Fuge, one of the 'wonderful creatures' of the *Gazette*, ageing, hardened, banal, but momentarily restored to the empire of romance by those unshed, glittering tears. As an experience it was worth having.

She could not speak, and we did not. I heard the commercial traveller reading: '"The motion was therefore carried by twenty-five votes to nineteen, and the Countess of Chell promised that the whole question of the employment of barmaids should be raised at the next meeting of the B.W.T.S." There! what do you think of that?'

Miss Annie Brett moved quickly towards the commercial traveller.

'I'll tell you what *I* think of it,' she said, with ecstatic resentment. 'I think it's just shameful! Why should the Countess of Chell want to rob a lot of respectable young ladies of their living? I can tell you they're just as respectable as the Countess of Chell is – yes, and perhaps more, by all accounts. I think people do well to call her "Interfering Iris". When she's robbed them of their living, what does she expect them to do? Is she going to keep them? Then what does she expect them to do?'

The commercial traveller was inept enough to offer a jocular reply, and then he found himself involved in the morass of 'the whole question'.

He, and we also, were obliged to hear in immense detail Miss Annie Brett's complete notions of the movement for the abolition of barmaids. The subject was heavy on her mind, and she lifted it off. Simon Fuge was relinquished; he dropped like a stone into the pool of forgetfulness. And yet, strange as it seems, she was assuredly not sincere in the expression of her views on the question of barmaids. She held no real views. She merely persuaded herself that she held them. When the commercial traveller, who was devoid of sense, pointed out that it was not proposed to rob anybody of a livelihood, and that existent barmaids would be permitted to continue to grace the counters of their adoption, she grew frostily vicious. The commercial traveller decided to retire and play billiards. Mr Brindley and I in our turn departed. I was extremely disappointed by this sequel.

'Ah!' breathed Mr Brindley when we were outside, in front of the Town Hall. 'She was quite right about that clock.'

After that we turned silently into a long illuminated street which rose gently. The boxes of light were flashing up and down it, but otherwise it seemed to be quite deserted. Mr Brindley filled a pipe and lit it as he walked. The way in which that man kept the match alight in a fresh breeze made me envious. I could conceive myself rivalling his exploits in cigarette-making, the purchase of rare books, the interpretation of music, even (for a wager) the drinking of beer, but I knew that I should never be able to keep a match alight in a breeze. He threw the match into the mud, and in the mud it continued miraculously to burn with a large flame, as though still under his magic dominion. There are some things that baffle the reasoning faculty.

'Well,' I said, 'she must have been a pretty woman once.'

'"Pretty," by God!' he replied, 'she was beautiful. She was considered the finest piece in Hanbridge at one time. And let me tell you we're supposed to have more than our share of good looks in the Five Towns.'

'What – the women, you mean?'

'Yes.'

'And she never married?'

'No.'

'Nor – anything?'

'Oh no,' he said carelessly.

'But you don't mean to tell me she's never – ' I was just going to exclaim, but I did not, I said: 'And it's her sister who is Mrs Colclough?'

'Yes.' He seemed to be either meditative or disinclined to talk. However, my friends have sometimes hinted to me that when my curiosity is really aroused, I am capable of indiscretions.

'So one sister rattles about in an expensive motor-car, and the other serves behind a bar!' I observed.

He glanced at me.

'I expect it's a bit difficult for you to understand,' he answered; 'but you must remember you're in a democratic district. You told me once you knew Exeter. Well, this isn't a cathedral town. It's about a century in front of any cathedral town in the world. Why, my good sir, there's practically no such thing as class distinction here. Both my grandfathers were working potters. Colclough's father was a joiner who finished up as a builder. If Colclough makes money and chooses to go to Paris and get the best motor-car he can, why in Hades shouldn't his wife ride in it? If he is fond of music and can play like the devil, that isn't his sister-in-law's fault, is it? His wife was a dressmaker, at least she was a dressmaker's assistant. If she suits him, what's the matter?'

'But I never suggested – '

'Excuse me,' he stopped me, speaking with careful and slightly exaggerated calmness, 'I think you did. If the difference in the situations of the two sisters didn't strike you as very extraordinary, what did you mean?'

'And isn't it extraordinary?' I demanded.

'It wouldn't be considered so in any reasonable society,' he insisted. 'The fact is, my good sir, you haven't yet quite got rid of Exeter. I do believe this place will do you good. Why, damn it! Colclough didn't marry both sisters. You think he might keep the other sister? Well, he might. But suppose his wife had half-a-dozen sisters, should he keep them all? I can tell you we're just like the rest of the world, we find no difficulty whatever in spending all the money we make. I dare say Colclough would be ready enough to keep his sister-in-law. I've never asked him. But I'm perfectly certain that his sister-in-law wouldn't be kept. Not much! You don't know these women down here, my good sir. She's earned her living at one thing or another all her life, and I reckon she'll keep on earning it till she drops. She is, without exception, the most exasperating female I ever came across, and that's saying something; but I will give her *that* credit: she's mighty independent.'

'How exasperating?' I asked, surprised to hear this from him.

'*I* don't know. But she is. If she was my wife I should kill her one night. Don't you know what I mean?'

'Yes, I quite agree with you,' I said. 'But you seemed to be awfully good friends with her.'

'No use being anything else. No woman that it ever pleased Providence to construct is going to frighten me away from the draught Burton that you can get at the Tiger. Besides, she can't help it. She was born like that.'

'She *talks* quite ordinarily,' I remarked.

'Oh! It isn't what she says, particularly. It's *her*. Either you like her or you don't like her. Now Colclough thinks she's all right. In fact, he admires her.'

'There's one thing,' I said, 'she jolly nearly cried tonight.'

'Purely mechanical!' said Mr Brindley with cruel curtness.

What seemed to me singular was that the relations which had existed between Miss Annie Brett and Simon Fuge appeared to have no interest whatever for Mr Brindley. He had not even referred to them.

'You were just beginning to draw her out,' I ventured.

'No,' he replied. 'I thought I'd just see what she'd say. No one ever did draw that woman out.'

I had completely lost my vision of her in the boat, but somehow that declaration of his, 'no one ever did draw that woman out', partially restored the vision to me. It seemed to invest her with agreeable mystery.

'And the other sister – Mrs Colclough?' I questioned.

'I'm taking you to see her as fast as I can,' he answered. His tone implied further: 'I've just humoured one of your whims, now for the other.'

'But tell me something about her.'

'She's the best bridge-player – woman, that is – in Bursley. But she will only play every other night for fear the habit should get hold of her. There you've got her.'

'Younger than Miss Brett?'

'Younger,' said Mr Brindley.

'She isn't the same sort of person, is she?'

'She is not,' said Mr Brindley. And his tone implied: 'Thank God for it!'

Very soon afterwards, at the top of a hill, he drew me into the garden of a large house which stood back from the road.

VII

It was quite a different sort of house from Mr Brindley's. One felt that immediately on entering the hall, which was extensive. There was far more money and considerably less taste at large in that house than in the other. I noticed carved furniture that must have been bought with a coarse and a generous hand; and on the walls a diptych by Marcus Stone portraying the course of true love clingingly draped. It was just like Exeter or Onslow Square. But the middle-aged servant who received us struck at once the same note as had sounded so agreeably at Mr Brindley's. She seemed positively glad to see us; our arrival seemed to afford her a peculiar and violent pleasure, as though the hospitality which we were about to accept was in some degree hers too. She robbed us of our hats with ecstasy.

Then Mr Colclough appeared.

'Delighted you've come, Mr Loring!' he said, shaking my hand again. He said it with fervour. He obviously was delighted. The exercise of hospitality was clearly the chief joy of his life; at least, if he had a greater it must have been something where keenness was excessive beyond the point of pleasure, as some joys are. 'How do, Bob? Your missis has just come.' He was still in his motoring clothes.

Mr Brindley, observing my gaze transiently on the Marcus Stones, said: 'I know what you're looking for; you're looking for "Saul's Soul's Awakening". We don't beep it in the window; you'll see it inside.'

'Bob's always rotting me about my pictures,' Mr Colclough smiled indulgently. He seemed big enough to eat his friend, and his rich, heavy voice rolled like thunder about the hall. 'Come along in, will you?'

'Half-a-second, Ol,' Mr Brindley called in a conspiratorial tone, and, turning to me: 'Tell him *the* Limerick. You know.'

'The one about the hayrick?'

Mr Brindley nodded.

There were three heads close together for a space of twenty seconds or so, and then a fearful explosion happened – the unique, tremendous laughter of Mr Colclough, which went off like a charge of melinite and staggered the furniture.

'Now, now!' a feminine voice protested from an unseen interior.

I was taken to the drawing-room, an immense apartment with an immense piano black as midnight in it. At the further end two women were seated close together in conversation, and I distinctly heard the name 'Fuge'. One of them was Mrs Brindley, in a hat. The other, a very big and stout woman, in an elaborate crimson garment that resembled a teagown, rose and came to meet me with extended hand.

'My wife – Mr Loring,' said Mr Oliver Colclough.

'So glad to meet you,' she said, beaming on me with all her husband's pleasure. 'Come and sit between Mrs Brindley and me, near the window, and keep us in order. Don't you find it very close? There are at least a hundred cats in the garden.'

One instantly perceived that ceremonial stiffness could not exist in the same atmosphere with Mrs Oliver Colclough. During the whole time I spent in her house there was never the slightest pause in the conversation. Mrs Oliver Colclough prevented nobody from talking, but she would gladly use up every odd remnant of time that was not employed by others. No scrap was too small for her.

'So this is the other one!' I said to myself. 'Well, give me this one!'

Certainly there was a resemblance between the two, in the general formation of the face, and the shape of the shoulders; but it is astonishing that two sisters can differ as these did, with a profound and vital difference. In Mrs Colclough there was no *coquetterie*, no trace of that more-than-half-suspicious challenge to a man that one feels always in the type to which her better belonged. The notorious battle of the sexes was assuredly carried on by her in a spirit of frank muscular gaiety – she could, I am sure, do her share of fighting. Put her in a boat on the bosom of the lake under starlight, and she would not by a gesture, a tone, a glance, convey mysterious nothings to you, a male. She would not be subtly changed by the sensuous influence of the situation; she would always be the same plump and earthly piece of candour. Even if she were in love with you, she would not convey mysterious nothings in such circumstances. If she were in love with you she would most clearly convey unmysterious and solid somethings. I was convinced that the contributing cause to the presence of the late Simon Fuge in the boat on Ilam Lake on the historic night was Annie the superior barmaid, and not Sally of the automobile. But Mrs Colclough, if not beautiful, was a very agreeable creation. Her amplitude gave at first sight an exaggerated impression of her age; but this departed after more careful inspection. She could not have been more than thirty. She was very dark, with plenteous and untidy black hair, thick eyebrows, and a slight moustache. Her eyes were very vivacious, and her gestures, despite that bulk, quick and graceful. She was happy; her ideals were satisfied; it was probably happiness that had made her stout. Her massiveness was apparently no grief to her; she had fallen into the carelessness which is too often the pitfall of women who, being stout, are content.

'How do, missis?' Mr Brindley greeted her, and to his wife, 'How do, missis? But, look here, bright star, this gadding about is all very well, but what about those precious kids of yours? None of 'em dead yet, I hope.'

'Don't be silly, Bob.'

'I've been over to your house,' Mrs Colclough put in. 'Of course it isn't mumps. The child's as right as rain. So I brought Mary back with me.'

'Well' said Mr Brindley, 'for a woman who's never had any children your knowledge of children beggars description. What you aren't sure you know about them isn't knowledge. However – '

'Listen,' Mrs Colclough replied, with a delightful throwing-down of the glove. 'I'll bet you a level sovereign that child hasn't got the mumps. So there! And Oliver will guarantee to pay you.'

'Aye!' said Mr Colclough; 'I'll back my wife any day.'

'Don't bet, Bob,' Mrs Brindley enjoined her husband excitedly in her high treble.

'I won't,' said Mr Brindley.

'Now let's sit down.' Mrs Colclough addressed me with particular, confidential grace.

We three exactly filled the sofa. I have often sat between two women, but never with such calm, unreserved, unapprehensive comfortableness as I experienced between Mrs Colclough and Mrs Brindley. It was just as if I had known them for years.

'You'll make a mess of that, Ol,' said Mr Brindley.

The other two men were at some distance, in front of a table, on which were two champagne bottles and five glasses, and a plate of cakes. 'Well,' I said to myself, 'I'm not going to have any champagne, anyhow. Mercurey! Green Chartreuse! Irish whisky! And then champagne! And a morning's hard work tomorrow! No!'

Plop! A cork flew up and bounced against the ceiling.

Mr Colclough carefully emptied the bottle into the glasses, of which Mr Brindley seized two and advanced with one in either hand for the women. It was the host who offered a glass to me.

'No, thanks very much, I really can't,' I said in a very firm tone.

My tone was so firm that it startled them. They glanced at each other with alarmed eyes, like simple people confronted by an inexplicable phenomenon.

'But look here, mister!' said Mr Colclough, pained, 'we've got this out specially for you. You don't suppose this is our usual tipple, do you?'

I yielded. I could do no less than sacrifice myself to their enchanting instinctive kindness of heart. 'I shall be dead tomorrow,' I said to myself; 'but I shall have lived tonight.' They were relieved, but I saw that I had given them a shock from which they could not instantaneously recover. Therefore I began with a long pull, to reassure them.

'Mrs Brindley has been telling me that Simon Fuge is dead,' said Mrs Colclough brightly, as though Mrs Brindley had been telling her that the price of mutton had gone down.

I perceived that those two had been talking over Simon Fuge, after their fashion.

'Oh yes,' I responded.

'Have you got that newspaper in your pocket, Mr Loring?' asked Mrs Brindley.

I had.

'No,' I said, feeling in my pockets; 'I must have left it at your house.'

'Well,' she said, 'that's strange. I looked for it to show it to Mrs Colclough, but I couldn't see it.'

This was not surprising. I did not want Mrs Colclough to read the journalistic obituary until she had given me her own obituary of Fuge.

'It must be somewhere about,' I said; and to Mrs Colclough: 'I suppose you knew him pretty well?'

'Oh, bless you, no! I only met him once.'

'At Ilam?'

'Yes. What are you going to do, Oliver?'

Her husband was opening the piano.

'Bob and I are just going to have another smack at that Brahms.'

'You don't expect us to listen, do you?'

'I expect you to do what pleases you, missis,' said he. 'I should be a bigger fool than I am if I expected anything else.' That he smiled at me. 'No! Just go on talking. Ol and I'll drown you easy enough. Quite short! Back in five minutes.'

The two men placed each his wine-glass on the space on the piano designed for a candlestick, lighted cigars, and sat down to play.

'Yes,' Mrs Colclough resumed, in a lower, more confidential tone, to the accompaniment of the music. 'You see, there was a whole party of us there, and Mr Fuge was staying at the hotel, and of course he knew several of us.'

'And he took you out in a boat?'

'Me and Annie? Yes. Just as it was getting dusk he came up to us and asked us if we'd go for a row. Eh, I can hear him asking us now! I asked him if he could row, and he was quite angry. So we went, to quieten him.' She paused, and then laughed.

'Sally!' Mrs Brindley protested. 'You know he's dead!'

'Yes.' She admitted the rightness of the protest. 'But I can't help it. I was just thinking how he got his feet wet in pushing the boat off.' She laughed again. 'When we were safely off, someone came down to the shore and shouted to Mr Fuge to bring the boat back. You know his quick way of talking.' (Here she began to imitate Fuge.) ' "I've quarrelled with the man this boat belongs to. Awful feud! Fact is, I'm in a hostile country here!" And a lot more like that. It seemed be had quarrelled with everybody in Ilam. He wasn't sure if the landlord of the hotel would let him sleep there again. He told us all about all his quarrels, until he dropped one of the oars. I shall never forget how funny he looked in the moonlight when he dropped the oar. "There, that's your fault!" he said. "You make me talk too much about myself, and I get excited." He kept striking matches to look for the oar, and turning the boat round and round with the other oar. "Last match!" he said. "We shall never see land tonight." Then he found the oar again. He considered we were saved. Then he began to tell us about his aunt. "You know, I'd no business to be here. I came down from London for my aunt's funeral, and here I am in a boat at night with two pretty girls!" He said the funeral had taught him one thing, and that was that black neckties were the only possible sort of necktie. He said the greatest worry of his life had always been neckties; but he wouldn't have to worry any more, and so his aunt hadn't died for nothing. I assure you he kept on talking about neckties. I assure you, Mr Loring, I went to sleep – at least I dozed – and when I woke up he was still talking about neckties. But then his feet began to get cold. I suppose it was because they were wet. The way he grumbled about his feet being cold! I remember he turned his coat collar up. He wanted to get on shore and walk, but he'd taken us a long way up the lake by that time, and he saw we were absolutely lost. So he put the oars in the boat and stood up and stamped his feet. It might have upset the boat.'

'How did it end?' I inquired.

'Well, Annie and I caught the train, but only just. You see it was a special train, so they kept it for us, otherwise we should have been in a nice fix.'

'So you have special trains in these parts?'

'Why, of course! It was the annual outing of the teachers of St Luke's Sunday School and their friends, you see. So we had a special train.'

At this point the duettists came to the end of a movement, and Mr Brindley leaned over to us from his stool, glass in hand.

'The railway company practically owns Ilam,' he explained, 'and so they run it for all they're worth. They made the lake, to feed the canals, when they bought the canals from the canal company. It's an artificial lake, and the railway runs alongside it. A very good scheme of the company's. They started out to make Ilam a popular resort, and they've made it a popular resort, what with special trains and things. But try to get a special train to any other place on their rotten system, and you'll soon see!'

'How big is the lake?' I asked.

'How long is it, Ol?' he demanded of Colclough. 'A couple of miles?'

'Not it! About a mile. Adagio!'

They proceeded with Brahms.

'He ran with you all the way to the station, didn't he?' Mrs Brindley suggested to Mrs Colclough.

'I should just say he did!' Mrs Colclough concurred. 'He wanted to get warm, and then he was awfully afraid lest we should miss it.'

'I thought you were on the lake practically all night!' I exclaimed.

'All night! Well, I don't know what you call all night. But I was back in Bursley before eleven o'clock, I'm sure.'

I then contrived to discover the *Gazette* in an unsearched pocket, and I gave it to Mrs Colclough to read. Mrs Brindley looked over her shoulder.

There was no slightest movement of depreciation on Mrs Colclough's part. She amiably smiled as she perused the *Gazette*'s version of Fuge's version of the lake episode. Here was the attitude of the woman whose soul is like crystal. It seems to me that most women would have blushed, or dissented, or simulated anger, or failed to conceal vanity. But Mrs Coclough might have been reading a fairy tale, for any emotion she displayed.

'Yes,' she said blandly; 'from the things Annie used to tell me about him sometimes, I should say that was just how he *would* talk. They seem to have thought quite a lot of him in London, then?'

'Oh, rather!' I said. 'I suppose your sister knew him pretty well?'

'Annie? I don't know. She knew him.'

I distinctly observed a certain self-consciousness in Mrs Colclough as she made this reply. Mrs Brindley had risen and with wifely attentiveness was turning over the music page for her husband.

VIII

Soon afterwards, for me, the night began to grow fantastic; it took on the colour of a gigantic adventure. I do not suppose that either Mr Brindley or Mr Colclough, or the other person who presently arrived, regarded it as anything but a pleasant conviviality, but to a man of my constitution and habits it was an almost incredible occurrence. The other person was the book-collecting doctor. He arrived with a discreet tap on the window at midnight, to spend the evening. Mrs Brindley had gone home and Mrs Colclough had gone to bed. The book-collecting doctor refused champagne; he was, in fact, very rude to champagne in general. He had whisky.

And those astonishing individuals, Messieurs Brindley and Colclough, secretly convinced of the justice of the attack on champagne, had whisky too. And that still most astonishing individual, Loring of the B.M., joined them. It was the hour of limericks. Limericks were demanded for the diversion of the doctor, and I furnished them. We then listened to the tale of the doctor's experiences that day amid the sturdy, natural-minded population of a mining village not far from Bursley. Seldom have I had such a bath in the pure fluid of human nature. All sense of time was lost. I lived to an eternity. I could not suggest to my host that we should depart. I could, however, decline more whisky. And I could, given the chance, discourse with gay despair concerning the miserable wreck that I should be on the morrow in consequence of this high living. I asked them how I could be expected, in such a state, to judge delicate points of expertise in earthenware. I gave them a brief sketch of my customary evening, and left them to compare it with that evening. The doctor perceived that I was serious. He gazed at me with pity, as if to say: 'Poor frail southern organism! It ought to be in bed, with nothing inside it but tea!' What he did actually say was: 'You come round to my place, I'll soon put you right!'

'Can you stop me from having a headache tomorrow?' I eagerly asked. 'I think so,' he said with calm northern confidence.

At some later hour Mr Brindley and I 'went round'. Mr Colclough would not come. He bade me good-bye, as his wife had done, with the most extraordinary kindness, the most genuine sorrow at quitting me, the most genuine pleasure in the hope of seeing me again.

'There are three thousand books in this room!' I said to myself, as I stood in the doctor's electrically lit library.

'What price this for a dog?' Mr Brindley drew my attention to an aristocratic fox-terrier that lay on the hearth. 'Well, Titus! Is it sleepy? Well, well! How many firsts has he won, doctor?'

'Six,' said the doctor. 'I'll just fix you up, to begin with,' he turned to me.

After I had been duly fixed up ('This'll help you to sleep, and this'll placate your "god",' said the doctor), I saw to my intense surprise that another 'evening' was to be instantly superimposed on the 'evening' at Mr Colclough's. The doctor and Mr Brindley carefully and deliberately lighted long cigars, and sank deeply into immense arm-chairs; and so I imitated them as well as I could in my feeble southern way. We talked books. We just simply enumerated books without end, praising or damning them, and arranged authors in neat pews, like cattle in classes at an agricultural show. No pastime is more agreeable to people who have the book disease, and none more quickly fleets the hours, and none is more delightfully futile.

Ages elapsed, and suddenly, like a gun discharging, Mr Brindley said – 'We must go!'

Of all things that happened this was the most astonishing.

We did go.

'By the way, doc.,' said Mr Brindley, in the doctor's wide porch, 'I forgot to tell you that Simon Fuge is dead.'

'Is he?' said the doctor.

'Yes. You've got a couple of his etchings, haven't you?'

'No,' said the doctor. 'I had. But I sold them several months ago.'

'Oh!' said Mr Brindley negligently; 'I didn't know. Well, so long!'

We had a few hundred yards to walk down the silent, wide street, where the gas-lamps were burning with the strange, endless patience that gas-lamps have. The stillness of a provincial town at night is quite different from that of London; we might have been the only persons alive in England.

Except for a feeling of unreality, a feeling that the natural order of things had been disturbed by some necromancer, I was perfectly well the same morning at breakfast, as the doctor had predicted I should be. When I expressed to Mr Brindley my stupefaction at this happy sequel, he showed a polite but careless inability to follow my line of thought. It appeared that he was always well at breakfast, even when he did stay up 'a little later than usual'. It appeared further that he always breakfasted at a quarter to nine, and read the *Manchester Guardian* during the meal, to which his wife did or did not descend – according to the moods of the nursery; and that he reached his office at a quarter to ten. That morning the mood of the nursery was apparently unpropitious. He and I were alone. I begged him not to pretermit his *Guardian*, but to examine it and give me the news. He agreed, scarcely unwilling.

'There's a paragraph in the London correspondence about Fuge,' he announced from behind the paper.

'What do they say about him?'

'Nothing particular.'

'Now I want to ask you something,' I said.

I had been thinking a good deal about the sisters and Simon Fuge. And in spite of everything that I had heard – in spite even of the facts that the lake had been dug by a railway company, and that the excursion to the lake had been an excursion of Sunday-school teachers and their friends – I was still haunted by certain notions concerning Simon Fuge and Annie Brett. Annie Brett's flush, her unshed tears; and the self-consciousness shown by Mrs Colclough when I had pointedly mentioned her sister's name in connection with Simon Fuge's: these were surely indications! And then the doctor's recitals of manners in the immediate neighbourhood of Bursley went to support my theory that even in Staffordshire life was very much life.

'What?' demanded Mr Brindley.

'Was Miss Brett ever Simon Fuge's mistress?'

At that moment Mrs Brindley, miraculously fresh and smiling, entered the room.

'Wife,' said Mr Brindley, without giving her time to greet me, 'what do you think he's just asked me?'

'*I* don't know.'

'He's just asked me if Annie Brett was ever Simon Fuge's mistress.'

She sank into a chair.

'Annie *Brett*?' She began to laugh gently. 'Oh! Mr Loring, you really are too funny!' She yielded to her emotions. It may be said that she laughed as they can laugh in the Five Towns. She cried. She had to wipe away the tears of laughter.

'What on earth made you think so?' she inquired, after recovery.

'I – had an idea,' I said lamely. 'He always made out that one of those two sisters was so much to him, and I knew it couldn't be Mrs Colclough.'

'Well,' she said, 'ask anybody down here, *any*-body! And see what they'll say.'

'No,' Mr Brindley put in, 'don't go about asking *any*-body. You might get yourself disliked. But you may take it it isn't true.'

'Most certainly,' his wife concurred with seriousness.

'We reckon to know something about Simon Fuge down here,' Mr Brindley added. 'Also about the famous Annie.'

'He must have flirted with her a good bit, anyhow,' I said.

'Oh, *flirt*!' ejaculated Mr Brindley.

I had a sudden dazzling vision of the great truth that the people of the Five Towns have no particular use for half-measures in any department of life. So I accepted the final judgement with meekness.

IX

I returned to London that evening, my work done, and the municipality happily flattered by my judgement of the slip-decorated dishes. Mr Brindley had found time to meet me at the midday meal, and he had left his office earlier than usual in order to help me to drink his wife's afternoon tea. About an hour later he picked up my little bag, and said that he should accompany me to the little station in the midst of the desert of cinders and broken crockery, and even see me as far as Knype, where I had to take the London express. No, there are no half-measures in the Five Towns. Mrs Brindley stood on her doorstep, with her eldest infant on her shoulders, and waved us off. The infant cried, expressing his own and his mother's grief at losing a guest. It seems as if people are born hospitable in the Five Towns.

We had not walked more than a hundred yards up the road when a motor-car thundered down upon us from the opposite direction. It was Mr Colclough's, and Mr Colclough was driving it. Mr Brindley stopped his friend with the authoritative gesture of a policeman.

'Where are you going, Ol?'

'Home, lad. Sorry you're leaving us so soon, Mr Loring.'

'You're mistaken, my boy,' said Mr Brindley. 'You're just going to run us down to Knype station, first.'

'I must look slippy, then,' said Mr Colclough.

'You can look as slippy as you like,' said Mr Brindley.

In another fifteen seconds we were in the car, and it had turned round, and was speeding towards Knype. A feverish journey! We passed electric cars every minute, and for three miles were continually twisting round the tails of ponderous, creaking, and excessively deliberate carts that dropped a trail of small coal, or huge barrels on wheels that dripped something like the finest Devonshire cream, or brewer's drays that left nothing behind them save a luscious odour of malt. It was a breathless slither over unctuous black mud through a long winding carion of brown-red houses and shops, with a glimpse here and there of a grey-green park, a canal, or a football field.

'I daredn't hurry,' said Mr Colclough, setting us down at the station. 'I was afraid of a skid.' He had not spoken during the transit.

'Don't put on side, Ol,' said Mr Brindley. 'What time did you get up this morning?'

'Eight o'clock, lad. I was at th' works at nine.'

He flew off to escape my thanks, and Mr Brindley and I went into the station. Owing to the celerity of the automobile we had half-an-hour to wait. We spent it chiefly at the bookstall. While we were there the extra-special edition of the *Staffordshire Signal*, affectionately termed 'the local rag' by its readers, arrived, and we watched a newsboy affix its poster to a board. The poster ran thus –

HANBRIDGE RATES
LIVELY MEETING

—

KNYPE F.C.
NEW CENTRE-FORWARD

—

ALL – WINNERS AND S.P.

Now, close by this poster was the poster of the *Daily Telegraph*, and among the items offered by the *Daily Telegraph* was: 'Death of Simon Fuge'. I could not forbear pointing out to Mr Brindley the difference between the two posters. A conversation ensued; and amid the rumbling of trains and the rough stir of the platform we got back again to Simon Fuge, and Mr Brindley's tone gradually grew, if not acrid, a little impatient.

'After all,' he said, 'rates are rates, especially in Hanbridge. And let me tell you that last season Knype Football Club jolly nearly got thrown out of the First League. The constitution of the team for this next season – why, damn it, it's a question of national importance! You don't understand these things. If Knype Football Club was put into the League Second Division, ten thousand homes would go into mourning. Who the devil was Simon Fuge?'

They joke with such extraordinary seriousness in the Five Towns that one is somehow bound to pretend that they are not joking. So I replied –

'He was a great artist. And this is his native district. Surely you ought to be proud of him!'

'He may have been a great artist,' said Mr Brindley, 'or he may not. But for us he was simply a man who came of a family that had a bad reputation for talking too much and acting the goat!'

'Well,' I said, 'we shall see – in fifty years.'

'That's just what we shan't,' said he. 'We shall be where Simon Fuge is – dead! However, perhaps we are proud of him. But you don't expect us to show it, do you? That's not our style.'

He performed the quasi-winking phenomenon with his eyes. It was his final exhibition of it to me.

'A strange place!' I reflected, as I ate my dinner in the dining-car, with the pressure of Mr Brindley's steely clasp still affecting my right hand, and the rich, honest cordiality of his *au revoir* in my heart. 'A place that is passing strange!'

And I thought further: He may have been a boaster, and a chatterer, and a man who suffered from cold feet at the wrong moments! And the Five Towns may have got the better of him, now. But that portrait of the little girl in the Wedgwood Institution is waiting there, right in the middle of the Five Towns. And one day the Five Towns will have to 'give it best'. They can say what they like! . . . What eyes the fellow had, when he was in the right company!

MARY MANN

Women o' Dulditch

Dinah Brome stood in the village shop, watching, with eyes keen to detect the slightest discrepancy in the operation, the weighing of her weekly parcels of grocery.

She was a strong, wholesome-looking woman of three- or four-and-forty, with a clean, red skin, clear eyes, dark hair, crinkling crisply beneath her sober, respectable hat. All her clothes were sober and respectable, and her whole mien. No one would have guessed from it that she had not a shred of character to her back.

The knowledge of this incontrovertible fact did not influence the demeanour of the shop-woman towards her. There was not better pay in the village, nor a more constant customer than Dinah Brome. In such circumstances, Mrs Littleproud was not the woman to throw stones.

'They tell me as how Depper's wife ain't a-goin' to get over this here sickness she've got,' she said, tucking in the edges of the whitey-brown paper upon the half-pound of moist sugar taken from the scales. 'The doctor, he ha'n't put a name to her illness, but 'tis one as'll carry her off, he say.'

'A quarter pound o' butter,' Dinah unmovedly said. 'The best, please. I don't fancy none o' that that ha' got the taste o' the shop in it.'

'Doctor, he put his hid in at the door this afternoon,' Mrs Littleproud went on; 'he'd got his monkey up, the old doctor had! " 'Tis a rank shame," he say, "there ain't none o' these here lazy women o' Dulditch with heart enough to go to help that poor critter in her necessity," he say.'

'Ler'm help her hisself,' said Mrs Brome, strong in her indifference. 'A couple o' boxes o' matches, Mrs Littleproud; and you can gi' me the odd ha'penny in clo' balls for the disgestion.'

'You should ha' heered 'm run on! "Where be that Dinah Brome?" he

410

say, "that ha' showed herself helpful in other folks' houses. Wha's she a-doin' of, that she can't do a neighbour's part here?"'

'And you telled 'm she was a-mindin' of 'er own business, I hope?' Mrs Brome suggested, in calmest unconcern.

'I'll tell you what I did say, Dinah, bor,' the shop-woman said, transferring the sticky clove-balls from their bottle to her own greasy palm. '"Dinah Brome, sir," I say, "is the most industrousest woman in Dulditch; arly and late," I say, "she's at wark; and as for her floors – you might eat off of 'em."' She screwed the half-dozen hard red balls in their bit of paper, and stowed them lightly in the customer's basket. 'That the lot this week, Dinah?'

Dinah removed her basket from counter to arm. 'What'd he got to say for hisself, then?' she asked.

'"A woman like that can allust make time," the old doctor he say. "Tell her to make time to help this here pore sufferin' woman." I'm a-sayin' it as he said it, Dinah. I ain't a-hintin' of it myself, bor.'

'Ler'm tell me, hisself, an old interfarin' old fule, and he'll ha' the rough side o' my tongue,' the customer said; and nodded an unsmiling good-afternoon, and went on her way.

Her way led her past the cottage of the woman of whom they had spoken. Depper's cottage, indeed, was the first in the row of which Dinah's was the last – a half-dozen two-roomed tenements, living-room below, bedroom above, standing with their backs to the road, from which they were divided by no garden, nor even so much as a narrow path. The lower window of the two allotted to each house was about four or five feet from the ground, and was of course the window of the living-room. Mrs Brome, as she passed that of the first house in the row, suddenly yielded to the impulse to stop and look within.

A small interior, with furniture much too big for it; a huge chest of drawers, of oak with brass fittings; a broken-down couch as big as a bed, covered with a dingy shawl, a man's greatcoat, a red flannel petticoat; a table cumbered with the remains of wretched meals never cleared away, and the poor cooking utensils of impoverished, shifty housekeeping.

The woman of whom they had been speaking stood with her back to the window. A stooping, drooping skeleton of a woman, who, with weak, shaking hands, kneaded some dough in which a few currants were stuck, before laying it on a black-looking baking tin.

'A fine time o' day to bake his fourses cake!' the woman outside commented, reaching on tiptoe, the better to look in at the window.

The tin having its complement of cakes, the sick woman essayed to carry it to the oven. But its weight was too much for her; it hung limply in her weak grasp; before the oven was reached the cakes were on the ragged carpet of the hearth.

'God in heaven!' ejaculated the woman looking in.

She watched while the poor woman within dropped on all-fours, feebly trying to gather up the cakes spreading themselves slowly over the dirty floor.

'If that don't make me sick!' said Dinah Brome to herself as she turned and went on her way.

The cottage of Dinah Brome, distant from that of Depper's wife by a score or so of yards, was, in its domestic economy, as removed from it as the North Pole from the South. Small wonder that Depper – his name was William Kittle, a fact of which the neighbourhood made no practical use, which he himself only recalled with an effort – preferred to the dirt, untidiness and squalor of his own abode the spick-and-span cleanliness of Dinah Brome's. Small wonder that in this atmosphere of wholesomeness and comfort, he chose to spend the hours of the Sabbath during which the public-house was closed; and other hours. Small wonder, looking at the fine, capable figure of the woman, now bustling about with teapot and cups, he should esteem Mrs Brome personally above the slatternly skeleton at his own hearth.

Having made a cup of tea and cut a couple of slices of bread-and-butter, the owner of the fresh-scrubbed bricks, the fresh polished furniture, the dazzlingly white hearth, turned her back on her household gods, and, plate and cup in hands, betook herself, by way of the uneven bricked passage separating the row of houses from their rows of gardens at the back, to the house of the wife of Depper.

'I swore I wouldn't,' she said to herself as she went along; 'but I'm dinged if the sight o' Depper's old woman a-crawlin' arter them mamucked up bits o' dough ha'n't tarned my stomach!'

She knocked at the door with the toe of her boot, her hands being full, and receiving no answer, opened it and went in.

Depper's old woman had fallen, a miserable heap of bones and dingy clothing, upon the broken-down couch, and had fainted there.

'I'd suner 'twas anyone in the warld than you a-waitin' on me like this,' she said, when, consciousness having returned during the ministrations of the other woman, her weary eyes opened upon the healthy face above her.

'And the las' time you told me to walk out o' your house, I swore I'd never set fut in it again,' Mrs Brome made answer. 'But I ha' swallered worse things in my time than my own wards, I make no doubt; and you ha' come to a pass, Car'line Kittle, when you ha' got to take what you can git and be thankful.'

'Pass? I ha' come to a pass, indeed!' the sick woman moaned. 'You're wholly right there, bor; wholly right.'

'So now you ha' got to drink this here cup o' hot tea I ha' brought ye; and let me help ye upstairs to yer bed as quick as may be.'

'When I ha' baked Depper's fourses cake, and sent it off by 'Meelyer's little gal – she ha' lent her to me to go back and forth to the harvest-field, 'Meelyer have – I kin go,' the wife said; 'not afore,' hiccoughing loudly over the tea she tried to drink; 'not afore – not afore! Oh, how I wish I could, bor; how I wish I could!'

'You're a-goin', this instant minute,' the masterful Dinah declared.

The other had not the strength to resist. 'I'm wholly done,' she murmured, helplessly, 'wholly done at last.'

'My! How ha' you got up these here stairs alone?' Dinah, having half-dragged, half-carried the feeble creature to the top, demanded of her, wiping her own brow.

'Crawled, all-fours.' Depper's wife panted out the explanation. 'And to git down 'em i' the mornin's – oh, the Lord alone knows how I ha' got down 'em i' th' mornin's. Thankful I'd be to know I'd never ha' to come down 'em agin.'

'You never will,' said Mrs Brome.

'I don't want to trouble you, no fudder. I can fend for myself now,' the poor woman said, when at length she lay at peace between the sheets; her face bathed, and the limp grimy fingers; the scant dry hair smoothed decently down the fallen temples. 'I'd rather it'd ha' been another woman that had done me the sarvice, but I ain't above bein' thankful to you, for all that. All I'll ask of ye now, Dinah Brome, is that ye'll have an eye to Depper's fourses cake in th' oven, and see that 'Meelyer's gal take it and his home-brew, comf'table, to th' field for 'm.'

Dinah, having folded the woman's clothes, spread them for additional warmth upon the poor bed-covering. 'Don't you worrit no more about Depper,' she said. 'Strike me, you're the one that want seein' to now, Car'line.'

The slow tears oozed beneath Car'line's closed lids. 'I kin fend for myself if Depper ain't put about,' she said.

When Depper returned, with the shades of night from the harvest-field, he might hardly have known his own living-room. The dirty rags of carpet had disappeared, the bricks were scrubbed, the dangerous-looking heap of clothing had been removed from the sofa, and a support added to its broken leg; the fireside chairs, the big chest of drawers, redo-lent of the turpentine with which they had been rubbed, shone in the candlelight; the kettle sang on the bars by the side of a saucepan of potatoes boiling for the meal. It was the sight of Dinah Brome at the head of affairs, however, which drew his attention from these details.

'Well, I'm jiggered!' Depper said, and paused, door in hand, on his own freshly-washed step.

'You wipe your feet, afore you come in,' said Mrs Brome, masterful as ever. 'Here's yer supper ready. I ain't a-goin' to ate it along of you, Depper; but I ha' got a ward or two to say to you afore I go.'

Depper entered, closed the door behind him, sat down, hat on head, in the freshly-polished chair by the hearth; he fixed his eyes, his mouth fallen open, on the fine form of Dinah standing before him, with hands on hips, arms akimbo, and the masterful gleam in her eyes.

'Depper, yer old woman's a-dyin' 'Dinah said.

'Marcy on us! Ye don't tell me that! Kind o' piney, like, fer the las' six months, my missus ha' bin', but – '

'Now she's a-dyin'. D'ye think I ha'n't got the right use o' my senses, arter all these years? Wheer ha' yer own eyes been? Look at 'er! No better'n a skeercrow of a woman, under yer very nose! She's a-dyin', I tell ye. And, Depper, what du I come here to find? I find a bare cupboard and a bare board. Not a mite o' nouragement i' th' house, sech as a pore suff'rin' woman like Car'line's in need of.'

'Car'line's a pore manager, as right well you know, Dinah. Ha'n't I telled ye – ?'

'You ha' telled me – yes. But have you played th' husban's part? You ha' telled me – and I ha' put the fault o' yer poverty home on ter yer pore missus's shoulders. But since I been here, I ha' seen 'er crawlin' on 'er han's and knees to wait on you, wi' yer fourses i' th' harvest-field. I ha' heered her manderin' on, "let things be comf'table for Depper," and let her fend for herself. And I can see with half an eye the bute is on t'other fut, Depper. And this here is what I'm a-goin' ter say to you, and don't you make no mistake about it: I'm yer wife's woman while she want me, and none o' yours.'

Depper was a small, well-made man, with a curling, grizzled head, and a well-featured face. It is possible that in his youth the word 'dapper' may have applied to him; a forgotten fact which perhaps accounted for his nickname. He gazed with an open mouth and puzzled, blear eyes at the woman before him.

'You and me,' he said slowly, with an utterance suspiciously slow and thick – 'you and me ha' kep' comp'ny, so to speak, fer a sight o' years, Dinah. We never had no fallin's out, this mander, afore, as I can call ter mind. I don't rightly onderstan' what you ha' got agin me – come ter put it into wards.'

'I ha' got this agin ye,' the valiant Dinah said: 'that you ha' nouraged yer own inside and let your missus's go empty. You ha' got too much drink aboard ye, now, an' her fit ter die for the want of a drop o' sperrits. And I ha' got this ter say: that we ha' come to a pass when I ha' got to make ch'ice twixt you and yer old woman. Arter wha's come and gone, we t'ree can't hob an' nob, as ye may say, together. My ch'ice is made, then, and this is how I ha' fixed it up. When yer day's wark is done, and you come home, I go out o' your house. Sune as yer up an' away i' th' mornin', I come in and ridd up yer missus and wait on 'er, while the woman's in need of me.'

Whether this plan met with Depper's approval or not, Dinah Brome did not wait to see. 'For Car'line's peace o' mind, arter wha's come and gone, 'tis th' only way,' she said to herself and to him; and by it he had to abide.

It was not for many weeks. The poor unlovely wife, lying in the dismantled four-poster in the only bedroom, was too far gone to benefit by the 'nouragement' Mrs Brome contrived to administer. The sixpenn'orths of brandy Depper, too late relenting, spared from the sum he had hitherto expended on his own beer – public-house brandy, poisonous stuff, but accredited by the labouring population of Dulditch with all but magical restorative powers – for once failed in its effect. Daily more of a skeleton, hourly feebler and feebler, grew Depper's old woman; clinging, for all that, desperately to life and the hope of recovery for the sake of Depper himself.

'Let go the things of this life, lay hold on those of Eternity,' the clergy-man said, solemnly reproving her for her worldly state of mind. 'Remember that there is no one in this world whose life is indispensable to the scheme of it. Try to think more humbly of yourself, my poor friend, less regretfully of the world you are hurrying from. Fix your eyes on the heavenly prospect. Try to join with me more heartily in the prayers for the dying.'

She listened to them, making no response, with slow tears falling from shut lids to the pillow. ' 'Tain't for myself I'm a-pinin', 'tis for Depper,' she said, the parson being gone.

'All the same, Car'line,' Mrs Brome said, sharply admonishing, 'I'd marmar a ward now and agin for myself, as the reverend ha' been advisin' of ye, if I was you. Depper he can look arter hisself; his time for prayin' ain't, so ter say, come yet. Yours is. I should like to hear a "Lord help me," now and agin from yer lips, when I tarn ye in the bed. I don't think but what yu'd be the better for it, pore critter. Your time's a-gettin' short, and 'tis best ter go resigned.'

'I cud go resigned if 'tweren't for Depper,' the dying woman made her moan.

'I can't think what he'll du all alone in th' house and me gone!' she often whimpered. 'A man can't fend for 'isself, like a woman can. They ha'n't the know ter du it. Depper, he ain't no better'n a child about makin' the kettle bile, and sechlike. It'll go hard, me bein' put out o' th' way, wi' Depper.'

'Sarve 'm right,' Mrs Brome always stoically said. 'He ha' been a bad man to you, Car'line. I don' know whu should speak to that if you and me don't, bor.'

'He ha'n't so much as laid a finger on me since I was ill,' Car'line said, making what defence for the absent man she could.

'All the same, when you're a-feelin' wholly low agin, jes' you say to yourself, "Th' Lord help me!"'Tis only dacent, you a dyin' woman, to do it. When ye ha'n't got the strength ter say it, I'll go on my knees and say it for ye, come to that, Car'line,' the notorious wrongdoer promised.

They sent for Depper to the White Hart to come home and see his wife die.

'I ain't, so ter say, narvish, bein' alone with 'er, and would as lief see the pore sufferin' critter draw her las' breath as not, but I hold 'tis dacent for man and wife to be together, come to th' finish; an' so I ha' sent for ye,' Mrs Brome told him.

Depper shed as many tears over his old woman as would have been expected from the best husband in the world; and Car'line let her dying gaze rest on him with as much affection, perhaps, as if he had indeed been that ideal person.

'There'll be money a-comin' in fro' th' club,' were almost her last words to him. She was speaking of the burial-club, into which she had always contrived to pay the necessary weekly pence; she knew it to be the surest consolation she could offer him.

Depper had made arrangements already for the payment of the eleven pounds from the burial-club; he had drunk a pint or two extra, daily, for the last week, the innkeeper being willing to trust him, in consideration of the expected windfall. The excitement of this handling of sudden wealth, and the dying of his wife, and the extra drink combined, completely upset his mental equilibrium. In the first moments of his widower-hood he was prostrate with emotion.

Dragged downstairs by the strong arm of Dinah Brome, he subsided into the chair on the hearth, opposite that for ever empty one of his old woman's; and with elbows on knees and head on hand he hiccoughed and moaned and wept aloud.

Above, Dinah Brome and that old woman who had a reputation in Dulditch for the laying-out of corpses, decked the poor cold body in such warmth of white flannelette, and such garniture of snipped-out frilling as, alive, Car'line Kittle could never have hoped to attain to.

These last duties achieved, Dinah descended, her arms full of blankets and pillows, no longer necessary above. These, with much banging and shaking, she spread upon the downstairs couch, indicating to the still weeping Depper it was there he was expected to pass the night.

'Bor, you may well blubber!' she said to him, with a kind of comfortable scorn of him and his sorrow. 'You 'ont ketch me a-dryin' yer tears for ye, and so I tell ye flat. A crule husban' yu ha' been as any woman ever had. If ever there was a wife who was kep' short, and used hard, that was *yer* wife, Depper, my man! Bad you ha' been to her that's gone to 'er account, in all ways; who should know that better'n me, I'll ask ye? An' if at las' 'tis come home to ye, sarve ye wholly right. Tha's all the comfort ye'll get from me, bor.'

'Stop along of me!' Depper cried, as, her work being finished, she moved to the door. ' 'Taint right as I should be left here alone; and me feelin' that low, and a'most dazed with affliction.'

'Tha's how you've a right to feel,' the stern woman said, unmoved by his tears.

'I keep a-thinkin' of wha's layin' up above theer, Dinah.'

'Pity you di'n't think on 'er more in 'er lifetime.'

' 'Taint nat'ral as I should be left wholly alone with a dead woman. 'Taint a nat'ral thing, I'm a-sayin', for me to du, Dinah, ter pass the night alone along o' my old missus's corp.'

'Bor, 'taint the fust onnat'ral thing you ha' done i' your life,' Mrs Brome said; and went out and shut the door.

An hour or so later Depper opened it, and going hurriedly past the intervening cottages, knocked stealthily upon the door of Dinah Brome.

She looked out upon him presently from her bedroom window, her dark, crinkled hair rough from the pillow, a shawl pulled over her nightgown.

'Whu's that a-distarbin' o' me, as ha'n't had a night's rest for a week, at this time o' night?' she demanded sharply.

'It's me; Depper,' the man's voice answered, whisperingly. 'Le' me in, Dinah. I daren't be alone along of 'er no longer. I ha' only got you, Dinah, now my old woman's gone! Le' me in!'

'You're a rum un ter call yerself a man and a husban' – you are!' Dinah Brome ejaculated; but she came downstairs and opened her door.

SAKI

Gabriel–Ernest

'There is a wild beast in your woods,' said the artist Cunningham, as he was being driven to the station. It was the only remark he had made during the drive, but as Van Cheele had talked incessantly his companion's silence had not been noticeable.

'A stray fox or two and some resident weasels. Nothing more formidable,' said Van Cheele. The artist said nothing.

'What did you mean about a wild beast?' said Van Cheele later, when they were on the platform.

'Nothing. My imagination. Here is the train,' said Cunningham.

That afternoon Van Cheele went for one of his frequent rambles through his woodland property. He had a stuffed bittern in his study, and knew the names of quite a number of wild flowers, so his aunt had possibly some justification in describing him as a great naturalist. At any rate, he was a great walker. It was his custom to take mental notes of everything he saw during his walks, not so much for the purpose of assisting contemporary science as to provide topics for conversation afterwards. When the bluebells began to show themselves in flower he made a point of informing every one of the fact; the season of the year might have warned his hearers of the likelihood of such an occurrence, but at least they felt that he was being absolutely frank with them.

What Van Cheele saw on this particular afternoon was, however, something far removed from his ordinary range of experience. On a shelf of smooth stone overhanging a deep pool in the hollow of an oak coppice a boy of about sixteen lay asprawl, drying his wet brown limbs luxuriously in the sun. His wet hair, parted by a recent dive, lay close to his head, and his light-brown eyes, so light that there was an almost tigerish gleam in them, were turned towards Van Cheele with a certain lazy watchfulness. It was an unexpected apparition, and Van Cheele found himself engaged in the novel process of thinking before he spoke. Where on earth could this wild-looking boy hail from? The miller's wife had lost a child some two months ago, supposed to have been swept away by the mill-race, but that had been a mere baby, not a half-grown lad.

'What are you doing there?' he demanded.

'Obviously, sunning myself,' replied the boy.

'Where do you live?'

'Here, in these woods.'

'You can't live in the woods,' said Van Cheele.

'They are very nice woods,' said the boy, with a touch of patronage in his voice.

'But where do you sleep at night?'

'I don't sleep at night; that's my busiest time.'

Van Cheele began to have an irritated feeling that he was grappling with a problem that was eluding him.

'What do you feed on?' he asked.

'Flesh,' said the boy, and he pronounced the word with slow relish, as though he were tasting it.

'Flesh! What flesh?'

'Since it interests you, rabbits, wild-fowl, hares, poultry, lambs in their season, children when I can get any; they're usually too well locked in at night, when I do most of my hunting. It's quite two months since I tasted child-flesh.'

Ignoring the chaffing nature of the last remark Van Cheele tried to draw the boy on the subject of possible poaching operations.

'You're talking rather through your hat when you speak of feeding on hares.' (Considering the nature of the boy's toilet the simile was hardly an apt one.) 'Our hillside hares aren't easily caught.'

'At night I hunt on four feet,' was the somewhat cryptic response.

'I suppose you mean that you hunt with a dog?' hazarded Van Cheele.

The boy rolled slowly over on to his back, and laughed a weird low laugh, that was pleasantly like a chuckle and disagreeably like a snarl.

'I don't fancy any dog would be very anxious for my company, especially at night.'

Van Cheele began to feel that there was something positively uncanny about the strange-eyed, strange-tongued youngster.

'I can't have you staying in these woods,' he declared authoritatively.

'I fancy you'd rather have me here than in your house,' said the boy.

The prospect of this wild, nude animal in Van Cheele's primly ordered house was certainly an alarming one.

'If you don't go I shall have to make you,' said Van Cheele.

The boy turned like a flash, plunged into the pool, and in a moment had flung his wet and glistening body half-way up the bank where Van Cheele was standing. In an otter the movement would not have been remarkable; in a boy Van Cheele found it sufficiently startling. His foot slipped as he made an involuntary backward movement, and he found himself almost prostrate on the slippery weed-grown bank, with those tigerish yellow eyes not very far from his own. Almost instinctively he half raised his hand to his throat. The boy laughed again, a laugh in which the snarl had nearly driven out the chuckle, and then, with another of his astonishing lightning movements, plunged out of view into a yielding tangle of weed and fern.

'What an extraordinary wild animal!' said Van Cheele as he picked himself up. And then he recalled Cunningham's remark, 'There is a wild beast in your woods.'

Walking slowly homeward, Van Cheele began to turn over in his mind various local occurrences which might be traceable to the existence of this astonishing young savage.

Something had been thinning the game in the woods lately, poultry had been missing from the farms, hares were growing unaccountably scarcer, and complaints had reached him of lambs being carried off bodily from the hills. Was it possible that this wild boy was really hunting the countryside in company with some clever poacher dog? He had spoken of hunting 'four-footed' by night, but then, again, he had hinted strangely at no dog caring to come near him, 'especially at night.' It was certainly puzzling. And then, as Van Cheele ran his mind over the various depredations that had been committed during the last month or two, he came suddenly to a dead stop, alike in his walk and his speculations. The child missing from the mill two months ago – the accepted theory was that it had tumbled into the mill-race and been swept away; but the mother had always declared she had heard a shriek on the hill side of the house, in the opposite direction from the water. It was unthinkable, of course, but he wished that the boy had not made that uncanny remark about child-flesh eaten two months ago. Such dreadful things should not be said even in fun.

Van Cheele, contrary to his usual wont, did not feel disposed to be communicative about his discovery in the wood. His position as a parish councillor and justice of the peace seemed somehow compromised by the fact that he was harbouring a personality of such doubtful repute on his property; there was even a possibility that a heavy bill of damages for raided lambs and poultry might be laid at his door. At dinner that night he was quite unusually silent.

'Where's your voice gone to?' said his aunt. 'One would think you had seen a wolf.'

Van Cheele, who was not familiar with the old saying, thought the remark rather foolish; if he *had* seen a wolf on his property his tongue would have been extraordinarily busy with the subject.

At breakfast next morning Van Cheele was conscious that his feeling of uneasiness regarding yesterday's episode had not wholly disappeared, and he resolved to go by train to the neighbouring cathedral town, hunt up Cunningham, and learn from him what he had really seen that had prompted the remark about a wild beast in the woods. With this resolution taken, his usual cheerfulness partially returned, and he hummed a bright little melody as he sauntered to the morning-room for his customary cigarette. As he entered the room the melody made way abruptly for a pious invocation. Gracefully asprawl on the ottoman, in an attitude of almost exaggerated repose, was the boy of the woods. He was drier than when Van Cheele had last seen him, but no other alteration was noticeable in his toilet.

'How dare you come here?' asked Van Cheele furiously.

'You told me I was not to stay in the woods,' said the boy calmly.

'But not to come here. Supposing my aunt should see you!'

And with a view to minimizing that catastrophe Van Cheele hastily obscured as much of his unwelcome guest as possible under the folds of a *Morning Post*. At that moment his aunt entered the room.

'This is a poor boy who has lost his way – and lost his memory. He doesn't know who he is or where he comes from,' explained Van Cheele desperately, glancing apprehensively at the waif's face to see whether he was going to add inconvenient candour to his other savage propensities.

Miss Van Cheele was enormously interested.

'Perhaps his underlinen is marked,' she suggested.

'He seems to have lost most of that, too,' said Van Cheele, making frantic little grabs at the *Morning Post* to keep it in its place.

A naked homeless child appealed to Miss Van Cheele as warmly as a stray kitten or derelict puppy would have done.

'We must do all we can for him,' she decided, and in a very short time a messenger, dispatched to the rectory, where a page-boy was kept, had returned with a suit of pantry clothes, and the necessary accessories of shirt, shoes, collar, etc. Clothed, clean, and groomed, the boy lost none of his uncanniness in Van Cheele's eyes, but his aunt found him sweet.

'We must call him something till we know who he really is,' she said. 'Gabriel-Ernest, I think; those are nice suitable names.'

Van Cheele agreed, but he privately doubted whether they were being grafted on to a nice suitable child. His misgivings were not diminished by the fact that his staid and elderly spaniel had bolted out of the house at the first incoming of the boy, and now obstinately remained shivering and yapping at the farther end of the orchard, while the canary, usually as vocally industrious as Van Cheele himself, had put itself on an allowance of frightened cheeps. More than ever he was resolved to consult Cunningham without loss of time.

As he drove off to the station his aunt was arranging that Gabriel-Ernest should help her to entertain the infant members of her Sunday-school class at tea that afternoon.

Cunningham was not at first disposed to be communicative.

'My mother died of some brain trouble,' he explained, 'so you will understand why I am averse to dwelling on anything of an impossibly fantastic nature that I may see or think that I have seen.'

'But what *did* you see?' persisted Van Cheele.

'What I thought I saw was something so extraordinary that no really sane man could dignify it with the credit of having actually happened. I was standing, the last evening I was with you, half-hidden in the hedge-growth by the orchard gate, watching the dying glow of the sunset.

Suddenly I became aware of a naked boy, a bather from some neighbouring pool, I took him to be, who was standing out on the bare hillside also watching the sunset. His pose was so suggestive of some wild faun of Pagan myth that I instantly wanted to engage him as a model, and in another moment I think I should have hailed him. But just then the sun dipped out of view, and all the orange and pink slid out of the landscape, leaving it cold and grey. And at the same moment an astounding thing happened – the boy vanished too!'

'What! vanished away into nothing?' asked Van Cheele excitedly.

'No; that is the dreadful part of it,' answered the artist; 'on the open hillside where the boy had been standing a second ago, stood a large wolf, blackish to colour, with gleaming fangs and cruel, yellow eyes. You may think – '

But Van Cheele did not stop for anything as futile as thought. Already he was tearing at top speed towards the station. He dismissed the idea of a telegram. 'Gabriel-Ernest is a werewolf' was a hopelessly inadequate effort at conveying the situation, and his aunt would think it was a code message to which he had omitted to give her the key. His one hope was that he might reach home before sundown. The cab which he chartered at the other end of the railway journey bore him with what seemed exasperating slowness along the country roads, which were pink and mauve with the flush of the sinking sun. His aunt was putting away some unfinished jams and cake when he arrived.

'Where is Gabriel-Ernest?' he almost screamed.

'He is taking the little Toop child home,' said his aunt. 'It was getting so late, I thought it wasn't safe to let it go back alone. What a lovely sunset, isn't it?'

But Van Cheele, although not oblivious of the glow in the western sky, did not stay to discuss its beauties. At a speed for which he was scarcely geared he raced along the narrow lane that led to the home of the Toops. On one side ran the swift current of the mill-stream, on the other rose the stretch of bare hillside. A dwindling rim of red sun showed still on the skyline, and the next turning must bring him in view of the ill-assorted couple he was pursuing. Then the colour went suddenly out of things, and a grey light settled itself with a quick shiver over the landscape. Van Cheele heard a shrill wail of fear, and stopped running.

Nothing was ever seen again of the Toop child or Gabriel-Ernest, but the latter's discarded garments were found lying in the road, so it was assumed that the child had fallen into the water, and that the boy had stripped and jumped in, in a vain endeavour to save it. Van Cheele and some workmen who were near by at the time testified to having heard a child scream loudly just near the spot where the clothes were found. Mrs Toop, who had eleven other children, was decently resigned to her bereavement, but Miss Van Cheele sincerely mourned her lost foundling. It was on her initiative that a memorial brass was put up in the parish church to 'Gabriel-Ernest, an unknown boy, who bravely sacrificed his life for another.'

Van Cheele gave way to his aunt in most things, but he flatly refused to subscribe to the Gabriel-Ernest memorial.

J. E. MALLOCH

Cheap Lodgings

It was morning. All night the trains had rushed groaning past the rows of stifled houses. Closed windows and drawn dirty blinds strove vainly to shut out soot or noise. And now the trains rushed still faster and more often, soiling the daybreak and silencing the dawn.

Lilian tossed uneasily on her bed. Her weariness was unashamed. In sleep she had not to smile and act and talk. Her thin cheeks were pale, and her thin fair hair scarcely shaded the pillow. Round her eyelids the lines were unnaturally deep, for the paint had not been taken off with care in the badly lit dressing-room; and companion lines ran as deeply from her nostrils to the corners of her hard, pretty mouth. Indeed, she wanted more sleep. Her part the night before had been long and wasteful, leaving her too weary even to wash her hands, which now lay limply, cigarette-stained, on the rough sheets. She had turned with her face window-wards. Daylight, stealing in, showed the table strewn with the relics of a dingy supper. The shell of a crab, some cheese, three black bottles were mixed up with gloves, hairpins, and a dog's collar, and the whole was bound together with tobacco ash. Noises outside began to increase, piling themselves up with stealthy additions from afar into the one great roar of London. Lilian stirred with physical irritation and kicked the fox-terrier who lay at her feet. He growled and sat up and wondered if he might go and lick her face. Then he looked dubiously at the other occupant of the bed, yawned, and curled up again to sleep.

A good deal more than half of the bed was filled by a large, heavy woman, whose auburn hair was brown at the roots. She sprawled on the pillow, and slept with her mouth open, snoring evenly.

A shriek from an engine awakened them both.

'Darling child,' said the elder woman, yawning, 'I do believe it's late. Just put out your hand and pull the bell.'

'No, damn! Let me sleep!' muttered Lilian.

'What a lazy child it is!' said the other good-naturedly, and there was silence again. The dog, tired of sleep, began to crawl up the bed, uncertain of his reception.

'What the devil's the matter with you, Spot?' said Lilian. And the other, sitting up, began to talk.

'There, there, what a pretty pet! Did he have a lazy mistress? Did he not like the dirty room? Eh? Never mind. His Aunt Marianne will give him his breakfast. *She* doesn't like the room either. My dear child, you can't imagine what this room means to me after eight servants and such a flat – the hall paper cost sixteen shillings a yard; and Bertram adored me both before our marriage and after. He really *did*.'

'Funny thing that he couldn't stay at home,' murmured Lilian sleepily.

'Ah, my dear, he changed – changed sadly. "Little woman," he used to say, "there may be others more beautiful than you, but there are none *like* you." And he meant it, I know he did.'

'But he was a bit of a brute, wasn't he?'

'He was sometimes brutal, my dear, but never a brute. No, I never forgot that he was a *gentleman*.'

'It seems *he* did, though.'

'Ah, you must make allowance, my dear, for a man. Wine and women – *Wein*, *Weib*, and song, as my dear father used to say, sitting in his library, surrounded by foreign books both dead and living. Yes, I think – excepting the one occasion when Bertram kicked me – and it was an awful kick; you remember, child, I was lying on the hearthrug – excepting that occasion Bertram never forgot what was due to his position as a great Shakespearian actor. And he *was* proud of me. "Have you seen my wife as Lady Macbeth?" he used to say. Oh, it *was* a most imposing performance, my dear. He wouldn't let the servants go to see it. "It isn't safe," he said; "they might be afraid to stay." And as we had eight, we had to be careful. Now, here goes!' and with a thump she was on the floor, pulling at the old bell-rope.

'I don't think Mrs Moore likes the way you ring that bell. She says she can always tell which of us has rung.'

'You see, my dear, she is accustomed to a very inferior class of people.'

A knock. 'There's Maud, beautiful Maud, with the tea! Come in, Maud.'

The door opened slowly and an old, weary-looking woman came in with two cups of milky tea on a tray.

'Hullo! it *isn't* Maud! Put it here, old lady.'

The old woman looked timidly at the chairs covered with clothing and the crowded table. Then she lifted two bottles off the table and pushed the small tray on to it.

'I say, there's some left, isn't there?'

'Yes, miss, I wasn't going to remove it. There's a half-glass, I should think' – and she held the bottle up to the light – 'or maybe more like a quarter.'

'Well, put it on the mantelpiece, will you, like a dear.'

The large lady was handing tea to the girl in bed. 'Here, Lil, see if this will rouse you. I wonder what's become of beautiful, slovenly Maud.'

Lilian sat up in bed wearily. 'O Lord what a rotten day! It's just the same colour as the curtains. I say, ma, I'm going to have these filthy rags pulled down.'

'We're only here for a week, child.'

'Are we! God knows a week's enough! What beastly tea – oh – oh – we're only play-actors, but we do enjoy life!' And she burst into a peal of laughter.

The elder lady, who had been dressing fitfully, was now putting up her hair with much dignity.

'How often have I told you, my dear, not to call me *ma?* I particularly dislike it. It's vulgar, and you know I am not old enough to be your mother. Ah, *my* dear mother, I can just remember her. How beautiful' (bursting into tears), 'how beautiful she was! Bertram always said you never would have thought she was my mother. Why are you laughing? He meant that she looked so young. We both did – always, always. There now, *that's* rather nice, I fancy – rather *recherché*. Eh, Lil? Just a little curl here to complete it? No; better not – so. Now, my dear, I flatter myself Charlie will think I look well to-day. My tea? Yes. *Very* good – but I was saying – call me *Marianne*, with *two* n's, or even Mrs Bertram Clark – but not *ma!*'

As she sailed out of the room in search of her boots the old weary woman returned bearing sticks and coal. She was followed by a gaily dressed girl with heavy black hair, fat cheeks, and a cast in one eye.

'Hullo, Maud!' Lilian greeted her, 'you *are* a swell to-day.'

'I suppose Oi may sometimes dress moiself in the morning as well as other people,' said Maud, tossing her head.

'Are you having a holiday, Maud? or are you going to do your work in your best frock?'

'No more work for me, thank God! No more coals, an' stairs an' tempers of people wot thinks they're lydies! No more sliving on twenty-foive people!'

'Twenty-five people in this hole of a house!' exclaimed Lilian.

'Yes, twenty-foive people. I suppose you and Mrs C. thought you 'ad the 'ouse to yourselves. But there's twenty-foive of you, all lodgers (darn them), except Mrs Moore, an the three kids, an' poor old Moore.'

'Good heavens, what a house! So you've given notice.'

'Rather! I'm off now. No work! No rows! No five bob a week – eh? Good, isn't it? Well, ta!'

And Maud, the lodging-house servant, had vanished.

The old woman was very carefully laying the fire. Her sooty hair straggled down her back as she bent in an attitude that seemed typical of her life.

'What's your name?' Lilian asked her, as she rose from her knees.

'Sarah, please, miss.'

'Well, so you've come to take Maud's place?'

'Yes, miss.'

'I hope you'll like it.'

'I hope to give satisfaction, miss.'

'I hope so, for your comfort. Mrs M.'s a stingy beast.' The old woman looked frightened. 'I say, Sarah, what's Maud going to do?'

'I don't know, I'm sure, miss.'

'Come, now, I'm sure you've an idea what's she's up to.'

'Well, miss, I think myself that she's up to no good. She's spending money, anyhow.'

'But you don't mean – oh, I say, impossible – beautiful Maud's never got a young man!'

'Well, miss – they do call her the Belle of Camberton.'

'What! Maud! So that's how she's gone.'

'Yes, miss, the streets.'

'Well, hang it all! I'd rather do that, though she is a nasty beast, than slave in a lodging-house.'

'Lilian!' said Mrs Clark's voice from the doorway, where she stood, boots in hand. 'How can you express sentiments so degrading to the name of woman! Maud is now an outcast from society, and as such deserves to be treated.'

'Society is kinder to its outcasts than to its inmates very often,' said Lilian hotly. 'What do you think, Sarah?'

'I think it's a bad business, miss.'

'Nonsense. You'd be very glad to be in Maud's shoes.'

'No, miss, I can't say that. I've always been respectable, and, please God, I'll die respectable. I'm sixty-eight now, so it can't be very long. I buried my 'usband twenty-two years ago, and I 'ope to meet him again.'

'And you are right,' said Mrs Clark impressively, '*you* Lilian, are not a true woman. You have none of a woman's feelings; you have never loved – as I loved Bertram – oh, what a deception! But a woman must conform to society.'

'When you put up your hair and put on your boots you grow mighty proper, ma. But what about Charlie, eh?'

'My dear, you know that in the sight of God, Charlie is my husband. Say no more. I am blameless. You know I am a Catholic and cannot be divorced.'

Mrs Bertram Clark crossed herself and bent down to the daily struggle with her boots. Speech became for her impossible and breathing a wrestle with facts. As her feet were large her boots had to be tight, and as her ankles were thick her heels had to be extra high. When she raised her fat face, purple with victory, the breakfast things were being taken away and Lilian was again questioning the sad old woman.

'I say, what good has virtue been to you? You are poor and old, and overworked and friendless. You'll have to slave morning and night in this beastly hole – '

'Everybody has to work, miss.'

'Yes, but look at me. I think I'm jolly ill-used, and I lie in bed like a pig, and you wait on me – and yet I *know* I'm ill-used. Always moving! always struggling, never enough – ugh! ugh! – Hand me those cigarettes, there's a dear. What do you think of Mrs Moore?'

'I think she means well, miss.'

'What does she mean to pay you?'

'I don't know, miss.'

'What! haven't you made terms with her?'

'No, miss. I hope – but I'm not sure – I hope for three-and-sixpence.'

'When do you come in the morning? When do you leave?'

'Six o'clock, and I go when the work's done. It may be eight, it may be nine.'

'Well, I think three-and-sixpence jolly little for a long day like that.'

The old woman astonished Lilian by bursting into a laugh. 'Three-and-sixpence a *day*, miss! It's a *week*.'

'What! Three-and-sixpence a *week!* What infamy! I'll tell Mrs Moore what I think of her. I'll go down this minute, and make her raise it to ten, jolly quick!'

And, lighting a cigarette hastily, she was off. But Sarah held her.

'In the name of God, miss, don't ruin me! It's little, I know, but it's something, and I'm not worth much. No one else would give me work. Look at me – I'm old, I'm rheumatic, I'm growing blind, I'm slow. I must take three-and-sixpence or starve. I've my son, too – 'e's soft-'eaded – 'e makes a little by mending chairs, but very little. We've our 'ome to keep together. Oh, miss, you mean kindness, but it would be ruin.'

'No, it would not be ruin, I'm damned if it would. I'll make the old cat feel what she's doing.'

'Oh dear, miss,' said the old woman in a quivering voice, 'don't! If you want to 'elp me, don't! If you ever had a 'ome of your own, or a son, don't.'

'Me! A son! O Lord!'

'Oh, miss, you've got a kind 'eart, I see. But don't lose me my work.'

'Very well then. See, there's sixpence. And look, I say, here's quite a drink of tea. Down with it! Now! And don't cry, old lady.'

A voice on the stairs crying 'Lil!' was the herald of Mrs Clark, followed by the landlady.

'My darling, oh! oh!' (with a little giggle), 'Charlie! Such a letter – he – But I see the things are not cleared away! Make haste, good woman. My dear, why will you talk so much to menials? Charlie's coming to take us both for a drive, and I've brought Mrs Moore up to see my new hat.'

Mrs Moore meantime was scolding Sarah for her slowness. 'Sarah's been doing something for me, Mrs Moore,' said Lilian shortly, trying to control her temper.

Sarah gave her a glance of entreaty, but Mrs Bertram Clark, passing her on the way to the cupboard where her hat was kept, touched her with her hand and whispered, 'My darling, you have a heart! So had my mother. You remind me of her just now – my sainted mother!' Her eyes filled with tears and she crossed herself hastily.

'What is it, Mrs C.?' asked the landlady, alarmed.

'Nothing – nothing! My dear mother is always with me, my sainted mother!' And she crossed herself again.

Mrs Moore winked at Lilian, and was surprised by her frown.

'I must warn you two ladies,' she said, 'that the stairs won't be very pleasant to-day. I'm having the walls and ceilings whitewashed.'

'Well, Mrs Moore,' said Lilian, 'I won't conceal from you that I think it's a good thing.'

'My dear Mrs Moore, what an expense!' said Mrs Bertram Clark.

'You may say so – and the funny thing is, that if every one paid their rent I couldn't afford it.'

'Come, Mrs Moore, it's early yet,' said Lilian.

'It's this way, ladies – there's that carpenter-painter lodger of mine, you know him?'

'No, I don't think so.'

'No? He has a room below this – thin man with a cough and not much else. Well, he's behind with his rent two weeks, so I'm taking it out of him this way. He's got the materials, and rather than leave a respectable house, he'll whitewash it. And then, of course, I'll get the rent out of him when he has work.'

'Poor man,' said Mrs Clark, her hand in a bandbox full of soft white paper. 'Has he a wife and any dear little children?'

'No, he's a bachelor. He's been out of work for a year nearly. Oh! what a lovely hat! Isn't she fine, miss?'

'Fine's not the word,' said Lilian, with a puff of smoke from her cigarette.

'My dear, do not smoke my hat. Oh, if Bertram could have seen this!'

'Look here,' said Lilian, 'I have seen that headdress before, and' (jamming on the hat) 'I'm going to take the dog for a run. Spot! That's right, old boy! Oh, what a beautiful hound! Make all the noise you can! *Come* along!'

The thin man on a ladder on the stair was wasting his one possession, his cough.

'Good-morning,' said Lilian; 'it's pretty cold.'

'Yes, miss, thank you.'

Lilian looked at him steadily for a second or two, and then said: 'Look here! No breakfast?'

The man blushed, and she was ashamed.

As she went downstairs she opened her purse. It contained sixpence. For a moment she looked at it doubtfully.

'Well, Spot, come!' she cried, and hurried out.

At the end of the street was a public-house. There she purchased as much brandy as you can get in a bottle for sixpence.

'That's my last penny, Spot,' she remarked cheerily as they turned back to the house.

Half-way upstairs Lilian took a sip from the bottle, a small sip. Then a party of people coming down in a hurry compelled her to stand aside. A door behind her opened, and she found herself in a very small room. It was almost dark, for the window, about a foot square, looked on to the landing, and was covered with dust. Evidently it did not open, and the room was close and evil-smelling. It had been intended for the bathroom of the house. The bath, with mildewed taps, was there, and in it lay the remains of an old and filthy mattress. The room contained nothing but some rags of carpet, a bit of mirror, and a pail of whitewash. A glance was enough. She came out half suffocated.

The man on the stair was still coughing.

'See here,' she said, and pressed the bottle into his hand.

Before he could thank her she was upstairs.

'Here! Ma! Mrs B. C.! Marianne! Lend me a tanner.'

'My dear child,' said the lady, with a simper, 'you may ask anything *to-day*. There is a shilling. Now, don't be rash. What will you do with it?'

'Get drunk! – drunk! Come along, you blasted dog!'

JOSEPH CONRAD

The Secret Sharer

On my right hand there were lines of fishing-stakes resembling a mysterious system of half-submerged bamboo fences, incomprehensible in its division of the domain of tropical fishes, and crazy of aspect as if abandoned for ever by some nomad tribe of fishermen now gone to the other end of the ocean; for there was no sign of human habitation as far as the eye could reach. To the left a group of barren islets, suggesting ruins of stone walls, towers, and blockhouses, had its foundations set in a blue sea that itself looked solid, so still and stable did it lie below my feet; even the track of light from the westering sun shone smoothly, without that animated glitter which tells of an imperceptible ripple. And when I turned my head to take a parting glance at the tug which had just left us anchored outside the bar, I saw the straight line of the flat shore joined to the stable sea, edge to edge, with a perfect and unmarked closeness, in one levelled floor half brown, half blue under the enormous dome of the sky. Corresponding in their insignificance to the islets of the sea, two small clumps of trees, one on each side of the only fault in the impeccable joint, marked the mouth of the river Meinam we had just left on the first preparatory stage of our homeward journey; and, far back on the inland level, a larger and loftier mass, the grove surrounding the great Paknam pagoda, was the only thing on which the eye could rest from the vain task of exploring the monotonous sweep of the horizon. Here and there gleams as of a few scattered pieces of silver marked the windings of the great river; and on the nearest of them, just within the bar, the tug steaming right into the land become lost to my sight, hull and funnel and masts, as though the impassive earth had swallowed her up without an effort, without a tremor. My eye followed the light cloud of her smoke, now here, now there, above the plain, according to the devious curves of the stream, but always fainter and farther away, till I lost it at last behind the mitre-shaped hill of the great pagoda. And then I was left alone with my ship, anchored at the head of the Gulf of Siam.

She floated at the starting-point of a long journey, very still in an immense stillness, the shadows of her spars flung far to the eastward by the setting sun. At that moment I was alone on her decks. There was not a sound in her – and around us nothing moved, nothing lived, not a canoe on the water, not a bird in the air, not a cloud in the sky. In this breathless pause at the threshold of a long passage we seemed to be measuring our fitness for a long and arduous enterprise, the appointed task of both our existences to be carried out, far from all human eyes, with only sky and sea for spectators and for judges.

There must have been some glare in the air to interfere with one's sight, because it was only just before the sun left us that my roaming eyes made out beyond the highest ridge of the principal islet of the group something which did away with the solemnity of perfect solitude. The tide of darkness flowed on swiftly; and with tropical suddenness a swarm of stars came out above the shadowy earth, while I lingered yet, my hand resting lightly on my ship's rail as if on the shoulder of a trusted friend. But, with all that multitude of celestial bodies staring down at one, the comfort of quiet communion with her was gone for good. And there were also disturbing sounds by this time – voices, footsteps forward; the steward flitted along the main-deck, a busily ministering spirit; a hand-bell tinkled urgently under the poop-deck . . .

I found my two officers waiting for me near the supper table, in the lighted cuddy. We sat down at once, and as I helped the chief mate, I said:

'Are you aware that there is a ship anchored inside the islands? I saw her mastheads above the ridge as the sun went down.'

He raised sharply his simple face, overcharged by a terrible growth of whisker, and emitted his usual ejaculations: 'Bless my soul, sir! You don't say so!'

My second mate was a round-cheeked, silent young man, grave beyond his years; I thought; but as our eyes happened to meet I detected a slight quiver on his lips. I looked down at once. It was not my part to encourage sneering on board my ship. It must be said, too, that I knew very little of my officers. In consequence of certain events of no particular significance, except to myself, I had been appointed to the command only a fortnight before. Neither did I know much of the hands forward. All these people had been together for eighteen months or so, and my position was that of the only stranger on board. I mention this because it has some bearing on what is to follow. But what I felt most was my being a stranger to the ship; and if all the truth must be told, I was somewhat of a stranger to myself. The youngest man on board (barring the second mate), and untried as yet by a position of the fullest responsibility, I was willing to take the adequacy of the others for granted. They had simply to be equal to their tasks; but I wondered how far I should turn out faithful to that ideal conception of one's own personality every man acts up for himself secretly.

Meantime the chief mate, with an almost visible effort of collaboration on the part of his round eyes and frightful whiskers, was trying to evolve a theory of the anchored ship. His dominant trait was to take all things into earnest consideration. He was of a painstaking turn of mind. As he used to say, he 'liked to account to himself' for practically everything that came in his way, down to a miserable scorpion he had found in his cabin a week before. The why and the wherefore of that scorpion – how it got on board and came to select his room rather than the pantry (which was a dark place and more what a scorpion would be partial to), and how on earth it managed to drown itself in the inkwell of his writing-desk – had exercised him infinitely. The ship within the islands was much more easily accounted for; and just as we were about to rise from table he made his pronouncement. She was, he doubted not, a ship from home lately arrived. Probably she drew too much water to cross the bar except at the top of spring tides. Therefore she went into that natural harbour to wait for a few days in preference to remaining in an open roadstead.

'That's so,' confirmed the second mate, suddenly, in his slightly hoarse voice. 'She draws over twenty feet. She's the Liverpool ship *Sephora* with a cargo of coal. Hundred and twenty-three days from Cardiff.'

We looked at him in surprise.

'The tugboat skipper told me when he came on board for your letters, sir,' explained the young man. 'He expects to take her up the river the day after tomorrow.'

After thus overwhelming us with the extent of his information he slipped out of the cabin. The mate observed regretfully that he 'could not account for that young fellow's whims'. What prevented him telling us all about her at once, he wanted to know.

I detained him as he was making a move. For the last two days the crew had had plenty of hard work, and the night before they had very little sleep. I felt painfully that I – a stranger – was doing something unusual when I directed him to let all hands turn in without setting an anchor-watch. I proposed to keep on deck myself till one o'clock or thereabouts. I would get the second mate to relieve me at that hour.

'He will turn out the cook and the steward at four.' I concluded, 'and then give you a call. Of course at the slightest sign of any sort of wind we'll have the hands up and make a start at once.'

He concealed his astonishment. 'Very well, sir.' Outside the cuddy he put his head in the second mate's door to inform him of my unheard-of caprice to take a five hours' anchor-watch on myself. I heard the other raise his voice incredulously – 'What? The Captain himself?' Then a few more murmurs, a door closed, then another. A few moments later I went on deck.

My strangeness, which had made me sleepless, had prompted that unconventional arrangement, as if I had expected in those solitary hours of the night to get on terms with the ship of which I knew nothing, manned by men of whom I knew very little more. Fast alongside a wharf, littered like any ship in port with a tangle of unrelated things, invaded by unrelated shore people, I had hardly seen her yet properly. Now, as she lay cleared for sea, the stretch of her main-deck seemed to me very fine under the stars. Very fine, very roomy for her size, and very inviting. I descended the poop and paced the waist, my mind picturing to myself the coming passage through the Malay Archipelago, down the Indian Ocean, and up the Atlantic. All its phases were familiar enough to me, every characteristic, all the alternatives which were likely to face me on the high seas – everything! . . . except the novel responsibility of command. But I took heart from the reasonable thought that the ship was like other ships, the men like other men, and that the sea was not likely to keep any special surprises expressly for my discomfiture.

Arrived at that comforting conclusion, I bethought myself of a cigar and went below to get it. All was still down there. Everybody at the after end of the ship was sleeping profoundly. I came out again on the quarter-deck, agreeably at ease in my sleeping-suit on that warm breathless night, bare-footed, a glowing cigar in my teeth, and, going forward, I was met by the profound silence of the fore end of the ship. Only as I passed the door of the forecastle I heard a deep, quiet, trustful sigh of some sleeper inside. And suddenly I rejoiced in the great security of the sea as compared with the unrest of the land, in my choice of that untempted life presenting no dis-quieting problems, invested with an elementary moral beauty by the absolute straightforwardness of its appeal and by the singleness of its purpose.

The riding-light in the fore-rigging burned with a clear, untroubled, as if symbolic, flame, confident and bright in the mysterious shades of the night. Passing on my way aft along the other side of the ship, I observed that the rope side-ladder, put over, no doubt, for the master of the tug when he came to fetch away our letters, had not been hauled in as it should have been. I became annoyed at this, for exactitude in small matters is the very soul of discipline. Then I reflected that I had myself peremptorily dismissed my officers from duty, and by my own act had prevented the anchor-watch being formally set and things properly attended to. I asked myself whether it was wise ever to interfere with the established routine of duties even from the kindest of motives. My action might have made me appear eccentric. Goodness only knew how that absurdly whiskered mate would 'account' for my conduct, and what the whole ship thought of that informality of their new captain. I was vexed with myself.

Not from compunction certainly, but, as it were mechanically, I pro-ceeded to get the ladder in myself. Now a side-ladder of that sort is a light affair and comes in easily, yet my vigorous tug, which should have brought it flying on board, merely recoiled upon my body in a totally unexpected jerk. What the devil! . . . I was so astounded by the immovableness of that ladder that I remained stock-still, trying to account for it to myself like that imbecile mate of mine. In the end, of course, I put my head over the rail.

The side of the ship made an opaque belt of shadow on the darkling glassy shimmer of the sea. But I saw at once something elongated and pale floating very close to the ladder. Before I could form a guess a faint flash of phosphorescent light, which seemed to issue suddenly from the naked body of a man, flickered in the sleeping water with the elusive, silent play of summer lightning in a night sky. With a gasp I saw revealed to my stare a pair of feet, the long legs, a broad livid back immersed right up to the neck in a greenish cadaverous glow. One hand, awash, clutched the bottom rung of the ladder. He was complete but for the head. A headless corpse! The cigar dropped out of my gaping mouth with a tiny plop and a short hiss quite audible in the absolute stillness of all things under heaven. At that I suppose he raised up his face, a dimly pale oval in the shadow of the ship's side. But even then I could only barely make out down there the shape of his black-haired head. However, it was enough for the horrid, frost-bound sensation which had gripped me about the chest to pass off. The moment of vain exclamations was past, too. I only climbed on the spare spar and leaned over the rail as far as I could, to bring my eyes nearer to that mystery floating alongside.

As he hung by the ladder, like a resting swimmer, the sea-lightning played about his limbs at every stir; and he appeared in it ghastly, silvery, fish-like. He remained as mute as a fish, too. He made no motion to get out of the water, either. It was inconceivable that he should not attempt to come on board, and strangely troubling to suspect that perhaps he did not want to. And my first words were prompted by just that troubled incertitude.

'What's the matter?' I asked in my ordinary tone, speaking down to the face upturned exactly under mine.

'Cramp,' it answered, no louder. Then slightly anxious, 'I say, no need to call anyone.'

'I was not going to,' I said.

'Are you alone on deck?'

'Yes.'

I had somehow the impression that he was on the point of letting go the ladder to swim away beyond my ken – mysterious as he came. But, for the moment, this being appearing as if he had risen from the bottom of the sea (it was certainly the nearest land to the ship) wanted only to know the time. I told him. And he, down there, tentatively:

'I suppose your captain's turned in?'

'I am sure he isn't,' I said.

He seemed to struggle with himself, for I heard something like the low, bitter murmur of doubt. 'What's the good?' His next words came out with a hesitating effort.

'Look here, my man. Could you call him out quietly?'

I thought the time had come to declare myself.

'*I* am the captain.'

I heard a 'By Jove!' whispered at the level of the water. The phosphorescence flashed in the swirl of the water all about his limbs, his other hand seized the ladder.

'My name's Leggatt.'

The voice was calm and resolute. A good voice. The self-possession of that man had somehow induced a corresponding state in myself. It was very quietly that I remarked:

'You must be a good swimmer.'

'Yes. I've been in the water practically since nine o'clock. The question for me now is whether I am to let go this ladder and go on swimming till I sink from exhaustion, or – to come on board here.'

I felt this was no mere formula of desperate speech, but a real alternative in the view of a strong soul. I should have gathered from this that he was young; indeed, it is only the young who are ever confronted by such clear issues. But at the time it was pure intuition on my part. A mysterious communication was established already between us two – in the face of that silent, darkened tropical sea. I was young, too; young enough to make no comment. The man in the water began suddenly to climb up the ladder, and I hastened away from the rail to fetch some clothes.

Before entering the cabin I stood still, listening in the lobby at the foot of the stairs. A faint snore came through the closed door of the chief mate's room. The second mate's door was on the hook, but the darkness in there was absolutely soundless. He, too, was young and could sleep like a stone. Remained the steward, but he was not likely to wake up before he was called. I got a sleeping-suit out of my room and, coming back on deck, saw the naked man from the sea sitting on the main-hatch, glimmering white in the darkness, his elbows on his knees and his head in his hands. In a moment he had concealed his damp body in a sleeping-suit of the same grey-stripe pattern as the one I was wearing and followed me like my double on the poop. Together we moved right aft, bare-footed, silent.

'What is it?' I asked in a deadened voice, taking the lighted lamp out of the binnacle, and raising it to his face.

'An ugly business.'

He had rather regular features; a good mouth; light eyes under somewhat heavy, dark eyebrows; a smooth, square forehead; no growth on his cheeks; a small, brown moustache, and a well-shaped, round chin. His expression was concentrated, meditative, under the inspecting light of the lamp I held up to his face; such as a man thinking hard in solitude might wear. My sleeping-suit was just right for his size. A well-knit young fellow of twenty-five at most. He caught his lower lip with the edge of white, even teeth.

'Yes,' I said, replacing the lamp in the binnacle. The warm, heavy tropical night closed upon his head again.

'There's a ship over there,' he murmured.

'Yes, I know. The *Sephora*. Did you know of us?'

'Hadn't the slightest idea. I am the mate of her – ' He paused and corrected himself. 'I should say I *was*.'

'Aha! Something wrong?'

'Yes. Very wrong indeed. I've killed a man.'

'What do you mean? Just now?'

'No, on the passage. Weeks ago. Thirty-nine south. When I say a man – '

'Fit of temper,' I suggested, confidently.

The shadowy, dark head, like mine, seemed to nod imperceptibly above the ghostly grey of my sleeping-suit. It was, in the night, as though I had been faced by my own reflection in the depths of a sombre and immense mirror.

'A pretty thing to have to own up to for a Conway boy,' murmured my double, distinctly.

'You're a Conway boy?'

'I am,' he said, as if startled. Then, slowly . . . 'Perhaps you too – '

It was so; but being a couple of years older I had left before he joined. After a quick interchange of dates a silence fell; and I thought suddenly of my absurd mate with his terrific whiskers and the 'Bless my soul – you don't say so' type of intellect. My double gave me an inkling of his thoughts by saying: 'My father's a parson in Norfolk. Do you see me before a judge and jury on that charge? For myself I can't see the necessity. There are fellows that an angel from heaven – And I am not that. He was one of those creatures that are just simmering all the time with a silly sort of wickedness. Miserable devils that have no business to live at all. He wouldn't do his duty and wouldn't let anybody else do theirs. But what's the good of talking! You know well enough the sort of ill-conditioned, snarling cur – '

He appealed to me as if our experience had been as identical as our clothes. And I knew well enough the pestiferous danger of such a character where there are no means of legal repression. And I knew well enough also that my double there was no homicidal ruffian. I did not think of asking him for details, and he told me the story roughly in brusque, disconnected sentences. I needed no more. I saw it all going on as though I were myself inside that other sleeping-suit.

'It happened while we were setting a reefed foresail, at dusk. Reefed foresail! You understand the sort of weather. The only sail we had left to keep the ship running; so you may guess what it had been like for days. Anxious sort of job, that. He gave me some of his cursed insolence at the sheet. I tell you I was overdone with this terrific weather that seemed to have no end to it. Terrific, I tell you – and a deep ship. I believe the fellow himself was half crazed with funk. It was no time for gentlemanly reproof, so I turned round and felled him like an ox. He up and at me. We closed just as an awful sea made for the ship. All hands saw it coming and took to the rigging, but I had him by the throat, and went on shaking him like a rat, the men above us yelling, "Look out! look out!" Then a crash as if the sky had fallen on my head. They say that for over ten minutes hardly anything was to be seen of the ship – just the three masts and a bit of the forecastle head and of the poop all awash driving along in a smother of foam. It was a miracle that they found us, jammed together behind the forebits. It's clear that I meant business, because I was holding him by the throat still when they picked us up. He was black in the face. It was too much for them. It seems they rushed us aft together, gripped as we were, screaming "Murder!" like a lot of lunatics, and broke into the cuddy. And the ship running for her life, touch and go all the time, any minute her last in a sea fit to turn your hair grey only a-looking at it. I understand that the skipper, too, started raving like the rest of them. The man had been deprived of sleep for more than a week, and to have this sprung on him at the height of a furious gale nearly drove him out of his mind. I wonder they didn't fling me overboard after getting the carcass of their precious ship-mate out of my fingers. They had rather a job to separate us, I've been told. A sufficiently fierce story to make an old judge and a respectable jury sit up a bit. The first thing I heard when I came to myself was the maddening howling of that endless gale, and on that the voice of the old man. He was hanging on to my bunk staring into my face out of his sou'wester.

'"Mr Leggatt, you have killed a man. You can act no longer as chief mate of this ship."'

His care to subdue his voice made it sound monotonous. He rested a hand on the end of the skylight to steady himself with, and all that time did not stir a limb, so far as I could see. 'Nice little tale for a quiet tea-party,' he concluded in the same tone.

One of my hands, too, rested on the end of the skylight; neither did I stir a limb, so far as I knew. We stood less than a foot from each other. It occurred to me that if old 'Bless my soul – you don't say so' were to put his head up the companion and catch sight of us, he would think he was seeing double, or imagine himself come upon a scene of weird witchcraft; the strange captain having a quiet confabulation by the wheel with his own grey ghost. I became very much concerned to prevent anything of the sort. I heard the other's soothing undertone.

'My father's a parson in Norfolk,' it said. Evidently he had forgotten he had told me this important fact before. Truly a nice little tale.

'You had better slip down into my stateroom now,' I said, moving off stealthily. My double followed my movements; our bare feet made no sound; I let him in, closed the door with care, and, after giving a call to the second mate, returned on deck for my relief.

'Not much sign of any wind yet,' I remarked when he approached.

'No, sir. Not much,' he assented, sleepily, in his hoarse voice, with just enough deference, no more, and barely suppressing a yawn.

'Well, that's all you have to look out for. You have got your orders.'

'Yes, sir.'

I paced a turn or two on the poop and saw him take up his position face forward with his elbow in the ratlines of the mizzen-rigging before I went below. The mate's faint snoring was still going on peacefully. The cuddy lamp was burning over the table on which stood a vase with flowers, a polite attention from the ship's provision merchant – the last flowers we should see for the next three months at the very least. Two bunches of bananas hung from the beam symmetrically, one on each side of the rudder-casing. Everything was as before in the ship – except that two of her captain's sleeping-suits were simultaneously in use, one motionless in the cuddy, the other keeping very still in the captain's stateroom.

It must be explained here that my cabin had the form of the capital letter L, the door being within the angle and opening into the short part of the letter. A couch was to the left, the bed-place to the right; my writing-desk and the chronometers' table faced the door. But anyone opening it, unless he stepped right inside, had no view of what I call the long (or vertical) part of the letter. It contained some lockers surmounted by a bookcase; and a few clothes, a thick jacket or two, caps, oilskin coat, and such like, hung on hooks. There was at the bottom of that part a door opening into my bath-room, which could be entered also directly from the saloon. But that way was never used.

The mysterious arrival had discovered the advantage of this particular shape. Entering my room, lighted strongly by a big bulkhead lamp swung on gimbals above my writing-desk, I did not see him anywhere till he stepped out quietly from behind the coats hung in the recessed part.

'I heard somebody moving about, and went in there at once,' he whispered.

I, too, spoke under my breath.

'Nobody is likely to come in here without knocking and getting permission.'

He nodded. His face was thin and the sunburn faded, as though he had been ill. And no wonder. He had been, I heard presently, kept under arrest in his cabin for nearly seven weeks. But there was nothing sickly in his eyes or in his expression. He was not a bit like me, really; yet, as we stood leaning over my bed-place, whispering side by side, with our dark heads together and our backs to the door, anybody bold enough to open it stealthily would have been treated to the uncanny sight of a double captain busy talking in whispers with his other self.

'But all this doesn't tell me how you came to hang on to our side-ladder,' I inquired, in the hardly audible murmurs we used, after he had told me something more of the proceeding on board the *Sephora* once the bad weather was over.

'When we sighted Java Head I had had time to think all those matters out several times over. I had six weeks of doing nothing else, and with only an hour or so every evening for a tramp on the quarter-deck.'

He whispered, his arms folded on the side of my bed-place, staring through the open port. And I could imagine perfectly the manner of this thinking out – a stubborn if not a steadfast operation; something of which I should have been perfectly incapable.

'I reckoned it would be dark before we closed with the land,' he continued, so low that I had to strain my hearing, near as we were to each other, shoulder touching shoulder almost. 'So I asked to speak to the old man. He always seemed very sick when he came to see me – as if he could not look me in the face. You know, that foresail saved the ship. She was too deep to have run long under bare poles. And it was I that managed to set it for him. Anyway, he came. When I had him in my cabin – he stood by the door looking at me as if I had the halter round my neck already – I asked him right away to leave my cabin door unlocked at night while the ship was going through Sunda Straits. There would be the Java coast within two or three miles, off Angier Point. I wanted nothing more. I've had a prize for swimming my second year in the Conway.'

'I can believe it,' I breathed out.

'God only knows why they locked me in every night. To see some of their faces you'd have thought they were afraid I'd go about at night strangling people. Am I a murdering brute? Do I look it? By Jove! if I had been he wouldn't have trusted himself like that into my room. You'll say I might have chucked him aside and bolted out, there and then – it was dark already. Well, no. And for the same reason I wouldn't think of trying to smash the door. There would have been a rush to stop me at the noise, and I did not mean to get into a confounded scrimmage. Somebody else might have got killed – for I would not have broken out only to get chucked back, and I did not want any more of that work. He refused, looking more sick

445

than ever. He was afraid of the men, and also of that old second mate of his who had been sailing with him for years – a grey-headed old humbug; and his steward, too, had been with him devil knows how long – seventeen years or more – a dogmatic sort of loafer who hated me like poison, just because I was the chief mate. No chief mate ever made more than one voyage in the *Sephora*, you know. Those two old chaps ran the ship. Devil only knows what the skipper wasn't afraid of (all his nerve went to pieces altogether in that hellish spell of bad weather we had) – of what the law would do to him – of his wife, perhaps. Oh, yes! she's on board. Though I don't think she would have meddled. She would have been only too glad to have me out of the ship in any way. The "brand of Cain" business, don't you see. That's all right. I was ready enough to go off wandering on the face of the earth – and that was price enough to pay for an Abel of that sort. Anyhow, he wouldn't listen to me. "This thing must take its course. I represent the law here." He was shaking like a leaf. "So you won't?" "No!" "Then I hope you will be able to sleep on that," I said, and turned my back on him. "I wonder that *you* can," cries he, and locks the door.

'Well, after that, I couldn't. Not very well. That was three weeks ago. We have had a slow passage through the Java Sea; drifted about Carimata for ten days. When we anchored here they thought, I suppose, it was all right. The nearest land (and that's five miles) is the ship's destination; the consul would soon set about catching me; and there would have been no object in bolting to these islets there. I don't suppose there's a drop of water on them. I don't know how it was, but tonight that steward, after bringing me my supper, went out to let me eat it, and left the door unlocked. And I ate it – all there was, too. After I had finished I strolled out on the quarter-deck. I don't know that I meant to do anything. A breath of fresh air was all I wanted, I believe. Then a sudden temptation came over me. I kicked off my slippers and was in the water before I had made up my mind fairly. Somebody heard the splash and they raised an awful hullabaloo. "He's gone! Lower the boats! He's committed suicide! No, he's swimming." Certainly I was swimming. It's not so easy for a swimmer like me to commit suicide by drowning. I landed on the nearest islet before the boat left the ship's side. I heard them pulling about in the dark, hailing, and so on, but after a bit they gave up. Everything quieted down and the anchorage became as still as death. I sat down on a stone and began to think. I felt certain they would start searching for me at daylight. There was no place to hide on those stony things – and if there had been, what would have been the good? But now I was clear of that ship, I was not going back. So after a while I took off all my clothes, tied them up in a bundle with a stone inside, and dropped them in the deep water on the outer side of that islet. That was suicide enough for me. Let them think what they liked, but I didn't mean to drown myself. I meant to swim till I sank – but that's not the same thing. I struck out for another of these little islands, and it was from that one that I first saw your riding-light. Something to swim for. I went on easily, and on the way I came upon a flat rock a foot or two above water. In the daytime, I dare say, you might make it out with a glass from your poop. I scrambled up on it and rested myself for a bit. Then I made another start. That last spell must have been over a mile.'

His whisper was getting fainter and fainter, and all the time he stared straight out through the port-hole, in which there was not even a star to be seen. I had not interrupted him. There was something that made comment impossible in his narrative, or perhaps in himself; a sort of feeling, a quality, which I can't find a name for. And when he ceased, all I found was a futile whisper: 'So you swam for our light?'

'Yes – straight for it. It was something to swim for. I couldn't see any stars low down because the coast was in the way, and I couldn't see the land, either. The water was like glass. One might have been swimming in a confounded thousand-feet deep cistern with no place for scrambling out anywhere; but what I didn't like was the notion of swimming round and round like a crazed bullock before I gave out; and as I didn't mean to go back . . . No. Do you see me being hauled back, stark naked, off one of these little islands by the scruff of the neck and fighting like a wild beast? Somebody would have got killed for certain, and I did not want any of that. So I went on. Then your ladder – '

'Why didn't you hail the ship?' I asked, a little louder.

He touched my shoulder lightly. Lazy footsteps came right over our heads and stopped. The second mate had crossed from the other side of the poop and might have been hanging over the rail, for all we knew.

'He couldn't hear us talking – could he?' My double breathed into my very ear, anxiously.

His anxiety was an answer, a sufficient answer, to the question I had put to him. An answer containing all the difficulty of that situation. I closed the port-hole quietly, to make sure. A louder word might have been overheard.

'Who's that?' he whispered then.

'My second mate. But I don't know much more of the fellow than you do.'

And I told him a little about myself. I had been appointed to take charge while I least expected anything of the sort, not quite a fortnight ago. I didn't know either the ship or the people. Hadn't had the time in port to look about me or size anybody up. And as to the crew, all they knew was that I was appointed to take the ship home. For the rest, I was almost as much of a stranger on board as himself, I said. And at the moment I felt it most acutely. I felt that it would take very little to make me a suspect person in the eyes of the ship's company.

He had turned about meantime; and we, the two strangers on the ship, faced each other in identical attitudes.

'Your ladder – ' he murmured, after a silence. 'Who'd have thought of finding a ladder hanging over at night in a ship anchored out here! I felt just then a very unpleasant faintness. After the life I've been leading for nine weeks, anybody would have got out of condition. I wasn't capable of swimming round as far as your rudder-chains. And, lo and behold! there was a ladder to get hold of. After I gripped it I said to myself, "What's the good?" When I saw a man's head looking over I thought I would swim away presently and leave him shouting – in whatever language it was. I didn't mind being looked at. I – I liked it. And then you speaking to me so quietly – as if you had expected me – made me hold on a little longer. It had been a confounded lonely time – I don't mean while swimming. I was glad to talk a little to somebody that didn't belong to the *Sephora*. As to asking for the captain, that was a mere impulse. It could have been no use, with all the ship knowing about me and the other people pretty certain to be round here in the morning. I don't know – I wanted to be seen, to talk with somebody, before I went on. I don't know what I would have said . . . "Fine night, isn't it?" or something of the sort.'

'Do you think they will be round here presently?' I asked with some incredulity.

'Quite likely,' he said, faintly.

He looked extremely haggard all of a sudden. His head rolled on his shoulders.

'H'm. We shall see then. Meantime get into that bed,' I whispered. 'Want help? There.'

It was a rather high bed-place with a set of drawers underneath. This amazing swimmer really needed the lift I gave him by seizing his leg. He tumbled in, rolled over on his back, and flung one arm across his eyes. And then, with his face nearly hidden, he must have looked exactly as I used to look in that bed. I gazed upon my other self for a while before drawing across carefully the two green serge curtains which ran on a brass rod. I thought for a moment of pinning them together for greater safety, but I sat down on the couch, and once there I felt unwilling to rise and hunt for a pin. I would do it in a moment. I was extremely tired, in a peculiarly intimate way, by the strain of stealthiness, by the effort of whispering and the general secrecy of this excitement. It was three o'clock by now and I had been on my feet since nine, but I was not sleepy; I could not have gone to sleep. I sat there, fagged out, looking at the curtains, trying to clear my mind of the confused sensation of being in two places at once, and greatly bothered by an exasperating knocking in my head. It was a relief to discover suddenly that it was not in my head at all, but on the outside of the door. Before I could collect myself the words 'Come in' were out of my mouth, and the steward entered with a tray, bringing in my morning coffee. I had slept, after all, and I was so frightened that I shouted, 'This way! I am here, steward,' as though he had been miles away. He put down the tray on the table next the couch and only then said, very quietly, 'I can see you are here, sir.' I felt him give me a keen look, but I dared not meet his eyes just then. He must have wondered why I had drawn the curtains of my bed before going to sleep on the couch. He went out, hooking the door open as usual.

I heard the crew washing decks above me. I knew I would have been told at once if there had been any wind. Calm, I thought, and I was doubly vexed. Indeed, I felt dual more than ever. The steward reappeared suddenly in the doorway. I jumped up from the couch so quickly that he gave a start.

'What do you want here?'

'Close your port, sir – they are washing decks.'

'It is closed,' I said, reddening.

'Very well, sir.' But he did not move from the doorway and returned my stare in an extraordinary, equivocal manner for a time. Then his eyes wavered, all his expression changed, and in a voice unusually gentle, almost coaxingly:

'May I come in to take the empty cup away, sir?'

'Of course!' I turned my back on him while he popped in and out. Then I unhooked and closed the door and even pushed the bolt. This sort of thing could not go on very long. The cabin was as hot as an oven, too. I took a peep at my double, and discovered that he had not moved, his arm was still over his eyes; but his chest heaved; his hair was wet; his chin glistened with perspiration. I reached over him and opened the port.

'I must show myself on deck,' I reflected.

Of course, theoretically, I could do what I liked, with no one to say nay to me within the whole circle of the horizon; but to lock my cabin door and take the key away I did not dare. Directly I put my head out of the companion I saw the group of my two officers, the second mate bare-footed, the chief mate in long india-rubber boots, near the break of the poop, and the steward half-way down the poop-ladder talking to them eagerly. He happened to catch sight of me and dived, the second ran down on the main-deck shouting some order or other, and the chief mate came to meet me, touching his cap.

There was a sort of curiosity in his eye that I did not like. I don't know whether the steward had told them that I was 'queer' only, or downright drunk, but I know the man meant to have a good look at me. I watched him coming with a smile which, as he got into point-blank range, took effect and froze his very whiskers. I did not give him time to open his lips.

'Square the yards by lifts and braces before the hands go to breakfast.'

It was the first particular order I had given on board that ship; and I stayed on deck to see it executed, too. I had felt the need of asserting myself without loss of time. That sneering young cub got taken down a peg or two on that occasion, and I also seized the opportunity of having a good look at the face of every foremast man as they filed past me to go to the after braces. At breakfast time, eating nothing myself, I presided with such frigid dignity that the two mates were only too glad to escape from the cabin as soon as decency permitted; and all the time the dual working of my mind distracted me almost to the point of insanity. I was constantly watching myself, my secret self, as dependent on my actions as my own personality, sleeping in that bed, behind that door which faced me as I sat at the head of the table. It was very much like being mad, only it was worse because one was aware of it.

I had to shake him for a solid minute, but when at last he opened his eyes it was in the full possession of his senses, with an inquiring look.

'All's well so far,' I whispered. 'Now you must vanish into the bath-room.'

He did so, as noiseless as a ghost, and then I rang for the steward, and facing him boldly, directed him to tidy up my stateroom while I was having my bath – 'and be quick about it'. As my tone admitted of no excuses, he said, 'Yes, sir,' and ran off to fetch his dust-pan and brushes. I took a bath and did most of my dressing, splashing, and whistling softly for the steward's edification, while the secret sharer of my life stood drawn up bolt upright in that little space, his face looking very sunken in daylight, his eyelids lowered under the stern, dark line of his eyebrows drawn together by a slight frown.

When I left him there to go back to my room the steward was finishing dusting. I sent for the mate and engaged him in some insignificant conversation. It was, as it were, trifling with the terrific character of his whiskers; but my object was to give him an opportunity for a good look at my cabin. And then I could at last shut, with a clear conscience, the door of my stateroom and get my double back into the recessed part. There was nothing else for it. He had to sit still on a small folding stool, half smothered by the heavy coats hanging there. We listened to the steward going into the bath-room out of the saloon, filling the water-bottles there, scrubbing the bath, setting things to rights, whisk, bang, clatter – out again into the saloon – turn the key – click. Such was my scheme for keeping my second self invisible. Nothing better could be contrived under the circumstances. And there we sat; I at my writing-desk ready to appear busy with some papers, he behind me out of sight of the door. It would not have been prudent to talk in daytime; and I could not have stood the excitement of that queer sense of whispering to myself. Now and then, glancing over my shoulder, I saw him far back there, sitting rigidly on the low stool, his bare feet close together, his arms folded, his head hanging on his breast – and perfectly still. Anybody would have taken him for me.

I was fascinated by it myself. Every moment I had to glance over my shoulder. I was looking at him when a voice outside the door said:

'Beg pardon, sir.'

'Well!' . . . I kept my eyes on him, and so when the voice outside the door announced. 'There's a ship's boat coming our way, sir,' I saw him give a start – the first movement he had made for hours. But he did not raise his bowed head.

'All right. Get the ladder over.'

I hesitated. Should I whisper something to him? But what? His immobility seemed to have been never disturbed. What could I tell him he did not know already? . . . Finally I went on deck.

2

The skipper of the *Sephora* had a thin red whisker all round his face, and the sort of complexion that goes with hair of that colour; also the particular, rather smeary shade of blue in the eyes. He was not exactly a showy figure; his shoulders were high, his stature but middling – one leg slightly more bandy than the other. He shook hands, looking vaguely around. A spiritless tenacity was his main characteristic, I judged. I behaved with a politeness which seemed to disconcert him. Perhaps he was shy. He mumbled to me as if he were ashamed of what he was saying; gave his name (it was something like Archbold – but at this distance of years I hardly am sure), his ship's name, and a few other particulars of that sort, in the manner of a criminal making a reluctant and doleful confession. He had had terrible weather on the passage out – terrible – terrible – wife aboard, too.

By this time we were seated in the cabin and the steward brought in a tray with a bottle and glasses. 'Thanks! No.' Never took liquor. Would have some water, though. He drank two tumblerfuls. Terrible thirsty work. Ever since daylight had been exploring the islands round his ship.

'What was that for – fun?' I asked, with an appearance of polite interest.

'No!' He sighed. 'Painful duty.'

As he persisted in his mumbling and I wanted my double to hear every word, I hit upon the notion of informing him that I regretted to say I was hard of hearing.

'Such a young man, too!' he nodded, keeping his smeary blue, unintelligent eyes fastened upon me. What was the cause of it – some disease? he inquired, without the least sympathy and as if he thought that, if so, I'd got no more than I deserved.

'Yes; disease,' I admitted in a cheerful tone which seemed to shock him. But my point was gained, because he had to raise his voice to give me his tale. It is not worth while to record that version. It was just over two months since all this had happened, and he had thought so much about it that he seemed completely muddled as to its bearings, but still immensely impressed.

'What would you think of such a thing happening on board your own ship? I've had the *Sephora* for these fifteen years. I am a well-known shipmaster.'

He was densely distressed – and perhaps I should have sympathized with him if I had been able to detach my mental vision from the unsuspected sharer of my cabin as though he were my second self. There he was on the other side of the bulkhead, four or five feet from us, no more, as we sat in the saloon. I looked politely at Captain Archbold (if that was his name), but it was the other I saw, in a grey sleeping-suit, seated on a low stool, his bare feet close together, his arms folded, and every word said between us falling into the ears of his dark head bowed on his chest.

'I have been at sea now, man and boy, for seven-and-thirty years, and I've never heard of such a thing happening in an English ship. And that it should be my ship. Wife on board, too.'

I was hardly listening to him.

'Don't you think,' I said, 'that the heavy sea which, you told me, came aboard just then might have killed the man? I have seen the sheer weight of a sea kill a man very neatly, by simply breaking his neck.'

'Good God!' he uttered, impressively, fixing his smeary blue eyes on me. 'The sea! No man killed by the sea ever looked like that.' He seemed positively scandalized at my suggestion. And as I gazed at him, certainly not prepared for anything original on his part, he advanced his head close to mine and thrust his tongue out at me so suddenly that I couldn't help starting back.

After scoring over my calmness in this graphic way he nodded wisely. If I had seen the sight, he assured me, I would never forget it as long as I lived. The weather was too bad to give the corpse a proper sea burial. So next day at dawn they took it up on the poop, covering its face with a bit of bunting; he read a short prayer, and then, just as it was, in its oilskins and long boots, they launched it among those mountainous seas that seemed ready every moment to swallow up the ship herself and the terrified lives on board of her.

'That reefed foresail saved you.' I threw in.

'Under God – it did.' he exclaimed fervently. 'It was by a special mercy, I firmly believe, that it stood some of those hurricane squalls.'

'It was the setting of that sail which – ' I began.

'God's own hand in it,' he interrupted me. 'Nothing less could have done it. I don't mind telling you that I hardly dared give the order. It seemed impossible that we could touch anything without losing it, and then our last hope would have been gone.'

The terror of that gale was on him yet. I let him go on for a bit, then said, casually – as if returning to a minor subject:

'You were very anxious to give up your mate to the shore people, I believe?'

He was. To the law. His obscure tenacity on that point had in it something incomprehensible and a little awful; something, as it were, mystical, quite apart from his anxiety that he should not be suspected of 'countenancing any doings of that sort'. Seven-and-thirty virtuous years at sea, of which over twenty of immaculate command, and the last fifteen in the *Sephora*, seemed to have laid him under some pitiless obligation.

'And you know,' he went on, groping shamefacedly among his feelings, 'I did not engage that young fellow. His people had some interest with my owners. I was in a way forced to take him on. He looked very smart, very gentlemanly, and all that. But do you know – I never liked him, somehow. I am a plain man. You see, he wasn't exactly the sort for the chief mate of a ship like the *Sephora*.'

I had become so connected in thoughts and impressions with the secret sharer of my cabin that I felt as if I, personally, were being given to understand that I, too, was not the sort that would have done for the chief mate of a ship like the *Sephora*. I had no doubt of it in my mind.

'Not at all the style of man. You understand,' he insisted, superfluously, looking hard at me.

I smiled urbanely. He seemed at a loss for a while.

'I suppose I must report a suicide.'

'Beg pardon?'

'Sui-cide! That's what I'll have to write to my owners directly I get in.'

'Unless you manage to recover him before tomorrow,' I assented, dispassionately . . . 'I mean, alive.'

He mumbled something which I really did not catch, and I turned my ear to him in a puzzled manner. He fairly bawled:

'The land – I say, the mainland is at least seven miles off my anchorage.'

'About that.'

My lack of excitement, of curiosity, of surprise, of any sort of pronounced interest, began to arouse his distrust. But except for the felicitous pretence of deafness I had not tried to pretend anything. I had felt utterly incapable of playing the part of ignorance properly, and therefore was afraid to try. It is also certain that he had brought some ready-made suspicions with him, and that he viewed my politeness as a strange and unnatural phenomenon. And yet how else could I have received him? Not heartily! That was impossible for psychological reasons, which I need not state here. My only object was to keep off his inquiries. Surlily? Yes, but surliness might have provoked a point-blank question. From its novelty to him and from its nature, punctilious courtesy was the manner best calculated to restrain the man. But there was the danger of his breaking through my defence bluntly. I could not, I think, have met him by a direct lie, also for psychological (not moral) reasons. If he had only known how afraid I was of his putting my feeling of identity with the other to the test! But, strangely enough – (I thought of it only afterwards) – I believe that he was not a little disconcerted by the reverse side of that weird situation, by something in me that reminded him of the man he was seeking – suggested a mysterious similitude to the young fellow he had distrusted and disliked from the first.

However that might have been, the silence was not very prolonged. He took another oblique step.

'I reckon I had no more than a two-mile pull to your ship. Not a bit more.'

'And quite enough, too, in this awful heat,' I said.

Another pause full of mistrust followed. Necessity, they say, is mother of invention, but fear, too, is not barren of ingenious suggestions. And I was afraid he would ask me point-blank for news of my other self.

'Nice little saloon, isn't it?' I remarked, as if noticing for the first time the way his eyes roamed from one closed door to the other. 'And very well fitted out, too. Here, for instance,' I continued, reaching over the back of my seat negligently and flinging the door open, 'is my bath-room.'

He made an eager movement, but hardly gave it a glance. I got up, shut the door of the bath-room, and invited him to have a look round, as if I were very proud of my accommodation. He had to rise and be shown round, but he went through the business without any raptures whatever.

'And now we'll have a look at my stateroom,' I declared, in a voice as loud as I dared to make it, crossing the cabin to the starboard side with purposely heavy steps.

He followed me in and gazed around. My intelligent double had vanished. I played my part.

'Very convenient – isn't it?'

'Very nice. Very comf . . .' He didn't finish and went out brusquely as if to escape from some unrighteous wiles of mine. But it was not to be. I had been too frightened not to feel vengeful; I felt I had him on the run, and I meant to keep him on the run. My polite insistence must have had something menacing in it, because he gave in suddenly. And I did not let him off a single item; mate's room, pantry, storerooms, the very sail-locker which was also under the poop – he had to look into them all. When at last I showed him out on the quarter-deck he drew a long, spiritless sigh, and mumbled dismally that he must really be going back to his ship now. I desired my mate, who had joined us, to see to the captain's boat.

The man of whiskers gave a blast on the whistle which he used to wear hanging round his neck, and yelled, '*Sephora*'s away!' My double down there in my cabin must have heard, and certainly could not feel more relieved than I. Four fellows came running out from somewhere forward and went over the side, while my own men, appearing on deck too, lined the rail. I escorted my visitor to the gangway ceremoniously, and nearly overdid it. He was a tenacious beast. On the very ladder he lingered, and in that unique, guiltily conscientious manner of sticking to the point:

'I say . . . you . . . you don't think that – '

I covered his voice loudly:

'Certainly not . . . I am delighted. Good-bye.'

I had an idea of what he meant to say, and just saved myself by the privilege of defective hearing. He was too shaken generally to insist, but my mate, close witness of that parting, looked mystified and his face took on a thoughtful cast. As I did not want to appear as if I wished to avoid all communication with my officers, he had the opportunity to address me.

'Seems a very nice man. His boat's crew told our chaps a very extraordinary story, if what I am told by the steward is true. I suppose you had it from the captain, sir?'

'Yes. I had a story from the captain.'

'A very horrible affair – isn't it, sir?'

'It is.'

'Beats all these tales we hear about murders in Yankee ships.'

'I don't think it beats them. I don't think it resembles them in the least.'

'Bless my soul – you don't say so! But of course I've no acquaintance whatever with American ships, not I, so I couldn't go against your knowledge. It's horrible enough for me . . . But the queerest part is that those fellows seemed to have some idea the man was hidden aboard here. They had really. Did you ever hear of such a thing?'

'Preposterous – isn't it?'

We were walking to and fro athwart the quarter-deck. No one of the crew forward could be seen (the day was Sunday), and the mate pursued:

'There was some little dispute about it. Our chaps took offence. "As if we would harbour a thing like that," they said. "Wouldn't you like to look for him in our coal-hole?" Quite a tiff. But they made it up in the end. I suppose he did drown himself. Don't you, sir?'

'I don't suppose anything.'

'You have no doubt in the matter, sir?'

'None whatever.'

I left him suddenly. I felt I was producing a bad impression, but with my double down there it was most trying to be on deck. And it was almost as trying to be below. Altogether a nerve-trying situation. But on the whole I felt less torn in two when I was with him. There was no one in the whole ship whom I dared take into my confidence. Since the hands had got to know his story, it would have been impossible to pass him off for anyone else, and an accidental discovery was to he dreaded now more than ever . . .

The steward being engaged in laying the table for dinner, we could talk only with our eyes when I first went down. Later in the afternoon we had a cautious try at whispering. The Sunday quietness of the ship was against us; the stillness of air and water around her was against us; the elements, the men were against us – everything was against us in our secret partnership; time itself – for this could not go on for ever. The very trust in Providence was, I suppose, denied to his guilt. Shall I confess that this thought cast me down very much? And as to the chapter of accidents which counts for so much in the book of success, I could only hope that it was closed. For what favourable accident could be expected?

'Did you hear everything?' were my first words as soon as we took up our position side by side, leaning over my bed-place.

He had. And the proof of it was his earnest whisper, 'The man told you he hardly dared to give the order.'

I understood the reference to be to that saving foresail.

'Yes. He was afraid of it being lost in the setting.'

'I assure you he never gave the order. He may think he did, but he never gave it. He stood there with me on the break of the poop after the main-topsail blew away, and whimpered about our last hope – positively whimpered about it and nothing else – and the night coming on! To hear one's skipper go on like that in such weather was enough to drive any fellow out of his mind. It worked me up into a sort of desperation. I just took it into my own hands and went away from him, boiling, and – But what's the use telling you? *You* know! . . . Do you think that if I had not been pretty fierce with them I should have got the men to do anything? Not it! The bo's'n perhaps? Perhaps! It wasn't a heavy sea – it was a sea gone mad! I suppose the end of the world will be something like that;

and a man may have the heart to see it coming once and be done with it – but to have to face it day after day – I don't blame anybody. I was precious little better than the rest. Only – I was an officer of that old coal-wagon, anyhow –'

'I quite understand,' I conveyed that sincere assurance into his ear. He was out of breath with whispering; I could hear him pant slightly. It was all very simple. The same strung-up force which had given twenty-four men a chance, at least, for their lives, had, in a sort of recoil, crushed an unworthy mutinous existence.

But I had no leisure to weigh the merits of the matter – footsteps in the saloon, a heavy knock. 'There's enough wind to get under way with, sir.' Here was the call of a new claim upon my thoughts and even upon my feelings.

'Turn the hands up,' I cried through the door. 'I'll be on deck directly.'

I was going out to make the acquaintance of my ship. Before I left the cabin our eyes met – the eyes of the only two strangers on board. I pointed to the recessed part where the little camp-stool awaited him and laid my finger on my lips. He made a gesture – somewhat vague – a little mysterious, accompanied by a faint smile, as if of regret.

This is not the place to enlarge upon the sensations of a man who feels for the first time a ship move under his feet to his own independent word. In my case they were not unalloyed. I was not wholly alone with my command; for there was that stranger in my cabin. Or rather, I was not completely and wholly with her. Part of me was absent. That mental feeling of being in two places at once affected me physically as if the mood of secrecy had penetrated my very soul. Before an hour had elapsed since the ship had begun to move, having occasion to ask the mate (he stood by my side) to take a compass bearing of the Pagoda, I caught myself reaching up to his ear in whispers. I say I caught myself, but enough had escaped to startle the man. I can't describe it otherwise than by saying that he shied. A grave, preoccupied manner, as though he were in possession of some perplexing intelligence, did not leave him henceforth. A little later I moved away from the rail to look at the compass with such a stealthy gait that the helmsman noticed it – and I could not help noticing the unusual roundness of his eyes. These are trifling instances, though it's to no commander's advantage to be suspected of ludicrous eccentricities. But I was also more seriously affected. There are to a seaman certain words, gestures, that should in given conditions come as naturally, as instinctively as the winking of a menaced eye. A certain order should spring on to his lips without thinking; a certain sign should get itself made, so to speak, without reflection. But all unconscious alertness had abandoned me. I had to make an effort of will to recall myself back (from the cabin) to the conditions of the moment. I felt that I was appearing an irresolute commander to those people who were watching me more or less critically.

And, besides, there were the scares. On the second day out, for instance, coming off the deck in the afternoon (I had straw slippers on my bare feet) I stopped at the open pantry door and spoke to the steward. He was doing something there with his back to me. At the sound of my voice he nearly jumped out of his skin, as the saying is, and incidentally broke a cup.

'What on earth's the matter with you?' I asked, astonished.

He was extremely confused. 'Beg pardon, sir. I made sure you were in your cabin.'

'You see I wasn't.'

'No, sir. I could have sworn I had heard you moving in there not a moment ago. It's most extraordinary . . . very sorry, sir.'

I passed on with an inward shudder. I was so identified with my secret double that I did not even mention the fact in those scanty, fearful whispers we exchanged. I suppose he had made some slight noise of some kind or other. It would have been miraculous if he hadn't at one time or another. And yet, haggard as he appeared, he looked always perfectly self-controlled, more than calm – almost invulnerable. On my suggestion he remained almost entirely in the bath-room, which, upon the whole, was the safest place. There could be really no shadow of an excuse for anyone ever wanting to go in there, once the steward had done with it. It was a very tiny place. Sometimes he reclined on the floor, his legs bent, his head sustained on one elbow. At others I would find him on the camp-stool, sitting in his grey sleeping-suit and with his cropped dark hair like a patient, unmoved convict. At night I would smuggle him into my bed-place, and we would whisper together, with the regular footfall of the officer of the watch passing and repassing over our heads. It was an infinitely miserable time. It was lucky that some tins of fine preserves were stowed in a locker in my stateroom; hard bread I could always get hold of; and so he lived on stewed chicken, pâté de foie gras, asparagus, cooked oysters, sardines – on all sorts of abominable sham delicacies out of tins. My early morning coffee he always drank; and it was all I dared do for him in that respect.

Every day there was the horrible manoeuvring to go through so that my room and then the bath-room should be done in the usual way. I came to hate the sight of the steward, to abhor the voice of that harmless man. I felt that it was he who would bring on the disaster of discovery. It hung like a sword over our heads.

The fourth day out, I think (we were then working down the east side of the Gulf of Siam, tack for tack, in light winds and smooth water) – the fourth day, I say, of this miserable juggling with the unavoidable, as we sat at our evening meal, that man, whose slightest movement I dreaded, after putting down the dishes ran up on deck busily. This could not be dangerous. Presently he came down again; and then it appeared that he had remembered a coat of mine which I had thrown over a rail to dry after having been wetted in a shower which had passed over the ship in the afternoon. Sitting stolidly at the head of the table I became terrified at the sight of the garment on his arm. Of course he made for my door. There was no time to lose.

'Steward,' I thundered. My nerves were so shaken that I could not govern my voice and conceal my agitation. This was the sort of thing that made my terrifically whiskered mate tap his forehead with his forefinger. I had detected him using that gesture while talking on deck with a confidential air to the carpenter. It was too far to hear a word, but I had no doubt that this pantomime could only refer to the strange new captain.

'Yes, sir,' the pale-faced steward turned resignedly to me. It was this maddening course of being shouted at, checked without rhyme or reason, arbitrarily chased out of my cabin, suddenly called into it, sent flying out of his pantry on incomprehensible errands, that accounted for the growing wretchedness of his expression.

'Where are you going with that coat?'

'To your room, sir.'

'Is there another shower coming?'

'I'm sure I don't know, sir. Shall I go up again and see, sir?'

'No! never mind.'

My object was attained, as of course my other self in there would have heard everything that passed. During this interlude my two officers never raised their eyes off their respective plates; but the lip of that confounded cub, the second mate, quivered visibly.

I expected the steward to hook my coat on and come out at once. He was very slow about it; but I dominated my nervousness sufficiently not to shout after him. Suddenly I became aware (it could be heard plainly enough) that the fellow for some reason or other was opening the door of the bath-room. It was the end. The place was literally not big enough to swing a cat in. My voice died in my throat and I went stony all over. I expected to hear a yell of surprise and terror, and made a movement, but had not the strength to get on my legs. Everything remained still. Had my second self taken the poor wretch by the throat? I don't know what I could have done next moment if I had not seen the steward come out of my room, close the door, and then stand quietly by the sideboard.

'Saved,' I thought. 'But, no! Lost! Gone! He was gone!'

I laid my knife and fork down and leaned back in my chair. My head swam. After a while, when sufficiently recovered to speak in a steady voice, I instructed my mate to put the ship round at eight o'clock himself.

'I won't come on deck,' I went on. 'I think I'll turn in, and unless the wind shifts I don't want to be disturbed before midnight. I feel a bit seedy.'

'You did look middling bad a little while ago,' the chief mate remarked without showing any great concern.

They both went out, and I stared at the steward clearing the table. There was nothing to be read on that wretched man's face. But why did he avoid my eyes, I asked myself. Then I thought I should like to hear the sound of his voice.

'Steward!'

'Sir!' Startled as usual.

'Where did you hang up that coat?'

'In the bath-room, sir.' The usual anxious tone. 'It's not quite dry yet, sir.'

For some time longer I sat in the cuddy. Had my double vanished as he had come? But of his coming there was an explanation, whereas his disappearance would be inexplicable . . . I went slowly into my dark room, shut the door, lighted the lamp, and for a time dared not turn round. When at last I did I saw him standing bolt-upright in the narrow recessed part. It would not be true to say I had a shock, but an irresistible doubt of his bodily existence flitted through my mind. Can it be, I asked myself, that he is not visible to other eyes than mine? It was like being haunted. Motionless, with a grave face, he raised his hands slightly at me in a gesture which meant clearly, 'Heavens! what a narrow escape!' Narrow indeed. I think I had come creeping quietly as near insanity as any man who has not actually gone over the border. That gesture restrained me, so to speak.

The mate with the terrific whiskers was now putting the ship on the other tack. In the moment of profound silence which follows upon the hands going to their stations I heard on the poop his raised voice: 'Hard alee!' and the distant shout of the order repeated on the maindeck. The sails, in that light breeze, made but a faint fluttering noise. It ceased. The ship was coming round slowly; I held my breath in the renewed stillness of expectation; one wouldn't have thought that there was a single living soul on her decks. A sudden brisk shout, 'Mainsail haul!' broke the spell, and in the noisy cries and rush overhead of the men running away with the main-brace we two, down in my cabin, came together in our usual position by the bed-place.

He did not wait for my question. 'I heard him fumbling here and just managed to squat myself down in the bath,' he whispered to me. 'The fellow only opened the door and put his arm in to hang the coat up. All the same –'

'I never thought of that,' I whispered back, even more appalled than before at the closeness of the shave, and marvelling at that something unyielding in his character which was carrying him through so finely. There was no agitation in his whisper. Whoever was being driven distracted, it was not he. He was sane. And the proof of his sanity was continued when he took up the whispering again.

'It would never do for me to come to life again.'

It was something that a ghost might have said. But what he was alluding to was his old captain's reluctant admission of the theory of suicide.

It would obviously serve his turn – if I had understood at all the view which seemed to govern the unalterable purpose of his action.

'You must maroon me as soon as ever you can get among these islands off the Cambodje shore,' he went on.

'Maroon you! We are not living in a boy's adventure tale,' I protested. His scornful whispering took me up.

'We aren't indeed! There's nothing of a boy's tale in this. But there's nothing else for it. I want no more. You don't suppose I am afraid of what can be done to me? Prison or gallows or whatever they may please. But you don't see me coming back to explain such things to an old fellow in a wig and twelve respectable tradesmen, do you? What can they know whether I am guilty or not – or of *what* I am guilty, either? That's my affair. What does the Bible say? "Driven off the face of the earth." Very well. I am off the face of the earth now. As I came at night so I shall go.'

'Impossible!' I murmured. 'You can't.'

'Can't? . . . Not naked like a soul on the Day of Judgement. I shall freeze on to this sleeping-suit. The Last Day is not yet – and . . . you have understood thoroughly. Didn't you?'

I felt suddenly ashamed of myself. I may say truly that I understood – and my hesitation in letting that man swim away from my ship's side had been a mere sham sentiment, a sort of cowardice.

'It can't be done now till next night,' I breathed out. 'The ship is on the off-shore tack and the wind may fail us.'

'As long as I know that you understand,' he whispered. 'But of course you do. It's a great satisfaction to have got somebody to understand. You seem to have been there on purpose.' And in the same whisper, as if we two whenever we talked had to say things to each other which were not fit for the world to hear, he added, 'It's very wonderful.'

We remained side by side talking in our secret way – but sometimes silent or just exchanging a whispered word or two at long intervals. And as usual he stared through the port. A breath of wind came now and again into our faces. The ship might have been moored in dock, so gently and on an even keel she slipped through the water, that did not murmur even at our passage, shadowy and silent like a phantom sea.

At midnight I went on deck, and to my mate's great surprise put the ship round on the other tack. His terrible whiskers flitted round me in

464

silent criticism. I certainly should not have done it if it had been only a question of getting out of that sleepy gulf as quickly as possible. I believe he told the second mate, who relieved him, that it was a great want of judgement. The other only yawned. That intolerable cub shuffled about so sleepily and lolled against the rails in such a slack, improper fashion that I came down on him sharply.

'Aren't you properly awake yet?'

'Yes, sir! I am awake.'

'Well, then, be good enough to hold yourself as if you were. And keep a look-out. If there's any current we'll be closing with some islands before daylight.'

The east side of the gulf is fringed with islands, some solitary, others in groups. On the blue background of the high coast they seem to float on silvery patches of calm water, arid and grey, or dark green and rounded like clumps of evergreen bushes, with the larger ones, a mile or two long, showing the outlines of ridges, ribs of grey rock under the dank mantle of matted leafage. Unknown to trade, to travel, almost to geography, the manner of life they harbour is an unsolved secret. There must be villages – settlements of fishermen at least – on the largest of them, and some communication with the world is probably kept up by native craft. But all that forenoon, as we headed for them, fanned along by the faintest of breezes, I saw no sign of man or canoe in the field of the telescope I kept on pointing at the scattered group.

At noon I gave no orders for a change of course, and the mate's whiskers became much concerned and seemed to be offering themselves unduly to my notice. At last I said:

'I am going to stand right in. Quite in – as far as I can take her.'

The state of extreme surprise imparted an air of ferocity also to his eyes, and he looked truly terrific for a moment.

'We're not doing well in the middle of the gulf,' I continued, casually. 'I am going to look for the land breezes tonight.'

'Bless my soul! Do you mean, sir, in the dark among the lot of all them blinds and reefs and shoals?'

'Well – if there are any regular land breezes at all on this coast one must get close inshore to find them, mustn't one?'

'Bless my soul!' he exclaimed again under his breath. All that afternoon he wore a dreamy, contemplative appearance which in him was a mark of perplexity. After dinner I went into my stateroom as if I meant to take some rest. There we two bent our dark heads over a half-unrolled chart lying on my bed.

'There,' I said. 'It's got to be Koh-ring. I've been looking at it ever since sunrise. It has got two hills and a low point. It must be inhabited. And on the coast opposite there is what looks like the mouth of a biggish river – with some town, no doubt, not far up. It's the best chance for you that I can see.'

'Anything. Koh-ring let it be.'

He looked thoughtfully at the chart as if surveying chances and distances from a lofty height – and following with his eyes his own figure wandering on the blank land of Cochin-China, and then passing off that piece of paper clean out of sight into uncharted regions. And it was as if the ship had two captains to plan her course for her. I had been so worried and restless running up and down that I had not had the patience to dress that day. I had remained in my sleeping-suit, with straw slippers and soft floppy hat. The closeness of the heat in the gulf had been most oppressive, and the crew were used to see me wandering in that airy attire.

'She will clear the south point as she heads now,' I whispered into his ear. 'Goodness only knows when, though, but certainly after dark. I'll edge her into half a mile, as far as I may be able to judge in the dark – '

'Be careful,' he murmured, warningly – and I realized suddenly that all my future, the only future for which I was fit, would perhaps go irretrievably to pieces in any mishap to my first command.

I could not stop a moment longer in the room. I motioned him to get out of sight and made my way on the poop. That unplayful cub had the watch. I walked up and down for a while thinking things out, then beckoned him over.

'Send a couple of hands to open the two quarter-deck ports,' I said, mildly.

He actually had the impudence, or else so forgot himself in his wonder at such an incomprehensible order, as to repeat:

'Open the quarter-deck ports! What for, sir?'

'The only reason you need concern yourself about is because I tell you to do so. Have them open wide and fastened properly.'

He reddened and went off, but I believe made some jeering remark to the carpenter as to the sensible practice of ventilating a ship's quarter-deck. I know he popped into the mate's cabin to impart the fact to him because the whiskers came on deck, as it were by chance, and stole glances at me from below – for signs of lunacy or drunkenness, I suppose.

A little before supper, feeling more restless than ever, I rejoined, for a moment, my second self. And to find him sitting so quietly was surprising, like something against nature, inhuman.

I developed my plan in a hurried whisper.

'I shall stand in as close as I dare and then put her round. I will presently find means to smuggle you out of here into the sail-locker, which communicates with the lobby. But there is an opening, a sort of square for hauling the sails out, which gives straight on the quarter-deck and which is never closed in fine weather, so as to give air to the sails. When the ship's way is deadened in stays and all the hands are aft at the mainbraces you will have a clear road to slip out and get overboard through the open quarter-deck port. I've had them both fastened up. Use a rope's end to lower yourself into the water so as to avoid a splash – you know. It could be heard and cause some beastly complication.'

He kept silent for a while, then whispered, 'I understand.'

'I won't be there to see you go,' I began with an effort. 'The rest . . . I only hope I have understood, too.'

'You have. From first to last' – and for the first time there seemed to be a faltering, something strained in his whisper. He caught hold of my arm, but the ringing of the supper bell made me start. He didn't, though; he only released his grip.

After supper I didn't come below again till well past eight o'clock. The faint, steady breeze was loaded with dew; and the wet, darkened sails held all there was of propelling power in it. The night, clear and starry, sparkled darkly, and the opaque, lightless patches shifting slowly against the low stars were the drifting islets. On the port bow there was a big one more distant and shadowily imposing by the great space of sky it eclipsed.

On opening the door I had a back view of my very own self looking at a chart. He had come out of the recess and was standing near the table.

'Quite dark enough.' I whispered.

He stepped back and leaned against my bed with a level, quiet glance.

I sat on the couch. We had nothing to say to each other. Over our heads the officer of the watch moved here and there, Then I heard him move quickly. I knew what that meant. He was making for the companion; and presently his voice was outside my door.

'We are drawing in pretty fast, sir. Land looks rather close.'

'Very well,' I answered. 'I am coming on deck directly.'

I waited till he was gone out of the cuddy, then rose. My double moved too. The time had come to exchange our last whispers, for neither of us was ever to hear each other's natural voice.

'Look here!' I opened a drawer and took out three sovereigns. 'Take this anyhow. I've got six and I'd give you the lot, only I must keep a little money to buy some fruit and vegetables for the crew from native boats as we go through Sunda Straits.'

He shook his head.

'Take it,' I urged him, whispering desperately. 'No one can tell what – '

He smiled and slapped meaningly the only pocket of the sleeping-jacket. It was not safe, certainly. But I produced a large old silk handkerchief of mine, and tying the three pieces of gold in a corner, pressed it on him. He was touched, I suppose, because he took it at last and tied it quickly round his waist under the jacket, on his bare skin.

Our eyes met; several seconds elapsed, till, our glances still mingled, I extended my hand and turned the lamp out. Then I passed through the cuddy, leaving the door of my room wide open . . . 'Steward!'

He was still lingering in the pantry in the greatness of his zeal, giving a rub-up to a plated cruet stand the last thing before going to bed. Being careful not to wake up the mate, whose room was opposite, I spoke in an undertone.

He looked round anxiously. 'Sir!'

'Can you get me a little hot water from the galley?'

'I am afraid, sir, the galley fire's been out for some time now.'

'Go and see.'

He flew up the stairs.

'Now,' I whispered, loudly, into the saloon – too loudly, perhaps, but I was afraid I couldn't make a sound. He was by my side in an instant – the double captain slipped past the stairs – through a tiny dark passage . . . a sliding door. We were in the sail-locker, scrambling on our knees over the sails. A sudden thought struck me. I saw myself wandering bare-footed, bareheaded, the sun beating on my dark poll. I snatched off my floppy hat and tried hurriedly in the dark to ram it on my other self. He dodged and fended off silently. I wonder what he thought had come to me before he understood and suddenly desisted. Our hands met gropingly, lingered united in a steady, motionless clasp for a second . . . No word was breathed by either of us when they separated.

I was standing quietly by the pantry door when the steward returned.

'Sorry, sir. Kettle barely warm. Shall I light the spirit-lamp?'

'Never mind.'

I came out on deck slowly. It was now a matter of conscience to shave the land as close as possible – for now he must go overboard whenever the ship was put in stays. Must! There could be no going back for him. After a moment I walked over to leeward and my heart flew into my mouth at the nearness of the land on the bow. Under any other circumstances I would not have held on a minute longer. The second mate had followed me anxiously.

I looked on till I felt I could command my voice.

'She may weather,' I said then in a quiet tone.

'Are you going to try that, sir?' he stammered out incredulously.

I took no notice of him and raised my tone just enough to be heard by the helmsman.

'Keep her good full.'

'Good full, sir.'

The wind fanned my cheek, the sails slept, the world was silent. The strain of watching the dark loom of the land grow bigger and denser was too much for me. I had shut my eyes – because the ship must go closer. She must! The stillness was intolerable. Were we standing still?

When I opened my eyes the second view started my heart with a thump. The black southern hill of Koh-ring seemed to hang right over the ship like a towering fragment of the everlasting night. On that enormous mass of blackness there was not a gleam to be seen, not a sound to be heard. It was gliding irresistibly towards us and yet seemed already within reach of the hand. I saw the vague figures of the watch grouped in the waist, gazing in awed silence.

'Are you going on, sir?' inquired an unsteady voice at my elbow.

I ignored it. I had to go on.

'Keep her full. Don't check her way. That won't do now,' I said, warningly.

'I can't see the sails very well,' the helmsman answered me, in strange, quavering tones.

Was she close enough? Already she was, I won't say in the shadow of the land, but in the very blackness of it, already swallowed up as it were, gone too close to be recalled, gone from me altogether.

'Give the mate a call,' I said to the young man who stood at my elbow as still as death. 'And turn all hands up.'

My tone had a borrowed loudness reverberated from the height of the land. Several voices cried out together! 'We are all on deck, sir.'

Then stillness again, with the great shadow gliding closer, towering higher, without light, without a sound. Such a hush had fallen on the ship that she might have been a bark of the dead floating in slowly under the very gate of Erebus.

'My God! Where are we?'

It was the mate moaning at my elbow. He was thunderstruck, and as it were deprived of the moral support of his whiskers. He clapped his hands and absolutely cried out, 'Lost!'

'Be quiet,' I said, sternly.

He lowered his tone, but I saw the shadowy gesture of his despair. 'What are we doing here?'

'Looking for the land wind.'

He made as if to tear his hair, and addressed me recklessly.

'She will never get out. You have done it, sir. I knew it'd end in something like this. She will never weather, and you are too close now to stay. She'll drift ashore before she's round. O my God!'

I caught his arm as he was raising it to batter his poor devoted head, and shook it violently.

'She's ashore already,' he wailed, trying to tear himself away.

'Is she? . . . Keep good full there!'

'Good full, sir,' cried the helmsman in a frightened, thin, child-like voice.

I hadn't let go the mate's arm and went on shaking it. 'Ready about, do you hear? You go forward' – shake – 'and stop there' – shake – 'and hold your noise' – shake – 'and see these head-sheets properly over-hauled' – shake, shake – shake.

And all the time I dared not look towards the land lest my heart should fail me. I released my grip at last and he ran forward as if fleeing for dear life.

I wondered what my double there in the sail-locker thought of this commotion. He was able to hear everything – and perhaps he was able to understand why, on my conscience, it had to be thus close – no less. My first order 'Hard alee!' re-echoed ominously under the towering shadow of Koh-ring as if I had shouted in a mountain gorge. And then I watched the land intently. In that smooth water and light wind it was impossible to feel the ship coming-to. No! I could not feel her. And my second self was making now ready to slip out and lower himself overboard. Perhaps he was gone already . . . ?

The great black mass brooding over our very mastheads began to pivot away from the ship's side silently. And now I forgot the secret stranger ready to depart, and remembered only that I was a total stranger to the ship. I did not know her. Would she do it? How was she to be handled?

I swung the mainyard and waited helplessly. She was perhaps stopped, and her very fate hung in the balance, with the black mass of Koh-ring like the gate of the everlasting night towering over her taffrail. What would she do now? Had she way on her yet? I stepped to the side swiftly, and on the shadowy water I could see nothing except a faint phosphorescent flash revealing the glassy smoothness of the sleeping surface. It was impossible to tell – and I had not learned yet the feel of my ship. Was she moving? What I needed was something easily seen, a piece of paper, which I could throw overboard and watch. I had nothing on me. To run down for it I didn't dare. There was no time. All at once my strained, yearning stare distinguished a white object floating within a yard of the ship's side. White on the black water. A phosphorescent flash passed under it. What was that thing? . . . I recognized my own floppy hat. It must have fallen off his head . . . and he didn't bother. Now I had what I wanted – the saving mark for my eyes. But I hardly thought of my other self, now gone from the ship, to be hidden for ever from all friendly faces, to be a fugitive and a vagabond on the earth, with no brand of the curse on his sane forehead to stay a slaying hand . . . too proud to explain.

And I watched the hat – the expression of my sudden pity for his mere flesh. It had been meant to save his homeless head from the dangers of the sun. And now – behold – it was saving the ship, by serving me for a mark to help out the ignorance of my strangeness. Ha! It was drifting forward, warning me just in time that the ship had gathered sternway.

'Shift the helm,' I said in a low voice to the seaman standing still like a statue.

The man's eyes glistened wildly in the binnacle light as he jumped round to the other side and spun round the wheel.

I walked to the break of the poop. On the overshadowed deck all hands stood by the forebraces waiting for my order. The stars ahead seemed to be gliding from right to left. And all was so still in the world that I heard the quiet remark 'She's round', passed in a tone of intense relief between two seamen.

'Let go and haul.'

The foreyards ran round with a great noise, amidst cheery cries. And now the frightful whiskers made themselves heard giving various orders. Already the ship was drawing ahead. And I was alone with her. Nothing! no one in the world should stand now between us, throwing a shadow on the way of silent knowledge and mute affection, the perfect communion of a seaman with his first command.

Walking to the taffrail, I was in time to make out, on the very edge of a darkness thrown by a towering black mass like the very gateway of Erebus – yes, I was in time to catch an evanescent glimpse of my white hat left behind to mark the spot where the secret sharer of my cabin and of my thoughts, as though he were my second self, had lowered himself into the water to take his punishment: a free man, a proud swimmer striking out for a new destiny.

MAX BEERBOHM

A. V. Laider

I unpacked my things and went down to await luncheon.

It was good to be here again in this little old sleepy hostel by the sea. Hostel I say, though it spelt itself without an s and even placed a circumflex above the o. It made no other pretension. It was very cosy indeed.

I had been here just a year before, in mid-February, after an attack of influenza. And now I had returned, after an attack of influenza. Nothing was changed. It had been raining when I left, and the waiter – there was but a single, a very old waiter – had told me it was only a shower. That waiter was still here, not a day older. And the shower had not ceased.

Steadfastly it fell on to the sands, steadfastly into the iron-grey sea. I stood looking out at it from the windows of the hall, admiring it very much. There seemed to be little else to do. What little there was I did. I mastered the contents of a blue hand-bill which, pinned to the wall just beneath the framed engraving of Queen Victoria's Coronation, gave token of a concert that was to be held – or rather, was to have been held some weeks ago – in the Town Hall, for the benefit of the Life-Boat Fund. I looked at the barometer, tapped it, was not the wiser. I glanced at a pamphlet about Our Dying Industries (a theme on which Mr Joseph Chamberlain was at that time trying to alarm us). I wandered to the letter-board.

These letter-boards always fascinate me. Usually some two or three of the envelopes stuck into the cross-garterings have a certain newness and freshness. They seem sure they will yet be claimed. Why not? Why *shouldn't* John Doe, Esq., or Mrs Richard Roe, turn up at any moment? I do not know. I can only say that nothing in the world seems to me more unlikely. Thus it is that these young bright envelopes touch my heart even more than do their dusty and sallow seniors. Sour resignation is less touching than impatience for what will not be, than the eagerness that has to wane and wither. Soured beyond measure these old envelopes are. They are not nearly so nice as they should be to the young ones. They lose no chance of sneering and discouraging. Such dialogues as this are only too frequent:

A Very Young Envelope. Something in me whispers that he will come to-day!

A Very Old Envelope. He? Well, that's good! Ha, ha, ha! Why didn't he come last week, when *you* came? What reason have you for supposing he'll ever come *now*? It isn't as if he were a frequenter of the place. He's never been here. His name is utterly unknown here. You don't suppose he's coming on the chance of finding *you*?

A. V. Y. E. It may seem silly, but – something in me whispers –

A. V. O. E. Something in *you*? One has only to look at you to see there's nothing in you but a note scribbled to him by a cousin. Look at *me*! There are three sheets, closely written, in *me*. The lady to whom I am addressed –

A. V. Y. E. Yes, sir, yes; you told me all about her yesterday.

A. V. O. E. And I shall do so to-day and tomorrow and every day and all day long. That young lady was a widow. She stayed here many times. She was delicate, and the air suited her. She was poor, and the tariff was just within her means. She was lonely, and had need of love. I have in me for her a passionate avowal and strictly honourable proposal, written to her, after many rough copies, by a gentleman who had made her acquaintance under this very roof. He was rich, he was charming, he was in the prime of life. He had asked if he might write to her. She had flutteringly granted his request. He posted me to her the day after his return to London. I looked forward to being torn open by her. I was very sure she would wear me and my contents next to her bosom. She was gone. She had left no address. She never returned . . . This I tell you, and shall continue to tell you, not because I want any of your callow sympathy, – no, *thank* you! – but that you may judge how much less than slight are the chances that you yourself –

But my reader has overheard these dialogues as often as I. He wants to know what was odd about this particular letter-board before which I was standing. At first glance I saw nothing odd about it. But presently I distinguished a handwriting that was vaguely familiar. It was mine.

I stared, I wondered. There is always a slight shock in seeing an envelope of one's own after it has gone through the post. It looks as if it had gone through so much. But this was the first time I had ever seen an envelope of mine eating its heart out in bondage on a letter-board. This was outrageous. This was hardly to be believed. Sheer kindness had impelled me to write to 'A. V. Laider, Esq.,' and this was the result! I hadn't minded receiving no answer. Only now, indeed, did I remember that. I hadn't received one. In multitudinous London the memory of A. V. Laider and his trouble had soon passed from my mind. But – well, what a lesson not to go out of one's way to write to casual acquaintances!

My envelope seemed not to recognize me as its writer. Its gaze was the more piteous for being blank. Even so had I once been gazed at by a dog that I had lost and, after many days, found in the Battersea Home. 'I don't know who you are, but whoever you are, claim me, take me out of this!' That was my dog's appeal. This was the appeal of my envelope.

I raised my hand to the letter-board, meaning to effect a swift and lawless rescue, but paused at sound of a footstep behind me. The old waiter had come to tell me that my luncheon was ready. I followed him out of the hall, not, however, without a bright glance across my shoulder to reassure the little captive that I should come back.

I had the sharp appetite of the convalescent, and this the sea-air had whetted already to a finer edge. In touch with a dozen oysters, and with stout, I soon shed away the unreasoning anger I had felt against A. V. Laider. I became merely sorry for him that he had not received a letter which might perhaps have comforted him. In touch with cutlets, I felt how sorely he had needed comfort. And anon, by the big bright fireside of that small dark smoking-room where, a year ago, on the last evening of my stay here, he and I had at length spoken to each other, I reviewed in detail the tragic experience he had told me; and I fairly revelled in reminiscent sympathy with him . . .

A. V. LAIDER – I had looked him up in the visitors' book on the night of his arrival. I myself had arrived the day before, and had been rather sorry there was no one else staying here. A convalescent by the sea likes to have some one to observe, to wonder about, at meal-time. I was glad when, on my second evening, I found seated at the table opposite to mine another guest. I was the gladder because he was just the right kind of guest. He was enigmatic. By this I mean that he did not look soldierly nor financial nor artistic nor anything definite at all. He offered a clean slate for speculation. And thank heaven! he evidently wasn't going to spoil the fun by engaging me in conversation later on. A decently unsociable man, anxious to be left alone.

The heartiness of his appetite, in contrast with his extreme fragility of aspect and limpness of demeanour, assured me that he, too, had just had influenza. I liked him for that. Now and again our eyes met and were instantly parted. We managed, as a rule, to observe each other indirectly. I was sure it was not merely because he had been ill that he looked interesting. Nor did it seem to me that a spiritual melancholy, though I imagined him sad at the best of times, was his sole asset. I conjectured that he was clever. I thought he might also be imaginative. At first glance I had mistrusted him. A shock of white hair, combined with a young face and dark eyebrows, does somehow make a man look like a charlatan. But it is foolish to be guided by an accident of colour. I had soon rejected my first impression of my fellow-diner. I found him very sympathetic.

Anywhere but in England it would be impossible for two solitary men, howsoever much reduced by influenza, to spend five or six days in the same hostel and not exchange a single word. That is one of the charms of England. Had Laider and I been born and bred in any other land we should have become acquainted before the end of our first evening in the small smoking-room, and have found ourselves irrevocably committed to go on talking to each other throughout the rest of our visit. We might, it is true, have happened to like each other more than any one we had ever met. This off-chance may have occurred to us both. But it counted for nothing as against the certain surrender of quietude and liberty. We slightly bowed to each other as we entered or left the dining-room or smoking-room, and as we met on the widespread sands or in the shop that had a small and faded circulating library. That was all. Our mutual aloofness was a positive bond between us.

Had he been much older than I, the responsibility for our silence would of course have been his alone. But he was not, I judged, more than five or six years ahead of me, and thus I might without impropriety have taken it on myself to perform that hard and perilous feat which English people call, with a shiver, 'breaking the ice.' He had reason, therefore, to be as grateful to me as I to him. Each of us, not the less frankly because silently, recognized his obligation to the other. And when, on the last evening of my stay, the ice actually was broken no ill-will rose between us: neither of us was to blame.

It was a Sunday evening. I had been out for a long last walk and had come in very late to dinner. Laider left his table almost immediately after I sat down to mine. When I entered the smoking-room I found him reading a weekly review which I had bought the day before. It was a crisis. He could not silently offer, nor could I have silently accepted, sixpence. It was a crisis. We faced it like men. He made, by word of mouth, a graceful apology. Verbally, not by signs, I besought him to go on reading. But this, of course, was a vain counsel of perfection. The social code forced us to talk now. We obeyed it like men. To reassure him that our position was not so desperate as it might seem, I took the earliest opportunity to mention that I was going away early next morning. In the tone of his 'Oh, are you?' he tried bravely to imply that he was sorry, even now, to hear that. In a way, perhaps, he really was sorry. We had got on so well together, he and I. Nothing could efface the memory of that. Nay, we seemed to be hitting it off even now. Influenza was not our sole theme. We passed from that to the aforesaid weekly review, and to a correspondence that was raging therein on Faith and Reason.

This correspondence had now reached its fourth and penultimate stage – its Australian stage. It is hard to see why these correspondences spring up; one only knows that they do spring up, suddenly, like street crowds. There comes, it would seem, a moment when the whole English-speaking race is unconsciously bursting to have its say about some one thing – the split infinitive, or the habits of migratory birds, or faith and reason, or what-not. Whatever weekly review happens at such a moment to contain a reference, however remote, to the theme in question reaps the storm. Gusts of letters blow in from all corners of the British Isles. These are presently reinforced by Canada in full blast. A few weeks later the Anglo-Indians weigh in. In due course we have the help of our Australian cousins. By that time, however, we of the Mother Country have got our second wind, and so determined are we to make the most of it that at last even the Editor suddenly loses patience and says 'This correspondence must now cease. – Ed.' and wonders why on earth he ever allowed anything so tedious and idiotic to begin.

I pointed out to Laider one of the Australian letters that had especially pleased me in the current issue. It was from 'A Melbourne Man,' and was of the abrupt kind which declares that 'all your correspondents have been groping in the dark' and then settles the whole matter in one short sharp flash. The flash in this instance was 'Reason is faith, faith reason – that is all we know on earth and all we need to know.' The writer then inclosed his card and was, etc., 'A Melbourne Man.' I said to Laider how very restful it was, after influenza, to read anything that meant nothing whatsoever. Laider was inclined to take the letter more seriously than I, and to be mildly metaphysical. I said that for me faith and reason were two separate things, and (as I am no good at metaphysics, however mild) I offered a definite example, to coax the talk on to ground where I should be safer. 'Palmistry, for example,' I said. 'Deep down in my heart I believe in palmistry.'

Laider turned in his chair. 'You believe in palmistry?'

I hesitated. 'Yes, somehow I do. Why? I haven't the slightest notion. I can give myself all sorts of reasons for laughing it to scorn. My common sense utterly rejects it. Of course the shape of the hand means something – is more or less an index of character. But the idea that my past and future are neatly mapped out on my palms – ' I shrugged my shoulders.

'You don't like that idea?' asked Laider in his gentle, rather academic voice.

'I only say it's a grotesque idea.'

'Yet you do believe in it?'

'I've a grotesque belief in it, yes.'

'Are you sure your reason for calling this idea "grotesque" isn't merely that you dislike it?'

'Well,' I said, with the thrilling hope that he was a companion in absurdity, 'doesn't it seem grotesque to *you*?'

'It seems strange.'

'You believe in it?'

'Oh, absolutely.'

'Hurrah!'

He smiled at my pleasure, and I, at the risk of re-entanglement in metaphysics, claimed him as standing shoulder to shoulder with me against 'A Melbourne Man.' This claim he gently disputed. 'You may think me very prosaic,' he said, 'but I can't believe without evidence.'

'Well, I'm equally prosaic and equally at a disadvantage: I can't take my own belief as evidence, and I've no other evidence to go on.'

He asked me if I had ever made a study of palmistry. I said I had read one of Desbarolles' books years ago, and one of Heron-Allen's. But, he asked, had I tried to test them by the lines on my own hands or on the hands of my friends? I confessed that my actual practice in palmistry had been of a merely passive kind – the prompt extension of my palm to any one who would be so good as to 'read' it and truckle for a few minutes to my egoism. (I hoped Laider might do this.)

'Then I almost wonder,' he said, with his sad smile, 'that you haven't lost your belief, after all the nonsense you must have heard. There are so many young girls who go in for palmistry. I am sure all the five foolish virgins were "awfully keen on it" and used to say "You can be led, but not driven," and "You are likely to have a serious illness between the ages of forty and forty-five," and "You are by nature rather lazy, but can be very energetic by fits and starts." And most of the professionals, I'm told, are as silly as the young girls.'

For the honour of the profession, I named three practitioners whom I had found really good at reading character. He asked whether any of them had been right about past events. I confessed that, as a matter of fact, all three of them had been right in the main. This seemed to amuse him. He asked whether any of them had predicted anything which had since come true. I confessed that all three had predicted that I should do several things which I had since done rather unexpectedly. He asked if I didn't accept this as at any rate a scrap of evidence. I said I could only regard it as a fluke – a rather remarkable fluke.

The superiority of his sad smile was beginning to get on my nerves. I wanted him to see that he was as absurd as I. 'Suppose,' I said, 'suppose for sake of argument that you and I are nothing but helpless automata created to do just this and that, and to have just that and this done to us. Suppose, in fact, we *haven't* any free will whatsoever. Is it likely or conceivable that the Power that fashioned us would take the trouble to jot down in cipher on our hands just what was in store for us?'

Laider did not answer this question, he did but annoyingly ask me another. 'You believe in free will?'

'Yes, of course. I'll be hanged if I'm an automaton.'

'And you believe in free will just as in palmistry – without any reason?'

'Oh, no. Everything points to our having free will.'

'Everything? What, for instance?'

This rather cornered me. I dodged out, as lightly as I could, by saying 'I suppose *you* would say it was written in my hand that I should be a believer in free will.'

'Ah, I've no doubt it is.'

I held out my palms. But, to my great disappointment, he looked quickly away from them. He had ceased to smile. There was agitation in his voice as he explained that he never looked at people's hands now. 'Never now – never again.' He shook his head as though to beat off some memory.

I was much embarrassed by my indiscretion. I hastened to tide over the awkward moment by saying that if *I* could read hands I wouldn't, for fear of the awful things I might see there.

'Awful things, yes,' he whispered, nodding at the fire.

'Not,' I said in self-defence, 'that there's anything very awful, so far as I know, to be read in *my* hands.'

He turned his gaze from the fire to me. 'You aren't a murderer, for example?'

'Oh, no,' I replied, with a nervous laugh.

'*I* am.'

This was a more than awkward, it was a painful, moment for me; and I am afraid I must have started or winced, for he instantly begged my pardon. 'I don't know,' he exclaimed, 'why I said it. I'm usually a very reticent man. But sometimes – ' He pressed his brow. 'What you must think of me!'

I begged him to dismiss the matter from his mind.

'It's very good of you to say that; but – I've placed myself as well as you in a false position. I ask you to believe that I'm not the sort of man who is "wanted" or ever was "wanted" by the police. I should be bowed out of any police-station at which I gave myself up. I'm not a murderer in any bald sense of the word. No.'

My face must have perceptibly brightened, for 'Ah,' he said, 'don't imagine I'm not a murderer at all. Morally, I am.' He looked at the clock. I pointed out that the night was young. He assured me that his story was not a long one. I assured him that I hoped it was. He said I was very kind. I denied this. He warned me that what he had to tell might rather tend to stiffen my unwilling faith in palmistry, and to shake my opposite and cherished faith in free will. I said 'Never mind.' He stretched his hands pensively toward the fire. I settled myself back in my chair.

'My hands,' he said, staring at the backs of them, 'are the hands of a very weak man. I dare say you know enough of palmistry to see that for yourself. You notice the slightness of the thumbs and of the two "little" fingers. They are the hands of a weak and over-sensitive man – a man without confidence, a man who would certainly waver in an emergency. Rather Hamlet-ish hands,' he mused. 'And I'm like Hamlet in other respects, too: I'm no fool, and I've rather a noble disposition, and I'm unlucky. But Hamlet was luckier than I in one thing; he was a murderer by accident, whereas the murders that I committed one day fourteen years ago – for I must tell you it wasn't one murder, but many murders that I committed – were all of them due to the wretched inherent weakness of my own wretched self.

'I was twenty-six – no, twenty-seven years old, and rather a nondescript person, as I am now. I was supposed to have been called to the Bar. In fact, I believe I *had* been called to the Bar. I hadn't listened to the call. I never intended to practise, and I never did practise. I only wanted an excuse in the eyes of the world for existing. I suppose the nearest I have ever come to practising is now at this moment: I am defending a murderer. My father had left me well enough provided with money. I was able to go my own desultory way, riding my hobbies where I would. I had a good stableful of hobbies. Palmistry was one of them. I was rather ashamed of this one. It seemed to me absurd, as it seems to you. Like you, though, I believed in it. Unlike you, I had done more than merely read a book or so about it. I had read innumerable books about it. I had taken casts of all my friends' hands. I had tested and tested again the points at which Desbarolles dissented from the gypsies, and – well, enough that I had gone into it all rather thoroughly, and was as sound a palmist as a man may be without giving his whole life to palmistry.

'One of the first things I had seen in my own hand, as soon as I had learned to read it, was that at about the age of twenty-six I should have a narrow escape from death – from a violent death. There was a clean break in the life-line, and a square joining it – the protective square, you know. The markings were precisely the same in both hands. It was to be the narrowest escape possible. And I wasn't going to escape without injury, either. That is what bothered me. There was a faint line connecting the break in the life-line with a star on the line of health. Against that star was another square. I was to recover from the injury, whatever it might be. Still, I didn't exactly look forward to it. Soon after I had reached the age of twenty-five, I began to feel uncomfortable. The thing might be going to happen at any moment. In palmistry, you know, it is impossible to pin an event down hard and fast to one year. This particular event was to be when I was *about* twenty-six; it mightn't be till I was twenty-seven; it might be while I was only twenty-five.

'And I used to tell myself that it mightn't be at all. My reason rebelled against the whole notion of palmistry, just as yours does. I despised my faith in the thing, just as you despise yours. I used to try not to be so ridiculously careful as I was whenever I crossed a street. I lived in London at that time. Motor-cars had not yet come in, but – what hours, all told, I must have spent standing on curbs, very circumspect, very lamentable! It was a pity, I suppose, that I had no definite occupation – something to take me out of myself. I was one of the victims of private means. There came a time when I drove in four-wheelers rather than in hansoms, and was doubtful of four-wheelers. Oh, I assure you, I was very lamentable indeed.

'If a railway-journey could be avoided, I avoided it. My uncle had a place in Hampshire. I was very fond of him and of his wife. Theirs was the only house I ever went to stay in now. I was there for a week in November, not long after my twenty-seventh birthday. There were other people staying there, and at the end of the week we all travelled back to London together. There were six of us in the carriage: Colonel Elbourn and his wife and their daughter, a girl of seventeen; and another married couple, the Blakes. I had been at Winchester with Blake, but had hardly seen him since that time. He was in the Indian Civil, and was home on leave. He was sailing for India next week. His wife was to remain in

England for some months, and then join him out there. They had been married five years. She was now just twenty-four years old. He told me that this was her age.

'The Elbourns I had never met before. They were charming people. We had all been very happy together. The only trouble had been that on the last night, at dinner, my uncle asked me if I still went in for "the gypsy business," as he always called it; and of course the three ladies were immensely excited, and implored me to "do" their hands. I told them it was all nonsense, I said I had forgotten all I once knew, I made various excuses; and the matter dropped. It was quite true that I had given up reading hands. I avoided anything that might remind me of what was in my own hands. And so, next morning, it was a great bore to me when, soon after the train started, Mrs Elbourn said it would be "too cruel" of me if I refused to do their hands now. Her daughter and Mrs Blake also said it would be "brutal"; and they were all taking off their gloves, and – well, of course I had to give in.

'I went to work methodically on Mrs Elbourn's hands, in the usual way, you know, first sketching the character from the backs of them; and there was the usual hush, broken by the usual little noises – grunts of assent from the husband, cooings of recognition from the daughter. Presently I asked to see the palms, and from them I filled in the details of Mrs Elbourn's character before going on to the events in her life. But while I talked I was calculating how old Mrs Elbourn might be. In my first glance at her palms I had seen that she could not have been less than twenty-five when she married. The daughter was seventeen. Suppose the daughter had been born a year later – how old would the mother be? Forty-three, yes. Not less than that, poor woman!'

Laider looked at me. 'Why "poor woman," you wonder? Well, in that first glance I had seen other things than her marriage-line. I had seen a very complete break in the lines of life and of fate. I had seen violent death there. At what age? Not later, not possibly *later*, than forty-three. While I talked to her about the things that had happened in her girlhood, the back of my brain was hard at work on those marks of catastrophe. I was horribly wondering that she was still alive. It was impossible that between her and that catastrophe there could be more than a few short months. And all the time I was talking; and I suppose I acquitted myself well, for I remember that when I ceased I had a sort of ovation from the Elbourns.

'It was a relief to turn to another pair of hands. Mrs Blake was an amusing young creature, and her hands were very characteristic, and prettily odd in form. I allowed myself to be rather whimsical about her nature, and, having begun in that vein, I went on in it – somehow – even after she had turned her palms. In those palms were reduplicated the signs I had seen in Mrs Elbourn's. It was as though they had been copied neatly out. The only difference was in the placing of them; and it was this difference that was the most horrible point. The fatal age in Mrs Blake's hands was – not past, no, for here *she* was. But she might have died when she was twenty-one. Twenty-three seemed to be the utmost span. She was twenty-four, you know.

'I have said that I am a weak man. And you will have good proof of that directly. Yet I showed a certain amount of strength that day – yes, even on that day which has humiliated and saddened the rest of my life. Neither my face nor my voice betrayed me when in the palms of Dorothy Elbourn I was again confronted with those same signs, She was all for knowing the future, poor child! I believe I told her all manner of things that were to be. And she had no future – none, none in *this* world – except –

'And then, while I talked, there came to me suddenly a suspicion. I wondered it hadn't come before. You guess what it was? It made me feel very cold and strange. I went on talking. But, also, I went on – quite separately – thinking. The suspicion wasn't a certainty. This mother and daughter were always together. What was to befall the one might anywhere – anywhere – befall the other. But a like fate, in an equally near future, was in store for that other lady. The coincidence was curious, very. Here we all were together – here, they and I – I who was narrowly to escape, so soon now, what they, so soon now, were to suffer. Oh, there was an inference to be drawn. Not a *sure* inference, I told myself. And always I was talking, talking, and the train was swinging and swaying noisily along – to what? It was a fast train. Our carriage was near the engine. I was talking loudly. Full well I had known what I should see in the Colonel's hands. I told myself I had not known. I told myself that even now the thing I dreaded was not sure to be. Don't think I was dreading it for myself. I wasn't so "lamentable" as all that – now. It was only of them that I thought – only for them. I hurried over the Colonel's character and career; I was perfunctory. It was Blake's hands that I wanted. *They* were the hands that mattered. If *they* had the marks – Remember, Blake was to start for India in the coming week, his wife was to remain in England. They would be apart. Therefore –

'And the marks were there. And I did nothing – nothing but hold forth on the subtleties of Blake's character. There was a thing for me to do. I wanted to do it. I wanted to spring to the window and pull the communication-cord. Quite a simple thing to do. Nothing easier than to stop a train. You just give a sharp pull, and the train slows down, comes to a standstill. And the Guard appears at your window. You explain to the Guard.

'Nothing easier than to tell him there is going to be a collision. Nothing easier than to insist that you and your friends and every other passenger in the train must get out at once . . . There *are* easier things than this? Things that need less courage than this? Some of *them* I could have done, I daresay. This thing I was going to do. Oh, I was determined that I would do it – directly.

'I had said all I had to say about Blake's hands. I had brought my entertainment to an end. I had been thanked and complimented all round. I was quite at liberty. I was going to do what I had to do. I was determined, yes.

'We were near the outskirts of London. The air was grey, thickening; and Dorothy Elbourn had said, "Oh, this horrible old London! I suppose there's the same old fog!" And presently I heard her father saying something about "prevention" and "a short act of Parliament" and "anthracite." And I sat and listened and agreed and – '

Laider closed his eyes. He passed his hand slowly through the air.

'I had a racking headache. And when I said so, I was told not to talk. I was in bed, and the nurses were always telling me not to talk. I was in a hospital. I knew that. But I didn't know why I was there. One day I thought I should like to know why, and so I asked. I was feeling much better now. They told me, by degrees, that I had had concussion of the brain. I had been brought there unconscious, and had remained unconscious for forty-eight hours. I had been in an accident – a railway accident. This seemed to me odd. I had arrived quite safely at my uncle's place, and I had no memory of any journey since that. In cases of concussion, you know, it's not uncommon for the patient to forget all that happened just before the accident; there may be a blank of several hours. So it was in my case. One day my uncle was allowed to come and see me. And somehow, suddenly, at sight of him, the blank was filled in. I remembered, in a flash, everything. I was quite calm, though. Or I made myself seem so, for I wanted to know how the collision had happened. My uncle told me that the engine-driver had failed to see a signal because of the fog, and our train had crashed into a goods-train. I didn't ask him about the people who were with me. You see, there was no need to ask. Very gently my uncle began to tell me, but – I had begun to talk strangely, I suppose. I remember the frightened look of my uncle's face, and the nurse scolding him in whispers.

'After that, all a blur. It seems that I became very ill indeed, wasn't expected to live. However, I live.'

There was a long silence. Laider did not look at me, nor I at him. The fire was burning low, and he watched it.

At length he spoke, 'You despise me. Naturally, I despise myself.'

'No, I don't despise you; but –'

'You blame me.' I did not meet his gaze. 'You blame me,' he repeated.

'Yes.'

'And there, if I may say so, you are a little unjust. It isn't my fault that I was born weak.'

'But a man may conquer weakness.'

'Yes, if he is endowed with the strength for that.'

His fatalism drew from me a gesture of disgust. 'Do you really mean,' I asked, 'that because you didn't pull that cord, you *couldn't* have pulled it?'

'Yes.'

'And it's written in your hands that you couldn't?'

He looked at the palms of his hands. 'They are the hands of a very weak man,' he said.

'A man so weak that he cannot believe in the possibility of free will for himself or for any one?'

'They are the hands of an intelligent man, who can weigh evidence and see things as they are.'

'But answer me: Was it fore-ordained that you should not pull that cord?'

'It was fore-ordained.'

'And was it actually marked in your hands that you were not going to pull it?'

'Ah, well, you see, it is rather the things one *is* going to do that are actually marked. The things one *isn't* going to do, – the innumerable negative things, – how could one expect *them* to be marked?'

'But the consequences of what one leaves undone may be positive?'

'Horribly positive,' he winced. 'My hand is the hand of a man who has suffered a great deal in later life.'

'And was it the hand of a man *destined* to suffer?'

'Oh, yes. I thought I told you that.'

There was a pause.

'Well,' I said, with awkward sympathy, 'I suppose all hands are the hands of people destined to suffer.'

'Not of people destined to suffer so much as I have suffered – as I still suffer.'

The insistence of his self-pity chilled me, and I harked back to a question he had not straightly answered. 'Tell me: Was it marked in your hands that you were not going to pull that cord?'

Again he looked at his hands, and then, having pressed them for a moment to his face, 'It was marked very clearly,' he answered, 'in *their* hands.'

Two or three days after this colloquy there had occurred to me in London an idea – an ingenious and comfortable doubt. How was Laider to be sure that his brain, recovering from concussion, had *remembered* what happened in the course of that railway-journey? How was he to know that his brain hadn't simply, in its abeyance, *invented* all this for him? It might be that he had never seen those signs in those hands. Assuredly, here was a bright loop-hole. I had forthwith written to Laider, pointing it out.

This was the letter which now, at my second visit, I had found miserably pent on the letter-board. I remembered my promise to rescue it. I arose from the retaining fireside, stretched my arms, yawned, and went forth to fulfil my Christian purpose. There was no one in the hall. The 'shower' had at length ceased. The sun had positively come out, and the front door had been thrown open in its honour. Everything along the sea-front was beautifully gleaming, drying, shimmering. But I was not to be diverted from my errand. I went to the letter-board. And – my letter was not there! Resourceful and plucky little thing – it had escaped! I did hope it would not be captured and brought back. Perhaps the alarm had already been raised by the tolling of that great bell which warns the inhabitants for miles around that a letter has broken loose from the letter-board. I had a vision of my envelope skimming wildly along the coast-line, pursued by the old but active waiter and a breathless pack of local wor-thies. I saw it out-distancing them all, dodging past coast-guards, doubling on its tracks, leaping breakwaters, unluckily injuring itself, losing speed, and at last, in a splendour of desperation, taking to the open sea. But suddenly I had another idea. Perhaps Laider had returned?

He had. I espied afar on the sands a form that was recognizably, by the listless droop of it, his. I was glad and sorry – rather glad, because he completed the scene of last year; and very sorry, because this time we should be at each other's mercy: no restful silence and liberty, for either of us, this time. Perhaps he had been told I was here, and had gone out to avoid me while he yet could. Oh weak, weak! Why palter? I put on my hat and coat, and marched out to meet him.

'Influenza, of course?' we asked simultaneously.

There is a limit to the time which one man may spend in talking to another about his own influenza; and presently, as we paced the sands, I felt that Laider had passed this limit. I wondered that he didn't break off and thank me now for my letter. He must have read it. He ought to have thanked me for it at once. It was a very good letter, a remarkable letter. But surely he wasn't waiting to answer it by post? His silence about it gave me the absurd sense of having taken a liberty, confound him! He was evidently ill at ease while he talked. But it wasn't for me to help him out of his difficulty, whatever that might be. It was for him to remove the strain imposed on myself.

Abruptly, after a long pause, he did now manage to say, 'It was – very good of you to – to write me that letter.' He told me he had only just got it, and he drifted away into otiose explanations of this fact. I thought he might at least say it was a remarkable letter; and you can imagine my annoyance when he said, after another interval, 'I was very much touched indeed.' I had wished to be convincing, not touching. I can't bear to be called touching.

'Don't you,' I asked, 'think it *is* quite possible that your brain invented all those memories of what – what happened before that accident?'

He drew a sharp sigh. 'You make me feel very guilty.'

'That's exactly what I tried to make you *not* feel!'

'I know, yes. That's why I feel so guilty.'

We had paused in our walk. He stood nervously prodding the hard wet sand with his walking-stick. 'In a way,' he said, 'your theory was quite right. But – it didn't go far enough. It's not only possible, it's a fact, that I didn't see those signs in those hands. I never examined those hands. They weren't there. *I* wasn't there. I haven't an uncle in Hampshire, even. I never had.'

I, too, prodded the sand. 'Well,' I said at length, 'I do feel rather a fool.'

'I've no right even to beg your pardon, but – '

'Oh, I'm not vexed. Only – I rather wish you hadn't told me this.'

'I wish I hadn't had to. It was your kindness, you see, that forced me. By trying to take an imaginary load off my conscience, you laid a very real one on it.'

'I'm sorry. But you, of your own free will, you know, exposed your conscience to me last year. I don't yet quite understand why you did that.'

'No, of course not. I don't deserve that you should. But I think you will. May I explain? I'm afraid I've talked a great deal already about my influenza, and I shan't be able to keep it out of my explanation. Well, my weakest point – I told you this last year, but it happens to be perfectly true that my weakest point – is my will. Influenza, as you know, fastens unerringly on one's weakest point. It doesn't attempt to undermine my imagination. That would be a forlorn hope. I have, alas! a very strong imagination. At ordinary times my imagination allows itself to be governed by my will. My will keeps it in check by constant nagging. But when my will isn't strong enough even to nag, then my imagination stampedes, I become even as a little child. I tell myself the most preposterous fables, and – the trouble is – I can't help telling them to my friends. Until I've thoroughly shaken off influenza, I'm not fit company for any one. I perfectly realize this, and I have the good sense to go right away till I'm quite well again. I come here usually. It seems absurd, but I must confess I was sorry last year when we fell into conversation. I knew I should very soon be letting myself go, or rather, very soon be swept away. Perhaps I ought to have warned you; but – I'm a rather shy man. And then you mentioned the subject of palmistry. You said you believed in it. I wondered at that. I had once read Desbarolles' book about it, but I am bound to say I thought the whole thing very great nonsense indeed.'

'Then,' I gasped, 'it isn't even true that you believe in palmistry?'

'Oh, no. But I wasn't able to tell you that. You had begun by saying that you believed in palmistry, and then you proceeded to scoff at it. While you scoffed I saw myself as a man with a terribly good reason for *not* scoffing; and in a flash I saw the terribly good reason; I had the whole story – at least I had the broad outlines of it – clear before me.'

'You hadn't ever thought of it before?' He shook his head. My eyes beamed. 'The whole thing was a sheer improvisation?'

'Yes,' said Laider, humbly, 'I am as bad as all that. I don't say that all the details of the story I told you that evening were filled in at the very instant of its conception. I was filling them in while we talked about palmistry in general, and while I was waiting for the moment when the story would come in most effectively. And I've no doubt I added some extra touches in the course of the actual telling. Don't imagine that I took the slightest pleasure in deceiving you. It's only my will, not my conscience, that is weakened after influenza. I simply can't help telling what I've made up, and telling it to the best of my ability. But I'm thoroughly ashamed all the time.'

'Not of your ability, surely?'

'Yes, of that, too,' he said with his sad smile. 'I always feel that I'm not doing justice to my idea.'

'You are too stern a critic, believe me.'

'It is very kind of you to say that. You are very kind altogether. Had I known that you were so essentially a man of the world – in the best sense of that term – I shouldn't have so much dreaded seeing you just now and having to confess to you. But I'm not going to take advantage of your urbanity and your easy-going ways. I hope that some day we may meet somewhere when I haven't had influenza and am a not wholly undesirable acquaintance. As it is, I refuse to let you associate with me. I am an older man than you, and so I may without impertinence warn you against having anything to do with me.'

I deprecated this advice, of course; but, for a man of weakened will, he showed great firmness. 'You,' he said, 'in your heart of hearts don't want to have to walk and talk continually with a person who might at any moment try to bamboozle you with some ridiculous tale. And I, for my part, don't want to degrade myself by trying to bamboozle any one – especially one whom I have taught to see through me. Let the two talks we have had be as though they had not been. Let us bow to each other, as last year, but let that be all. Let us follow in all things the precedent of last year.'

With a smile that was almost gay he turned on his heel, and moved away with a step that was almost brisk. I was a little disconcerted. But I was also more than a little glad. The restfulness of silence, the charm of liberty – these things were not, after all, forfeit. My heart thanked Laider for that; and throughout the week I loyally seconded him in the system he had laid down for us. All was as it had been last year. We did not smile to each other, we merely bowed, when we entered or left the dining-room or smoking-room, and when we met on the widespread sands or in that shop which had a small and faded, but circulating, library.

Once or twice in the course of the week it did occur to me that perhaps Laider had told the simple truth at our first interview and an ingenious lie at our second. I frowned at this possibility. The idea of any one wishing to be quit of *me* was most distasteful. However, I was to find reassurance. On the last evening of my stay, I suggested, in the small smoking-room, that he and I should, as sticklers for precedent, converse. We did so, very pleasantly. And after a while I happened to say that I had seen this afternoon a great number of sea-gulls flying close to the shore.

'Sea-gulls?' said Laider, turning in his chair.

'Yes. And I don't think I had ever realized how extraordinarily beautiful they are when their wings catch the light.'

'Beautiful?' Laider threw a quick glance at me and away from me. 'You think them beautiful?'

'Surely.'

'Well, perhaps they are, yes; I suppose they are. But – I don't like seeing them. They always remind me of something – rather an awful thing – that once happened to me.' . . .

It was a very awful thing indeed.

E. M. FORSTER

The Celestial Omnibus

I

The boy who resided at Agathox Lodge, 28, Buckingham Park Road, Surbiton, had often been puzzled by the old sign-post that stood almost opposite. He asked his mother about it, and she replied that it was a joke, and not a very nice one, which had been made many years back by some naughty young men, and that the police ought to remove it. For there were two strange things about this sign-post: firstly, it pointed up a blank alley, and, secondly, it had painted on it, in faded characters, the words, 'To Heaven'.

'What kind of young men were they?' he asked.

'I think your father told me that one of them wrote verses, and was expelled from the University and came to grief in other ways. Still, it was a long time ago. You must ask your father about it. He will say the same as I do, that it was put up as a joke.'

'So it doesn't mean anything at all?'

She sent him upstairs to put on his best things, for the Bonses were coming to tea, and he was to hand the cake-stand.

It struck him, as he wrenched on his tightening trousers, that he might do worse than ask Mr Bons about the sign-post. His father, though very kind, always laughed at him – shrieked with laughter whenever he or any other child asked a question or spoke. But Mr Bons was serious as well as kind. He had a beautiful house and lent one books, he was a church-warden, and a candidate for the County Council; he had donated to the Free Library enormously, he presided over the Literary Society, and had Members of Parliament to stop with him – in short, he was probably the wisest person alive.

Yet even Mr Bons could only say that the sign-post was a joke – the joke of a person named Shelley.

'Of course!' cried the mother; 'I told you so, dear. That was the name.'

'Had you never heard of Shelley?' asked Mr Bons.

'No,' said the boy, and hung his head.

'But is there no Shelley in the house?'

'Why, yes!' exclaimed the lady, in much agitation. 'Dear Mr Bons, we aren't such Philistines as that. Two at the least. One a wedding present, and the other, smaller print, in one of the spare rooms.'

'I believe we have seven Shelleys,' said Mr Bons, with a slow smile. Then he brushed the cake crumbs off his stomach, and, together with his daughter, rose to go.

The boy, obeying a wink from his mother, saw them all the way to the garden gate, and when they had gone he did not at once return to the house, but gazed for a little up and down Buckingham Park Road.

His parents lived at the right end of it. After No. 39 the quality of the houses dropped very suddenly, and 64 had not even a separate servants' entrance. But at the present moment the whole road looked rather pretty, for the sun had just set in splendour, and the inequalities of rent were drowned in a saffron afterglow. Small birds twittered, and the breadwinners' train shrieked musically down through the cutting – that wonderful cutting which has drawn to itself the whole beauty out of Surbiton, and clad itself, like any Alpine valley, with the glory of the fir and the silver birch and the primrose. It was this cutting that had first stirred desires within the boy – desires for something just a little different, he knew not what, desires that would return whenever things were sunlit, as they were this evening, running up and down inside him, up and down, up and down, till he would feel quite unusual all over, and as likely as not would want to cry. This evening he was even sillier, for he slipped across the road towards the sign-post and began to run up the blank alley.

The alley runs between high walls – the walls of the gardens of 'Ivanhoe' and 'Bella Vista' respectively. It smells a little all the way, and is scarcely twenty yards long, including the turn at the end. So not unnaturally the boy soon came to a standstill. 'I'd like to kick that Shelley,' he exclaimed, and glanced idly at a piece of paper which was pasted on the wall. Rather an odd piece of paper, and he read it carefully before he turned back. This is what he read:

S. AND C.R.C.C.
Alteration in Service

Owing to lack of patronage the Company are regretfully compelled to suspend the hourly service, and to retain only the

Sunrise and Sunset Omnibuses,

which will run as usual. It is to be hoped that the public will patronize an arrangement which is intended for their convenience. As an extra inducement, the Company will, for the first time, now issue

Return Tickets!

(available one day only), which may be obtained of the driver. Passengers are again reminded that *no tickets are issued at the other end,* and that no complaints in this connexion will receive consideration from the Company. Nor will the Company be responsible for any negligence or stupidity on the part of Passengers, nor for Hailstorms, Lightning, Loss of Tickets, nor for any Act of God.

§ For the Direction.

Now, he had never seen this notice before, nor could he imagine where the omnibus went to. S. of course was for Surbiton, and R.C.C. meant Road Car Company. But what was the meaning of the other C.? Coombe and Malden, perhaps, or possibly 'City'. Yet it could not hope to compete with the South-Western. The whole thing, the boy reflected, was run on hopelessly unbusinesslike lines. Why no tickets from the other end? And what an hour to start! Then he realized that unless the notice was a hoax, an omnibus must have been starting just as he was wishing the Bonses good-bye. He peered at the ground through the gathering dusk, and there he saw what might or might not be the marks of wheels. Yet nothing had come out of the alley. And he had never seen an omnibus at any time in the Buckingham Park Road. No: it must be a hoax, like the sign-posts, like the fairy-tales, like the dreams upon which he would wake suddenly in the night. And with a sigh he stepped from the alley – right into the arms of his father.

Oh, how his father laughed! 'Poor, poor Popsey!' he cried. 'Diddums! Diddums! Diddums think he'd walky-palky up to Evvink!' and his mother, also convulsed with laughter, appeared on the steps of Agathox Lodge. 'Don't, Bob!' she gasped. 'Don't be so naughty! Oh, you'll kill me! Oh, leave the boy alone!'

But all that evening the joke was kept up. The father implored to be taken too. Was it a very tiring walk? Need one wipe one's shoes on the door-mat? And the boy went to bed feeling faint and sore, and thankful for only one thing – that he had not said a word about the omnibus. It was a hoax, yet through his dreams it grew more and more real, and the streets of Surbiton, through which he saw it driving, seemed instead to become hoaxes and shadows. And very early in the morning he woke with a cry, for he had had a glimpse of its destination. He struck a match, and its light fell not only on his watch but also on his calendar, so that he knew it to be half an hour to sunrise. It was pitch dark, for the fog had come down from London in the night, and all Surbiton was wrapped in its embraces. Yet he sprang out and dressed himself, for he was determined to settle once for all which was real: the omnibus or the streets. 'I shall be a fool one way or the other,' he thought, 'until I know.' Soon he was shivering in the road under the gas lamp that guarded the entrance to the alley.

To enter the alley itself required some courage. Not only was it horribly dark, but he now realized that it was an impossible terminus for an omnibus. If it had not been for a policeman, whom he heard approaching through the fog, he would never have made the attempt. The next moment he had made the attempt and failed. Nothing. Nothing but a blank alley and a very silly boy gaping at its dirty floor. It *was* a hoax. 'I'll tell papa and mamma,' he decided. 'I deserve it, I deserve that they should know. I am too silly to be alive.' And he went back to the gate of Agathox Lodge.

There he remembered that his watch was fast. The sun was not risen;

it would not rise for two minutes. 'Give the bus every chance,' he thought cynically, and returned into the alley.

But the omnibus was there.

II

It had two horses, whose sides were still smoking from their journey, and its two great lamps shone through the fog against the alley's walls, changing their cobwebs and moss into tissues of fairyland. The driver was huddled up in a cape. He faced the blank wall, and how he had managed to drive in so neatly and so silently was one of the many things that the boy never discovered. Nor could he imagine how ever he would drive out.

'Please,' his voice quavered through the foul brown air. 'Please, is that an omnibus?'

'Omnibus est,' said the driver, without turning round. There was a moment's silence. The policeman passed, coughing, by the entrance of the alley. The boy crouched in the shadow, for he did not want to be found out. He was pretty sure, too, that it was a Pirate; nothing else, he reasoned, would go from such odd places and at such odd hours.

'About when do you start?' He tried to sound nonchalant.

'At sunrise.'

'How far do you go?'

'The whole way.'

'And can I have a return ticket which will bring me all the way back?'

'You can.'

'Do you know, I half think I'll come.' The driver made no answer. The sun must have risen, for he unhitched the brake. And scarcely had the boy jumped in before the omnibus was off.

How? Did it turn? There was no room. Did it go forward? There was a blank wall. Yet it was moving – moving at a stately pace through the fog, which had turned from brown to yellow. The thought of warm bed and warmer breakfast made the boy feel faint. He wished he had not come. His parents would not have approved. He would have gone back to them if the weather had not made it impossible. The solitude was terrible; he was the only passenger. And the omnibus, though well-built, was cold and somewhat musty. He drew his coat round him, and in so doing chanced to feel his pocket. It was empty. He had forgotten his purse.

'Stop!' he shouted. 'Stop!' And then, being of a polite disposition, he glanced up at the painted notice-board so that he might call the driver by name. 'Mr Browne! stop; oh, do please stop!'

Mr Browne did not stop, but he opened a little window and looked in at the boy. His face was a surprise, so kind it was and modest.

'Mr Browne, I've left my purse behind. I've not got a penny. I can't pay for the ticket. Will you take my watch, please? I am in the most awful hole.'

'Tickets on this line,' said the driver, 'whether single or return, can be purchased by coinage from no terrene mint. And a chronometer, though it had solaced the vigils of Charlemagne or measured the slumbers of Laura, can acquire by no mutation the doublecake that charms the fangless Cerberus of Heaven!' So saying, he handed in the necessary ticket, and, while the boy said 'Thank you,' continued: 'Titular pretensions, I know it well, are vanity. Yet they merit no censure when uttered on a laughing lip, and in an homonymous world are in some sort useful, since they do serve to distinguish one Jack from his fellow. Remember me, therefore, as Sir Thomas Browne.'

'Are you a Sir? Oh, sorry!' He had heard of these gentlemen drivers. 'It *is* good of you about the ticket. But if you go on at this rate, however does your bus pay?'

'It does not pay. It was not intended to pay. Many are the faults of my equipage; it is compounded too curiously of foreign woods; its cushions tickle erudition rather than promote repose; and my horses are nourished not on the evergreen pastures of the moment, but on the dried bents and clovers of Latinity. But that it pays! – that error at all events was never intended and never attained.'

'Sorry again,' said the boy rather hopelessly. Sir Thomas looked sad, fearing that, even for a moment, he had been the cause of sadness. He invited the boy to come up and sit beside him on the box, and together they journeyed on through the fog, which was now changing from yellow to white. There were no houses by the road; so it must be either Putney Heath or Wimbledon Common.

'Have you been a driver always?'

'I was a physician once.'

'But why did you stop? Weren't you good?'

'As a healer of bodies I had scant success, and several score of my patients preceded me. But as a healer of the spirit I have succeeded beyond my hopes and my deserts. For though my draughts were not better nor subtler than those of other men, yet, by reason of the cunning goblets wherein I offered them, the queasy soul was ofttimes tempted to sip and be refreshed.'

'The queasy soul,' he murmured; 'if the sun sets with trees in front of it, and you suddenly come strange all over, is that a queasy soul?'

'Have you felt that?'

'Why yes.'

After a pause he told the boy a little, a very little, about the journey's end. But they did not chatter much, for the boy, when he liked a person, would as soon sit silent in his company as speak, and this, he discovered, was also the mind of Sir Thomas Browne and of many others with whom he was to be acquainted. He heard, however, about the young man Shelley, who was now quite a famous person, with a carriage of his own, and about some of the other drivers who are in the service of the Company. Meanwhile the light grew stronger, though the fog did not disperse. It was now more like mist than fog, and at times would travel quickly across them, as if it was part of a cloud. They had been ascending, too, in a most puzzling way; for over two hours the horses had been pulling against the collar, and even if it were Richmond Hill they ought to have been at the top long ago. Perhaps it was Epsom, or even the North Downs; yet the air seemed keener than that which blows on either. And as to the name of their destination, Sir Thomas Browne was silent.

Crash!

'Thunder, by Jove!' said the boy, 'and not so far off either. Listen to the echoes! It's more like mountains.'

He thought, not very vividly, of his father and mother. He saw them sitting down to sausages and listening to the storm. He saw his own empty place. Then there would be questions, alarms, theories, jokes, consolations. They would expect him back at lunch. To lunch he would not come, nor to tea, but he would be in for dinner, and so his day's truancy would be over. If he had had his purse he would have bought them presents – not that he should have known what to get them.

Crash!

The peal and the lightning came together. The cloud quivered as if it were alive, and torn streamers of mist rushed past. 'Are you afraid?' asked Sir Thomas Browne.

'What is there to be afraid of? Is it much farther?'

The horses of the omnibus stopped just as a ball of fire burst up and exploded with a ringing noise that was deafening but clear, like the noise of a blacksmith's forge. All the cloud was shattered.

'Oh, listen, Sir Thomas Browne! No, I mean look; we shall get a view at last. No, I mean listen; that sounds like a rainbow!'

The noise had died into the faintest murmur, beneath which another murmur grew, spreading stealthily, steadily, in a curve that widened but did not vary. And in widening curves a rainbow was spreading from the horses' feet into the dissolving mists.

'But how beautiful! What colours! Where will it stop? It is more like the rainbows you can tread on. More like dreams.'

The colour and the sound grew together. The rainbow spanned an enormous gulf. Clouds rushed under it and were pierced by it, and still it grew, reaching forward, conquering the darkness, until it touched something that seemed more solid than a cloud.

The boy stood up. 'What is that out there?' he called. 'What does it rest on, out at that other end?'

In the morning sunshine a precipice shone forth beyond the gulf. A precipice – or was it a castle? The horses moved. They set their feet upon the rainbow.

'Oh, look!' the boy shouted. 'Oh, listen! Those caves – or are they gateways? Oh, look between those cliffs at those ledges. I see people! I see trees!'

'Look also below,' whispered Sir Thomas. 'Neglect not the diviner Acheron.'

The boy looked below, past the flames of the rainbow that licked against their wheels. The gulf also had cleared, and in its depths there flowed an everlasting river. One sunbeam entered and struck a green pool, and as they passed over he saw three maidens rise to the surface of the pool, singing, and playing with something that glistened like a ring.

'You down in the water – ' he called.

They answered, 'You up on the bridge – ' There was a burst of music. 'You up on the bridge, good luck to you. Truth in the depth, truth on the height.'

'You down in the water, what are you doing?'

Sir Thomas Browne replied: 'They sport in the mancipiary possession of their gold'; and the omnibus arrived.

III

The boy was in disgrace. He sat locked up in the nursery of Agathox Lodge, learning poetry for a punishment. His father had said, 'My boy! I can pardon anything but untruthfulness,' and had caned him, saying at each stroke, 'There is *no* omnibus, *no* driver, *no* bridge, *no* mountain; you are a *truant*, a *guttersnipe*, a *liar*.' His father could be very stern at times. His mother had begged him to say he was sorry. But he could not say that. It was the greatest day of his life, in spite of the caning and the poetry at the end of it.

He had returned punctually at sunset – driven not by Sir Thomas Browne, but by a maiden lady who was full of quiet fun. They had talked of omnibuses and also of barouche landaus. How far away her gentle voice seemed now! Yet it was scarcely three hours since he had left her up the alley.

His mother called through the door. 'Dear, you are to come down and to bring your poetry with you.'

He came down, and found that Mr Bons was in the smoking-room with his father. It had been a dinner party.

'Here is the great traveller!' said his father grimly. 'Here is the young gentleman who drives in an omnibus over rainbows, while young ladies sing to him.' Pleased with his wit, he laughed.

'After all,' said Mr Bons, smiling, 'there is something a little like it in Wagner. It is odd how, in quite illiterate minds, you will find glimmers of Artistic Truth. The case interests me. Let me plead for the culprit. We have all romanced in our time, haven't we?'

'Hear how kind Mr Bons is,' said his mother, while his father said, 'Very well. Let him say his Poem, and that will do. He is going away to my sister on Tuesday, and *she* will cure him of this alley-sloping.' (Laughter.) 'Say your Poem.'

The boy began. '"Standing aloof in giant ignorance."'

His father laughed again – roared. 'One for you, my son! "Standing aloof in giant ignorance!" I never knew these poets talked sense. Just describes you. Here, Bons, you go in for poetry. Put him through it, will you, while I fetch up the whisky?'

'Yes, give me the Keats,' said Mr Bons. 'Let him say his Keats to me.'

So for a few moments the wise man and the ignorant boy were left alone in the smoking-room.

'"Standing aloof in giant ignorance, of thee I dream and of the Cyclades, as one who sits ashore and longs perchance to visit – "'

'Quite right. To visit what?'

'"To visit dolphin coral in deep seas,"' said the boy, and burst into tears.

'Come, come! why do you cry?'

'Because – because all these words that only rhymed before, now that I've come back they're me.'

Mr Bons laid the Keats down. The case was more interesting than he had expected. '*You?*' he exclaimed. 'This sonnet, *you?*'

'Yes – and look, farther on: "Aye, on the shores of darkness there is light, and precipices show untrodden green." It *is* so, sir. All these things are true.'

'I never doubted it,' said Mr Bons, with closed eyes.

'You – then you believe me? You believe in the omnibus and the driver and the storm and that return ticket I got for nothing and – '

'Tut, tut! No more of your yarns, my boy. I meant that I never doubted the essential truth of Poetry. Some day, when you have read more, you will understand what I mean.'

'But, Mr Bons, it *is* so. There *is* light upon the shores of darkness. I have seen it coming. Light and a wind.'

'Nonsense,' said Mr Bons.

'If I had stopped! They tempted me. They told me to give up my ticket – for you cannot come back if you lose your ticket. They called from the river for it, and indeed I was tempted, for I have never been so happy as among those precipices. But I thought of my mother and father, and that I must fetch them. Yet they will not come, though the road starts opposite our house. It has all happened as the people up there warned me, and Mr Bons has disbelieved me like everyone else. I have been caned. I shall never see that mountain again.'

'What's that about me?' said Mr Bons, sitting up in his chair very suddenly.

'I told them about you, and how clever you were, and how many books you had, and they said, "Mr Bons will certainly disbelieve you."'

'Stuff and nonsense, my young friend. You grow impertinent. I – well – I will settle the matter. Not a word to your father. I will cure you. To-morrow evening I will myself call here to take you for a walk, and at sunset we will go up this alley opposite and hunt for your omnibus, you silly little boy.'

His face grew serious, for the boy was not disconcerted, but leapt about the room singing, 'Joy! joy! I told them you would believe me. We will drive together over the rainbow. I told them that you would come.'

After all, could there be anything in the story? Wagner? Keats? Shelley? Sir Thomas Browne? Certainly the case was interesting.

And on the morrow evening, though it was pouring with rain, Mr Bons did not omit to call at Agathox Lodge.

The boy was ready, bubbling with excitement, and skipping about in a way that rather vexed the President of the Literary Society. They took a turn down Buckingham Park Road, and then – having seen that no one was watching them – slipped up the alley. Naturally enough (for the sun was setting) they ran straight against the omnibus.

'Good heavens!' exclaimed Mr Bons. 'Good gracious heavens!'

It was not the omnibus in which the boy had driven first, nor yet that in which he had returned. There were three horses – black, grey, and white, the grey being the finest. The driver, who turned round at the mention of goodness and of heaven, was a sallow man with terrifying jaws and sunken eyes. Mr Bons, on seeing him, gave a cry as if of recognition, and began to tremble violently.

The boy jumped in.

'Is it possible?' cried Mr Bons. 'Is the impossible possible?'

'Sir; come in, sir. It is such a fine omnibus. Oh, here is his name – Dan someone.'

Mr Bons sprang in too. A blast of wind immediately slammed the omnibus door, and the shock jerked down all the omnibus blinds, which were very weak on their springs.

'Dan . . . Show me. Good gracious heavens! we're moving.'

'Hooray!' said the boy.

Mr Bons became flustered. He had not intended to be kidnapped. He could not find the door-handle, nor push up the blinds. The omnibus was quite dark, and by the time he had struck a match, night had come on outside also. They were moving rapidly.

'A strange, a memorable adventure,' he said, surveying the interior of the omnibus, which was large, roomy, and constructed with extreme regularity, every part exactly answering to every other part. Over the door (the handle of which was outside) was written, '*Lasciate ogni baldanza voi che entrate*' – at least, that was what was written, but Mr Bons said that it was Lashy arty something, and that baldanza was a mistake for speranza. His voice sounded as if he was in church. Meanwhile, the boy called to the cadaverous driver for two return tickets. They were handed in without a word. Mr Bons covered his face with his hand and again trembled. 'Do you know who that is!' he whispered, when the little window had shut upon them. 'It is the impossible.'

'Well, I don't like him as much as Sir Thomas Browne, though I shouldn't be surprised if he had even more in him.'

'More in him?' He stamped irritably. 'By accident you have made the greatest discovery of the century, and all you can say is that there is more in this man. Do you remember those vellum books in my library, stamped with red lilies? This – sit still, I bring you stupendous news! – *this is the man who wrote them.*'

The boy sat quite still. 'I wonder if we shall see Mrs Gamp?' he asked, after a civil pause.

'Mrs – ?'

'Mrs Gamp and Mrs Harris. I like Mrs Harris. I came upon them quite suddenly. Mrs Gamp's bandboxes have moved over the rainbow so badly. All the bottoms have fallen out, and two of the pippins off her bedstead tumbled into the stream.'

'Out there sits the man who wrote my vellum books!' thundered Mr Bons, 'and you talk to me of Dickens and of Mrs Gamp?'

'I know Mrs Gamp so well,' he apologized. 'I could not help being glad to see her. I recognized her voice. She was telling Mrs Harris about Mrs Prig.'

'Did you spend the whole day in her elevating company?'

'Oh, no. I raced. I met a man who took me out beyond to a race-course. You run, and there are dolphins out at sea.'

'Indeed. Do you remember the man's name?'

'Achilles. No; he was later. Tom Jones.'

Mr Bons sighed heavily. 'Well, my lad, you have made a miserable mess of it. Think of a cultured person with your opportunities! A cultured person would have known all these characters and known what to have said to each. He would not have wasted his time with a Mrs Gamp or a Tom Jones. The creations of Homer, of Shakespeare, and of Him who drives us now, would alone have contented him. He would not have raced. He would have asked intelligent questions.'

'But, Mr Bons,' said the boy humbly, 'you will be a cultured person. I told them so.'

'True, true, and I beg you not to disgrace me when we arrive. No gossiping. No running. Keep close to my side, and never speak to these Immortals unless they speak to you. Yes, and give me the return tickets. You will be losing them.'

The boy surrendered the tickets, but felt a little sore. After all, he had found the way to this place. It was hard first to be disbelieved and then to be lectured. Meanwhile, the rain had stopped, and moonlight crept into the omnibus through the cracks in the blinds.

'But how is there to be a rainbow?' cried the boy.

'You distract me,' snapped Mr Bons. 'I wish to meditate on beauty. I wish to goodness I was with a reverent and sympathetic person.'

The lad bit his lip. He made a hundred good resolutions. He would imitate Mr Bons all the visit. He would not laugh, or run, or sing, or do any of the vulgar things that must have disgusted his new friends last time. He would be very careful to pronounce their names properly, and to remember who knew whom. Achilles did not know Tom Jones – at least, so Mr Bons said. The Duchess of Malfi was older than Mrs Gamp – at least, so Mr Bons said. He would be self-conscious, reticent, and prim. He would never say he liked anyone. Yet when the blind flew up at a chance touch of his head, all these good resolutions went to the winds, for the omnibus had reached the summit of a moonlit hill, and there was the chasm, and there, across it, stood the old precipices, dreaming, with their feet in the everlasting river. He exclaimed, 'The mountain! Listen to the new tune in the water! Look at the camp-fires in the ravines.' and Mr Bons, after a hasty glance, retorted, 'Water? Camp-fires? Ridiculous rubbish. Hold your tongue. There is nothing at all.'

Yet, under his eyes, a rainbow formed, compounded not of sunlight and storm, but of moonlight and the spray of the river. The three horses put their feet upon it. He thought it the finest rainbow he had seen, but did not dare to say so, since Mr Bons said that nothing was there. He leant out – the window had opened – and sang the tune that rose from the sleeping waters.

'The prelude to Rhinegold?' said Mr Bons suddenly. 'Who taught you these *leit motifs*?' He, too, looked out of the window. Then he behaved very oddly. He gave a choking cry, and fell back on to the omnibus floor. He writhed and kicked. His face was green.

'Does the bridge make you dizzy?' the boy asked.

'Dizzy!' gasped Mr Bons. 'I want to go back. Tell the driver.'

But the driver shook his head.

'We are nearly there,' said the boy. 'They are asleep. Shall I call? They will be so pleased to see you, for I have prepared them.'

Mr Bons moaned. They moved over the lunar rainbow, which ever and ever broke away behind their wheels. How still the night was! Who would be sentry at the Gate?

'I am coming,' he shouted, again forgetting the hundred resolutions. 'I am returning – I, the boy.'

'The boy is returning,' cried a voice to other voices, who repeated, 'The boy is returning.'

'I am bringing Mr Bons with me.'

Silence.

'I should have said Mr Bons is bringing me with him.'

Profound silence.

'Who stands sentry?'

'Achilles.'

And on the rocky causeway, close to the springing of the rainbow bridge, he saw a young man who carried a wonderful shield.

'Mr Bons, it is Achilles, armed.'

'I want to go back,' said Mr Bons.

The last fragment of the rainbow melted, the wheels sang upon the living rock, the door of the omnibus burst open. Out leapt the boy – he could not resist – and sprang to meet the warrior, who, stopping suddenly, caught him on his shield.

'Achilles!' he cried, 'let me get down, for I am ignorant and vulgar, and I must wait for that Mr Bons of whom I told you yesterday.'

But Achilles raised him aloft. He crouched on the wonderful shield, on heroes and burning cities, on vineyards graven in gold, on every dear passion, every joy, on the entire image of the Mountain that he had discovered, encircled, like it, with an everlasting stream. 'No, no,' he protested, 'I am not worthy. It is Mr Bons who must be up here.'

But Mr Bons was whimpering, and Achilles trumpeted and cried, 'Stand upright upon my shield!'

'Sir, I did not mean to stand! Something made me stand. Sir, why do you delay? Here is only the great Achilles, whom you knew.'

Mr Bons screamed, 'I see no one. I see nothing. I want to go back.' Then he cried to the driver, 'Save me! Let me stop in your chariot. I have honoured you. I have quoted you. I have bound you in vellum. Take me back to my world.'

The driver replied, 'I am the means and not the end. I am the food and not the life. Stand by yourself, as that boy has stood. I cannot save you. For poetry is a spirit; and they that would worship it must worship in spirit and in truth.'

Mr Bons – he could not resist – crawled out of the beautiful omnibus. His face appeared, gaping horribly. His hands followed, one gripping the step, the other beating the air. Now his shoulders emerged, his chest, his stomach. With a shriek of 'I see London,' he fell – fell against the hard, moonlit rock, fell into it as if it were water, fell through it, vanished, and was seen by the boy no more.

'Where have you fallen to, Mr Bons? Here is a procession arriving to honour you with music and torches. Here come the men and women whose names you know. The mountain is awake, the river is awake, over the race-course the sea is awaking those dolphins, and it is all for you. They want you – '

There was the touch of fresh leaves on his forehead. Some one had crowned him.

ΤΕΛΟΣ

From the *Kingston Gazette, Surbiton Times, and Raynes Park Observer.*

The body of Mr Septimus Bons has been found in a shockingly mutilated condition in the vicinity of the Bermondsey gas-works. The deceased's pockets contained a sovereign-purse, a silver cigar-case, a bijou pronouncing dictionary, and a couple of omnibus tickets. The unfortunate gentleman had apparently been hurled from a considerable height. Foul play is suspected, and a thorough investigation is pending by the authorities.

WYNDHAM LEWIS

Brotcotnaz

Madame Brotcotnaz is orthodox: she is the Breton woman at forty-five, from La Basse-Bretagne, the heart of Old Brittany, the region of the great Pardons. Frans Hals also would have passed from the painting of the wife of a petty burgess to Madame Brotcotnaz without any dislocation of his formulas or rupture of the time-sense. He would still have seen before him the black and white – the black broadcloth and white coiffe or caul; and for the white those virgated, slate-blue surfaces, the cold ink-black for the capital masses of the picture, would have appeared without a hitch. On coming to the face Frans Hals would have found his favourite glow of sallow-red, only deeper than he was accustomed to find in the flemish women. He would have gone to that part of the palette where the pigment lay for the men's faces at forty-five, the opposite end to the monticules of olive and sallow peach for the *juniors,* or the virgins and young wives.

The distillations of the breton orchard have almost subdued the obstinate yellow of jaundice, and Julie's face is a dull claret. In many tiny strongholds of eruptive red the more recent colour has entrenched itself. Her hair is very dark, parted in the middle, and tightly brushed down upon her head. Her eyebrows arc for ever raised. She could not depress them, I suppose, any more, if she wanted to. A sort of scaly rigor fixes the wrinkles of the forehead into a seriated field of what is scarcely flesh, with the result that if she pulled her eyebrows down, they would fly up again the moment she released the muscles. The flesh of the mouth is scarcely more alive: it is parched and pinched in, so that she seems always hiding a faint snicker by driving it primly into her mouth. Her eyes are black and moist, with the furtive intensity of a rat. They move circumspectly in this bloated shell. She displaces herself also more noiselessly than the carefulest nun, and her hands are generally decussated, drooping upon the ridge of her waist-line, as though fixed there with an emblematic nail, at about the level of her navel. Her stomach is, for her, a kind of exclusive personal 'calvary.' At its crest hang her two hands, with the orthodox decussation, an elaborate ten-fingered symbol.

Revisiting the home of the Brotcotnazes this summer, I expected to find some change: but as I came down the steep and hollow ramp leading from the cliffs of the port, I was reassured at once. The door of the *débit* I perceived was open, with its desiccated bush over the lintel. Julie, with her head bound up in a large surgical bandage, stood there peering out, to see if there were any one in sight. No one was in sight. I had not been noticed; it was not from the direction of the cliffs that she redoubted interruption. She quickly withdrew. I approached the door of the *débit* in my noiseless *espadrilles* (that is, the hemp and canvas shoes of the country), and sprang quickly in after her. I snapped her with my eye while I shouted:

'Madame Brotcotnaz! Attention!'

She was behind the bar-counter, the fat medicine-glass was in the air, reversed. Her head was back, the last drops were trickling down between her gum and underlip, which stuck out like the spout of a cream-jug. The glass crashed down on the counter; Julie jumped, her hand on her heart. Beneath, among tins and flagons, on a shelf, she pushed at a bottle. She was trying to get it out of sight. I rushed up to her and seized one of her hands.

'I am glad to see you, Madame Brotcotnaz!' I exclaimed. 'Neuralgia again?' I pointed to the face.

'Oh, que vous m'avez fait peur, Monsieur Kairor!'

She placed her hand on her left breast, and came out slowly from behind the counter.

'I hope the neuralgia is not bad?'

She patted her bandage with a sniff.

'It's the erysipelas.'

'How is Monsieur Brotcotnaz?'

'Very well, thank you, Monsieur Kairor!' she said in a subdued sing-song. 'Very well,' she repeated, to fill up, with a faint prim smile. 'He is out with the boat. And you, Monsieur Kairor? Are you quite well?'·

'Quite well. I thank you, Madame Brotcotnaz,' I replied, 'except perhaps a little thirsty. I have had a long walk along the cliff. Could we have a little glass together, do you think?'

'Why, yes, Monsieur Kairor.' She was more reserved at once. With a distant sniff, she turned half in the direction of the counter, her eyes on the wall before her. 'What must I give you now?'

'Have you any *pur jus*, such as I remember drinking the last time I was here?'

'Why, yes.' She moved silently away behind the wooden counter. Without difficulty she found the bottle of brandy, and poured me out a glass.

'And you, Madame? You will take one with me, isn't that so?'

'Mais, je veux bien!' she breathed with muted dignity, and poured herself out a small glass. We touched glasses.

'A votre santé, Madame Brotcotnaz!'

'A la vôtre, Monsieur Kairor!'

She put it chastely to her lip and took a decent sip, with the expression reserved otherwise for intercourse with the sacrament.

'It's good.' I smacked my lips.

'Why, yes. It is not at all bad,' she said, turning her head away with a faint sniff.

'It's good *pur jus*. If it comes to that, it is the best I have tasted since last I was here. How is it your *pur jus* is always of this high quality? You have taste where this drink is concerned, about that there can be no two opinions.'

She very softly tossed her head, wrinkled her nose on either side of the bridge, and appeared about to sneeze, which was the thing that came next before a laugh.

I leant across and lightly patted the bandage. She withdrew her head.

'It is painful?' I asked with commiseration.

My father, who, as I believe I have said, is a physician, once remarked in my hearing at the time my mother was drinking very heavily, prior to their separation, that for the management of alcoholic poisoning there is nothing better than koumiss.

'Have you ever tried a mixture of fermented mare's milk? Ordinary buttermilk will do. You add pepsin and lump sugar and let it stand for a day and a night. That is a very good remedy.'

She met this with an airy mockery. She dragged her eyes over my face afterwards with suspicion.

'It's excellent for erysipelas.'

She mocked me again. I told myself that she might at any moment find koumiss a useful drink, though I knew that she was wounded in the sex-war now only, and so required a management of another sort. I enjoyed arousing her veteran's contempt. She said nothing, but sat with resignation on the wooden bench at the table.

'I remember well these recurrent indispositions before, Madame Brot-cotnaz,' I said. She looked at me in doubt for a moment, then turned her face quickly towards the door, slightly offended.

Julie was, of course, secretive, but as it had happened, she was forced to hug her secrets in public like two dolls that every one could see. I pretended to snatch first one, then the other. She looked at me and saw that I was not serious. She was silent in the way a child is: she just silently looked at me with a primitive coquetry of reproach, and turned her side to me. – Underneath the counter on the left hand of a person behind it was the bottle of eau-de-vie. When every one else had gone to the river to wash clothes, or had collected in the neighbouring inn, she approached the bottle on tiptoe, poured herself out several glasses in succession, which she drank with little sighs. Everybody knew this. That was the first secret. I had ravished it impetuously as described. Her second secret was the periodic beatings of Brotcotnaz. They were of very great severity. When I had occupied a room there, the crashing in the next apartment at night lasted sometimes for twenty minutes. The next day Julie was bandaged and could hardly limp downstairs. That was the erysipelas. Every one knew this, as well: yet her secretiveness had to exercise itself upon these scandalously exposed objects. I just thought I would stroke the second of them when I approached my hand to her bandaged face. These intrusions of mine into a *public* secret bored her only. She knew as well as I did when a thing was secret and when it was not. *Qu'est-ce qu'il a, cet homme?* she would say to herself.

'When do you expect Nicholas?' I asked.

She looked at the large mournful clock.

'Il ne doit pas tarder.'

I lifted my glass.

'To his safe return.'

The first muscular indications of a sneeze, a prim depression of the mouth, and my remark had been acknowledged, while she lifted her glass and took a solid sip.

Outside it was a white calm: I had seen a boat round the corner, with folded sails, beneath the cliff. That was no doubt Brotcotnaz. As I passed. they had dropped their oars out.

He should be here in a moment.

'Fill up your glass, Madame Brotcotnaz,' I said.

She did not reply. Then she said in an indifferent catch of the breath,

'Here he is!' Hands folded, or decussated as I have said they always were, she left him to me. She had produced him with her exclamation, '*Le v'là!*'

A footfall, so light that it seemed nothing, came from the steps outside. A shadow struck the wall opposite the door. With an easy, dainty, and rapid tread, with a coquettishly supple giving of the knees at each step, and a gentle debonair oscillation of the massive head, a tall heavily-built fisherman came in. I sprang up and exclaimed:

'Ah! Here is Nicholas! How are you, old chap?'

'Why, it is Monsieur Kairor!' came the low caressing buzz of his voice. 'How are you? Well, I hope?'

He spoke in a low indolent voice. He smiled and smiled. He was dressed in the breton fashion.

'Was that you in the boat out there under the cliff just now?' I asked.

'Why, yes, Monsieur Kairor, that must have been us. Did you see us?' he said, with smiling interest.

I noted his child's pleasure at the image of himself somewhere else, in his boat, observed by me. It was as though I had said, Peep-oh! I see you, and we were back in the positions we then had occupied. He reflected a moment.

'I didn't see you. Were you on the cliff? I suppose you've just walked over from Loperec?'

His instinct directed him to account for my presence, here, and then up on the cliff. It was not curiosity. He wished to have cause and effect properly displayed. He racked his brains to see if he could remember having noticed a figure following the path on the cliff.

'Taking a little walk?' he added then.

He sat on the edge of a chair, with the symmetrical propriety of his healthy and powerful frame, the balance of the seated figure of the natural man, of the european type, found in the quattrocento frescoes. Julie and he did not look at each other.

'Give Monsieur Brotcotnaz a drink at once,' I said.

Brotcotnaz made a deprecatory gesture as she poured it, and continued to smile abstractedly at the table.

The dimensions of his eyes, and their oily suffusion with smiling-cream, or with some luminous jelly that seems still further to magnify them, are very remarkable. They are great tender mocking eyes that express the coquetry and contentment of animal fats. The sides of his massive forehead are often flushed, as happens with most men only in moments of embarrassment. Brotcotnaz is always embarrassed. But the flush with him, I think, is a constant affluence of blood to the neighbour-hood of his eyes, and has something to do with their magnetic machinery. The tension caused in the surrounding vessels by this aesthetic concentration may account for it. What we call a sickly smile, the mouth remaining lightly drawn across the gums, with a slight painful contraction – the set suffering grin of the timid – seldom leaves his face.

The tread of this timid giant is softer than a nun's – the supple quick-giving at the knees at each step that I have described is the result no doubt of his fondness for the dance, in which he was so rapid, expert, and resourceful in his youth. When I first stayed with them, the year before, a man one day was playing a pipe on the cliff into the hollow of which the house is built. Brotcotnaz heard the music and drummed upon the table. Then, lightly springing up, he danced in his tight-fitting black clothes a finicky hornpipe, in the middle of the *débit*. His red head was balanced in the air, face downwards, his arms went up alternately over his head, while he watched his feet like a dainty cat, placing them lightly and quickly here and there, with a ceremonial tenderness, and then snatching them away.

'You are fond of dancing,' I said.

His large tender steady blue eyes, suffused with the witchery of his secret juices, smiled and smiled: he informed me softly:

J'suis maître danseur. C'est mon plaisir!'

The buzzing breton drawl, with as deep a 'z' as the dialect of Somerset, gave a peculiar emphasis to the *C'est mon plaisir!* He tapped the table, and gazed with the full benignity of his grin into my face.

'I am master of all the breton dances,' he said.

'The aubade, the gavotte – ?'

'Why, yes, the breton gavotte.' He smiled serenely into my face. It was a blast of innocent happiness.

I saw as I looked at him the noble agility of his black faun-like figure as it must have rushed into the dancing crowd at the Pardon, leaping up into the air and capering to the *biniou* with grotesque elegance, while a crowd would gather to watch him. Then taking hands, while still holding their black umbrellas, they would spread out in chains, jolting in a dance confined to their rapidly moving feet. And still like a black fountain of movement, its vertex the flat, black, breton hat, strapped under the chin, he would continue his isolated performance. – His calm assurance of mastery in these dances implied such a position in the past in the festal life of the pagan countryside.

'Is Madame fond of dancing?' I asked.

'Why, yes. Julie can dance.'

He rose, and extending his hand to his wife with an indulgent gallantry, he exclaimed:

'Viens donc, Julie! Come then. Let us dance.'

Julie sat and sneered through her vinous mask at her fascinating husband. He insisted, standing over her with one toe pointed outward in the first movement of the dance, his hand held for her to take in a courtly attitude.

'Viens donc, Julie! Dansons un peu!'

Shedding shamefaced, pinched, and snuffling grins to right and left as she allowed herself to be drawn into this event, she rose. They danced a sort of minuet for me, advancing and retreating, curtseying and posturing, shuffling rapidly their feet. Julie did her part, it seemed, with understanding. With the same smile, at the same pitch, he resumed his seat in front of me.

'He composes verses also, to sing,' Julie then remarked.

'Songs for gavotte-airs, to be sung – ?'

'Why, yes. Ask him!'

I asked him.

'Why, yes,' he said. 'In the past I have written many verses.'

Then, with his settled grin, he intoned and buzzed them through his scarcely parted teeth, whose tawny rows, he manipulating their stops with his tongue, resembled some exotic musical instrument.

Brotcotnaz is at once a fisherman, *débitant* or saloon-keeper, and 'cultivator.' In spite of this trinity of activities, he is poor. To build their present home he dissipated what was then left of Julie's fortune, so I was told by the postman one evening on the cliff. When at length it stood complete, beneath the little red bluff hewn out for its reception, brightly whitewashed, with a bald slate roof, and steps leading up to the door from the steep and rugged space in front of it, he celebrated its completion with an expressive house-warming. Now he has the third share in a fishing boat, and what trade comes his way as a saloon-keeper, but it is very little.

His comrades will tell you that he is a '*charmant garçon, mais jaloux.*' They call him '*traître.*' He has been married twice. Referring to this, gossip tells you he gave his first wife a hard life. If this is true, and by analogy, he may have killed her. In spite of this record, poor Julie 'would have him.' Three times he has inherited money which was quickly spent. Such is his bare history and the character people give him.

The morning after a beating – Julie lying seriously battered upon their bed, or sitting rocking herself quietly in the *débit*, her head a turban of bandages, he noiselessly attends to her wants, enquires how she feels, and applies remedies. It is like a surgeon and a patient, an operation having just been successfully performed. He will walk fifteen miles to the nearest large town and back to get the necessary medicines. He is grave, and receives pleasantly your commiserations on her behalf, if you offer them. He has a delicate wife, that is the idea: she suffers from a chronic complaint. He addresses her on all occasions with a compassionate gentleness. There is, however, something in the bearing of both that suggests restraint. They are resigned, but none the less they remember the cross they have to bear. Julie will refer to his intemperance, casually, sometimes. She told me on one occasion, that, when first married, they had had a jay. This bird knew when Brotcotnaz was drunk. When he came in from a wake or 'Pardon,' and sat down at the *débit* table, the jay would hop out of its box, cross the table, and peck at his hands and fly in his face.

The secret of this smiling giant, a year or two younger, I daresay, than his wife, was probably that he intended to kill her. She had no more money. With his reputation as a wife-beater, he could do this without being molested. When he went to a 'Pardon,' she on her side knew he would try to kill her when he came back. That seemed to be the situation. If one night he did succeed in killing her, he would sincerely mourn her. At the *fiançailles* with his new bride he would see this one on the chair before him, his Julie, and, still radiating tolerance and health, would shed a melancholy smiling tear.

'You remember, Nicholas, those people that called on Thursday?' she now said.

He frowned gently to recall them.

'Ah, yes, I know – the Parisians that wanted the room.'

'They have been here again this afternoon.'

'Indeed.'

'I have agreed to take them. They want a little cooking. I've consented to do that. I said I had to speak to my husband about it. – They are coming back.'

He frowned more heavily, still smiling. He put his foot down with extreme softness:

'Julie, I have told you that I won't have that! It is useless for you to agree to do cooking. It is above your strength, my poor dear. You must tell them you can't do it.'

'But – they are returning. They may be here at any moment, now. I can do what they wish quite easily.'

With inexorable tenderness he continued to forbid it. Perhaps he did not want people in the house.

'Your health will not permit of your doing that, Julie.'

He never ceased to smile, but his brows remained knit. This was almost a dispute. They began talking in breton.

'Nicholas, I must go,' I said, getting up. He rose with me, following me up with the redoubled suavity of his swimming eyes.

'You must have a drink with me, Monsieur Kairor. Truly you must! Julie! Another glass for Monsieur Kairor.'

I drank it and left, promising to return. He came down the steps with me, his knee flexing with exaggerated suppleness at each step, placing his feet daintily and noiselessly on the dryest spaces on the wet stones. I watched him over my shoulder returning delicately up the steps, his massive back rigid, inclined forward, as though he were being steadily hauled up with a cord, only his feet working.

It was nearly three weeks later when I returned to Kermanec. It was in the morning. This time I came over in a tradesman's cart. It took me to the foot of the rough ascent, at the top of which were Brotcotnaz's steps. There seemed to be a certain animation. Two people were talking at the door, and a neighbour, the proprietress of the successful *débit*, was ascending the steps. The worst had happened. *Ça y est.* He had killed her! Taking this for granted, I entered the *débit*, framing my *condoléances*. She would be upstairs on the bed. Should I go up? There were several people in the room. As I entered behind them, with a start of surprise I recognized Julie. Her arm was in a large sling. From beneath stained cloths, four enormously bloated and discoloured fingers protruded. These the neighbours inspected. Also one of her feet had a large bandage. She looked like a beggar at a church door: I could almost hear the familiar cry of the '*droit des pauvres!*' She was speaking in breton, in her usual tone of '*miséricorde*,' with her ghostly sanctimonious snigger. In spite of this, even if the circumstances had not made this obvious, the atmosphere was very different from that to which I had been accustomed.

At first I thought: She has killed Brotcotnaz, it must be that. But that hypothesis was contradicted by every other fact that I knew about them. It was possible that he had killed himself by accident. But, unnoticed, in the dark extremity of the *débit*, there he was! On catching sight of his dejected figure, thrust into the darkest shadow of his saloon, I received my second shock of surprise. I hesitated in perplexity. Would it be better to withdraw? I went up to Julie, but made no reference to her condition, beyond saying that I hoped she was well.

'As well as can be expected, my poor Monsieur Kairor!' she said in a sharp whine, her brown eyes bright, clinging and sad.

Recalling the events of my last visit and our conversation, in which I had tapped her bandages, I felt these staring fingers, thrust out for inspection, were a leaf taken out of my book. What new policy was this? I left her and went over to Brotcotnaz. He did not spring up: all he did was to smile weakly, saying:

'*Tiens! Monsieur Kairor, vous voilà.* – Sit down, Monsieur Kairor!'

I sat down. With his elbows on the table he continued to stare into space. Julie and her women visitors stood in the middle of the *débit*; in subdued voices they continued their discussion. It was in breton, I could not follow it easily.

This situation was not normal: yet the condition of Julie was the regular one. The intervention of the neighbours and the present dejection of Brotcotnaz was what was unaccountable. Otherwise, for the cause of the mischief there was no occasion to look further; a solution, sound, traditional, and in every way satisfying, was there before me in the person of Nicholas. But he whom I was always accustomed to see master of the situation was stunned and changed, like a man not yet recovered from some horrid experience. He, the recognized agent of Fate, was usually so above the mêlée. Now he looked another man, like somebody deprived of a coveted office, or from whom some privilege had been withheld. Had Fate acted without him? Such necessarily was the question that at this point took shape.

Meanwhile I no doubt encountered in turn a few of the perplexities, framing the same dark questions, that Brotcotnaz himself had done. He pulled himself together now and rose slowly,

'You will take something, Monsieur Kairor!' he said, habit operating, with a thin unction.

'Why, yes, I will have a glass of cider,' I said. 'What will you have, Nicholas?'

'Why, I will take the same, Monsieur Kairor,' he said. The break or give at the knee as he walked was there as usual, but mechanical, I felt. Brotcotnaz would revive, I hoped, after his drink. Julie was describing something: she kept bending down to the floor, and making a sweeping gesture with her free hand. Her guests made a chuckling sound in their throats like 'hoity-toity.'

Brotcotnaz returned with the drinks.

'*A la vôtre, Monsieur Kairor!*' He drank half his glass. Then he said:

'You have seen my wife's fingers?'

I admitted guardedly that I had noticed them.

'Higher up it is worse. The bone is broken. The doctor says that it is possible she will lose her arm. Her leg is also in a bad state.' He rolled his head sadly.

At last I looked at him with relief. He was regaining his old composure. I saw at once that a very significant thing had happened for him, if she lost her arm, and possibly her leg. He could scarcely proceed to the destruction of the trunk only. It was not difficult at least to appreciate the sort of problem that might present itself.

'Her erysipelas is bad this time, there is no use denying it,' I said.

A look of confusion came into his face. He hesitated a moment. His ill-working brain had to be adjusted to a past time, when what now possessed him was not known. He disposed himself in silence, then started in an astonished voice, leaning over the table:

'It isn't the erysipelas, Monsieur Kairor! Haven't you heard?'

'No, I have heard nothing. In fact, I have only just arrived.'

Now I was going to hear some great news from this natural casuist: or was I not? It was *not* erysipelas.

Julie had caught the word 'erysipelas' whispered by her husband. She leered round at me, standing on one leg, and tossed me a desperate snigger of secretive triumph, very well under control and as hard as nails.

Brotcotnaz explained.

The baker had asked her, on driving up the day before, to put a stone under the wheel of his cart, to prevent it from moving. She had bent down to do so, pushing the stone into position, but suddenly the horse backed: the wheel went over her hand. That was not all. At this she slipped on the stony path, blood pouring from her fingers, and went partly under the cart. Bystanders shouted, the horse started forward, and the cart went over her arm and foot in the reverse direction.

He told me these facts with astonishment – the sensation felt by him when he had heard them for the first time. He was glad to tell me. There was a misunderstanding, or half misunderstanding, on the part of his wife and all the others in this matter. He next told me how he had first heard the news.

At the time this accident had occurred he had been at sea. On landing he was met by several neighbours.

'Your wife is injured! She has been seriously injured!'

'What's that? My wife injured? My wife seriously injured!' – Indeed I understood him! I began to feel as he did. 'Seriously' was the word stressed naïvely by him. He repeated these words, and imitated his expression. He reproduced for me the dismay and astonishment, and the shade of over-powering suspicion, that his voice must originally have registered.

It was now that I saw him encountering all the notions that had come into my own mind a few minutes before, on first perceiving the injured woman, the visiting neighbours and his dejected form thrown into the shade by something.

'Your wife is seriously injured!' I stood there altogether upset – *tout à fait bouleversé*.

The familiar image of her battered form as seen on a *lendemain de Pardon* must have arisen in his mind. He is assailed with a sudden incapacity to think of injuries in his wife's case except as caused by a human hand. He is solicited by the reflection that he himself had not been there. There was, in short, the effect, but not the cause. Whatever his ultimate intention as regards Julie, he is a '*jaloux.*' All his wild jealousy surges up. A cause, a rival cause, is incarnated in his excited brain, and goes in an overbearing manner to claim its effect. In a second a man is born. He does not credit him, but he gets a foothold just outside of reason. He is a rival! – another Brotcotnaz: all his imagination is sickened by this super-Brotcotnaz, as a woman who had been delivered of some hero, already of heroic dimensions, might nat-urally find herself. A moment of great weakness and lassitude seizes him. He remains powerless at the thought of the aggressive actions of this hero. His mind succumbs to torpor, it refuses to contemplate this figure.

It was at this moment that some one must have told him the actual cause of the injuries. The vacuum of his mind, out of which all the machinery of habit had been momentarily emptied, filled up again with its accustomed furniture. But after this moment of intense void the fur-niture did not quite resume its old positions, some of the pieces never returned, there remained a blankness and desolate novelty in the destiny of Brotcotnaz. That was still his state at present.

I then congratulated Julie upon her escape. Her eyes peered into mine with derision. What part did I play in this? She appeared to think that I too had been outwitted. I sauntered over to the counter and withdrew the bottle of *eau-de-vie* from its hiding-place.

'Shall I bring it over to you?' I called to Brotcotnaz. I took it over. Julie followed me for a moment with her mocking gaze.

'I will be the *débitant*!' I said to Brotcotnaz.

I poured him out a stiff glass.

'You live too near the sea,' I told him.

'Needs must,' he said, 'when one is a fisherman.'

'Ahès!' I sighed, trying to recall the famous line of the armorican song, that I was always meeting in the books that I had been reading. It began with this whistling sigh of the renegade king, whose daughter Ahès was.

'Why, yes,' Brotcotnaz sighed politely, supposing I had complimented the lot of the fisherman in my exclamation, doing the devil's tattoo on the table, as he crouched in front of me.

'Ahès, *bréman* Mary Morgan.' I had got it.

'I ask your pardon, Monsieur Kairor?'

'It is the lament of your legendary king for having been instrumental in poisoning the sea. You have never studied the lore of your country?'

'A little,' he smiled.

The neighbours were leaving. We three would now be alone. I looked at my watch. It was time to rejoin the cart that had brought me.

'A last drink, Madame Brotcotnaz!' I called.

She returned to the table and sat down, lowering herself to the chair, and sticking out her bandaged foot. She took the drink I gave her, and raised it almost with fire to her lips. After the removal of her arm, and possibly a foot, I realized that she would be more difficult to get on with than formerly. The bottle of *eau-de-vie* would remain no doubt in full view, to hand, on the counter, and Brotcotnaz would be unable to lay a finger on her: in all likelihood she meant that arm to come off.

I was not sorry for Nicholas; I regarded him as a changed man. Whatever the upshot of the accident as regards the threatened amputations, the disorder and emptiness that had declared itself in his mind would remain.

'To your speedy recovery, Madame Brotcotnaz,' I said.

We drank to that, and Brotcotnaz came to the door. Julie remained alone in the *débit*.

E. F. BENSON

The Bus-Conductor

My friend, Hugh Grainger, and I had just returned from a two days' visit in the country, where we had been staying in a house of sinister repute which was supposed to be haunted by ghosts of a peculiarly fearsome and truculent sort. The house itself was all that such a house should be, Jacobean and oak-panelled, with long dark passages and high vaulted rooms. It stood, also, very remote, and was encompassed by a wood of sombre pines that muttered and whispered in the dark, and all the time that we were there a south-westerly gale with torrents of scolding rain had prevailed, so that by day and night weird voices moaned and fluted in the chimneys, a company of uneasy spirits held colloquy among the trees, and sudden tattoos and tappings beckoned from the window-panes. But in spite of these surroundings, which were sufficient in themselves, one would almost say, to spontaneously generate occult phenomena, nothing of any description had occurred. I am bound to add, also, that my own state of mind was peculiarly well adapted to receive or even to invent the sights and sounds we had gone to seek, for I was, I confess, during the whole time that we were there, in a state of abject apprehension, and lay awake both nights through hours of terrified unrest, afraid of the dark, yet more afraid of what a lighted candle might show me.

Hugh Grainger, on the evening after our return to town, had dined with me, and after dinner our conversation, as was natural, soon came back to these entrancing topics.

'But why you go ghost-seeking I cannot imagine,' he said, 'because your teeth were chattering and your eyes starting out of your head all the time you were there, from sheer fright. Or do you like being frightened?'

Hugh, though generally intelligent, is dense in certain ways; this is one of them.

'Why, of course, I like being frightened,' I said. 'I want to be made to creep and creep and creep. Fear is the most absorbing and luxurious of emotions. One forgets all else if one is afraid.'

'Well, the fact that neither of us saw anything,' he said, 'confirms what I have always believed.'

'And what have you always believed?'

'That these phenomena are purely objective, not subjective, and that one's state of mind has nothing to do with the perception that perceives them, nor have circumstances or surroundings anything to do with them either. Look at Osburton. It has had the reputation of being a haunted house for years, and it certainly has all the accessories of one. Look at yourself, too, with all your nerves on edge, afraid to look round or light a candle for fear of seeing something! Surely there was the right man in the right place then, if ghosts are subjective.'

He got up and lit a cigarette, and looking at him – Hugh is about six feet high, and as broad as he is long – I felt a retort on my lips, for I could not help my mind going back to a certain period in his life, when, from some cause which, as far as I knew, he had never told anybody, he had become a mere quivering mass of disordered nerves. Oddly enough, at the same moment and for the first time, he began to speak of it himself.

'You may reply that it was not worth my while to go either,' he said, 'because I was so clearly the wrong man in the wrong place. But I wasn't. You for all your apprehensions and expectancy have never seen a ghost. But I have, though I am the last person in the world you would have thought likely to do so, and, though my nerves are steady enough again now, it knocked me all to bits.'

He sat down again in his chair.

'No doubt you remember my going to bits,' he said, 'and since I believe that I am sound again now, I should rather like to tell you about it. But before I couldn't; I couldn't speak of it at all to anybody. Yet there ought to have been nothing frightening about it; what I saw was certainly a most useful and friendly ghost. But it came from the shaded side of things; it looked suddenly out of the night and the mystery with which life is surrounded.'

'I want first to tell you quite shortly my theory about ghost-seeing,' he continued, 'and I can explain it best by a simile, an image. Imagine then that you and I and everybody in the world are like people whose eye is directly opposite a little tiny hole in a sheet of cardboard which is continually shifting and revolving and moving about. Back to back with that sheet of cardboard is another, which also, by laws of its own, is in perpetual but independent motion. In it too there is another hole, and when, fortuitously it would seem, these two holes, the one through which we are always looking, and the other in the spiritual plane, come opposite one another, we see through, and then only do the sights and sounds of the spiritual world become visible or audible to us. With most people these holes never come opposite each other during their life. But at the hour of death they do, and then they remain stationary. That, I fancy, is how we 'pass over.'

'Now, in some natures, these holes are comparatively large, and are constantly coming into opposition. Clairvoyants, mediums are like that. But, as far as I knew, I had no clairvoyant or mediumistic powers at all. I therefore am the sort of person who long ago made up his mind that he never would see a ghost. It was, so to speak, an incalculable chance that my minute spy-hole should come into opposition with the other. But it did: and it knocked me out of time.'

I had heard some such theory before, and though Hugh put it rather picturesquely, there was nothing in the least convincing or practical about it. It might be so, or again it might not.

'I hope your ghost was more original than your theory,' said I, in order to bring him to the point.

'Yes, I think it was. You shall judge.'

I put on more coal and poked up the fire. Hugh has got, so I have always considered, a great talent for telling stories, and that sense of drama which is so necessary for the narrator. Indeed before now, I have suggested to him that he should take this up as a profession, sit by the fountain in Piccadilly Circus, when times are, as usual, bad, and tell stories to the passers-by in the street, Arabian fashion, for reward. The most part of mankind, I am aware, do not like long stories, but to the few, among whom I number myself, who really like to listen to lengthy accounts of experiences, Hugh is an ideal narrator. I do not care for his theories, or for his similes, but when it comes to facts, to things that happened, I like him to be lengthy.

'Go on, please, and slowly,' I said. 'Brevity may be the soul of wit, but it is the ruin of story-telling. I want to hear when and where and how it all was, and what you had for lunch and where you had dined and what – '

Hugh began:

'It was the 24th of June, just eighteen months ago,' he said. 'I had let my flat, you may remember, and came up from the country to stay with you for a week. We had dined alone here – '

I could not help interrupting.

'Did you see the ghost here?' I asked. 'In this square little box of a house in a modern street?'

'I was in the house when I saw it.'

I hugged myself in silence.

'We had dined alone here in Graeme Street,' he said, 'and after dinner I went out to some party, and you stopped at home. At dinner your man did not wait, and when I asked where he was, you told me he was ill, and, I thought, changed the subject rather abruptly. You gave me your latch-key when I went out, and on coming back, I found you had gone to bed. There were, however, several letters for me, which required answers. I wrote them there and then, and posted them at the pillar-box opposite. So I suppose it was rather late when I went upstairs.

'You had put me in the front room, on the third floor, overlooking the street, a room which I thought you generally occupied yourself. It was a very hot night, and though there had been a moon when I started to my party, on my return the whole sky was cloud-covered, and it both looked and felt as if we might have a thunderstorm before morning. I was feeling very sleepy and heavy, and it was not till after I had got into bed that I noticed by the shadows of the window-frames on the blind that only one of the windows was open. But it did not seem worth while to get out of bed in order to open it, though I felt rather airless and uncomfortable, and I went to sleep.

'What time it was when I awoke I do not know, but it was certainly not yet dawn, and I never remember being conscious of such an extraordinary stillness as prevailed. There was no sound either of foot-passengers or wheeled traffic; the music of life appeared to be absolutely mute. But now instead of being sleepy and heavy, I felt, though I must have slept an hour or two at most, since it was not yet dawn, perfectly fresh and wide-awake, and the effort which had seemed not worth making before, that of getting out of bed and opening the other window, was quite easy now, and I pulled up the blind, threw it wide open, and leaned out, for somehow I parched and pined for air. Even outside the oppression was very noticeable, and though, as you know, I am not easily given to feel the mental effects of climate, I was aware of an awful creepiness coming over me. I tried to analyse it away, but without success; the past day had been pleasant, I looked forward to another pleasant day to-morrow, and yet I was full of some nameless apprehension. I felt, too, dreadfully lonely in this stillness before the dawn.

'Then I heard suddenly and not very far away the sound of some approaching vehicle; I could distinguish the tread of two horses walking at a slow foot's pace. They were, though yet invisible, coming up the street, and yet this indication of life did not abate that dreadful sense of loneliness which I have spoken of. Also in some dim unformulated way that which was coming seemed to me to have something to do with the cause of my oppression.

'Then the vehicle came into sight. At first I could not distinguish what it was. Then I saw that the horses were black and had long tails, and that what they dragged was made of glass, but had a black frame. It was a hearse. Empty.

'It was moving up this side of the street. It stopped at your door.

'Then the obvious solution struck me. You had said at dinner that your man was ill, and you were, I thought, unwilling to speak more about his illness. No doubt, so I imagined now, he was dead, and for some reason, perhaps because you did not want me to know anything about it, you were having the body removed at night. This, I must tell you, passed through my mind quite instantaneously, and it did not occur to me how unlikely it really was, before the next thing happened.

'I was still leaning out of the window, and I remember also wondering, yet only momentarily, how odd it was that I saw things – or rather the one thing I was looking at – so very distinctly. Of course, there was a moon behind the clouds, but it was curious how every detail of the hearse and the horses was visible. There was only one man, the driver, with it, and the street was otherwise absolutely empty. It was at him I was looking now. I could see every detail of his clothes, but from where I was, so high above him, I could not see his face. He had on grey trousers, brown boots, a black coat buttoned all the way up, and a straw hat. Over his shoulder there was a strap, which seemed to support some sort of little bag. He looked exactly like – well, from my description what did he look exactly like?'

'Why – a bus-conductor,' I said instantly.

'So I thought, and even while I was thinking this, he looked up at me. He had a rather long thin face, and on his left cheek there was a mole with a growth of dark hair on it. All this was as distinct as if it had been noonday, and as if I was within a yard of him. But – so instantaneous was all that takes so long in the telling – I had not time to think it strange that the driver of a hearse should be so unfunereally dressed.

'Then he touched his hat to me, and jerked his thumb over his shoulder.'

'"Just room for one inside, sir," he said.

'There was something so odious, so coarse, so unfeeling about this that I instantly drew my head in, pulled the blind down again, and then, for what reason I do not know, turned on the electric light in order to see what time it was. The hands of my watch pointed to half-past eleven.

'It was then for the first time, I think, that a doubt crossed my mind as to the nature of what I had just seen. But I put out the light again, got into bed, and began to think. We had dined; I had gone to a party, I had come back and written letters, had gone to bed and had slept. So how could it be half-past eleven? . . . Or – *what* half-past eleven was it?

'Then another easy solution struck me; my watch must have stopped. But it had not; I could hear it ticking.

'There was stillness and silence again. I expected every moment to hear muffled footsteps on the stairs, footsteps moving slowly and smally under the weight of a heavy burden, but from inside the house there was no sound whatever. Outside, too, there was the same dead silence, while the hearse waited at the door. And the minutes ticked on and ticked on, and at length I began to see a difference in the light in the room, and knew that the dawn was beginning to break outside. But how had it happened then that if the corpse was to be removed at night it had not gone, and that the hearse still waited, when morning was already coming?

'Presently I got out of bed again, and with the sense of strong physical shrinking I went to the window and pulled back the blind. The dawn was coming fast; the whole street was lit by that silver hueless light of morning. But there was no hearse there.

'Once again I looked at my watch. It was just a quarter-past four. But I would swear that not half an hour had passed since it had told me that it was half-past eleven.

'Then a curious double sense, as if I was living in the present and at the same moment had been living in some other time, came over me. It was dawn on June 25th, and the street, as was natural, was empty. But a little while ago the driver of a hearse had spoken to me, and it was half-past eleven. What was that driver, to what plane did he belong? And again *what* half-past eleven was it that I had seen recorded on the dial of my watch?

'And then I told myself that the whole thing had been a dream. But if you ask me whether I believed what I told myself, I must confess that I did not.

'Your man did not appear at breakfast next morning, nor did I see him again before I left that afternoon. I think if I had, I should have told you about all this, but it was still possible, you see, that what I had seen was a real hearse, driven by a real driver, for all the ghastly gaiety of the face that had looked up to mine, and the levity of his pointing hand. I might possibly have fallen asleep soon after seeing him, and slumbered through the removal of the body and the departure of the hearse. So I did not speak of it to you.'

There was something wonderfully straightforward and prosaic in all this; here were no Jacobean houses oak-panelled and surrounded by weeping pine-trees, and somehow the very absence of suitable surroundings made the story more impressive. But for a moment a doubt assailed me.

'Don't tell me it was all a dream,' I said.

'I don't know whether it was or not. I can only say that I believe myself to have been wide awake. In any case the rest of the story is – odd.'

'I went out of town again that afternoon,' he continued, 'and I may say that I don't think that even for a moment did I get the haunting sense of what I had seen or dreamed that night out of my mind. It was present to me always as some vision unfulfilled. It was as if some clock had struck the four quarters, and I was still waiting to hear what the hour would be.

'Exactly a month afterwards I was in London again, but only for the day. I arrived at Victoria about eleven, and took the underground to Sloane Square in order to see if you were in town and would give me lunch. It was a baking hot morning, and I intended to take a bus from the King's Road as far as Graeme Street. There was one standing at the corner just as I came out of the station, but I saw that the top was full, and the inside appeared to be full also. Just as I came up to it the conductor who, I suppose, had been inside, collecting fares or what not, came out on to the step within a few feet of me. He wore grey trousers, brown boots, a black coat buttoned, a straw hat, and over his shoulder was a strap on which hung his little machine for punching tickets. I saw his face, too; it was the face of the driver of the hearse, with a mole on the left cheek. Then he spoke to me, jerking his thumb over his shoulder.

' "Just room for one inside, sir," he said.

'At that a sort of panic-terror took possession of me, and I know I gesticulated wildly with my arms, and cried, 'No, no!' But at that moment I was living not in the hour that was then passing, but in that hour which had passed a month ago, when I leaned from the window of your bedroom here just before the dawn broke. At this moment too I knew that my spy-hole had been opposite the spy-hole into the spiritual world. What I had seen there had some significance, now being fulfilled, beyond the significance of the trivial happenings of to-day and to-morrow. The Powers of which we know so little were visibly working before me. And I stood there on the pavement shaking and trembling.

'I was opposite the post-office at the corner, and just as the bus started my eye fell on the clock in the window there. I need not tell you what the time was.

'Perhaps I need not tell you the rest, for you probably conjecture it, since you will not have forgotten what happened at the corner of Sloane Square at the end of July, the summer before last. The bus pulled out from the pavement into the street in order to get round a van that was standing in front of it. At the moment there came down the King's Road a big motor going at a hideously dangerous pace. It crashed full into the bus, burrowing into it as a gimlet burrows into a board.'

He paused.

'And that's my story,' he said.

KATHERINE MANSFIELD

The Woman at the Store

All that day the heat was terrible. The wind blew close to the ground; it rooted among the tussock grass, slithered along the road, so that the white pumice dust swirled in our faces, settled and sifted over us and was like a dry-skin itching for growth on our bodies. The horses stumbled along, coughing and chuffing. The pack-horse was sick – with a big open sore rubbed under the belly. Now and again she stopped short, threw back her head, looked at us as though she were going to cry, and whinnied. Hundreds of larks shrilled; the sky was slate colour, and the sound of the larks reminded me of slate pencils scraping over its surface. There was nothing to be seen but wave after wave of tussock grass, patched with purple orchids and manuka bushes covered with thick spider webs.

Jo rode ahead. He wore a blue galatea shirt, corduroy trousers and riding boots. A white handkerchief, spotted with red – it looked as though his nose had been bleeding on it – was knotted round his throat. Wisps of white hair straggled from under his wideawake hat – moustache and eyebrows were called white – he slouched in the saddle, grunting. Not once that day had he sung

> 'I don't care, for don't you see,
> My wife's mother was in front of me!'

It was the first day we had been without it for a month, and now there seemed something uncanny in his silence. Jim rode beside me, white as a clown; his black eyes glittered and he kept shooting out his tongue and moistening his lips. He was dressed in a Jaeger vest and a pair of blue duck trousers, fastened round the waist with a plaited leather belt. We had hardly spoken since dawn. At noon we had lunched off fly biscuits and apricots by the side of a swampy creek.

'My stomach feels like the crop of a hen,' said Jo. 'Now then, Jim, you're the bright boy of the party – where's this 'ere store you kep' on talking about. "Oh yes," you says, "I know a fine store, with a paddock for the horses and a creek runnin' through, owned by a friend of mine who'll give yer a bottle of whisky before 'e shakes hands with yer." I'd like ter see that place – merely as a matter of curiosity – not that I'd ever doubt yer word – as yer know very well – *but . . .*'

Jim laughed. 'Don't forget there's a woman too, Jo, with blue eyes and yellow hair, who'll promise you something else before she shakes hands with you. Put that in your pipe and smoke it.'

'The heat's making you balmy,' said Jo. But he dug his knees into the horse. We shambled on. I half fell asleep and had a sort of uneasy dream that the horses were not moving forward at all – then that I was on a rocking-horse, and my old mother was scolding me for raising such a fearful dust from the drawing-room carpet. 'You've entirely worn off the pattern of the carpet,' I heard her saying, and she gave the reins a tug. I snivelled and woke to find Jim leaning over me, maliciously smiling.

'That was a case of all but,' said he. 'I just caught you. What's up? Been bye-bye?'

'No!' I raised my head. 'Thank the Lord we're arriving somewhere.'

We were on the brow of the hill, and below us there was a whare roofed with corrugated iron. It stood in a garden, rather far back from the road – a big paddock opposite, and a creek and a clump of young willow trees. A thin line of blue smoke stood up straight from the chimney of the whare; and as I looked a woman came out, followed by a child and a sheep dog – the woman carrying what appeared to me a black stick. She made gestures at us. The horses put on a final spurt, Jo took off his wideawake, shouted, threw out his chest, and began singing 'I don't care, for don't you see . . . ' The sun pushed through the pale clouds and shed a vivid light over the scene. It gleamed on the woman's yellow hair, over her flapping pinafore and the rifle she was carrying. The child hid behind her, and the yellow dog, a mangy beast, scuttled back into the whare, his tail between his legs. We drew rein and dismounted.

'Hallo,' screamed the woman. 'I thought you was three 'awks. My kid comes runnin' in ter me. "Mumma," says she, "there's three brown things comin' over the 'ill," says she. An' I comes out smart, I can tell yer. "They'll be 'awks," I says to her. Oh, the 'awks about 'ere, yer wouldn't believe.'

The 'kid' gave us the benefit of one eye from behind the woman's pinafore – then retired again.

'Where's your old man?' asked Jim.

The woman blinked rapidly, screwing up her face.

'Away shearin'. Bin away a month. I suppose ye're not goin' to stop, are yer? There's a storm comin' up.'

'You bet we are,' said Jo. 'So you're on your lonely, missus?'

She stood, pleating the frills of her pinafore, and glancing from one to the other of us, like a hungry bird. I smiled at the thought of how Jim had pulled Jo's leg about her. Certainly her eyes were blue, and what hair she had was yellow, but ugly. She was a figure of fun. Looking at her, you felt there was nothing but sticks and wires under that pinafore – her front teeth were knocked out, she had red, pulpy hands and she wore on her feet a pair of dirty Bluchers.

'I'll go and turn out the horses,' said Jim. 'Got any embrocation? Poi's rubbed herself to hell!'

' 'Arf a mo!' The woman stood silent a moment, her nostrils expanding as she breathed. Then she shouted violently, 'I'd rather you didn't stop . . . You *can't*, and there's the end of it. I don't let out that paddock any more. You'll have to go on; I ain't got nothing!'

'Well, I'm blest!' said Jo heavily. He pulled me aside. 'Gone a bit off 'er dot,' he whispered. 'Too much alone, *you know*,' very significantly. 'Turn the sympathetic tap on 'er, she'll come round all right.'

But there was no need – she had come round by herself.

'Stop if yer like!' she muttered, shrugging her shoulders. To me – 'I'll give yer the embrocation if yer come along.'

'Right-o, I'll take it down to them.' We walked together up the garden path. It was planted on both sides with cabbages. They smelled like stale dish-water. Of flowers there were double poppies and sweet-williams. One little patch was divided off by paua shells – presumably it belonged to the child – for she ran from her mother and began to grub in it with a broken clothes-peg. The yellow dog lay across the doorstep, biting fleas; the woman kicked him away.

'Gar-r, get away, you beast . . . the place ain't tidy. I 'aven't 'ad time ter fix things to-day – been ironing. Come right in.'

It was a large room, the walls plastered with old pages of English periodicals. Queen Victoria's Jubilee appeared to be the most recent number. A table with an ironing board and wash-tub on it, some wooden forms, a black horsehair sofa and some broken cane chairs pushed against the walls. The mantel-piece above the stove was draped in pink paper, further ornamented with dried grasses and ferns and a coloured print of Richard Seddon. There were four doors – one, judging from the smell, led into the 'Store,' one on to the 'backyard,' through a third I saw the bedroom. Flies buzzed in circles round the ceiling, and treacle papers and bundles of dried clover were pinned to the window curtains.

I was alone in the room; she had gone into the store for the embrocation. I heard her stamping about and muttering to herself: 'I got some, now where did I put that bottle? . . . It's behind the pickles . . . no, it ain't.' I cleared a place on the table and sat there, swinging my legs. Down in the paddock I could hear Jo singing and the sound of hammer strokes as Jim drove in the tent pegs. It was sunset. There is no twilight in our New Zealand days, but a curious half-hour when everything appears grotesque – it frightens – as though the savage spirit of the country walked abroad and sneered at what it saw. Sitting alone in the hideous room I grew afraid. The woman next door was a long time finding that stuff. What was she doing in there? Once I thought I heard her bang her hands down on the counter, and once she half moaned, turning it into a cough and clearing her throat. I wanted to shout 'Buck up!' but I kept silent.

'Good Lord, what a life!' I thought. 'Imagine being here day in, day out, with that rat of a child and a mangy dog. Imagine bothering about ironing. *Mad*, of course she's mad! Wonder how long she's been here – wonder if I could get her to talk.'

At that moment she poked her head round the door.

'Wot was it yer wanted?' she asked.

'Embrocation.'

'Oh, I forgot. I got it, it was in front of the pickle jars.'

She handed me the bottle.

'My, you do look tired, you do! Shall I knock yer up a few scones for supper? There's some tongue in the store, too, and I'll cook yer a cabbage if you fancy it.'

'Right-o.' I smiled at her. 'Come down to the paddock and bring the kid for tea.'

She shook her head, pursing up her mouth.

'Oh no. I don't fancy it. I'll send the kid down with the things and a billy of milk. Shall I knock up a few extry scones to take with yer ter-morrow?'

'Thanks.'

She came and stood by the door.

'How old is the kid?'

'Six – come next Christmas. I 'ad a bit of trouble with 'er one way an' another. I 'adn't any milk till a month after she was born and she sickened like a cow.'

'She's not like you – takes after her father?' Just as the woman had shouted her refusal at us before, she shouted at me then.

'No, she don't! She's the dead spit of me. Any fool could see that. Come on in now, Else, you stop messing in the dirt.'

I met Jo climbing over the paddock fence.

'What's the old bitch got in the store?' he asked.

'Don't know – didn't look.'

'Well, of all the fools. Jim's slanging you. What have you been doing all the time?'

'She couldn't find this stuff. Oh, my shakes, you are smart!'

Jo had washed, combed his wet hair in a line across his forehead, and buttoned a coat over his shirt. He grinned.

Jim snatched the embrocation from me. I went to the end of the paddock where the willows grew and bathed in the creek. The water was clear and soft as oil. Along the edges held by the grass and rushes white foam tumbled and bubbled. I lay in the water and looked up at the trees that were still a moment, then quivered lightly and again were still. The air smelt of rain. I forgot about the woman and the kid until I came back to the tent. Jim lay by the fire watching the billy boil.

I asked where Jo was, and if the kid had brought our supper.

'Pooh,' said Jim, rolling over and looking up at the sky.

'Didn't you see how Jo had been titivating? He said to me before he went up to the whare, "Dang it! she'll look better by night light – at any rate, my buck, she's female flesh!"'

'You had Jo about her looks – you had me too.'

'No – look here. I can't make it out. It's four years since I came past this way and I stopped here two days. The husband was a pal of mine once, down the West Coast – a fine, big chap, with a voice on him like a trombone. She'd been barmaid down the Coast – as pretty as a wax doll. The coach used to come this way then once a fortnight, that was before they opened the railway up Napier way, and she had no end of a time! Told me once in a confidential moment that she knew one hundred and twenty-five different ways of kissing!'

'Oh, go on, Jim! She isn't the same woman!'

' 'Course she is . . . I can't make it out. What I think is the old man's cleared out and left her: that's all my eye about shearing. Sweet life! The only people who come through now are Maoris and sundowners!'

Through the dark we saw the gleam of the kid's pinafore. She trailed over to us with a basket in her hand, the milk billy in the other. I unpacked the basket, the child standing by.

'Come over here,' said Jim, snapping his fingers at her.

She went, the lamp from the inside of the tent cast a bright light over her. A mean, undersized brat, with whitish hair and weak eyes. She stood, legs wide apart and her stomach protruding.

'What do you do all day?' asked Jim.

She scraped out one ear with her little finger, looked at the result and said, 'Draw.'

'Huh! What do you draw? Leave your ears alone!'

'Pictures.'

'What on?'

'Bits of butter paper an' a pencil of my Mumma's.'

'Boh! What a lot of words at one time!' Jim rolled his eyes at her. 'Baa-lambs and moo-cows?'

'No, everything. I'll draw all of you when you're gone, and your horses and the tent, and that one' – she pointed to me – 'with no clothes on in the creek. I looked at her where she couldn't see me from.'

'Thanks very much. How ripping of you,' said Jim. 'Where's Dad?'

The kid pouted. 'I won't tell you because I don't like yer face!' She started operations on the other ear.

'Here,' I said. 'Take the basket, get along home and tell the other man supper's ready.'

'I don't want to.'

'I'll give you a box on the ear if you don't,' said Jim savagely.

'Hie! I'll tell Mumma. I'll tell Mumma.' The kid fled.

We ate until we were full, and had arrived at the smoke stage before Jo came back, very flushed and jaunty, a whisky bottle in his hand.

' 'Ave a drink – you two!' he shouted, carrying off matters with a high hand. ' 'Ere, shove along the cups.'

'One hundred and twenty-five different ways,' I murmured to Jim.

'What's that? Oh! stow it!' said Jo. 'Why 'ave you always got your knife into me. You gas like a kid at a Sunday School beano. She wants us to go there to-night and have a comfortable chat. I' – he waved his hand airily – 'I got 'er round.'

'Trust you for that,' laughed Jim. 'But did she tell you where the old man's got to?'

Jo looked up. 'Shearing! You 'eard 'er, you fool!'

The woman had fixed up the room, even to a light bouquet of sweet-williams on the table. She and I sat one side of the table, Jo and Jim the other. An oil lamp was set between us, the whisky bottle and glasses, and a jug of water. The kid knelt against one of the forms, drawing on butter paper; I wondered, grimly, if she was attempting the creek episode. But Jo had been right about night time. The woman's hair was tumbled – two red spots burned in her cheeks – her eyes shone – and we knew that they were kissing feet under the table. She had changed the blue pinafore for a white calico dressing-jacket and a black skirt – the kid was decorated to the extent of a blue sateen hair ribbon. In the stifling room, with the flies buzzing against the ceiling and dropping on to the table, we got slowly drunk.

'Now listen to me,' shouted the woman, banging her fist on the table. 'It's six years since I was married, and four miscarriages. I says to 'im, I says, what do you think I'm doin' up 'ere? If you was back at the Coast I'd 'ave you lynched for child murder. Over and over I tells 'im – you've broken my spirit and spoiled my looks, and wot for – that's wot I'm driving at.' She clutched her head with her hands and stared round at us. Speaking rapidly, 'Oh, some days – an' months of them – I 'ear them two words knockin' inside me all the time – "Wot for!" but sometimes I'll be cooking the spuds an' I lifts the lid off to give 'em a prong and I 'ears, quite suddin again, "Wot for!" Oh! I don't mean only the spuds and the kid – I mean – I mean,' she hiccoughed – 'you know what I mean, Mr Jo.'

'I know,' said Jo, scratching his head.

'Trouble with me is,' she leaned across the table, 'he left me too much alone. When the coach stopped coming, sometimes he'd go away days, sometimes he'd go away weeks, and leave me ter look after the store. Back 'e'd come – pleased as Punch. "Oh, 'allo,"'e'd say. " 'Ow are you gettin' on? Come and give us a kiss." Sometimes I'd turn a bit nasty, and then 'e'd go off again, and if I took it all right, 'e'd wait till 'e could twist me round 'is finger, then 'e'd say, "Well, so long, I'm off," and do you think I could keep 'im? – not me!'

'Mumma,' bleated the kid, 'I made a picture of them on the 'ill, an' you an' me an' the dog down below.'

'Shut your mouth!' said the woman.

A vivid flash of lightning played over the room – we heard the mutter of thunder.

'Good rhing that's broke loose,' said Jo. 'I've 'ad it in me 'ead for three days.'

'Where's your old man now?' asked Jim slowly.

The woman blubbered and dropped her head on to the table. 'Jim, 'e's gone shearin' and left me alone again,' she wailed.

' 'Ere, look out for the glasses,' said Jo. 'Cheer-o, 'ave another drop. No good cryin' over spilt 'usbands! You, Jim, you blasted cuckoo!'

'Mr Jo,' said the woman, drying her eyes on her jacket frill, 'you're a gent, an' if I was a secret woman I'd place any confidence in your 'ands. I don't mind if I do 'ave a glass on that.'

Every moment the lightning grew more vivid and the thunder sounded nearer. Jim and I were silent – the kid never moved from her bench. She poked her tongue out and blew on her paper as she drew.

'It's the loneliness,' said the woman, addressing Jo – he made sheep's eyes at her – 'and bein' shut up 'ere like a broody 'en.' He reached his hand across the table and held hers, and though the position looked most uncomfortable when they wanted to pass the water and whisky, their hands stuck together as though glued. I pushed back my chair and went over to the kid, who immediately sat flat down on her artistic achievements and made a face at me.

'You're not to look,' said she.

'Oh, come on, don't be nasty!' Jim came over to us, and we were just drunk enough to wheedle the kid into showing us. And those drawings of hers were extraordinary and repulsively vulgar. The creations of a lunatic with a lunatic's cleverness. There was no doubt about it, the kid's mind was diseased. While she showed them to us, she worked herself up into a mad excitement, laughing and trembling, and shooting out her arms.

'Mumma,' she yelled. 'Now I'm going to draw them what you told me I never was to – now I am.'

The woman rushed from the table and beat the child's head with the flat of her hand.

'I'll smack you with yer clothes turned up if yer dare say that again,' she bawled.

Jo was too drunk to notice, but Jim caught her by the arm. The kid did not utter a cry. She drifted over to the window and began picking flies from the treacle paper.

We returned to the table – Jim and I sitting one side, the woman and Jo, touching shoulders, the other. We listened to the thunder, saying stupidly, 'That was a near one,' 'There it goes again,' and Jo, at a heavy hit, 'Now we're off,' 'Steady on the brake,' until rain began to fall, sharp as cannon shot on the iron roof.

'You'd better doss here for the night,' said the woman.

'That's right,' assented Jo, evidently in the know about this move.

'Bring up yer things from the tent. You two can doss in the store along with the kid – she's used to sleep in there and won't mind you.'

'Oh, Mumma, I never did,' interrupted the kid.

'Shut yer lies! An' Mr Jo can 'ave this room.'

It sounded a ridiculous arrangement, but it was useless to attempt to cross them, they were too far gone. While the woman sketched the plan of action, Jo sat, abnormally solemn and red, his eyes bulging, and pulling at his moustache.

'Give us a lantern,' said Jim, 'I'll go down to the paddock.' We two went together. Rain whipped in our faces, the land was light as though a bush fire was raging. We behaved like two children let loose in the thick of an adventure, laughed and shouted to each other, and came back to the whare to find the kid already bedded in the counter of the store. The woman brought us a lamp. Jo took his bundle from Jim, the door was shut.

'Good night all,' shouted Jo.

Jim and I sat on two sacks of potatoes. For the life of us we could not stop laughing. Strings of onions and half-hams dangled from the ceiling – wherever we looked there were advertisements for 'Camp Coffee' and tinned meats. We pointed at them, tried to read them aloud – overcome with laughter and hiccoughs. The kid in the counter stared at us. She threw off her blanket and scrambled to the floor, where she stood in her grey flannel night-gown rubbing one leg against the other. We paid no attention to her.

'Wot are you laughing at?' she said uneasily.

'You!' shouted Jim. 'The red tribe of you, my child.'

She flew into a rage and beat herself with her hands. 'I won't be laughed at, you curs – you.' He swooped down upon the child and swung her on to the counter.

'Go to sleep, Miss Smarty – or make a drawing – here's a pencil – you can use Mumma's account book.'

Through the rain we heard Jo creak over the boarding of the next room – the sound of a door being opened – then shut to.

'It's the loneliness,' whispered Jim.

'One hundred and twenty-five different ways – alas! my poor brother!'

The kid tore out a page and flung it at me.

'There you are,' she said. 'Now I done it ter spite Mumma for shutting me up 'ere with you two. I done the one she told me I never ought to. I done the one she told me she'd shoot me if I did. Don't care! Don't care!'

The kid had drawn the picture of the woman shooting at a man with a rook rifle and then digging a hole to bury him in.

She jumped off the counter and squirmed about on the floor biting her nails.

Jim and I sat till dawn with the drawing beside us. The rain ceased, the little kid fell asleep, breathing loudly. We got up, stole out of the whare, down into the paddock. White clouds floated over a pink sky – a chill wind blew; the air smelled of wet grass. Just as we swung into the saddle Jo came out of the whare – he motioned to us to ride on.

'I'll pick you up later,' he shouted.

A bend in the road, and the whole place disappeared.

REBECCA WEST

Indissoluble Matrimony

When George Silverton opened the front door he found that the house
was not empty for all its darkness. The spitting noise of the striking of
damp matches and mild, growling exclamations of annoyance told him
that his wife was trying to light the dining-room gas. He went in and
with some short, hostile sound of greeting lit a match and brought brightness into the little room. Then, irritated by his own folly in bringing
private papers into his wife's presence, he stuffed the letters he had brought
from the office deep into the pockets of his overcoat. He looked at her
suspiciously, but she had not seen them, being busy in unwinding her
orange motor veil. His eyes remained on her face to brood a little sourly
on her moving loveliness, which he had not been sure of finding: for she
was one of those women who create an illusion alternately of extreme
beauty and extreme ugliness. Under her curious dress, designed in some
pitifully cheap and worthless stuff by a successful mood of her indiscreet
taste – she had black blood in her – her long body seemed pulsing with
some exaltation. The blood was coursing violently under her luminous
yellow skin, and her lids, dusky with fatigue, drooped contentedly over
her great humid black eyes. Perpetually she raised her hand to the mass
of black hair that was coiled on her thick golden neck, and stroked it with
secretive enjoyment, as a cat licks its fur. And her large mouth smiled
frankly, but abstractedly, at some digested pleasure.

There was a time when George would have looked on this riot of
excited loveliness with suspicion. But now he knew it was almost certainly
caused by some trifle – a long walk through stinging weather, the report
of a Socialist victory at a by-election, or the intoxication of a waltz refrain
floating from the municipal band-stand across the flats of the local

recreation ground. And even if it had been caused by some amorous interlude he would not have greatly cared. In the ten years since their marriage
he had lost the quality which would have made him resentful. He now
believed that quality to be purely physical. Unless one was in good condition and responsive to the messages sent out by the flesh, Evadne could
hardly concern one. He turned the bitter thought over in his heart and
stung himself by deliberately gazing unmoved upon her beautiful joyful
body.

'Let's have supper now!' she said rather greedily.

He looked at the table and saw she had set it before she went out. As
usual she had been in an improvident hurry: it was carelessly done.
Besides, what an absurd supper to set before a hungry solicitor's clerk! In
the centre, obviously intended as the principal dish, was a bowl of plums,
softly red, soaked with the sun, glowing like jewels in the downward
stream of the incandescent light. Besides them was a great yellow melon,
its sleek sides fluted with rich growth, and a honeycomb glistening on a
willow-pattern dish. The only sensible food to be seen was a plate of
tongue laid at his place.

'I can't sit down to supper without washing my hands!'

While he splashed in the bathroom upstairs he heard her pull in a chair
to the table and sit down to her supper. It annoyed him. There was no
ritual about it. While he was eating the tongue she would be crushing
honey on new bread, or stripping a plum of its purple skin and holding
the golden globe up to the gas to see the light filter through. The meal
would pass in silence. She would innocently take his dumbness for a sign
of abstraction and forbear to babble. He would find the words choked on
his lips by the weight of dullness that always oppressed him in her presence. Then, just about the time when he was beginning to feel able to
formulate his obscure grievances against her, she would rise from the table
without a word and run upstairs to her work, humming in that uncanny,
negro way of hers.

And so it was. She ate with an appalling catholicity of taste, with a
nice child's love of sweet foods, and occasionally she broke into that
hoarse, beautiful croon. Every now and then she looked at him with too
obvious speculations as to whether his silence was due to weariness or
uncertain temper. Timidly she cut him an enormous slice of the melon,

which he did not want. Then she rose abruptly and flung herself into the rocking chair on the hearth. She clasped her hands behind her head and strained backwards so that the muslin stretched over her strong breasts. She sang softly to the ceiling.

There was something about the fantastic figure that made him feel as though they were not properly married.

'Evadne?'

' 'S?'

'What have you been up to this evening?'

'I was at Milly Stafordale's.'

He was silent again. That name brought up the memory of his courting days. It was under the benign eyes of blonde, plebeian Milly that he had wooed the distracting creature in the rocking chair.

Ten years before, when he was twenty-five, his firm had been reduced to hysteria over the estates of an extraordinarily stupid old woman, named Mrs Mary Ellerker. Her stupidity, grappling with the complexity of the sources of the vast income which rushed in spate from the properties of four deceased husbands, demanded oceans of explanations even over her weekly rents. Silverton alone in the office, by reason of a certain natural incapacity for excitement, could deal calmly with this marvel of imbecility. He alone could endure to sit with patience in the black-panelled drawing-room amidst the jungle of shiny mahogany furniture and talk to a mass of darkness, who rested heavily in the window-seat and now and then made an idiotic remark in a bright, hearty voice. But it shook even him. Mrs Mary Ellerker was obscene. Yet she was perfectly sane and, although of that remarkable plainness noticeable in most oft-married women, in good enough physical condition. She merely presented the loathsome spectacle of an ignorant mind, contorted by the artificial idiocy of coquetry, lack of responsibility, and hatred of discipline, stripped naked by old age. That was the real horror of her. One feared to think how many women were really like Mrs Ellerker under their armour of physical per- fection or social grace. For this reason he turned eyes of hate on Mrs Ellerker's pretty little companion, Milly Stafordale, who smiled at him over her embroidery with wintry northern brightness. When she was old she too would be obscene.

This horror obsessed him. Never before had he feared anything. He had never lived more than half-an-hour from a police station, and, as he had by some chance missed the melancholy clairvoyance of adolescence, he had never conceived of any horror with which the police could not deal. This disgust of women revealed to him that the world is a place of subtle perils. He began to fear marriage as he feared death. The thought of intimacy with some lovely, desirable and necessary wife turned him sick as he sat at his lunch. The secret obscenity of women! He talked darkly of it to his friends. He wondered why the Church did not provide a service for the absolution of men after marriage. Wife desertion seemed to him a beautiful return of the tainted body to cleanliness.

On his fifth visit to Mrs Ellerker he could not begin his business at once. One of Milly Stafordale's friends had come in to sing to the old lady. She stood by the piano against the light, so that he saw her washed with darkness. Amazed, of tropical fruit. And before he had time to apprehend the sleepy wonder of her beauty, she had begun to sing. Now he knew that her voice was a purely physical attribute, built in her as she lay in her mother's womb, and no index of her spiritual values. But then, as it welled up from the thick golden throat and clung to her lips, it seemed a sublime achievement of the soul. It was smouldering contralto such as only those of black blood can possess. As she sang her great black eyes lay on him with the innocent shamelessness of a young animal, and he remembered hopefully that he was good looking. Suddenly she stood in silence, playing with her heavy black plait. Mrs Ellerker broke into silly thanks. The girl's mother, who had been playing the accompaniment, rose and stood rolling up her music. Silverton, sick with excitement, was introduced to them. He noticed that the mother was a little darker than the conventions permit. Their name was Hannan – Mrs Arthur Hannan and Evadne. They moved lithely and quietly out of the room, the girl's eyes still lingering on his face.

The thought of her splendour and the rolling echoes of her voice disturbed him all night. Next day, going to his office, he travelled with her on the horse-car that bound his suburb to Petrick. One of the horses fell lame, and she had time to tell him that she was studying at a commercial college. He quivered with distress. All the time he had a dizzy illusion that she was nestling up against him. They parted shyly. During the next few days they met constantly. He began to go and see them in the evening at their home – a mean flat crowded with cheap glories of bead curtains and Oriental hangings that set off the women's alien beauty. Mrs Hannan was a widow and they lived alone, in a wonderful silence. He talked more than he had ever done in his whole life before. He took a dislike to the widow, she was consumed with fiery subterranean passions, no for guardian for the tender girl.

Now he could imagine with what silent rapture Evadne had watched his agitation. Almost from the first she had meant to marry him. He was physically attractive, though not strong. His intellect was gently stimulating like a mild white wine. And it was time she married. She was ripe for adult things. This was the real wound in his soul. He had tasted of a divine thing created in his time for dreams out of her rich beauty, her loneliness, her romantic poverty, her immaculate youth. He had known love. And Evadne had never known anything more than a magnificent physical adventure which she had secured at the right time as she would have engaged a cab to take her to the station in time for the cheapest excursion train. It was a quick way to light-hearted living. With loathing he remembered how in the days of their engagement she used to gaze purely into his blinking eyes and with her unashamed kisses incite him to extravagant embraces. Now he cursed her for having obtained his spiritual revolution on false pretences. Only for a little time had he had his illusion, for their marriage was hastened by Mrs Hannan's sudden death. After three months of savage mourning Evadne flung herself into marriage, and her excited candour had enlightened him very soon.

That marriage had lasted ten years. And to Evadne their relationship was just the same as ever. Her vitality needed him as it needed the fruit on the table before him. He shook with wrath and a sense of outraged decency.

'O George!' She was yawning widely.

'What's the matter?' he said without interest.

'It's so beastly dull.'

'I can't help that, can I?'

'No.' She smiled placidly at him. 'We're a couple of dull dogs, aren't we? I wish we had children.'

After a minute she suggested, apparently as an alternative amusement, 'Perhaps the post hasn't passed.'

As she spoke there was a rat-tat and the slither of a letter under the door. Evadne picked herself up and ran out into the lobby. After a second or two, during which she made irritating inarticulate exclamations, she came in reading the letter and stroking her bust with a gesture of satisfaction.

'They want me to speak at Longton's meeting on the nineteenth,' she purred.

'Longton? What's he up to?'

Stephen Longton was the owner of the biggest iron works in Petrick, a man whose refusal to adopt the livery of busy oafishness thought proper to commercial men aroused the gravest suspicions.

'He's standing as Socialist candidate for the town council.'

'. . . Socialist!' he muttered.

He set his jaw. That was a side of Evadne he considered as little as possible. He had never been able to assimilate the fact that Evadne had, two years after their marriage, passed through his own orthodox Radicalism to a passionate Socialism, and that after reading enormously of economics she had begun to write for the Socialist press and to speak successfully at meetings. In the jaundiced recesses of his mind he took it for granted that her work would have the lax fibre of her character: that it would be infected with her Oriental crudities. Although once or twice he had been congratulated on her brilliance, he mistrusted this phase of her activity as a caper of the sensualist. His eyes blazed on her and found the depraved, over-sexed creature, looking milder than a gazelle, holding out a hand-bill to him.

'They've taken it for granted!'

He saw her name – his name –

MRS EVADNE SILVERTON.

It was at first the blaze of stout scarlet letters on the dazzling white ground that made him blink. Then he was convulsed with rage.

'Georgie dear!'

She stepped forward and caught his weak body to her bosom. He wrenched himself away. Spiritual nausea made him determined to be a better man than her.

'A pair of you! You and Longton – !' he snarled scornfully. Then, seeing her startled face, he controlled himself.

'I thought it would please you,' said Evadne, a little waspishly.

'You mustn't have anything to do with Longton,' he stormed.

A change passed over her. She became ugly. Her face was heavy with intellect, her lips coarse with power. He was at arms with a Socialist lead. Much he would have preferred the bland sensualist again.

'Why?'

'Because' – his lips stuck together like blotting-paper – 'he's not the sort of man my wife should – should – '

With movements which terrified him by their rough energy, she folded up the bills and put them back in the envelope.

'George. I suppose you mean that he's a bad man.' He nodded.

'I know quite well that the girl who used to be his typist is his mistress.' She spoke it sweetly, as if reasoning with an old fool. 'But she's got consumption. She'll be dead in six months. In fact, I think it's rather nice of him. To look after her and all that.'

'My God!' He leapt to his feet, extending a shaking forefinger. As she turned to him, the smile dying on her lips, his excited weakness wrapped him in a paramnesic illusion: it seemed to him that he had been through all this before – a long, long time ago. 'My God, you talk like a woman off the streets!'

Evadne's lips lifted over her strong teeth. With clever cruelty she fixed his eyes with hers, well knowing that he longed to fall forward and bury his head on the table in a transport of hysterical sobs. After a moment of this torture she turned away, herself distressed by a desire to cry.

'How can you say such dreadful, dreadful things!' she protested, chokingly.

He sat down again. His eyes looked little and red, but they blazed on her. 'I wonder if you are,' he said softly.

'Are what?' she asked petulantly, a tear rolling down her nose.

'You know,' he answered, nodding.

'George, George, George!' she cried.

'You've always been keen on kissing and making love, haven't you, my precious? At first you startled me, you did! I didn't know women were like that.' From that morass he suddenly stepped on to a high peak of terror. Amazed to find himself sincere, he cried – 'I don't believe good women are!'

'Georgie, how can you be so silly!' exclaimed Evadne shrilly. 'You know quite well I've been as true to you as any woman could be.' She sought his eyes with a liquid glance of reproach. He averted his gaze, sickened at having put himself in the wrong. For even while he degraded his tongue his pure soul fainted with loathing of her fleshliness.

'I – I'm sorry.'

Too wily to forgive him at once, she showed him a lowering profile with downcast lids. Of course, he knew it was a fraud: an imputation against her chastity was no more poignant than a reflection on the cleanliness of her nails – rude and spiteful, but that was all. But for a time they kept up the deception, while she cleared the table in a steely silence.

'Evadne, I'm sorry. I'm tired.' His throat was dry. He could not bear the discord of a row added to the horror of their companionship. 'Evadne, do forgive me – I don't know what I meant by – '

'That's all right, silly!' she said suddenly and bent over the table to kiss him. Her brow was smooth. It was evident from her splendid expression that she was pre-occupied. Then she finished clearing up the dishes and took them into the kitchen. While she was out of the room he rose from his seat and sat down in the armchair by the fire, setting his bull-dog pipe alight. For a very short time he was free of her voluptuous presence. But she ran back soon, having put the kettle on and changed her blouse for a loose dressing-jacket, and sat down on the arm of his chair. Once or twice she bent and kissed his brow, but for the most part she lay back with his head drawn to her bosom, rocking herself rhythmically. Silverton, a little disgusted by their contact, sat quite motionless and passed into a doze. He revolved in his mind the incidents of his day's routine and remembered a snub from a superior. So he opened his eyes and tried to think of something else. It was then that he became conscious that the rhythm of Evadne's movement was not regular. It was broken as though she rocked in time to music. Music? His sense of hearing crept up to hear if there was any sound of music in the breaths she was emitting rather heavily every now and then. At first he could hear nothing. Then it struck him that each breath was a muttered phrase. He stiffened, and hatred flamed through his veins. The words came clearly through her lips . . . 'The present system of wage-slavery . . . '

'Evadne!' He sprang to his feet. 'You're preparing your speech!'

She did not move. 'I am,' she said.

'Damn it, you shan't speak!'

'Damn it, I will!'

'Evadne, you shan't speak! If you do I swear to God above I'll turn you out into the streets – ' She rose and came towards him. She looked black and dangerous. She trod softly like a cat with her head down. In spite of himself, his tongue licked his lips in fear and he cowered a moment before he picked up a knife from the table. For a space she looked down on him and the sharp blade.

'You idiot, can't you hear the kettle's boiling over?'

He shrank back, letting the knife fall on the floor. For three minutes he stood there controlling his breath and trying to still his heart. Then he followed her into the kitchen. She was making a noise with a basinful of dishes.

'Stop that row.'

She turned round with a dripping dish-cloth in her hand and pondered whether to throw it at him. But she was tired and wanted peace: so that she could finish the rough draft of her speech. So she stood waiting.

'Did you understand what I said then? If you don't promise me here and now – '

She flung her arms upwards with a cry and dashed past him. He made to run after her upstairs, but stumbled on the threshold of the lobby and sat with his ankle twisted under him, shaking with rage. In a second she ran downstairs again, clothed in a big cloak with a black bundle clutched to her breast. For the first time in their married life she was seized with a convulsion of sobs. She dashed out of the front door and banged it with such passion that a glass pane shivered to fragments behind her.

'What's this? What's this?' he cried stupidly, standing up. He perceived with an insane certainty that she was going out to meet some unknown lover. 'I'll come and tell him what a slut you are!' he shouted after her and stumbled to the door. It was jammed now and he had to drag at it.

The night was flooded with the yellow moonshine of midsummer: it seemed to drip from the lacquered leaves of the shrubs in the front garden. In its soft clarity he could see her plainly, although she was now two hundred yards away. She was hastening to the north end of Sumatra Crescent, an end that curled up the hill like a silly kitten's tail and stopped abruptly in green fields. So he knew that she was going to the young man who had just bought the Georgian Manor, whose elm trees crowned the hill. Oh, how he hated her! Yet he must follow her, or else she would cover up her adulteries so that he could not take his legal revenge. So he began to run – silently, for he wore his carpet slippers. He was only a hundred yards behind her when she slipped through a gap in the hedge to tread a field path. She still walked with pride, for though she was town-bred, night in the open seemed not at all fearful to her. As he shuffled in pursuit his carpet slippers were engulfed in a shining pool of mud: he raised one with a squelch, the other was left. This seemed the last humiliation. He kicked the other one off his feet and padded on in his socks, snuffling in anticipating of a cold. Then physical pain sent him back to the puddle to pluck out the slippers; it was a dirty job. His heart battered his breast as he saw that Evadne had gained the furthest hedge and was crossing the stile into the lane that ran up to the Manor gates.

'Go on, you beast!' he muttered. 'Go on, go on!' After a scamper he climbed the stile and thrust his lean neck beyond a mass of wilted hawthorn bloom that crumbled into vagrant petals at his touch.

The lane mounted yellow as cheese to where the moon lay on the iron tracery of the Manor gates. Evadne was not there. Hardly believing his eyes he hobbled over into the lane and looked in the other direction. There he saw her disappearing round the bend of the road. Gathering himself up to a run, he tried to think out his bearings. He had seldom passed this way, and like most people without strong primitive instincts he had no sense of orientation. With difficulty he remembered that after a mile's mazy wanderings between high hedges this lane sloped suddenly to the bowl of heather overhung by the moorlands, in which lay the Petrick reservoirs, two untamed lakes.

'Eh! she's going to meet him by the water!' he cursed to himself. He remembered the withered ash tree, seared by lightning to its root, that stood by the road at the bare frontier of the moor. 'May God strike her like that, he prayed,' 'as she fouls the other man's lips with her kisses. O God! let me strangle her. Or bury a knife deep in her breast.' Suddenly he broke into a lolloping run. 'O my Lord, I'll be able to divorce her. I'll be free. Free to live alone. To do my day's work and sleep my night's sleep without her. I'll get a job somewhere else and forget her. I'll bring her to the dogs. No clean man or woman in Petrick will look at her now. They won't have her to speak at that meeting now!' His throat swelled with joy, he leapt high in the air.

'I'll be about her. If I can prove that she's wrong with this man they'll believe me if I say she's a bad woman and drinks. I'll make her name a joke. And then – '

He flung wide his arms in ecstasy: the left struck against stone. More pain than he had thought his body could hold convulsed him, so that he sank on the ground hugging his aching arm. He looked backwards as he writhed and saw that the hedge had stopped; above him was the great stone wall of the county asylum. The question broke on him – was there any lunatic in its confines so slavered with madness as he himself? Nothing but madness could have accounted for the torrent of ugly words, the sea of uglier thoughts that was now a part of him. 'O God, me to turn like this!' he cried, rolling over full-length on the grassy bank by the roadside. That the infidelity of his wife, a thing that should have brought out the stern manliness of his true nature, should have discovered him as lecherous-lipped as any pot-house lounger, was the most infamous accident of his married life. The sense of sin descended on him so that his tears flowed hot and bitterly. 'Have I gone to the Unitarian chapel every Sunday morning and to the Ethical Society every evening for nothing?' his spirit asked itself in its travail. 'All those Browning lectures for nothing . . . ' He said the Lord's Prayer several times and lay for a minute quietly crying. The relaxation of his muscles brought him a sense of rest which seemed forgiveness falling from God. The tears dried on his cheeks. His calmer consciousness heard the sound of rushing waters mingled with the beating of blood in his ears. He got up and scrambled round the turn of the road that brought him to the withered ash tree.

He walked forward on the parched heatherland to the mound whose scarred sides, heaped with boulders, tufted with mountain grasses, shone before him in the moonlight. He scrambled up to it hurriedly and hoisted himself from ledge to ledge till he fell on his knees with a squeal of pain. His ankle was caught in a crevice of the rock. Gulping down his agony at this final physical humiliation he heaved himself upright and raced on to the summit, and found himself before the Devil's Cauldron, filled to the brim with yellow moonshine and the fiery play of summer lightning.

The rugged crags opposite him were a low barricade against the stars to which the mound where he stood shot forward like a bridge. To the left of this the long Lisbech pond lay like a trailing serpent: its silver scales glittered as the wind swept down from the vaster moorlands to the east. To the right under a steep drop of twenty feet was the Whimsey pond, more sinister, shaped in an unnatural oval, sheltered from the wind by the high ridge so that the undisturbed moonlight lay across it like a sharp-edged sword.

He looked about for some sign of Evadne. She could not be on the land by the margin of the lakes, for the light blazed so strongly that each reed could be clearly seen like a black dagger stabbing the silver. He looked down Lisbech and saw far east a knot of red and green and orange lights. Perhaps for some devilish purpose Evadne had sought Lisbech railway station. But his volcanic mind had preserved one grain of sense that assured him that, subtle as Evadne's villainy might be, it would not lead her to walk five miles out of her way to a terminus which she could have reached in fifteen minutes by taking a train from the station down the road. She must be under cover somewhere here. He went down the gentle slope that fell from the top of the ridge to Lisbech pond in a disorder of rough heather, unhappy patches of cultivated grass, and coppices of silver birch, fringed with flaming broom that seemed faintly tarnished in the moonlight. At the bottom was a roughly hewn path which he followed in hot aimless hurry. In a little he approached a riot of falling waters. There was a slice ten feet broad carved out of the ridge, and to this narrow channel of black shining rock the floods of Lisbech leapt some feet and raced through to Whimsey. The noise beat him back. The gap was spanned by a gaunt thing of paint-blistered iron, on which he stood dizzily and noticed how the wide step that ran on each side of the channel through to the other pond was smeared with sinister green slime. Now his physical distress reminded him of Evadne, whom he had almost forgotten in contemplation of these lonely waters. The idea of her had been present but obscured, as sometimes toothache may cease active torture. His blood lust set him on and he staggered forward with covered ears. Even as he went something caught his eye in a thicket high up on the slope near the crags. Against the slender pride of some silver birches stood a gnarled hawthorn tree, its branches flattened under the stern moorland winds so that it grew squat like an opened umbrella. In its dark shadows, faintly illumined by a few boughs of withered blossom, there moved a strange bluish light. Even while he did not know what it was it made his flesh stir.

The light emerged. It was the moonlight reflected from Evadne's body. She was clad in a black bathing dress, and her arms and legs and the broad streak of flesh laid bare by a rent down the back shone brilliantly white, so that she seemed like a grotesquely patterned wild animal as she ran down to the lake. Whirling her arms above her head she trampled down into the water and struck out strongly. Her movements were full of brisk delight and she swam quickly. The moonlight made her the centre of a little feathery blur of black and silver, with a comet's tail trailing in her wake.

Nothing in all his married life had ever staggered Silverton so much as this. He had imagined his wife's adultery so strongly that it had come to be. It was now as real as their marriage; more real than their courtship. So this seemed to be the last crime of the adulteress. She had dragged him over those squelching fields and these rough moors and changed him from a man of irritations, but no passions, into a cold designer of murderous treacheries, so that he might witness a swimming exhibition! For a minute he was stunned. Then he sprang down to the rushy edge and ran along in the direction of her course, crying – 'Evadne! Evadne!' She did not hear him. At last he achieved a chest note and shouted – 'Evadne! come here!' The black and silver feather shivered in mid-water. She turned immediately and swam back to shore. He suspected sullenness in her slowness, but was glad of it, for after the shock of this extraordinary incident he wanted to go to sleep. Drowsiness lay on him like lead. He shook himself like a dog and wrenched off his linen collar, winking at the bright moon to keep himself awake. As she came quite near he was exasperated by the happy, snorting breaths she drew, and strolled a pace or two up the bank. To his enragement the face she lifted as she waded to dry land was placid, and she scrambled gaily up the bank to his side.

'O George, why did you come!' she exclaimed quite affectionately, laying a damp hand on his shoulder.

'O damn it, what does this mean!' he cried, committing a horrid tenor squeak. 'What are you doing?'

'Why, George,' she said,' 'I came here for a bathe.'

He stared into her face and could make nothing of it. It was only sweet surfaces of flesh, soft radiances of eye and lip, a lovely lie of comeliness. He forgot this present grievance in a cold search for the source of her peculiar hatefulness. Under this sick gaze she pouted and turned away with a peevish gesture. He made no sign and stood silent, watching her saunter to that gaunt iron bridge. The roar of the little waterfall did not disturb her splendid nerves and she drooped sensuously over the hand-rail, sniffing up the sweet night smell; too evidently trying to abase him to another apology.

A mosquito whirred into his face. He killed it viciously and strode off towards his wife, who showed by a common little toss of the head that she was conscious of his coming.

'Look here, Evadne!' he panted. 'What did you come here for? Tell me the truth and I promise I'll not – I'll not – '

'Not WHAT, George?'

'O please, please tell me the truth, do Evadne!' he cried pitifully.

'But, dear, what is there to carry on about so? You went on so queerly about my meeting that my head felt fit to split, and I thought the long walk and the dip would do me good.' She broke off, amazed at the wave of horror that passed over his face.

His heart sank. From the loose-lipped hurry in the telling of her story, from the bigness of her eyes and the lack of subtlety in her voice, he knew that this was the truth. Here was no adulteress whom he could accuse in the law courts and condemn into the street, no resourceful sinner whose merry crimes he could discover. Here was merely his good wife, the faithful attendant of his hearth, relentless wrecker of his soul.

She came towards him as a cat approaches a displeased master, and hovered about him on the stone coping of the noisy sluice.

'Indeed!' he found himself saying sarcastically. 'Indeed!'

'Yes, George Silverton, indeed!' she burst out, a little frightened. 'And why shouldn't I? I used to come here often enough on summer nights with poor Mamma – '

'Yes!' he shouted. It was exactly the sort of thing that would appeal to that weird half-black woman from the back of beyond. 'Mamma!' he cried tauntingly, 'Mamma!'

There was a flash of silence between them before Evadne, clutching her breast and balancing herself dangerously on her heels on the stone coping, broke into gentle shrieks. 'You dare talk of my Mamma, my poor Mamma, and she cold in her grave! I haven't been happy since she died and I married you, you silly little misery, you!' Then the rage was suddenly wiped off her brain by the perception of a crisis.

The trickle of silence overflowed into a lake, over which their spirits flew, looking at each other's reflection in the calm waters: in the hurry of their flight they had never before seen each other. They stood facing one another with dropped heads, quietly thinking.

The strong passion which filled them threatened to disintegrate their souls as a magnetic current decomposes the electrolyte, so they fought to organize their sensations. They tried to arrange themselves and their lives for comprehension, but beyond sudden lyric visions of old incidents of hatefulness – such as a smarting quarrel of six years ago as to whether Evadne had or had not cheated the railway company out of one and eightpence on an excursion ticket – the past was intangible. It trailed behind this intense event as the pale hair trails behind the burning comet. They were pre-occupied with the moment. Quite often George had found a mean pleasure in the thought that by never giving Evadne a child he had cheated her out of one form of experience, and now he paid the price for this unnatural pride of sterility. For now the spiritual offspring of their intercourse came to birth. A sublime loathing was between them. For a little time it was a huge perilous horror, but afterwards, like men aboard a ship whose masts seek the sky through steep waves, they found a drunken pride in the adventure. This was the very absolute of hatred. It cheapened the memory of the fantasias of irritation and ill-will they had performed in the less boring moments of their marriage, and they felt dazed, as amateurs who had found themselves creating a masterpiece. For the first time they were possessed by a supreme emotion and they felt a glad desire to strip away restraint and express it nakedly. It was ecstasy; they felt tall and full of blood.

Like people who, bewitched by Christ, see the whole earth as the breathing body of God, so they saw the universe as the substance and the symbol of their hatred. The stars trembled overhead with wrath. A wind from behind the angry crags set the moonlight on Lisbech quivering with rage, and the squat hawthorn-tree creaked slowly like the irritation of a dull little man. The dry moors, parched with harsh anger, waited thirstily and, sending out the murmur of rustling mountain grass and the cry of wakening fowl, seemed to huddle closer to the lake. But this sense of the earth's sympathy slipped away from them and they loathed all matter as the dull wrapping of their flame-like passion. At their wishing matter fell away and they saw sarcastic visions. He saw her as a toad squatting on the clean earth, obscuring the stars and pressing down its hot moist body on the cheerful fields. She felt his long boneless body coiled round the roots of the lovely tree of life. They shivered fastidiously. With an uplifting sense of responsibility they realized that they must kill each other.

A bird rose over their heads with a leaping flight that made it seem as though its black body was bouncing against the bright sky. The foolish noise and motion precipitated their thoughts. They were broken into a new conception of life. They perceived that God is war and his creatures are meant to fight. When dogs walk through the world cats must climb trees. The virgin must snare the wanton, the fine lover must put the prude to the sword. The gross man of action walks, spurred on by the bloodless bodies of the men of thought, who lie quiet and cunningly do not tell him where his grossness leads him. The flesh must smother the spirit, the spirit must set the flesh on fire and watch it burn. And those who were gentle by nature and shrank from the ordained brutality were betrayers of their kind, surrendering the earth to the seed of their enemies. In this war there is no discharge. If they succumbed to peace now, the rest of their lives would be dishonourable, like the exile of a rebel who has begged his life as the reward of cowardice. It was their first experience of religious passion, and they abandoned themselves to it so that their immediate personal qualities fell away from them. Neither his weakness nor her prudence stood in the way of the event.

They measured each other with the eye. To her he was a spidery thing against the velvet blackness and hard silver surfaces of the pond. The light soaked her bathing dress so that she seemed, against the jagged shadows of the rock cutting, as though she were clad in a garment of dark polished mail. Her knees were bent so clearly, her toes gripped the coping so strongly. He understood very clearly that if he did not kill her instantly she would drop him easily into the deep riot of waters. Yet for a space he could not move, but stood expecting a degrading death. Indeed, he gave her time to kill him. But she was without power too, and struggled weakly with a hallucination. The quarrel in Sumatra Crescent with its suggestion of vast and unmentionable antagonisms; her swift race through the moon-drenched countryside, all crepitant with night noises: the swimming in the wine-like lake and the isolation of the moor, which was expressedly hostile to them, as nature always is to lonely man: and this stark contest face to face, with their resentments heaped between them like a pile of naked swords – these things were so strange that her civilized self shrank back appalled. There entered into her the primitive woman who is the curse of all women: a creature of the most utter femaleness, useless, save for childbirth, with no strong brain to make her physical weakness a light accident, abjectly and corruptingly afraid of man. A squaw, she dared not strike her lord.

The illusion passed like a moment of faintness and left her enraged at having forgotten her superiority even for an instant. In the material world she had a thousand times been defeated into making prudent reservations and practising unnatural docilities. But in the world of thought she had maintained unfalteringly her masterfulness in spite of the strong yearning of her temperament towards voluptuous surrenders. That was her virtue. Its violation whipped her to action and she would have killed him at once, had not his moment come a second before hers. Sweating horribly, he had dropped his head forward on his chest: his eyes fell on her feet and marked the plebeian moulding of her ankle, which rose thickly over a crease of flesh from the heel to the calf. The woman was coarse in grain and pattern.

He had no instinct for honourable attack, so he found himself striking her in the stomach. She reeled from pain, not because his strength overcame hers. For the first time her eyes looked into his candidly open, unveiled by languor or lust: their hard brightness told him how she despised him for that unwarlike blow. He cried out as he realized that this was another of her despicable victories and that the whole burden of the crime now lay on him, for he had begun it. But the rage was stopped on his lips as her arms, flung wildly out as she fell backwards, caught him about the waist with abominable justness of eye and evil intention. So they fell body to body into the quarrelling waters.

The feathery confusion had looked so soft, yet it seemed the solid rock they struck. The breath shot out of him and suffocation warmly stuffed his ears and nose. Then the rock cleft and he was swallowed by a brawling blackness in which whirled a vortex that flung him again and again on a sharp thing that burned his shoulder. All about him fought the waters, and they cut his flesh like knives. His pain was past belief. Though God might be war, he desired peace in his time, and he yearned for another God – a child's God, an immense arm coming down from the hills and lifting him to a kindly bosom. Soon his body would burst for breath, his agony would smash in his breast bone. So great was his pain that his consciousness was strained to apprehend it, as a too tightly stretched canvas splits and rips.

Suddenly the air was sweet on his mouth. The starlight seemed as hearty as a cheer. The world was still there, the world in which he had lived, so he must be safe. His own weakness and loveableness induced enjoyable tears, and there was a delicious moment of abandonment to comfortable whining before he realized that the water would not kindly buoy him up for long, and that even now a hostile current clasped his waist. He braced his flaccid body against the sucking blackness and flung his head back so that the water should not bubble so hungrily against the cords of his throat. Above him the slime of the rock was sticky with moonbeams, and the leprous light brought to his mind a newspaper paragraph, read years ago, which told him that the dawn had discovered floating in some oily Mersey dock, under walls as infected with wet growth as this, a corpse whose blood-encrusted finger-tips were deeply cleft. On the instant his own finger-tips seemed hot with blood and deeply cleft from clawing at the impregnable rock. He screamed gaspingly and beat his hands through the strangling flood. Action, which he had always loathed and dreaded, had broken the hard mould of his self-possession, and the dry dust of his character was blown hither and thither by fear. But one sharp fragment of intelligence which survived this detrition of his personality perceived that a certain gleam on the rock about a foot above the water was not the cold putrescence of the slime, but certainly the hard and merry light of a moon-ray striking on solid metal. His left hand clutched upwards at it, and he swung from a rounded projection. It was, his touch told him, a leaden ring hanging obliquely from the rock, to which his memory could visualize precisely in some past drier time when Lisbech sent no flood to Whimsey, a waterman mooring a boat strewn with pale-bellied perch. And behind the stooping waterman he remembered a flight of narrow steps that led up a buttress to a stone shelf that ran through the cutting. Unquestionably he was safe. He swung in a happy rhythm from the ring, his limp body trailing like a caterpillar through the stream to the foot of the steps, while he gasped in strength. A part of him was in agony, for his arm was nearly dragged out of its socket and a part of him was embarrassed because his hysteria shook him with a deep rumbling chuckle that sounded as though he meditated on some unseemly joke: the whole was pervaded by a twilight atmosphere of unenthusiastic gratitude for his rescue, like the quietly cheerful tone of a Sunday evening sacred concert. After a minute's deep breathing he hauled himself up by the other hand and prepared to swing himself on to the steps.

But first, to shake off the wet worsted rags, once his socks, that now stuck uncomfortably between his toes, he splashed his feet outwards to midstream. A certain porpoise-like surface met his left foot. Fear dappled his face with goose flesh. Without turning his head he knew what it was. It was Evadne's fat flesh rising on each side of her deep-furrowed spine through the rent in her bathing dress.

Once more hatred marched through his soul like a king: compelling service by his godhead and, like all gods a little hated for his harsh lien on his worshipper. He saw his wife as the curtain of flesh between him and celibacy, and solitude and all those delicate abstentions from life which his soul desired. He saw her as the invisible worm destroying the rose of the world with her dark secret love. Now he knelt on the lowest stone step watching her wet seal-smooth head bobbing nearer on the waters. As her strong arms, covered with little dark points where her thick hairs were clotted with moisture, stretched out towards safety he bent forward and laid his hands on her head. He held her face under water. Scornfully he noticed the bubbles that rose to the surface from her protesting mouth and nostrils, and the foam raised by her arms and her thick ankles. To the end the creature persisted in turmoil, in movement, in action . . .

She dropped like a stone. His hands, with nothing to resist them, slapped the water foolishly and he nearly overbalanced forward into the stream. He rose to his feet very stiffly. 'I must be a very strong man,' he said, as he slowly climbed the steps. 'I must be a very strong man,' he repeated, a little louder, as with a hot and painful rigidity of the joints he stretched himself out at full length along the stone shelf. Weakness closed him in like a lead coffin. For a little time the weakness of his clothes persisted in being felt: then the sensation oozed out of him and his body fell out of knowledge. There was neither pain nor joy nor any other reckless ploughing of the brain by nerves. He knew unconsciousness, or rather the fullest consciousness he had ever known. For the world became nothingness, and nothingness which is free from the yeasty nuisance of matter and the ugliness of generation was the law of his being. He was absorbed into vacuity, the untamed substance of the universe, round which he conceived passion and thought to circle as straws caught up by the wind. He saw God and lived.

In Heaven a thousand years are a day. And this little corner of time in which he found happiness shrank to a nut-shell as he opened his eyes again. This peace was hardly printed on his heart, yet the brightness of the night was blurred by the dawn. With the grunting carefulness of a man drunk with fatigue, he crawled along the stone shelf to the iron bridge, where he stood with his back to the roaring sluice and rested. All things seemed different now and happier. Like most timid people he disliked the night, and the commonplace hand which the dawn laid on the scene seemed to him a sanctification. The dimmed moon sank to her setting behind the crags. The jewel lights of Lisbech railway station were weak, cheerful twinklings. A steaming bluish milk of morning mist had been spilt on the hard silver surface of the lake, and the reeds no longer stabbed it like little daggers, but seemed a feathery fringe, like the pampas grass in the front garden in Sumatra Crescent. The black crags became brownish, and the mist disguised the sternness of the moor. This weakening of effects was exactly what he had always thought the extinction of Evadne would bring the world. He smiled happily at the moon.

Yet he was moved to sudden angry speech. 'If I had my time over again,' he said. ' I wouldn't touch her with the tongs.' For the cold he had known all along he would catch had settled in his head, and his handkerchief was wet through.

He leaned over the bridge and looked along Lisbech and thought of Evadne. For the first time for many years he saw her image without spirits, and wondered without indignation why she had so often looked like the cat about to steal the cream. What was the cream? And did she ever steal it? Now he would never know. He thought of her very generously and sighed over the perversity of late in letting so much comeliness.

'If she had married a butcher or a veterinary surgeon she might have been happy,' he said, and shook his head at the glassy black water that slid under the bridge to that boiling sluice.

A gust of ague reminded him that wet clothes clung to his fevered body and that he ought to change as quickly as possible, or expect to be laid up for weeks. He turned along the path that led back across the moor to the withered ash tree, and was learning the torture of bare feet on gravel when he cried out to himself: 'I shall be hanged for killing my wife.' It did not come as a trumpet call, for he was one of those people who never quite hear what is said to them, and this deafishness extended in him to emotional things. It stole on him calmly, like a fog closing on a city. When he first felt hemmed in by this certainty he looked over his shoulder to the crags, remembering tales of how Jacobite fugitives had hidden on the moors for many weeks. There lay at least another day of freedom. But he was the kind of man who always goes home. He stumbled on, not very unhappy, except for his feet. Like many people of weak temperament he did not fear death. Indeed, it had a peculiar appeal to him; for while it was important, exciting, it did not, like most important and exciting things try to create action. He allowed his imagination the vanity of painting pictures. He saw himself standing in their bedroom, plotting this last event, with the white sheet and the highlights of the mahogany wardrobe shining ghostly at him through the darkness. He saw himself raising a thin hand to the gas bracket and turning on the tap. He saw himself staggering to their bed while death crept in at his nostrils. He saw his corpse lying in full daylight, and for the first time knew himself certainly, unquestionably dignified.

He threw back his chest in pride: but at that moment the path stopped and he found himself staggering down the mound of heatherland and boulders with bleeding feet. Always he had suffered from sore feet, which had not exactly disgusted but, worse still, disappointed Evadne. A certain wistfulness she had always evinced when she found herself the superior animal had enraged and humiliated him many times. He felt that sting him now, and flung himself down the mound cursing. When he stumbled up to the withered ash tree he hated her so much that it seemed as though she were alive again, and a sharp wind blowing down from the moor terrified him like her touch.

He rested there. Leaning against the stripped grey trunk, he smiled up at the sky, which was now so touched to ineffectiveness by the dawn that it looked like a tent of faded silk. There was the peace of weakness in him, which he took to be spiritual, because it had no apparent physical justification: but he lost it as his dripping clothes chilled his tired flesh. His discomfort reminded him that the phantasmic night was passing from him. Daylight threatened him: the daylight in which for so many years he had worked in the solicitor's office and been snubbed and ignored. '"The garish day,"' he murmured disgustedly, quoting the blasphemy of some hymn writer. He wanted his death to happen in this phantasmic night.

So he limped his way along the road. The birds had not yet begun to sing, but the rustling noises of the night had ceased. The silent highway was consecrated to his proud progress. He staggered happily like a tired child returning from a lovely birthday walk: his death in the little bedroom, which for the first time he would have to himself, was a culminating treat to be gloated over like the promise of a favourite pudding for supper. As he walked he brooded dozingly on large and swelling thoughts. Like all people of weak passions and enterprise he loved to think of Napoleon, and in the shadow of the great asylum wall he strutted a few steps of his advance from murder to suicide, with arms crossed on his breast and thin legs trying to strut massively. He was so happy. He wished that a military band went before him, and pretended that the high hedges were solemn lines of men, stricken in awe to silence as their king rode out to some nobly self-chosen doom. Vast he seemed to himself, and magnificent like music, and solemn like the Sphinx. He had saved the earth from corruption by killing Evadne, for whom he now felt the unremorseful pity a conqueror might bestow on a devastated empire. He might have grieved that his victory brought him death, but with immense pride he found that the occasion was exactly described by a text, 'He saved others. Himself

He could not save.' He had missed the stile in the field above Sumatra Crescent and had to go back and hunt for it in the hedge. So quickly had his satisfaction borne him home.

The field had the fantastic air that jerry-builders give to land poised to the knife-edge of town and country, so that he walked in romance to his very door. The unmarred grass sloped to a stone-hedge of towers of loose brick, trenches and mounds of shining clay, and the fine intentful spires of the scaffording round the last unfinished house. And he looked down on Petrick. Though to the actual eye it was but a confusion of dark distances through the twilight, a breaking of velvety perspectives, he saw more intensely than ever before its squalid walls and squalid homes where mean men and mean women enlaced their unwholesome lives. Yet he did not shrink from entering for his great experience: as Christ did not shrink from being born in a stable. He swaggered with humility over the trodden mud of the field and the new white flags of Sumatra Crescent. Down the road before him there passed a dim figure, who paused at each lamp post and raised a long wand to behead the yellow gas-flowers that were now wilting before the dawn: a ghostly herald preparing the world to be his deathbed. The Crescent curved in quiet darkness, save for one house. where blazed a gas-lit room with undrawn blinds. The brightness had the startling quality of a scream. He looked in almost anxiously as he passed, and met the blank eyes of a man in evening clothes who stood by the window shaking a medicine. His face was like a wax mask softened by heat: the features were blurred with the suffering which comes from the spectacle of suffering. His eyes lay unshiftingly on George's face as he went by and he went on shaking the bottle. It seemed as though he would never stop.

In the hour of his grandeur George was not forgetful of the griefs of the little human people, but interceded with God for the sake of this stranger. Everything was beautiful, beautiful, beautiful.

His own little house looked solemn as a temple. He leaned against the lamp-post at the gate and stared at its empty windows and neat bricks. The disorder of the shattered pane of glass could be overlooked by considering a sign that this house was a holy place: like the Passover blood on the lintel. The propriety of the evenly drawn blind pleased him enormously. He had always known that this was how the great tragic things of the world had accomplished themselves: quietly. Evadne's raging activity belonged to trivial or annoying things like spring-cleaning or thunder storms. Well, the house belonged to him now. He opened the gate and went up the asphalt path, sourly noticing that Evadne had as usual left out the lawn-mower, though it might very easily have rained, with the wind coming up as it was. A stray cat that had been sleeping in the tuft of pampas grass in the middle of the lawn was roused by his coming, and fled insolently close to his legs. He hated all wild homeless things, and bent for a stone to throw at it. But instead his fingers touched a slug, which reminded him of the feeling of Evadne's flesh through the slit in her bathing dress. And suddenly the garden was possessed by her presence: she seemed to amble there as she had so often done, sowing seeds unwisely and tormenting the last days of an ailing geranium by insane transplantation, exclaiming absurdly over such mere weeds as morning glory. He caught the very clucking of her voice . . . The front door opened at his touch.

The little lobby with its closed doors seemed stuffed with expectant silence. He realized that he had come to the theatre of his great adventure. Then panic seized him. Because this was the home where he and she had lived together so horribly he doubted whether he could do this splendid momentous thing, for here he had always been a poor thing with the habit of failure. His heart beat in him more quickly than his raw feet could pad up the oil-clothed stairs. Behind the deal door at the end of the passage was death. Nothingness! It would escape him, even the idea of it would escape him if he did not go to it at once. When he burst at last into its presence he felt so victorious that he sank back against the door waiting for death to come to him without turning on the gas. He was so happy. His death was coming true.

But Evadne lay on his deathbed. She slept there soundly, with her head flung back on the pillows so that her eyes and brow seemed small in shadow, and her mouth and jaw huge above her thick throat in the light. Her wet hair straggled across the pillow on to a broken cane chair covered with her tumbled clothes. Her breast, silvered with sweat, shone in the ray of the street lamp that had always disturbed their nights. The counterpane rose enormously over her hips in rolls of glazed linen. Out of mere innocent sleep her sensuality was distilling a most drunken pleasure.

Not for one moment did he think this a phantasmic appearance. Evadne was not the sort of woman to have a ghost.

Still leaning against the door, he tried to think it all out: but his thoughts came brokenly, because the dawnlight flowing in at the window confused him by its pale glare and that lax figure on the bed held his attention. It must have been that when he laid his murderous hands on her head she had simply dropped below the surface and swum a few strokes under water as any expert swimmer can. Probably he had never even put her into danger, for she was a great lusty creature and the weir was a little place. He had imagined the wonder and peril of the battle as he had imagined his victory. He sneezed exhaustingly, and from his physical distress realized how absurd it was ever to have thought that he had killed her. Bodies like his do not kill bodies like hers.

Now his soul was naked and lonely as though the walls of his body had fallen in at death, and the grossness of Evadne's sleep made him suffer more unlovely a destitution than any old beggarwoman squatting by the roadside in the rain. He had thought he had had what every man most desires: one night of power over a woman for the business of murder or love. But it had been a lie. Nothing beautiful had ever happened to him. He would have wept, but the hatred he had learnt on the moors obstructed all tears in his throat. At least this night had given him passion enough to put an end to it all.

Quietly he went to the window and drew down the sash. There was no fire place, so that sealed the room. Then he crept over to the gas bracket and raised his thin hand, as he had imagined in his hour of vain glory by the lake.

He had forgotten Evadne's thrifty habit of turning off the gas at the main to prevent leakage when she went to bed.

He was beaten. He undressed and got into bed: as he had done every night for ten years, and as he would do every night until he died. Still sleeping, Evadne caressed him with warm arms.

JAMES JOYCE

An Encounter

It was Joe Dillon who introduced the Wild West to us. He had a little library made up of old numbers of *The Union Jack, Pluck* and *The Halfpenny Marvel*. Every evening after school we met in his back garden and arranged Indian battles. He and his fat young brother Leo the idler held the loft of the stable while we tried to carry it by storm; or we fought a pitched battle on the grass. But, however well we fought, we never won siege or battle and all our bouts ended with Joe Dillon's war dance of victory. His parents went to eight-o'clock mass every morning in Gardiner Street and the peaceful odour of Mrs Dillon was prevalent in the hall of the house. But he played too fiercely for us who were younger and more timid. He looked like some kind of an Indian when he capered round the garden, an old tea-cosy on his head, beating a tin with his fist and yelling:

– Ya! yaka, yaka, yaka!

Everyone was incredulous when it was reported that he had a vocation for the priesthood. Nevertheless it was true.

A spirit of unruliness diffused itself among us and, under its influence, differences of culture and constitution were waived. We banded ourselves together, some boldly, some in jest and some almost in fear: and of the number of these latter, the reluctant Indians who were afraid to seem studious or lacking in robustness, I was one. The adventures related in the literature of the Wild West were remote from my nature but, at least, they opened doors of escape. I liked better some American detective stories which were traversed from time to time by unkempt fierce and beautiful girls. Though there was nothing wrong in these stories and though their intention was sometimes literary they were circulated secretly at school. One day when Father Butler was hearing the four pages of Roman History, clumsy Leo Dillon was discovered with a copy of *The Halfpenny Marvel*.

– This page or this page? This page? Now, Dillon, up! *Hardly had the day* . . . Go on! What day? *Hardly had the day dawned* . . . Have you studied it? What have you there in your pocket?

Everyone's heart palpitated as Leo Dillon handed up the paper and everyone assumed an innocent face. Father Butler turned over the pages, frowning.

– What is this rubbish? he said. *The Apache Chief!* Is this what you read instead of studying your Roman History? Let me not find any more of this wretched stuff in this college. The man who wrote it, I suppose, was some wretched scribbler that writes these things for a drink. I'm surprised at boys like you, educated, reading such stuff. I could understand it if you were . . . National School boys. Now, Dillon, I advise you strongly, get at your work or . . .

This rebuke during the sober hours of school paled much of the glory of the Wild West for me and the confused puffy face of Leo Dillon awakened one of my consciences. But when the restraining influence of the school was at a distance I began to hunger again for wild sensations, for the escape which those chronicles of disorder alone seemed to offer me. The mimic warfare of the evening became at last as wearisome to me as the routine of school in the morning because I wanted real adventures to happen to myself. But real adventures, I reflected, do not happen to people who remain at home: they must be sought abroad.

The summer holidays were near at hand when I made up my mind to break out of the weariness of school-life for one day at least. With Leo Dillon and a boy named Mahony I planned a day's miching. Each of us saved up sixpence. We were to meet at ten in the morning on the Canal Bridge. Mahony's big sister was to write an excuse for him and Leo Dillon was to tell his brother to say he was sick. We arranged to go along the Wharf Road until we came to the ships, then to cross in the ferryboat and walk out to see the Pigeon House. Leo Dillon was afraid we might meet Father Butler or someone out of the college; but Mahony asked, very sensibly, what would Father Butler be doing out at the Pigeon House. We were reassured: and I brought the first stage of the plot to an end by collecting sixpence from the other two, at the same time showing them my own sixpence. When we were making the last arrangements on the eve we were all vaguely excited. We shook hands, laughing, and Mahony said:

– Till to-morrow, mates.

That night I slept badly. In the morning I was first-comer to the bridge as I lived nearest. I hid my books in the long grass near the ashpit at the end of the garden where nobody ever came and hurried along the canal bank. It was a mild sunny morning in the first week of June. I sat up on the coping of the bridge admiring my frail canvas shoes which I had diligently pipeclayed overnight and watching the docile horses pulling a tram-load of business people up the hill. All the branches of the tall trees which lined the mall were gay with little light green leaves and the sunlight slanted through them on to the water. The granite stone of the bridge was beginning to be warm and I began to pat it with my hands in time to an air in my head. I was very happy.

When I had been sitting there for five or ten minutes I saw Mahony's grey suit approaching. He came up the hill, smiling, and clambered up beside me on the bridge. While we were waiting he brought out the catapult which bulged from his inner pocket and explained some improvements which he had made in it. I asked him why he had brought it and he told me he had brought it to have some gas with the birds. Mahony used slang freely, and spoke of Father Butler as Old Bunser. We waited on for a quarter of an hour more but still there was no sign of Leo Dillon. Mahony, at last, jumped down and said:

'Come along. I knew Fatty'd funk it.'

'And his sixpence . . . ?' I said.

'That's forfeit,' said Mahony. 'And so much the better for us – a bob and a tanner instead of a bob.'

We walked along the North Strand Road till we came to the Vitriol Works and then turned to the right along the Wharf Road. Mahony began to play the Indian as soon as we were out of public sight. He chased a crowd of ragged girls, brandishing his unloaded catapult and, when two ragged boys began, out of chivalry, to fling stones at us, he proposed that we should charge them. I objected that the boys were too small and so we walked on, the ragged troop screaming after us: *'Swaddlers! Swaddlers!'*

thinking that we were Protestants because Mahony, who was dark-complexioned, wore the silver badge of a cricket club in his cap. When we came to the Smoothing Iron we arranged a siege; but it was a failure because you must have at least three. We revenged ourselves on Leo Dillon by saying what a funk he was and guessing how many he would get at three o'clock from Mr Ryan.

We came then near the river. We spent a long time walking about the noisy streets flanked by high stone walls, watching the working of cranes and engines and often being shouted at for our immobility by the drivers of groaning carts. It was noon when we reached the quays and, as all the labourers seemed to be eating their lunches, we bought two big currant buns and sat down to eat them on some metal piping beside the river. We pleased ourselves with the spectacle of Dublin's commerce – the barges signalled from far away by their curls of woolly smoke, the brown fishing fleet beyond Ringsend, the big white sailing-vessel which was being discharged on the opposite quay. Mahony said it would be right skit to run away to sea on one of those big ships and even I, looking at the high masts, saw, or imagined, the geography which had been scantily dosed to me at school gradually taking substance under my eyes. School and home seemed to recede from us and their influences upon us seemed to wane.

We crossed the Liffey in the ferryboat, paying our toll to be transported in the company of two labourers and a little Jew with a bag. We were serious to the point of solemnity, but once during the short voyage our eyes met and we laughed. When we landed we watched the discharging of the graceful threemaster which we had observed from the other quay. Some bystander said that she was a Norwegian vessel. I went to the stern and tried to decipher the legend upon it but, failing to do so, I came back and examined the foreign sailors to see had any of them green eyes for I had some confused notion . . . The sailors' eyes were blue and grey and even black. The only sailor whose eyes could have been called green was a tall man who amused the crowd on the quay by calling out cheerfully every time the planks fell:

'All right! All right!'

When we were tired of this sight we wandered slowly into Ringsend. The day had grown sultry, and in the windows of the grocers' shops musty biscuits lay bleaching. We bought some biscuits and chocolate which we ate sedulously as we wandered through the squalid streets where the families of the fishermen live. We could find no dairy and so we went into a huckster's shop and bought a bottle of raspberry lemonade each. Refreshed by this, Mahony chased a cat down a lane, but the cat escaped into a wide field. We both felt rather tired and when we reached the field we made at once for a sloping bank over the ridge of which we could see the Dodder.

It was too late and we were too tired to carry out our project of visiting the Pigeon House. We had to be home before four o'clock lest our adventure should be discovered. Mahony looked regretfully at his catapult and I had to suggest going home by train before he regained any cheerfulness. The sun went in behind some clouds and left us to our jaded thoughts and the crumbs of our provisions.

There was nobody but ourselves in the field. When we had lain on the bank for some time without speaking I saw a man approaching from the far end of the field. I watched him lazily as I chewed one of those green stems on which girls tell fortunes. He came along by the bank slowly. He walked with one hand upon his hip and in the other hand he held a stick with which he tapped the turf lightly. He was shabbily dressed in a suit of greenish-black and wore what we used to call a jerry hat with a high crown. He seemed to be fairly old for his moustache was ashen-grey. When he passed at our feet he glanced up at us quickly and then continued his way. We followed him with our eyes and saw that when he had gone on for perhaps fifty paces he turned about and began to retrace his steps. He walked towards us very slowly, always tapping the ground with his stick, so slowly that I thought he was looking for something in the grass.

He stopped when he came level with us and bade us good-day. We answered him and he sat down beside us on the slope slowly and with great care. He began to talk of the weather, saying that it would be a very hot summer and adding that the seasons had changed greatly since he was a boy – a long time ago. He said that the happiest time of one's life was undoubtedly one's schoolboy days and that he would give anything to be young again. While he expressed these sentiments which bored us a little we kept silent. Then he began to talk of school and of books. He asked us whether we had read the poetry of Thomas Moore or the works of Sir Walter Scott and Lord Lytton. I pretended that I had read every book he mentioned so that in the end he said:

– Ah, I can see you are a bookworm like myself. Now, he added, pointing to Mahony who was regarding us with open eyes, he is different; he goes in for games.

He said he had all Sir Walter Scott's works and all Lord Lytton's works at home and never tired of reading them. Of course, he said, there were some of Lord Lytton's works which boys couldn't read. Mahony asked why couldn't boys read them – a question which agitated and pained me because I was afraid the man would think I was as stupid as Mahony. The man, however, only smiled. I saw that he had great gaps in his mouth between his yellow teeth. Then he asked us which of us had the most sweethearts. Mahony mentioned lightly that he had three totties. The man asked me how many had I. I answered that I had none. He did not believe me and said he was sure I must have one. I was silent.

– Tell us, said Mahony pertly to the man, how many have you yourself?

The man smiled as before and said that when he was our age he had lots of sweethearts.

– Every boy, he said, has a little sweetheart.

His attitude on this point struck me as strangely liberal in a man of his age. In my heart I thought that what he said about boys and sweethearts was reasonable. But I disliked the words in his mouth and I wondered why he shivered once or twice as if he feared something or felt a sudden chill. As he proceeded I noticed that his accent was good. He began to speak to us about girls, saying what nice soft hair they had and how soft their hands were and how all girls were not so good as they seemed to be if one only knew. There was nothing he liked, he said, so much as looking at a nice young girl, at her nice white hands and her beautiful soft hair. He gave me the impression that he was repeating something which he had learned by heart or that, magnetized by some words of his own speech, his mind was slowly circling round and round in the same orbit. At times he spoke as if he were simply alluding to some fact that everybody knew, and at times he lowered his voice and spoke mysteriously as if he were telling us something secret which he did not wish others to overhear. He repeated his phrases over and over again, varying them and surrounding them with his monotonous voice. I continued to gaze towards the foot of the slope, listening to him.

After a long while his monologue paused. He stood up slowly, saying that he had to leave us for a minute or so, a few minutes, and, without changing the direction of my gaze, I saw him walking slowly away from us towards the near end of the field. We remained silent when he had gone. After a silence of a few minutes I heard Mahony exclaim:

– I say! Look what he's doing!

As I neither answered nor raised my eyes Mahony exclaimed again:

– I say . . . He's a queer old josser!

– In case he asks us for our names, I said, let you be Murphy and I'll be Smith.

We said nothing further to each other. I was still considering whether I would go away or not when the man came back and sat down beside us again. Hardly had he sat down when Mahony, catching sight of the cat which had escaped him, sprang up and pursued her across the field. The man and I watched the chase. The cat escaped once more and Mahony began to throw stones at the wall she had escaladed. Desisting from this, he began to wander about the far end of the field, aimlessly.

After an interval the man spoke to me. He said that my friend was a very rough boy and asked did he get whipped often at school. I was going to reply indignantly that we were not National School boys to be *whipped*, as he called it; but I remained silent. He began to speak on the subject of chastising boys. His mind, as if magnetized again by his speech, seemed to circle slowly round and round its new centre. He said that when boys were that kind they ought to be whipped and well whipped. When a boy was rough and unruly there was nothing would do him any good but a good sound whipping. A slap on the hand or a box on the ear was no good: what he wanted was to get a nice warm whipping. I was surprised at this sentiment and involuntarily glanced up at his face. As I did so I met the gaze of a pair of bottle-green eyes peering at me from under a twitching forehead. I turned my eyes away again.

The man continued his monologue. He seemed to have forgotten his recent liberalism. He said that if ever he found a boy talking to girls or having a girl for a sweetheart he would whip him and whip him; and that would teach him not to be talking to girls. And if a boy had a girl for a sweetheart and told lies about it then he would give him such a whipping as no boy ever got in this world. He said that there was nothing in this world he would like so well as that. He described to me how he would whip such a boy as if he were unfolding some elaborate mystery. He would love that, he said, better than anything in this world; and his voice, as he led me monotonously through the mystery, grew almost affectionate and seemed to plead with me that I should understand him.

I waited till his monologue paused again. Then I stood up abruptly. Lest I should betray my agitation I delayed a few moments pretending to fix my shoe properly and then, saying that I was obliged to go, I bade him good-day. I went up the slope calmly but my heart was beating quickly with fear that he would seize me by the ankles. When I reached the top of the slope I turned round and, without looking at him, called loudly across the field:

– Murphy!

My voice had an accent of forced bravery in it and I was ashamed of my paltry stratagem. I had to call the name again before Mahony saw me and hallooed in answer. How my heart beat as he came running across the field to me! He ran as if to bring me aid. And I was penitent; for in my heart I had always despised him a little.

D. H. LAWRENCE

The Prussian Officer

I

They had marched more than thirty kilometres since dawn, along the white, hot road, where occasional thickets of trees threw a moment of shade, then out into the glare again. On either hand, the valley, wide and shallow, glistered with heat; dark green patches of rye, pale young corn, fallow and meadow and black pine-woods spread in a dull, hot diagram under a glistening sky. But right in front the mountains ranged across, pale blue and very still, the snow gleaming gently out of the deep atmosphere. And towards the mountains, on and on, the regiment marched between the rye-fields and the meadows, between the scraggy fruit-trees set regularly on either side the highroad. The burnished, dark green rye threw off a suffocating heat, the mountains drew gradually nearer and more distinct. While the feet of the soldiers grew hotter, sweat ran through their hair under their helmets, and their knapsacks could burn no more in contact with their shoulders, but seemed instead to give off a cold, prickly sensation.

He walked on and on in silence, staring at the mountains ahead, that rose sheer out of the land, and stood fold behind fold, half earth, half heaven, the heaven, the barrier with slits of soft snow in the pale, bluish peaks.

He could now walk almost without pain. At the start, he had determined not to limp. It had made him sick to take the first steps, and during the first mile or so, he had compressed his breath, and the cold drops of sweat had stood on his forehead. But he had walked it off. What were they after all but bruises! He had looked at them, as he was getting up:

deep bruises on the backs of his thighs. And since he had made his first step in the morning, he had been conscious of them, till now he had a tight, hot place in his chest, with suppressing the pain, and holding himself in. There seemed no air when he breathed. But he walked almost lightly.

The captain's hand had trembled in taking his coffee at dawn: his orderly saw it again. And he saw the fine figure of the captain wheeling on horseback at the farm-house ahead, a handsome figure in pale blue uniform with facings of scarlet, and the metal gleaming on the black helmet and the sword scabbard, and dark streaks of sweat coming on the silky bay horse. The orderly felt he was connected with that figure moving so suddenly on horseback: he followed it like a shadow, mute and inevitable and damned by it. And the officer was always aware of the tramp of the company behind, the march of his orderly among the men.

The captain was a tall man of about forty, grey at the temples. He had a handsome, finely-knit figure, and was one of the best horsemen in the West. His orderly, having to rub him down, admired the amazing riding-muscles of his loins.

For the rest, the orderly scarcely noticed the officer any more than he noticed himself. It was rarely he saw his master's face: he did not look at it. The captain had reddish-brown, stiff hair, that he wore short upon his skull. His moustache also was cut short and bristly over a full, brutal mouth. His face was rather rugged, the cheeks thin. Perhaps the man was the more handsome for the deep lines in his face, the irritable tension of his brow, which gave him the look of a man who fights with life. His fair eyebrows stood bushy over light blue eyes that were always flashing with cold fire.

He was a Prussian aristocrat, haughty and overbearing. But his mother had been a Polish Countess. Having made too many gambling debts when he was young, he had ruined his prospects in the army, and remained an infantry captain. He had never married: his position did not allow it, and no woman had ever moved him to it. His time he spent riding – occasionally he rode one of his own horses at the races – and at the officers' club. Now and then he took himself a mistress. But after such an event, he returned to duty with his brow still more tense, his eyes still more hostile and irritable. With the men, however, he was merely impersonal, though a devil when roused, so that on the whole they feared him but had no great aversion from him. They accepted him as the inevitable.

To his orderly he was at first cold and just and indifferent: he did not fuss over trifles. So that his servant knew practically nothing about him, except just what orders he would give, and how he wanted them obeyed. That was quite simple. Then the change gradually came.

The orderly was a youth of about twenty-two, of medium height, and well-built. He had strong, heavy limbs, was swarthy, with a soft, black, young moustache. There was something altogether warm and young about him. He had firmly marked eyebrows over dark, expressionless eyes, that seemed never to have thought, only to have received life direct through his senses, and acted straight from instinct.

Gradually the officer had become aware of his servant's young, vigorous, unconscious presence about him. He could not get away from the sense of the youth's person, while he was in attendance. It was like a warm flame upon the older man's tense, rigid body, that had become almost unliving, fixed. There was something so free and self-contained about him, and something in the young fellow's movement, that made the officer aware of him. And this irritated the Prussian. He did not choose to be touched into life by his servant. He might easily have changed his man, but he did not. He now very rarely looked direct at his orderly, but kept his face averted, as if to avoid seeing him. And yet as the young soldier moved unthinking about the apartment, the elder watched him, and would notice the movement of his strong young shoulders under the blue cloth, the bend of his neck. And it irritated him. To see the soldier's young, brown, shapely peasants' hands grasp the loaf or the wine-bottle sent a flash of hate or of anger through the elder man's blood. It was not that the youth was clumsy: it was rather the blind, instinctive sureness of movement of an unhampered young animal that irritated the officer to such a degree.

Once, when a bottle of wine had gone over, and the red gushed out onto the table-cloth, the officer had started up with an oath, and his eyes, bluey like fire, had held those of the confused youth for a moment. It was a shock for the young soldier. He felt something sink deeper, deeper into his soul, where nothing had ever gone before. It left him rather blank and wondering. Some of his natural completeness in himself was gone, a little uneasiness took its place. And from that time an undiscovered feeling had held between the two men.

Henceforward the orderly was afraid of really meeting his master. His subconsciousness remembered those steely blue eyes and the harsh brows, and did not intend to meet them again. So he always stared past his master, and avoided him. Also, in a little anxiety, he waited for the three months to have gone, when his time would be up. He began to feel a constraint in the captain's presence, and the soldier even more than the officer wanted to be left alone in his neutrality as servant.

He had served the captain for more than a year, and knew his duty. This he performed easily, as if it were natural to him. The officer and his commands he took for granted, as he took the sun and the rain, and he served as a matter of course. It did not implicate him personally.

But now if he were going to be forced into a personal interchange with his master, he would be like a wild thing caught, he felt he must get away.

But the influence of the young soldier's being had penetrated through the officer's stiffened discipline, and perturbed the man in him. He, however, was a gentleman, with long fine hands and cultivated movements, and was not going to allow such a thing as the stirring of his innate self. He was a man of passionate temper, who had always kept himself suppressed. Occasionally there had been a duel, an outburst before the soldiers. He knew himself to be always on the point of breaking out. But he kept himself hard to the idea of the Service. Whereas the young soldier seemed to live out his warm, full nature, to give it off in his very movements, which had a certain zest, such as wild animals have in free movement. And this irritated the officer more and more.

In spite of himself, the captain could not regain his neutrality of feeling towards his orderly. Nor could he leave the man alone. In spite of himself, he watched him, gave him sharp orders, tried to take up as much of his time as possible. Sometimes he flew into a rage with the young soldier, and bullied him. Then the orderly shut himself off, as it were out of earshot, and waited with sullen, flushed face, for the end of the noise. The words never pierced to his intelligence, he made himself, protectively, impervious to the feelings of his master.

He had a scar on his left thumb, a deep seam going across the knuckle. The officer had long suffered from it, and wanted to do something to it.

Still it was there, ugly and brutal on the young, brown hand. At last the captain's reserve gave way. One day, as the orderly was smoothing out the table-cloth, the officer pinned down his thumb with a pencil, asking:

'How did you come by that?'

The young man winced and drew back at attention.

'A wood-axe, Herr Hauptmann,' he answered.

The officer waited for further explanation. None came. The orderly went about his duties. The elder man was sullenly angry. His servant avoided him. And the next day he had to use all his will-power to avoid seeing the scarred thumb. He wanted to get hold of it and – A hot flame ran in his blood.

He knew his servant would soon be free, and would be glad. As yet, the soldier had held himself off from the elder man. The captain grew madly irritable. He could not rest when the soldier was away, and when he was present, he glared at him with tormented eyes. He hated those fine black brows over the unmeaning dark eyes, he was infuriated by the free movement of the handsome limbs, which no military discipline could make stiff. And he became harsh and cruelly bullying, using contempt and satire. The young soldier only grew more mute and expressionless.

'What cattle were you bred by, that you can't keep straight eyes. Look me in the eyes when I speak to you.'

And the soldier turned his dark eyes to the other's face, but there was no sight in them: he stared with the slightest possible cast, holding back his sight, perceiving the blue of his master's eyes, but receiving no look from them. And the elder man went pale, and his reddish eyebrows twitched. He gave his order, barrenly.

Once he flung a heavy military glove into the young soldier's face. Then he had the satisfaction of seeing the black eyes flare up into his own, like a blaze when straw is thrown on a fire. And he had laughed with a little tremor and a sneer.

But there were only two months more. The youth instinctively tried to keep himself intact: he tried to serve the officer as if the latter were an abstract authority, and not a man. All his instinct was to avoid personal contact, even definite hate. But in spite of himself the hate grew, responsive to the officer's passion. However, he put it in the background. When he had left the army he could dare acknowledge it. By nature he was active, and had many friends. He thought what amazing good fellows they were. But, without knowing it, he was alone. Now this solitariness was intensified. It would carry him through his term. But the officer seemed to be going irritably insane, and the youth was deeply frightened.

The soldier had a sweetheart, a girl from the mountains, independent and primitive. The two walked together, rather silently. He went with her, not to talk, but to have his arm round her, and for the physical contact. This eased him, made it easier for him to ignore the captain; for he could rest with her held fast against his chest. And she, in some unspoken fashion, was there for him. They loved each other.

The captain perceived it, and was mad with irritation. He kept the young man engaged all the evenings long, and took pleasure in the dark look that came on his face. Occasionally, the eyes of the two men met, those of the younger sullen and dark, doggedly unalterable, those of the elder sneering with restless contempt.

The officer tried hard not to admit the passion that had got hold of him. He would not know that his feeling for his orderly was anything but that of a man incensed by his stupid, *perverse* servant. So, keeping quite justified and conventional in his consciousness, he let the other thing run on. His nerves, however, were suffering. At last he slung the end of a belt in his servant's face. When he saw the youth start back, the pain-tears in his eyes and the blood on his mouth, he had felt at once a thrill of deep pleasure, and of shame.

But this, he acknowledged to himself was a thing he had never done before. The fellow was too exasperating. His own nerves must be going to pieces. He went away for some days with a woman.

It was a mockery of pleasure. He simply did not want the woman. But he stayed on for his time. At the end of it, he came back in an agony of irritation, torment, and misery. He rode all the evening, then came straight in to supper. His orderly was out. The officer sat with his long, fine hands lying on the table, perfectly still, and all his blood seemed to be corroding.

At last his servant entered. He watched the strong, easy young figure, the fine eyebrows, the thick black hair. In a week's time the youth had got back his old well-being. The hands of the officer twitched, and seemed to be full of mad flame. The young man stood at attention, unmoving, shut off.

The meal went in silence. But the orderly seemed eager. He made a clatter with the dishes.

'Are you in a hurry?' asked the officer, watching the intent, warm face of his servant. The other did not reply.

'Will you answer my question?' said the captain.

'Yes, Sir,' replied the orderly, standing with his pile of deep army plates. The captain waited, looked at him, then asked again:

'Are you in a hurry?'

'Yes, Sir,' came the answer, that sent a flash through the listener.

'For what?'

'I was going out, Sir.'

'I want you this evening.'

There was a moment's hesitation. The officer had a curious stiffness of countenance.

'Yes, Sir,' replied the servant, in his throat.

'I want you tomorrow evening also – in fact you may consider your evenings occupied, unless I give you leave.'

— The mouth with the young moustache set close.

'Yes, Sir,' answered the orderly, loosening his lips for a moment.

He again turned to the door.

'And why have you a piece of pencil in your ear?'

The orderly hesitated, then continued on his way without answering. He set the plates in a pile outside the door, took the stump of pencil from his ear, and put it in his pocket. He had been copying a verse for his sweetheart's birthday-card. He returned to finish clearing the table. The officer's eyes were dancing, he had a little, eager smile.

'Why have you a piece of pencil in your ear?' he asked.

The orderly took his hands full of dishes. His master was standing near the great green stove, a little smile on his face, his chin thrust forward. When the young soldier saw him his heart suddenly ran hot. He felt blind. Instead of answering, he turned dazedly to the door. As he was crouching to set down the dishes, he was pitched forward by a kick from behind. The pots went in a stream down the stairs, he clung to the pillar of the banisters. And as he was rising he was kicked heavily again, and again, so that he clung sickly to the post for some moments. His master had gone swiftly into the room and closed the door. The maid-servant downstairs looked up the staircase and made a mocking face at the crockery disaster.

The officer's heart was plunging. He poured himself a glass of wine, part of which he spilled on the floor, and gulped the remainder, leaning against the cool, green stove. He heard his man collecting the dishes from the stairs. Pale, as if intoxicated, he waited. The servant entered again. The captain's heart gave a pang, as of pleasure, seeing the young fellow bewildered and uncertain on his feet, with pain.

'Schöner!' he said.

The soldier was a little slower in coming to attention.

'Yes, Sir!'

The youth stood before him, with pathetic young moustache, and fine eyebrows very distinct on his forehead of dark marble.

'I asked you a question.'

'Yes, Sir.'

The officer's tone bit like acid.

'Why had you a pencil in your ear?'

Again the servant's heart ran hot, and he could not breathe. With dark, strained eyes, he looked at the officer, as if fascinated. And he stood there sturdily planted, unconscious. The dithering smile came into the captain's eyes, and he lifted his foot.

'I – I forgot it – Sir,' panted the soldier, his dark eyes fixed on the other man's dancing blue ones.

'What was it doing there?'

He saw the young man's breast heaving as he made an effort for words.

'I had been writing.'

'Writing what?'

Again the soldier looked him up and down. The officer could hear him panting. The smile came into the blue eyes. The soldier worked his dry throat, but could not speak. Suddenly the smile lit like a flame on the officer's face, and a kick came heavily against the orderly's thigh. The youth moved a pace sideways. His face went dead, with two black, staring eyes.

'Well?' said the officer.

The orderly's mouth had gone dry, and his tongue rubbed in it as on dry brown paper. He worked his throat. The officer raised his foot. The servant went stiff.

'Some poetry, Sir,' came the crackling, unrecognizable sound of his voice.

'Poetry, what poetry?' asked the captain, with a sickly smile.

Again there was the working in the throat. The captain's heart had suddenly gone down heavily, and he stood sick and tired.

'For my girl, Sir,' he heard the dry, inhuman sound.

'Oh!' he said, turning away. 'Clear the table.'

'Click!' – went the soldier's throat; then again, 'click!'; and then the half articulate:

'Yes, Sir.'

The young soldier was gone, looking old, and walking heavily. The officer, left alone, held himself rigid, to prevent himself from thinking. His instinct warned him that he must not think. Deep inside him was the intense gratification of his passion, still working powerfully. Then there was a counteraction, a horrible breaking down of something inside him, a whole agony of reaction. He stood there for an hour motionless, a chaos of sensations, but rigid with a will to keep blank his consciousness, to prevent his mind grasping. And he held himself so until the worst of the stress had passed, when he began to drink, drank himself to an intoxication, till he slept obliterated. When he woke in the morning he was shaken to the base of his nature. But he had fought off the realization of what he had done. He had prevented his mind from taking it in, had suppressed it along with his instincts, and the conscious man had nothing to do with it. He felt only as after a bout of intoxication, weak, but the affair itself all dim and not to be recovered. Of the drunkenness of his passion he successfully refused remembrance. And when his orderly appeared with coffee, the officer assumed the same self he had had the morning before. He refused the event of the past night – denied it had ever been – and was successful in his denial. He had not done any such thing – not he himself. Whatever there might be lay at the door of a stupid, insubordinate servant.

The orderly had gone about in a stupor all the evening. He drank some beer because he was parched, but not much, the alcohol made his feeling come back, and he could not bear it. He was dulled, as if nine-tenths of the ordinary man in him were inert. He crawled about disfigured. Still, when he thought of the kicks, he went sick, and when he thought of the threats of more kicking, in the room afterwards, his heart went hot and faint, and he panted, remembering the one that had come. He had been forced to say 'For my girl'. He was much too done even to want to cry. His mouth hung slightly open, like an idiot's. He felt vacant, and wasted. So, he wandered at his work, painfully, and very slowly and clumsily, fumbling blindly with the brushes, and finding it difficult, when he sat down, to summon the energy to move again. His limbs, his jaw were slack and nerveless. But he was very tired. He got to bed at last and slept inert, relaxed, in a sleep that was rather stupor than slumber, a dead night of stupefaction shot through with gleams of anguish.

In the morning were the manœuvres. But he woke even before the bugle sounded. The painful ache in his chest, the dryness of his throat, the awful steady feeling of misery made his eyes come awake and dreary at once. He knew without thinking, what had happened. And he knew that the day had come again, when he must go on with his round. The last bit of darkness was being pushed out of the room. He would have to move his inert body and go on. He was so young, and had known so little trouble, that he was bewildered. He only wished it would stay night, so that he could lie still, covered up by the darkness. And yet nothing would prevent the day from coming, nothing would save him from having to get up, and saddle the captain's horse, and make the captain's coffee. It was there, inevitable. And then, he thought, it was impossible. Yet they would not leave him free. He must go and take the coffee to the captain. He was too stunned to understand it. He only knew it was inevitable – inevitable, however long he lay inert.

At last, after heaving at himself, for he seemed to be a mass of inertia, he got up. But he had to force every one of his movements from behind, with his will. He felt lost, and dazed, and helpless. Then he clutched hold of the bed, the pain was so keen. And looking at his thighs, he saw the darker bruises on his swarthy flesh and he knew that, if he pressed one of his fingers on one of the bruises, he should faint. But he did not want to faint – he did not want anybody to know. No one should ever know. It was between him and the captain. There were only the two people in the world now – himself and the captain.

Slowly, economically, he got dressed and forced himself to walk. Everything was obscure, except just what he had his hands on. But he managed to get through his work. The very pain revived his dulled senses. The worst remained yet. He took the tray and went up to the captain's room. The officer, pale and heavy, sat at the table. The orderly, as he saluted, felt himself put out of existence. He stood still for a moment submitting to his own nullification – then he gathered himself, seemed to regain himself, and then the captain began to grow vague, unreal, and the younger soldier's heart beat up. He clung to this sensation – that the captain did not exist, so that he himself might live. But when he saw his officer's hand tremble as he took the coffee, he felt everything falling shattered. And he went away, feeling as if he himself were coming to pieces, disintegrated. And when the captain was there on horseback, giving orders, while he himself stood, with rifle and knapsack, sick with pain, he felt as if he must shut his eyes – as if he must shut his eyes on everything. It was only the long agony of marching with a parched throat that filled him with one single, sleep-heavy intention: to save himself.

2

He was getting used even to his parched throat. That the snowy peaks were radiant among the sky, that the whitey-green glacier river twisted through its pale shoals, in the valley below, seemed almost supernatural. But he was going mad with fever and thirst. He plodded on, uncomplaining. He did not want to speak, not to anybody. There were two gulls, like flakes of water and snow, over the river. The scent of green rye soaked in sunshine came like a sickness. And the march continued, monotonously, almost like a bad sleep.

At the next farm-house, which stood low and broad near the highroad, tubs of water had been put out. The soldiers clustered round to drink. They took off their helmets, and the steam mounted from their wet hair. The captain sat on horseback, watching. He needed to see his orderly. His helmet threw a dark shadow over his light, fierce eyes, but his moustache and mouth and chin were distinct in the sunshine. The orderly must move under the presence of the figure of the horseman. It was not that he was afraid, or cowed. It was as if he were disembowelled, made empty, like an empty shell. He felt himself as nothing, a shadow creeping under the sunshine. And, thirsty as he was, he could scarcely drink, feeling the captain near him. He would not take off his helmet to wipe his wet hair. He wanted to stay in shadow, not to be forced into consciousness. Starting, he saw the light heel of the officer prick the belly of the horse; the captain cantered away, and he himself could relapse into vacancy.

Nothing, however, could give him back his living place in the hot, bright morning. He felt like a gap among it all. Whereas the captain was prouder, overriding. A hot flash went through the young servant's body. The captain was firmer and prouder with life, he himself was empty as a shadow. Again the flash went through him, dazing him out. But his heart ran a little firmer.

The company turned up the hill, to make a loop for the return. Below, from among the trees, the farm-bell clanged. He saw the labourers mowing barefoot at the thick grass leave off their work and go downhill, their scythes hanging over their shoulders, like long, bright claws curving down behind them. They seemed like dream-people, as if they had no relation to himself. He felt as in a blackish dream: as if all the other things were there and had form, but he himself was only a consciousness, a gap that could think and perceive.

The soldiers were tramping silently up the glaring hillside. Gradually his head began to revolve slowly, rhythmically. Sometimes it was dark before his eyes, as if he saw this world through a smoked glass, frail shadows and unreal. It gave him a pain in his head to walk.

The air was too scented, it gave no breath. All the lush green-stuff seemed to be issuing its sap, till the air was deathly, sickly with the smell of greenness. There was the perfume of clover, like pure honey and bees. Then there grew a faint acrid tang – they were near the beeches; and then a queer clattering noise, and a suffocating, hideous smell: they were passing a flock of sheep, a shepherd in a black smock, holding his hook. Why should the sheep huddle together under this fierce sun? He felt that the shepherd could not see him, though he could see the shepherd.

At last there was the halt. They stacked rifles in a conical stack, put down their kit in a scattered circle around it, and dispersed a little, sitting on a small knoll high on the hillside. The chatter began. The soldiers were steaming with heat, but were lively. He sat still, seeing the blue mountains rise upon the land, twenty kilometres away. There was a blue fold in the ranges, then out of that, at the foot, the broad pale bed of the river, stretches of whitey-green water between pinkish-grey shoals among the dark pine-woods. There it was, spread out a long way off. And it seemed to come downhill, the river. There was a raft being steered, a mile away. It was a strange country. Nearer, a red-roofed, broad farm with white base and square dots of windows crouched beside the wall of beech-foliage on the wood's edge. There were long strips of rye and clover and pale green corn. And just at his feet, below the knoll, was a darkish bog, where globe flowers stood breathless still on their slim stalks. And some of the pale gold bubbles were burst, and a broken fragment hung in the air. He thought he was going to sleep.

Suddenly something moved into this coloured mirage before his eyes. The captain, a small, light blue and scarlet figure, was trotting evenly between the strips of corn, along the level brow of the hill. And the man making flag-signals was coming on. – Proud and sure moved the horse-man figure, the quick, bright thing in which was concentrated all the light of this morning, which for the rest lay a fragile, shining shadow. Submissive, apathetic, the young soldier sat and stared. But as the horse slowed to a walk, coming up the last steep path, the great flash flared over the body and soul of the orderly. He sat waiting. The back of his head felt as if it were weighted with a heavy piece of fire. He did not want to eat. His hands trembled slightly as he moved them. Meanwhile the officer on horseback was approaching slowly and proudly. The tension grew in the orderly's soul. Then again, seeing the captain ease himself on the saddle, the flash blazed through him.

The captain looked at the patch of light blue and scarlet, and dark heads, scattered closely on the hillside. It pleased him. The command pleased him. And he was feeling proud. His orderly was among them in common subjection. The officer rose a little on his stirrups to look. The young soldier sat with averted, dumb face. The captain relaxed on his seat. His slim-legged, beautiful horse, brown as a beech nut, walked proudly uphill. The captain passed into the zone of the company's atmosphere: a hot smell of men, of sweat, of leather. He knew it very well. After a word with the lieutenant, he went a few paces higher, and sat there, a dominant figure, his sweat-marked horse swishing its tail, while he looked down on his men, on his orderly, a nonentity among the crowd.

The young soldier's heart was like fire in his chest, and he breathed with difficulty. The officer, looking downhill, saw three of the young soldiers, two pails of water between them, staggering across a sunny green field. A table had been set up under a tree, and there the slim lieutenant stood importantly busy. Then the captain summoned himself to an act of courage. He called his orderly.

The flame leapt into the young soldier's throat as he heard the command, and he rose blindly, stifled. He saluted, standing below the officer. He did not look up. But there was the flicker in the captain's voice.

'Go to the inn and fetch me –' the officer gave his commands. 'Quick!' he added.

At the last word, the heart of the servant leapt with a flash, and he felt the strength come over his body. But he turned in mechanical obedience, and set off at a heavy run downhill, looking almost like a bear, his trousers bagging over his military boots. And the officer watched this blind, plunging run all the way.

But it was only the outside of the orderly's body that was obeying so humbly and mechanically. Inside had gradually accumulated a core into which all the energy of that young life was compact and concentrated. He executed his commission, and plodded quickly back uphill. There was a pain in his head, as he walked, that made him twist his features unknowingly. But hard there in the centre of his chest was himself, himself, firm, and not to be plucked to pieces.

The captain had gone up into the wood. – The orderly plodded through the hot, powerfully smelling zone of the company's atmosphere. He had a curious mass of energy inside him now. The captain was less real than himself. He approached the green entrance to the wood. There, in the half-shade, he saw the horse standing, the sunshine and the flickering shadow of leaves dancing over his brown body. There was a clearing where timber had lately been felled. Here, in the gold-green shade beside the brilliant cup of sunshine, stood two figures, blue and pink, the bits of pink showing out plainly. The captain was talking to his lieutenant.

The orderly stood on the edge of the bright clearing, where great trunks of trees, stripped and glistening, lay stretched like naked, brown-skinned bodies. Chips of wood littered the trampled floor, like splashed light, and the bases of the felled trees stood here and there, with their raw, level tops. Beyond was the brilliant, sunlit green of a beech.

'Then I will ride forward,' the orderly heard his captain say. The lieutenant saluted and strode away. He himself went forward. A hot flash passed through his belly, as he tramped towards his officer.

The captain watched the rather heavy figure of the young soldier stumble forward, and his veins too ran hot. This was to be man to man between them. He yielded before the solid, stumbling figure with bent head. The orderly stooped and put the food on a level-sawn tree-base. The captain watched the glistening, sun-inflamed, naked hands. He wanted to speak to the young soldier, but could not. The servant propped a bottle against his thigh, pressed open the cork, and poured out the beer into the mug. He kept his head bent. The captain accepted the mug.

'Hot!' he said, as if amiably.

The flame sprang out of the orderly's heart, nearly suffocating him.

'Yes, Sir,' he replied, between shut teeth.

And he heard the sound of the captain's drinking, and he clenched his fists, such a strong torment came into his wrists. Then came the faint clang of the closing of the pot-lid. He looked up. The captain was watching him. He glanced swiftly away. Then he saw the officer stoop and take a piece of bread from the tree-base. Again the flash of flame went through the young soldier, seeing the stiff body stoop beneath him, and his hands jerked. He looked away. He could feel the officer was nervous. The bread fell as it was being broken. The officer ate the other piece. The two men stood tense and still, the master laboriously chewing his bread, the servant staring with averted face, his fists clenched.

Then the young soldier started. The officer had pressed open the lid of the mug again. The orderly watched the lid of the mug, and the white hand that clenched the handle, as if he were fascinated. It was raised. The youth followed it with his eyes. And then he saw the thin, strong throat of the elder man moving up and down as he drank, the strong jaw working. And the instinct which had been jerking at the young man's wrists suddenly jerked free. He jumped, feeling as if he were rent in two by a strong flame.

The spur of the officer caught in a tree-root, he went down backwards with a crash, the middle of his back thudding sickeningly against the sharp-edged tree-base, the pot flying away. And in a second the orderly, with serious, earnest young face, and underlip between his teeth, had got his knee in the officer's chest and was pressing the chin backward over the farther edge of the tree-stump, pressing, with all his heart behind in a passion of relief, the tension of his wrists exquisite with relief. And with the base of his palms he shoved at the chin, with all his might. And it was pleasant too to have that chin, that hard jaw already slightly rough with beard, in his hands. He did not relax one hair's-breadth but, all the force of all his blood exulting in his thrust, he shoved back the head of the other man, till there was a little 'cluck' and a crunching sensation. Then he felt as if his heart went to vapour. Heavy convulsions shook the body of the officer, frightening and horrifying the young soldier. Yet it pleased him too to repress them. It pleased him to keep his hands pressing back the chin, to feel the chest of the other man yield in expiration to the weight of his strong young knee, to feel the hard twitching of the prostrate body jerking his own whole frame, which was pressed down on it.

But it went still. He could look into the nostrils of the other man, the eyes he could scarcely see. How curiously the mouth was pushed out, exaggerating the full lips, and the moustache bristling up from them. Then, with a start, he noticed the nostrils gradually filled with blood. The red brimmed, hesitated, ran over, and went in a thin trickle down the face to the eyes.

It shocked and distressed him. Slowly, he got up. The body twitched and sprawled there inert. He stood and looked at it in silence. It was a pity it was broken. It represented more than the thing which had kicked and bullied him. He was afraid to look at the eyes. They were hideous now, only the whites showing, and the blood running to them. The face of the orderly was drawn with horror at the sight. Well, it was so. In his heart he was satisfied. He had hated the face of the captain. It was extinguished now. There was a heavy relief in the orderly's soul. That was as it should be. But he could not bear to see the long, military body lying broken over the tree-base, the fine fingers crisped. He wanted to hide it away.

Quickly, busily, he gathered it up and pushed it under the felled tree-trunks, which rested their beautiful smooth length either end on logs.

The face was horrible with blood. He covered it with the helmet. Then he pushed the limbs straight and decent, and brushed the dead leaves off the fine cloth of the uniform. So, it lay quite still in the shadow under there. A little strip of sunshine ran along the breast, from a chink between the logs. The orderly sat by it for a few moments. Here his own life also ended.

Then, through his daze, he heard the lieutenant, in a loud voice, explaining to the men outside the wood that they were to suppose the bridge on the river below was held by the enemy. Now they were to march to the attack in such and such a manner. The lieutenant had no gift of expression. The orderly, listening from habit, got muddled. And when the lieutenant began it all again, he ceased to hear.

He knew he must go. He stood up. It surprised him that the leaves were glittering in the sun, and the chips of wood reflecting white from the ground. For him a change had come over the world. But for the rest it had not – all seemed the same. Only he had left it. And he could not go back. – It was his duty to return with the beer-pot and the bottle. He could not. He had left all that. The lieutenant was still hoarsely explaining. He must go, or they would overtake him. And he could not bear contact with anyone now.

He drew his fingers over his eyes, trying to find out where he was. Then he turned away. He saw the horse standing in the path. He went up to it and mounted. It hurt him to sit in the saddle. The pain of keeping his seat occupied him as they cantered through the wood. He would not have minded anything, but he could not get away from the sense of being divided from the others. The path led out of the trees. On the edge of the wood he pulled up and stood watching. There in the spacious sunshine of the valley soldiers were moving in a little swarm. Every now and then, a man harrowing on a strip of fallow shouted to his oxen, at the turn. The village and the white-towered church was small in the sunshine. And he no longer belonged to it – he sat there, beyond, like a man outside in the dark. He had gone out from everyday life into the unknown, and he could not, he even did not want to go back.

Turning from the sun-blazing valley, he rode deep into the wood. Tree-trunks, like people standing grey and still, took no notice as he went. A doe, herself a moving bit of sunshine and shadow, went running through the flecked shade. There were bright green rents in the foliage. Then it was all pine-wood, dark and cool. And he was sick with pain, he had an intolerable great pulse in his head, and he was sick. He had never been ill in his life. He felt lost, quite dazed with all this.

Trying to get down from the horse, he fell, astonished at the pain and his lack of balance. The horse shifted uneasily. He jerked its bridle and sent it cantering jerkily away. It was his last connection with the rest of things.

But he only wanted to lie down and not be disturbed. Stumbling through the trees, he came on a quiet place where beeches and pine trees grew on a slope. Immediately he had lain down and closed his eyes, his consciousness went racing on without him. A big pulse of sickness beat in him as if it throbbed through the whole earth. He was burning with dry heat. But he was too busy, too tearingly active in the incoherent race of delirium, to observe.

3

He came to with a start. His mouth was dry and hard, his heart beat heavily, but he had not the energy to get up. His heart beat heavily. Where was he? – the barracks, – at home? There was something knocking. And, making an effort, he looked round – trees, and glitter of greenery, and reddish bright, still pieces of sunshine on the floor. He did not believe he was himself, he did not believe what he saw. Something was knocking. He made a struggle towards consciousness, but relapsed. Then he struggled again. And gradually his surroundings fell into relationship with himself. He knew, and a great pang of fear went through his heart. Somebody was knocking. He could see the heavy, black rags of a fir-tree overhead. Then everything went black. Yet he did not believe he had closed his eyes. He had not. Out of the blackness sight slowly emerged again. And someone was knocking. Quickly, he saw the blood-disfigured face of his captain, which he hated. And he held himself still with horror. Yet, deep inside him, he knew that it was so, the captain should be dead. But the physical delirium got hold of him. Someone was knocking. He lay perfectly still, as if dead, with fear. And he went unconscious.

When he opened his eyes again, he started, seeing something creeping swiftly up a tree-trunk. It was a little bird. And a bird was whistling overhead. Tap-tap-tap – it was the small, quick bird rapping the tree-trunk with its beak, as if its head were a little round hammer. He watched it curiously. It shifted sharply, in its creeping fashion. Then, like a mouse, it slid down the bare trunk. Its swift creeping sent a flash of revulsion through him. He raised his head. It felt a great weight. Then, the little bird ran out of the shadow across a still patch of sunshine, its little head bobbing swiftly, its white legs twinkling brightly for a moment. How neat it was in its build, so compact, with pieces of white on its wings. There were several of them. They were so pretty – but they crept like swift, erratic mice, running here and there among the beech-mast.

He lay down again exhausted, and his consciousness lapsed. He had a horror of the little creeping birds. All his blood seemed to be darting and creeping in his head. And yet he could not move.

He came to with a further ache of exhaustion. There was the pain in his head, and the horrible sickness, and his inability to move. He had never been ill in his life. He did not know where he was or what he was. Probably he had got sunstroke. Or what else? – he had silenced the captain for ever – some time ago – oh, a long time ago. There had been blood on his face, and his eyes had turned upwards. It was all right, somehow. It was peace. But now he had got beyond himself. He had never been here before. Was it life, or not-life? He was by himself. They were in a big, bright place, those others, and he was outside. The town, all the country, a big bright place of light: and he was outside, here, in the darkened open beyond, where each thing existed alone. But they would all have to come out there sometime, those others. Little, and left behind him, they all were. There had been father and mother and sweetheart. What did they all matter. This was the open land.

He sat up. Something scuffled. It was a little brown squirrel running in lovely, undulating bounds over the floor, its red tail completing the undulation of its body – and then, as it sat up, furling and unfurling. He watched it, pleased. It ran on again, friskily, enjoying itself. It flew wildly at another squirrel, and they were chasing each other, and making little scolding, chattering noises. The soldier wanted to speak to them. But only a hoarse sound came out of his throat. The squirrels burst away – they flew up the trees. And then he saw the one peeping round at him, half way up a tree-trunk. A start of fear went through him, though, in so far as he was conscious, he was amused. It still stayed, its little keen face staring at him half way up the tree-trunk, its little ears pricked up, its clawey little hands clinging to the bark, its white breast reared. He started from it in panic.

Struggling to his feet, he lurched away. He went on walking, walking, looking for something – for a drink. His brain felt hot and inflamed for want of water. He stumbled on. Then he did not know anything. He went unconscious as he walked. Yet he stumbled on, his mouth open.

When, to his dumb wonder, he opened his eyes on the world again, he no longer tried to remember what it was. There was thick, golden light behind golden-green glitterings, and tall, grey-purple shafts, and dark-nesses further off, surrounding him, growing deeper. He was conscious of a sense of arrival. He was amid the reality, on the real, dark bottom. But there was the thirst burning in his brain. He felt lighter, not so heavy. He supposed it was newness. The air was muttering with thunder. He thought he was walking wonderfully swiftly and was coming straight to relief – or was it to water?

Suddenly he stood still with fear. There was a tremendous flare of gold, immense – just a few dark trunks like bars between him and it. All the young level wheat was burnished, gold glaring on its silky green. A woman, full-skirted, a black cloth on her head for head dress, was passing like a block of shadow through the glistering green corn, into the full glare. There was a farm, too, pale blue in shadow, and the timber black. And there was a church spire nearly fused away in the gold. The woman moved on, away from him. He had no language with which to speak to her. She was the bright, solid unreality. She would make a noise of words that would confuse him, and her eyes would look at him without seeing him. She was crossing there to the other side. He stood against a tree.

When at last he turned, looking down the long, bare grove whose fore bed was already filling dark, he saw the mountains in a wonder-light, not far away, and radiant. Behind the soft, grey ridge of the nearest range the further mountains stood golden and pale grey, the snow all radiant like pure, soft gold. So still, gleaming in the sky, fashioned pure out of the ore of the sky, they shone in their silence. He stood and looked at them, his face illuminated. And like the golden, lustrous gleaming of the snow he felt his own thirst bright in him. He stood and gazed, leaning against a tree. And then everything slid away into space.

During the night the lightning fluttered perpetually, making the whole sky white. He must have walked again. The world hung livid around him for moments, fields a level sheen of grey-green light, trees in dark bulk, and a range of clouds black across a white sky. Then the darkness fell like a shutter, and the night was whole. A faint flutter of a half-revealed world, that could not quite leap out of the darkness! – Then there again stood a sweep of pallor for the land, dark shapes looming, a range of clouds hanging overhead. The world was a ghostly shadow, thrown for a moment upon the pure darkness, which returned ever whole and complete.

And the mere delirium of sickness and fever went on inside him – his brain opening and shutting like the night – then sometimes convulsions of terror from something with great eyes that stared round a tree – then the long agony of the march, and the sun decomposing his blood – then the pang of hate for the captain, followed by a pang of tenderness and ease. But everything was distorted, born of an ache and resolving into an ache.

In the morning he came definitely awake. Then his brain flamed with the sole horror of thirstiness. The sun was on his face, the dew was steaming from his wet clothes. Like one possessed, he got up. There, straight in front of him, blue and cool and tender, the mountains ranged across the pale edge of the morning sky. He wanted them – he wanted them alone – he wanted to leave himself and be identified with them. They did not move, they were still and soft, with white, gentle markings of snow. He stood still, mad with suffering, his hands crisping and clutching. Then he was twisting in a paroxysm on the grass.

He lay still, in a kind of dream of anguish. His thirst seemed to have separated itself from him, and to stand apart, a single demand. Then the pain he felt was another single self. Then there was the clog of his body, another separate thing. He was divided among all kinds of separate beings. There was some strange, agonized connection between them, but they were drawing further apart. Then they would all split. The sun, drilling down on him, was drilling through the bond. Then they would all fall, fall through the everlasting lapse of space.

Then again his consciousness reasserted itself. He roused onto his elbow and stared at the gleaming mountains. There they ranked, all still and wonderful between earth and heaven. He stared till his eyes went black, and the mountains as they stood in their beauty, so clean and cool, seemed to have it, that which was lost in him.

4

When the soldiers found him, three hours later, he was lying with his face over his arm, his black hair giving off heat under the sun. But he was still alive. Seeing the open, black mouth the young soldiers dropped him in horror.

He died in the hospital at night, without having seen again.

The doctors saw the bruises on his legs, behind, and were silent.

The bodies of the two men lay together, side by side, in the mortuary, the one white and slender, but laid rigidly at rest, the other looking as if every moment it must rouse into life again, so young and unused, from a slumber.

Biographies

(JOSEPH) RUDYARD KIPLING (1865–1936) was born in Bombay. The painter Edward Burne-Jones was his uncle; Stanley Baldwin, the Prime Minister, was his first cousin. He was sent back to England at six, where the cruelty and neglect of his paid guardians left a lasting mark. He returned to India to work as a journalist at sixteen, and very quickly made a huge popular impact with the vividness and range of his writing. He was one of the first truly global writers, with his subjects reflecting periods living in America and South Africa as well as India, and the first English writer to be awarded the Nobel Prize in Literature. His reputation was, and remains, the subject of fierce controversy.

THOMAS HARDY (1840–1928) was born in Higher Bockhampton, Dorset. The son of a jobbing stonemason, he was apprenticed to architectural practices in Dorset and London. (A rare witness to his architectural practice is his house, Max Gate, near Dorchester, built much later and a work of stunning incompetence.) He began to publish novels in 1871, becoming successful with *Far from the Madding Crowd*, published by the *Cornhill Magazine* in 1874. Short fiction remained an important sideline for Hardy in the early years of the boom. Over the next twenty years, Hardy published fiction that often raised protests because of its tendency to violence and sexual frankness. After *Jude the Obscure* (1895) Hardy renounced fiction in favour of poetry.

W(ILLIAM) S(CHWENK) GILBERT (1836–1911), although now mostly remembered for his collaborations with the composer Arthur Sullivan, was a professional writer of considerable range and extensive practice, including short fiction. Born in London, his writing career began as a contributor of fillers and squibs, often in verse, to comic magazines, including *Punch*. He met his greatest success as a dramatist of comedies, pantomimes and serious drama on social themes, among other distinctions introducing the can-can to the British stage. He was highly litigious by temperament, and the successful Gilbert and Sullivan collaborations came to an end over a court case. He died of heart failure, trying to save a girl who he thought was drowning. Leaving £118,028 at his death – perhaps £14m in today's values – he may be the most financially successful writer in this anthology.

OLIVE SCHREINER (1855–1920) was born in Basutoland in the Cape Colony, the daughter of a missionary. Her early ambition to be a doctor was frustrated by the limitations of her education at home. Soon after arriving in England in 1881, she published her most successful novel, *The Story of an African Farm*. She was quickly accepted into the most radical intellectual circles, including Edward Carpenter, Eleanor Marx and Havelock Ellis, and was one of the first movers of the women's liberation movement and what would be called the 'New Woman'. She returned to South Africa in 1889, continuing to argue for idealistic causes. When she died, her will funded a scholarship for women medical students at what would become the University of Cape Town, irrespective of race or religion, intended to favour the poor.

OSCAR WILDE (1854–1900) was born in Dublin, the son of a surgeon and a writer. Soon after arriving in London in 1879, he had become so celebrated that Gilbert and Sullivan could portray him in *Patience* (1881); when the operetta transferred to America, the promoters paid for Wilde to give a lecture tour so that audiences would understand the object of the satire. Celebrated as a conversationalist, reviewer, essayist, lecturer and writer of fiction, his greatest fame was to come as a dramatist. He first went to bed with a man (Robert Ross) shortly after his marriage; thereafter his sexual behaviour grew so reckless by the standards of the time that he was jailed and cast out from society.

GEORGE MOORE (1852–1933) was born at Moore Hall, County Mayo, the son of Irish gentry, and barely educated. After he inherited the family estates in 1870, he went to Paris with the intention of becoming an artist. He was a favourite subject for caricaturists – Yeats said he looked as if he were 'carved from a turnip' – but scrupulous and exquisite as a writer. In 1879 falling revenues from the estate obliged him to move to London, where he made a reputation as an original, often outrageous, English disciple of Zola and other French realists. He played an important part in the establishment of an Irish national culture after 1900, happy to cause controversy with his writings to the end.

BARRY PAIN (1864–1928) was born in Cambridge, the son of a linen draper. He is the epitome of the writer created by the boom in periodical publication. On moving to London in 1890, he quickly found a market for short comic pieces, short fiction and ingenious parodies, especially with *Black and White* and the *Cornhill Magazine*. An industrious man, he published some sixty books of extraordinary range; the *Eliza* books, which are occasionally still read, are by no means his best.

ELLA D'ARCY (1857?–1937) was born in Pimlico, the daughter of a corn chandler. She had some private income from her father's Irish estate, and trained as an artist before starting to publish short fiction. 'Irremediable' was printed in the first issue of *The Yellow Book*, where she worked in some unofficial editorial capacity. In person, she was variously described by her contemporaries as 'a mouse-mannered piece of sex', the laziest woman they had ever met, and a 'goblin' for her habit of turning up unannounced. In later life, she lived in Paris. The very first paperback published by Penguin, André Maurois' *Ariel*, was in her translation.

H[ERBERT] G[EORGE] WELLS (1866–1946) was born in Bromley, the son of an unsuccessful shopkeeper and a lady's maid. His education was fiercely fought for against circumstances and poor health.

He started to publish short stories, often in the form of scientific romances, in the late 1880s. His fiction was balanced between these and realistic fiction, often informed by Wells' 'commitment to Fabian socialism. He was both a celebrated philanderer, and a proponent of sexual freedoms. In later years he was a substantial public figure who was welcomed by both Roosevelts, Lenin and Stalin as a visiting dignitary, never losing his taste for controversy or brisk vituperation.

HENRY JAMES (1843–1916) was born in New York City, the son of a writer and the grandson of a cotton merchant who had amassed one of the largest fortunes in America. He was the brother of the philosopher William James and of the diarist Alice James. He started to publish in 1864. After 1869 he was increasingly in Europe, and from 1876 permanently in London. He had a gift for friendship, and the ever-increasing analytical expertise of his fiction raised him high in the estimation of successive generations, through the 1890s aesthetes and even modernists like Ezra Pound. He never, however, had a large popular success. In 1914 he became a British citizen, and shortly before his death was awarded the Order of Merit.

'GEORGE EGERTON' (1859–1945) was the pen-name of Mary Chavelita Dunne. She was born in Melbourne, Australia, the daughter of a Captain Dunne of Irish descent. She moved to London to be the companion of a Mrs Whyte-Melville, whose husband she soon ran off with to Norway. She was familiar with new Norwegian writers, including Ibsen and Knut Hamsun, with whom she had an affair and whose novel *Hunger* she translated. Her first fiction was immediately successful. She was strongly associated with the 'New Woman' of the 1890s, and when intellectual fashion moved on, her reputation and popularity declined.

ARTHUR MORRISON (1863–1945) was born in East London, the son of an engine-fitter – he later attempted to conceal his working-class origins. He became a journalist and the clerk to a charity before starting to publish his tales of working-class life in 1891. His fiction was controversial because of its realistic and unvarnished approach to serious social issues. After 1913 he stopped writing fiction and journalism, and devoted himself to the collection of Chinese and Japanese art. The study of his life, obscure both in its early and later years, has been made more difficult by his wife's obeying his instruction to burn all his papers on his death.

GEORGE GISSING (1857–1903) was born in Wakefield, the son of a pharmaceutical chemist. Brilliant promise as a pupil and student was brought to an abrupt end when he was found to have stolen from fellow students to support his indigent girlfriend, and sent to prison. His two marriages were both disastrous; his prolific career was conducted under constant money worries. He began writing short stories in 1893; his gloomy analysis of the literary scene that flourished after the explosion of periodicals in his novel *New Grub Street* primarily reflects his idiosyncratic analysis of his own experience.

ARTHUR CONAN DOYLE (1859–1930) was born in Edinburgh, the son of an artist and draughtsman. He trained as a doctor, and entered general practice while starting to write fiction as a sideline. The stories of his creation, Sherlock Holmes, started to be published in 1887, but became hugely successful after they were taken up by *The Strand* in July 1891. Despite the immense fees that the Holmes stories were soon commanding, Conan Doyle killed his hero off, only later to resurrect him, inspired by the offer of a colossal sum. In later years, he was an energetic proponent of spiritualism, and the ingenuous advocate of the small girls who perpetrated the 'Cottingley fairies' hoax.

E[RNEST] W[ILLIAM] HORNUNG (1866–1921) was born in Middlesbrough, the son of a very successful iron, coal and timber merchant. Suffering poor health, he was sent to Australia to convalesce. He made an initial mark on his return with stories and novels with an Australian setting before marrying Arthur Conan Doyle's sister, and creating the anti-Sherlock Holmes, Raffles. The Raffles books sold in large quantities, despite their outrageous amorality and open suggestions of a homosexual *ménage*; Hornung's writing after the first three of them underwent a sad decline in quality.

SOMERVILLE AND ROSS (Edith Somerville (1858–1959) and 'Martin Ross', the pen-name of Violet Martin (1862–1915)) were second cousins and literary collaborators, and perhaps secretly married to each other. Edith Somerville was born in Corfu but grew up in Ireland. She was a dedicated sportswoman and suffragist. Violet Martin was born in Connemara, County Galway, the youngest of sixteen children. They began to collaborate soon after their meeting in 1886. They were politically divergent; Somerville was a nationalist, Martin a Unionist, but agreed on women's suffrage. After Martin's death in 1915, Edith Somerville continued to write as 'Somerville and Ross'.

CHARLOTTE MEW (1869–1928) was born in London, the daughter of an architect. The fear of inherited madness bore heavily on her all her life. She was an early contributor to *The Yellow Book*, and fell in love with Ella D'Arcy on its staff. A later passion for May Sinclair ended humiliatingly. She turned to poetry in 1909, and was promoted and admired by Harold Monro and Thomas Hardy. Her extreme poverty in a life shared with her sister was alleviated by a small civil-list pension. After her sister died of cancer, Mew committed suicide, using the cheapest poison available.

M[ONTAGUE] R[HODES] JAMES (1862–1936) was born in Good-nestone in Kent, the son of a Church of England vicar. As a scholar first at Eton and then at King's College, Cambridge, he developed a fascination for mediaeval arcana, particularly manuscripts. At King's he became a fellow, then Dean, then Provost, and from 1893 director of the Fitzwilliam Museum. His scholarly work, including substantial catalogues of manuscript collections, remains important. The ghost stories started to be written in the 1890s, and were first collected in 1904. His last years were spent as Provost of Eton. He was awarded the Order of Merit in 1930.

G[ILBERT] K[EITH] CHESTERTON (1874–1936) was born in London, the son of an estate agent. Although his disorganized temperament was not conducive to success in education, by the 1890s he found himself ideally suited to supplying short pieces and reviews to the new periodical press. By the beginning of the new century, he was a celebrated figure as well as a writer of fiction, journalism and polemics. In 1909 he and his wife moved to Beaconsfield. He took a strongly Christian position, revelling in paradox, and converted to Roman Catholicism in 1922; his later years, burdened by editorial roles he was ill-suited to maintain, failed to sustain the brilliant unpredictability of his pre-war writing.

MAY SINCLAIR (1863–1946) was born near Birkenhead, the daughter of a shipping contractor. She started to publish poetry in 1886, and fiction in 1897. She was identified with a certain sexual frankness in writing and with 'New Woman' and suffragist movements. Her books sold very well, enabling her to support the children of two of her siblings. She moved in advanced intellectual circles, promoting various new movements in thought, including Tagore's mysticism, psychoanalysis and even parapsychology, all of which are reflected in her fiction. After 1920 ill health affected the quality of her writing and eventually forced her retirement.

ISRAEL ZANGWILL (1864–1926) was born in East London, the son of an itinerant pedlar who had fled Baltic Russia at the age of twelve. His ability at the Jewish Free School and at London University, where he took evening classes, enabled him to become first a teacher, then a journalist. His writing raised international interest, and by the new century he had become a prominent voice in the developing Zionist cause. He eventually refused to support the Balfour Declaration on the grounds that it made inadequate provision for the existing Arab population in Palestine.

ARNOLD BENNETT (1864–1931) was born in Burslem, the son of a (in succession) master potter, weaver, pawnbroker, and solicitor – his father was in constant financial worries. Bennett's first literary success was with a story in *The Yellow Book*, and afterwards he pursued a distinctive vein of French-influenced realism. A decade living in Paris after 1902 sealed his literary sophistication and elegance; by 1912 he was in a position to buy a yacht and a Queen Anne house in the country. Throughout the 1920s he maintained an interest in very advanced younger writers; a toxic but naïve essay about his ingenious and well-made work by Virginia Woolf continues to mislead readers about its profound merits. He died of typhoid after drinking tap water in France.

MARY MANN (1848–1929) was born in Norwich, the daughter of a successful merchant. She married a yeoman farmer, and took up a good number of prominent parochial and local positions of authority. She began to write in the 1880s, publishing the first of many novels in 1883. Her reputation rests on the short stories which she supplied to magazines in the period, gaining some important proponents, such as D. H. Lawrence.

'SAKI' (Hector Hugh Munro) (1870–1916) was born in Burma, the son of the Burmese Inspector General of Police. He was brought up by forceful aunts in Devon. In 1900 he began to write for the *Westminster Gazette* under his celebrated pseudonym, taken from the *Rubáiyát* of Omar Khayyám. His was the epitome of the exquisite but heartless comedy that homosexual writers specialized in. He enlisted in the ranks at the outbreak of the Great War, and was killed by a sniper's bullet at the Battle of the Ancre. His body was never recovered.

J[ANE] E[SDON] MALLOCH (1874–1937) better known under her married name, Jane Brailsford, was a militant campaigner for women's suffrage. She was born in Renfrewshire, the daughter of a cotton manufacturer. She studied philosophy and Greek at Glasgow University under Gilbert Murray, to whom she was passionately attached without return. She married her philosophy tutor, soon to become a radical journalist, Henry Brailsford, never concealing her contempt

for him. She was sent to prison for the violence of her suffrage protests. She suffered from depressive and physical breakdowns, and
severe alcoholism. In 1921 she permanently separated from her husband, finally dying of cirrhosis in Kew. The story here printed may
be her only published work of fiction. The discovery of 'J. E. Malloch''s identity was made by Dr Charlotte Jones of Queen Mary,
University of London, to whom the editor is very grateful.

JOSEPH CONRAD (1857–1924), formerly Jozef Korzeniowski, was born
in what is now Ukraine, the son of a Polish nobleman. From 1874 to
1894 he was engaged in a career as a mariner, including spells running guns for the Carlists and seeing the brutality of Belgian colonial
rule at first hand. After 1894 he settled in Britain, of which he had
become a citizen, and embarked on a peerless series of novels and
short stories. Despite the acknowledged excellence of his fiction, he
had no big popular success until *Chance* in 1916. Although even the
most sophisticated and challenging of his novels were serialized in
periodicals, including *Nostromo*, his debts rose to terrifying levels.
Chance changed his fortunes, and by 1919 film producers were paying
£3,000 for the film rights to his books. His personality, after much
investigation, remains cryptic.

MAX BEERBOHM (1872–1956) was born in London, the son of a prosperous corn merchant. While at Oxford, he was taken up by Oscar
Wilde's circle, and became well known as a brilliant caricaturist.
Amusingly publishing a volume entitled *The Works of Max Beerbohm*
at twenty-six, he became celebrated as an artist, essayist, peerless
literary parodist and writer of fiction. His private life is described by
his biographer as 'peculiar'. He married in 1910 and settled in Rapallo,
Italy. He never learnt to speak Italian, though he lived there the rest
of his life. In later years he became an admired broadcaster, was given
a knighthood and buried in St Paul's Cathedral.

E[DWARD] M[ORGAN] FORSTER (1879–1970) was born in London,
the son of an architect. His father died the year after his birth,

leaving the family, along with a later bequest from an aunt, comfortably supplied. He disliked school, but was very happy at Cambridge,
to which his fiction repeatedly returns. He started publishing novels
in 1904, and short fiction shortly thereafter. He came to terms, slowly,
with his homosexuality, writing one of his best novels, *Maurice,* on
the subject in 1911 (it was not published until 1971). After 1912 he
travelled to India and Egypt. *A Passage to India* was the last of his
novels, but he lived almost another half century, increasingly celebrated and fêted. He refused a knighthood, but was awarded the
Order of Merit and made a Companion of Honour.

(PERCY) WYNDHAM LEWIS (1882–1957) was born on his father's yacht off
the coast of Nova Scotia. His father was a soldier. He grew up in
England, training to be an artist. He moved to Paris and advanced
artistic circles – he would have been aware of Picasso's *Les Demoiselles
d'Avignon* during its creation. After 1909 he returned to England,
devoting his energies both to writing and to an exceptionally bold
painting style, identified with Vorticism. His high point of influence
came at the outbreak of World War One in 1914, which saw him
produce and edit the most extreme of modernist journals, *Blast*, and
decorate an entire dining room in a London restaurant. His argu-
mentative temperament kept him prominent for many years; his
catastrophically ill-judged publication of a pro-Hitler polemic in 1931
had a justifiably negative effect on his reputation, though he continued
to write and paint with a startling, idiosyncratically mannered style.

E[DWARD] F[REDERIC] BENSON (1867–1940) was born at Wellington College, the son of the headmaster and subsequently Archbishop of
Canterbury. He, his mother and at least four of his five siblings, all
remarkable in different ways, were homosexual. He was a brilliant
classicist, and after university worked in Athens and Egypt. After 1893,
his fiction achieved great success, both in short and long forms. From
a staggeringly prolific oeuvre, the *Mapp and Lucia* novels are the best
remembered. From 1918 he lived in Henry James's former house, Lamb
House in Rye, and served as the town's mayor in the 1930s.

KATHERINE MANSFIELD (1888–1923) was born Kathleen Beauchamp in Wellington, New Zealand, the daughter of a prosperous businessman. In 1903 her education was concluded in London, and she finally moved permanently from New Zealand in 1908. She was disinherited by her mother on the grounds of a lesbian attachment, and started to suffer serious health problems early. After the publication of her first book, she met John Middleton Murry, and they began a fruitful editorial collaboration. She was closely associated with D. H. Lawrence and Virginia Woolf; her short fiction was immensely influential during her lifetime and afterwards.

REBECCA WEST (1892–1983) was born Cicily Fairfield in London, the daughter of an Anglo-Irish adventurer with a very varied life, and a talented pianist. She saw very early that her birth name would not do for a serious writer, and took her pseudonym from Ibsen's heroine. She began professional life as a social commentator along socialist and feminist lines, arousing H. G. Wells's interest. He became her lover and the father of her son. She went on writing fiction alongside the classics of reportage, such as *Black Lamb and Grey Falcon*, which turned her into an international intellectual of unassailable eminence. In later years she was a prominent polemicist against communism, often being identified as an apologist for McCarthyism.

JAMES JOYCE (1882–1941) was born in Dublin, the son of an unsuccessful speculative businessman and rates collector. He was schooled at a boarding school run along Jesuit lines and studied at University College, Dublin. His earliest writings baffled all his readers. In June 1904, he met Nora Barnacle, and soon afterwards set off for Paris, Zurich and finally Trieste, where they settled. His first book, the collection *Dubliners*, went into print only after the most protracted struggle with the publisher. In 1915 the Joyces moved to Zurich, where much of *Ulysses* was written; it started to be published, like all Joyce's work, in periodicals. After the publication of *Ulysses* in 1922, Joyce's fame was secured, although the novel went on being suppressed on the grounds of obscenity for at least another decade. He benevolently and immediately used his celebrity to promote the literary work of one of his Trieste patrons, the novelist Italo Svevo.

D[AVID] H[ERBERT] LAWRENCE (1885–1930) was born in Eastwood in Nottinghamshire, the son of a coalminer. He won a county scholarship to Nottingham High School and, though he did not excel at school, managed to qualify as a schoolteacher. After 1909, he started to attract attention as a writer. In 1912, his meeting with the German-born Frieda Weekley, née von Richthofen, broadened his horizons considerably. He struggled a good deal with prosecutions for obscenity. After the war, the couple led a peripatetic existence that took them across the world in search of new ways of living. His last years were spent under the shadow of the tuberculosis that killed him. His real fame was achieved only after his death.

THE PENGUIN BOOK OF
THE BRITISH SHORT STORY:
VOLUME 1: FROM DANIEL DEFOE
TO JOHN BUCHAN

'The Boy-scouts mistook my signal, and have killed the postman.
I've had very little practice in this sort of thing, you see'

The British short story tradition is probably the richest, most
varied and historically extensive in the world. This new anthology
celebrates the full diversity and energy of its writers, subjects and
tones, from the story's origins with Defoe, Swift and Fielding, to
the 'golden age' of the fin de siècle and Edwardian period, ending
with the First World War. Including the most famous authors as
well as some magnificent, little-known stories never republished
since their first appearance in magazines and periodicals, these
stories are by turns topical and playful, ghostly and theatrical,
rumbustious and sublime.

Edited with an introduction by Philip Hensher

ISBN: 978 0 141 39600 2

THE PENGUIN BOOK OF
THE BRITISH SHORT STORY:
VOLUME 2: FROM P.G. WODEHOUSE
TO ZADIE SMITH

'She would tear the house down – shatter the windows, slash the
furniture, flood the baths, fire the curtains!'

Hilarious, exuberant, surreal, subtle, tender, brutal, spectacular
and above all unexpected: this extraordinary selection celebrates
the British short story from the 1920s to the present day. From
Angela Carter to V. S. Pritchett, Elizabeth Taylor to J. G. Ballard,
Ali Smith to a host of little-known works from magazines and
periodicals, and including tales of air-raids, phone sex, snobbery,
modern-day slavery, grief, desire, the familiar and the strange,
here is the short story in all its limitless possibilities.

Edited with an introduction by Philip Hensher

ISBN: 978 0 141 39602 6

THE PENGUIN BOOK OF THE CONTEMPORARY SHORT STORY

'Like its predecessors, this volume is a feast, and every morsel worth savouring' Edmund Gordon, *Literary Review*

We are living in a particularly rich period for British short stories. Despite the relative lack of places in which they can be published, the challenge the medium represents has attracted a host of remarkable, subversive, entertaining and innovative writers. Philip Hensher, following the success of his definitive *Penguin Book of British Short Stories*, has scoured a vast trove of material and chosen thirty great stories for this new volume of works written between 1997 and the present day.

Edited with an Introduction by Philip Hensher

ISBN: 978 0 141 98621 0

THE PENGUIN BOOK OF
JAPANESE SHORT STORIES

'Filling up with sugar – what a lovely way to die!'

This is a celebration of the Japanese short story from its modern origins in the nineteenth century to remarkable contemporary works. It includes the most well-known Japanese writers – Akutagawa, Murakami, Mishima, Kawabata - but also many surprising new pieces, from Yuko Tsushima's 'Flames' to Banana Yoshimoto's 'Bee Honey'. Ranging over myth, horror, love, nature, modern life, a diabolical painting, a cow with a human face and a woman who turns into sugar, *The Penguin Book of Japanese Short Stories* is filled with fear, charm, beauty and comedy.

Edited by Jay Rubin with an introduction by Haruki Murakami

ISBN: 978 0 241 31190 5

THE PENGUIN BOOK OF
ITALIAN SHORT STORIES

'An enticing collection . . . the tales are by turns startling, moving,
intriguing and provocative' *Times Literary Supplement*

Jhumpa Lahiri's landmark collection brings together forty writers
that reflect over a hundred years of Italy's vibrant and diverse
short story tradition, including well known authors such as Italo
Calvino, Elsa Morante and Luigi Pirandello, alongside many cap-
tivating rediscoveries. Poets, journalists, visual artists, musicians,
editors, critics, teachers, scientists, politicians, translators: the
writers that inhabit these pages represent a dynamic cross section
of Italian society.

Edited with an introduction and selected translations
by Jhumpa Lahiri

ISBN: 978 0 241 29985 2

THE PENGUIN BOOK OF
CHRISTMAS STORIES

'Bring out the tall tales now that we told by the fire as the
gaslight bubbled...'

This is a collection of the most magical, moving, chilling and
surprising Christmas stories from around the world, taking us
from frozen Nordic woods to glittering Paris, a New York speak-
easy to an English country house, bustling Lagos to midnight mass
in Rio, and even outer space. Here are classic tales from writers
including Truman Capote, Shirley Jackson, Dylan Thomas, Saki
and Chekhov, as well as little-known treasures such as Italo
Calvino's wry sideways look at Christmas consumerism, Selma
Lagerlof's enchanted forest in Sweden, and Irène Nemerovsky's
dark family portrait. Featuring santas, ghosts, trolls, unexpected
guests, curmudgeons and miracles, here is Christmas as imagined
by some of the greatest short story writers of all time.

ISBN: 978 0 241 39670 4

THE PENGUIN BOOK OF
SPANISH SHORT STORIES

This collection celebrates the richness and variety of the Spanish short story, from the nineteenth century to the present day. Featuring over fifty stories selected by revered translator Margaret Jull Costa, it blends old favourites and hidden gems – many of which have never before been translated into English – and introduces readers to surprising new voices as well as giants of Spanish literary culture, from Emilia Pardo Bazán and Leopoldo Alas, through Mercè Rodoreda and Manuel Rivas, to Ana Maria Matute and Javier Marías.

Brimming with romance, horror, history, farce, strangeness and beauty, and showcasing alluring hairdressers, war defectors, vampiric mothers, and talismanic mandrake roots, the daring and entertaining assortment of tales in *The Penguin Book of Spanish Short Stories* will be a treasure trove for readers.

Edited by Margaret Jull Costa

ISBN: 978 0 241 39047 4

THE PENGUIN BOOK OF OULIPO: QUENEAU, PEREC, CALVINO AND THE ADVENTURE OF FORM

'A superb selection . . . Lovers of word games and literary puzzles will relish this indispensable anthology' *Guardian*

This anthology brings together the work of one of the most curious and playful literary groups of the twentieth century, who revelled in puzzles, problems, literary constraints and trickery. Here are poems, stories, word games and conundrums by famous Oulipians including Georges Perec and Italo Calvino, interwoven with pieces by 'anticipatory' wordsmiths and fellow travellers from Jonathan Swift to Lewis Carroll.

Edited by Philip Terry

ISBN: 978 0 241 37845 8